Hope and Lies

Book One of the Abredea Series

C.H. Lyn

Horizon Publishing

Contents

Content Warnings   VIII

Dedication   IX

1. Chapter 1   1

2. Chapter 2   19

3. Chapter 3   34

4. Chapter 4   42

5. Chapter 5   54

6. Chapter 6   63

7. Chapter 7   71

8. Chapter 8   80

9. Chapter 9   85

10. Chapter 10   90

11. Chapter 11   96

12. Chapter 12   107

13. Chapter 13   125

14. Chapter 14   132

15. Chapter 15   143

16. Chapter 16   153

17. Chapter 17   166

18. Chapter 18   174

19.	Chapter 19	184
20.	Chapter 20	196
21.	Chapter 21	211
22.	Chapter 22	217
23.	Chapter 23	230
24.	Chapter 24	244
25.	Chapter 25	265
26.	Chapter 26	277
27.	Chapter 27	287
28.	Chapter 28	289
29.	Chapter 29	304
30.	Chapter 30	315
31.	Chapter 31	329
32.	Chapter 32	338
33.	Chapter 33	351
34.	Chapter 34	361
35.	Chapter 35	364
36.	Chapter 36	377
37.	Chapter 37	389
38.	Chapter 38	405
39.	Chapter 39	416
40.	Chapter 40	427
41.	Chapter 41	439
42.	Chapter 42	449
43.	Chapter 43	451

44. Chapter 44   458

45. Chapter 45   467

46. Chapter 46   480

47. Chapter 47   488

48. Chapter 48   500

49. Chapter 49   504

Content Warnings

Violence
Child Harm
Mention of Sexual Assault

Dedication

To the empaths like Cho, who feel everything.
To the fighters like Maybelle, who never give up.
And to the lost souls like Juliana, you aren't nothing, and you will find your way.

Country of Pangaea

The Dugout

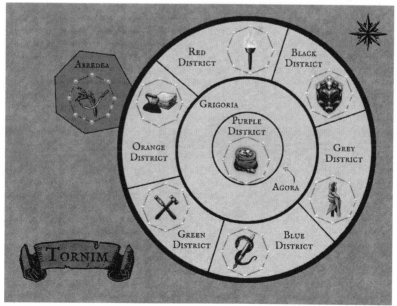

City of Tornim

Grey-Stars:
Government

 Black-Stars:
Military

 Blue-Stars:
Doctors & Research

 Red-Stars:
Emergency Personnel

 Purple-Stars:
Merchants

 Green-Stars:
Skilled Craftsmen

 Orange-Stars:
City Laborers

 White-Stars:
Undesirables

Chapter One

70 Years Ago - Beyond the Grey-Star Military Compound Wall

The sun shone bright across the early morning sky and a chill cut the air. Boots were necessary to walk across the dew-coated fields without soaking one's pants to the knee. In the distance, a long wall separated the wilderness from the elite. Skyscrapers, coated in glass and white concrete, peaked out from the center of the city. The rising sun glinted across the windows, blinding those who stared too long.

A truck, sporting the emblem of a Grey-Star medical unit, idled on the gravel road halfway between the city and the forest. The trees encroached slowly. It had been many decades since men thrived from destroying them. It would be many decades more before those who remained grew concerned about the dangers of the wilderness. The Grey-Stars, and their allies, had other worries at the moment.

The convoy truck honked a whiny horn and a couple, standing a few feet away, parted. The shorter of the two waved a hand in the direction of the med-unit transport. Then she turned back and shook her head as the man opened his mouth.

Maybelle pressed a delicate finger to Ben's lips. "Don't. I'll see you soon. I promise."

"I don't like you going out again, not after last time."

She sighed, brushing a hand through her short, black hair and pulled her thin navy jacket tighter around her torso. "I'm not going because I want to. It's my assignment."

"I can get you out of it," Ben murmured through pale lips.

Maybelle rolled her eyes. She glanced at the truck. They had been on their way when Ben flagged them down. Her unit commander was not pleased with the delay, but Ben outranked him. "Little late for that, don't you think?"

He ran a hand across his face, rubbing the sleep from his eyes. "Yeah, I suppose you're right. Take this with you. For me."

He pressed a golden locket—etched with ornate, detailed lines—into her hands. She took it, glancing up at him.

"I didn't want to bring it on a mission, it's so beautiful."

"It'll make you think of me while you're out there. If anything goes wrong," Ben's square jaw tightened, "I'll be there for you. Be careful, all right?"

"I'll see you soon." Maybelle went on her toes to peck his cheek, then turned without another word and jogged to the truck. She slipped the chain, thicker than the jewelry she was used to, over her head.

The high cheek-boned, strong jawed, immaculately eyebrowed, dark brown head of Kate popped out through the opening in the tarp that protected those riding in the bed from the elements. "Took you long enough," she said with a wry grin. "We ready to go yet?"

"Yes."

Kate reached out a hand, Maybelle grasped it, and her friend pulled her up. Their unit commander, a gruff, weathered man with grey hair and a constant severe expression, slammed a palm on the window to the cab. The truck lurched forward.

A dozen people sat comfortably along the thick benches lining either side of the truck bed: the six members of the Grey-Star med-unit with their packed medical bags, and the Black-Star security force with their long, heavy plasma guns.

"What did he want?" Kate asked as the two women settled into seats near the tarp flap.

"Just to say bye. And give me something."

Kate raised an eyebrow.

Maybelle pulled the chain forward and showed Kate the locket. "He gave it to me last night, but I left it in my dorm."

"He stopped the truck just to bring you a locket?"

"Yeah... I think he's worried. After last time..."

Maybelle clenched her jaw and Kate's gaze fell. Their last mission, also their first mission, had been an utter failure. It's hard to heal people who are already dead. And by the time they'd arrived at the Black-Star outpost, everyone had been dead.

"I'll talk to him when we get back. He can't..." she sighed. "If things are going to get serious between us, he can't pull rank that way."

"Serious? Haven't they already gotten serious? He spent the night in your room last week."

Maybelle gave Kate a significant "shut up" look. "That was because of the nightmares. Nothing happened."

Kate unsuccessfully covered a mischievous grin. "Whatever you say."

"I love you like a sister, but please stop talking."

Kate raised her hands in defeat and looked away.

Maybelle leaned back. The truck went over a bump. She closed her eyes and took a deep breath. After almost thirty years of friendship, Kate still didn't know how to hold her tongue. It had gotten the two of them in trouble more times than Maybelle could count.

Her temple itched. She reached a manicured finger and scratched at the place where her skin met the circular gemstone embedded in the soft space between her eye and hairline. Once she scratched the itch away, she absentmindedly stroked the cut grey stone, barely larger than her com-piece.

Recalling the long list of research transmissions she still needed to listen to, Maybelle pulled the small black device from her pocket and tucked it into her ear. She took out a piece of glass the size of her ID card, tapped on the screen for a moment, and turned up the volume as the truck's engine revved. They were going up an incline. Her heartbeat quickened, as it always did when they went into the mountains.

She took a deep breath and concentrated on the low female voice, dripping like honey into her left ear.

"Trial number 4629. Subject responded positively to the first series of injections. Fetus reached 16 weeks." A heavy sigh. *"The miscarriage was worse than last time. I have concerns about the rate of injections... and the priorities of my superiors. The mother must remain healthy during the process."*

The truck hit another bump and Kate grabbed Maybelle's knee. Grey eyes met. Maybelle took her friend's hand and held it as they rumbled through the forest, the doctor's voice still going over results from the latest tests.

The med-truck jerked to a stop. They reversed, turned, and moved down the dirt road they had missed.

"We're a few minutes out," the unit commander said.

Maybelle pulled her med-bag between her legs and double checked the contents. Kate clenched and unclenched her hands. After a few sharp turns, the truck stopped.

The six members of the security force went first, returning quickly to give the all clear for the Grey-Stars. Maybelle and Kate jumped from the bed. The Black-Star recruit who had driven hurried around the side of the truck and unloaded their bags. Maybelle picked up hers and waited for Kate.

Kate, dark braids dancing around her shoulders, flashed a grin at the Black-Star. He was young, maybe twenty-two or twenty-three. Fresh from training and not used to working with Grey-Stars yet; his wide blue eyes watched Kate's every move.

A ripple went through the air. A fluctuation that Maybelle noticed and the Black-Star did not. She shot Kate a dark look as the rookie lunged forward.

"Let me!" He picked up her bag, his eyes wide, his hands fumbling in his hurry to please.

"Can't you turn it off once in a while?" Maybelle muttered as Kate walked by.

"It's harmless. They like the feeling." Kate waved a hand loftily through the air.

"It's manipulative."

Kate shook her head and marched away, calling over her shoulder. "We're meant to use our gift to make life easier."

Something heavy and unpleasant thunked in the pit of Maybelle's stomach as the Black-Star scurried behind her friend. She grimaced and followed them, gripping the strap of her own bag between pale fingers.

Leaves crunched under their feet. Twigs snapped with each step. But beyond the sounds made by the med-unit, the forest was unnervingly silent. No birds zipped through the trees, no rodents danced under the brush. Maybelle swallowed. The unpleasant feeling in her stomach moved up to her chest.

The path ended suddenly, dumping the group in a clearing.

Kate gasped. A shudder went through Maybelle; her throat clenched, and her ears rang. The Black-Star dropped the bag he carried, turned around, and emptied the contents of his stomach behind a bush.

Blood. It dripped from the trees, auburn and brown leaves speckled with crimson. Red splattered the barracks wall; small spots followed by gentle drips, and finally huge splashes coated the white paint. The stench worked its way into Maybelle's nose, through her throat, and to her tongue. The metallic taste of the air had her doubled over, swallowing repeatedly to avoid throwing up.

The clearing was carved out of a dense section of forest. The trees surrounding them towered high, letting in only the occasional beam of direct sunlight. Three buildings: a mess hall, a barracks for the Black-Star trainees, and housing for the Grey-Star instructors, sat against three sides of the woods. The barracks was the largest, sleeping forty Black-Stars, fresh from the Coding.

They were all dead.

Their bodies littered the training field. The stench of blood, soot, and burned flesh, engulfed the air.

Tears welled in Maybelle's eyes. A shudder wracked her body, and her hands shook before she clenched them into white-knuckled fists. These Black-Stars were practically children. Twenty-year-olds, barely out of school, the gemstones on their temples hardly used to being that shiny black color.

A girl lay a few feet away. Her body was twisted, and closer than the rest, as though she had been running for the path before being struck down. The gemstone on her right temple was barely visible beneath strands of blonde hair, stuck to the blood matted across her face. A jagged slice ran from the top of her eyebrow and down past her jaw. It cut straight through her brilliant blue eye, leaving a glassy, empty stare that Maybelle could not break from.

After a moment, tears cascading down her cheeks, Maybelle turned away. She met Kate's gaze and saw her own fear reflected in their dark depths. They couldn't win this war if the rebels kept murdering new recruits.

A sharp voice broke her out of the despair encompassing her mind.

"Look for survivors," the unit commander barked.

She clenched her jaw and looked closer at the bodies. Some were moving. As the ringing in her ears diminished, she heard the moans of the injured.

She rushed forward.

Movement to her right pulled her attention. A young man, another Black-Star, with sandy hair and thin arms, opened his mouth and closed it, over and over. She knelt and rummaged through her bag.

His forehead was split open, blood dribbling down his cheek. He kept trying to speak. Maybelle put a gentle finger to his lips.

"Shh, it's all right. I'm here. I've got you." She pulled a small cannister from the bag, popped the lid, and sprayed it directly into his wound.

He cried out in pain.

Once the cut was disinfected, Maybelle used a second cannister to spray foam into the slice. It would only take a few moments for the inflamed red swelling to reduce back to its normal size and color. His cry turned into a soft whimper.

She squeezed his shoulder, meeting his eye and speaking in a low voice. "This will cool and numb the wound, and it should start the healing process. I'm going to wrap you up, then we'll get you home, all right?"

He didn't answer, but there was less fear in his gaze. She glanced back and noted the Black-Star rookie who had accompanied their med-unit was still crouched over next to the bush.

"Come help me get him up. We should get him into the truck."

The boy quivered, his gaze fixed on a shredded limb a few feet away.

"Hey!" Maybelle snapped. His eyes turned to her. She took a deep breath, concentrated, and a familiar warmth filled her chest. As she exhaled, the air between herself and the rookie warped just enough to bend the light filtering through the trees.

The Black-Star stood, his face suddenly alert. He went to her, ready to please, needing to please. Needing to do whatever was necessary to keep her happy.

"How can I help?" he asked, his voice weak but determined.

"Get this one to the truck, then come back."

He gave a sharp nod and gently helped the injured boy stand. They both hesitated for a moment, wearing matching expressions of rapture and awe.

Maybelle clenched her jaw and turned away. Kate may enjoy having people stare at her with that unwavering loyalty and admiration, but it made Maybelle uncomfortable. It didn't feel real to her. Perhaps because it wasn't.

She picked her way through the bodies, searching for another injured person. Around her, and further in the clearing, the rest of the med-unit was doing the same. Kate knelt near the trees, over a body not wearing the standard trainee tactical gear.

"Our own come first," another member of the unit called to her, not unkindly.

Kate stood and walked toward the center of the clearing, though her face wore a troubled expression. She bent again, this time at the body of a trainee, when the unit commander started toward her, his face contorted in contempt and derision.

"Grey-Stars before Black!" he snapped. "You can't be that—"

He froze, his words hanging in the air. A spurt of red blossomed on the chest of his tan uniform. He looked down. He fell.

Kate screamed.

Maybelle stood, rooted to the ground, as figures appeared from between the trees. Men and women surrounded them; guns drawn. Their clothes were mismatched, hardly uniforms, but each bore their insignia. A single red handprint. That handprint had haunted Maybelle's nightmares since the start of the uprising.

Several things happened at once. The Black-Stars traveling with the med-unit raised their plasma guns. They traded half a dozen shots before being struck down. Old fashioned weapons, with crude metal projectiles that ripped apart flesh, slaughtered them where they stood. The Black-Star trainee with a bandage around his head fell, his stomach torn open.

Kate panicked and tried to run. A rebel, one with orange gemstones, took two short steps and slammed the butt of his gun into the back of her head. She dropped to the ground.

Maybelle's heart clenched with fear. She started toward her friend when something hard pressed into the small of her back.

"Don't," a female voice, shallow and muffled, said.

She froze. Part of her wanted to ignore the order, regardless of the weapon currently jutting against her spine. Her gaze was still fixed on Kate's form. Her friend stirred and Maybelle let out the breath she had been holding.

"Don't move," the woman said again. "I don't want to shoot you."

Around them, the rest of the medical unit was being held at gunpoint. A young man with dark hair, his gun slung across his shoulder, poked the dead unit-commander with his foot.

"Did you hear him?" the boy sneered. "Grey-Stars before Black-Stars," he said in a crude, yet accurate, impression of the dead man. "What a piece of shit."

"That's enough." A voice, one that reminded Maybelle of deep caverns and dark trenches, carried through the air.

She looked to its owner and her pulse, already thundering with fear, sped up.

The man was a mountain; tall and broad, with dark cargo-pants, thick boots, and a black shirt decorated with the red handprint of the rebels, though his had two white lines painted across the four fingers. Twin green gemstones glistened against his temples, in sharp contrast to his dark red hair which had been cut short on the sides and left longer at the top. The hair on his head matched a full beard which hung down to his chest as well as the curly strands which could have been mistaken for sleeves on his arms. In one massive hand he clenched a three-foot-long blade, serrated on one side, the darkened color of wet metal. In the other, he held a plasma gun. Small red netting covered both his nostrils.

He strode toward the dark-haired man, an annoyed look on his face. "Put your mask on; what are you thinking?"

The younger man did as he was told, pulling out a sheer red device about the size of Maybelle's palm, and fitting it over his nose and mouth. With a glance, Maybelle realized each of the rebels had some form of netting or mask covering their faces. She frowned, a thought attempting to force its way through the fear muddling her brain.

"Get them moving. I don't like being out in the open," the man with the red beard said.

The weapon at her back nudged her forward. She let it move her toward the trees, but when they drew level with Kate, she dropped and scurried to her friend.

The woman behind her gave a shout of surprise and footsteps sounded in her wake. The man who had knocked Kate to the ground raised his gun. Maybelle didn't care.

She reached her friend and grabbed Kate's thin hand. Slender fingers weakly squeezed her own. Maybelle brushed a hand across her forehead. It came away wet with blood.

Kate was alive. She was breathing. Maybelle pulled her up, putting an arm around her waist and straightening.

The woman who had followed her stared grimly at them both. She was a White-Star. Pearly gemstones glinted against her tanned skin. Short, with blonde hair and an oval face, she too wore a red mask across her nose and mouth.

Maybelle fixed her with a hard glare.

"Let's go." The woman gestured with her gun.

They followed the rest of the rebels, and the remaining Grey-Stars, into the trees. Kate gained coherence as they walked, eventually leaning less on Maybelle for support and more for comfort.

Shudder after shudder ran through Maybelle. So many bodies. So many dead. And they were next.

She'd heard the stories, the rumors, the detailed accounts of what happened when the rebels took prisoners. It was rare. Those who fell on the battlefield died where they lay, left for the scavengers. Those unfortunate civilians who got in their way were left for their families to find.

The last she'd heard of Grey-Stars taken prisoner involved torture, imprisonment, and ultimately a cruel and horrible death.

"They're going to kill us," Kate mumbled, her voice shook with gasping breaths. Her body trembled.

Maybelle tightened her grip around Kate's waist. "No. They aren't. They would have done it back there."

Kate's charcoal grey eyes, wide and bloodshot, met Maybelle's lighter ones. "Then what..."

They stopped. The rebels had found a clear space between the trees. The three remaining Grey-Stars were already lined up on their knees. Maybelle and Kate were led to the far end and shoved to the ground. Maybelle took the opportunity to check Kate's head. A jagged cut, about the length of her thumb, ran along her hairline. It was shallow, though blood still pooled and dribbled from the edge.

They waited on their knees on the damp ground as a few of the rebels, including the large man, Red-Beard, spoke in hushed tones a few yards away. The rest of the rebel group, almost a dozen men and women, watched the prisoners, weapons at the ready.

The women wore their hair cropped short or in tight braids with strands falling around their weary faces. The men's clothes were patched and frayed, covered in dirt and blood.

Hard hands held guns, axes, and knives. Gemstones; white, orange, green, and even purple, glistened against dark, tan, and pale temples. They turned as one when Red-Beard walked toward the Grey-Stars, his hand on his gun.

"We need to get moving." He looked at the people on their knees. "Cooperate and we won't hurt you."

The Grey-Star at the end of the line, a man older than Maybelle and Kate who had been friends with the unit-commander, gave a derisive snort.

Red-Beard faced him. "Something to say?"

The older man struggled to his feet, the contempt on his face palpable. A few of the rebels near them inched forward with wary expressions.

The top of the Grey-Star's head barely reached Red-Beard's nose, but he faced the rebel nonetheless, head raised, teeth barred, and hands clenched into tight fists.

"We will never cooperate with murderers, cowards, and criminals. You aren't worth the time it takes to kill you."

He spit; the blob of mucus and saliva landed with an audible splat on Red-Beard's cheek.

A gunshot rang through the air, the Grey-Star's body dropped, and Kate screamed. Maybelle reached out a hand and grabbed Kate's. She tightened her fingers, pressing into the grooves between Kate's knuckles. After a moment of ragged breaths and terrified sobs, her friend returned the pressure.

Red-Beard turned, his expression livid, to the young rebel who had fired.

"What in the *depths* was that?"

"He..." The boy faltered under Red-Beard's glare. The excited, victorious look melted into fear and regret. "He spat at you... I..."

"You proved him right. Hand off your weapon. I'll deal with you when we get back to base." He let out a sigh and ran a hand through his beard. His gaze drifted down, scanning the remaining four prisoners.

Cold malice stared back at him from the eyes of the first two Grey-Stars. Kate looked at the ground, tears still marking tracks down her cheeks. Maybelle met his gaze, holding it even as fear coursed through her body, until he looked away.

He gestured to the short blonde woman. "Get the wounded and the prisoners loaded up. We've been here too long already."

She gave a sharp jerk of the head. "What about the dead?"

"Leave them," he said, not meeting her eyes.

She opened her mouth, but he held up a hand.

"I said, leave them. We don't have time."

Her lip curled up in a snarl, but she didn't speak.

The prisoners were moved, shoved through the forest for what seemed like an hour, until they came upon a rocky dirt road.

Maybelle kept her fingers locked in Kate's until the last possible moment when the rebels loaded them into transport trucks very similar to their own. Two older women searched them for weapons, bound their hands, and tied them to steel loops drilled into the bed of the truck. The rebels loaded the other two members of their unit into the second truck.

Several people piled into the truck, sitting as far to the back and away from Maybelle and Kate as possible. Red-Beard and the short woman joined them as well. The truck lurched forward. Maybelle swallowed. Her eyes darted around, searching for a way out, or at least something to look at to distract her mind from the horrible scenarios it kept playing out.

They drove for hours. At a certain point the adrenaline from the mayhem, death, and fear faded away. Maybelle struggled to keep her eyes open. Kate slumped against her shoulder, head lolling with every pothole and rock they drove over.

Streaks of orange, red, and pink crisscrossed the western horizon by the time the truck pulled to a stop. If she had a better sense of direction, Maybelle may have been able to guess that their journey through the mountains led them north and that, though they had traveled for over half the day, they weren't nearly as far from the main Grey-Star compound as it seemed.

However, Maybelle's sense of direction barely told her where "up" was, and as far as she was concerned, they could have been halfway across the country for all it mattered.

They would be dead soon, no matter which direction they'd gone.

She and Kate were released from the truck. Their hands remained tied in front of them. They'd parked along the edge of a cleared-out space, roughly the size of a small city block. Forest surrounded them. To the east, massive mountains climbed up, up, up, their tips obscured by the clouds. To the west, dwindling light carved monstrous shadows from the trees.

A building, barely fit to be called such, stood in the center of the clearing. There were four walls, a tin roof, one door, and no windows. Trucks, wooden boxes, fuel containers, weapons, and an assortment of other gear, sat sprawled around the shed.

Small clusters of warm bodies surrounded a dozen dug-out fires. The chatter in the air died as Maybelle and Kate were pushed toward the small building. Several people stood and walked closer, gawking at them, and murmuring to each other, hands going to their weapons.

Anxiety grew in Maybelle as they approached the building. Her footsteps faltered. A gun dug into her lower back, and she picked up her pace. Kate's body shook next to her.

"No, no, no, no..." her friend whispered.

"Shh." Maybelle gave her the smallest nudge with her shoulder.

Kate quieted, though her whimpers continued unabated. The door to the shed opened. Maybelle blinked in the darkness, waiting for her eyes to adjust. Where she expected to see chains, bars, and instruments of torture, there were stairs. Massive black steps led into the earth until Maybelle couldn't even make out their outline.

She froze.

"Let's go." Red-Beard's deep voice sounded from just outside the door. The person behind her pushed once again and, hands still bound before her, she carefully stepped onto the first stair.

Blackness came at her from every angle. She reached out and brushed her knuckles against the wall, just to reassure herself it existed. After a moment, a faint green light behind them made the going slightly easier.

They walked down the stairs for five full minutes. The scent of earth, rich and overpowering, surrounded them. Walls faded from stone to rock and from rock to hard packed dirt. The stairwell grew brighter until they rounded a sharp turn and came to level ground. Above them, three glowing orbs, roughly the size of truck tires, hung from the high ceiling. They lit up the room, showing three brick archways, one on either side of the stairwell and one across the way. Smaller globes, like the ones which hung along the streets back in the city, illuminated the creeping corridors.

Kate and Maybelle were jostled to the side as the majority of the rebels made their way through the right-most arch. A few remained behind, weapons still drawn and pointed at the Grey-Stars.

"This way," the blonde woman said, jerking her head to the left.

They followed her, the other rebels taking up the rear. After another several minutes of twists, turns, doorways, and forks, they reached a large metal door.

The room was bright. White walls offset the dark ceiling. Cement coated the floor, with small drains spaced evenly along the center. A long silver table sat in the middle and along the walls...

Maybelle squinted. Along the walls were glass enclosures. She couldn't call them cages, as there were no bars, but they were certainly designed to keep their occupants inside. There were a dozen, six on either side of the room. Each contained a white cot, a grey blanket, and a bucket the purpose of which Maybelle desperately did not want to think about.

She turned her focus to the rebels already sitting at the metal table. Their faces were vaguely familiar. Red-Beard stepped forward. He set his gun on the table and walked down the length of the room, eyeing each glass box.

When he reached the far wall he turned, eyebrows drawn tightly together, jaw clenched at an angle.

"Where are they?" he growled.

A woman sitting at the table cast her eyes down, a heavy—almost sad—sigh escaping through her trembling lips.

The man across from her clenched his hands on the tabletop. Red stained his skin. A stone-like weight settled in Maybelle's stomach.

"One of them got ahold of a blade," the woman said, still not looking at Red-Beard.

There was silence in the room. The heaviness of it pressed against Maybelle's shoulders and chest. Kate's shuddering breaths broke it, followed by a crash as Red-Beard gripped the back of a chair and hurled it against a wall.

"Two," he shouted. "Two of the *five* we were supposed to bring back. I *told* you, I told you how important this is."

His large palm covered his face, dragging at his skin until he gave his beard a sharp tug and released it. He rested both hands on the table and stared at the three people responsible for killing the remaining members of the med-unit.

"Go. Get some food in you. We de-brief in an hour."

They scrambled away, leaving Red-Beard, the blonde woman, and two more rebels from the group who had transported Kate and Maybelle.

"Someone needs to tell Command," the woman said, turning to the door. "I have to check on the girls anyway."

Red-Beard shook his head with a sigh. "Thanks, Sam. I'll be up there in a bit." She nodded and left.

"Believe it or not," he looked at Kate and Maybelle, "we didn't plan on hurting any of you. These deaths," he shook his head again, "they were needless. Wasteful. If you cooperate with us, you will be kept safe."

They said nothing. Kate stared at the floor; Maybelle watched the man. A long moment passed.

"Get them in the cells."

Their bonds were cut. Maybelle's jaw clenched. Her hands itched with the desire to fight, or at least flee. But there was no way she would remember how to get to the surface, even if she somehow managed to get herself and Kate out of the room.

A woman pushed Maybelle into an enclosure, shut the door, and did up the latch. Cold air, blowing down on her from a vent in the wall above, sent a shiver down her spine. She went to the cot and sat, staring out at the murderers who held them captive.

Red-Beard and the remaining rebels held a short, muttered conversation. Maybelle couldn't make out the muffled words through the glass. They left the room, shutting off the lights and leaving Maybelle and Kate in the dim glow of a small blue orb left on the table.

Maybelle closed her eyes and took a breath. The sudden flux of adrenaline had, once again, left her exhausted. She looked up at the sound of crying.

Kate sat on the concrete next to the wall joining their cells. Her forehead, stained even darker than usual with blood and sweat, leaned against the glass. Soft sobs filtered into Maybelle's cell through small holes in the glass, evenly spaced along the top, bottom, and middle.

Maybelle went to her, sitting on the floor and pressing a palm on the glass. After a moment, Kate pressed her palm likewise and looked up at her friend.

"How did this happen?" she sniffed. Her voice echoed a bit as though she were down a long tunnel rather than a few inches away.

"I don't know." Maybelle shook her head. "The area was supposed to be cleared. I don't..."

"They're going to kill us."

"Not right away."

Kate looked at her and Maybelle immediately regretted her words. Then again, it wasn't anything Kate didn't know.

"What are we going to do?" Kate leaned her head against the glass once more.

"I don't know," Maybelle said again.

They sat that way, in silent darkness, for a while. Eventually, Kate fell asleep, curled up against the glass like a cat against a warm body. Maybelle stayed awake, unable to close her eyes for more than a few seconds without horrific images filtering across her vision.

She clenched and unclenched her fingers, trying to bring warmth to their thin, pale forms. Her tan pants, heavily pocketed and coated in grim, along with the light top and thin jacket she wore, did little to protect her skin from the chilly air still blowing in from the *nacra* vent. Her legs ached, both from slamming into the ground in the forest, and climbing down the mountain of stairs. Knots started in her lower back and stretched up to just below her hairline. She rolled her head; rubbed the back of her neck.

Her hand brushed against a thick chain, and she paused. She drew the locket out from underneath her shirt. Ben.

She hadn't let herself think about him... about the fact that she'd never see him again, never be pulled tight into his arms again. Tears formed and fell down her cheeks, their warmth disappearing by the time they reached her jaw, leaving cold tracks upon her face.

She tried to open the golden oval in her palm. It was heavy, and larger than most of her jewelry. She might get to see Ben's face again, staring out at her from the picture she hoped was inside.

But it would not open. After a moment of trying, she let the locket thunk against her chest. Her hands fell to her sides, fingertips brushing against the cold floor. Her mind drifted.

Maybelle urged her body to relax. Her fears about the next day would be somewhat lessened if she could get some sleep. She took a deep breath, but it only brought a fresh wave of tears. The image of the Black-Star girl's eye, broken and blank, came to the front of her mind. She shuddered.

Maybelle closed her eyes, leaned her head back against the glass, and wished she could go home. A strange sensation, similar to missing a step, or leaning back too far in a chair, went through her stomach. Wind rushed past her ears.

Warmth hugged at her skin. Her fingers twitched as they recognized plush carpet in place of concrete. Her next breath brought with it the scent of jasmine.

Maybelle opened her eyes.

She sat against a firm wooden door. The cozy, comfortable room held a bed decorated with fluffy pillows, a sink and mirror, a small desk, a dresser, and a nightstand. Hairclips, knickknacks, a candle, and a few bracelets cluttered the top of the nightstand. Framed pictures sat atop the dresser. Her and Kate at ten-years-old, still in their primary school uniforms. Her and Kate again, graduating tech-school at 24, two years early. Her and Kate in their first laboratory at the research facility they were both accepted to. And one newer photo, her and Ben, sitting together on a park bench.

Maybelle stood slowly, her head reeling; her breath came in shallow, fearful gasps. She put a tentative hand on the bed, confirming with her touch that it was, in fact, really in front of her. She walked to the sink and turned a handle. Water flowed, circling until it disappeared down the drain.

Not even Grey-Stars had the tech for this level of hologram. It had to be real. She had to be home.

She glanced at herself in the mirror and nearly screamed. Her eyes... her eyes were... wrong.

Her irises, grey with flecks of black, were gone. Only the pupil remained, a tiny black dot in the center of her white eye. Her fingers shook as she reached up a hand, pulling back one of her eyelids for a better look.

As she stared into the glass, the space around her pupil darkened, the white returning to grey once more.

She pressed cold fingers to her lips. The fear which had filled her before was nothing compared to the petrifying terror flowing through her now. This was strange. Different. Bad. There was something wrong with her.

Maybelle rubbed the grey gemstones on her temples; at least they were still normal.

Maybelle's gaze drifted to the pictures on her dresser. She didn't know how she got home. She didn't know what was wrong with her eyes. And she didn't know what would happen to her if someone saw them that way. But that wasn't important now.

Kate's face grinned up at her from the pictures, mischievous smile in place as usual. Her friend was still in that place.

Maybelle inched open the door. The hallway was dark; the bright light from her room seemed to disrupt the stillness of the night. She slid the door shut behind her and made her way out of the Grey-Star Standard Dorm building. Ben would be asleep, or maybe still awake and waiting to hear word of their return. Either way, he'd be in the officer's quarters, closer to the center of the city.

After the noise, fear, and smells of the forest, she found herself unsettled by the stillness of the night. The scent of cement and steel, the quiet of the outside world, pressed upon her senses.

Being uncomfortable in the place she called home made her even more uncomfortable. She shook her head, rolled her shoulders back, and walked quickly, keeping to the shadows of the buildings. There would be many questions when she found Ben, but he would understand. He would know they needed to get Kate before they figured out what was wrong with her.

The officer's quarters were a few minutes' walk. Maybelle slid open the familiar door, hurried to the stairwell, and sped up to the third floor. Ben's room was at the end of the hallway. She knocked.

No answer.

He had fallen asleep. Good, the poor man needed to rest with all that was going on. She knocked again, a little louder.

Still no answer.

She gave it one more try, knocking loud enough that she heard someone move around in the room next door. Scurrying back to the stairs, she realized her mistake and sighed. Of course, he wasn't home sleeping. He would be in the library, working until she returned safely to the city.

Maybelle went back to the main floor and walked briskly down yet another hallway. Halfway to the library, she slowed to quietly go around an open door.

She hadn't yet reached the beam of light coming through the opening when she paused. A familiar voice caught her ear.

"—have to wait. We need to be sure, absolutely sure, they arrived before it turns on."

Ben.

Maybelle reached for the doorknob when a second voice in the room spoke, and she froze.

"It's been hours since confirmed capture. How long could it take?"

The voice was male. Old and gruff, his tone implied impatience. His words implied something else. Maybelle waited for Ben's response, holding her breath.

"I'm not willing to risk blowing the entire operation with a rush job. We wait the original thirty-six hours." Something clinked, glass on glass. "You trusted me with this operation. They were captured just as I said they would be. Trust me a little longer."

That couldn't be right. Maybelle peeked her head around the door and glanced into the room.

It was an office. Maps of the old world, before the plague, lined a far wall. Bookshelves, filled with hardbacks, statues, and pictures sat against two other walls. A massive metal desk sat in the center of the room. Four thick beige armchairs rested before it. Ben was there, leaning against one of the chairs. His back was to her. He held a drink in his hand. Her expectation, that he would be pacing the room with feverish worry, perhaps angrily demanding they be rescued immediately, was shattered.

The man sitting behind the desk seemed more agitated than Ben. Short, wide, and significantly older, he ran a hand across his forehead, brushing past the grey gemstones on his temples. Maybelle knew his face, but not his name.

Twelve Grey-Star Commanders ran the war. This man was one of them.

"How do you know they weren't killed on sight?"

Ben stood and walked around the desk. He leaned down and pointed to a glass tablet on the desk.

"This group has been trying to get their hands on a med-unit for months now. But... not just any med-unit. They're only going for units with former researchers on the team."

Maybelle didn't understand. Or... she didn't want to. Because she certainly understood what his words *meant*. What they insinuated.

Their capture hadn't been an accident.

Maybelle wanted to go in, find out what was going on, and demand help for Kate, but something in the back of her mind cautioned against it. She stood just outside the line of light, listening intently.

"I don't like it. What if the locator malfunctions? What if she opens it early?"

"The locket is sealed shut. It won't open until it's time."

Maybelle's hand flew to her throat. She closed her fingers around the piece of gold dangling from her neck. This was wrong, so wrong.

"You know... they won't survive." The commander no longer sounded anxious. His tone became taunting.

"Obviously."

The dismissal in Ben's voice sent a shard of ice through Maybelle's heart. Her mouth was dry, she couldn't swallow. Her breath was shallow, she couldn't fill her lungs. The muscles in her arms flexed as her hands clenched. She forced herself to concentrate, listen to the rest of the conversation. She peeked her head back around the door.

"It's two lives." Ben waved a hand, his voice unconcerned. "Two little lives to win a war."

Kate.

Rushing filled Maybelle's ears. The ground opened before her, her stomach rolled, and she screamed.

When she opened her eyes, dim blue light greeted her. Cold air pressed against her skin. Her limbs weighed a thousand pounds and she collapsed to her knees, gasping for breath.

"How in the *depths* did you do that?"

Kate's voice filtered into her ringing ears. She looked up.

She was in Kate's cell. Kate sat on the cot staring, somewhat fearfully, at Maybelle. When her gaze reached Maybelle's eyes, the fear on her face magnified.

"What's wrong with your eyes?"

Maybelle shook her head. Tears, furious tears that stung with the burn of betrayal, squeezed from her eyes, and dripped down her cheeks.

"It was all on purpose."

"What?" Kate left the cot, going to her knees in front of Maybelle and grabbing her hand. Concern rapidly replaced her fear.

"Everything that happened," Maybelle choked out, nearly sobbing. "The Black-Stars, the trainees, our unit. He... he knew they were going to die. He knows *we're* going to die. He planned the whole thing."

"Maybelle, what... what are you talking about?"

In a voice that went from shaking with tears to shaking with anger, Maybelle told Kate what had happened; from appearing in her dorm to thinking about her friend and falling through the ground.

"So, you can... you can just," Kate snapped her fingers, "and be somewhere else?"

Maybelle squinted at her friend. "Is that the most important part of this? Our own people sent us to *die*."

"Yes, but now," her friend gave her a significant look, reminiscent of the times she knew the answer to a problem long before Maybelle and was impatient for her to get it as well, "we don't have to die because *you* can get us out of here."

Maybelle blinked. "Right."

"Your eyes are back to normal by the way."

"Where are we going to go?" Maybelle realized she was on the floor and stood up. Kate followed her to the cot, and they sat side by side. Kate's warm hand still squeezed Maybelle's frozen fingers.

"Back home?" Kate frowned at her.

Maybelle frowned back. "Didn't you hear what I said? Ben sent us to die. He plans on the rebels killing us, and he doesn't care."

Kate's mouth twisted to the side, and she raised a shoulder. "It's been an exhausting, incomprehensible day. Is it possible you didn't hear things quite right? You said you were outside the room."

Maybelle clamped down on the frustration threatening to snap out of her. She couldn't blame Kate for hoping she was wrong. She hoped she was wrong. But she wasn't in the habit of doubting herself.

"I heard the words that came out of his mouth. Clear as I hear you now."

Kate shook her head and waved a hand. "That isn't really the problem, anyway. What are we going to *say* about how we got home? About... about your..."

"My eyes. My... whatever this is?"

"Your... zapping ability. I like that. Zapping." Kate met her eye with a grin before a serious note took over. "We can't tell anyone about this."

"I know."

Kate's fingers tightened around Maybelle's hand. "You know what they'll do to you."

"I know."

"I can't let that happen. We can't tell anyone."

Appreciation for this girl, this woman before her, who had endured a nightmare of a day; who had grown up in the same strict world of right and wrong, good and bad, normal and different that she had; who had been her friend so long she couldn't remember a time without her, filled her to the core. Kate wasn't afraid of her... ability. She wasn't going to turn her in when they finally went home. She would protect her, as much as she could. Tears filled Maybelle's eyes again.

She brushed them away and wrapped Kate in a hug, squeezing her until the tears stopped.

"I have a plan."

Kate raised an eyebrow.

Chapter Two

Present Day - Late Spring - Blue-Star District in Tornim

J uliana bent forward and brushed her fingers through her hair. She flipped her head back up and gave the floor length mirror a sidelong glance. She frowned and put a finger on the small gemstone pressed into her right temple. It swirled with color, rapidly switching from sunset orange to vibrant pink. Juliana faced the Coding today, and the thought made her stomach roil with anxiety and excitement.

She turned away from the mirror, gazing instead out the large window letting in the morning light. Long neon purple curtains fluttered as a light breeze drifted through the room. Beautiful, bright blues, greens, and purples coated every surface, a sharp contrast to the metallic silver which had been the fashion only a month ago.

"Hurry up so we can see your outfit!" Moniqua squealed from the chat-screen consuming the wall next to her closet.

Juliana straightened her top. Wide sleeves of sea blue went to her wrists. A long hood hung down the back; the neckline left just enough room for the birthday necklace her parents planned on giving her that night. Her pair of plain black pants ended with laced up boots.

"All right." She danced to the side, spreading her arms as she stepped out. The large screen, separated into four squares, hung from the wall. A small camera in the middle stared down at her as she did a twirl for her friends.

"It's fantasia." Moniqua tossed her black braids over her shoulder and stepped away from her camera, coming back with sage green nail polish. Brilliant blue gemstones on her temples glistened against her dark skin. Moniqua was one of the oldest in their class; she'd gone through the Coding a few months earlier.

"Agreed." Alex's red, cropped haircut jerked in and out of the screen. His homework was spread all across the bed and he kept jumping around to find some book or another to reference.

He paused for a moment to stare at the screen, his green eyes bright against his pale skin. His own gemstones glinted dark purple with blue accents, the usual color for his gems when he studied. As with everyone under twenty, his gemstones swirled in an array of colors depending on his mood. "You look wonderful."

"Thanks." Juliana moved a few boxes off her bed and sat. "Do you think I need to get my hair done?"

The handsome, square-jawed blond staring at her from the top right corner of the screen grinned. "You look amazing, I think your hair is perfect."

Heat rushed to Juliana's cheeks. "Thanks, Don."

He winked. "I've got to head out, my qualifying exam is Friday and I really need to put in some study hours. Happy birthday."

His screen went dark and Moniqua cackled wickedly.

"He likes you." She did a little dance in her chair and Juliana rolled her eyes. "But you definitely should get your hair done."

"You think?" Juliana tugged at the blond strands.

"Yes. But please make sure you go to one of the malls in Grigoria. It's honestly embarrassing going into Agora."

Alex looked up from his work and glared at the screen. "Right, because the ones who work in Agora aren't good enough to style hair." Sarcasm and disdain dripped from his voice and Moniqua straightened.

"That's not what I said. But Juliana's going to be a Blue-Star as of four o'clock today, and she needs to shop for her station."

"There is nothing wrong with a Blue-Star shopping in Agora." Alex's cheeks flushed, his eyes narrowing as his voice grew harsh.

"Friends, let's take a break." Juliana glanced at the digital readout on her desk and stood up. She needed to get going, and Alex and Moniqua weren't going to stop arguing this point anytime soon. The caste separation was a heated debate whenever the two of them got into it, and she didn't care enough to be involved in the discussion.

"Moniqua, I'll set an appointment to get my hair styled in Grigora before my event tonight. And Alex, you and I can go get celebratory sleeve temporaries tomorrow morning, in Agora. Deal?"

"Deal," Moniqua said right away. "Call me after your Star Appointment and I'll meet you. I want to add some green to the end of my braids to match my nails."

Alex sighed. "Deal." A smile broke across his face. "Have fun today, and good luck!"

Juliana gave them both a little wave and disconnected. She pocketed her card, ear-piece, and the pamphlet she'd been sent from the Star-Office, and headed to the door. Her hand rested on one of the many boxes scattered around the room. An Orange-Star was scheduled to come pack up her things after the Star Appointment. They'd move her into an apartment in the twenty to twenty-eight-year-old complex.

Her twentieth birthday felt like it had taken forever to get there, but the last week had flown by. Final exams took place two weeks before each person's birthday, and she'd aced hers. The last several days were comprised of scheduling her move, organizing the party taking place after her appointment, fending off matchmakers, and scheduling herself for classes in her preferred Blue-Star field. Tomorrow she'd start her medic courses, and in two years' time, she'd start out as a mid-level Medical in Tornim's hospital.

Juliana glanced at the holo-screen on the wall next to the door. A string of shells hung around the edges. Images of Juliana and her parents at Mendax, a resort for the top three tiers of society, flashed on the screen. They were followed by pictures of a trip much longer ago. Her parents wore less lines around their eyes, Juliana's hair done up in braids, her gemstones too big on her eight-year-old face.

Her chest tightened. Her life as a child was ending. After today she'd be an adult, officially placed in her caste and ready to live the life of a Blue-Star. It was daunting and thrilling all at once.

She danced down the polished staircase and paused on her way through the kitchen. A note and a small blue box had been left on the usually spotless counter.

Darling, sorry we couldn't spend the morning with you on such a special day. Take all our love with you to the Star Office. As well as these, for luck. – Love, Mom and Dad

She lifted the lid and let out a low gasp. Resting on a cushion of white cotton sat a pair of stunning earrings. Silver. Long and pointed at the ends with dazzling blue sapphires embedded into the metal, ten on each earring. She slid them on, the weight tugging gently at her earlobes.

With a happy sigh, she hurried out the front door. Juliana tapped a round button next to the door, calling herself a private transport, and sat on the stone bench near the street.

Her lips moved silently as she went through a list of government officials during the wait, from the governor of Tornim to the chancellor of Pangaea. A short exam took place before the Coding. Juliana didn't have access to the list of questions, but her older friends and teachers assured her that knowing the government and history of Pangaea was an important aspect.

A few minutes passed and a small grey hydro-car pulled up to the house. The driver's window rolled down and a dark-haired man glanced out. Twin orange gemstones on his temples perfectly matched his vibrant button up shirt and black tie.

"Pick up for the Foster house?"

"Yes." Juliana opened the door and rested herself comfortably in the back seat. Another thing that would change when she became an official Blue-Star, her drivers would get the door for her.

"Where to, ma'am?" A tenseness accented the driver's voice.

"The Star Office."

"Ahh." The driver glanced at her from the rearview mirror, a grin splaying across his face. "Happy birthday."

"Thank you." Juliana shifted in her seat. Nerves tingled down her arms. Only a few hours to go.

They cruised in silence. The Orange-Star expertly guided them through the lite traffic of early afternoon in the Blue-District. As they neared the center of the city the houses and yards shrank.

Juliana's home sat in the middle of the district. Wealthier homes reached farther out, approaching the wall surrounding Tornim.

A silver fence came up on their left. Three tall buildings and a maze of gardens and fountains sat comfortably within the space. A massive, ornate gate opened up on the cross street and Juliana couldn't help turning and staring as they passed it by. As of tomorrow, she'd begin her lessons at the Blue-Star technical school.

A few minutes passed and they reached the vast, wide streets of Grigoria. The Outer Market ran in a thick circle along the inner edges of the districts and completely surrounded the Inner Market, Agora.

They drove under a crimson archway, part of the wall that circled Grigoria. Multitudes of cars, hydro and solar, were parked along the sidewalks. Massive structures, built of concrete and glass, stretched several stories into the air.

Shopping centers for the higher classes opened up into gorgeous emerald-green gardens with flowers, trees, and bushes in every color of the rainbow. Research facilities, government buildings, the Black-Star training compound, and the city's hospital all claimed homes within Grigoria's borders.

The driver turned onto the main street leading to Agora when the car slowed and approached the curb.

"Why are we stopping?" Juliana demanded.

"Sorry, miss. Red-Stars." A quiver laced the driver's voice. His hand shook as he adjusted the mirror and nodded behind them.

A Red-Star patrol car parked behind them.

Juliana rolled her eyes as two men got out and sauntered over to the Orange-Star's transport. "This is ridiculous," she said. "What did you do?"

"Nothing, miss. Honest."

A tall man tapped on the driver's window. Twin red gemstones glistened from his temples. A shadow traced his jaw, and tinges of purple underlined his drooping eyes. The wrinkled uniform did nothing to improve his appearance. The second man stood near the back of the car.

The window rolled down and the driver offered up a nervous smile.

"How can I help you today, sir?"

"Where are you going?" His voice was as tired as he appeared.

"Taking this young lady to the other side of Grigoria."

The Red-Star leaned in, taking a quick look at Juliana before speaking.

"Looks like you've got a flat tire."

A loud pop sounded behind them, and the back-right corner of the car dropped several inches. Juliana jumped and turned in her seat as the second Red-Star straightened and moved to the passenger window.

The Orange-Star opened his mouth, but the man in the uniform spoke again.

"I'm afraid you'll be fined for that. And you can't drive on designated roads until you get it fixed." He pulled a handheld tablet from his belt and typed in a few numbers.

Juliana gave an audible sigh; the Orange-Star put up a hesitant hand.

"Sir, I've got a customer. I need to drive her to the Star Office."

"Ah." The Red-Star grinned and turned to leer at Juliana from the back window. "Happy birthday."

Juliana's eyebrows drew together at his mocking tone. She slid across the seat, opened the door, and stepped out of the car, coming face-to-face with the man delaying her trip.

"Thank you," sarcasm dripped from her voice, "it *was* a happy birthday, until you needlessly pulled over my transport and harassed my driver."

The cocky smile slid from his face and a hand reached toward his club.

"That's not a good tone to take with me," he growled.

Juliana's eyebrows rose incredulously. This man was forgetting one important question. Fortunately for him, his partner remembered it.

"Excuse me." The second man stepped around the front of the car and put a hand on his partner's shoulder. "What Star are your parents?"

Juliana leaned back on one foot, put a hand on her hip, and flashed her biggest, brightest, and bitchiest smile. "Blue."

Both men took a step back.

"Our apologies, miss," the partner said.

Juliana sighed and shook her head. "Maybe next time do some actual patrol work. And verify people's class before you delay them." She leaned over the driver's window.

A bead of sweat clung to the man's face. He gave her a weak smile. "I'm terribly sorry about the inconvenience, miss."

"I'll walk from here. And I'll call another transport for my return trip. I expect at least half a refund since you didn't manage to get me to the Star Office in the first place."

"Of course, Miss Foster. My apologies."

Juliana turned from the car to find both Red-Stars still gawking at her. She shook her head, brushed a hand through her hair, and marched away down the street toward Agora.

"May we offer you a ride?" one of the Red-Stars shouted after her.

She ignored them.

Only a few minutes passed before Agora loomed ahead of her. A brick wall, as tall as a house, surrounded Agora, separating it from the rest of the city. Four large archways, one for each direction on a compass, rested above ornate twisting metal gates the color of rusted iron. The gates stood open for the public from the early hours of the morning to late at night.

Purple-Stars lived here, many above the restaurants, shops, salons, and cafés they owned, still others in little houses scattered throughout the district.

A Red-Star stood on either side of the Southgate as Juliana walked through, her head held high. The streets here were smaller, more intricate, and less refined. Most people parked their cars along the outer edge. Many of the inner alleys were cobblestone or too small for modern vehicles. Only the main roads, connecting the gates in an X through the market, were large enough to drive down.

Moniqua may not enjoy shopping in the Inner Market, but Juliana couldn't get enough of it. Every color gemstone entered Agora. It was the only place in the city to find the freshest food, newest trends, and the most beautiful architecture.

Concrete and glass made rare appearances in Agora. Most of the buildings sang of the old world. Brick and decorative woodwork laced throughout the short structures, none more than three or four stories high.

Juliana strolled down the street, winding her way through the bustle of people doing their shopping. A stall rested on either side of an outdoor seating space for a small café. One was covered in colorful scarves, the other displaying a new design for summer sandals. As with most shopkeepers in Agora, the owners had purple gemstones on each temple. On the other side of the small road an old man offered passersby cups of freshly squeezed juice. A girl, likely in the green or orange class, sang in a loud, ringing voice, as a tall woman dropped a few trading coins into an upturned pink, flowery hat.

A hundred smells assaulted Juliana's nose as she moved farther into Agora. The scent of freshly baked bread wafted out an open door. Sizzling meat sent flurries of crispy, spiced smoke through the air. Juliana paused at an intersection, one smell eclipsing the rest.

Down the alley to her left was a small stall; an elderly woman with purple gemstones sat on a wobbly stool behind the table. Sticky buns, coated in a white, lemony smelling glaze, sent tendrils of steam rising into the air.

Juliana turned and let the scent guide her forward. A plump woman stood in front of the stand; a black and orange bug barrette pinned back her brown hair.

Matching orange gemstones on her temples glimmered against the sunlight. A gaggle of children clustered around her. Tiny fingers grasped at the table as she continually smacked them away.

The elderly Purple-Star passed her a box and the woman turned away, the children close on her tail.

Juliana stepped up, admiring the small square cloths hanging from the edges of the stand. They fluttered in the breeze. A trio of black birds flew against different colored backgrounds on each piece.

The old woman smiled at Juliana; crooked front teeth set off her aging face.

"What can I get for you?"

Juliana closed her eyes and breathed deep through her nose. She grinned and pointed to a particularly glazy roll. "One of those looks delicious, please."

The woman rolled up her sleeves and gently set the roll in a box. A tattoo on her left wrist caught Juliana's gaze. A mountain, encircled by a thin purple line.

"Anything to drink, dear?"

Juliana returned her focus to the food. "Umm, yes. Do you have any coffee? I need a jolt of energy."

"Of course." She poured a slow, thick stream of the rich caffeine into a small cup and handed it and the box to Juliana.

Juliana paid with a few coins she'd tucked into her pockets and turned away, strolling down the street to find a place to sit. Juliana picked an outdoor table at a quint midday restaurant on the corner and sat down. She pulled out the roll and licked the glaze off her fingers.

She ate the bun slowly, pealing the layers into thin strips. The coffee brought a wave of warmth through her chest every time she took a sip. The chill of the late spring afternoon sent an occasional shiver down her spine.

A few friends stopped by, to say hi or wish her luck. After what seemed like no time at all, she stood, placed the box and cup in a recycle container on the street, and made her way to the far side of Agora.

As she neared the Star Office, a nervous pounding pressed against her stomach. She tapped her fingers against her thumb, one after another back and forth.

She stepped through the Northgate into Grigoria and there it was. The building was dark, a stark contrast to the white, tan, and glass which towered above on either side.

A narrow set of stone steps led her to a pair of black double doors. A stoic Red-Star stood to the left of the entrance, his arms folded, a thin line where a smile might have been. Juliana showed him the pamphlet and he opened the door for her.

Dim lights hung from the ceiling. Uncomfortable looking maroon chairs and benches lined the edges of the long, rectangular room. Even more filled the middle, running in rows facing each other. Over a dozen people sat, scattered around the furniture, some in groups of two or three, and a few alone. Six holo-screens hung from the walls, advertisements flashing silently across them.

A set of seven windows made up the right-hand wall. Bright signs atop each window announced which class they served. A family of four stood at the Green-Star window, the parents eagerly urging their son to the front. Juliana made her way down to the third window from the end.

Blue-Stars.

A large woman sat on the other side of the glass. Orange gemstones shone from her temples. A pair of oversized front teeth jutted out past her bottom lip. Straight, plain brown hair hung just above her shoulders, accentuating the width of her neck. A tablet sat propped up on the desk; her short round fingers poked at the glass.

Juliana waited in front of the window for a moment. When the woman didn't seem to see her, she tapped a finger on the glass.

Only the woman's eyes moved, glancing up briefly before looking back at her screen. She held up one finger, her nail protruding like a pink tinged turret.

Juliana sighed and leaned back, resting her weight on her left leg. The longer she waited the more nervous she felt. Her fingers tapped back and forth against her thumb. Finally, the window opened and the woman gestured her forward.

"Welcome to the Star Office. Thank you for responding to your summons in a timely manner."

Juliana gritted her teeth at the woman's nasally voice. She handed over her pamphlet.

"You are reminded to leave any and all electronics at the front window." She looked up at Juliana. "That's with me."

Juliana nodded, lips tight.

"You will first take the standard exam, then an aptitude test, and lastly, we will administer the Coding. Each of these processes is very important and it's vital for you to do your best at each step. Please hand over electronics, then sit and wait." She squinted. "Those might interfere with the process." She pointed to Juliana's ears.

Juliana passed over her card and ear-piece, removed her earrings and tucked them into her pants pocket, and then moved to the far end of the room. A series of doors opposite the entrance led back into the main sections of the Star Office.

Juliana breathed deep. She leaned against the stiff chair and closed her eyes, attempting to relax.

A giggle broke her concentration.

She opened an eye to find a young woman sitting in the chair across from her. A pair of dazzling gemstones flashed on her temples, changing color from bright pink to sunset orange. Juliana self-consciously put a finger to her own gems, wondering if their color changed as rapidly.

"Hello." The girl's bright voice echoed through the quiet room. It rang with enthusiasm.

Juliana offered a tentative smile. These were the final moments before she became a Blue-Star. She had to be wary of who she associated with. Being too friendly with anyone from the lower classes could impede her future.

"Hello," she responded, her voice neutral.

"I'm so excited. It feels like this day took forever getting here. Are your parents coming by?" She glanced around the room, as though she expected them to appear through a wall. "My parents are coming in a few minutes. They should be finishing up at the Separation Seminar."

"No." Juliana's eyebrows drew together in annoyance. Some people brought their parents to hold their hands through the Coding. She wasn't a child anymore; she didn't need anyone walking her through life.

"Oh." Her face drooped. "Sorry, I'm really excited."

At the disappearance of the girl's smile, Juliana took a deep breath. "No, I'm sorry. I don't mean to be rude. I'm... nervous."

The girl grinned again. "What caste are you expecting?"

"Blue." The word brought contentment to Juliana's mind and a smile to her lips.

"Woah. I've never spoken to a Blue-Star in person before."

Juliana's smile widened. "What about you?"

"My whole family is Red-Stars. My mom is an emergency medical helper, and my dad works a patrol."

Juliana nodded. "Red isn't too bad."

"Yeah." She shook her head. "I don't really want to be one though. I'd prefer being a Purple-Star."

Juliana's face pinched in a frown. "You'd rather drop a caste than be a Red-Star?"

"Well, it's not that far of a drop, just one class. I really don't fit in with my family. I've never wanted to do anything in the Red-Star bracket. I've always loved the markets though. I think I could really excel as a Purple-Star."

"You'd never excel as far as the lowest Red-Star, though." Juliana shook her head.

She nodded, looking away. "It's not as big for us, the lower classes. You know, unless—"

"You won't be able to see your family," Juliana interrupted. "You won't live in the same district. It's incredibly unlikely you'll be in a different caste than your parents. Unless you did something insane." Juliana's voice grew harsh. Frustration at this girl's naivety caused her hands to shake.

The girl glanced over at her. "I don't mean any offense here, but you wouldn't understand. Blue-Stars have a wide range of possible career choices. Red-Stars don't." Her right shoulder lifted in an apologetic shrug. "I'd be happy as a Purple-Star. Honestly," she shook her head, gazing at the far wall, "as long as I don't get White-Star, I probably won't mind."

Juliana's eyes widened and a gasp escaped her lips. She stood and walked away, picking a new seat across of the room.

It was foolish to even mention the White-Stars on a day like this. To be Coded as a White-Star, a Moon, an Undesirable...

A shudder went through her shoulders and down her spine at the thought. It was unfathomable to her that someone would want to be Coded into a lower caste.

That girl was exactly the sort of person Moniqua constantly warned her about. She shook her head again and focused her gaze on the holo-screen pressed into the right wall.

Images flashed across it, advertising full body celebratory tattoos, matchmaking companies for each district, places to buy hydro and solar-cars, and custom Home-Artificials.

People filtered in and out of the waiting room. A large family took up a corner for a few minutes, before the twin twenty-year-old boys were called back to go through their appointment. They returned almost forty-five minutes later, both beaming, wearing matching green gemstones. Their father, still in his saw-dusty work clothes, grasped them both in a tight hug before they made their way out.

The girl across the way went in. She glanced at Juliana as she said goodbye to her parents.

Still Juliana waited. Her fingers fidgeted. Her foot tapped on the ground. It wasn't supposed to take this long.

Another hour passed, and the girl returned from her appointment. Her parents stood quickly and went to her, joy on their faces. Glistening red gemstones shone from each temple. Her body trembled; red streaks crossed her pale face where she'd rubbed her eyes.

Finally, a warm, female voice called Juliana's name.

Juliana rose and strode to the open door. She froze at the sight of the tall, thin woman waiting for her in the doorway.

Grey gemstones, the color of monstrous thunder clouds, glimmered on her temples. Juliana's eyes widened and her legs stopped working for a second.

"Hello," she managed. A small, nervous smile crossed her lips.

The woman took a step back, letting Juliana enter the small corridor. A wave of bliss hit her as the door closed. It flowed over her head, crashing onto her shoulders and rushing through to her feet. Concern melted away as she stared at the Grey-Star.

She appeared to be in her late forties or fifties. A calm, nonchalant smile pressed laugh lines up, onto her high cheekbones. Grey eyes, matching the gemstones, held a kind warmth that spread to Juliana. Her hair was pinned up in a loose bun, wisps of black and grey falling down around her face.

A loud click broke Juliana's trance. The door latched into place, and the feeling diminished. Juliana's nerves returned, anxiety quickening her heartbeat.

"My name is Ms. Wolfe."

Juliana's nerves settled like waves after a storm, calming once again at the Grey-Star's voice. She exhaled, a smile crossing her face.

"It's an honor to meet you, ma'am."

Ms. Wolfe's eyes glinted; the warmth flickered for a moment. It returned just as quickly. The woman put a hand on Juliana's shoulder and smiled down at her.

"Follow me, dear. Let's get you going."

Juliana nodded and did as she was told, keeping close on Wolfe's heels as they clicked down the tile floor. They passed through another door and into a cold room with a simple table and chair. A screen, pressed into the table, illuminated the room with the words Standard Exam.

Wolfe nodded to the chair and Juliana sat. She cast a wobbly smile at Wolfe, who returned it with one exuding comfort.

Off-white walls with pale pink trim closed in around her. A small door on the opposite side of the room opened and a plump, kind-looking attendant with orange gemstones jostled in.

She caught sight of Wolfe and paused, a nervous chuckle rushing from her lips.

"Oh, hello, ma'am."

Wolfe smiled, and the woman's shoulders dropped. Her anxious, tight lips relaxed into a serene grin.

"I... I need to administer the standard exam," the Orange-Star said.

Wolfe nodded.

"It shouldn't take too long." The attendant turned her attention to Juliana. "Just highlight the bubble you think is right; don't leave any blank. The questions are basic, and they are not dependent on caste."

"All right." Juliana straightened in her chair, confidence returning. She'd studied for this.

"You have removed your ear-piece and card?"

"Yes."

"Do you have any other outside electronic or Artificial devices?"

"No."

"Excellent. Then we shall begin." The attendant left the room.

Wolfe leaned in and whispered, "Good luck," before following, closing the door with a click behind her.

A shiver went through Juliana. She looked down and pulled all her focus to the test.

Who was responsible for saving Pangaea from the plague?

- *Grey-Stars.*

How did the current Chancellor ascend to the position?

- *Jackie Collette stepped into the role of Chancellor, coming from an advisor position, after her husband died.*

How many members of Congress serve Pangaea?

- *Two for every city and two for the Capital, or 22.*

Juliana went through the fifty questions and leaned back in her chair with a self-satisfied smile. Moniqua finished the standard in thirty minutes, it only took Juliana twenty-six.

The door popped open, and Wolfe's heels clicked into the room.

"How did it go?"

Juliana stood and grinned hopefully at the Grey-Star. "I did well. None of my friends finished as quickly."

Wolfe's long fingers wrapped around her arm and gave a light squeeze. "Let's find out your score."

Juliana's gaze caught on the storm of grey pressed against Wolfe's temples. A hint of unease went through her gut. She cleared her throat.

"I don't..." She bit her lip. "I greatly appreciate your presence at this important time, but I'd be remiss not to ask why I'm being graced by your escort."

A light laugh, bubbled up from the Grey-Star's lips.

"Juliana, you have to know you're someone we'd pay attention to. You have some of the highest marks of your year. You come from powerful stock. I run an exclusive research facility and I hope to work with you in the future."

Any anxiety within Juliana evaporated. Pride welled in her.

"Well done!" The attendant returned, bouncing into the room with a bright grin. "You didn't miss a single question. And you finished so fast, almost a record."

Juliana's smile grew. One step of the appointment done, only three more and she'd be a Blue-Star.

"On to the blood test." Wolfe opened the second door and marched down a new corridor.

Juliana hurried behind.

The blood testing room boasted rose colored walls and plush gel-chairs. A male attendant with cropped black hair and red gemstones stood to the side. A metallic smell filled Juliana's nostrils, leaving a coppery taste in her mouth. She sucked on her tongue to get rid of the flavor.

"Welcome." The attendant gave them a pleasant grin and gestured to the chairs. "Please, have a seat." He turned to Wolfe. "Is there anything I can get you?"

"No, thank you. I'm simply here to escort Miss Foster through her appointment."

He nodded, confusion flashing across his face before he turned back to Juliana. "This is a basic portion of the process. It won't take very long. We ask that you try to relax."

Juliana bobbed her head up and down, nerves tying up her tongue despite the confidence she'd felt only moments before. She bunched up the wave of fabric cascading down her arm and rested her bare skin against the side of the chair.

The attendant cleansed her skin, then pierced the pale flesh with a needle and waited patiently as blood flooded a small vial.

"All done." He removed the needle and wiped her skin with a small cloth. A dot of healing ointment followed, and as he rubbed it into her arm the pinprick from the needle disappeared.

Juliana stood. Her vision went spotty for a moment. She rested a hand on the chair, steadying herself before standing straight.

Wolfe waited at the door, a calm smile on her lips. Juliana followed her out, thanking the man on the way. The two of them clicked and padded down the hall. Wolfe in her heels, Juliana in her low boots.

They stopped outside an orange door.

"Aptitude test," Wolfe said. "Next step is the Coding."

Juliana inhaled. "And then I'm a Blue-Star."

Wolfe tilted her head a fraction to the side, and then turned and opened the door. The room was similar to the standard exam room. A Red-Star attendant waited inside. He nodded to Wolfe and offered her a seat in the next room, then turned to Juliana.

"Welcome, this is the last step before the Coding. Make sure you take your time and complete every question. There are no correct answers; use your best judgement. The questions will be used after the Coding to determine the best career for you in whichever caste you are placed."

"Blue," Juliana whispered under her breath. An ear-to-ear grin spread across her face. She was so close.

"Good luck."

Juliana bowed her head and stared at the screen.

If a pre-Coded person is found having sexual relations, what do you do?

Juliana filled in the obvious answer: immediately inform the authorities.

What is the best response to discovering a family member, or friend, has been Coded as a White-Star?

Juliana shuddered. The answer to this one also came easily. You cut them from your life, destroy all pictures and any evidence of their being. You pretend they never existed. It was a nightmare possibility for every twenty-year-old.

If a lower caste is found loitering in one of the top three districts, what is the best response?

Simple, you put in a call to a Red-Star patrol and they handle it.

Similar questions followed, then a few puzzles and mind games. Juliana solved them all with ease. Fifteen minutes flew by. Then the time was up; the questions were done. The Coding was next.

The door opened. Wolfe clicked into the room, her eyes on a tablet in her hands.

"Interesting answers." She slid her finger up the glass, her gaze scanning the words.

Juliana swallowed, a flood of nerves thundering in her stomach.

Wolfe's grey eyes met hers and another wave of calm coated her skin, soothing down the little hairs which had been standing on end. "Time for the final step. Let's get you where you belong."

Juliana nodded, her lips tight together.

They moved down yet another corridor; this one had white lights above white walls above white tile. A black door awaited them at the end.

Wolfe remained a comforting presence behind her as she pulled the door open. A round room greeted her. A sheet of black glass, a window to the observation room, made up a third of the wall. The crisscross grated floor clanked with each step.

In the middle of the room a massive, metallic chair sat heavy and bolted to the ground. Juliana took a tentative step, her legs shaking. Excitement drained from her mind, leaving fear and anxiety in its wake.

A short, dark-skinned Blue-Star attendant joined them from a second door. She nodded politely to Wolfe, and then gestured to the chair.

"Please, have a seat."

Juliana's lips trembled as she attempted to smile at the woman. She made her way to the chair and sat. Clamps snapped over her wrists and ankles. She inhaled sharply and the attendant put a hand on her arm.

"I know it is unsettling. But the Coding is a quick process. Make sure you stay as still as possible."

Juliana nodded and cleared her throat. She didn't speak, but the excitement returned, fighting against her nerves.

"Remember, be still." The Blue-Star's silky-smooth voice brought a drop of comfort to Juliana. The woman turned and opened the door for Wolfe.

The Grey-Star smiled again at Juliana before turning and clicking into the other room. The attendant followed, leaving Juliana alone.

She closed her eyes, pushing away the fear and focusing instead on what would come tomorrow. The new apartment, the new classes, the start of her life.

Blood pounded in her ears as the chair rose into the air. A metal clamp went across her chest. The chill of it went through the fabric of her shirt. She shuddered.

Whirring sounded from above. A large machine lowered from the ceiling, needles extending from either side. It dropped down, coming to a stop directly above her head. The needles slid close, the tips pressing against her gemstones.

Her body trembled even as she held as still as possible. She gritted her teeth at the pressure on her temples. Shallow breaths slid through her lips as her chest shuddered with each passing second.

"Blue," she chanted, closing her eyes and barely opening her mouth as she repeated the word over and over.

The whirring stopped. The needles slid from her gemstones. The chair sank back to the ground, and the clamp over her chest returned to its original position. Her heart swelled. It was done. Her smile was impossible to stop.

She moved to stand, but the clamps around her wrists and ankles remained in place. The door behind her opened.

"Finally," she sang, shimmying her shoulders. "Let's get these restraints off so I can go celebrate!" She cast a grin at the attendant, but her smile faltered as she saw the woman's face.

Horror filled the woman's wide brown eyes. Fingers pressed against the top lip of her open mouth. A few seconds passed in silence before the horror turned into something else. Something closer to hate.

"What is it?" A weight settled on Juliana's chest.

"Oh," Wolfe approached from behind the attendant, a mournful furrow between her brows and sadness in her gaze. "I'm so sorry, dear."

Juliana shook her head. "No."

The Blue-Star moved in front of her and held up a mirror.

A scream ripped through Juliana's throat as her gaze caught the reflection of two pearly white gemstones pressed into her temples.

She was a Moon.

Chapter Three

Present Day - Late Spring - The Star Office in Grigoria

There was a speck on the wall. Not a speck, a scratch. A place where the paint was peeling away from the surface beneath. Juliana stared at it, at the tinge of grey peaking from behind the russet paint, curling at the edges.

She was unmoving. Frozen. If she didn't move, time didn't move. If time didn't move, maybe she wouldn't be taken from the room. She wouldn't be put in the car. She wouldn't be taken to the wall, and then to the camp. If time didn't move, maybe it was a dream.

Maybe none of this was real.

She hadn't spoken a word. Not a single syllable to bring realism to this nightmare. Her skin tingled. Buzzing filled her ears. Silence filled her mind and heart. Silence and disbelief.

The door slammed open. Juliana blinked. Time continued on.

She'd sat alone in the small office for over an hour. Now, a muscular man in a too-large suit shuffled in, duffle bag in his hands.

He tossed the bag onto the desk; its brass buckles clunked against the wood. He stared hard at Juliana. Red gemstones glistened from his temples. Dark, stringy hair receded toward the back of his head. The oversized cuffs of his jacket hung down to the middle of his sausage-like fingers.

She bowed her head, letting her long blonde hair cover the pearly white gemstones imbedded in her temples.

"Are you listening?"

His harsh, grating voice startled her. She nodded fervently.

"Good. As a White-Star, you will be sent to your district tonight. Your parents have been notified."

Heat rushed to her cheeks as shame filled her.

"They will bring whatever clothing you need. Any items you take need to fit in this bag. No electronic devices or Artificials are allowed in the *camp*."

Juliana flinched at the word.

"Your parents will be here in a few minutes. You'll have fifteen minutes to say goodbye. Assuming they wish to see you."

Icy fear sliced through her chest. What if they didn't want to see her? It wasn't unheard of for parents of a Moon to drop off their belongings and get as far away from the Star Office as possible.

"Please," panic sent a tremor through her voice, "there's been some kind of mistake. I'm not—"

"Quiet. I don't want to hear it. You're a White-Star. Stand."

Her breath caught. She blinked away the tears threatening to spill from her eyes. Heat drove out the ice in her chest, giving her the courage to speak again. "There was a Grey-Star, Ms. Wolfe; I need to speak to her."

The man's lip curled in incredulous disgust. "A Grey-Star, talk to you? Absurd. Now, stand up."

Juliana obeyed, her movements stiff as she took the bag and followed the man out the door and down the dark hallway.

They entered a small room. A set of thick black couches sat in the center, a plain wooden table between them. Additional Red-Stars held position on either side of the door. They stared at Juliana as she walked by, and she ducked her head again.

"Sit." The man glared at her, and a shiver went down her back. She sat, bunching up the bag in her lap.

The Red-Star left, saying something unintelligible to the guards in the hallway. The door clicked closed. Muffled voices and laughter sounded from the other side. Juliana pinched her eyes shut and shook her head.

This wasn't happening. This wasn't real. She'd wake up. She'd wake up to Moniqua calling her, yelling at her for not getting up early on the day of her appointment. Alex would join the call. They would talk and laugh and make plans for the next few weeks. She'd talk to Don. They'd go on a few dates.

Tears flowed from her eyes, cascading down her cheeks and dripping off her chin. Her breath came in short bursts.

This wasn't right.

A new set of voices sounded behind her.

She turned as the door opened again. A tall woman entered. Her pale blue eyes were red and puffy around the edges. Immaculate lipstick matched the purple streaks in her cropped blond hair. A nose ring connected a small golden chain to a tiny magnet on her blue gemstone. She caught sight of Juliana and gasped.

Juliana stood; fear stopped her from running to her mother. Her fingers trembled, eyes burning. Then her father stepped forward, a wobbly version of his jovial smile in place. A large bag hung from his shoulder. "Hey, sweetie." He winked at her.

She went to them, falling into her mother's arms and burying her head into her shoulder as the tears continued to flow. After a moment they made their way to the couches.

"I don't understand," Juliana whimpered into her mother's shirt. "How did this happen?"

"Oh honey," her father ran his hand up and down her arm, "I'm so sorry. This isn't right. This shouldn't be—"

"Henry," Juliana's mother snapped. Her icy gaze darted to the open door.

Henry moved to close it.

A Red-Star on the other side took a step toward him. "I'm sorry, sir. But you can't shut this door."

"Why the *nacra* not?"

Juliana glanced up, eyes wide. Her father, a short, happy man with dirty blonde hair and a nonchalant smile, rarely cursed.

"Well, sir, that is..." the taller man stammered. Brown eyes glanced at the glistening blue gemstones on Henry's temples.

The Red-Star's partner came to his rescue. "She's dangerous, sir. A Moon, you know."

Henry was a genius of a man who often forgot to take off his lab coat before leaving work. He enjoyed muffins more than cupcakes and tea more than coffee. He stood a head shorter than his wife and had distanced himself so fully from his familial history of a short temper that Juliana had difficulty remembering a time she'd actually seen him angry.

At the Red-Star's words, Henry's eyes narrowed. His shoulders drew back, and an invisible force seemed to sweep through the room. As the men before him drew themselves back and away from his wrath, he seemed to tower over them.

"I am a Blue-Star of the Foster family. My work guarantees your caste medical help when you deal with actual criminals. *Not* people like my daughter." Henry's voice softened to a hiss as he took a step toward them, his hand on the edge of the door. "I will do as I please in saying goodbye to my only child. And *you* will stay out of my way. Your supervisor will receive a formal complaint for your tone when speaking to a superior. You're lucky I'm not the kind of man who would demand you lose your job."

He slammed the door in their faces.

"Why did this happen?" Juliana muttered as her father rejoined them on the couch. "I never did anything wrong. I've been good."

"Marissa?" Henry glanced at his wife.

She sat with her arm looped around Juliana's. Pain radiated from her features, but her lips were pressed together in a thin line, the muscles in her jaw tight under her skin.

"We don't have long, love." Henry put a hand on her knee. "You want to start?"

Marissa sucked in a breath through clenched teeth. Juliana looked from one to the other, confusion etched across her face.

"Our family has dealt with this before," Marissa murmured, barely opening her mouth. Her cheek twitched in something close to a wince.

"What do you mean?" Juliana frowned.

"I had a sister. A twin sister." A tight smile crossed her mother's lips. "We were incredibly close. We set our appointments at the same time. I became a Blue-Star immediately. She... she came out a White-Star."

A cold weight set in Juliana's chest. "You never said... I didn't know I had an aunt."

"You don't," Marissa snapped.

Juliana's bottom lip quivered.

"*Marissa.*" Henry frowned at his wife, then took his daughter's hand and met her eyes. "It's not because she became a White-Star. It's because she died. In the camp, a few years after their birthday."

Marissa sniffed and Juliana leaned into her mother's side.

"Why are you telling me this?" Juliana asked. "Did you find a way to get her out? Before she died?"

Henry shook his head, sadness in his eyes. "No. There is no way out of the camp. When you are there," he swallowed, "you are there for life."

Juliana's body shook. Her mother squeezed her tighter.

"Then why?" she said through gritted teeth.

"Brenna was always the one to make friends." Marissa kissed Juliana's forehead. "I hope you can find some of them. Maybe they can keep you safe."

"They didn't keep her safe." Juliana sat up, grasping her father's hand in a panic. "How did she die?"

"We don't know." Henry patted her hand.

"So, there's nothing." Juliana glanced at each of them, hope dying inside her. "There's nothing you can do? I thought maybe... I thought maybe it was all a mistake. Maybe they got it wrong." Her shoulders went forward, her chest contracted as all the air left her body. Her jaw clenched. She took a sharp breath through her nose, releasing it with a shudder.

"No, sweetie." Henry looked down, studying the floor. "There's nothing we can do. They don't make mistakes like this."

Juliana nodded. The buzzing had returned to her ears. She cleared her throat. She stared at the small table in the middle, examining the surface, taking in each scratch and dent. A thought sparked across her mind.

"There was a Grey-Star."

Her parents looked at her.

"A woman, at the Coding, Ms. Wolfe. I don't know her first name. But she said she was there because she wanted to work with me in the future."

Henry frowned and Marissa's brow furrowed as she bit the edge of her lip.

"I thought... maybe..." Juliana glanced from one parent to the other and back.

Marissa squeezed her hand. "We'll look into it. But I don't..." She swallowed and gave Henry a pained look.

"We wouldn't want to get your hopes up, Jules. Or our own."

Juliana sniffed and nodded.

They sat in silence. The minutes passed like seconds, Juliana cuddled between her parents like a child who'd had a nightmare. Like a child still going through the nightmare.

"Thank you for coming. To say goodbye." Juliana's lips barely moved.

"Of course." Marissa lifted her chin with two fingers. "You are our daughter. Of course we came."

"Even though I'm... a Moon." Heat rushed to her cheeks. Fury and embarrassment raced across her flushed skin.

Henry sighed. "It doesn't matter how many Separation Seminars we go to, Jules. You will always be our daughter. And we will always love you."

Marissa pulled over the large bag they had brought and removed clothes and supplies from it, shoving them into the tan bag on the table. Each piece of fabric caught Juliana's eye. They were dark, dull, not the normal bright colors she wore. Her throat caught as her hairbrush and toothbrush followed a pair of rolled up socks into the bag. Not everything fit.

Henry pulled a blue box, wrapped with a white bow, from his pocket and handed it to Juliana.

"This was for your celebration."

In the box sat a beautiful, ornate silver locket. The letter J, surrounded by roses, was etched into the front. Juliana opened it, and a holographic image of her parents smiled up at her. She shook, tears spilling once more.

Henry took the locket from her and latched it around her neck, gently pulling her hair through the chain so it sat comfortably on her chest.

"It's almost time," Marissa said, buckling up the bag and handing it to Juliana. Someone knocked on the door.

Juliana's eyes went wide, and her chest pounded. "No. We have more time. This can't be it."

Her parents stood and Juliana stood with them. Her voice was high, hands trembling with panic. "This isn't right. This isn't what was supposed to happen."

"We know." Henry blinked, tears dripping from his eyes.

They pulled her to them and held her close. The door opened. Juliana bit back sobs as Red-Stars took her arms. They pried her away. The blurred image of her parents, both shedding distraught tears, stuck in her mind as the Red-Stars dragged her from the room. She didn't struggle; her limp hands clung to the strap of her bag.

They took her down a hallway, out a door, and into the frigid spring night.

Orbs dangled above the sidewalks, lighting the way for the few people still out and about. Juliana gazed up at one, caught in the sparkle of its light.

A van idled on the side of the road. The Red-Stars marched her to it, opened the back door, and shoved her inside.

A spark of fury ignited her limbs. She yanked her arms away from the men. Turning to gracefully take her seat, she glared at them in silence.

A young man climbed into the driver's seat. Orange gemstones were barely visible on his temples. A tattoo Artificial in the shape of a howling wolf obscured much of his right cheek and forehead. Frizzy bright green hair covered his head.

One of the Red-Stars sat in the passenger seat, another climbed into the back and sat facing Juliana. She gritted her teeth and sat rigid against the rough fabric, clenching her bag in her lap like a lifeline.

They drove, rumbling along the smooth streets of Grigoria. After a short time, they passed under the arch to the Orange-Star district. The roads deteriorated, shaking the van more and more as they approached the wall.

All of Tornim was enclosed by a wall, but the section which bordered the camp was higher, thicker, and designed to keep White-Stars from entering the city. Juliana had seen it from a distance whenever the family left the city for a vacation. But she'd never entered the Orange-Star district; she'd never seen it up close.

The darkness of the concrete was accentuated by the growing night. A street separated the Wall from the homes in the district. The van parked in front of the houses. Juliana didn't move.

"Out." The driver glared at her in the mirror.

A heavy, angry sigh escaped Juliana's clenched teeth. She jerked on the handle and stepped out of the van, slinging her bag across her shoulder.

The Red-Stars moved in on either side of her. One grabbed her upper arm and pulled her forward.

"I don't need help walking," she snapped.

He stared at her for a moment, then squeezed her arm uncomfortably tight and continued across the street. She bit back a whimper.

Four more Red-Stars stood by a small brick guard house built into the side of the wall. A tall woman with midnight skin, flowing braids, and a small glass tablet in her hands seemed to be the one in charge. She typed a note into it as Juliana and her escort approached.

When they came to a stop, the Red-Star's grip on her arm loosened. She wrenched free and straightened her sleeve.

"Juliana Foster?" one of the men asked.

Juliana nodded, untucking a lock of hair from behind her ear and maneuvering it to cover her temple.

"No Artificials in the camp," the tall woman said, glancing at Juliana's bag.

"There aren't any. It's clothes and a hairbrush."

Someone grabbed the bag and yanked it roughly off her shoulder. She took a step toward him, but another Red-Star shoved her back. He hit the same shoulder and she winced.

"That's mine," she growled through gritted teeth.

"We have to check it. Moons aren't known for telling the truth." The one who shoved her, a short man with a black beard, smirked.

He and another Red-Star dropped the bag and opened it, tossing her clothes across the ground. Her nostrils flared, jaw locked, fingernails digging into her palms. Embarrassment churned in her stomach. Helplessness she'd never experienced encompassed her body.

"It's clean." The bearded man looked up at the woman.

She nodded and glanced at Juliana. "Get your things."

Angry tears threatened to overcome Juliana as she bent and shoved the last pieces of her old life back into the bag. She stood, pulling the strap onto her shoulder with a pained grimace. The woman gestured to the wall and Juliana followed her, head down in case her tears escaped.

They paused at the brick building. The woman typed a note into her tablet, and then turned and looked Juliana up and down.

Her gaze paused at Juliana's neckline.

"What is that?"

Juliana's hand leapt to her throat, clutching the locket tightly. "A necklace."

The woman took a step and grabbed the chain, yanking it from Juliana's grasp. The metal ripped at her neck as it broke apart. Juliana's eyes blazed with fury.

"Give it back." She lunged forward and grabbed at the locket.

The same bearded Red-Star jammed his palm against her shoulder again. She stumbled to the side, missing the chain by inches.

The woman turned away and clicked the locket open.

Juliana wiped her eyes furiously. "It's not an Artificial." Her voice cracked. "I want it back."

"Get used to wanting things you won't get."

Juliana's hands trembled. Her jaw clenched so tight her teeth hurt. Her breath came in short, ragged, bursts. Tears burned behind her eyes, but she did not let them spill.

Someone grabbed her by the elbow and led her to the center of the wall. They pressed a paper into her hand.

Rumbling filled the air. A crack appeared in the wall, a seam which grew as two sections of concrete slid apart to reveal a narrow walkway. The darkness of the night was overshadowed by the overwhelming black of the entrance.

Juliana swallowed, and a breath of fear escaped her lips.

"Go on, then," a voice behind her snapped.

The muscles in her legs refused to respond. A hand on her lower back propelled her forward. She stepped into the black. A shiver flew across her skin; inside the wall was several degrees colder than the air outside. She took another step. Loud rumbling sounded again as the door behind her slid shut.

She was alone in the dark.

Fear flooded her, clenching at her chest and clawing at her legs. She dragged her feet across the ground, inching, bit by bit, forward.

After a few feet she stopped. When she closed her eyes, the darkness was the same. Tears streamed down her cheeks. Her fingers clutched at the smooth walls on either side. The cold concrete seemed to crawl up her arms and into her chest.

Maybe she should stay here.

Disappear in the wall.

Fade into nothing.

Ahead of her was a grating, crunching sound. A crack of light appeared, a line in the wall. Whispers of wind swirled around her. She took a shuddering breath and clambered to her feet.

Juliana made her way forward as the door inched open. Harsh light burned her eyes, the brilliant white of it reminding her just how far she'd fallen.

Chapter Four

Present Day - Mid Summer - Agora- Inner Market of Tornim

A red ceramic mug held dark, rich liquid; steam rose in perfect waves from its surface. Sticky sweet, with just enough bitterness to keep it drinkable, this was Chogan's favorite place to order hot chocolate. He raised the mug to his lips, puffed a gentle bit of air onto the still surface, and watched the miniature ripples of sweetness sweep out before sipping a sizeable mouthful.

Warmth seeped down his throat, the temperature spreading as it settled in his stomach. The café was chilly, the vents strategically placed along the ceiling overcompensating for the hot summer day.

Cho smiled up at the waitress, who'd just brought over his bagel and drink, and passed over three of the coins his brother had given him.

The smile, and the money, caused a shift in the emotions emanating from her. Tension, which had tugged at Cho's mind since he'd entered the café and ordered his treat, eased. Tendrils of pleasure settled around him. His smile shifted, eased into something more genuine as the woman returned to her post behind the counter at the far end of the little building.

Cho leaned back into his booth. Pleasure was not a particularly specific emotion. He sighed, the momentary relaxation lapsing back into his usual state of anxiety. He flicked a strand of black hair away from his forehead and glared at the hot chocolate.

As far as bribes go, it was a good one. His brother knew him well. They didn't have the money for this sort of thing very often and one of the few aspects Cho missed about his old life were the weekly hot chocolates their mother used to make. It was just about the only thing that could have convinced him to leave the safety of their group and practice his ability in a public place with no safety net.

Cho's sharp gaze darted around. The waitress wiped down the front counter with a grey cloth, then moved to put out more pastries. A couple sat at a round, mosaic table near the door. They both wore thick pants, a leather bag of tools on the ground between their seats. Shining green gemstones glinted from their temples.

Three teenagers around his age, with their gemstones swirling in an array of color, chatted happily a few tables away.

Happy. Another rather vague emotion.

Cho heaved a sigh, tugged down the edges of his dark red knitted cap, took a bite of his bagel, and closed his eyes. Within his mind a blossom of saffron gold light glinted and spun. The thick, wood-looking chest he'd created for it stood open, the orb of light spinning above it like a dog pleased to greet its owner at the front door. This particular dog, his power, had been firmly locked in the chest that morning during mediation. Going above ground, being around other people, had popped the open and let it out. He grimaced.

Waves of emotion from the teenagers' table hit him. All three at once.

With a wince, he tightened control of his light. His power. The chest shook as he pressed the orb into it and shut the lid. The waves died down to gentle laps against the shore of his mind.

Happy.

He concentrated; eyes still closed. One of them was happy. The emotion was strong, overpowering hints of anxiety from the second person, and rumblings of anger from the third.

Closer. Tighter.

Cho plucked a piece of light from the chest in his mind and held it close. He opened his eyes for a moment, making sure no one was paying him too much attention. His fingers closed around the warm mug, and he went to work.

The little light grew within him. He pulled the emotions toward him, letting them filter through his handful of power as each one reached him. His heartbeat quickened. Giddy joy warred with his already present anxiety. Anger flitted through his chest. He gritted his teeth and clamped down on the feelings that were not his to stop them from taking him over.

Pushing away the other two, Cho focused on the girl bubbling with happiness. He filtered through her emotion as it crowded into his mind, filling him like a public transport with too many people.

There. Between jolts of joy, he felt a hint of nerves. Anticipation. Excitement about something coming. Something big and expected to be good. But... another shift as someone at the table said something. The excitement dimmed as more nerves spiked. So not necessarily good.

Cho swallowed and pulled his power back, away from the girl's emotions. The yellow light fought him, pulling and ripping, sticking to the girl's emotions and trying to dig into his mind with the intrusive feelings. With a snarl, Cho yanked his power into the box and slammed the lid.

Like a magnet, the girl's cloud of emotions surrounded the chest. Cho gritted his teeth, his fingers going white against the ceramic mug. He sucked in a few deep breaths and let them out, willing the unwanted emotions to leave with each exhale.

He finished the exercise just in time to watch the girl, whose happiness had crumbled into a wreck of nerves and frustration, rise from her table and storm out of the café.

One of the boys remaining shrugged and continued to eat. The other's cheeks reddened. He glanced around and pushed his plate away. Cho caught the tail end of his sentence, "... didn't have to be such an asshole about it."

Cho took another gulp of his hot chocolate and leaned against his seat again. An exercise like that, one where he allowed someone's emotions fully into his mind to analyze them and get better at differentiating between anger and hate, fear and anxiety, happiness and anticipation, was draining, to say the least.

He finished the first half of his bagel and pictured what his brother would say if he were there.

What was she feeling?

Happy. Again, too vague.

Why happy, what else?

The nerves indicated anticipation. Excitement, a more specific emotion than happy.

What happened?

Something made her nerves spike. The asshole probably said something to piss her off. Cho pictured his older brother shaking his head and leaning in.

Get more specific. What can you infer from her feelings?

At which point Cho would suggest that Ichiro just read her nacra mind so he could go back to his book. Ichi would get frustrated—which Cho would notice—and the two would argue about the importance of practice, training, and the morals of violating people's minds.

Cho gritted his teeth and drank more of his chocolate. His wards were strong. Stronger than they'd ever been thanks to his training and the policies his brother kept in place to protect their group. Ichiro had the best mental defenses of anyone in Haven. But he was Cho's brother, and they could read each other like open books, powers or not.

He'd done it though. Cho couldn't help the grin sliding across his lips. He'd fully read someone's emotions and successfully gotten them back out without Ichi or Elaine there to help him put his power back in the box. He hadn't cracked, hadn't laughed or cried, hadn't betrayed the truth; that each emotion he analyzed were felt by him as though they were his own.

He glanced at the watch on his wrist. Plenty of time. Did he really need to keep practicing though? One was probably enough to earn him the chocolate.

His gaze darted to the remaining half of the bagel.

The bell above the café door tinkled. A Red-Star family of three strode to the counter and perused the selection of pastries in the display window.

The boys near him stood and left. They cast a glance down each side of the street before one shoved the other and they half-jogged away.

The Red-Star girl, no more than thirteen or fourteen with long blonde braids, left her parents at the counter and found a table in the center of the room.

Cho pulled his shoulder bag from the tile floor under his table and fished out a book.

The waitress cast a raised eyebrow his direction as she brought the Red-Stars their drinks but said nothing. It wasn't abnormal for the higher classes to use old fashioned paper, and he'd tipped her well enough that she might think he was from a wealthier caste. In contrast, his clothes and the face that he'd used cash said otherwise. But beyond a curious look or two, reading a book with actual pages wouldn't draw more attention than he could handle. Besides, he'd done enough training for the day and didn't need to meet with the others for another thirty minutes.

The second hand on Cho's watch ticked absently as he engrossed himself in the novel. His power was stored away, but the emotions of the people around him still buffeted against his mind. Reading took longer than it used to.

He'd just raised his mug to drain the dregs of his chocolate when piercing fear split his gut. Every hair stood on end. His skin buzzed; a muscle twitched in his cheek.

The book hit the table with a solid thunk, and the waitress glanced in his direction.

Cho slid his plate and cup away. He focused on controlling his breathing and heart rate. His hands stopped shaking. His pulse stopped pounding in his ears. The muscles in his back relaxed.

But the Red-Star girl at the table did not relax.

Her fear, a sharp spear at first, now a dull throb against the warding in his mind, remained intact and pungent.

Cho picked up his book again, moving with deliberate ease. Gazing over the top of the yellowing pages, he studied the family. Both parents chatted between sips of their drinks and nibbles of their food. Under the current of fear, he felt their contentment, perhaps some unease about things outside of their control, but nothing with the intensity of the girl's emotion.

Her back was to him. The floral print tank-top and loosely knitted dark green sweater did not hide how rigid she sat. How still she'd become in the last few seconds. His gaze darted to every corner of the café. He took in every face, every window.

He saw nothing to explain it.

So, he stared. Even as the fear subsided to a low murmur. Even as the girl rose, putting a hand out as her father gave her a questioning look. As she took her mug to the little table on the side of the café, the one with a tub for dirty dishes. As she glanced back, ensured her parents weren't watching, and then poured what appeared to be a chunk of black ice from her mug into the trash basket.

It landed with a thud and Cho's eyes widened, his nostrils flaring. He rose. Too quickly, he realized, as the girl shot him a look and hurried back to her table. He picked up his dishes and walked them to the tub. The trash was difficult to glance into, but the only other dish in the tub was a little blue mug.

A little blue mug with ice lining the handle and the rim.

Cho squeezed his eyes shut. His jaw ached and he reminded himself to stop clenching his teeth. Returning to his table, he checked his watch.

He was going to be late.

Cho followed the family through Agora. His loose button-up shirt buffeted against the wind; the side bag thudded against his hip and his red knit cap warmed the tips of his ears beyond the point of comfort in the warm mid-summer heat.

There were dozens of hats scattered around his home. Ichiro and Elaine were both well into their twenties, as were Jason and Samaira. The twins could pass for pre-Coded, but Ichiro and his girlfriend would attract unwanted attention if they ventured out without their gemstones covered. It was easier in the winter. The two of them rarely went out during hot summer months.

The Red-Star family stopped again, at a jewelry store this time. Cho turned and pretended to survey the array of silk scarves before him. The Purple-Star manning the stall gave him a friendly nod which he returned.

His jaw ached again.

Sitting in a mostly empty café was one thing, wandering the busy streets of Agora without any of his family there to help was another. Exhaustion was setting in. The strain of keeping the whirlwind of other people's emotions from overtaking his own sucked away his energy.

A pair of dirty-blond braids bobbed along past the jewelry store. The parents went inside. The girl turned and wandered down a smaller alley.

Cho swept away from the scarf stall and hurried after her. He glanced in the store window in time to see the Purple-Star shop keeper pull something sparkly from a case. He hoped that meant they'd be there a while.

He swung around the building. This alley was smaller with fewer stalls. There were glass blown baubles, polished stones, beaded jewelry, and—for some reason—a vegetable stand.

The girl stood a few yards away, holding a necklace up to the light. Cho slowed his pace as he approached her. The stall owner gave him a sidelong glance but said nothing.

"Excuse me," Cho murmured.

She jumped at his raspy voice.

He cleared his throat and tried again. "Sorry, excuse me, I was hoping I could speak to you for a moment?"

Brown eyes, glinting with flecks of hazel, widened as she looked at him. She was younger than he'd thought, maybe twelve. Recognition crossed her features. Her mouth opened in an exhale and Cho fought to keep his expression neutral. The fear emanating from her threatened to overcome him once again.

"You were," she glanced at the man behind the stall and set the necklace down, "you were at the café."

Cho nodded and gestured for her to step away with him. "If I could just speak to you for a quick moment. I wanted to—"

"My parents are right around the corner." Her gaze darted to the main road. She took a step back, her hands clenched into fists.

Her knuckles grew white, then whiter still as frost crawled across her skin.

Cho grimaced and stepped back. "I know that."

Her eyebrows came together in a frown.

"I mean, I'm not here to hurt you. I just..." Cho glanced at the stall owner who was watching the conversation with avid curiosity. "I need to ask you about something that happened at the café. Something I saw you do." He shot a pointed glance at her hands.

The fear in the air splintered and refracted, morphing into anger, anxiety, disbelief, and back to fear again. Cho put a hand to his temple and pressed against it through the fabric of his cap. His wards were cracking.

"What did you..." The girl also darted a look at the stall owner. She clenched her jaw, pulled her thin sweater tight around her torso, and stepped toward Cho.

He gave a fraction of a nod and moved back down the alley toward the main road. They stopped between two tented stalls.

She dropped her voice to a whisper. "Whatever you think you saw in that café, you *didn't*."

He met her eye and held her gaze. "I saw you turn your drink to ice. And I see the cold on your knuckles as we speak."

She swallowed, glanced at her hands, and shoved them into the pockets of her sweater. Cho winced at the fresh wave of fear.

"You can't prove anything." Her voice shook. "You could tell who-whoever you want, but-but it doesn't matter. My parents are Red-Stars and unless your—"

She stopped at Cho's raised hand. "I don't care what your parents are," he said with a shake of his head. "I don't want to tell anyone about you. About your gift."

His composure escaped him then. A brief twitch flashed in his mind and across his face as he called it a gift.

She stared at him, tears glistening at the corners of her eyes.

"I want to help you," he said. "I've been in your position. I know what it's like, having to hide who you are, what you can do. I understand your fear."

She was silent for a few seconds. Then, "you can... what can you do?"

He shook his head with a tight smile. "Nothing as impressive as turning things to ice. But I get by. Listen," he leaned in, "you're in danger. If anyone finds out about you. About your power—"

Her braids dangled back and forth as she shook her head. "No one's going to find out."

Cho raised his eyebrows. "I found out."

"Well," she chewed on her bottom lip, "I won't make a mistake like that again. I can control it. No one will know."

"I didn't follow you to give you a warning. I followed you to give you an offer. If your parents, or friends, or teachers, realize what you can do... they'll send you away. Somewhere bad." He paused. He'd never been present for one of his brother's introductory speeches, besides his own, and that had been a unique case. He was pretty sure this wasn't part of Ichi's script.

The girl's eyes widened again, fear splayed across her face.

"It's okay though. There's a place. A safe place for people like us. Kids with power. You can come with me—"

She was already shaking her head. "No. No, I'm not going with you. I'm not leaving my parents." She held up her hands. "Look, see? Gone already."

The frost had disappeared. Melted, from the look of her damp pockets.

"You won't be able to hide it forever. They'll see it."

She clenched her jaw. "They won't care."

He scoffed before he could stop himself.

Her indignant expression turned to an angry one. "They *won't*. I'm their daughter. They love me. Different or not."

Cho pursed his lips and clenched the strap of his bag. He gave a small nod. "I think you're wrong."

She opened her mouth, but he continued, not letting her speak.

"But I'm not going to try and make you come with me. And not just because I don't want to end up a popsicle."

The hint of a smile flickered across her lips.

"We don't do things like that. It's not who we are. But," he sighed, "I do think you're putting yourself in danger. So, I'm going to do something I'll probably regret."

He dug through his bag. Ripping a small scrap of paper from his book, he scrawled a number on it and handed it to her.

"I could have just put this in my com." She raised an eyebrow at him.

Cho shook his head. "Don't put that number in your com unless you absolutely need to call me. *Life or death* need to call. Otherwise, if you change your mind, or just want to talk, I'll be at that café every other day at the same time for the next couple weeks."

He'd have to check the schedule, but hopefully that timeline would work. If not, he'd be doing dishes or laundry for a month to pay someone back for covering for him.

She pocketed the slip of paper. Cho's gaze caught a flash of red behind her. He put a soft hand on her upper arm and gave a gentle squeeze.

"Good luck..."

"Claire," she answered his pause. "I won't need it..."

He grinned. "Cho."

Without another word, he strode past her and away through the crowd, moving around her parents as they scanned the alley for their daughter.

Agora was called the inner market because it sat in the center of the city. A massive circle, ringed by Grigoria, it was the focal point for the lower castes. The term market, however, was somewhat deceptive. Agora behaved more like a miniature city within Tornim. The Purple-Stars lived there. Some in apartments above their shops or restaurants, most in neighborhoods lining the wall separating Agora from Grigoria. After all, the towering glass and concrete malls, restaurants, and entertainment centers in Grigoria required Purple-Stars to own and run them as well.

The wall between the two markets was mostly decorative. Four arched gateways, one for each point on a compass, remained open most of the time. Shoppers easily moved between the markets, and those who wanted a direct route from one side of Grigoria to the other often took a short cut through Agora.

At the far end of a narrow street near one of the entrances to Grigoria, a group of boys knelt together around a pile of marbles. A few yards away, a fourteen-year-old watched them with sharp black eyes. She leaned her lanky form against the wall, arms crossed, jaw tight, and brow furrowed as usual.

Cho glanced at his watch as he hurried toward her. He was an hour late.

Jane was many things, forgiving wasn't one of them.

Neither was patient.

"Where in the *depths* have you been?" she hissed, pushing off against the wall as he approached.

One of the boys glanced back at them. She waved a hand at him, and he went back to his game.

"I'm sorry, Jane. There was something I needed to deal with." Cho dropped his voice. "How'd the watch go? Anything new?"

Jane glared at him. "Where were you?"

Cho took a deep breath and pushed away the hints of worry and anger coming from Jane. Her mental wards were usually enough, but after practice he was extra sensitive. His own frustration and anxiety were enough to deal with.

"Let's talk on the way, yeah?"

"Oh, *now* we're in a hurry." Jane gave a disgruntled shake of her head, blew her bangs out of her eyes, and called to her brother, "Hey, let's go."

Tommy scooped his marbles and darted from the ground faster than most kids run to dinner. His easy smile met Cho, who returned the grin.

One of the other children piped up from behind them. "Hey, kid, what's your name, so we can find you to play again?"

Tommy opened his mouth, but Jane put a hand on his shoulder and gave a small shake of her head. Tommy's stomach sunk with disappointment. Cho swallowed, gritted his teeth, and roughly shoved the emotion away.

He kept pace with Jane through the maze of streets which made up Agora. As they wound further away from the Star Office where Tommy and Jane had spent the past few hours on watch, Jane filled him in on what he'd missed.

"No changes, that I can tell. But I want to get in there before they go for it. Get a map of the interior." She pulled her hair back as they walked, tying it in a tight pony-tail. Her rail-straight bangs dipped just below her eyebrows. "Do you think you can talk to Ichi about letting Tommy and me do a run?"

Cho heaved a sigh and rubbed the back of his neck. "That's a lot, Jane. By yourselves? Giving you a watch was more than Elaine was comfortable with."

She rolled her eyes. "Elaine would be happy to stay home all day and never let anyone leave."

"That's not true." Cho grimaced. "She wants everyone safe."

"Tommy and I were safe enough before you all found us. We were careful getting into that building this morning. We'd be safe doing a run to make sure the inside is what we think it is."

Cho shook his head. The corporate building Jane and Tommy had snuck into that morning wasn't crawling with Red-Stars; the Star-Office was. He hooked a thumb around the strap of his bag and glanced back to make sure Tommy was on their tail. Sure enough, the boy followed Jane like a duckling. His sandy-brown hair flopped this way and that as he bounded along behind them.

"I think Ichi will agree with you that it's necessary, but it's not up to me. I'm not the right person to ask to talk to him about it."

Jane pursed her lips. The three of them entered an indoor market and Tommy's hands found Cho's and Jane's. Scents of every spice and sweetness pummeled Cho's nostrils as intensely as the emotions pummeled his mind and heart.

Places like this, they were the worst. People pressed together. Buying dinner on their way home. Selling the last of their wares before returning to their shops. Arguing over the price of chicken. Growing more and more frustrated as people didn't hear them, didn't move quickly enough, didn't pay attention.

A worried one bumped his shoulder. The one at the corner stall fumed with barely suppressed rage. Three ran past, the sound of their laughter barely noticeable compared to the excitement pumping through their veins. A hundred emotions all at once.

Cho's grip on Tommy's hand tightened. The boy returned the pressure and Cho looked down. Dark eyes met his, warm where his sisters were cold. Something thrummed in Cho's hand. They stopped, only a few yards from the exit, as the way became too congested with people for them to continue forward.

Cho's palms were damp, his hands shaking. Tommy kept his gaze and, as Cho felt his heart might explode at the speed it was pounding, a stream of calm trundled up his arm. Tommy took a deep breath and release it. The calm grew. Tommy squeezed his hand again. Another feeling, not calm exactly, but something like content, something mild, pushed in as well.

Cho looked up and caught Jane's gaze. He pulled his friends emotions close, using them like a shield against the onslaught of the marketplace. Once his hands stopped shaking and the ringing in his ears dimmed, he gave her a sharp nod.

She returned it, and by then the crowd had disbursed. They crossed to the exit and were dumped into a different part of Agora, close to Grigoria, but on the opposite side from where they'd come.

Cho dropped Tommy's hand and the shield broke. He stepped away from them. As they walked toward the sewer grate only a few blocks away Cho's power shrunk back into its box. He was once again able to pick out his emotions from the ones around him.

"You good?" Jane asked a few minutes later.

Cho nodded, his voice low. "I just hate it."

"Yeah."

She didn't bother reminding him they *needed* to go through a crowded place before going home, and for that he was grateful. There was no coddling with Jane. No attempting to ease the struggle with the burning knowledge that it was to keep their family safe.

He already knew that. He understood. He wasn't complaining, and he didn't need anyone telling him it was a necessary pain.

"Thank you," Cho muttered. He glanced at Tommy, still holding Jane's hand. "Both of you."

Tommy nodded with a grin. Jane pretended she hadn't heard him.

"I heard something else while we were covering your watch," she said as they made the last turn.

Cho raised an eyebrow.

"A score. It'd pay something between three and five."

"Hundred?" Cho's pulse quickened. He looked at Jane with wide eyes. "That would be..."

"Yeah," she huffed out a chuckle. "I've got to get Ichi on board."

Cho held his hands up. "Again, don't ask me about it. I'm not my brother, I don't run the ship. I'm not in charge of anything."

Her bangs dangled from side to side as she shook her head. Between them, Tommy dropped her hand. The boy was small. Smaller looking still, with a sister so tall. He yawned and Cho glanced to the west. The sun sank toward the building tops. The day had been long.

Jane knelt and gestured to her brother. He clambered onto her back, latching his hands around her pale neck. She tucked her hands under his knees and stood back up, giving him a quick hitch until he settled into place with a grin on his face.

Jane hurried on and Cho rushed to keep up.

He glanced around as they reached their stopping point. The streets were deserted here. There were no cameras glinting from orbs lighting the way, because there were no orbs in this part of Agora. A heavy man-hole grate sat a little crooked on the ground before them.

"Want to try and move it? Or should we do this the easy way?" Jane asked with a rare grin.

Cho exhaled in a combination of a laugh and a sigh. "You're not supposed to drop anyone but you and Tommy."

Jane's nose wrinkled. "It was *one* time. Not my fault Jason can't keep his balance."

There was no mistaking Cho's laugh this time. He snorted and shook his head. "I don't want anyone getting in trouble."

"I'll only get in trouble if you rat me out." Jane raised an eyebrow. "Make a decision; I'm tired. And I don't really want to stand here and watch you fight to pick that thing up by yourself."

Cho opened his mouth to defend himself, crooked his jaw to the side, and clicked his teeth together. "I figured you'd help," he grumbled.

Jane turned and Cho let out another chuckle. Tommy's head lolled against Jane's shoulder, a trickle of drool sliding down his chin. Cho hadn't noticed her arms shift around to support Tommy's weight behind her back.

"Fine."

"Grab my elbow, don't move, and don't let go," Jane commanded.

Cho nodded. She took a step forward, planting herself firmly on the cover. Cho followed suit, moving a half-step when she directed him to.

He took hold of her elbow, closed his eyes, and sucked in a deep breath.

The panicked feeling of falling barely had time to reach his stomach before his feet hit solid ground again. He exhaled and opened his eyes.

Jane stood in the same position as before, but the world around them had gone dark. He glanced up at the manhole cover, then met Jane's shadowed grin with one of his own.

"Nice work."

She shrugged the shoulder not soaked in drool and led the way down the dimly lit sewer tunnel.

"So, you gonna tell me why you were so late meeting us?"

Cho pinched the bridge of his nose before hurrying after her. "Yeah. I found a kid. A kid with power."

Jane turned; her dark eyes wide when they met his. She paused, then heaved a sigh. "Well, *nacra.*"

Chapter Five

Present Day - Mid Summer - Deep in the Sewers of Agora

C ho waited as Jane tucked Tommy into the bottom bunk in the room the siblings shared. She closed the thick metal door and the two of them made their way to Ichiro's study.

The halls of Haven were narrow, but the ceilings stretched nearly twenty feet high. With numerous branching corridors and dozens of rooms in a variety of sizes, it gave one the feeling of walking through a maze. Small lights, round orbs of soft yellow, sat in brackets along the walls. Shadows flickered on either side of them.

The central hall they walked down bloomed before them into a massive open space. Stairs took up much of the far wall, leading up to the lowest levels of Tornim's sewers. To their left heavy pots in a multitude of colors held plants of every variety. Sky, a small girl a barely older than Tommy, stood with her hands plunged into the soil of a wilted and sad looking peach tree. As Cho and Jane moved around her toward a second hallway the leaves shimmered and shook as though a gentle breeze had broken the stillness of the room.

Branches rose, a few of the flowers spread their petals, and Sky pulled her hands from the dirt, giving the trunk a tender pet before tending to a row of tomatoes.

Other children milled around the family room. Some cradled cracked, mismatched bowls of stew, a few read under the light of larger orbs dangling from hooks on the walls, and several practiced with their powers.

Cho caught a whiff of the stew, a thick vegetable dish stuffed with faux-meat and spices. His stomach rumbled, the snack from the café a distant memory when compared to Elaine and Jason's cooking.

"You can eat after the meeting." Jane flashed an eye roll in his direction.

Cho raised his hands with a shrug. "I didn't even say anything."

"Your stomach is loud," Jane said as they strode a few yards down the side hallway. She reached out and knocked on the only wooden door in Haven.

A few seconds later the door creaked open. Cho suppressed his sigh as a bright eyed, exuberant, and annoying face poked around the doorway.

"*Finally.* You know you're both late, right?" Jason asked.

Jane glared and stalked past him, not bothering to respond.

Cho moved to step into the room, but Jason's thick arm, a dozen shades darker than his own, flashed up to block his way.

Cho gritted his teeth. He scowled at the bird tattooed on Jason's forearm; an elegant thing, wrapped in flames as it seemed to soar across his skin.

"Jason," Samaira's voice, similar to her brother's if an octave higher, sounded from within the room, "quit being a dick."

Jason grinned, white teeth flashing as he pushed off the doorframe and stepped back to let Cho in. As Cho moved into the room, Jason took up his usual place, balanced on top of the wooden side table against the far wall. It was a marvel that the thing hadn't yet collapsed under his weight.

His twin sister, Samaira, leaned against the wall next to the door. She raised a hand coated in twisting black ink and brushed it across the tight spirals of her cropped hair. "You *are* late though." She grinned the same grin as her brother, but without the mischievous glint in her eyes.

Elaine sprawled on a maroon couch across the room. She pulled her long legs in to make space as Jane walked over. Golden beads at the ends of her thin box braids clicked together in a sound so familiar, so associated with comfort, that Cho's stomach unknotted and his tense shoulders dropped.

Jane perched herself on the armrest of the couch; she lifted her bare feet onto the soft fabric and pulled a fraying pillow to her chest. Elaine leaned across and murmured something to her. The edge of Jane's mouth twitched as though she'd just managed not to smile.

Elaine caught Cho's eye and winked. His lips, pressed tight to avoid telling Jason to do something anatomically impossible, eased into a smile. His sister—well, his brother's girlfriend, but she was basically his sister at this point—had been trying to win Jane over since the moment she and Tommy had arrived.

It had taken a while, but Jane's icy exterior was starting to melt.

Someone shifted, and Cho's attention turned to his brother, seated at the chair behind his desk.

Ichi stood and went to Cho, clapping a hand around his back and giving a quick squeeze. "We worried when you didn't return on time." The hint of their mother's accent, one from a language forgotten generations ago, danced across his tongue as he spoke.

Cho returned the hug before stepping back. He sat in the unoccupied chair in front of the desk and exhaled a groan. "We came back as quick as we could. It was my fault we were late." He met Ichi's eye. "I'll explain after, if that's all right."

Ichi's eyes narrowed a fraction, but he nodded and turned to Jane. "How'd it go?"

Jane reached into the pocket of her long grey sweater and produced a black device no larger than Cho's thumb. "This has shipping routes from Inka Tech. For the last five years." She passed it to Elaine.

Jason barked out a laugh and clapped his hands. "*Shit*, we should have had them on it from the start, Ichi. Walking through walls... who knew?" He shook his head with a smirk drawn across his face.

Samaira laughed as well. She looked at Jane. "That's *nacra* impressive, kid."

The beginning of a smile tightened on Jane's face. "Thanks," she said through half-clenched teeth. "It wasn't just me who got it. Tommy played a huge part."

Ichi nodded, stroking the sharp edges of his jaw where a stubble of coarse black hair grew. "I imagine you had to go invisible once you got inside?"

Jane jerked her head in the affirmative.

"You were careful though?" Elaine's eyes, pools of black framed by smooth skin almost the color of night, widened. Her wards were stronger than anyone else's in Haven, even Ichi's, but Cho didn't need his power to read the concern on her face.

"Yeah. We did Inka Tech first, before our turn to watch the Star Office. Cho was there to keep lookout while the floor went on their lunch break. It only took a couple minutes since we knew where we were going."

Ichiro moved to Elaine's side and squeezed her shoulder. "Jane knows how to stay safe."

Elaine's fingers entwined with his for a brief moment before she handed him the chip and he returned to the desk.

Jane looked ready to burst with barely contained pride. Her emotion seeped through the defenses in her mind as it grew.

"This is excellent," Samaira said. She pushed off the wall and went to Ichi's desk.

Cho scootched his chair out of her way as she stepped in front of him.

Her long fingers, scarred and calloused, flattened a rumpled sheet of paper taking up most of the wooden surface. "With their routes, we should have most of the picture. Looks like," she pointed to seven spots, "these will be the safest."

"I've been thinking about water," Jason cut in next to her. He shook his head as he took in a few of the places she'd mentioned. "These don't have any access, according to this map."

Elaine and Jane rose from the couch and joined Ichi on the far side of the desk. Cho stood as well, positioned himself at the end, and fiddled with a small potted fern.

"This one is not as new as I'd like." Elaine took up a corner of the paper in her fingers. "I want to find one made in the last few years before we actually go."

"I have a lead on a few new maps we can pick up in the next week or so. Besides, this intel will probably change up the places we'd likely get discovered,"

Ichi replied. "We should wait to choose any possible locations until we've added the last of the details."

Cho stared down at the map before them. Pangaea spread across the table. Ocean lined the west, massive mountain ranges to the north and south, and a deep gorge and river formed the eastern border. In the center was the country that claimed them, the cities they survived in, and maybe, somewhere on that paper, was a home.

Haven kept them safe, warm, alive... but many of the children didn't see sunshine for days, sometimes weeks at a time. They stole to have enough to eat. And they were constantly hounded by the fear of being discovered.

"Have you decided who you'll be taking?" Jason asked. He leaned into the desk, his eyes alight at the prospect of being among the first to leave Tornim.

Ichi grinned. "No. But I'll let you all know by the time we get these taken care of." He tapped the gemstone on his temple, still swirling with color even as he approached his twenty-fifth birthday.

Elaine's fingers twisted the ends of her navy-blue scarf. She chewed on her bottom lip until she spotted Cho watching her. Then she flashed him a sweet smile and stopped the fidgeting.

"Anything new on that front?" Ichi asked Jane. "And thank you for taking over Cho's watch."

She nodded, first at Ichi, then at Cho. "It was good to have him as look out this morning at the Tech company. Me and Tommy didn't notice anything at the Star Office. Red-Stars switched out at the usual time. Regular number of people going in and out. It was normal."

"Good." Ichi looked over at Cho, but before he spoke Jane piped up again.

"There is something else though. I... that is, we, Tommy and I overheard some people. We have a lead on a score."

Jason clapped his hands and rubbed them together. Samaira met her brother's eye with an excited grin.

Ichi tilted his head at Jane. "How much?"

"Over three hundred."

There was an intake of breath from several members of the group.

"When?"

"A couple weeks; it shouldn't take much surveillance to nail down the details."

Ichiro's reaction was more muted than the twins', but Cho knew his brother. He knew from the twitch of his cheek and the tug of his ear how excited he really was.

Three hundred coins would buy new shoes for the kids whose toes were poking out of theirs. It would buy food for a month or more. It would be used as bribes for Red-Stars to look the other direction. It would mean a world of difference in getting out of the city.

"It's late," Ichi said. "But tomorrow during breakfast, first thing, you and I will sit down and talk details. I want you planning the job with me." Finally, a grin slid across his face. "If you think you're up for it."

Jane's eyes widened. "That would... yeah. That would be great."

Ichi folded up the map, tucking it into the top drawer of his old wooden desk. "It's getting late. You should all—"

"Oh yeah." Jason turned to Cho.

Cho did not suppress his eye roll.

"Why is it so late, Cho?" Jason nudged Cho with his elbow. "What slowed you down today? A cute girl? Get lost? Problems with your power, maybe?"

Samaira clapped a hand on the back of her brother's neck. "You need food, Jace."

"What?" Jason looked at her like she'd grown horns.

"You need food. You turn into a nacra asshole when you're hungry."

"I'm not—" Jason's look of indignation, as well as whatever response he was working on, were quelled as Samaira opened the door with one hand and propelled her six-foot-three brother out of it with the other.

"Wait for me," Jane called after them. She gave Ichi the slightest of smiles, met Cho's gaze, shrugged, and took off after the twins.

"Well," Elaine's dazzling white smile softened the atmosphere in the room, "I'm also curious about what made you late. Though I hope not to be an asshole about asking."

Cho snorted.

"Sit, brother." Ichi gestured to the couch and produced a stack of oat raisin cookies from another drawer in his desk.

Cho crossed the room and sat. Elaine joined him, and Ichi dragged a ripped and stained emerald-colored armchair in front of them and sank into it. The three sat in silence for a moment. Cho picked at his cookie, pulling the raisins out and eating them one by one.

"What happened?" Ichi asked. He leaned forward, resting his elbows on his thighs and staring at his brother. "Was it your gift?"

Cho shook his head, thought about it, and shrugged. "Not like you mean. Practice actually went pretty good."

Elaine patted his knee. "That's great to hear. Your wards are holding?"

"Yeah, I'm getting better at telling the difference in similar emotions. The trouble is separating theirs from mine. And getting the information to my body."

Ichi ran a hand down the edge of his jaw. "Heightened heart rate? Sweating?"

"Damp palms, hair on end, shivers," Cho nodded, "all the usual."

"That's a good focus for us to work on during tomorrow's meditation," Elaine mumbled around a mouthful of oats.

"So, what was it then?"

"There was a girl. She can freeze things."

Ichiro crumpled into his chair with a heavy sigh, exhaustion lining his face.

Elaine reached out her hand. Ichi sat back up, taking her fingers in his and holding them as Cho explained everything that had happened in the café and afterwards.

"I'm sorry, Ichi. I know I should have done more to get her to come with me. She was... she was being stubborn. And foolish." Cho's stomach tensed. "I don't... why does she think she'll be able to keep it hidden?"

At this, Ichi and Elaine exchanged a glance. Heat bloomed at the back of Cho's neck.

Ichi leaned in wearing a sad sort of smile. "You remember how it was three years ago. You thought it could stay hidden as well. You thought you could keep your ability from mother and father."

Cho's eyes burned. He clenched his fist and gritted his teeth.

Elaine gently released Ichi's hand and pressed her fingers into Cho's upper back, rubbing little circles along his shoulder blades.

"That was different," Cho muttered, his jaw still clenched. "Mine isn't physical. And I didn't know there was somewhere to go."

Silence spread through the room like smoke.

It was strange. These two people were the only humans Cho could be around and truly feel like himself. Elaine and Ichi had the strongest minds of anyone he knew. They alone kept all their emotions within their own selves. When it was just the three of them the only feelings he felt were his.

Sometimes he wished they weren't.

"You only spoke to her today. She might change her mind." Ichi met Cho's gaze. "Take all the time you need for this. You said every other day? I think you're on watch a few nights this week, but we'll take you off completely if that will help."

Cho shook his head. "I don't think that'll be necessary. I'll keep an eye out in that area of Agora. And," he sighed, "it'll give me a good excuse to keep practicing in public."

"Watch for Black-Stars." Elaine stood and moved across the room. Her long skirt, forest green with hand embroidered violet flowers, swayed as she circled Ichi's desk and opened yet another drawer.

Her clothes, like everything in Haven, were old but well cared for. When she wasn't rebinding the covers of every book they managed to find, she was sewing patches onto pants and shirts, or detailing a dress into something new for one of the children. Her hands, dark enough to blend into the deepest ocean, aged her beyond her twenty-six years. Even with the silk gloves Ichi had stolen for their third anniversary, and the lotion derived from one of Sky's succulents, the work Elaine put into Haven showed in the scratches and scars, dry skin, and burns.

Elaine and Ichi had found each other fourteen years ago, and founded Haven not long after. Their blood, sweat, and tears were poured into every scrap of cloth, every painting on the wall, every child's safe and warm bed.

"Take this with you." Elaine glanced at Ichi. When he nodded, she pulled a black object from the drawer and returned to Cho, handing it to him. "We don't want you caught with no way to defend yourself. Jason and Samaira will be busy these next few weeks, months really. Jane has her score to contend with, and no one else with an active power is old enough to go with you to wait on this girl."

It was a knife. Tucked down into a frame of metal, but Cho found the switch within a few seconds and the blade revealed itself. He ran a finger along the edge. The silver color was distorted; a rainbow of wave-like patterns, like oil stains on the street, lined the metal.

"This is..."

"Super illegal," Ichi filled in, "yeah. So be careful. Don't get caught with it. But, if a Black-Star is after you..." he shook his head, the smile fading as something between fear and anger flashed across his eyes. "We've lost a lot of kids over the years 'cause we didn't get to them fast enough. Once a Black-Star finds one of us, it's too late to help. Maybe if we knew where they took them—"

Ichi's voice broke, and he clamped his lips together. Elaine walked around behind his chair. She leaned down, tucking her head into the crook of his neck and draping her long arms around his chest.

"Don't get caught," Ichi repeated after a moment. "And do what you need to to keep this girl and yourself safe."

Cho nodded and closed the knife. He slid it into his pocket, the weight reassuring against his leg.

"Hey," Ichi patted Elaine's arm and murmured something into her ear.

She nodded, straightening. "I'm off to bed. Ichi, you'll make sure the kids are going to sleep before you come in?"

"Of course."

She went to Cho and he stood as she pulled him into a tight hug. "I'm glad you're back home safe." Her kiss landed on his hat just above his right gemstone. With a wave to them both, she disappeared out the door.

"What is it?" Cho asked as Ichi rose from his chair with a groan.

"Just some things I need to talk with you about. I'll make it quick, I'm sure you're starving."

Cho said nothing. His stomach, which had indeed been grumbling about the lack of food, was back to clenching with nerves.

"We're making so much progress." Ichi pulled the armchair back to its spot in the corner of the room and began straightening the papers on his desk. "If my timeline moves as planned, we'll be able to start scouting places within the next few months."

Cho followed him across the room, the anxiety not letting him stand still any longer. He already knew this. What was his brother getting at?

At Cho's silence, Ichi plowed on. "I told Jason I don't know who's coming yet, and that's mostly true. But I do know..." he licked his lips and grimaced. "I know who I'm leaving here. I know who we're leaving in charge while we're gone."

Cho's stomach stopped churning. It stopped doing anything. It disappeared as a pit opened up and seemed to swallow all of his insides.

"Elaine and I need someone we trust implicitly. Someone who can read other people. Someone who can lead."

His head was shaking even as he raised his hands to object. "I can't—"

"You *can*, Cho. You really can."

"No, Ichi. I can't. I don't want to *be* able to read people. I don't want to lead. I don't want to be in charge while you're gone for," Cho's heartbeat thundered in his ears as his voice grew louder, "... how long? A week, at least?"

"Probably closer to three."

Cho sucked in breath through his teeth and turned in a circle. This wasn't happening. This was the worst idea his brother had ever had.

"This is the worst idea you've ever had. What about Samaira? Jason even?" Cho pleaded. "They're older, more experienced. They have physical powers."

Ichi raised an eyebrow. "I'm pretty sure they'll both be coming with me. But even if they don't..." He rubbed a hand across his forehead. "They're fighters, Cho. You know I love them. You know they're family. But Samaira has a one-track mind, and Jason..." He sighed and gave Cho an incredulous shrug.

"Yeah, I get that... I just..." Cho's eyes narrowed as he pinched his lips together. "*Shit.*"

"I know it isn't ideal. But it won't be for long."

Cho scoffed. He shook his head, the edge of his thumbnail trembling between his front teeth.

"And," Ichi continued as though he hadn't heard the noise, "we have time for me to help prepare you. Get you ready to take care of everyone."

Cho swallowed and gave Ichi a pleading look.

"I've made up my mind, Cho. This is the plan. We'll start getting together in the evenings, when you don't have watch, to go over the actual running of Haven."

Ichi walked around the desk and put a hand on Cho's shoulder. He leaned forward. Cho clenched his jaw, but matched his brother's movement, pressing his forehead against Ichi's.

"We've got a lot of work to do, brother."

"Yeah," Cho mumbled, pulling away. "Night."

He turned and left the study, no longer all that hungry for food, but ravenous for time alone.

Chapter Six

70 Years Ago - Rebel Hide Out

T he beginning of Maybelle's plan failed utterly and completely.

She grasped Kate's hand and squeezed her eyes shut, picturing her dorm room. When she pinched open one eye to check where they were, cold glass, concrete, and blue light sunk her heart.

"I must be too tired?" She glanced at Kate. "I'm sorry, I don't... I don't know how I did it."

"It's all right. You said we have thirty-six hours before the tracker goes live. That'll give us until about midday tomorrow. You can rest tonight and get us out of here first thing in the morning."

Maybelle nodded. "I'll drop us right outside the city—if I can. Then I'll go in and find Ben. I can pretend I escaped."

"You can find out if he plans on coming to get me or not." Kate frowned. "Actually, you'd better leave me here. With the locket. If what you heard is true then that's all he'll be worried about. If he doesn't make any plans to come get me," she shrugged, "we'll know."

Maybelle shook her head, incredulous. "I'm not *leaving* you here. What happens if I can't 'zap' back? Or if I don't have the energy to take you with me when I do get back?"

"We'll still have time, and we don't know if you'd be able to take me anyway. You getting to Ben might be the only way for us to get out of here."

A sigh blew through Maybelle's gritted teeth. "I don't like it."

"You don't have to like it. But that's the plan." Kate's voice held its signature finality.

"Fine." Maybelle squeezed Kate's hand. "I'm going to try and get back into my own cell. Something tells me they'll be suspicious if I'm in here with you when they come back in the morning."

Kate laughed.

Maybelle stared at her cot. Nothing happened.

She squinted her eyes, took a deep breath, and blinked. Kate stared back at her from the other side of the glass.

"That's so strange," Kate muttered, gazing at her eyes.

"Yeah," Maybelle mumbled. She yawned, exhaustion pulling at every part of her body. "I'm going to... I want to lay down."

She sank onto the cot and slumped sideways, her head thudding on the canvas. She shivered. A blanket sat folded at the end of the bed. Her arms were too tired... too tired to reach it.

"Maybelle?"

She forced her eyes to open.

Kate stared with a furrowed brow and narrowed eyes; her hand pressed up against the glass. "Are you alright?"

"I'm tired," Maybelle slurred.

"Get that blanket over you. It's cold."

"Yeah, cold."

She reached a limp arm down, grasped the edge of the scratchy, checkered blanket, and slowly pulled it over her legs.

"Are you sure you're alright?"

"Just tired," Maybelle said through a yawn.

At the edge of her fading vision, she thought she saw Kate grin.

"I'll see you in the morning. Get some rest."

Her head bobbed in agreement. Then, pulling her arms to her chest and turning her head toward the wall, she slipped into sleep.

She woke without opening her eyes. Darkness caressed her lids. The cool air felt good against her pounding head. The gemstones in her temples burned against her skin. Every muscle in her body screamed its displeasure at the events of the day before.

She moaned, rolled a little to release her arm from under her chest, and tried to go back to sleep. Someone turned on a light in the room. The red glow through her eyelids seemed to blind her.

The immediate instinct, which was to open her eyes, only made the problem worse. She winced and put a hand over her face. People out there, in the world beyond her aching head, were making noise—too much noise.

"Get up," a feminine voice demanded.

Maybelle winced again but pulled herself up, sitting on the cot with her legs dangling over the side. A hand grabbed her arm. She flinched, knocking it away.

"Fine. Get yourself up."

Footsteps, heavy boots on concrete, indicated the person was leaving. The temptation to collapse back onto the bed overwhelmed Maybelle. Instead, she glanced over at Kate's cell. Kate stood at the glass, watching her with wary eyes.

"You alright?"

Maybelle lowered her jaw in a half-nod.

"Let's go!"

The shout made Kate jump. Maybelle forced herself to stand. Her legs barely held her weight and as she stepped forward she grabbed the wall to steady herself.

"What's wrong with her?" the woman from before, Sam, growled to Kate. Kate flinched.

"Nothing," Maybelle murmured. "Tired."

They left the cells and sat at the long metal table. Maybelline leaned a forearm against the steel. The cold against her skin felt so good she dropped her torso and rested her forehead on the surface.

Kate's hand found hers under the table. Her friend's long fingernails gently scratched the skin on the top of her hand. The familiar feeling took Maybelle away from the table, the cells, the rebel base. This was what Kate always did to help Maybelle cope, whether it was before final exams, laboratory inspections, funding meetings...

It drew some of the weariness from Maybelle's mind, clearing it enough for her to raise her head and survey the room.

Sam stood at the head of the table. She wore a clean combat uniform. Her cropped blonde hair looked damp. Hatred seeped from her gaze as she glared at the two Grey-Stars.

The other rebels in the room seemed more at ease. Though they held weapons, their gear had been replaced with more neutral clothes. After a moment of silence the door flew open. Maybelle winced as it slammed against the wall; the sound reverberated through her skull.

Red-Beard walked in and plunked himself into a chair across the table from Maybelle.

"Good morning."

He too wore a more relaxed uniform, though he and the others still had masks over their noses and mouths.

The blood had been washed from his face and Maybelle only saw one blade on his belt. The red handprint, two strips of white across the fingers, was smaller on his grey shirt. It sat just below his left shoulder.

She and Kate did not respond to his greeting. He glanced at Sam.

She shrugged and gestured at each of them in turn. "This one seems hungover and that one is scared of her own shadow."

As if to exemplify her point, Kate winced and tried to make herself as small as possible.

"Have they had any food?" Red-Beard asked.

"No." Sam sneered.

"Well, let's get them some food." He waved a hand at one of the other rebels. "Go, breakfast platter, quickly."

The man scurried off and the rest sat in uncomfortable silence for a few minutes. Sam stared at Red-Beard. Red-Beard seemed to be purposefully avoiding her gaze.

After a moment she stalked forward, leaned close, and hissed his ear. "Red, we shouldn't give them anything until they've agreed."

Maybelle squinted at the two of them and caught Sam's gaze for a brief second before the other woman scowled and turned away.

"They won't be any help in this state," he said with a wave of his meaty hand.

"It's a waste of resources," she growled.

Maybelle's lip twitched as the meaning of their words filtered into her sluggish mind. "Red?"

The man glanced at her and raised an eyebrow.

"Your name?"

He nodded.

"Because of that," she gestured to his beard, her words slightly slurred, "or something else?"

There was a pause. Sam stared at her with a deep frown creased between her eyebrows. Kate tilted her head, concerned.

Red barked out a laugh which made them all jump.

"Something else," he grunted, still chuckling. "But this helps, don't it?" He gave his beard a tender stroke.

His gaze flicked to Sam and the rage roiling in her eyes. He straightened and cleared his throat.

The rebel returned bearing a massive plate of food. Fruit, toast, a grainy substance in a bowl, and two steaming mugs of brown liquid plunked onto the table before them. Kate straightened and reached out a hand.

Maybelle grabbed her knee and squeezed. When Kate looked at her, she shook her head.

"Ha." Red nodded. "Smart girl. I can't blame you for that one, but it isn't poisoned."

"You'll have to forgive me if I don't take your word for it." Maybelle gritted her teeth. The effort of speaking sent another round of throbbing through her temples.

He nodded, reached forward, and grabbed a few berries, a slice of toast, and one of the bowls. After taking a few bites of everything he gestured with a massive hand.

"See?"

Maybelle looked pointedly at the mugs.

He chuckled and, after taking a sip from each mug, inclined his head.

Maybelle pulled the platter forward, grabbed a piece of toast, and shoved half of it into her mouth. Only when the bread touched her lips did she realize a good half of her discomfort stemmed from draining hunger.

She and Kate finished the platter in minutes. She downed the mug; strong, dark caffeine flooding her veins. Her headache faded with each gulp.

She set it on the table with a clunk and Red straightened up. "Excellent. Let's get to it then."

Kate's mug fell from her hands and shattered on the concrete floor.

The big man stared at her. After a pause, he faced Maybelle instead. "I want to start by, well, by offering my condolences. We didn't mean for so many of your unit to..." he clenched his teeth awkwardly, "to not make it here. We hoped to have more of you to work on this project."

"Project..." Maybelle said.

"Yes. It wasn't an accident we captured *your* group. We know you were working in research before the war. We'd like... we need... for you to do some research for us."

Maybelle cocked her head. "What kind of research?"

Kate shot her a sideways glance at the same time that Maybelle realized what she had asked.

Red fiddled with a small spoon from the tray. "We want you to find a way to suppress the Grey-Stars'... Suggestion? Influence? I'm not sure what you call it. We call it Manipulation."

The blood drained from Maybelle's face. A chill went through her chest and her eyes widened. After a few seconds, she licked her lips and shook her head. "I don't know what you're talking about."

"Don't lie," Sam snapped. She crossed her arms and glared at Maybelle.

"Listen," Red continued. "We know about it, so there's no point in you trying to cover. Why do you think we have these?" He gestured to the red netting on his nose.

Maybelle took a few breaths, her skin tingling. *Suggestion*, or "manipulation" as the rebels apparently called it, was the Grey-Stars' greatest weapon. And one of their most guarded secrets.

"How do you know about it?" she asked, her gaze drawn to the netting.

He shook his head and waved a hand. "That part doesn't matter. What matters is that we can't win a war if you Grey-Stars can walk through a city and get everyone on your side."

"But you have that netting," Kate said. Her dark skin flushed as Red glanced at her.

"Yeah. But that's a quick fix, not a solution. We need you two to create an aerosol, something we can use in the field to limit Grey-Star influence over your soldiers. Something we can use in cities, to show people *how* they're being manipulated. Once they realize what you do to them, they'll join us."

Maybelle swallowed. Her head moved back and forth, almost on its own, in a disbelieving shake. "No. No, we can't do that. We have *suggestion* for a reason. We keep the peace."

Sam let out a furious growl. She slammed her hand onto the table, leaned in, and faced Maybelle with rage in her eyes. "*Keep the peace?*" she spat. "You don't keep the peace. You control people."

"Sam," Red interrupted.

Sam turned on him. "I told you this was a waste of time."

"That's enough." The man's tone commanded silence. The other rebels in the room shifted uncomfortably.

Sam planted her fists on her hips and paced the room. Red watched her for a moment before turning to Maybelle.

"I don't think you understand what we're saying. You don't have a choice." His voice was solemn, his eyes grave as he looked from Maybelle to Kate and back. "We brought you here for a reason, and this is it. You'll be starting tomorrow."

Maybelle's chest constricted. They couldn't do this; there would be total chaos in the cities. Everything would shut down. People would get hurt, maybe die. The Grey-Stars ran things for a reason, how could these people not understand that?

She shook her head, fingers absentmindedly stroking the gem on her right temple. "We can't do that," she murmured.

"Why do you even want it?" Kate's voice shook, but she got out the words. "Why are you doing any of this? The Grey-Stars help people. We make the world a better place."

Sam whirled around and strode back across the room. "You help *your* people. You make *your* world a better place. The rest of us are stuck with what we can get, what we're born into. And how about the White-Stars? How is what you're doing now helping them?" She planted her fists on the table, her voice growing louder the longer she spoke. One hand lifted, pointing at the gleaming white gems on her temples. "I had a good life." She gritted her teeth, hatred gleaming through her eyes as she stared at Maybelle. "You took that from me, from my daughters." Tears glittered in her eyes.

Red stood and grabbed her arms, pulling her away from the table. "That's enough. Get some air." He led her to the door and gently pushed her outside. He returned to his seat and sighed, running his hand down his beard.

"What did she mean about the White-Stars?" Maybelle asked. She'd heard reports of outlying villages being harmed during fighting, but that violence was at the hands of the rebels.

"Don't play dumb." He shook his head. "I was hoping this would be easier. I hoped you'd be more cooperative."

Maybelle shook her head. "We can't. We can't betray our people like that. Not for murderers."

His face darkened, his hands forming fists on the table. A moment passed in silence before he relaxed. His eyes still glinted with shadow as he stood to leave.

"I've been given one week to make you cooperate my way. The next guy's not as nice as I am."

He nodded at the two rebels next to the wall. Maybelle and Kate Grey-Stars were returned to their cages, the glass doors sealing behind them.

The rebels left the room. Red stood at the door for a moment as he looked back at them. His voice came in clearly through the speakers built into the glass.

"I'll have more food brought to you this evening. I sincerely hope you've reconsidered by then."

He shut the door leaving them in semi-darkness.

"How can they expect us to do that?" Kate murmured, a tremor in her voice.

"What did the woman, Sam, mean about the White-Stars?"

Kate shrugged, her gaze distant and distracted. She sat on her cot.

Maybelle sat on hers as well. She pulled the locket from under her pillow and stared at it. She turned it over and over in her hands. The memory of the night Ben had given it to her was fresh in her mind. With it came the feeling of betrayal again, but this time it was joined by doubt. What if Kate was right? What if she had heard Ben wrong? If she hadn't... where would they go when they escaped?

"How are you feeling?" Kate asked.

"I think I can do it again." Maybelle stood, stretching her arms out and flexing her muscles. "The food helped, and the sleep."

"What are you going to do?" Kate raised a tentative eyebrow.

"I think you're right. I need to talk to Ben. I need to see if he really was trying to get us killed. If he was..." She clenched her teeth.

"You can't tell him about your... zapping, whatever it is. If any of the Command finds out—"

"I know." Maybelle sighed.

"I mean, *I* don't think it's bad." Kate smiled weakly. "But with so many of our kind being born without *suggestion*, and then you have... this. It's so much more. I don't want to think about what they'd do to find out how you got it."

Maybelle ran a hand through her hair. "I don't know how I got it."

"I know."

She looked at her friend through the glass. The understanding in Kate's eyes filled Maybelle with warmth even in the cold chamber.

"The plan then." Kate clapped her hands, taking a brisk tone. "You're leaving the locket here with me."

Maybelle nodded.

"You shouldn't zap right into the city, that won't make any sense. Come up from the woods, tell Ben you ran away from the fight. You got lost and found your way back. Tell him I was captured. If he talks about a rescue mission or something, we know you misheard him. If he just asks about the locket..."

"We know he only needed us for one thing," Maybelle finished for her. "I don't like leaving you here."

"You won't. Either Ben will be the Grey-Star we hope he is, or you'll figure out the truth and come back for me."

"What if I don't have the strength to get us both out when I get back?"

"Then we'll wait until evening. We will still have some time on the locket. As long as the rebels don't find out, we'll be able to escape tonight."

Maybelle shook her head, her grey eyes hooded with doubt. "What if I can't... what if I'm not strong enough? I can't leave you here."

The corners of Kate's mouth twitched as she gave Maybelle a reassuring smile. "You won't. You'll come back for me. I know it."

Maybelle closed her eyes and concentrated on her friend. A second later she was in Kate's cell and hugging her with all her strength.

"*Oomph.*" After a confused pause, Kate hugged her back.

They stood for a moment and then Maybelle slid away, leaving the thick locket in Kate's hand. She sniffed, her eyes burning.

"I'm scared," she whispered. "What if we can't go home?"

Kate's eyes glistened. Maybelle's own tears trickled down her cheeks.

"Go find out," her friend said.

Maybelle closed her eyes again and was gone.

Chapter Seven

Present Day - Late Spring - The Wall Between Tornim and the Camp

A tall, reedy man stood a foot from the opening in the wall between Tornim and the camp. Light emanated from a white orb resting comfortably in his palm. Thin grey hair coated his round skull; the color matched his wispy goatee. His wide grin showed a few silver teeth, and as it stretched across his face, a multitude of creases appeared in his skin. Pearly white gemstones rested on his temples.

Juliana winced at the brightness of the light. Her footsteps faltered once she passed the opening. The ground here was soft dirt, not the stiff concrete her feet were used to.

Beyond the pool of light in the man's hand, darkness engulfed them. Buildings, barely visible in the black, rose no more than two stories in the sky. Only faint light was visible from a few dirty windows. Juliana swallowed. Already everything was so different. Her fingers trembled. She tapped them against her thumb in a steadying rhythm.

"Welcome to the camp." The man gestured around as if Juliana were viewing a magnificent park. He had a jovial lilt to his voice.

Eyes burning, she said nothing.

"My name is James Montague. I'm the town hall keeper, records keeper, and resident tour guide." He grinned again.

She stared at him. A rushing sound muffled all outside noise. Though her chest rose and fell with deep breaths, the oxygen in her lungs didn't seem to be functioning properly. Her head spun.

"Well," the man turned, "let's get you settled in for the night, shall we? Then tomorrow we can take care of the paperwork and get you into a house."

Juliana watched her feet while they made their way farther into the camp. They'd reached the buildings. Shadows danced off the short wooden structures. Juliana shivered, though the late spring air was not particularly cold. Ice flowed through her body, chilling her to the bone.

"Here we are."

Montague gestured toward the largest of the buildings around them. Concrete steps rose up several feet until they reached a columned archway. Juliana shuffled behind him, through a set of glass and wooden double doors. He led her down a hallway, shadows flickering around dim orbs fixed to the walls.

"You can sleep here tonight." He took a right into a small room.

A cot, less than half the size of Juliana's bed, sat in the corner. She walked to the middle of the room and the bag of her things slid off her shoulder, landing on the wooden floor with a thump.

"I'll be back in the morning, first thing, to give you the introduction packet and..." he faltered a bit, "and get you all settled."

She was going to be alone. Her gaze flicked to the hall.

"Uhm." He took a step to the left, positioning himself in the doorway. "There's a curfew at ten. And that's in," he looked down at a time piece on his wrist, "about fifteen minutes. It's not a good idea for you to wander around tonight. You'll have plenty of time to explore tomorrow."

Her eyebrows furrowed. A blush of heat rushed to her cheeks. Explore? She didn't want to explore this place. She wanted to leave it.

"I'll see you in the morning." He turned to go. "Please, don't try to go outside." He pulled the door closed.

Juliana watched him go without a word.

Her hands clenched; fingernails dug into her skin. Her mind buzzed frantically. Only one thought was getting through the haze in her mind. *I don't belong here.*

She crossed to the door. The handle turned with ease, and she pulled it open. The lights in the hallway had gone out. She took a step into the darkness. Her ears rang, hands shook, breath coming in shallow gasps.

This was stupid. Where would she go? She knew nothing about the camp. Nothing that would help her escape, and even if she got out, she couldn't go back to Tornim. Couldn't go to any city. There was nowhere for her. It wasn't even that she didn't belong *here*. She just didn't belong.

Tears sprang from her eyes, and she hurriedly wiped them away. Her feet moved backward, bringing her back into the room and to the cot. She collapsed onto it, curled into a ball.

The lights across the room blurred in her teary vision. The emptiness inside her grew, encompassing her stomach and leaving a heavy stone in its wake, overcoming her lungs and deflating them like a dying balloon, attaching to her heart and shriveling it like a leaf in autumn. Nothing felt real. Nothing felt whole.

She closed her eyes. Perhaps, when she woke, this would all have been a nightmare. If not... then maybe she'd die in her sleep. Either way.

A drop slid down her cheek and soaked into the rough fabric of the pillowcase.

The night passed at an agonizingly slow pace. Juliana did not sleep, but dozed restlessly every hour or so. Each time her mind sunk into slumber visions of her family and friends, furious and hateful, swam before her.

Moniqua screamed at her, long, green-painted nails clawed at her face. Alex shook his head from a distance, backing away each time she neared him and not meeting her eyes. Her parents stepped out of the Separation Center a hundred times, steadily growing more and more distant. Until, just as dawn began to paint the windows gold, they exited the center, saw her, and proclaimed in furious voices that they'd never had a daughter. A pair of faceless Red-Stars grabbed her arms. She struggled against them and they laughed. They dragged her to a massive pit in the center of the street and flung her into the black.

She jerked upright, panting, sweating, and shaking. A stream of light hit the wall across from the window. There was movement outside her door. Voices chattered, seemingly oblivious to her presence.

Juliana raised a trembling hand to her forehead and wiped away the sweat. Her tired eyes were tight and dry. Her body ached from laying on the ridiculous cot. She stood, pulled her hair forward so it covered her temples, and lifted her bag from the floor where she had dropped it last night.

It had to be early. The sun barely peaked over the horizon. The man from the night before, Montague, stood behind a raised desk in the front room. His pale blue suit was baggy on his thin frame. His ancient face broke into a smile when he saw her, and he gestured her over with a small wave.

Two people stood behind the desk with him, chatting animatedly in the early morning.

"Miss Juliana, glad to see you're up so early." He grinned down at her. "We've got a busy day here, so it'll be good to get you all taken care of quickly."

Juliana remained silent. The buzzing in her ears had faded slightly, but a storm of fury now clouded her mind. She stepped up to the desk and stared across it at him.

"I've got a few things here for you." He pushed a stack of papers across the desk toward her.

The others with him, a tall, lanky young man with coal black skin and pinched brown eyes, and an older woman with wispy brown hair, turned to watch. White gemstones glinted from both their temples.

"What is this?" Juliana's lips barely parted as she spoke. She lifted a corner of the papers and let them fall. She hadn't seen actual paper, outside of a textbook, since primary school.

Weight pressed on her chest.

"A welcome packet of my own making." His chest puffed out a bit. "I've included a list of rules, regulations, a map, job opportunities for newcomers, and a full list of banned items in Abredea."

Juliana's gaze snapped up to the man. "What's that?"

His eyebrows drew together in a confused frown. "I don't—"

"Abredea." She glanced at the people behind him.

The crinkle around the young man's eyes made his smile feel judgmental.

She swallowed and tried to calm herself. Sweat beaded on her palms. Her fingers tapped against her thumb in a rapid rhythm.

"Ahh, of course." Montague offered her a reassuring nod and a wrinkled grin. "Abredea is what we here call the camp."

Juliana inhaled sharply. The instinct to shudder at the mention of the camp zipped through her spine. She pushed it down, knowing how it might look in front of these strangers.

"Anyway," he plunged on, looking slightly disappointed with the conversation. "I'll give you a quick run-through of the paperwork, then we can walk you over to your new home."

Panic, the combination of her fear and anger, rose up inside her. Her clothes were constricting and tight. Though the morning was quite cool, heat flushed her cheeks and chest.

Juliana's gaze rose slowly. "I—" she faltered. "I'd rather look this over later."

"Well," Montague glanced at the woman behind him. She nodded and pulled the man away. "That should be fine. You can come back here with it, if need be, or May can help you."

Juliana swallowed again. Not another new person. "Who?"

"May. You'll be staying with her."

Juliana's lips trembled. She clenched them together and nodded, her expression stiff.

He stepped around the desk, nabbing her papers and pressing them into her hands. His thin fingers brushed against hers and she took a hurried step back.

"Let's go," he said to her, with an attempt at a reassuring smile as he led the way out of the building.

She followed him. One hand clenched the papers to her chest, the other tightened around the strap on her bag. The thick fabric banged against her thigh with every other step she took.

He took her southwest, away from the city wall and further into the camp. Juliana shook her head just enough to let her hair hide her face. Her gaze stayed fixed on Montague's feet, kicking up dust ahead of her with his brisk pace.

Before long, the cobblestones crumbled away to dirt. Her black boots, flexible with a sturdy heel, darkened with red as the ground of the camp coated them. Blurry figures spoke to her, or maybe to Montague, as they walked. None of it penetrated her mind.

Almost twenty minutes passed before Montague spoke again.

"Almost there."

Juliana looked up. Scattered trees lined the narrow road they now walked down. The pit in her stomach grew at the sight of the houses around them. These were worse than the Orange-Star district. None were taller than one story with no yards to speak of. Stone or brick trails led through dirt and patchy weeds to front doors. There were dusty windows, tattered walls, and random pieces of junk scattered around. Make-shift covered porches—planks of wood with questionable stability—decorated a few of the homes.

They turned down a winding path. There were fewer houses here. Tall, stringy grass encroached over much of the road and after several tight turns, they reached a small stretch with one structure at the end.

Juliana winced. This had to be it. There were no more houses, no more roads to turn down.

It was small, this little wooden hut she was to live in. A covered porch extended about four feet from the door, wooden supports on each corner. Glass bottles, in many shapes and colors, hung from the edges, strings of twine tightly wrapped around their necks. A faded blue rocking chair sat to the left of the door. On the ground next to it lay a bundle of dark brown yarn in a pale wicker basket.

Brilliant green vines grew from the center of black tires, half buried in the dirt at the edges of the porch. Tendrils covered in tiny white star-shaped blooms crawled up to the roof, a scattered pattern against the green. As Juliana passed them, the scent of jasmine surrounded her.

Montague reached the door and looked back at her with a grin. He knocked and waited. After some time, a voice called them inside.

Montague pushed the door open and held it for Juliana. A woman stood across the room from them in what appeared to be the kitchen, though it was smaller than any kitchen Juliana had ever seen. Her back to them, she spoke with a deliberate, strong voice.

"Thank you for bringing her, Montague."

"Not a problem, Miss May. Can I leave her with you, then? I've got to get back to work."

Juliana's eyes widened. She glanced at the elderly man and shook her head the tiniest bit. He gave her a quick nod and another smile.

"Of course." The woman still had not turned. She was shorter than Juliana, with long, storm cloud grey hair tied in a braid that nearly reached her waist. "We've got it from here."

Juliana took a shallow breath. This was too much, too new.

"I'll be at town hall all day if you have any issues. Have to start getting things ready for the new captain."

He left.

The room dimmed once the door closed. A solitary light hung from the ceiling in the kitchen. The side walls each had a small window, and above the kitchen sink a longer window gave a dusty view of the outside.

Juliana took a hesitant step forward. The house was larger than it appeared. On one side of the room, a bed sat squished into the corner. A thick wooden trunk rested at the foot. It had been painted an array of messy colors, as though by a child. A thick blanket, pale blue and coated with tiny pink flowers, sat folded at the end of the bed.

To Juliana's right, a wider bed sat against the other wall. Another blanket, red with gigantic purple roses, lay across the top, tucked neatly into the sides and matching the pillowcase at the head. A tall chest of drawers stood against the same wall; another colorful mass of vibrant swirls coated the wood. Past the chest, in a small break between the kitchen and the main room, a short hallway led to a minuscule bathroom, its door sitting open.

The distance between beds left a fair space to walk through the room. Juliana inched closer to the kitchen. A small table with three chairs, sat to the side. Dark green covered the wooden legs, making it appear as though vines had sprouted from the ground and grown into furniture. A lush jungle was painted into the top of the wood; brightly colored animals and birds poked out from behind the foliage. The chairs were painted to match, though each seemed to have its own specific animal theme.

The woman before Juliana had not turned. Water flowed in a broken stream from the sink below the window. The countertop and cabinets on either side of her were coated in black and decorated with swirling suns, moons, and galaxies.

Juliana gritted her teeth. She hoisted the bag off her shoulder and dumped it onto the table, tossing the information packet down beside it. The woman still did not move.

A sigh of frustration hissed through Juliana's clenched teeth. She waited, one hand on her hip, the other clenched at her side. After what felt like several long minutes, the woman faced her.

Juliana stepped back so quickly her hip rammed into the chair decorated with elephants.

A jagged scar ravaged the woman's face. It fell from the edge of her hairline, down her left cheek to the tip of her jaw. There was a small space under her pearly white gemstone where the blade must have bounced off the stone before plunging even deeper into her flesh. Almost half an inch thick at the spot just above her cheekbone, the white scar stole Juliana's gaze for a long moment.

The woman waited, a serene steadiness in her grey eyes. They were crinkled around the edges and below them the skin was darker, like many sleepless nights had left her weary. On the unmarred side of her face, an uneven row of wrinkles sprung into place when her lips turned up in a soft half-smile.

"Welcome to my home, Juliana."

Juliana swallowed. Never had she seen a face like this woman's. Fear erupted through her.

"I understand the shock of arriving in Abredea, especially coming from such a distinguished caste." May's gaze flicked to Juliana's gemstones. "I hope I can help to ease your transition."

"Tran—transition?" Juliana found her voice. The word came out in a broken laugh. She swallowed again, her mouth dry. "It's not a transition. It's a *frosted disaster.*"

The grey in May's eyes darkened at Juliana's words, but her smile remained soft and kind. Her head tilted in a gentle nod. "It *is* a disaster. To be torn from your home, your life, and brought here when you were expecting something so different."

Fire filled Juliana. It melted the numbness and fear. Fury raged through her mind and body; her hands clenched into fists at her sides.

"You know nothing of my life." She sneered at the old woman. "I'm *not* supposed to be here. I'm better than this. Better than living in this," she gestured around the single-room home, "hovel. Better than speaking to the people here, than breathing the same air. Better than being a—" she stopped, choking on her anger. The word refused to slip past her lips. It was too unreal that she was actually here, in this place. Alone. She slammed her hand on the table, the sting on her palm a tangible comfort.

May remained unmoved. Her eyes darkened farther still, but she did not speak or yell or throw Juliana from her home for saying such things.

Juliana's fingers trembled on the tabletop. She clenched them together again to stop them from moving. She swallowed. "Better than being a Moon," she murmured.

The heat which had flared inside her so quickly, died. In its place smoky, black emptiness consumed her. She stared at May with no idea what to do or say next.

"Sit," the old woman said.

Juliana sat, folding her hands together in her lap, and stared down at them. May joined her at the table. She tugged her braid over her shoulder and let it fall across her chest as she gazed at Juliana.

"It's been a long time since I have helped a new White-Star." Her words came slow, her voice aging her more than the grey hair and wrinkled skin.

Juliana raised her eyes. May's scar caught her attention once again before she forced her gaze elsewhere.

"I don't believe the last one was raised in the same caste as yourself. Blue?" she asked.

Juliana nodded.

"It is going to take a while, but eventually this will feel like home."

Juliana shuddered, her fingers curling to fists again. "This will never be my home."

May patted the table with a wrinkled hand. A sigh passed her lips as she looked at Juliana. "You're exhausted. I doubt they fed you at town hall." She stood and turned toward the kitchen. "And you can't have gotten much sleep last night."

Juliana's eyebrows drew together. She opened her mouth slightly. Before she uttered a word, May opened a cabinet and pulled down a pan.

"You get changed into some fresh clothes and unpack." She gestured to the bed with the colorful trunk. "Shower if you'd like. I'll have some breakfast ready before you're done."

Juliana stood numbly. She wanted to ask where this kindness came from, but the longer she waited the more her curiosity dimmed. Cold and hollow, she took a long sleeve brown shirt and a pair of matching soft pants from her bag.

"Bathroom's at the end of that hall," May said over her shoulder, still bustling around the kitchen.

Juliana avoided looking at the mirror until she finished changing. She leaned forward, turning her head from side to side for a better view of the gemstones. They glinted in the light, pearly white and shimmering.

Her fingers pressed against the edges of her temple and, for the first time, she slid her nails against the edge of the gemstone. It was smooth with her flesh, her nails unable to catch on the surface.

Something thudded in the kitchen and Juliana's hand fell to the side. She shivered.

Upon her re-entry into the kitchen, May informed her that the bunk bed and trunk were hers. The thought of how horrific this was, to be sharing not only a house but a room with this person, flashed through Juliana's mind for a brief moment before it died in the void that consumed her.

She dumped her dirty clothes and the items her parents had brought her into the trunk and tucked the empty bag under the bed.

May gestured her to the table and they ate. Breakfast consisted of a grey eggshell-colored mushy porridge and a single slice of bread.

A spark of anger flamed in Juliana at the state of her food. She glared across the table at May, her jaw tensed.

The anger ebbed away as fast as it had come. Her shoulders slumped. She took a few bites from her bowl then went to her bed.

Juliana curled into a ball, facing the wall. A few tugs pulled the blanket completely over her and buried her in darkness. She closed her eyes and succumbed to the emptiness inside.

Chapter Eight

Present Day - Late Spring - Abredea Town Square

"**N**ope!" Anthony caught Jimmy before he could run to the fountain, lifted him into the air and swung him in a long arc before planting him on the ground. "Yer not allowed in the fountain today. Yer mom'll kill me."

"Aww, come on. Yeh always do stuff yer not allowed," Jimmy pleaded, his lilting accent matching his older cousin's.

Anthony sighed and ran a hand through his hair. The thick black strands were getting too long, almost past his eyes. He'd have to get May to cut it soon.

"Listen, kid." He knelt and looked his cousin in the eye. "I can't argue with yer logic, but if yeh get all soakin' wet, we'll both be in trouble."

"I'm up for it if you are!" Jimmy sang with a gleam in his eyes.

Anthony squinted at him. "... Fine."

A yelp of joy erupted through the air as the six-year-old took off. Anthony stood, picking up Jimmy's books and tucking them under his arm.

Small arcs of water sprayed through the air in the center of the square. They crisscrossed each other, creating a web shape when viewed from above. A few sandy-haired children also splashed through the fountain; several more little ones stared longingly at the fun as their parents pulled them away.

Two-story buildings surrounded the square. Unlike most of Abredea, these buildings were constructed from brick and stone rather than wood. Little shops left their doors open during the day, wishing for both a breeze and customers. The owners would lock up and climb to their homes above once the sun set.

People bustled along the cobblestone. A few walking their children home from school. A gaggle of women washed laundry in the free basins at the edge of the square. One of them glanced up at the squeal of joy and Anthony winced under the harsh gaze of his aunt.

"I said not today!" she thundered across the square at him. The women around her chuckled.

Anthony put up his hands and shrugged while he walked over.

"I couldn't help it, he's too cute askin'." He bent and kissed Naya's cheek.

"Aye, tha's true." She glared at him. A reluctant grin spread across her drawn face as Jimmy jumped up and down in a particularly deep puddle of water. "But you get tah clean him up tonight before dinner. I'm not dealin' with tha' mess." She pointed.

Jimmy waved ferociously at them. Bits of red mud, currently coating the majority of his body, flew off his hand.

Anthony nodded. "Tha's fair."

"Thanks for pickin' him up for me. I've got tah get this done."

The anxiety in her voice made Anthony pause. He raised an eyebrow.

"The mayor wants all his things finished before the meetin's start for this new captain."

"Oh yeah." Anthony frowned. "Thought tha' wasn't for another month or so?"

She nodded, casting a glance at the mayor's house. "But Masterson's tah meet with Captain Durang, the new captain, the Red-Star patrollers, *and* a whole basket ah colorful city folk before things get finalized."

Anthony rubbed his hands together, his thoughts drifting away.

Naya dropped her wash and turned to face him, wet hands going to her hips. "Get tha' look off yer face."

"What look?" He grinned sheepishly. He picked up the pants she had set down and scrubbed them against the ribbed metal.

"I know yeh. I know yeh think this'll be some kinda challenge. But it won't. It better not."

He frowned at her. "I honestly have no idea what yer talkin' about."

"This captain is rumored tah be much worse than Durang."

"Worse how?" he asked with a jerk of his head.

"Stricter. More aggressive. Pays more attention." Worry lined her voice and her eyes, enhancing the wrinkles which had recently begun to surround them.

"Come on, Naya." Anthony's tone sounded a lot like Jimmy's earlier. "It'd be pretty nacra hard for him tah pay less attention than Durang. I'll be fine." He winked.

She lowered her voice, leaning in so the other people washing wouldn't hear. "I don' want yeh hunting once this new person arrives. Not 'til we know what kinda man he is."

He dropped the wash.

"I'm serious." She put her hands together and held them before her.

"Naya, stop." His voice held no humor.

"Yeh need tah listen tah me for once."

"No." Anthony stuck his hands deep in his pockets. "I'm not gonna stop, Naya. We need tha' food. The way things are goin'..." He sighed, jaw tight. "The packets shrunk again not even two months ago."

"I can't lose you too, Tony." A sad sort of fear shadowed her hazel eyes.

A pang went through Anthony's chest. He pinched his lips together, jaw clenched, and swallowed the lump in his throat.

"We'll see." He glanced over at Jimmy still happily dancing through the water. "I'll ask about gettin' a few more hours in the fields."

"I'm glad he has yeh." Naya patted his cheek.

"I'm glad he has his mother." Anthony kissed her forehead. He turned away and went to get his cousin. "Oy!" he shouted at the mud-covered child. "Let's get yeh cleaned up and start homework."

Jimmy groaned, but leapt to his feet and raced toward Anthony. A small grimy hand wormed its way into Anthony's large, calloused palm. Anthony swung his arm as they followed the dust-coated cobblestones down the central road which cut a line through most of Abredea.

They stopped along the way a few times. Jimmy's friends, walking home from school with parents or older siblings, wanted to say hi. Anthony waited under one of the massive trees growing throughout Abredea while the children played.

He leaned against the rough bark. Stop hunting. It was laughable. Naya and Jimmy depended on the food he brought in. They, along with several other families on the west end, would go hungry without his almost weekly hunting trips.

As he thought it, two Orange-Stars strode up the path lugging a handcart stacked with plain wooden crates. A Red-Star followed close behind, her gaze fixing on Anthony while they passed.

Anthony sighed as the Orange-Star hefted one of the crates and dropped it at the door of a house across the way, next to a similar—empty—crate. The other marked a note on a flat glass tablet.

Mush packets were said to carry all the protein and nutrients Moons needed. Two packets a day, smaller than his fist...

Anthony ran his tongue along the inner edge of his teeth, frustration coursing through his veins as the Orange-Stars took the empty crate from last week and moved on to the next house on their list.

Jimmy shouted and Anthony looked up. His little cousin had trekked down the road without him. The boy waved his arms at Anthony, yelling for him to hurry up.

They continued down the road. Houses shrank as they headed west. The cobblestone crumbled giving way to a simple dirt path. Less people walked with them now. A few waved. A few threw dirty looks at Jimmy's messy state.

Veering right, they followed a thin winding trail for several minutes. Finally, they arrived at a one-bedroom home. Tall ivory flowers led them to the chipped wooden door. A tree stump sat below a small window a few feet from the entrance.

"Let's get yeh cleaned up. I've only got an hour or so before I need tah get tah work."

Jimmy raced inside and stripped in the small bathroom.

Different sized rugs covered the floor. Thinner, hand sewn runners in pale colors lined a minuscule hallway connecting the bathroom and Jimmy's bedroom to the main room. Other rugs, in darker colors and woven rather than sewn, covered the hard floor in the kitchen area. Anthony's favorite, a deep midnight blue one and the softest of them all, lay next to Naya's bed, tucked in the corner of the main room.

Jimmy stuck a muddy face out the bathroom door. "Yeh work tonight?" A sideways frown crossed his oval-shaped face.

"Aye. Don't worry about it. Now, hop in tha' tub before I get in there."

A squeal of giggles spun from his cousin's mouth and a splash of water sounded as Jimmy turned the nozzle.

"It's cold!" he yelped.

"Give it a sec tah warm up," Anthony called to him. He came in to find Jimmy huddled at the edge of the bathtub lowering his toes a little at a time into the chilly water. A few moments passed and Jimmy gave Anthony a fat lipped pout.

"Hang on." Anthony strode outside, stepped onto the stump, and hoisted himself up to the roof. Shiny solar panels covered the cheap wooden slats. A leafy branch from a nearby tree lay on a good third of the grid. Thick green leaves blocked the sun's rays.

Anthony swore and threw the sticky branch off the roof. It landed next to the house with a thud. A spiderweb fracture, about the size of his palm, radiated across one of the panels where the branch had struck. Pinching his eyes closed, Anthony sighed.

He swung down from the roof and made his way into the bathroom. Jimmy sat in the tub, his deep olive skin finally becoming visible underneath all that mud. Steam whispered up into the air, fogging the mirror in the corner.

Enough panels were clear that there was hot water. He probably wouldn't need to get the broken one replaced until it started getting truly cold outside. He doubted he'd even have to tell Naya about it. She didn't need the extra worry.

"All right." Anthony plucked his clean cousin from the water, draped a towel around him, and pointed to his room. "Get on some clean clothes."

He sat at the table in the kitchen and rested his elbows on the hard surface. A new solar panel, even just the square that broke, would cost a good month's worth of pay. An angry sigh escaped through his clenched teeth.

He glanced up at the only framed picture in the house. It hung from the kitchen wall, well dusted and spotless. His uncle grinned heartily from the frame; one arm wrapped around his wife, the other resting on his baby boy's blanket. A younger version of Anthony stood in the foreground glancing up at his overjoyed relatives. He saw himself in his uncle. In the dark eyes, the hair, the crooked grin.

The bite of loss clutched at Anthony's chest. It had been six months, but Dave's death swirled around him like an angry wind. Life seemed so easy before his passing.

Jimmy skipped into the room. His dress shirt, still a bit big for him, hung open and unbuttoned. He'd rolled the sleeves up to his elbows and chosen with a pair of checkerboard shorts that almost reached his ankles. Wild, unkempt black hair stood on end, still wet from the bath.

Anthony chuckled at the six-year-old's outfit choices, flicked open the crumbling math book, and got down to working through subtraction homework.

When Naya arrived nearly forty minutes later, Anthony and Jimmy had gotten through all his assignments and were building a massive structure out of hand-carved building blocks. She set her basket of laundry on the table and took the pins from her hair. Dark brown curls cascaded around her face, falling to her shoulders.

Anthony stood and stretched.

"I gotta get goin'." He hugged her.

"Already? I was gonna keep yeh for dinner. Fallsworthy gave me an extra couple rolls for mendin' his wife's dress when I did their last load."

"I got stuff tah get done."

She stared at him.

"What?"

"What stuff?" Her eyebrows climbed toward her hairline.

"I'm getting' some supplies," he responded blandly.

"Hmm."

"What?" he asked again, exasperation coming through his voice this time.

She crossed her arms. "Curfew is at ten."

"I won' be out after ten."

Her shoulders slumped, lips pressed in a stern frown.

"Bye," he said quickly. He gave Jimmy a kiss on the head and left.

Naya's lectures took too much time. When Dave died, he'd stepped in to help as much as possible while Naya grieved. Now that she was back on her feet she actually paid attention to where he went... and how often he broke the law.

Chapter Nine

Present Day - Late Spring - May's House, West End of Abredea

Juliana woke to a cloud of emptiness still consuming her mind. She rolled, stretching an arm over her head and curled her toes under the blanket. This bed was half the size of hers, and much less comfortable.

A stab of realization pierced the cloud. This *was* her bed now. A shiver ran through her, ruining the stretch.

She lay on her back and stared at the afternoon light hitting the ceiling. The words she'd spoken to May reverberated through her mind. *This will never be my home.*

A door in the kitchen opened and closed. Footsteps clicked along on the wooden slat floor. Juliana shut her eyes. Pain sprung up in her chest, climbing to her throat and clamping as though someone were choking her. It slithered down as well, cramping her stomach in tight knots and filling it with fire. Tears filled her closed eyes and she hastily lifted the blanket over her face.

She would not cry. Not when someone might hear. She wouldn't show that weakness. Her jaw clenched and she glared at the covers over her head.

Waves of terror, pain, and anger broke over her, each worse than the last. Fury welled inside her—desperate hatred for the old woman she was forced to live with, for the people who administered the Coding, and for her parents, who should have gotten her out of this.

Despair overwhelmed the anger. Her mind flew through what she'd lost. Long days in Grigoria with Moniqua and Alex, the one kiss Don had stolen in the park last week, studying late into the night, picking out furniture for her new apartment, her bedroom, the shells strung along the walls, the kitchen, baking cookies on rainy days with her father, the sound of her mother's laugh.

This will never be my home.

She had no home. Tornim would never let her back.

Eventually her eyes closed and she drifted back to sleep. Mountains loomed through her dreams, vast and mysterious. Nightmares crept in: she fell through pits of black, strangers ripped the gems from her temples, her parents pushed her away.

The house was dark when she woke. Deep breathing across the room suggested that May had gone to bed. Juliana grudgingly appreciated not being woken throughout the day. Stronger than her desire for anything, apart from going home, was the desire to avoid speaking to anyone, ever again.

She slid from the bed, lacing her feet back into her black boots and tugging her pant cuffs down over them. The front door opened in silence. A cascade of chirps and buzzing met her ears the moment she stepped outside. Night was more alive here.

She quietly shut the door and stepped off the roughly hewn wooden porch. Her eyes adjusted to the night. A half-moon, nearly over her head, bathed the earth in an eerie glow. Specks of light dotted the sky, clustered particularly close together in a thick line stretching from one edge of the horizon to the other. She stared up at them and, for a moment, Juliana enjoyed the stars.

Cool air nipped at her fingers. She tucked her hands into the oversized front pocket of her sweater. Her feet moved forward, propelling her along the path to a destination yet unknown.

Voices grew and faded in the dark as she passed other homes. Her path met up with the main road and she took it west, away from the square.

Steady streams of light fell from the windows in the houses lining the path; they left little patches of yellow on the rocky dirt. One by one, in no particular order, they shut off.

She continued walking. The houses grew further apart and, eventually, the path she was on became undistinguishable from the dirt on either side. She passed through a clustered row of trees. Weeds grew up, clawing her knees. They tugged at her pants and grabbed at her feet. She slowed, taking care to avoid the larger shrubs and patches of grass. Their darker shadows left her uneasy.

Quite suddenly the weeds ended. A section of bare dirt, five feet across and stretching farther than she could see to the left and right, separated her from a tall, chain-link fence.

Juliana took a step, her foot landing in the soft dirt without a sound. She reached out a tentative hand and touched the metal. The cold kissed her fingers. She really was trapped here... for the rest of her life.

It was too much. Her knees thudded against the ground as she fell. Tears blurred her vision before they poured down her cheeks. She put her free hand over her mouth to muffle the sobs; the other clutched so tight to the fence her knuckles went white. Minutes passed in silence, the only sound coming from her gasping breath and the rustle of the wind through the trees.

A soft crack in the distance made her stand. She looked toward the camp, but nothing came out of the darkness.

Juliana wiped the tears from her cheeks with the back of her sleeve. She clutched at the chain-link, glancing up at the fence. The climb wasn't far.

She squinted into the darkness. Her neck prickled, her chest tight. No eyes appeared in the shadows.

Fury, fear, and frustration flooded her once again. She didn't belong here. Her fingers tightened around the metal; her right foot found a hold in one of the slots. She hefted. Her body rose and she latched her left foot farther up the fence.

Her fingers found new homes and she was pulling up once again when a voice behind her made her freeze.

"I... wouldn' be doin' tha' if I were yeh."

Juliana turned her head just enough to see a dark man standing behind her. His arms were crossed over his chest and, though Juliana couldn't make out his face, she thought she heard amusement in his voice.

"Well, I'm not you, am I?" she snapped. But she'd stopped the climb.

"Suit yourself, but the guards do their walkthrough at curfew. Tha' started about ten minutes ago. They'll be comin' 'round here pretty soon."

There was a soft lilt to his voice. He almost seemed to sing each word, the sound a contrast to the other White-Stars she's heard.

Juliana pressed her forehead against the cold fence. The chill filled her, helping her anger die down. She jumped from the fence, landing squarely on her feet, and facing the stranger.

He stood a few feet away, as tall as she was and darker. His sharp jawline was less obscured by shadow from a level height. She made out full lips and shaggy black hair which hung down just below his eyebrows. Dark eyes, from the night or genetics, glinted as the moonlight hit them.

Her upper lip curled as she clenched her fists at her sides. "It's rude to stare at people, you know." She squinted at him. Something was missing from his features, but she couldn't figure out what.

The man gave a small nod. "Just givin' a warnin' is all."

"I didn't ask for any warning," she snapped.

He remained silent, watching her.

Her jaw clenched and she tucked a strand of hair behind her ear in a quick, flustered movement. "What do you mean by guard?" There was an unintentional bite to her words. Her voice was different here, harsh and cold; another piece of this place that was unfamiliar.

He grinned. His smile was crooked, curving all the way up on the right, but not quite as high on the left. It gave him a mischievous look. "Guards, as in, the

Red-Stars assigned tah Abredea. They'll be passin' by here any minute." His smile faltered and his gaze darted down and back up again.

Juliana followed his glance; a small canvas bag sat in the dirt next to him. It bulged at the sides.

"So?" she asked, taking a step away from him and his cheerful smile.

"Well, it's after curfew." He shook his head with a soft sigh. "Yeh don' wanna be caught outside after curfew."

That, at least, was something she understood. Curfew for underage Blue-Stars in the city was midnight. She took a heavy breath. "All right then."

Juliana turned and walked away. The weeds slowed her trek, and she frowned in frustration at the unmistakable sound of footsteps behind her.

"Are yeh stayin' with May?" the man asked as he caught up with her.

Juliana whipped around. "How do you know that?" she demanded.

"My cousin and me helped her set up for a new Moon a few days ago. And," he added as an afterthought, "everyone from Abredea knows not tah be out this late."

She stuck her hand on her hip and jutted out her chin. "You're out."

He nodded. His fingers fiddled with the strap of the bag slung over his shoulder. "Tha's true." His teeth gleamed as his crooked-smile came back. "But I never get caught."

Something itched at the back of Juliana's mind; what was off about his face? She clenched her hands, trying to figure out what had her so on edge. Besides *everything*.

Footsteps crunched behind them, from the outer edge of the fence. The man's eyes went wide.

"I need tah keep up tha' streak. Let's go." He held out a hand, gesturing for her to go first.

She hesitated, confused by his kind manner after her blatant rudeness.

"Sorry." He glanced back at the fence before looking her in the eye. His voice dropped to a loud whisper. "When I said, 'let's go', I should 'ave said, let's go, *quickly*."

The footsteps grew louder, and with them came the low rumble of voices.

Juliana moved, and the two made their way back to the main road in silence.

Juliana's brain hurt. The whiplash between feeling too much and feeling nothing created a very real ache across the back of her neck and deep into her shoulders. Confusion addled her head.

She'd been nothing short of rude to both May and this man, and yet, they'd shown her not only kindness, but a willingness to help her; with no apparent benefit to themselves. Had she spoken that way to anyone from her caste in the Tornim...

Her right eye twitched. Just behind it, throbbing pain pounded against her temple.

They came to the turn off she'd taken from May's and the man stopped. "I'll see yeh 'round, I guess." He offered her a smile.

She returned it with a wary one. He walked away and she pinched her lips together with uncertainty. Pain thundered against her temple again.

"Hey, um." She cleared her throat, tapping her fingers against her thumb in rapid succession. "Sorry, for before. I uh, I was rude."

He'd glanced back when she spoke. A few seconds passed in silence. Then he nodded and continued on his way.

It wasn't until she'd walked back to the house, slipped inside, latched the door, and crawled into her bed that she realized what was missing. His temples, where she'd seen gemstones on every person in her life, were bare.

She rolled over and focused on May's steady breathing. Questions swirled around her mind; questions she wouldn't likely receive answers to. Behind these, tucked away in the back of her thoughts, fury burned low like hot coals. She couldn't convince herself to be horrible to May; it wasn't the old woman's fault Juliana ended up in the camp. Nor could she blame her parents or the people who sent her here. What could they have done?

No, the hatred in her heart was for herself. She'd done something, at some point or other in her life, to end up here. Something so horrible it deemed her unworthy, unfit to live with her loved ones. Undesirable. A Moon.

Chapter Ten

70 Years Ago - Beyond the Grey-Star Military Compound Wall

Maybelle disappeared from the rebel base and materialized at the edge of the woods near one of the entrances to the main Grey-Star military compound. A field stretched from the trees to the concrete wall which surrounded the city. Dew licked her shins as she strode through the grass. She'd traveled just as far last night, but this time felt different. Perhaps because she'd zapped or teleported or whatever it was on purpose, but she felt stronger.

When Maybelle reached shouting distance from the wall she broke into a run, screaming for help.

A squad of Black-Stars guarded the gate. One hurried toward her, his weapon drawn. She fell into his arms and gasped, panting for breath.

"I need to see Ben. General Benedict Jacobson. Right away."

The guard shouted to his men and one of them raced away through the entrance.

"Let's get you inside, ma'am," the senior officer said, glancing at her gems.

"Thank you," she breathed. Her skin crawled with nerves.

After fifteen minutes, two new Black-Stars showed up in a hydro-car. They gently helped her into the back seat and took off. They arrived in front of the officer's building minutes later.

Ben was waiting when she got out of the car. His military uniform was pressed and crisp as ice. The usually firm hair was rumpled and soft, as though he'd dragged a hand through it many times. Silver and grey streaked earrings were a match for the glinting grey gemstones on his temples. A panel of symbols was pinned to his black jacket, just above his heart.

He ran to her, pulling her into his arms, his thick eyebrows drawn together with concern.

A familiar flutter went through her stomach as she looked up at him, but the conversation she'd overheard rang through her ears. She pulled away.

"Can we talk?" She touched his forearm. "Somewhere private?"

He hesitated. "We need to debrief with Command. You've been missing for two days, we thought..."

She swallowed. She hadn't planned on seeing the twelve commanders running the war. That would take longer than she wanted to leave Kate alone.

"Please, Ben? I've been so scared, I just... I need to talk to you." She moved her hand from his forearm to his chest, putting a light pressure on his spotless uniform.

His shoulders went back, chin rising as he nodded. He dismissed the Black-Stars and took Maybelle through a pair of swinging glass doors into the entrance hall of the officer's quarters. She gritted her teeth, thinking of the last time she'd been there.

He led her to a small room off the hallway. A bay window overlooked a quiet courtyard. Half a dozen armchairs sat against the walls. A wooden table took up the center of the room. She sank into a cushy armchair, and he wrapped a blanket around her shoulders.

"What happened?" he asked in a tight, gravelly voice. He pulled a chair so close their knees almost touched. "I thought they captured you."

She shook her head, trying to read his face and be convincing at the same time. "No, I got away. They started shooting and I... I ran. There were so many dead, Ben. So many, and the people I helped, the ones I healed." She swallowed. "They killed them too, and the Black-Stars in our guard." She searched his eyes, hoping to see some sorrow, some small hint of grief for the one's they'd lost.

"How did you get away?" There was concern in his voice and a frown on his face, but his eyes were still impossible to read.

"I told you; I ran... I heard gun shots and I panicked. I didn't know what to do."

"That's all right, it's all right." He patted her leg, clicking his teeth together as he stared at a spot to her left. He stood and paced the room. "No one expects you to hold it together when the shooting starts; that's why you're in the medical unit."

Maybelle pressed her lips together, biting down the flare of anger his words sparked. "They have Kate. What are we doing to get her back?"

He chewed on his thumb nail as he surveyed her. His gaze slid down, landing at a spot beneath her chin.

"Where's your locket?" he asked, reaching toward her and tugging her shirt to the side, revealing her creamy skin.

"I was showing it to Kate when we got there..." Maybelle's heartbeat quickened as she leaned away from his hand. "She must still have it."

He nodded calmly, but a smile crossed his lips. His eyes brightened. "Good, good," he muttered to himself.

Maybelle couldn't get enough oxygen in her next breath. Her eyes burned as she stared up at his calm expression.

Her lower lip quivered as she spoke. "Why is that good?"

He paused, tilting his head slightly as he surveyed her.

He sat back down, leaning toward Maybelle. "I didn't tell you before, but there's a tracker in that locket. We will find out where the rebels are holding Kate. I promise."

"And then you'll go get her." Maybelle caught his eye and didn't look away.

He didn't respond.

"You'll go get her. As soon as you can."

Ben frowned when she didn't break eye-contact. Then he let out a sigh that morphed into a chuckle. He leaned back in his chair, his hands resting on his lap, front teeth clicking together as he stared at her.

"You already knew." He shook his head. "I knew you were too smart." He waved a finger at her. "I even told the—" He broke off, a resigned expression on his face.

"What?" She gazed at him, keeping her face as calm as her body would let her. "What is it I already knew?"

"You already knew the locket is a tracker." He stood and strode in a circle. A frustrated breath hissed from between his clenched teeth. "You have to understand, Maybelle, this is for the good of all of us. We have to win this war."

"You knew I was going to be captured." Her face was still serene. Her heart beat slower now, almost as if this confrontation calmed her nerves.

He scoffed. "Knew? I planned the frosted thing. This is *my* operation."

"You knew the tracker would be found, and I'd be killed." She breathed slowly, watching him pace the room.

"Found? I'm sure whatever was left of it would've been buried." He paused, staring at her. "*Will* be buried."

Maybelle was on her feet before she realized she'd moved. The blanket fell from her shoulders as she stared up at Ben, fear cutting through her calm.

"What do you mean buried?"

"You think I'd send a simple tracking device when I knew they would take you to their main base? That locket will destroy two city blocks worth of our enemy." He laughed; the sound echoed in Maybelle's ears as her eyes widened in horror.

"It's a bomb," she breathed.

The words barely escaped her lips when the door burst open. A tall, skinny Grey-Star holding a clipboard stood in the doorway.

"General Jacobson." He nodded his head respectfully. "You were supposed to bring her up for debriefing."

Ben regained his composure, straightening his uniform and smoothing his features. "We were on our way. Inform the commanders we will arrive shortly."

The man disappeared down the hall.

Ben looked at Maybelle. His cold eyes didn't match the sincerity in his voice. "You understand. It's a necessary loss."

"You're going to kill her." Maybelle shook her head. She couldn't feel her fingers, her whole body tingled with nerves. "Your bomb is going to kill Kate too."

"It's a necessary loss," he repeated. His voice was hard now. He grabbed her upper arm and steered her out of the room.

They walked down the hallway. Images flashed through Maybelle's mind: Kate healing the wounded, Red laughing at her comment about his beard, Sam's expression when she talked about her children. Horror filled her as she imagined their gruesome deaths at the hands of a massive explosion.

"You were going to kill me. I thought... I thought I meant something to you."

He said nothing but gripped her arm tighter and pulled her toward the stairs. When they reached the top, he wheeled her around so her body was right in front of his.

"You were a *means* to an *end*. I was going to blow you up too." He spoke slowly, the words dripping like poison from his lips. "We need to win this war. I'll do whatever is necessary to make that happen."

Maybelle shook her head, ignoring the hurt from his words.

"Those people don't deserve to die that way," she murmured.

He froze. There was fire in his wide alert eyes as he studied her face.

She swallowed. Her heartbeat thundered in her ears. She was too aware of her breathing, too aware of the way his eyes bored into her.

"Those people?" He took a step back. "You've met them... You *were* captured."

He glanced toward the end of the hall where the commanders waited for them. "Did you escape?" He took another step back. "Or did they let you go? Why? Why would they let you go?" Comprehension dawned on his face. His eyebrows narrowed as he gazed at her in disgust.

Maybelle put her hands up, shaking her head. "It's not what you think, I'm not—"

He reached for his gun.

She broke off, turned, and sprinted down the hall. A plasma bolt missed her head by inches. Shouts of confusion, then anger, sounded behind her as Ben screamed her disloyalty into the air. Doors slammed open as people filled the hall, searching for the source of the noise.

"I hope you said goodbye to Kate," he screamed. "She'll be dead in minutes, you traitorous bitch!"

His fury reverberated down the hall. Footsteps pounded behind Maybelle. She flew down the stairs, taking the steps three at a time. She rounded a corner and pressed herself against the wall.

She closed her eyes and willed herself to be anywhere but there.

When she opened them, she stood in the field just outside the wall. She gulped down heavy breaths. Her eyes took a moment to focus.

Ben's last words echoed in her ears. How long would it take to activate the locket?

She closed her eyes again, concentrating this time, thinking only of Kate.

"Give it to me!" Maybelle shouted as she zapped into Kate's cell.

Her friend looked up, terror on her face. "It's you." She sighed, fear melting into relief. "What happened with—"

"Kate, give me the locket. Now." Her head was already dizzy. If she stopped now, she wouldn't be able to keep going.

Kate frowned and pulled the locket from under her pillow. Maybelle snatched it and zapped again. She concentrated on the forest, hoping to end up far away from the rebel base.

She opened her eyes and saw—to her horror—she stood right outside the little building that led underground.

Rebels surrounded her, some tending to the trucks, some huddled around small fires, others patrolling the forest edge. She closed her eyes, willing herself to be farther away. But her head swam, her heart pounded, and her breath was coming faster than she could control.

She snapped her eyes open and ran, pushing her legs to fly. She had to get away from the base; she had to get away from Kate.

Thinking about her friend's life made her run faster, but shouting filled the air. The rebels had noticed her.

They didn't understand, they couldn't stop her. If they stopped her, they'd all be dead.

She glanced back, at least a dozen of the rebels were chasing her, but she didn't stop. She couldn't stop.

She faced forward and ran smack into someone's very thick torso.

It was Red. He stared down at her with a bemused expression on his face. A sharp pain stabbed through her temples.

"You don't understand," she gasped, but her words were too quiet. Her body sank as her legs buckled.

The man's bemused expression turned into a curious frown. He grabbed her arms with thick gloved hands, forcing her body upright. Rebels circled them, muttering amongst themselves.

"What's going on?"

"—in the depths did she get out?"

"—her eyes?"

"Hush." Red's tone silenced their voices.

"You have to get rid of it." Maybelle shoved the golden locket into his chest. It glowed hot; the metal seared the skin on her hands.

Red took the locket and let go of her arms. She fell to her knees. Buzzing filled her ears and her vision blurred. He crouched next to her; his eyes focused on hers.

"You have to... It's a... bomb..." she whispered. Her head hit the ground with a thump and darkness swallowed her.

Chapter Eleven

Present Day - Late Spring
- May's House

Juliana woke to humming. She rolled over slowly, having spent the night curled as tight to the wall as possible. May wandered through the backdoor into the kitchen, her arms loaded with leafy greens. She dumped them on the counter and paused, pain twisting her expression as she rubbed her hip. A moment passed, then she turned back to the vegetables.

"It's rude to stare, you know."

Juliana flushed as May repeated her own words from the night before.

"I'm sorry," she mumbled, climbing from the cot and getting fresh clothes from her trunk. She regretted dumping everything in as soon as she opened the lid. It was a mess.

She glanced toward the kitchen. "Are you alright?" she asked, a tentative waver in her voice.

"I'm fine." May ran the water, rinsing purple roots before placing them on a towel laid out on the counter. "It's just age finally catching up to me. About time." She chuckled.

Juliana swallowed, said nothing, and hurried to the bathroom to change. She came out and, not knowing what to do, stood in the kitchen next to May for a while. Guilty waves collided with her hatred. She felt, if possible, even worse about being a Moon after she'd been so rude to May the day before.

"About yesterday, what I said..." She glanced at May, half hoping the woman wouldn't catch her eye, but May looked up and watched her silently. "I didn't mean it. I know it was, um, inappropriate and rude and... and horrible. I'm sorry."

"I know." May turned back to the radishes and scrubbed at a spot of dirt on one. "Things are going to be hard for a while."

Juliana shivered. She clenched her fist to stop her hand from shaking. "I don't want to be here." Her eyes burned. "I don't want to be one of them," she whispered.

"I know." May shut off the water and dried her wrinkled hands on a rag hanging from a hook on the cabinet. Her steady voice calmed Juliana's heart. "But things will get better. It won't feel this way forever."

Juliana bent her head to hide the tears forming in her eyes.

During breakfast May suggested that Juliana spend the day exploring the camp. She even offered to come along and introduce her to a few people. Juliana declined as politely as she could, her skin crawling at the thought.

She helped with the dishes and once May went outside to work in her garden, Juliana left. She wandered the same path she had the night before. It looked less foreboding in the daylight. Those scary bushes were blooming with pink and purple flowers. A few larger shrubs with darker leaves sprouted stalks of bright yellow petals.

There it was. The fence.

Juliana stared at it. Stared at the forest beyond. She'd never been in a forest like that; a natural one. Further west, beyond the tips of the trees, mountains towered above it all.

The horizon had never captured her attention in the city. Why would it?

As she followed the mountains up, her gaze lit on a cloud, then another. From here... looking up at the brilliant blue sky... she could almost pretend she was home.

Hours passed as she sat, then lay, then sat again, near the western edge of the camp. It wasn't until the sky began to dim as the sun sank toward the horizon, that Juliana trudged back to May's.

The next day she borrowed a rough woven blanket and returned to her spot.

And the day after.

And the day after that.

The emptiness which tugged at her belly never left. It grew. Consuming her lungs, her heart, her mind. She went over every moment of her life, from the earliest memories of her childhood to every step she had taken in the Star Office.

Which of them had ruined her?

The time she'd taken an extra cupcake in her second-year class.

Or maybe stealing her mother's favorite bracelet when she was seven—each time she thought she was numb, a memory of her parents shot pain through her once more.

Something more recent, like the kiss she and Don had shared in the park only a few weeks before her Coding? It wasn't against the law, but maybe they thought something more had happened.

What had she done to deserve this fate?

She ran out of tears on the fourth day. By the fifth she'd grown tired of simply laying on the ground and had taken to climbing one of the large trees that obscured her little field from the rough path leading back into the camp.

From there she could see the mountains more clearly. They'd been in her dreams again, off and on between the nightmares which kept her tossing and turning for hours. Though, maybe they weren't these mountains. These didn't have any snow.

On the sixth day, only a few hours into her solitary vigil, something new happened.

Juliana had fallen into an uneasy doze on her blanket. Sun poured down, only the tree branches above stopping her pale skin from burning to a crisp. She woke with a start and sat upright. A few yards away, under the branches of a flowering tree, sat a girl.

Juliana blinked a few times, bit the inside of her cheek to make sure she really had woken up, and squinted at the girl.

She was maybe 16 or 17, with long brown hair and a field of freckles across her slightly hooked nose and rosy cheeks. She wasn't looking at Juliana. Her gaze was fixed on her hands where a row of flowers were threaded together at the stems.

Juliana watched her for a long moment.

The girl finished tying the ends of her flowers together, slipped the circlet around her wrist, and briefly caught Juliana's eye. "Hi." Her voice was light, like a little bird.

Heat thrummed through Juliana's chest. She swallowed and gritted her teeth. This was just what she was trying to avoid. Her temper had spiked so high with May, with the man at the fence... she wasn't willing to make a fool of herself, or worse, say the wrong thing to the wrong person and get herself—and May—in trouble.

"Hello," Juliana returned.

The girl looked away, plucked a flower from the grass beside her, and gazed out at the forest. Juliana followed her line of sight, wondering if she'd seen something.

After a few long seconds Juliana glanced back at the girl. A book had replaced the flowers. She was leaning against the base of Juliana's climbing tree and seemed to be completely ignoring her.

Juliana held her breath for a moment, unsure of more than just herself for the first time in days. Eventually, flustered and frustrated, she stood, shook out her blanket, and went back to May's.

On her return to the field the next day, Juliana breathed a sigh of relief to find herself alone once more. She spread out in her spot, lay back, and stared at the same sky she used to watch from home. For the first time, she considered it might be nice to have something to read.

Juliana was in the tree that afternoon when the girl showed up again. After a quick perusal of the area, and spotting Juliana in the tree, she gave a little wave and settled herself under a different tree not too far away.

Juliana did not wave back, but she didn't leave either. The two stayed under the trees, only the wind and the birds disrupting the stillness, until the sun touched the mountains.

Two days later, Juliana asked for her name.

"Daisy," the girl said with a grin. "It's nice to meet you. I wanted to introduce myself that first day, but I didn't want to disturb you."

Though Daisy had been born in the camp—as evidenced by the lack of gemstones on her temples—her accent was similar to Juliana's. The words came out light, dancing across the air like leaves on the wind.

"I'm Juliana." Her own voice felt forced and tight.

After introductions, the two sat in silence again. Daisy read her book. Juliana watched the sky and the mountains.

The next day, Daisy brought a surprise.

"Here." She pulled two books from a small satchel at her waist. "I finished this one. You can borrow it if you want, or I have this other one."

Juliana stared.

"Or neither," Daisy said, her pitch rising as the words tumbled from her lips. "I like reading, but not everyone does. It doesn't matter." She shook her head, the locks of brown hair falling around her heart-shaped face.

Juliana reached out and took the book Daisy had finished. "Thank you. I... I like reading too."

Juliana waited until Daisy had settled into the new book to open her own. She ran a hand over the hard cover, thick and worn, edges frayed, and colors fading. Tears sprang into the corners of her eyes. She let out a wavering exhale and jerked her gaze back to the clouds.

As a Blue-Star, her family owned a small collection of physical books. It was a privilege she hadn't even considered in her days spent reviewing the things she'd lost.

This same book sat on the shelf in her mother's study.

She traced the dragon on the cover, flipped to the first page, and read through the steady stream of tears flowing down her cheeks.

"This one's for you." Juliana tossed Daisy a floral print blanket as the younger girl stepped delicately through the field.

"Ah," Daisy hummed. "Thank you." Her smile cut through the grey of the first stormy afternoon since Juliana's arrival.

"You know…" Juliana hesitated. "I get here in the mornings. If you wanted to come earlier…"

Daisy sighed and shook her head as she flung the blanket out next to Juliana's. "I can't. I have school until two, six days a week."

"Six? We only do four in the city."

"Really?" Daisy's eyes widened, curiosity flashing in her smile. "What else… that is, if you don't mind talking about it?"

Juliana gave half a shrug.

"What else is different about Abredea?"

Juliana blinked. Someone else had said that word. *Abredea*. A second passed before it clicked. They called the camp Abredea. Montague had told her the first day; and the man had said it again the night she'd run to the fence.

"A lot," Juliana murmured. The tips of her fingers brushed against her thumb.

A breeze blew past them, carrying the scent of smoke, hints of jasmine, and thick pine. Daisy watched her, but Juliana found she didn't mind the gaze. There was no malice in Daisy's eyes, no expectation in her stare.

"I think…" Juliana glanced at Daisy before looking out at the forest. "I think the biggest change is in my head."

"What do you mean?" Daisy asked after a pause.

She sighed. "Just that," her fingers grasped at a long strand of grass and she ripped it from the ground, "there wasn't time in Tornim. Not for sitting still like this. There was always something to do. An assignment, a function, going into the market with friends, school. I've never had to just… sit with myself." She clenched her jaw. The blade of grass was now a dozen smaller pieces.

Daisy nodded, also keeping her hands busy as she wove together flower stems. "I felt the opposite when my mom died."

Juliana's head snapped in Daisy's direction, her eyes wide. A cold breath of air filled her lungs as an ache went through her chest.

"There was," Daisy continued, "too much to do. She was really sick, you know, before she passed and... there was always so much time to sit with her. Father hired help so I could focus on taking care of her." She swallowed and glanced up for a moment. Tears glistened in her eyes, but a smile nudged at the edges of her mouth. "She'd pull me into bed with her, tuck me under the blankets, and I'd read to her. Even when I was little and needed help sounding out the words. She called me her little bird."

The smile faltered. The tears overflowed, streaming down her cheeks. She sniffed. "When it got really bad and noise hurt her head, we would just sit in silence. I never wanted to be away. She liked holding my hand."

Juliana's gut clenched at the pain on Daisy's face. She hesitated but doing *nothing* in this moment... this moment of sorrow she'd been wallowing in for days, mirrored on Daisy, wasn't something she could stomach.

Tentative fingers reached out, cuticles scabbed from picking at them throughout her sleepless nights. Daisy bit her lip and took the offered hand. Juliana's squeeze was returned.

They stayed there, hands clasped and resting on the ground between them, until the sky blossomed with red and purple. The sun dipped below the mountains, the clouds above them splintering with light.

The next few weeks passed more quickly than Juliana expected.

Her afternoons with Daisy melted from icy silence to rivers of laughter, and sometimes tears. The emptiness inside diminished when she told Daisy about her family, her friends, the things she missed about her home.

It shrunk even more when Daisy shared as well. Her mother had died a few years ago, and she'd been holding an emptiness inside too. They discussed loss. They shared stories of happier times in their childhood. Daisy explained basics of living in Abredea, things Juliana should have read in the welcome packet she'd shoved into her trunk.

Juliana's path from May's to the field became worn. Weeds grew up on the side, knowing their lives would be short if they tried to thrive where footsteps treaded so often. But the rest of the camp remained strange to her.

The one-month anniversary of Juliana's Coding did not creep up on her. She saw it coming a week in advance, then days in advance, and the night before was filled with nightmares.

She woke late that morning. May had already begun her trimming and weeding in the garden. A bowl of mush, the grainy, oatmeal-like substance which was their only guaranteed food, sat cold on the table. Beside it, a small wicker basket held a handful of strawberries; a slip of paper stuck out from under it.

I expect today will be difficult. Hopefully these can sweeten the bitterness of being so far from home.

Juliana swallowed down her mush, gripped the note in one clenched fist and the basket in the other, and fled to the field with tears in her eyes.

Pain from May's kindness thrummed like a punch to the gut. Every unearned word of comfort or gesture of caring left her with the sensation of ants crawling up her spine.

Daisy would like the strawberries, though. Juliana's grimace slid into a smile as she pushed through the trees and laid out her blanket. She eyed the juicy red fruit, then set the basket further away to avoid the temptation.

The lack of food, readily available and in surplus as it had been her entire life, was the most notable physical change from living in the city. Government food, the mush packets, were delivered once a week. Each individual in Abredea received two per day.

It seemed that Juliana had been fortunate in being placed with May. Her garden, especially in the spring, was a source of sustenance they would not otherwise have. Juliana knew, from offhand remarks and uncomfortable conversations with Daisy, that she hadn't eaten what Juliana considered a proper meal since before her mother died.

She was looking forward to sharing this gift with her friend.

Daisy, however, did not show up that afternoon.

Juliana read the newest book Daisy had borrowed from school for her, climbed the tree, stared at the clouds, and even tried her hand at a flower bracelet. A pile of petals dirtied her blanket as the sun arced through the sky. With a frown, Juliana stood. She scooped up the basket of fruit and took a breath.

She let it out through pursed lips, drummed the tips of her fingers against the tip of her thumb, and tightened her grip on the wicker handle. One foot in front of the other she made her way past the turn to May's house and deeper into Abredea.

Though she'd been here before, nothing was familiar. Her only guide was the road, which had turned from dirt to cobblestone, and the knowledge that the school was near the main square.

She expected stares and feared what they might mean.

The road widened; paths and trails branched from either side. Homes grew larger and more plentiful as she made her way east and, a few minutes beyond the path to May's, Juliana encountered people.

Nerves jangled in her stomach. She stared straight ahead, catching only a glimpse of the little family walking by. A glint of white drew her gaze. Gemstones, on the temples of the adults.

A woman caught her eye. She swallowed and hurried down the road.

The closer she got to the square, the more people crowded the road. There seemed to be a shift change going on, and the school day had recently ended. Women carried baskets of clothes and brown paper bags from the grocer. Men hitched up their overalls and tugged wide-brimmed hats over their sun worn skin.

Juliana shared the awkward experience of moving at the same pace as the people around her and found herself just behind a group discussing a possible uptick in government provided food. One laughed, teasing the others at their hopefulness.

As much as her fear of catching attention tightened her chest, it seemed she was as interesting as the cobblestones. No one paid her any mind.

She'd almost arrived in the square—the unmistakable sound of a crowd of people gathering, playing, and shopping evident ahead—when a yelp reached her ears.

She paused, making the family behind her swerve as she hesitated in the center of the road. A winding path twisted between a collection of larger homes; down it, someone cried out again.

Juliana frowned. She glanced back at the square, memories of being in Agora with her friends splashing against her mind in unrelenting waves. She winced, tightened her grip on the basket, and turned toward the welcome distraction.

The chatter from the main road grew quiet as she moved between the houses and trees. She rounded a bend and halted.

A blonde boy leaned, panting, against the trunk of a thick tree. Blood dripped from his nose. Swirling gemstones gleamed from his temples, their colors moving fast. Three others, their backs to Juliana, stood around him. To the side, a tall girl had an arm wrapped around Daisy's chest, holding her back.

"—him alone," Daisy snarled. She glanced up at the crunch of leaves under Juliana's feet and fear flashed across her face.

The bleeding boy pushed off the tree. His fist whirled wildly through the air and his attackers cackled with laughter.

Fury erupted in her chest. She drew herself up, chin rising, lip curled, as the basket hit the ground. She stalked forward.

"What are you doing?" Juliana demanded. A splinter of doubt cut through her as the three boys turned. She shoved it away.

The attacker's temples were bare of gemstones, same as Daisy. Eyes widened, one took a full step back and another swallowed. The last quickly masked his fear and scoffed.

"None of yer business, city bitch."

Juliana's expression shifted. A grin grew across her lips, full and dangerous as she recalled the power she'd held as a Blue-Star. These children, and they were that, none of them looked as old as Daisy, didn't know what they were getting into. "That's not something you should say to me." Her voice cut through the air like ice.

The girl holding Daisy released her and moved toward the boy who had spoken, wrapping her fingers around his forearm.

"Why not?" He shook off the girl and stepped toward Juliana, scorn twisting across his dusty face. "Yer the same as us now. Those don' make you special 'ere." He tapped a dirty finger against his empty temple. He gestured back toward the boy at the tree.

Daisy had hurried to him and slung one of his arms around her shoulders.

The one in front of Juliana spit at her feet. "Acting high and mighty, like yer better than us, won' get you shite."

Juliana glanced past him, ignoring the words coming out of his uncivilized mouth as she watched her friend. Daisy, whose smile rarely slipped, even when she and Juliana talked about the worst times of their lives, wore a mask of rage. She put tender fingers to a slice on the boy's eyebrow.

Juliana looked back at the bully with a pitying shake of her head. "It's a shame you don't understand how insignificant you are in this world. *Playing* at power doesn't give it to you. It makes you look weak."

Her words carried a ring of truth, and with it a sting that shook his bravado. The girl grabbed his arm again, standing on her toes and whispering something in his ear.

His eyes widened, his sneer slipping. He waved a hand and the others hurriedly followed as he backed away.

Juliana frowned, watching them skirt the side of a house and disappear. "What was that?"

"Well," Daisy moved toward her, the boy limping along, "you *do* have a way with words. But I think Beatrice probably reminded him that you live with May."

Juliana raised an eyebrow.

The boy chuckled and winced. "They live in the west end too. Don' wanna be responsible for their families l... loo... missin' out on the food she gives 'em."

A lock of blonde hair fell across Juliana's face as she shook her head. "May wouldn't stop helping because of me."

Daisy shrugged. "Probably depends on how much she likes you. But," her usual bright smile returned, "they don't know that."

Juliana chuckled and turned to look at Daisy's friend. "Hi."

Daisy slapped a hand to her forehead. "Right, you two haven't met. Juliana, this is Taz. Taz, this is Juliana."

Taz grinned; his smile was just as wide, but somehow wilder than Daisy's. With a nod, he held out a hand.

Juliana took it, covering her cringe at the unmistakable feeling of dirt and sweat on his palm with a cough.

"Thanks," Taz said. "I o...owe... owe yeh..." He clenched his jaw and inhaled. With deliberate slowness, he spoke again. "I owe yeh one."

"Juliana would you," Daisy hesitated, then plowed on, "would you be okay with Taz joining us this afternoon?"

A shiver ran down Juliana's back and trepidation seized her. Someone new. Again.

But Daisy had become a welcome relief to the isolation, the darkness; and this Taz was clearly important to her. Juliana gave a nod, her jaw tight, and led the way as they hobbled toward the main street.

She picked up the strawberries and laughed aloud at Daisy's exclamation of excitement.

The three made their way to the field. The blankets lay where Juliana had left them, just as undisturbed as everything else in their little sanctuary. Strawberry juice ran like blood and laughter echoed like screams.

Taz joined them most days after that. He worked a few afternoons a week at the bakery, but for the most part the three of them spent their time together.

He and Daisy had been friends for years, since his arrival in Abredea when he was only five. Juliana gaped at this information. She stared at the stones on his temples, their color swirling faster than any she'd seen before.

"What about before?" she quizzed. "What where your parents?"

Taz shrugged a bony shoulder. "I don' remember. I don' remember anythin' before Montague talkin' tah me at town hall."

"But..." Juliana opened her mouth, closed it again, and grunted. "That's not possible. Everyone is accounted for. A missing child would be... well. *Impossible.*"

Daisy leaned in and put an arm around Juliana, squeezing her in a half-hug where they sat. "I don't think..." She hesitated, then squeezed again and said, "I don't think things in the city were always the way you thought they were. I think maybe some things were different from what you were led to believe."

Juliana's skin tingled. Her fingertips pressed against her thumb—pointer, ring, pinky, middle, over and over as her mind tried to wrap around the thought of a child mysteriously ending up in the camp.

The conversation continued, morphing into a discussion on the rumors of more food supplements, as she tried to process Taz's story. Eventually, she pushed it from her mind and returned to the present.

Juliana's initial fear, that Daisy and Taz's friendship would have no room for an intruder like her, eased within the first week of this new routine. It wasn't long before she was venturing closer and closer to the square, waiting for them just beyond the bend in the road so they could all walk together.

She went to the field alone less and less. Some mornings, after particularly vivid dreams of mountains, she'd go out, climb the tree, and stare at the peaks sticking out from beyond the forest, searching for the snow she kept seeing in her sleep.

Most of the time she spent her mornings at home with May. Gardening became a comfort. The steady movement of her body, weeding, planting, watering, and harvesting. She helped May prepare baskets which were picked up in the afternoons, always after she'd gone to meet her friends.

Life was nothing like she'd expected. She wasn't *happy*, exactly. But the despair in her chest, the screaming void telling her over and over how much of a failure she was, grew quieter around these people. Their voices drowned out the pain. At least, a little.

Chapter Twelve

Present Day - Early Fall - Red-Star District in Tornim

J ared Dilenski woke in the early hours of the morning. His wife rolled over, curling herself into the pillow she preferred to him, and would continue to sleep well into the day before starting her shift at the city gate.

Had Jared taken his current position, transporting coins to be converted into digital currency, to be gone by the time she awoke and in bed by the time she got home on purpose? Or had his job and hers been the fault of their strained relationship?

Or maybe it was the fact that they'd found each other through a matchmaker and wed shortly after their Coding ceremonies to escape their parents' houses?

Either way, Jared downed his black coffee, pulled his keys from the dish by the door, and left their small home without saying goodbye. Stars speckled the night sky. There were more up there, but they were hard to see in the Red-Star district with so many lights along the streets. Safety. That's what the lights provided. Red-Stars might not be able to boast being one of the top three classes, but there was no crime in their district.

It was probably the same in the Black-Star district, but Jared had never been invited there.

He clambered into his truck, started the engine, and pulled the lever which folded the solar panels on the roof inward on themselves. Jared navigated the smooth streets until he reached the gate to Grigoria. He flashed his pass, the one allowing him to be out after curfew, and the fellow Red-Star manning the gate waved him through.

At the main office, Jared checked in and got his list of shops for the shift. Over a dozen stops today, collecting the coins traded amongst the lower classes and then taking them to the government's central banking building deep in Grigoria. From there, they'd be converted into electronic funds to be deposited into the shopkeeper's accounts.

"Who's riding with me today, Gladys?" he asked, scanning down the tablet with one hand and bringing an apple fritter to his lips with the other.

The woman behind the counter, a Red-Star with greying hair shaved close to her scalp and sporting a dizzying array of Tattoo Artificials across her face, gave him an apologetic shrug. "No one."

"What?" Apple fritter sprayed across the countertop. Jared coughed, swallowed, and wiped the crumbs onto the ground. An Orange-Star emptying the waste basket across the room flashed a glare at him. Jared raised an eyebrow and the man got back to his business.

Jared looked at Gladys. "What do you mean, *no one?* This is a two-person job, minimum. I'm not even going to be able to lift the frosted box once I get there if I'm by myself."

Gladys shrugged again; the apologetic look replaced with a more apathetic one. "Tanner called out. His wife is having the baby."

Jared locked his jaw, gripped the tablet, and turned on his heel.

It was going to be a long day.

Two hours in, the earliest beams of sunrise illuminated the horizon to the east. Jared's arms were sore from lifting bags of coins into the massive chest in the back of his fortified truck. His mind was sore from the continuous counting, checking, and double counting to ensure none of the lower castes were trying to cheat the system. And his temper was sore from the constant delays which would not have been happening if he'd had a partner.

Glancing at the digital clock on the dash of his truck, Jared muttered, "*Nacra* Tanner, useless as frosted Moon," and flicked the wheel to the left.

Agora wasn't like the Red-Star district. Or any district, really, even though it was *technically* the Purple-Star district. The main streets were lit, but the rest was dark. Alleys, hiding spots, empty buildings, and a plethora of other lapses in management which were safety hazards.

However, the maze of crisscrossing paths, dead ends, and narrow backstreets offered plenty of opportunities for shortcuts his bosses back at the main office didn't take into account when they planned his routes. They shaved precious minutes off his workday.

Jared angled the truck between two brick buildings and bounced along, tires bumping over cobblestone. Emergency escape ladders dangled below shuttered windows on the outsides of the three-story apartment buildings. Jared scanned both sides of the alley for signs of troublemakers out after curfew. The buildings were home to unmarried Purple-Stars and sometimes he'd spot a few of the residents, in their twenties, out on the grated metal landings drinking and smoking. A shadow flickered above him, barely outlined in the greying light of the sky. But a closer look gave him nothing to report.

Gripping the wheel with a sigh, Jared leaned back in his seat and thought of the meal waiting for him at the end of his shift. Maybe Lenora would be waitressing at his usual spot. She was a Purple, but she always slipped him an extra biscuit.

Something thudded on the roof of the truck.

Jared jerked straight up. He took his foot off the accelerator and glanced in his mirrors. Nothing.

Maybe a bird?

Something thudded again. This time inside the armored, locked back of the truck. He thought he heard a voice, but that was impossible.

He focused on the road ahead, heart pounding. He'd get out of this alley and make straight for the emergency post only a few blocks away. Whoever was stationed there would help him detain any person who'd gotten into his truck.

He pressed the pedal, but the truck did not move. Knuckles white on the steering wheel, Jared uttered a disbelieving grunt as the entire front end of the truck was lifted off its wheels. Open mouthed and terrified, Jaren gaped as the driver's side door was wrenched open.

He looked into the night expecting a monster of a man or a crew of Oranges looking for trouble.

The sight of nothing at all was doubly horrifying.

"Ugh, Red," came a disembodied voice. There was a chuckle. "You're definitely losing your job."

Then something slammed into Jared's nose with enough force to crack the cartilage. Blood spurted down the front of him, leaving stains of warmth and wetness. Dazed and confused, Jared put one hand to his nose before he realized a rope had appeared around the other.

By the time he knew he should be struggling, his left hand was fastened to the steering wheel and something was jerking his right there as well. An unseen force clicked a button on the dashboard.

The engine shut off.

"You're gonna take a little nap now," the disembodied voice said.

Jared's eyes widened in fear as the voice chuckled. Something sharp stabbed into his arm. A few seconds passed, and then everything went still and dark as Jared slumped sideways in his seat, very much unconscious.

One minute earlier...

Cho clung tight to the rough edges of the bricks beside him. He was well hidden, a long black cloak covering his clothes, hood up to conceal his face. None of the windows lining the alley were lit, and because they weren't on any sort of main road there were no streetlights to illuminate the area.

Far above him, Jane perched at the edge of the apartment building roof, her steely gaze fixed on an armored truck turning into the alleyway. Across from them Tommy and Jason hid behind a set of garbage cans, out of sight for the moment. On the second-story landing, pressed into the shadows, two twelve-year-old girls held hands.

The twins, Luna and Nova, stood perfectly still. Wind whipped their outfits, pulling at their matching blonde braids. Cho held his breath as the truck passed over the marker.

A shape fell from the sky.

In unison, Luna and Nova reached out their hands and slowed Jane's descent. She landed on the back of the truck, her own black cloak billowing around her. She wobbled for a moment as the truck suddenly slowed. A second later, she appeared to melt into the roof.

Cho moved.

He scurried down the ladder to his left, clamping each hand around the cold rust-colored rungs with all the strength in his fingers. A sigh of relief followed his first footstep on solid ground.

A few yards away, the truck had slowed to a halt. Cho glanced up. Luna and Nova were locked in concentration, staring at the front wheels of the vehicle as they used their power of levitation to keep the tires from finding purchase.

Jason and Tommy ran toward the driver's side door. Jason held out a hand and Tommy's small one clasped it tight. They both disappeared.

Cho hurried to the back of the truck. As expected, the doors were sealed with both a digital and physical lock.

A few agonizing seconds passed. Every gust of wind heightened Cho's anxiety.

Jane had planned this well. He'd helped with the recon, weeks of watching and waiting, following people, finding the right driver at the right time. Yet, it could still all go wrong in a second.

Fear had stalked him since they'd left Haven earlier that night.

Cho bit at the edge of his nail, then the metal making up the door of the truck seemed to bend. The side of a box emerged, sliding through the door as though it were made of liquid concrete.

Once it had reached six or so inches beyond the edge of the truck Cho tucked his hands under the side of the box and helped pull, preparing himself for the weight of it once Jane pushed it all the way through.

Though he'd braced, it still nearly knocked him to his knees. The chest, as long as his leg and as wide as the length of his arm, weighed a lot more than they'd anticipated.

Jane's head and torso leaned out of the truck. Her body slid through the metal as easily as a knife through warm butter. She bent awkwardly, half of her still within the door, as she tried to help Cho lower the box to the ground.

Cho's breath caught as an edge slipped from his fingers. The box landed on the ground with a loud thud.

He froze. The sound echoed across the bricks, reverberating in his ears as he imagined every light going on and a horde of Red-Stars descending upon them.

A few seconds passed during which Jane jumped down from the truck and stood in front of him. Sweat lined her brow. Her breath was unsteady and she winced, flexing her fingers. "Frosted thing is heavy."

They stared at the chest sitting on the cobblestones.

Cho looked up. Jane had a gleam in her eye.

"You want to open it," he said.

"Don't you?"

"I think we should wait until we get somewhere safe." Cho startled himself with his decisive tone.

From Jane's expression, she was surprised as well. "Fine then. Let's get going."

"Aw, come on, Cho."

Cho's eye twitched at Jason's voice. The older man slapped his shoulder and crouched by the chest.

"Don't be such a Red. Take a risk for once."

Cho gaped at him. He could remind Jason they were already taking a risk even being there, but he knew it would go unheard; so he stood with his arms crossed and teeth gritted as Jason and Jane pried open the box.

Luna and Nova floated down from their perch to join the group. They cast nervous glances around, but the excitement in their eyes grew as the hinges on the chest whined in the early morning air.

The lid fell open and Cho sucked in a cold breath. Someone whistled softly. Jason swore.

There were bags and bags. Over a dozen. Cho did quick math in his head. More than the two or three hundred they thought they were stealing. By a lot.

"Let's get this to Haven." Jane's face was flushed with success. Pride shook in her voice as she nodded to Jason and Cho.

The two gripped a pair of metal handles on the sides of the chest and heaved. Getting this thing home was not going to be a short walk through Agora.

Light, true light rather than grey streaks, announced the arrival of dawn. Their group had traveled far but had farther still to go before they'd be able to lower the chest into the sewers. Luna and Nova grew paler after each turn carrying it. Cho's biceps burned. His stomach clenched at the thought of how far they had left. It would be easier if they could make a straight shot through Agora and get down to the sewers as quickly as possible. But that would mean going through the busiest sections of the market where Purple-Stars would be setting up their wares.

Jane darted ahead of them, Tommy's hand clenched in her own as the two made sure the way was clear. Behind them, Luna and Nova shuffled along with weary footsteps.

Shrill beeping filled the air.

Cho dropped his side of the chest. He spun in panic before realization hit him and he hurriedly patted at his pockets.

Jane whirled around, fury in her gaze.

The beeping stopped as Cho pulled a small circular com device from his back pocket. The thing was old, a model from almost a decade ago, but it worked just as well as the new ones. Its usual home, the back of a drawer in his bedroom, had been replaced with his pocket after his conversation with Claire a few weeks ago.

As he clicked a button on the side to answer the call, a chill sank down his spine.

Breathing, sharp, shallow, and terrified; Cho didn't need his power to feel the emotion on the other end.

"Claire?" he murmured.

Jane's expression, one of murderous intent, shifted to confusion as she stopped her march toward him and brought her hands to her hips a few feet away. Jason, who had set his end of the box down and also looked furious, swept the perimeter with his dark gaze.

"*Cho. I need help. You said... you said I could call if I needed help.*"

Her sentences were panicked and fast. Sniffs, gulps of air, and chattering teeth broke up the words.

"Where are you?" Cho glanced at Jane as he asked.

She widened her eyes and shook her head.

He frowned at her.

"*I'm... I'm at home. My mom. She found... she saw me this morning. I was practicing. I was just trying to learn to control it better.*" Claire's voice broke into sobs.

Cho's gaze darted around. With Jane leading the way, his focus had been on carrying the box. Now he took in his surroundings. They were near the northern entrance to Grigoria, and from there it wasn't far to the Red-Star district.

"We're close," he said to Claire, and also to Jane as he met her eye.

"No." Jane took a step away from him, gesturing at the chest.

"*What do I do?*" Claire asked at the same time. "*My parents are downstairs. They locked me in my room. They said... they said Black-Stars are coming to take me away to...*" She sucked in a ragged breath. "*To fix me... Are they going to fix me?*"

The terror in her voice cut through Cho's stomach like a blade. He shook his head, ignoring Jane.

"No. They can't fix you. We can't let them get to you." He filtered through ideas, discarding each one as more dangerous than the last. "You need to come to us."

"What in the *depths* are you doing, Cho?" Jane demanded.

"Hang on, Claire."

Cho muted his com device.

"What am I doing?" He met Jane's gaze and held it fast, his dark eyes boring into hers. "The same thing Ichi does. Helping someone who needs it."

She inhaled through her teeth. Fists clenched and unclenched at her sides as she closed her eyes and let out a string of curses under her breath.

"Where is she?" Jason asked.

"Red-Star district," Cho responded.

Claire's rapid breathing still sounded through the com in his ear.

Jason swore again. "Cho, we can't get in there. Not just us. Not in daylight. There'll be a dozen guards at the gate."

"We can't leave her." Cho glared at him, but hesitated and licked his dry lips before he spoke again. "Black-Stars are on their way."

Tommy, who had been watching the scene unfold with vague concern and curiosity, rushed to Jane's side and snatched her hand tight to his chest. Luna and Nova moved closer to the rest of them, grey eyes darting around as though the military arm of the Grey-Stars might step out of any doorway.

Jason met Cho's glare with a sneer, though a hint of fear flickered in his black eyes. "I don't need to be reminded that we don't leave people behind."

"Even *dumbass* frosts who don't have the brains to run away when they had the chance," Jane snarled. She looked past Cho at the twins. "Can you two make this thing easier for them to carry?"

The girls nodded.

Cho opened his mouth to object, but Jane cut him off.

"I'm *not* losing a score this big to a dipshit. Obviously, we aren't going to abandon her either. I can't drop it here. Underneath us right now is at least six feet of dirt. I can't get through that, not with this kind of mass." She scowled. "I know a place. It's on the way."

Cho unmuted his com as Jane delivered the plan to the group. He and Jason lifted the chest, Luna and Nova doing their best to make the load lighter. Tommy walked just behind them, his small fingers pressed against the metal to keep it invisible as they ventured onto higher traffic streets.

"We're on the way, Claire. But I need you to listen to me carefully. There's a few things you need to do."

"All right. I'm... I'm ready."

They reached the wall separating Grigoria and the districts almost ten minutes later. Jane had dropped the chest of coins through the street and into sewer tunnel down a side alley off one of the busiest roads in the market. She climbed back up through the grate with a line of sweat along her forehead. They'd have a difficult time getting to it later, but at least no one was likely to opened up a sewer grate and poke around in a place with so much foot traffic.

"Is she in place?" Jason glanced at Cho.

The shadow of the wall covered them, crouched forty or so yards from the northern gate. The entrance to the Red-Star district was the most heavily fortified of the lower casts. Gate houses sat on either side of the four-lane road, with a third, small guard post in the middle. Vehicles were stopped upon entering, either for gemstone verification or for the driver to submit proof they were allowed in the district. The same process took place on the wide sidewalks as pedestrians made their way in and out.

Guards armed with shock clubs strode between the few cars driving in at what was still an early hour. The district itself had only just opened its gates to incoming traffic from Grigoria. Most of the cars at this hour would be delivery and maintenance personal; Orange and Green-Stars on their way to do some job or another.

"*I'm here, but I don't know if this... there's a lot of guards.*" Claire had heard Jason through the com Cho still wore in his ear.

Cho nodded to Jason and whispered to Claire, "It'll work. Just be ready."

Behind the men, Luna and Nova crouched on the balls of their feet, jaws locked, and brows furrowed in identical expressions of determination.

They waited for a lull in the cars. After a few minutes only one vehicle still idled at the gate. A black truck, with a canvas covered bed and markings along the side Cho couldn't make out from their distance.

"Now," Jason muttered.

Luna and Nova groaned in unison. Cho's gaze darted back and forth between the girls and the truck. They repeated their move from earlier that morning, lifting the front tires off the asphalt. This time barely half an inch off the ground. A hopefully imperceptible amount.

The Red-Star at the center guardhouse waved for the truck to continue through. The front tires rotated through the air, spinning in place. The vehicle didn't move.

The Red-Star stepped out and walked to the driver's side of the vehicle. Tinted windows stopped Cho from seeing anything more.

He glanced back at the twins, a twinge of worry stabbing his gut. Blood dripped from Luna's nose, a few drops at first, then a steady rivulet which soaked into her flowing ivory dress. The twins' knuckles were white, their hands clenched so tightly together they were shaking.

"Now, Jason."

Jason shook his head, tugging at the side of the knit cap hiding his gemstones, frustration in his voice. "I can't yet. There's still someone inside."

"The twins—"

"I know," Jason snapped, taking his eyes off the guardhouse for a brief second to shoot the girls a worried look. "Give it another... there we go."

His worry melted into a smile as the second Red-Star stepped out of the small building and strode toward the still immobile truck. The front wheels, which had stopped spinning after a few seconds of no forward progress, spun again as the driver pressed the accelerator.

Jason placed a knee on the ground and inhaled through flared nostrils. He brought his hands together. As he pulled them apart, fire bloomed between his palms. Red flames licked the air around his fingers, not burning or even touching his skin.

The ball of fire was small. Jason watched it for a heartbeat before his gaze flicked back to the guardhouse. He shoved his right hand forward, extending through his elbow and shoulder.

Fire shot through the air. Barely two feet above the ground, the size of Jason's fist, the small fireball met its mark dead on. Behind it, three more bolts followed only half a second apart.

A scorching hole appeared in the side of the guardhouse. Then the building was on fire.

Someone shouted. Flames danced up the walls, growing with the breeze coming in through the window and open door. Boots pounded pavement. Red-Stars scrambled to put out the fire, their confusion and anger spreading in a wave that nearly knocked Cho off balance.

He slammed his defenses into place. A wall staggered into formation around the sparking, spinning yellow of his power. Emotions struck, and though it was poorly formed, the wall kept the worst of the storm of feelings from taking control.

As the Red-Stars focused on the fire, the twins dropped the truck. The driver had not lifted his foot from the accelerator and the thing shot forward, smashing through the barrier which had lowered back into place.

More Red-Stars hurried their posts. Shouts of fury and indignation echoed through the still morning air.

"If you aren't already, get a move on," Cho said into his com.

Jason flashed a white, toothy grin at him. "This is fun. I'll help you rescue strays any day."

Cho rolled his eyes, then glanced at Luna and Nova. Luna lay slumped in Nova's arms, her eyes closed.

"She's all right," Nova panted, catching his gaze. "We just... we need a break."

He nodded and nudged Jason. There were more important things to do than watch chaos unfold. Jason caught sight of Luna and went to her with no hesitation. Staying low, he lifted the unconscious girl from her sister's arms.

"See you in a sec," he said to Cho with a jerk of his head. He carried Luna along the wall until they were across the street from a glass and concrete office building. Darting a shifty glance around, Jason crossed the street at a brisk stride and slipped behind the building.

Cho returned his attention to the gate. Claire had to be coming now. He glanced at Nova, resolutely waiting beside him.

He tapped the side of his com. "Claire?"

Where was she?

A figure darted out from around the nearest gatehouse. Claire ran towards them. She wore fluffy purple pajamas with a thin sweater pulled over the top. Even from the distance Cho noted her red, puffy eyes, a smear of snot across her cheek.

Cho exhaled. Nova grinned over at him, flecks of dried blood on her top lip he hadn't noticed before.

Claire was yards from them, relief splintering through the fear on her face. Cho's gaze slipped past her. To the chaos at the gate. To the truck they'd plowed into the barrier. To the men exiting the truck. Men with plasma guns holstered at their hips.

Men with black gemstones shining on their temples.

Cho's stomach sank like a stone. He went numb as Claire reached them, wrapping trembling arms around his neck as he stood to meet her. He put a hand around her, his arm supporting her weight as she slumped with a sudden loss of adrenaline.

Her emotions flooded him. They warred in his mind and body, pushing against his own cold terror. The barrier in his mind cracked.

The Black-Stars weren't looking at the gate, the truck, or the fire. They were staring at Cho and the girls.

No. They were *striding toward* Cho and the girls.

"Cho..." Nova's soft voice, high and sweet like her sister's, was a whimper.

"I see. Get ready." He tightened his grip, shifting so he had his right shoulder under Claire's left, taking even more of her weight. "Claire, in a second we need to run. Stay with me."

Cho clenched a trembling hand. Something popped in the fire at the guardhouse. A few of the Black-Stars turned at the noise.

"*Go.*"

Nova launched from the wall, sprinting faster than the wind. Her feet didn't seem to completely touch the ground as she made for the building Jason and Luna had disappeared behind.

Cho followed her, half carrying Claire for a few seconds before she lurched away and ran on her own. He reached for her hand, and she took it, clasping his like a lifeline as they sped toward the towering structure.

They swung around the corner and came face to face with the rest of the group. As planned, Jane and Tommy were waiting. Jane held out her hand. Cho took it, keeping a tight grip on Claire's as he pulled her closer. The entire group vanished.

Cho heard Claire's intake of breath but, though he felt her hand in his and heard her whimper of fear, he could not see her. Or anyone else.

"Claire," he whispered, "close your eyes."

Heavy footfalls sounded from around the corner of the building. Jane tugged his hand. He took a deep breath and followed her through a solid wall. Claire squeezed his fingers so hard he was sure one would snap, but when he hauled on her arm, she moved with him.

They emerged in a small office space. A long table sat in the center of a windowless room. Squares and circles decorated the thin carpet; a picture of a tree hung from a wall.

The room was deserted. Jane dropped Cho's hand and he and Claire instantly became visible. The others did as well; only Jane and Tommy remained unseen.

Nova rushed to the door, which led to equally empty hallway, and closed it with a soft click. Claire released Cho's hand, her fingers trembling as she took repeated deep breaths.

"Hey, it's okay now." Jane's disembodied voice came from a far corner, gentler than Cho had ever heard.

Tommy's sobs punctuated the silence.

"Tommy," Jane whispered. "We're safe here. I promise."

Slowly, as though melting into existence, Jane and her brother reappeared. Tears streamed down Tommy's face, thinning the snot at his nose, and dripping onto the carpet. Jane cradled him to her chest, stroking his dirty blonde hair and continuing to murmur in his ear.

"What do we..." Nova stared at them from across the room. "What do we do?"

"I take it you all saw—"

"The Black-Stars?" Jason interrupted Cho as he moved toward one of the thick black chairs set around the long table. He kicked it out with one leg and lowered Luna onto the cushions.

Cho strode toward her, reaching her at the same time as her sister. Nova knelt and put a hand to Luna's forehead.

"She's all right."

As if in agreement, Luna's pale eyes flickered open, and she sat up with a low groan.

"We need to get home," Cho said, glancing at Jane.

"Home..." Claire murmured. She hadn't moved away from the beige wall behind her. The cuffs of her fuzzy pajama pants were dirty, clay-colored mud caked at the edges. She'd managed to put on a pair of running shoes before freezing the lock on her bedroom door, breaking it open, and sneaking out the back door of her family's home; all while muttering to Cho in her com as they planned her escape.

Her fingers shook. She stared at them as ice grew across her skin, horror in her eyes. Her gaze darted up and met Cho staring at her.

"What... what did I do?" she whimpered.

He hurried over and took hold of her wrists. They didn't have time for this. Not to mention the danger Claire's power could cause if she wasn't able to control herself.

He'd heard plenty of disaster stories from when Samaira and Jason were still learning to use their ability to create and control fire.

The moment his skin made contact with hers, the impact of her emotions tripled against his fractured warding. Sweat seeped from his pores. His lips trembled, forehead and palms damp. The muscles in his stomach clenched, his guts squirming with fear, anxiety, and shame.

Embrace it. If it must control you for it to end, let it control you. Let it control you for a few painful seconds, then shove it completely from your mind.

Elaine's words were easier said than done, but she'd helped him practice this new technique every morning for the last three weeks. As Claire's emotions slammed him like waves against sea cliffs, he released the walls protecting his mind.

The flood left him light-headed, dizzy, and short of breath. Oxygen wasn't reaching his lungs.

Cho closed his eyes. He sucked in several deep breaths before he opened them again. He reached within and grasped the frantic emotions that flooded him from Claire's touch. Pulling her emotions away from his own saffron power, he separated the two and shoved his power back into the safety of the ornate chest in his mind. Cho pushed the last of Claire's emotions away with another exhale.

The creeping cold which had begun at his palms wound up his wrists stopped. The ice which had whitened his brown skin melted and dripped to the ground, leaving spots on the carpet.

Claire met his gaze. Fear still clouded the hazel of her eyes, but she had control of herself again. She shook free of his hands and clenched her fingers into fists. The remaining ice shattered and fell.

"It's going to be all right," Cho said, first to her, then again to the group at large.

"How?" Jane snapped. She stood, keeping a hand on Tommy's shoulder. "How are we getting out of this? I don't have the energy to drop us from here, not unless you want me looking like Luna."

Nova grunted, a scowl on her face as she watched Jane.

"Jane's right." Jason stretched his arms, loosening his shoulders and wrists with the look of someone preparing for a fight. "There's no easy way out of here. Might have to put down some Black-Stars to get home."

"No." Cho glared at him.

A sneer crossed Jason's smooth skin. "Scared?"

"Who's going to fight with you, Jason?" Cho clenched his jaw, struggling against his own anger now. "Luna and Nova are drained, Jane just said she's low on power, and I don't have an active ability."

Jason's expression faltered, but a flicker of fire still gleamed in his eyes. "She's got an active power." He jutted his chin at Claire.

Cho gave him an incredulous glare, then turned to Jane. "We're going to have to come back for the coins."

She nodded. "It's way too dangerous to try and get it with Black-Stars crawling around Grigoria. Not to mention how impossible it would be to carry it home right now."

Relief flared through Cho's chest. The idea of trying to drag Jane away from that much money, after all the work she put into getting it, was not something he wanted to deal with on top of their current problems.

"So... what do we do then?" Claire's voice, deeper than the twins' but a child's voice nonetheless, shook with fear.

"How's Tommy holding up?" Cho glanced at the boy. His hair was matted with sweat, the front of his shirt dirty from wiping nervous fingers across it.

Jane gave Cho a cutting look. "He's as tired as the rest of us."

"But in a pinch?" Jason asked.

Tommy nodded, his eyes wide. "I haven't done too much yet."

"I don't want you doing too much at all." Jane took up his little hand and clenched it in hers.

"We'll take the long way." Cho sighed. "The really long way. Hopefully we won't need him." Cho strode across the room and knelt, coming level with Tommy's innocent gaze. "You'll be our back-up plan, all right?"

Tommy's excited grin peeked through his worried expression.

"Let's go."

Getting out of the building was easier than Cho expected.

They moved down the windowed halls, past offices and storage closets, and into a lobby filled with towering large-leaf plants in clay pots. The walls and doors were made of glass, textured so passing pedestrians would have to press their noses to it to see in.

The area was still deserted. Cho glanced up at a clock on the wall above a receptionist's desk. It was barely seven in the morning.

Exhaustion would have drawn his mouth into a wide yawn, but the adrenaline in his system kept him going. He led the others through the lobby and halted at the bolted double doors. The glass panes were lined with metal; square bars of steel forming structured designs to reinforce and decorate the entrance.

Cho held up a hand, motioning for the others to pause at the door. He looked along the street outside, searching. A few long seconds passed. Jason heaved a sigh and adjusted his grip under Luna's knees. She clung to his back, arms wrapped around his neck, ankles crossed in front of his torso.

Just as Cho's fingers grasped the heavy knob to unlock the door, movement caught his eye. A squadron of Black-Stars marched—jogged—into view as they turned the corner at the top of the street. There were eight of them side-by-side, heavy plasma guns in their hands, pace uniform, and heads on swivels, scanning the streets for any sign of the children.

Cho froze. Fear flooded his system as the others saw the squad.

He bit down on the emotion and waited. The Black-Stars didn't stop as they hurried down the street and rounded a building a block away.

"Now," Cho murmured. He unbolted the door, and they slipped out.

Staying close to the walls, they made their way deeper into Grigoria. If they could get to Agora, they'd have a better chance of staying inconspicuous. The hustle and bustle of the inner market started at the crack of dawn. It wasn't so strange for children to be running around: getting to school, going on errands for their parents, or causing general mischief.

Each step reverberated up Cho's legs, his feet aching against the cold concrete beneath him. They'd been up since midnight. The others' fatigue clung to him like dirt on the cuff of a pair of pants. There was no shaking it off anymore, not until they got to Haven. Any effort he put into protecting himself from the group would only drain him more.

Footsteps pounded toward them. Someone gripped Cho's forearm and he glanced up at Jason, scanning the area and jerking his head at the intersection behind them. Cho stepped away, Jason's fingers slipping from his arm, and whispered to the group.

"This way." They darted down a side street. It was smaller than the wide metropolitan avenues that took up much of Grigoria. A short-cut. One of many Cho had found in the days before his power emerged.

They ran. Each time Cho thought they'd lost the Black-Stars, the thundering of boots on pavement would reach their ears. Was it coincidence? Bad luck that the Black-Stars grid search kept running into them? He thought he'd kept them on enough of a divergent path that they'd be safe.

He snorted to himself, earning a curious glance from Jane as they crouched behind a low brick wall.

"Sorry," he whispered as the sound of the Black-Stars faded further down the street.

Safe. A foolish hope, but one he clung to as they continued to evade the people who wanted them dead.

A final turn onto one of the four main boulevards which crossed through Grigoria brought the gate into sight. It loomed ahead of them, a quarter mile away. There was nothing but grassy parks between them and Agora.

Cho's gaze slid over the families starting their day with an early morning picnic. A few children scrambled across a playground. The bejeweled hanging lights, ones which kept the wealthier areas of the city alight in a warm glow even through the night, had yet to be shut off.

His chest clenched, a surge of bitter anger spiking through him. His gaze fixed on a small black orb embedded into the light post. Beneath the glass... a small red light shifted his direction.

"*Nacra,*" he growled. Stupid. Cameras were everywhere in Grigoria. How could he think they'd be able to lose the Black-Stars before reaching Agora with camera surveillance feeding their location at every turn.

"Cameras?" Jason murmured just behind him.

"Yeah. We *have* to get into Agora or we're never going to lose them."

Jane panted on Cho's left, clutching her side with a grimace. "Got a plan for getting past *them*?" She gestured with her free hand and Cho gritted his teeth.

Two figures stood on either side of the eastern gate to Agora. Cho couldn't make out their gemstones yet, but they wore the red uniforms of Red-Star patrollers. Not as dangerous as Black-Stars—they weren't permitted to carry plasma-guns—but they'd likely been warned to keep an eye out for the group.

Even if not, they'd ask questions. Jason was too old. If they made him take off his cap, they'd see the swirling color of his gemstones.

Cho motioned for everyone to keep moving forward and ducked down to crouch alongside Tommy as they jogged along.

"Hey, you ready?"

Tommy swallowed and glanced at his sister. Jane's expression was pinched with worry.

He nodded.

"Right. Climb up," Cho said. He stopped running long enough for Tommy to jump onto his back. Tucking his hands under the boy's knees, they caught up to the rest of the group. Cho filled them in, his voice hoars and out of breath. "Stay close. Nova—you're responsible for keeping everyone connected. Hold onto Claire. Jane, you keep a grip on Jason and Tommy. Remember, if anyone lets go..."

He grimaced. They didn't need an explanation of the danger, not with the amount of fear he felt coursing through them all.

Tommy's fingers clasped around his neck. Nova's hand gripped the boy's left ankle, Jane—his right. They locked hands with the rest of the group.

"Wait for it," Cho muttered to Tommy. They slowed now, keeping a quick pace, but not running. This had to be timed right. Tommy wouldn't be able to keep them invisible for long, but if they got too close and the Red-Stars closed ranks...

Twenty yards from the entrance, a Red-Star wearing a cap matching his gem-stones put up a hand and took a few steps toward them.

"Hold on there, kids. There's a security threat going on. We need some—"

He fell silent, his jaw dropping into astonishment as Cho gave the word and they disappeared.

"What..." The Red-Star took a faltering step back. His fellow guards let out gasps; one shouted.

Cho kept pace; fear of losing one of the others stopped him from breaking into a sprint to get through the gate. The shadow of the wall passed over them and then...

They were through. Red-Stars shouted behind them, confusion and fear in their voices.

The wall surrounding Agora was high. Cho led them across the street, ducked into the closest alley they found, and paused.

A glance down told him Tommy had released his power. The boy's legs were visible. Upon turning, the fist-like tension in Cho's gut unclenched with relief. Everyone was still there.

Jane hurried to his side and prodded the boy on his back. "Tommy?" she whispered.

"What is it?" Cho asked, concern lacing his voice.

"He'll be all right." Jason had already started moving further into the alley. They had a ways to go still before they could safely enter the sewers. "The kid fell asleep."

"He's drained," Jane snapped. She bared her teeth at Cho, her furrowed brow just visible under her bangs. "I told you he didn't have enough energy."

Cho bit the inside of his lip to keep from growling back at her. He shifted, gently moving Tommy around front, and letting his head loll onto his shoulder.

"He did though," Cho responded softly. "He got us through the gate."

She opened her mouth, but he cut her off.

"We need to go. Tommy bought us time, let's use it."

Jane snarled, looking more animal than girl for a moment before she turned from him and followed Jason down the alley. Nova gave Cho a half-shrug and kept pace with the others.

Claire took a hesitant step forward, waiting for him. The frustration in his chest diminished for a moment, replaced with pity and pride. Tangled strands of dirty hair had escaped from her braids. The skin on her hands was bright red—from her icy power or the way she clenched them together, he wasn't sure.

But she was here. She'd kept up. The others' powers hadn't scared her away.

He gave a brisk nod, and they followed the group.

The rest of the way home was a test in patience and pacing. Agora didn't have as many cameras as Grigoria, but there were enough that the group had to take lengthy roundabout paths to get to the nearest safe and unattended sewer grate. Beyond city surveillance, they'd become a beyond-disheveled group at that point, and while it wasn't unusual for children to wander alone in Agora, they stood out.

Eventually, they made their way down a thin alley between two restaurants, too narrow for cars. A large metal grate—meant for flushing rainwater out of the city—sat in the center of the patchy cobblestone ground.

Jason reached the grate and hesitated—Luna still slumped on his back—before Nova's soft voice told him to step aside. She held up shaking hands and the grate wobbled. Blood dripped from her nose.

Jane touched her shoulder and then knelt. The two of them grunted with effort as the edge of the grate lifted. Claire inched forward uncertainly, then joined them. The three girls pushed the grate to the side, leaving an opening large enough for even Jason carrying Luna to climb down.

Jane and Nova went first, looking up to guide Jason and Luna, then Cho and Tommy. Claire brought up the rear, her braids bobbing in the air as she looked into the hole with trepidation. Once she joined them at the bottom, Jason gently lowered Luna to the ground. She stood, swaying, and clinging to her sister as he replaced the grate, disguising their escape.

"Now," Cho said, pulling a small blue orb from his pocket and handing it to Jane. Light filled the dark sewer tunnel as she flicked the switch on the bottom and held it aloft. "Let's go home."

Chapter Thirteen

Present Day - Early Fall - Haven, Home for Lost Children

They entered Haven at the height of morning activity. Children raced through the main room; eating, laughing, practicing their letters, reading, and interrupting meditation practice.

Cho wanted nothing more than to slump against the solid metal door as it closed behind them, but Tommy—still asleep—had grown quite heavy, and they *had* to report to Ichiro as soon as possible.

Their arrival hadn't gone unnoticed. The sound of the heavy latch sliding into place and their footsteps on the grated metal stairs caught Elaine's attention. She spoke to the children attempting mediation in the petite garden area of Sky's plant corner, and then rose to meet Cho's group at the bottom of the staircase.

"You're late," she murmured, her sharp gaze taking in Luna—sagging on her sister as the twins struggled to stay awake, Tommy—fully asleep and drooling on Cho's shoulder, and Claire—standing behind them all, shrinking in on herself with the air of someone who wanted to disappear.

"Things didn't exactly..." Cho began, not sure what to say, or how much to say in front of everyone before he had a chance to talk to Ichi.

"Go according to plan," Jane finished for him, her voice dry. As exhausted as she was, she still managed the energy to throw Cho a dirty look.

"Get the little ones into bed," Elaine said, looking at Cho and Jane, "then come to the study. We will meet you there."

Jason bent, planted a kiss on Luna's forehead, then Nova's, and then turned and strode toward the hall leading to the study.

Elaine's gaze lingered on Claire. "You can come with me, child. Unless you're more comfortable waiting for the others." The warmth of the words, of Elaine's voice, slammed Cho with memory.

Claire's wide eyes shone with tears. Cho offered up a weak smile; the morning's toll on his power combined with carrying Tommy didn't leave him with energy for anything more. "It's all right," he mumbled. "You can go with her. I'll be there in just a minute."

With trembling steps, Claire allowed Elaine to lead her toward the study. Cho and Jane joined them a few minutes later. The twins had fully collapsed in their bed, not worried in the slightest about being left out of the meeting. Tommy barely stirred when they laid him down and the only delay was Jane glancing nervously back at him, not wanting to leave the room.

Ichi was on him the instant Cho stepped through the doorway. His brother's strong arms pulled him into a tight embrace. Even through Ichi's rock-solid defenses, the mix of fear, anxiety, and finally relief at the return of everyone, overwhelmed him. He squeezed Ichi back before prying himself out of his brother's grasp.

"Sorry," Ichi murmured in his ear as he stepped away. He raised his voice, turning to the others. "It's been a tense few hours. Samaira was about to go and find you."

Cho glanced at the tall woman, her black skin rippling with tight muscles clenched in both of her crossed arms. She stood against the wall in a blood red tank top. Her expression was a mask of calm, but her eyes glinted. Jason stood next to her, visibly exhausted, but staying close to his sister. Their arms touched as they leaned, half on the wall, half on each other.

Claire perched on the edge of the couch, her Red-Star upbringing evident in her rigid back, raised chin, and planted feet. Her fear only showed on her face and the wringing of her hands. Elaine kept a comfortable distance between them, not settling back in a way that might startle the girl from her seat.

Ichi leaned against his desk, Jane took the chair in front of it, and Cho slunk into the chair behind the desk. The room was silent for several long seconds. Cho closed his eyes, embracing the quiet.

Ichiro shifted, the movement bumping the desk against Cho's chair. Cho cracked open his eyes. His older brother watched him. Their almond brown gazes met.

"Jason filled us in while you put the younger ones to bed," Ichi said. He gestured to Claire. "Your new friend hasn't said a word."

Elaine leaned in and whispered something to Claire.

"Black-Stars..." Ichi shook his head. He pressed two fingers to the space between his eyebrows. "That's..." a heavy sigh, "*not* ideal."

Samaira shifted. Cho glanced over in time to catch the sharing of a nervous glance between her and Jason. Elaine cleared her throat looking pointedly at Ichi.

"But that can wait." Ichi forced a smile and turned his gaze to Claire. "We have a new arrival. Welcome, Claire. Cho has told us a little bit about you, but it is lovely to get to meet you. I cannot express how glad I am that our family was able to get you out."

Claire watched him for a long moment. "Those..." she swallowed. "Those Black-Stars were coming for me."

It wasn't a question, though it might have been. She had known they were coming, had told Cho about overhearing her parents' conversation. But the statement seemed to solidify something inside her. The fear in her eyes melted into something harder. Anger, or resolve. She met Cho's gaze and he nodded in confirmation.

"If they had taken you," Elaine murmured, "it would have been impossible for us to reach you."

"The last... many children we've encountered with abilities—"

"The ones who don't come with us right away," Jason interrupted Ichi with a glare, first pointing at Claire, then at his sister when Samaira elbowed him in the side.

Ichi continued as if Jason hadn't spoken. "...have been taken."

"How... how often does this happen?" Claire's voice trembled. "How many of us are there?"

Ichi sighed, and lines of weariness replaced his smile. "More often than I'd like. From what I can tell—what *we* can tell." He gestured to Elaine. "Three or four children present abilities every year. Sometimes less, sometimes more."

"That doesn't..." Claire frowned.

"Seem like a lot?" Samaira finished for her. She unfolded her arms and pulled forth a small ball of flame into her palm.

Jason tilted his head, resting it against her broad shoulder.

"In a city this size," Elaine said, folding her hands across her lap, "it doesn't seem like much. We are rare, Claire. Most people like us... most people with abilities, powers, don't manifest them until much later in life."

"And for them," Ichi strode across the room, reaching out a hand for Elaine to hold, "it's too late. They've already been taken."

"But... but taken by who? Why?" Claire's voice rose an octave as panic once again laced through her words.

"By those same *frosted* Black-Stars who tried to take all of us this morning," Jane bit the words out, but her anger wasn't directed at Claire. The younger girl seemed to notice the difference and gave Jane a slow nod.

"Language," Elaine murmured.

Jane's jaw clenched, a muscle in her neck throbbing.

"That will do on this topic for now," Ichi said.

The room fell back into something close to silence. There was a thrum as Claire ran her nails across the rivets on the couch. Crackling, from the small handful of fire now dancing in Samaira's hand. Squeaking, from Jane's chair as she shifted, her eyelids drooping heavily.

"Let's get the lot of you to bed," Elaine stood, squeezed Ichi's hand, then moved away from him toward the door.

Claire darted a nervous glance at Cho, but followed Elaine across the room.

Jane stood as well, she, Jason, and Samaira joining the others at the door. Cho exhaled a sigh of relief. Every fiber of his body was exhausted. Every inch of him craved the isolation of his small, dark room.

"I need Cho and the twins to stay," Ichi cut in as Elaine opened the door.

Cho's stomach sank as he lowered himself back into the chair. Sleep. He just wanted to sleep.

Jane's head whipped around, the hurt expression on her face quickly shifting to anger as she met Ichi's sharp eye.

"I'll fill you in after you get a few hours of sleep, Jane. Go. Be with Tommy."

A flicker of understanding split through the anger. Still, she stormed past Elaine and Claire, shoved the door open and disappeared down the hall without another word.

"They need rest, Ichi." Elaine grimaced at Ichi's pained expression. She sighed and put a gentle hand on Claire's shoulder. "Let's at least get you to bed. Everyone will be eager to meet you once you've had a chance to get settled."

The door closed behind them. Cho knew, from his own experience arriving in Haven all those years ago, that Elaine would give Claire the welcome speech on their way to the nearest empty room.

You're safe here, Cho. This is a place where you can be you. Unabashed, unashamed, unafraid. We will do everything we can to teach you how to control your gift.

Cho had snorted at that and let out a laugh that sounded more like a cry.

Well, whatever you'd like to call it is fine. But for us, and especially for the younger children, we call it a gift. Take a few days to yourself, Cho. Take some time away from everyone to heal. Then, I know Ichi is eager to give you a tour of the home we've built. He's been waiting for you.

Granted, Elaine's little talk with Claire would probably go differently. But the important stuff, being safe, being yourself, having a family, and learning control would all be in there.

Jason's voice rocked Cho from his memory.

"So, the Black-Stars, Ichi? Figure that's what you want to talk about?"

Ichi nodded.

Cho looked up at him from the desk.

Jason sighed and slumped onto the couch, sprawling with both feet up and crossed at the ankles. Samaira paced her usual track around the office, wearing a trail into the carpet.

"I never expected them to come at us in this way. So public, so brazen." Ichi shook his head. He lifted a small square of pale pink paper from his desk and folded it in half. "There are things I need to tell you. Pieces of the puzzle Elaine and I have recently pieced together."

Samaira kept pacing, though her stride slowed.

Cho sat up in his chair watching his brother. What puzzle?

"You already know what happens to those of us who don't exhibit powers before the Coding." Ichi turned to Cho.

"They get taken to the camp."

Ichi nodded.

Jason grunted from the couch. "They aren't usually snatched by Black-Stars though. From what we've seen, it's Reds who facilitate the move for new White-Stars." He scratched his chin. "I still don't get how they stop abilities from showing up once they get there though."

"That's a small piece of our problem. And not what I'm worried about at the moment."

Cho frowned. The camp was an issue they'd discussed hundreds of times. Ichi and Elaine had discovered the truth behind the Coding long ago—it found people with latent powers. How, they weren't sure. Why was less of a mystery. To put them in the camp. Not everyone there had power; plenty were political dissidents, lawbreakers, or unfortunate children whose families had made the wrong person angry.

They'd thought about going in. Thought about trying to rescue children taken by Black-Stars. There were two problems with this idea. First, getting out of the city—let alone into the camp—was nearly impossible. Second, no one there had powers; Ichi had yet to discover why.

"What does that have to do with the Black-Stars this morning?" Cho asked.

Ichi turned to him. "That's what I want to talk about. Before today I'd never dream the Black-Stars would come at us in that way. Storming Grigoria? Marching through Agora hunting you? That's not their usual method." He ran his nails across the edge of the paper in his hands, sealing the crease. "The lack of secrecy concerns me. If they've decided they don't care about people finding out about us? If they don't need to use caution in the city anymore..." He swallowed. "Their desire for our existence to remain hidden is one of the only things that's kept us alive this long."

Jason scoffed. "We're also good at fighting... and hiding," he added grudgingly.

Ichi gave his old friend a long stare. "If they'd caught you. Or, more likely if they'd caught Claire, they wouldn't have taken her to the camp."

Cho's eyes widened.

Samaira stopped pacing and fixed a quizzical frown at Ichi.

"Where then?" Jason stretched, flexing his biceps and forearms. A collection of burns crisscrossed a pattern along his skin, scars from over a decade ago when his and Samaira's powers first emerged and they weren't in control of their flames.

"The children they catch, the ones who survive the hunt, are taken to a research facility somewhere in Pangaea. It's run by a Grey-Star."

A chill ran across Cho's skin. Samaira and Jason shared an identical intake of air.

"So that's..." Cho hesitated, not wanting to voice his thoughts. "That's who actually wants us? The Grey-Stars?"

Ichi ran a hand across his face. "We've thought this whole time that they wanted to take us to the camps. To hide us like they hide the Moons. Keep us walled off from the rest of the world and restrict our abilities. But that's not it. The Grey-Stars are *different*. Not like us, but not like everyone else either. I don't know what it is. Elaine doesn't know."

"She's seen one, right?" Samaira broke in. "A Grey-Star. In person?"

Ichi nodded. "She remembers a Grey-Star. It's one of the few memories I've been able to access. What she remembers is not... it's not pleasant."

Samaira's jaw clenched, her muscles tight. The room was silent for a few seconds.

Ichi cleared his throat. "This Grey-Star is the one who wants us. Not for the camps, but for whatever this facility is. It's why I've been so adamant about getting ahold of any children we discover." He looked to Cho. "It's why I told you not to hold back with Claire."

"What do we..." Cho swallowed. "What do we do then?"

Ichi gave him a long look. Cho was grateful his brother's mental wards kept his emotions in check, but he wouldn't mind knowing what Ichi was thinking in this moment.

"We move up the timeline."

Cho's chest tightened.

Jason sat upright. "When?"

"I was hoping for tonight, but after seeing Jane's state I think we should wait a day. Tomorrow night. Then Elaine and I will leave a few days later."

Cho's mouth ran dry.

Samaira and Jason glanced at him before sharing a look.

"You're still only taking Samaira?" Jason asked.

Ichi nodded. The two stared at each other for a moment. Cho studied Jason's expression. The man didn't look any happier about staying behind than Cho was about being left in charge. Eventually, Jason stood, breaking eye contact and returning to his sister's side.

"We've got work to do then," Samaira stated. She latched an arm around Jason's. "Let's get you rested up; we have details to pin down if this is finally happening."

The twins left the room, Jason sporting a sour expression.

"Is this why you're so anxious to leave?" Cho voiced the thought which had been stirring in his mind during the conversation. "Because the Black-Stars are getting more direct?"

Ichi turned to face him. "Yes. They won't..." He sighed, fingers still fiddling with the small paper. "They won't stop hunting us, Cho. I thought... years ago I thought if we hid, stayed out of the way, didn't disturb the *proper* citizens, they'd leave us alone. Sure, they kept going after new kids who demonstrated power, but we thought they were going to the camps."

Cho nodded. It was a fear they all held, even in the safety of Haven. Going to the camp, having their power taken, or suppressed, or whatever it was that stopped the White-Stars from using their abilities.

If he was honest, it was something he used to daydream about. The camps were known to be horrible, dangerous places where there wasn't enough food, the people were cruel and unlawful, and a wrong look could get you killed. But... a place where he didn't have his power.

There was a time when that was all he wanted.

"They need us." Ichi broke the silence. "I don't know why, but they do. And they won't stop hunting us until they get what they want. *That's* why I want to get us out of here. *That's* why I want to find us a home where we don't have to be constantly on alert, on the run."

Cho picked at the skin around his thumb nail.

Ichi clapped a hand on his shoulder. "Get to bed. You should rest a few hours before meditation today. And you'll definitely need to get a full night's sleep before tomorrow."

Cho's eyebrows crinkled. "I'm still going?"

"If you're up for it."

Cho stood, pushing himself up with a groan and passing his brother to reach the door. "I'm up for it, Ichi." He paused. "Maybe talk to Jane, soon. She had more hurt than anger when you sent her out."

Ichi gave him a rueful smile. "I know."

Cho was pulled in for one more bone-shattering hug. When they parted, Cho walked away with a small pale pink paper crane cradled in his palm.

Chapter Fourteen

Present Day - Mid Summer - May's House

Juliana scowled at the bowl of grey mush on the table before her. A little painted jungle cat of some kind—black with yellow spots—peaked out from behind a dark green leaf next to her wooden bowl. She lifted a glob with her spoon.

Her lip curled in disgust as it plunked back into the bowl.

"Not as good without the extras, is it?"

Juliana glanced up hopefully. Two months had passed since her Coding, and during that time she'd only had to eat plain mush packets a handful of times. Now, however, she was on day three of grey goop in her bowl. Not a strawberry or spoonful of sugar in sight.

"It's disgusting," Juliana grumbled, slouching back down into her chair as May hobbled over with her own bowl. Her hope, that May would open a cupboard and produce a hidden pouch of sweet crystals, was dashed.

May chuckled as she eased into her seat. "Come winter you'll be happy for anything to warm your belly, disgusting or not."

"When do we get more sugar from the square?" Juliana fiddled with her spoon.

The berry patches in May's garden had been picked clean. It would be days still until more were ripe. May had mentioned wild berries—plump black things juicier than she could imagine—but they were in the forest. Outside the fence. In a place Juliana would never be allowed to go.

May tisked and her grey eyes flickered like a storm. "That sugar was a gift, Juliana."

Juliana straightened, warmth reddening her cheeks.

"It cost Anthony a full rabbit and a basket of mushrooms to get me that little bag from the grocers. An absolute racket if you ask me," she murmured as an aside, "but a wonderful birthday present just the same."

The sinking pit in her stomach—which had shrunk considerably the more time Juliana spent with Taz and Daisy—grew again. It sucked down the sunlight, leaving Juliana feeling cold in the early morning warmth of the kitchen.

"Oh, don't you worry, dear." May grinned at her. The skin around her scar stretched and twisted, shinning white. "I don't mind sharing. Especially with a sweetie like you."

Juliana shook her head, unable to stop the smile.

"But... if you want more of that kind of thing. And other spices, bread, cheese, meat. Anything besides these," she tapped her spoon against the side of her bowl, "then you'll need to find work."

"What kind of—"

Someone knocked on the door.

May blinked and exchanged a quizzical glance with Juliana. Their early morning routine had fallen into place a few weeks prior. It was new for Juliana—just like everything else—this rising with the sun. But something about perching next to May's old rocking chair, a steaming mug of lightly minted water in hand, and watching the sun rise over the city skyline, brought peace to her day.

It also meant she and May were awake and eating their breakfast long before most of the camp—Abredea—woke up.

"Who in the *depths*?"

"I can get it," Juliana said. "You just sat down." She rose, not giving May time to object as she strode across the room and undid the little latch on the front door.

She blinked up in surprise. Montague stood before her, fully dressed for the day in the same worn suit he'd had on when she arrived. He clutched a hat in one hand and rubbed the sleep from his eyes with the other.

"Um, hello." Juliana hesitated.

"Open the door girl, let him in," May called.

Juliana swung the door wide, and Montague bobbled past her with a nod.

"Thank you, Miss Juliana. And good morning, to both of you."

May raised an eyebrow. "It is a good morning, James. Would you care for a cup of tea, something to warm your hands?"

Juliana followed Montague across the room as he settled himself into one of the dining table chairs.

"The offer is appreciated, Miss May. But as I'm sure you know, the new captain will be arriving in the next few days and we have quite a lot to be getting on with."

Juliana's stomach churned. Something about her schedule these last few weeks had been keeping her together. The same people, the same places, even the same disgusting food, for some reason made being at the camp seem less real.

Each day felt the same. Each night was a blur of nightmares, dreams about snow-capped mountains, and empty blackness.

Almost like time was standing still. This intrusion sped things up again.

"What brings you to our home at this early hour?" May asked.

Our... home...

Juliana's ears rang. She braced a hand on the wall.

"... got word last night, late. I didn't want to wake you both, so I hoofed it down here first thing."

"Oh my."

Juliana darted a glance at May. Her face had gone pale. She trailed a gnarled finger up the edge of her scar to her gemstone.

"What do they..." May cleared her throat and a forced smile parted her lips. "What do they require?"

Montague gestured to Juliana with a little nod of his head. "They want to speak to you."

Juliana blinked and shook her head. "I'm sorry, what's going on? I was... distracted for a moment."

"A Grey-Star, Miss Juliana." Montague watched her. "A Grey-Star has commanded your presence at town hall."

Juliana gaped at him.

"The Abredea town hall, of course," he said, as though that would clear up her confusion.

A thrumming mix of excitement and nerves started in Juliana's chest. Her skin tingled, little bolts of electricity seeming to flow through her veins.

"Who?" Juliana's parents' faces swam before her as she tried to imagine them going to one of their superiors in an attempt to have a Grey-Star intervene on her behalf.

It was difficult to picture.

A more probable answer rested in the woman she'd met at the Coding. Though, why Ms. Wolfe would bother with her now that she was a Moon...

"When?" Juliana demanded before Montague had time to answer her first question.

"They didn't specify, Miss Juliana. A Blue-Star assistant contacted us late last night and said the Grey would be arriving sometime today. I thought it best to fetch you as early as possible so we might not keep them waiting."

Juliana nodded. There, at least, was something they were doing right. Juliana would never dream of keeping a Grey-Star waiting.

She rushed to the chest at the foot of her cot and pulled her nicest outfit from it.

"I'll be ready in just a moment," Juliana called to Montague as she scurried into the bathroom to change.

A harsh scraping of wood made Juliana glance back. May stood, eyes wide, palms on the table. She leaned against it, her brow furrowed as she hissed something at Montague.

Juliana brushed aside her curiosity and dressed. The same blue flowing sleeves she'd worn to the Coding, the soft fabric skimming her belly button, high pants hugging her waist.

It felt odd to wear now. Her skin had grown used to the strange clothes her parents packed and the outfits May lent her.

She ran a comb through her hair, pulled the strands—longer than they'd been in years—into a braid, and tied it with a small circle of elastic.

Double-checking herself in the mirror, she hurried back out. "I'm ready."

Montague gave her an acknowledging nod and continued his conversation with a tense-looking May.

Juliana clenched her jaw. She strode to the door and opened it, waiting. Her stomach churned with curiosity about what the Grey-Star could want.

Hope fluttered in the depths of that pit. She squashed it.

No one left the camps. Ever.

Juliana held her temper and impatience as long as she could, a good thirty seconds, before she stalked out the door and let it slam shut behind her. Montague had come to fetch her with the purpose of getting to town hall as quickly as possible. It didn't make any sense for them to dawdle so he could have a conversation with May.

The two of them could talk anytime. This was more important.

She'd gone twenty yards or so when huffing and hurried footsteps sounded behind her. Montague caught up, out of breath by the time he reached her. The mirror effect of their outfits, their direction, and their pace was not lost on Juliana.

Her fingers tapped against her thumb. The sun lit their way. White-Stars shuffled about in the early morning. Men and women in overalls, thick pants, and layered tops made their way to the transport hubs on the northern end of the camp. They'd work anywhere between six and twelve hours in the fields, mines, or factories before being shipped back home.

Juliana's chest tightened and her pace quickened. May had mentioned work...

Did she mean for Juliana to throw on a pair of boots and bend her back throughout the hottest parts of the day? Or to dive beneath the ground and let her eyes grow accustomed to the dark?

Taz worked at the bakery. He spent two afternoons a week helping clean up, kneading bread, and running sacks of flour and other ingredients from the grocers to the bakers. He didn't make much, from what Juliana gathered, but he lived in the orphanage and was able to put away any leftover money he didn't spent on food.

According to Daisy, he'd be able to get full time work once he turned eighteen. This was an oddity to Juliana. She'd become an adult on her twentieth birthday. But here, children were expected to care for themselves at a much younger age.

Thinking of Taz led Juliana down a different train of thought. The story of how Taz arrived in Abredea. She couldn't fathom how a five-year-old child could just appear. No memories, no family, no documentation to show where he should be.

He had gemstones, he must have had a caste—one in the city, not the camp.

And yet he'd fallen through cracks Juliana hadn't even known existed.

Her brow furrowed as she and Montague passed the fountain and climbed the concrete steps of town hall.

"She's... they've not yet arrived, correct?" Juliana asked.

"I certainly hope not," Montague wheezed. He sucked in a few breaths at the top of the stairs and then straightened and held open the door for her.

Juliana squared her shoulders and raised her chin. She walked through the doors, gaze darting around the room.

The lobby was empty.

Juliana let out a small breath of relief. Keeping a Grey-Star waiting wouldn't help her chances.

She bit the inside of her lip. There was no chance, she reminded the small quiver of hope in her stomach. No chance of leaving the camp. To hope for it was inviting pain.

The interior of the town hall was cleaner than she expected. Her attention had been elsewhere the last time she'd been in the building. Now she had nothing to do but wait.

She walked the edges of the room, examining the architecture and the paintings hung at even intervals. Wooden benches lined the walls, some with faded cushions, all with intricately carved designs along the edges: swirling shapes of clouds, birds, and treetops.

"If you'll excuse me, Miss Juliana," Montague said from the front desk.

Juliana turned. His forehead glistened with sweat. The white gemstones on his temples gleamed in the yellowish light.

"I've some paperwork to attend to, and hopefully finish, before the Grey-Star arrives. I expect them to enter through the main doors, likely with an entourage of Black and Blue-Stars. I might suggest you keep alert so you're ready to greet them."

Juliana nodded.

"I will, of course, also come out to greet them. And," his neutrally kind expression flickered for a moment, "I expect the mayor will have heard about this by now. He will likely make an appearance."

Juliana frowned.

"There is nothing to be done about that," Montague sighed. "But if the Grey-Star wishes to speak to you alone, there are plenty of rooms available and

Mr. Marsterson isn't..." he clicked his teeth, seeming to search for the right word, "foolish enough to ignore an order from someone like that."

"I..." Juliana clenched her jaw. "Thank you," she said, her voice clipped.

Montague nodded and disappeared down the corridor behind the desk.

Juliana stood in the room for a long moment. Her gaze stuck on the open hallway remembering where she'd been led, where she'd spent her first night, where the dreams and nightmares had started.

Time passed slowly. Juliana paced the floor. Her palms went damp, and she waved them through the air to avoid staining her clothes with sweat. The adrenaline from her initial anticipation peaked and waned.

She examined the images hung on the walls; a collection from many sources it seemed. There were charcoal sketches, mostly locations in Abredea that she recognizes—the school, the square, the town hall. More intriguing were the colorful pieces. She wondered, vaguely, how the artist knew to draw such things. Perhaps it was someone who had grown up in Tornim, only to be expelled on their twentieth birthday. There were paintings of jungles, a vast stretch of ocean lined with rocky cliffs, and mountains far greater than the ones she viewed from her little field on the west end of Abredea.

Hours passed and Juliana's stomach rumbled. She pictured the small bowl of grey mush at May's table. A scowl crossed her lips, accompanying a particularly loud growl from her belly.

She stood at the windows for some time, watching the square fill, then empty again as people took their children to school, went off to work, and ran their errands through the morning. She spotted Daisy and Taz walking to school together.

A brief thought—hope that she'd be done in time to spend her afternoon with them—caused a crease in her forehead and a twinge in her gut. She should be focused on her meeting. It didn't matter how long it took.

Montague returned, having completed his paperwork. He gave her an apologetic smile and offered her a slice of stale bread he'd had in his office.

Juliana took it.

Well after midday there was a commotion near the wall. People in the square turned their gazes east, staring between the mayor's house and the hall. Juliana paced along the windowed wall looking out onto the camp.

The urge to rush outside and confirm her suspicion was strong, but she held her composure.

A pair of Red-Stars came into view. Juliana recognized one of them, a shorter man with a full blonde mustache and a pair of thick silver glasses, as a guard she'd seen around the camp.

A pair of Blue-Stars strode behind the Reds. Both were women, their suits pressed and clean, hair in immaculate buns, and wary gazes analyzing the people around them.

Juliana's stomach clenched. She glanced down at her own outfit, glad she hadn't stained the cloth with sweat, but unable to ignore the caking of russet-colored dust on her boots and the cuffs of her pants.

A Black-Star came next, followed closely by...

It was her. Ms. Wolfe.

Montague cleared his throat next to Juliana. She glanced at him. A small sheen glimmered across his forehead and his hands trembled slightly as he shot her a nervous
smile.

Two additional Black-Stars flanked Ms. Wolfe as the Red-Stars brought everyone up the steps of the building. They held open the doors and the troop flowed in. Two of the Black-Stars immediately strode through the building.

There was a pause, a holding of sorts as the sound of doors opening and closing, papers shuffling, and a few startled gasps from the people working in the back rooms, reached them.

The Black-Stars returned, gave their fellow caste member a nod, and positioned themselves on either side of the large front doors.

Juliana hesitated. Wolfe had come for *her*. To speak with *her*.

Why?

What was she worth to someone like this? Someone with so much power and influence when she had none.

She recalled their conversation at the Star Office. Wolfe's claim that Juliana had caught her attention through hard work and intelligence.

The glimmer of hope twinkled within her once again.

"Well, we've been to worse places, I suppose," one of the Blue-Stars said.

The other chuckled.

Montague stepped forward, wiping his palm across his pants before sticking it out to Wolfe. "Ma'am, thank you for gracing us with your presence. The newest member of our community is here as you requested. Is there anything I might offer to make your visit more comfortable?"

His tone was smooth, the traces of nerves only visible in his still trembling hand. He sounded... well, he sounded like he was from the city.

Juliana wondered, for the first time, which caste he had held before his Coding. She would bet it wasn't one of the lower three.

"No," Wolfe said.

A shiver ran up Juliana's spine. Then the Grey-Star turned to her.

The air in the room became warm in Juliana's lungs. The people around them, Blue, Black, Red, and Montague, seemed to relax. A breath of ease blew through the lobby.

"Juliana," Wolfe purred, "it's lovely to see you again. You're looking well, all things considered."

The smile spreading across Juliana's face faltered. She held it in place, nodding a thanks for what might have been a compliment but felt like a reminder of how far she'd fallen.

"Thank you, Ms. Wolfe. And thank you for the visit. I... I'm... was honored to hear of your wish to see me." Juliana's gaze darted to those around them, but no one appeared to have noticed her stumbling sentence.

They grinned blandly at Wolfe, ignoring Juliana entirely.

"Let's talk elsewhere, shall we?" Wolfe turned to Montague. "There is a room we might have?"

He nodded vigorously and led them down the hall to a small office space. There were two cushy chairs in front of a wooden desk, a third chair behind it.

"No one is using my office at the moment," Montague said. "Please, let me know if there is anything else I can do for you." He stood in the doorway, staring at Wolfe with an expression between admiration and worship.

Juliana's forehead pinched into a frown. Her fingertips thrummed against her thumb in a rapid pattern. Did she look like that when she talked to Wolfe? Perhaps she'd made a fool of herself at the Star Office?

But then, why...

"Thank you, I will call you should we need anything." Wolfe closed the door.

Juliana swallowed, her skin tingling with nerves. Pressure built in her head, causing a ringing in her ears.

"Shall we sit?"

Juliana flinched before correcting her expression into a neutral smile. She nodded and took the cushy chair Wolfe gestured to.

"Oh, Juliana," Wolfe sat as well, leaning in, and resting her forearms on her crossed knee, "I was so upset that day. I'm sorry I couldn't see you off, there was simply too much to do."

"Of course." Juliana disguised her sigh of relief as a shaky exhale and widened her smile. "I hoped, but couldn't *expect* someone of your station to have time for me after... what happened."

"My poor dear, how far you've fallen." Her tone was sympathetic, pitying.

Juliana concentrated on her even breathing. One wrong word or motion, and her chances of getting out...

She cleared the thought from her mind.

"I'm curious what I can do for you, in the state I currently find myself."

Wolfe reached out a hand. Her nails were manicured to perfection, small slivers of white accenting the tips with a clear sheen coating the rest.

Juliana took it, her own nails bitten to nubs, palms calloused from her past few weeks in the garden.

"I wanted to check on you." Wolfe squeezed Juliana's hand.

A flood of warmth filled the room. The tightness in Juliana's chest eased, her stomach unclenched, her heartbeat slowed. A flash of her mother's face crossed her mind. That comfort, belonging, the feelings she associated with the city, the Blue-Star district, her family...

Tears pricked at the edges of her eyes.

"Oh, darling," Wolfe murmured. "I feel so bad about this, dear. I'm sure *whatever* you did before isn't worth this punishment."

Juliana swallowed and nodded. A low whimper escaped her as Wolfe pulled her hand away. The warmth, however, remained. Juliana basked in it.

"Is there... is there anything to be done? Am I here forever?"

Wolfe patted Juliana's shoulder. "I can't say..." She sighed. "All I know is that exceptional people don't often remain in such dire places. Yet, you were placed here for a reason."

They sat quietly for a few minutes. Juliana felt Wolfe's gaze. She avoided meeting it, choosing instead to examine Montague's desk. He had a collection of small baubles decorating the corners. One, a miniature mountain with a waterfall of tiny metallic beads, uttered a low hum from the motor keeping the waterfall moving.

She bit her lip, thinking of her dreams, and looked out the small window on the far wall instead. It was minuscule, offering only the simplest of views. A tree. Light green leafy buds growing from skinny brown branches. A late blossom, somewhat left behind.

"I had a question, if that's all right?" Juliana looked back at Wolfe.

The woman nodded.

Juliana sighed, not sure how to start. "I know the Coding process is foolproof. The system has been in place for over a century and it doesn't make mistakes. But..."

Wolfe raised her eyebrows and Juliana hurried on.

"There's a boy here, he's young, only sixteen. But he has gemstones. He was *found* you see... as a small child. I'm curious how that could happen... Surely someone should have missed him. An alert would have gone out, and the Red-Stars would have searched. I don't..." Juliana shook her head, trying to find the correct words. "I suppose I don't understand how someone could fall through the cracks in such a way. How could someone end up here without going through the Coding?"

Wolfe's grey eyes were wide, fixed on Juliana. After a few seconds their intensity softened.

"I'm sure someone has documentation of his arrival, where he came from, and an appointment set for his twentieth birthday. There is no need to worry, my dear. You're correct in thinking we don't make mistakes like that. If he doesn't remember, well, that's a shame. But someone is watching out for him, rest assured."

Juliana's heart leapt to her throat. Taz... able to go through the Coding. He had a chance, a chance to get into Tornim.

She suddenly itched with the urge to leave, to meet him and Daisy and rush them to the field so they could bask in the news.

"As far as you're concerned..." Wolfe gave Juliana a pointed look and a wry smile. "I suggest you focus on being the best version of yourself. I'm working on things from my end, but you do everything you can to stay on the right side of the right people here. Not that there are many," she chuckled, and Juliana forced out a smile, "but you're a smart girl. You know who the important people are."

Juliana nodded. She pulled at the sleeves of her shirt, aware now of how cold she was. It felt as though someone had opened the window, chasing away the warmth.

Wolfe stood. "I'm glad to see you're doing... as well as can be expected. I'll try to check in on you again soon, and hopefully I'll have an update by then."

Hope flared bright and hot in Juliana's chest. She stood as well.

"I wondered, before you go..."

Wolfe tilted her head.

"Have you heard anything about my family? You mentioned before that you knew of my parents. I... I'm wondering how they are."

Wolfe was silent for a few seconds. "I haven't, I'm afraid. But I'm sure they're doing well."

Juliana widened her eyes to stop them from burning with tears. "Thank you," she said as they left the room and followed the hallway back to the lobby. "I appreciate your attention."

"Take care of yourself, dear." Wolfe smiled down at her as they reached the group of Black and Blue-Stars near the front doors.

Montague bobbed out from behind the front desk. "Is there anything else I might offer before you depart?"

Wolfe shook her head. "We have other appointments today. Thank you, for your..." she glanced around the mostly empty lobby, "hospitality."

And with that, they left.

Juliana stood at the window, watching the group stride back towards the city. A figure appeared in the doorway of the mayor's house and a large man she didn't recognize—though assumed must be Mayor Marsterson—jostled toward the Grey-Star.

The Black-Stars slammed into place in front of her, fully blocking her from the approaching Moon. Juliana raised an eyebrow as the man gesticulated with his hands, expressing an impressive level of excitement as he tried to speak to Wolfe.

"Every time," Montague muttered from her side.

She glanced over at him in time to see him shaking his head.

"Every time someone from Tornim comes, he does this. If you ask me, he thinks he's going to be a Purple again someday." He scoffed and waved a hand through the air. "Preposterous."

Juliana lifted a hand to her temple, feeling the gemstone pressed to her skin. "Is it so wrong? To want to be what you were?"

"Wrong? No, I don't believe so." Montague's voice softened. "However," he gestured out the window and Juliana looked out to see the Red-Stars now firmly walking the mayor backwards as Wolfe and her people continued toward the wall, "if it ends like that every time, one might consider changing their approach."

A half-chuckle snorted out before Juliana could stop it. She lifted a hand to her mouth, too late to hide her smile. Beside her, Montague was grinning as well.

"I'm sure you have much to do, Miss Juliana. I hope whatever that was, it went well."

"Thank you," she said, and then she left.

Chapter Fifteen

Present Day - Mid Summer - Field on the Western End of Abredea

"**I** can't understand why you're not excited."

Taz shrugged and took a bite out of his apple large enough to almost cut the little thing in half. Daisy giggled beside him, her laugh like a singing bird.

"I don' see what the big deal is," he said through a mouthful of apple. "I'm gonna end up a Moon, almost for sure." The color on his gemstones twirled and spun, cycling through the rainbow in an almost hypnotic way.

Juliana shook her head, rolling her own apple around in her hands. "The *chance* though, the chance to go to the city. To live... even as an Orange-Star." She gave a wistful sigh.

Daisy raised an eyebrow. "You're starting to sound like my father."

"Ugh!" Her lip curled. "How did I *not know* you're the mayor's daughter?"

"Well, you saw him yesterday. I don't exactly broadcast it."

Juliana laughed.

"Tha's why," Taz swallowed, "tha's why... why those kids sometimes go at Daisy instead... instead... instead of me."

Juliana's laugh died in her throat. She turned to catch her friend's eye. "How often does that happen?"

Daisy shrugged. "Not enough to worry about. Especially lately, since Taz and I don't hang around the square like we used to. No one's walking all the way out here to pick a fight," she said with a smile.

"*Hey!*"

All three heads turned at the shout. A figure marched toward them. Taller than Daisy and Taz, vaguely familiar to Juliana, a man with shaggy black hair strode right up to them, took in the blankets and picnic basket, and promptly sat on the blanket between Daisy and Taz.

Juliana eyed the mud and plant stains caked across his hands. The clothes he wore matched those of the people who worked in the fields. His skin was either naturally brown or he spent every spare moment of his life under the sun.

Perhaps both.

"So," the man began talking as soon as he sat, "first I lose Daisy." He faced the giggling girl. "I only see yeh in the mornin' now, and always when I 'ave tah leave and yeh 'ave school. And now," he turned to Taz, "you've abandoned me too!"

Taz grinned his wild grin and gave the man a playful shove.

"Stop smilin'!" he demanded, though there was laughter in his voice. "I miss yeh both. Is this where you've been this whole time?" He gestured around the field. His arm nearly clipped Juliana, who leaned back with an eyebrow raised. "Is there a reason I wasn't invited tah yer little picnic?" Daisy held out an apple and he took it. "And who's this?"

Juliana stared, the eyebrow still raised, her thundering heartbeat slowing, and the initial panic of someone new slowly fading.

"Hi, Anthony." Daisy's birdsong voice chittered through the air.

"Hi," he grumbled.

"This is Juliana," Taz said with a sweeping, seated bow.

Anthony squinted. He tilted his head. His gaze flicked to Juliana's temples. The look of recognition crossed his face at the same moment she realized who he was.

The man from the fence, her second night in Abredea.

Anthony nodded. "Right, we've met."

Heat rose in Juliana's cheeks. She nodded. "I had just arrived and... it was... I was not at my best."

He raised an eyebrow. "I wouldn' expect yeh tah be."

The heat slid from her cheeks to her belly as her eyes widened and her lip curled into a snarl.

Daisy and Taz sat very still, watching both of them.

Anthony went on, seemingly unperturbed. "I mean, who would expect yeh tah be all put together and not flustered or anythin' after goin' through the Codin'."

Juliana clenched her jaw.

"I heard," Taz broke in with a glance at Daisy, "the Codin' hurts. Is tha' true?" His hazel eyes shone with concern as he turned to Juliana.

"No," she said. She moved her attention to her friend and attempted to give him a comforting look even as anger roiled in her belly. "It doesn't hurt. They do strap you down, and the machine itself is... unnerving to say the least. But it's not actually painful."

"They strap yeh down?" Anthony demanded. He lifted a grubby hand to a scar on his left temple and rubbed the skin. He let out a sigh and a half-smile. "Glad *we* don' 'ave tah worry about tha'." He nudged Daisy.

Her grin was smaller than usual.

Anthony studied her. "Yer father again?"

Juliana watched as Taz and Anthony shifted their attention to Daisy, concern in the lines on their faces. Daisy nodded.

"He's trying to get me gemstones," she explained to Juliana. "Every time someone from the city comes to Abredea he harasses them about it."

Juliana frowned. "It sounds like he's trying to get you a better life."

Anthony scoffed loudly.

Daisy shook her head and Juliana recognized the bitter sadness on her face. It was the same expression she wore when she talked of her mother's death.

"It's not like that. It's not for me."

Juliana tilted her head, confused.

"Mayor Marsterson thinks if Daisy gets a chance at the Codin', and she gets intah the city, she'll be able tah get *him* out of Abredea." Anthony's voice was dry and flat. His dark eyes narrowed as he stared past Juliana, back up the path toward the square.

Juliana shook her head. "That's ridiculous. And impossible. Gemstones are placed within the first few days after birth, a week or two at most."

Taz lifted a finger to touch his own gemstone, the colors still shifting faster than Juliana had ever seen.

"I didn' know tha'." Anthony clicked his tongue against his teeth.

They sat for a few seconds, Juliana contemplating the possibility of someone Daisy's age getting gemstones, the others lost in their own thoughts. The wind picked up, showering them with flower petals from the tree above.

In the past few days their little field had blossomed. The trees bloomed in pinks and purples. Yellow flowers poured from stalk-like bushes. Darker yellow flowers sprouted from the ground out of bright green patches scattered among the long strands of wild grass. May called them dandelions, and the two of them had made tea with the flowers a few times.

The mountains, far beyond the fence and the forest between them, had shifted from brown to green. Maybe the snows came in the winter. Her dreams...

"There's also," Juliana interrupted her own thoughts, "the matter of anyone in the city having *any* influence at all when it comes to who lives here." Her stomach clenched as she said this. She had not told her friends what Wolfe said in regard to her own status as a Moon. She looked at Taz. "Even if you came out a Black-Star, you wouldn't be able to affect who goes in and comes out of the camp."

Anthony hissed through his teeth.

She looked at him.

"It's Abredea," he growled.

Juliana's jaw tightened again. She clenched a hand at her side and held his gaze. "In the city, they call it the camp."

After a pause, Anthony turned to Taz. "What's she talkin' about anyway? Yer doin' the Codin'?"

Taz shrugged. "I don'... don'..." he sucked in a steadying breath, "don' know if I'll even be able to."

"But yeh wanna?" Anthony's expression twisted as he studied his friend.

Juliana thought she caught a hint of hurt in his narrowed eyes and pinched lips.

Taz shrugged again. "I don' even know what caste I'm from, let alone where I'd be able tah do anything. I... I like it *here*. Even when it's hard."

This time Juliana was sure she spotted a flash of pain cross Anthony's features. His hands, elbows wrapped around his tucked-up knees, clenched. The sharp edge of his jaw tightened.

"Are yeh gettin' enough tah eat?" he murmured, so low Juliana almost didn't hear him over the breeze.

Taz gave a wobbly version of his usual grin and bumped his shoulder against Anthony's. "Yeah, I'd tell yeh if I wasn't."

Anthony shifted his focus to Daisy. "And you?"

Her smile was also muted. Juliana's frowned down at the grass and made a note to thank May—again—for the extra food she'd occasionally been able to bring to their afternoon get togethers.

Daisy nodded.

Anthony darted a glance at Juliana before speaking to the others again, his voice still a quiet rumble. "I'm sorry, I know I've been workin' a lot lately. I 'aven' had time tah... well, yeh know. Naya's got a panel busted on her roof. I've been tryin' tah save up enough tah get it fixed before fall."

"Anthony," Daisy sang, looping her small arm through his darker and more muscular one, "don't worry so much about us. We can handle ourselves. Besides," her full grin fell into place, "you've got enough to worry about."

Anthony frowned at her. "What's tha' supposed tah mean?"

"The new captain is... is... is comin' tomorrow," Taz snorted. "We've been takin' bets on how long it'll take before yeh do... do somethin' dumb and dangerous."

Juliana clamped her lips together as her eyes widened. A laugh bubbled up in her throat, but she held it down, watching for Anthony's reaction.

He pressed a hand to his chest, an overly dramatic wounded expression on his face. "Me? Do somethin' dangerous? How dare yeh suggest—"

"Naya's got you down for three days," Daisy interrupted.

Anthony's jaw dropped as both Daisy and Taz burst into laughter. Juliana watched Anthony mimic a fish, opening and closing his mouth a few times, before she had to join in.

The conversation slowly shifted, and Juliana found herself with an easy smile on her lips. She'd never sat like this with her friends from the city. They'd never talked about their fears, only their ambitions. They'd never discussed their families, only their futures.

And they'd certainly never leaned in as Daisy was doing now and whispered to her to make sure she was alright. To make sure this extra person wasn't too much and offer to go somewhere less stimulating.

Juliana rubbed a palm against her eye, forcing back tears as she shot Daisy a thankful smile and shook her head.

Daisy popped back into the conversation with a fervent opinion. Her fingers drifted through the grass, finding Juliana's and squeezing them.

Juliana sat in silence, observing the way these three interacted, and thinking about just how much her life had changed.

The afternoon passed quickly. With the arrival of the new captain in Abredea the next day, both Taz and Daisy had to leave earlier than usual. The baker had an hour of work for Taz; they were setting up a display in the window. Daisy's father wanted the house cleaned and his best suit pressed for the arrival.

Juliana's look of disgust when Daisy mentioned this was matched by Taz and Anthony.

"Can't he do his own suit?" Juliana asked incredulously.

Daisy rolled her eyes. "It was always something my mother did for him. He never learned."

Anthony opened his mouth, but Juliana's tongue was quicker.

"He's a frosted adult, it's not like he can't learn now."

Taz's cheeks puffed up and he expelled a shout of laughter. Anthony chuckled as well, nodding in agreement.

Daisy grinned at Juliana. "If only." She stood, lifted her blanket, and shook out the bits of leaves and dirt sticking to it.

Juliana rose as well, squeezing her friend in a quick hug before taking the blanket Daisy offered. "See you tomorrow?"

"I won' be able tah meet," Taz said. "I'm workin' all afternoon up tah the ceremony."

Anthony snorted. "Ceremony? Is tha' what we're callin' it?"

"Announcement?" Taz suggested.

"It's already been announced since we know about it," Juliana pointed out.

"Assembly?" Daisy asked.

Taz shrugged. "We do all *'ave* tah assemble."

Anthony shook his head and gave them a dry smirk. "It's a show."

They stared at him and his smirk faded.

"It's a show of force. Makin' everyone gather together tah watch this new captain make a speech and parade his guards aroun'." He gave an angry jerk of his head, dark hair falling across his eyes. "It's tah make it clear we have tah do what they say."

Juliana swallowed. Her fingers met the tip of her thumb again. Her memory flashed to the Orange-Star she'd hired to drive her to the Star Office on her birthday. The Red-Stars pulling him over and damaging his car, then fining him.

A show of force.

Making it clear he had to do what they said.

Her gut churned.

"Well, show of force or n... no... not, I'm callin' it a ceremony. Ceremonies mean the baker goes overboard and *tha'* means he burns somethin' and *tha'* means free food." Taz shook out his blanket, folded it up, and handed it to Juliana as well. "Thanks for the apples." He grinned, winked at her, grabbed Daisy, and the two of them trotted off toward the square.

Juliana blinked.

She and Anthony stood alone in the little field. Two blankets were draped over her arm, a third still on the ground next to her empty basket.

Anthony bent, lifted her blanket, and shook it out. She held out her arm. He set it atop the others, grabbed her basket, and looked at her.

His eyes were dark, as dark as when they met at the fence so many weeks ago, but she hadn't been sure if that was the night. It wasn't. They were black, the iris almost invisible.

"So, tah May's?"

Juliana's forehead creased. "I... yes, that's where I'm headed."

He nodded, brushing his free hand through his hair. "Me too."

Juliana's frown deepened as they made for the small path leading into Abredea.

They moved in silence for a few moments, questions nagging at Juliana. Biting her lip, she finally voiced one.

"Is it really a show of force?" she asked. "Not just a way for everyone to meet the new captain and get an understanding of, perhaps, the different methods they have?"

Anthony eyed her as they walked. "I doubt it. I was only five last time we got a new guard captain, but from what I remember there was a lot of unnecessary talkin', struttin' around, and threatenin'."

"Threatening?" Juliana said with alarm.

Anthony chuckled. "They really don' like it when we break their rules."

"They?"

He slowed to a stop and stared at her. "The Stars. The people in the city. The government. The ones who control Abredea."

Juliana gave a slow nod. "They don't like rule-breaking in the city either," she said.

He shrugged. "I doubt anyone in the city has 'ad tah steal food tah survive."

Juliana's throat went dry. Her stomach, not satiated after only her mush packet and two apples, rumbled. "No, I doubt that as well." Her voice was soft as she recalled her family's pantry, shelves stocked with flour, rice, meats and cheeses, a hundred kinds of snacks her parents would take to work, and a constant surplus of cookies their Orange-Star cook would make when she prepared their meals for the week.

After a few seconds of silence, Juliana continued down the dirt path, Anthony close behind her.

"Daisy does everything in that house, doesn't she?" she asked, partially to change the subject.

"Aye." Anthony kicked a clump of dirt off the road. "She always has, since we were kids. I remember her mom getting' sick. Her dad paid for some 'elp, but when her mom died, tha' was kinda tha'. She took over everythin' her mom did 'cause if she didn', they wouldn' eat."

Juliana's free hand tightened into a fist at her side. "Absolutely ridiculous," she muttered.

He nodded. "Marsterson was a Purple-Star. Apparently, tha' means he had lots of servants who worked around the house. Naya mentioned it once, he tried tah have some of the Moon-borns do his washin', cookin', and cleanin', without payin' 'em. It didn' last long and he was pretty mad about it."

"I don't..." Juliana faltered, blonde locks falling across her face as she shook her head. "I don't know how to express how much bullshit that is."

Anthony burst out a laugh.

"Really," Juliana looked at him, her eyes wide, "he was a Purple-Star? My family is Blue. We had a couple... a few Orange-Stars help out once or twice a week, usually cooking or cleaning, but my father certainly knows how to do his own laundry. And how to cook. And how to dress himself."

"And how tah treat his daughter, it sounds like."

Juliana's words fell short as a pang struck her chest. She chewed on her cheek, a mournful smile crossing her lips. "Yeah. They both did."

She picked up her pace. Not to leave Anthony behind, but to take the time to hide the tears burning her eyes. His boots crunched behind her, but he didn't seem to be trying to catch up.

They reached May's a minute later. Juliana strode through the open door and set the blankets on top of May's tall dresser.

"You're back early," came the weathered voice from the kitchen.

Juliana smiled. May leaned against the sink, a mug of tea warming her hands. Her white hair hung in a loose braid, the end reaching past her lower back. She grinned as Juliana stepped into the kitchen and pulled a second mug from the cupboard.

Juliana crossed, took the mug, and poured herself what smelled like dandelion-mint tea from the steaming pot on the stove.

"And you've brought company," May said, pulling another mug from the shelf as Anthony stepped into the kitchen. "You're early too, dear boy." May crossed to him and he bent as she kissed his cheek.

"They cut my hours again." He shrugged, but there was a sting in the words.

May frowned. "Should I have a word with the foreman? I knew him when he was a youngling. I'm sure I can remind him how to treat his hardest workers."

Anthony shook his head.

Juliana moved aside as May filled Anthony's mug with tea and handed it to him.

"It's not his fault," he said. He took a sip of the tea and grimaced. "It's Captain Durang. He puts extra Red-Stars on shift when I'm there and it makes everyone else nervous."

May clenched her mug. Her jaw, nearly as sharp as Anthony's, went taut. "Ohh, if I were a few years younger... that man would face what's coming to him."

Anthony smiled, and Juliana couldn't help the light chuckle that escaped her.

"Oh, you two." May glared at both of them. Then her glare slipped into a grin. "It's about time you met. Two months and I don't know how you haven't crossed paths yet."

Juliana flushed.

"Well, we met briefly." Anthony sipped his tea, meeting Juliana's eye over the rim of his steaming mug.

May raised an eyebrow but didn't press. "I've got your things on the table." She gestured to three large baskets taking up most of the tabletop filled with apples, onions, potatoes, tomatoes, radishes, and a few leafy greens.

Juliana blinked, realization hitting her as she looked at Anthony. He was nodding and listing out families to May.

"You're the one who delivers the produce every day," Juliana interrupted.

They both looked at her.

"Aye." Anthony finished his list and asked May if there was anyone he was missing.

Juliana quietly reassessed her first—and second—impressions of the man. She recalled his comment about stealing food, his bragging about never getting caught by the guards. Her eyes widened in realization, and she tightened her grip on her mug.

Anthony left not long after, taking the baskets with him and offering a polite goodbye which Juliana returned.

Once he was gone, she looked at May. "He's the one who delivers the food."

"That has been established, yes." May raised an eyebrow.

"He's also the one who brings us that fresh meat? And the mushrooms? And those tiny sweet onions we make soup with?"

May's grey eyes darkened. "Yes," she said slowly. "But that bit stays between us."

Juliana's heartrate doubled. "Because he's stealing that food?" She almost didn't want to know the answer.

May sighed. "There was a time it wasn't classified as stealing. But that is, technically, what he's doing. He hunts."

Juliana frowned, confused.

"He goes beyond the fence and hunts in the forest. Finds mushrooms and onions growing wild, catches fish from the river, and hunts rabbits, squirrels, even a deer once." A wistful smile crossed her lips. "That was a plentiful winter."

"But that's... that's illegal. And dangerous." Fear rippled through her. If Wolfe found out she knew someone who was breaking the law...

May leaned on the counter, surveying Juliana with a sharp gaze. "Anthony's mother died when he was young. Many people on our end of Abredea did what they could to help him. He does this to pay them back. To return a debt he *thinks* he owes."

Juliana gave a slight shake of her head, a heavy breath escaping her lungs.

May raised an eyebrow, her voice stern. "Darling girl, how well do you think you'd be holding up without the *actual* meal we have the privilege of eating a few times a week?"

Juliana opened her mouth, closed it again, took a sip of her tea, and changed the subject. "Do we need to prepare for tomorrow?"

May gave her a puzzled look.

"The new captain, the ceremony, or whatever it is, that's tomorrow."

"Ahh." May nodded. She crossed to the table and sank into one of the chairs. "Nothing special. Wear something nice, but comfortable. Most people will have time to clean up; they make everyone leave work early so the entirety of Abredea will be present."

Juliana's heart sank and she swallowed a shudder.

"Not to worry, we'll find a place at the edge of the crowd." May offered her a bitter smile, running a finger along her scar. "I don't like being surrounded either."

They talked a while longer. Juliana avoided the subject of Anthony and his illegal activities, though the hunger in her stomach warred with her common sense as they ate a dinner of steamed carrots and a bowl of mush. May's casual comment that Anthony would likely go hunting the next day, because he didn't have a shift in the fields, only served to give Juliana a stomachache.

When she worked up the courage, Juliana asked May about work in Abredea. They discussed a few options, from fieldwork to office work, possibly with Montague. Juliana made a note to talk with him about a possible job soon.

She swallowed down a spoonful of sticky grey goop with a grimace. She wanted that sugar.

Chapter Sixteen

Present Day - Mid Summer - The Forest West of Abredea

S unlight streamed through branches, lighting up bright green patches of grass, purple and yellow flowers blooming at every angle. The creek rushed by, still full from winter snows and spring rains.

Anthony strode through the forest, following the rough trail he'd inherited from his uncle. Three rabbits, full grown and fat and tied together on a tick rope, hung from his shoulder. His thick canvas bag was slung across his shoulder, bulging with wild onions. It kept rhythm as he walked, smacking his thigh with every other step.

Orange and red lit the sky behind him. The sun approached the mountains, ducking behind clouds and transforming the afternoon into a world of gold.

Anthony inhaled that raw scent of trees, dirt, and crisp and clean air that kept him going when it felt like everything would fall apart. Three shifts a week, down from the six he'd managed to talk the foreman into after finding Naya's broken panel.

He'd only saved up half of what he needed to get it replaced.

Anthony lifted his face as he stepped into a large beam of light. The sun caressed his skin. At least he had the whole summer to get a new panel before she and Jimmy really needed it.

He contemplated telling her. But she'd insist on helping pay for it—or worse would insist on paying for it herself. He didn't want to think about how long that might take.

No, he would find a way to make up the extra money from those missing shifts. He could pick up work here and there, and with more time to hunt he might be able to talk the grocer into buying some meat.

Anthony pushed past a thick set of brambles encroaching on his trail. This is what happened when he only had one day a week to sneak into the forest. He paused, his gaze catching the blackberries dangling, tantalizingly, from the prickly bushes.

With a glance at the sun—he needed to get back to Abredea—he pulled out a small pouch and stuffed it with thick berries.

Ten minutes later, hands stained with pinpricks of blood and berry juice, he jogged through the dense trees. The guards would be in the square, most of them anyway, preparing for the assembly. Still, he hesitated at the edge of the woods, watching. All was still and silent.

He slid through the gap in the fence. Thick bushes, currently bursting with yellow flowers, hid the slit his uncle had cut decades ago. Anthony did another check, but at this end of Abredea he was alone. Anthony hauled the two sides of chain-link fence together and twisted thick wires into place at the top, bottom, and middle, effectively sealing the gap until his next hunting trip.

He stopped at May's first. She was on his way home anyway and had an icebox. Something he didn't—and likely wouldn't ever—have the coin for.

The new girl, Juliana, was in the shower when he arrived. May gave him the usual peck on the cheek and was happy to store his catch until he had time to cut everything up. It wouldn't be that night. He barely had time to get home and change before he was required to be in the square.

He gave May a one-armed hug and left as she reminded him not to be late.

By the time he approached the square, the sun was almost touching the tips of the trees behind him. A few stragglers joined him on the road. They exchanged wary, lightly exasperated looks. For those missing a shift in the mines, fields, or factories this was a major inconvenience.

Anthony heaved an angry sigh as he spotted the Clearnecks, a family of six, making their way to the *ceremony*. They'd just had a baby and he knew John couldn't afford to miss a shift. He jogged a bit to catch up with them and scooped the second youngest onto his shoulders. They chatted about the weather, the lightness of spring rains, and the possibility of a third packet of government nutrients in the near future. The baby, wrapped tight to Violet's chest, fell asleep before they reached the crowded square.

Anthony parted from the family, letting the kids know he'd bring Jimmy by to play sometime soon.

The square was packed with hundreds of people. The bakery door was wide open, those with extra money—the Moons from the eastern end of Abredea—getting themselves little snacks to celebrate the afternoon off work and school. He caught sight of Taz wiping down the counter as he walked by, and they exchanged a wave. Everyone working in the square would have to stop soon. They'd lock up and join the rest in welcoming the new captain.

Tired of wading through the mass of people, Anthony moved to the edge of an alley and climbed onto a crate. He scanned the crowd. After a moment he spotted Naya and Jimmy at the far edge of the square with May and the new girl. He frowned. He thought Daisy would have been with her friend. His dark gaze did another pass over the crowd.

Movement at the town hall steps—not far from his perch—caught his attention. Mayor Marsterson, greasy as ever, stood a few yards from a podium they'd erected for the occasion. Montague stood with him, a clipboard in hand and a sour expression on his weathered face. Captain Durang was there as well. His red gemstones glinted in the early evening light. A few of his regular guards hovered on either side of the steps, but they seemed bored rather than alert.

He caught sight of Daisy sandwiched between her father and Captain Durang. She leaned on her leg, wringing her hands and darting her gaze across the crowd. Anthony grimaced as Durang leaned in and muttered something in her ear. Daisy winced, shrinking away from the pale man's thin mouth. Montague stepped forward, wedging himself between the two of them with a placating smile to Durang. Anthony made a mental note to bring the records keeper some blackberries.

A bell rang, echoing around the square and causing silence to fall. Montague straightened his shoulders and stepped up to the podium.

Juliana held tighter to May's arm than was probably necessary. The older woman was practically jogging and each step made Juliana's heart jump with fear that she'd fall.

They hurried toward the square, May muttering about always being late and Juliana scanning the ground for rocks or sticks while noting with bemusement that plenty of other people were still making their way to the event. An immense wave of sound rolled over them as they rounded the last bend to the square.

Juliana stopped dead in her tracks, losing her grip on May's arm. She stood frozen, heart thundering, throat dry, breath shallow.

So many people. There were so many... Moons here.

Juliana hadn't thought about the sheer volume of bodies that would be in the square. Hundreds, possibly over a thousand people crowded together on the dusty cobblestones. Bodies jammed between buildings, in alleyways and doorways, and filled the road in front of them all the way to the steps of town hall.

Her vision blurred as fear overtook her. She clenched her hands to stop the shaking, but her entire body trembled.

Two decades of living with the knowledge that White-Stars—Moons—were dangerous, troublesome people who stole, destroyed, and attacked without provocation triggered every self-preservation instinct she had.

Her feet took her backwards, several steps until she thudded against something. "Ouch."

She flinched and spun. White gemstones glistened against skin the dark, red-dish color of the clay-packed earth in Abredea. The man before her wore lightly stained tan overalls and a concerned look on his face.

"Yeh all righ' there?" He held up his hands, a soothing gesture. Lines of ink caught Juliana's focus. A tattoo of a mountain, on his wrist, with three black birds flying across the outline, traced where his veins met his palm.

The tattoo sparked a glimmer of recognition. The puzzle of it, of remembering how she knew this design, distracted her from her fear.

"She's a bit nervous, thanks, Darryl." May materialized at her elbow. A wrin-kled hand took Juliana's forearm with gentle pressure and pulled her away.

Juliana took a few stumbling steps before she found her feet. Shaky breaths didn't capture enough air and her vision went spotty.

"Breathe, Juliana," May commanded. Her voice, low in Juliana's ear left no room for argument. "In through the nose... that's it. And out. Nice and slow. Here, walk with me and we'll find a spot a bit less crowded."

Juliana didn't have the oxygen to give an incredulous snort, so she followed May, letting the woman pull her by the arm until they reached a small open space on the left side of the crowd.

"In and out... good, through the nose is key. I've got to teach you meditation one of these days. It'll help."

Juliana barely heard May's words. She focused on the breathing, on pulling in the bristles of anxiety shooting across her skin.

"Ahh, there's Daisy. Poor girl."

Juliana looked up, her vision back to normal. She glanced at May. The older woman's grey eyes met her blue ones and May pointed a gnarled finger toward the town hall steps.

Daisy stood at the top. Her pale pink dress was thin; the fabric did nothing to keep the evening breeze from chilling her arms. Her hair, usually in twin braids with strands of brown framing her heart-shaped face, was up in a tight bun similar to the one Ms. Wolfe wore. Daisy's hands were folded in front of her. The man next to her—not the one Juliana recognized as the mayor—leaned in and whispered something in her ear.

Juliana squinted, heat flooding her chest and stomach as Daisy's knuckles went white and she shied away from him. She winced, then quickly regained the bland smile which did not reach her eyes.

"Who's that man?" Juliana said with a growl.

"Captain Durang," a new voice said beside her.

She turned. A thin woman, darker than Anthony with long wavy black hair, stood with a young boy, maybe five or six, clenching her hand.

"Juliana," May turned and formed a little circle of the three women, "this is Naya. Naya, this is the girl I've been telling you about."

Juliana nodded, but her attention was fixed on Daisy. "Is she all right up there?" she asked May.

Again, Naya answered. "She'll be all right. Poor thing is used tah this. Her father parades her around at every opportunity. He wouldn' miss this one."

"Why is he..." Juliana snarled, but before she finished her question, Montague wedged himself between Daisy and the captain. The wash of relief in her gut matched the relief on her friend's soft face. Daisy's hands relaxed.

"I imagine he wanted tah get in a few last words before bein' replaced," Naya said. The sound was hypnotic, her lilting tone similar to Anthony's, but with a sharp edge that Anthony's did not have.

"He's been after Daisy for years now." May's tone was colder than ice. "Ever since her mother died. I think the girl was barely fourteen when he started coming around."

The roiling fire in Juliana's belly grew to a raging inferno as May's meaning slammed into her. Her eyes widened, mouth dry.

A hand touched her shoulder. Naya glanced up at her with tired brown eyes. "Her father would never let it 'appen. Not unless he 'ad somethin' to gain, and Durang has never 'ad *that* kind of power."

Juliana nodded, lips pressed tight together.

"Mama, where's Tony?"

Naya smiled down at the boy. "I'm sure he's 'ere somewhere." Under her breath Juliana heard, "he better be."

May laughed. "Don't mother hen about it, Naya. He's here. Stopped by the house before he headed over. This is Jimmy, by the way." She directed to Juliana. "Jimmy, this is our new friend Juliana."

Jimmy squinted up at her. It was an appraising look. Juliana straightened her shoulders a bit, unsure why, but feeling the need with those olive eyes fixed upon her so intently.

"You live with May."

Juliana nodded.

"She said yeh read a lot."

Juliana's gaze flicked to May. The woman's lips were pressed together in a way which told Juliana she was barely holding back a laugh.

"I do," Juliana replied, looking back at the boy.

"Will yeh read tah me? I'm not fast enough yet."

Naya heaved a sigh and gave Juliana an apologetic smile. "He loves stories, I just don' always 'ave the time…"

Juliana closed her eyes. Every limb felt stretched to the breaking point. Her muscles ached with exhaustion she didn't understand. Her mind scrambled, the rapid shift from fear to anger to this innocent conversation had drained her ability to respond normally. She feared herself. Her words. What might come out of her mouth without a strict reign on the horrid, intrusive thoughts stemming from her life in the city.

She clenched her jaw, but before she could speak, a thunderous bell rang out.

The crowd went silent. Naya and May turned, facing town hall. Naya pulled Jimmy in front of her and placed her hands protectively over his shoulders.

Montague stepped up to the podium, laid his clipboard on the wood, and cleared his throat. The sound echoed through the square, emanating from hidden speakers that must have been affixed to the different buildings around them.

"Greetings, people of Abredea." His voice carried a tremor, slight and minimal, but audible enough that Juliana felt a twinge of sympathy. "Thank you for being here on this lovely evening to welcome the new captain of the guard."

A ripple went through the crowd. Juliana glanced around as Naya rolled her eyes.

"I won't take up much time. I wanted to thank you all for your support during this change. We are a community, and by working together there is much we can achieve."

"Any word on the packets?" a voice shouted from somewhere near the center of the crowd.

Juliana blinked in surprise.

At the podium, Montague winced. Behind him the mayor's face reddened. Captain Durang waved a lazy hand as Marsterson looked to him.

"Nothing as of yet," Montague replied. "Please bring your questions to town hall after we are done here."

Mayor Marsterson strode forward and muttered something to Montague. The slender man nodded with a tight smile.

"Now, to introduce our new captain, I present to you your esteemed leader," there was another ripple through the crowd, "Mayor Marsterson."

Daisy's father didn't seem to notice the air of hostility which had risen with his introduction. Juliana looked at May.

May eyed her back and muttered out of the side of her mouth, "Everyone else likes Marsterson about as much as we do. This sort of thing doesn't do much to help his image."

"Hello," boomed Marsterson. His voice reverberated through the speakers, louder than Montague's and with an air of superiority which did not match his fraying suit jacket and slightly miscolored pants. "Thank you, thank you."

Juliana raised an eyebrow. The scattering of polite, obligatory applause quickly faded.

"As you all know, today we say goodbye to Captain Durang." He gestured behind him to the Red-Star. "He and his men will be leaving us for greener pastures in the city. And while we will miss them—"

Juliana almost missed the next few words at the bursts of laughter dotted through the crowd.

"—I am pleased to announce an upgrade to our guard."

Beside her, May tensed.

Juliana frowned. "What does he mean? An upgrade?"

May shook her head. "I'm not sure, but it doesn't sound good."

Behind Marsterson, Durang's face twisted into a scowl. His Red-Star guards didn't look pleased either.

"So, let's say farewell to Captain Durang and welcome Captain Steel to our camp!"

Light applause was accompanied by a furious hissing through the crowd. Juliana glanced around in alarm. The Moons stared at their mayor with fury on their faces.

In the midst of the upset, the doors to town hall slammed open. Daisy flinched and scurried to the side, pressing herself against the windowed wall of the building.

A Black-Star strode through the doors.

Juliana swallowed.

He wore black, from his weathered jacket to his boots. Gemstones gleamed on his temples, standing out against his sandy skin. Matching tattoos marked his face, a set of black dagger-shaped designs rising from the edge of his jaw to the bottom of the gems. His head and face were clean shaven, but it did nothing to make him appear younger. He was large, towering above Marsterson as he approached the podium.

Perhaps more disorienting was what followed him. Captain Steel was muscular, but the men and women in his unit certainly *looked* as though they could easily put him to shame.

Through the doors behind him, spreading out until their formation occupied the platform, came three dozen Black-Stars. Dressed like their commander, with shock-sticks and plasma guns fixed to their sides, the new guard looked ready for battle.

Alarm shot through Juliana. This was wrong. Red-Stars guarded the camps. Sometimes led by a Black-Star, if the camp was particularly dangerous, but never occupied by Black-Stars like this.

May gripped Juliana's arm, her fingers trembling. Juliana put her hand on May's.

On the steps of town hall, Daisy and Montague had squeezed themselves as far back as possible to make room for the new guards. The Red-Stars shifted uncomfortably.

Captain Steel stopped his stride once he reached the podium. With a single glance, Mayor Marsterson moved to the side with a half-bow.

"Thank you, Mayor." Steel's voice echoed through the square. Shifting bodies and murmuring voices ceased. "Durang," Steel barely spared a glance at the Red-Star, "you and your men are dismissed."

Durang looked as though he'd like nothing better than to take one of the plasma guns around him and direct a shot straight into one of Steel's glistening gemstones. Envy and scorn flickered across his face as he rested a hand on his shock-stick, gave Steel a forced deferential nod, and turned on his heel. The other Red-Stars followed, striding down the steps, around the edge of the building, and disappearing from sight in the direction of the wall.

"People of the camp," no whispers this time, no movement as Steel began his speech, "I have no doubt you've curiosities and questions. I hope to answer them all here and now to avoid any... confusion."

May's grip on Juliana's arm tightened. Naya lifted Jimmy into her arms, as though having him on the ground wasn't close enough, safe enough.

"There will be changes in the coming days. My unit and I will be staying in the city for the next week while our sleeping quarters are erected. From then on, we will be living in the camp."

The fearful silence dissolved into a storm of whispers.

Steel held up a black-gloved hand. "This is to ensure the safety and wellbeing of you all. Order has been... lax in this camp as of late. Rules and laws which are in place to keep people safe and secure will be enforced in a way the previous captain did not deem necessary."

Juliana's head bobbed in a light nod. This, at least, she was familiar with. It was the same way in the city; rules and laws in place to keep people safe.

Beside her, Naya let out a whimper.

"Over the next few days, we will maintain the regular watch and guard rotation. Expect my unit to wander. To ask you questions as we settle into our new positions. We are hopeful that with your cooperation, this transition period will go smoothly."

He stepped away from the podium; rather abruptly, and it took a few seconds for the mayor to realize the microphone was his again.

He scrambled forward, clenching the podium with both hands. "Thank you, Captain Steel. We all look forward to your protection in the coming days."

Steel's unit remained where they stood, but Steel positioned himself to the right and just ahead of Marsterson. The mayor's gaze kept darting to the Black-Star as he spoke.

"Have a wonderful evening everyone, and let's give a big hand for our new captain."

Juliana clapped her hands together a few times, as did the rest of the square. The sound died quickly.

The Black-Stars filed down the steps, circling the crowd and standing at attention as people moved toward the main road and their homes. Little pockets of space formed as the guards strode through. The people of Abredea gave a wide birth.

Juliana craned her neck as people moved around her, trying to spot Daisy and catch her friend's attention. At the podium, the mayor was trying to engage Steel in conversation. The Black-Star turned away mid-sentence and strode down the steps; two of the remaining guards flanked him.

Mayor Marsterson turned; he spat a few words at Daisy—who had stepped forward once the Black-Stars moved away—and marched toward their house. Daisy squeezed her eyes closed for a brief moment, then looked out, scanning the crowd.

Juliana waved a hand as her gaze reached them. Daisy caught her eye, nodded, and made her way to the edge of the square.

"Tha' was... interestin'."

Juliana jumped. Anthony stood next to Naya, hands in his pockets, a thoughtful expression on his face.

"Interestin'?" Naya demanded, a high pitch to her voice. "It was a frosted *warnin'*, Tony. And ye'd better heed it."

Anthony shifted on his feet, a stiff smile on his lips.

May gave Juliana's arm a squeeze and released her. "It was certainly something different."

"'ave yeh ever seen a Black-Star run Abredea?" Naya asked.

"Not in years and years," May murmured. Sadness shone in her eyes, dragging at her weathered face.

They were silent for a moment. Juliana winced as the press of people around them ebbed and flowed. The square emptied out quickly. A few families—wealthier, she assumed—remained behind, shopping and chatting together near the fountain.

Daisy joined their little group, shivering in the fading light. Juliana wrapped an arm around her friend. "Do you want to come back to May's for a bit?" She glanced at May. "If that's all right?"

"Of course!" May gave her a wide grin, the skin around her scar stretching. "Let's get back and have some tea. Warm up a bit." She turned to Naya, Jimmy, and Anthony. "You're coming as well. We have a bit of food, plenty of hot water, and it's been far too long since we've spent an evening together."

Juliana's heart sank. She glanced at Daisy and, seeing her friend's excited grin back in place, forced a smile onto her face.

"Excellent." Anthony rubbed his hands together. "I'll tell Taz. We'll meet yeh there."

Naya's eyes narrowed. "Yer just tellin' Taz? Tha's it?"

"Yeah," Anthony replied in an incredulous tone. "What else would I do?"

Juliana's tight smile relaxed into something real as she recalled the bet Taz and Daisy made on how soon Anthony would do something dumb and dangerous. Beside her, Daisy giggled. Then she shivered. The summer day had been warm, but with the sun gone the air took on a sharp chill.

"Let's go." Juliana led the way, weaving through the straggling remains of the short assembly. Steel's words occupied her thoughts as she walked, arm around Daisy. He wasn't demanding much. Obeying the rules is what kept things in the city running smoothly; she couldn't imagine it was so different here.

There was something odd about it all though. Something that made her gut churn. So many Black-Stars, and for one of the smallest camps in Pangaea.

Her brow furrowed until Daisy gave her a curious look. She shook her head and relaxed her face into a neutral expression. This wasn't anything for her to worry about. She thought of what Wolfe had said, hope stirring in her chest. With any luck, or justice, she'd be back in Tornim soon. Well before she had to worry about associating with a rule-breaker.

She shot a glare at Anthony's back as he headed toward the bakery.

Then her stomach rumbled. She sighed.

Interesting. Certainly one way to describe what just happened. Anthony ran a hand through his hair.

He needed another cut. May had been in a hurry a few weeks ago and used her garden sheers. He'd resembled a shaggy wolf ever since.

He jogged across the square. Dinner at May's was just what he—and everyone else—needed. If he got there quick enough, he could gut and skin one of the rabbits. Though, fish would cook faster. His mouth watered.

Anthony slowed a few yards from the bakery. The display was still in the window, though many of the items had sold. Standing before it, speaking to one of his men, was Captain Steel.

They murmured together, facing the square and subtly pointing to different buildings and people as they hurried by.

Anthony spotted Taz inside. His friend's gaze repeatedly darted out at the Black-Stars as he boxed up an order for one of the White-Stars who worked at town hall. Anthony continued forward. His heartbeat sped up, but he kept his face neutral, his stride even.

There was a shout to his left. He whipped around as a young girl, maybe two or three, sprinted past him. The woman shouting after her jogged to catch up, but a swollen pregnant belly slowed her down.

The girl tripped. Her pale dress flew out as she sprawled across the cobblestones stopping inches from Captain Steel's shiny black boots. Dirt and dust spiraled into the air, settling on his immaculate pants.

Tears sprang into the eyes of the child, and she began to wail. The Black-Star beside Steel—a man of equal height with jet black hair and a tattoo trailing up his neck—stooped, gripped the girl by the arm, and lifted her into the air.

Anthony froze. The girl's mother skidded to a halt, terror splashed across her face. The few people around them slowed to a stop, watching the interaction with wary eyes.

Anthony scanned the surroundings. One guard and Steel. The other Black-Stars had melted into Abredea. The little girl sobbed, wriggling against the large hand holding her up. Anthony's jaw clenched, his eyes narrow.

Steel lifted his leg and flicked a clump of dirt from his boot. "That was clumsy." His voice was even, but something in it made Anthony's skin crawl.

Anthony stepped forward, achingly loosening his features and forcing his hands to stop being fists. "An accident, I'm sure yeh agree Captain Steel."

Steel turned to him. Anthony met the cold gaze with a half-nod and a steady stare. When Steel didn't speak, Anthony took a few steps forward. He reached out, slow and careful, as though dealing with a wild animal rather than a man. The Black-Star beside Steel watched, confusion etched across his face, as Anthony gripped the child under her arms and gently pulled her from his grip.

The guard's hand tightened around her wrist for a brief second. His gaze darted to Steel. The captain jerked his head and the man let go.

Anthony shifted the girl, resting her on his hip. Her fingers curled tight into his shirt.

"What's your name, boy?" Steel asked.

"Anthony," he responded, voice clear and unafraid despite the shudder running down his back.

Steel's lip curled, twisting the tattoo on his cheek. "Anthony what?"

"Clearwater."

Steel stared him down. Anthony held the gaze, highly aware of the guard at Steel's side, the gun at his hip, and the thin braided whip dangling from Steel's belt.

After a long moment Steel nodded. "Clearwater. I'm sure we'll meet again."

"Welcome tah Abredea," Anthony said.

Steel's brow furrowed, but he said nothing else. Instead, he gestured for his guard and the two strode away, headed toward town hall.

Anthony watched them go, waited as they climbed the steps, and only breathed again when they entered the building.

The mother dashed forward, pulling the girl from his arms, and sobbing with relief as she thanked him repeatedly.

He nodded, forcing a tight smile as his breath caught up to him.

The other White-Stars moved on, a few he knew from the fields giving him sharp nods as they made their way home. Several minutes passed before he moved again. Recalling what he was supposed to be doing, he turned and bumped into Taz.

"Oof," Taz grunted, tripping backwards, and clutching the bag he held to his chest.

"Sorry." Anthony reached out, steadying his friend. "I was just comin' tah get yeh. We're doin' dinner at May's."

Taz raised a sandy eyebrow. "What're we eatin'?"

His tone brought a smile back to Anthony's face. "Oh, yeh know... a few things I picked up here and there."

The wild grin on Taz's face made Anthony chuckle. He gestured to the bag.

"Yeh got somethin' tah pitch in?"

Taz laughed and the two fell into stride together. Anthony's steps were shorter than usual to accommodate his smaller friend.

"I do, in fact. They were expectin' a bit... bit... bit more business today, but they didn' get it. I've got the extras." His eyes glinted with excitement. Then they dimmed. "What was tha'? With the new captain?"

Anthony sighed. "The usual."

"So, I win the bet? Yeh did somethin' dumb and dangerous already?"

Anthony rolled his eyes. "What'll it take for yeh to *not* tell Naya and May about it?"

Taz clicked his teeth, thinking hard. "Take me out with yeh. Just once."

Anthony stopped walking. "Taz..."

"Come on," Taz almost whined. "I'm older than ye... you were when yeh started goin'. I can 'elp."

"It's *too* dangerous."

Taz rolled his eyes and waved a hand through the air. "And yet, yeh con... cont... continue to go. Every week."

"Because I *'ave* to."

"Because yeh love it," Taz shot back.

Anthony grimaced. "Fine. Tell Naya. I'm not takin' yeh. Especially not now. New captain? Black-Stars crawlin' all over?"

Taz hesitated, shifting from foot to foot. The color in his gemstones shifted rapidly, orange to pink to yellow. Colors Anthony had long associated with nerves.

"I won... I won't..." Taz chewed his lip. When he spoke again, his voice was quiet. "I won't mess it up."

Anthony rubbed the bridge of his nose. "I know." He put a hand on Taz's shoulder and met his friend's gaze. "I'm not worried about yeh messin' anythin' up, Taz. I..." he swallowed. "I won't put yeh in a situation where yeh could get hurt."

Taz grimaced. Then he cast a glance towards Daisy's house and nodded. "I guess I... I understand."

"When things change, Taz. When the world is different and it's not..." Anthony growled. The weight of the child in his arms came back to him. She was so light. So thin. "When it's not like this, I'll take yeh every frosted day."

Taz nodded; his jaw tight.

"I won't tell Naya," he said.

Anthony threw an arm over Taz's shoulder with an off-kilter grin. "A true friend. Let's hurry. I'm hungry."

Chapter Seventeen

70 Years Ago - The Warren - Main Rebel Base

Maybelle stared at the screen. Her eyes clouded with tears as she took in the images before her. Her pounding headache faded into the background at the horror she witnessed. Eventually, the screams subsided and the screen faded to black.

Lights in the room came up. White walls gleamed around them. A sterile smell overwhelmed the space. Whether it was some sort of office, holding cell, or meeting place, was unclear.

Maybelle clenched her hands tightly in her lap. Kate sat a few spaces away, her head bent. Her body shook with gentle sobs.

Red stood behind them, his hand on the light-switch. Sam leaned against the wall to his left, her face marred with fury.

Maybelle stood, the feet of her chair scrapping against the ground. She turned to face the rebels.

Her voice shook. "We didn't know." A tear slid down her cheek.

"I'm aware." Red's gruff voice was thick. "If you'd have already known, you wouldn't have warned us about that bomb. If you'd have known, you probably wouldn't be here. Not given... what you can do."

Kate nodded furiously in her chair, her back still to the rest of them.

"How is this happening?" Maybelle gestured to the screen. "*Why* is this happening?"

Sam scoffed. She shook her head in disgust. Her light brown eyes blazed with anger; lips pressed together in a tight line.

"Fair is fair, Sam." Red walked to the middle of the room and pulled a chair forward. He turned and straddled it, facing Maybelle and Kate. "They told us their end; we tell them ours."

"*I* still don't know they're telling the truth."

Maybelle faced Sam, her hands crossed in front of her chest. "We are telling the truth. Why else would I warn you about a bomb in your base?"

"To save your own selfish skin." Sam stepped closer to Maybelle. Her hands clenched into fists at her side.

Maybelle sighed; Sam had said nothing else for the past three days.

The bomb had gone off. There was nothing Maybelle could have done to stop it. But Red believed her. In those precious few seconds, he'd believed her.

He'd put the locket on a transport and shot it away. Less than a minute later, it exploded. The massive crater left behind showed what the devastation could have been.

The underground base had tunnels spreading out for miles. The ones destroyed in the blast had been uniform and gear repair centers. Only ten rebel lives were lost, though nearly forty were injured. A small number compared to the nearly two thousand who lived at the base.

All of the survivors had been evacuated. Kate informed Red about the tracker in the bomb while Maybelle was unconscious. They'd started the move as soon as the bodies were burned.

Maybelle awoke after they arrived at the new base, almost two days later.

She told Red everything, including her ability to move from one place to another in the blink of an eye. As Kate pointed out, she had no choice if she wanted to properly explain their story. He hadn't said a word about her ability while they waited to hear what the rebel command wanted to do with them. And now Maybelle knew why.

The footage was horrific. Rebel spies managed to smuggle the images out of one of the leading research facilities in Pangaea. Kate and Maybelle had been on the waitlist to interview before the war started. They'd thought the facility was tackling the sterility problem in Grey-Stars.

The footage showed something quite different. Children, some as young as seven or eight, being tortured and experimented on. There were adults too, people with abilities like Maybelle. A woman in her thirties was controlling the flow of water, until the Grey-Stars on the screen injected her with something that unleashed uncontrollable, gut-wrenching screams.

"Who are those people?" Kate whimpered. "Why are they like Maybelle?"

"We don't know why these people have abilities, why their DNA has been altered. As far as *who* they are... we call them *alters* and we haven't found a common factor among them, but there are certainly many. We have over twenty here at the base."

Sam cleared her throat meaningfully.

"That's enough, Sam." Red frowned at her, the annoyance in his voice reaching its peak. "I outrank you. We're doing this my way, so stop whining about not trusting them and *help* me. You know as well as I do, they could be the key to ending this war."

She huffed, her face flushing. Lips pinched together, she grabbed a chair, yanked it away from the table, collapsed into it, and crossed her arms, glaring at Red.

"All right." Red sighed. "Back to it. We started this rebellion to overthrow the caste system. But the more we learned about Grey-Stars," he looked pointedly at Maybelle and Kate, "the more we came to realize there is more wrong with our country than just the castes. The images you saw are just a small part of the evidence we have of Grey-Stars torturing people with powers."

"Why haven't we heard of this?" Kate's low voice shook as she spoke. "We're Grey-Stars."

"How old are you?" Sam asked scornfully. "Twenty-one? Twenty-two? The government isn't going to tell every Grey-Star kid around."

"We're thirty-three," Maybelle said. She jerked her head toward Kate. "Thirty-four next month."

Red's eyebrows raised, a confused look on his face.

She explained the longevity of the Grey-Stars, her stomach in knots as she gave up one of her people's secrets to a man she'd met only days before.

"Only you?" He asked. "Only the Grey-Stars have this long life? What about Black-Stars?"

Maybelle shook her head. "Just us."

"Why haven't we heard about this?" Kate asked again. Her voice was thick with tears.

"It's a long story." Red leaned back in his chair.

"Right at the beginning of the rebellion, people started coming to us. There weren't many, only about a dozen in the first few years. They were like you. They had abilities we couldn't explain. And they didn't bend to the will of you Grey-Stars like the rest of us."

Guilt flowed through Maybelle. She lowered her eyes, hands clenched.

"We tried to keep them out of the fighting at first, but eventually it became clear we needed their help. That's when *you* found out about them." Sam leaned forward in her chair, her tone accusatory. "That's when you started *taking* them."

"I didn't take anyone." Maybelle's voice was calm, but her jaw clenched in frustration. "I'm not..." she gestured to Kate, "we're not, responsible for the actions of every Grey-Star. We didn't know this was happening. I doubt many do. Our people use *suggestion* to keep the peace, to keep people content in their stations."

"*Content in their stations?*" Sam repeated, disbelief etched across her face. There was acid in her voice. "What is content about a life of forced labor? Knowing your children will suffer for every choice you make? What's content about watching infants get sick and die because they aren't 'high' enough for expensive medicine?"

Kate flinched but Sam continued.

"How *content* would you feel, watching the women you care about be used for sex by Grey-Stars? Then when they come out of the trance, they can't even look in the mirror." The fury in her voice reached a peak. She stood and kicked her chair away. Her body shook, tears pouring down her face.

There was silence for several seconds. When she spoke again, her voice was barely a whisper. "What's content about losing the man you love because of the *frosted* color on your temple?"

Her voice demanded answers, but Maybelle had none. She sat in silent shock, processing the words. She ran a hand through her hair, strands catching on her dried and cracked skin. Fresh tears burned at her eyes, but she blinked them away.

Maybelle glanced at Kate; her friend's face had been a mask of horror since the images had started on the screen. Now her lip was curled, brows furrowed in unwavering anger.

The Grey-Stars, their own people, lied to them, betrayed them. Kate and Maybelle worked day and night before the war to fix their people, to help them. Children... Children were the most important commodity in the world to Grey-Stars. The protection of young life was above all else for Kate and Maybelle. And they'd been letting babies go without medicine; children get punished for their parents' mistakes, and the experimentation... She shuddered.

Beyond the children was the blatant manipulation of people. Maybelle had been taught from her first day in school their power was there to help the people. The thought of Grey-Stars, using their power to sexually abuse people... Maybelle swallowed several times to keep the vomit down.

She sat in silence. Kate took deep, shuddering, angry breaths. Sam left the room, slamming the door behind her. Red stared up at the lights. A tear slid down his cheek and disappeared into his beard. Had he lost someone to a different caste after the Coding? Or had someone he cared about been used? Or did he have children? And if so, were they...

She stopped thinking.

She wanted to call it all a lie. But the pain in Sam's voice, the tear on Red's cheek, and the images of those children, they weren't a lie. And they weren't going away.

She raised her head, looking at Kate. Her best friend since childhood, the one person she could always count on. Kate met her gaze, her eyes blazing with betrayal. She nodded.

Maybelle stood. Her voice shook slightly as she turned to Red. "What can we do?"

Red watched her, thoughtfully stroking his beard. "We need to know about you, about your kind. There are gaps in our knowledge, so many secrets you hold within your class. And we need help with the people, a serum to prevent the Grey-Stars from using their power."

"We call it *suggestion*." Kate stood also, crossing her arms tight over her chest. Red nodded.

"You don't need to keep wearing those." Kate's voice was harsh. Her gaze flickered back to the dark screen. "We can turn it off. We'll keep it off while we're around you."

"I'll let the leaders know, but I think we'll keep using them for a little while."

Maybelle nodded. "We'll tell you everything we know. And we can start working on a counteragent for *suggestion* as soon as we have a place to work."

Red stared from one to the other and back again. "We'll get you set up as soon as possible. You'll have a lab in the next few days."

Some of the tension in Maybelle's stomach eased. "We need to come up with a list of supplies."

Red stood, gesturing for them to follow him out of the room. "You can get it to me tomorrow. We need to get you two back to your cell for the night."

Maybelle frowned.

"Once we know you can be trusted you'll be given regular quarters. As it stands, we don't have enough for the refugees."

He led the way to their cell. In this new complex they shared a small concrete chamber with two beds and a tiny bathroom stall.

He bid them goodnight and promised to send food shortly. Maybelle sat on her cot. Her head was throbbing again, but this had nothing to do with her newfound ability.

"Why?"

Maybelle looked up. Kate sat against the wall, pawing at her face to wipe away the tears.

"They were so small, Maybelle. So young…" The hopelessness in her voice sent sharp pangs of ice through Maybelle's heart. Kate's shoulders shook. Her breathing turned to sobs as she stopped trying to stem the flow of tears.

Maybelle crossed the room, kneeling down beside her friend. She put a hand behind Kate's head and pulled her into her shoulder, stroking her hair. Kate's hands slid up from the ground and circled Maybelle.

They sat together; Kate mourning for the children lost, for the pain they endured before the end.

Thoughts and memories swirled through Maybelle's mind. Her life as a Grey-Star, Ben, her *purpose*… She was supposed to save them, to find a cure for Gery-Star infertility and save *her people*.

Images flashed across her vision, and tears burned in her eyes. The Black-Star recruit, eyes glazed as he did her bidding. The fallen girl at the battlefield, eye sliced in half. The pain on Sam's face.

Maybelle's stomach boiled. Fury pounded through her chest, and each beat of her heart sent strength and focus, narrowing her intent.

She'd help these rebels. She'd stop the atrocities. She'd exact brutal revenge against her people for what they'd done.

Six months passed in the blink of an eye.

Maybelle shoveled spoonsful of gravy into her mouth, occasionally coming out of the bowl for a bite of biscuit. She tucked her hair, cut along her jawline, behind her ears to keep it out of the food. Around her, fellow researchers ate with just as much vigor.

Kate scowled, dropped her spoon, and slumped into her chair.

"What?" Maybelle asked after swallowing a particularly hot chunk of meat. She grimaced and reached for her water.

"I don't understand how you can eat this."

Maybelle grinned at her friend. "It's been months, Kate. You'll get used to the food... eventually."

Kate shook her head. The purple-tinged bags under her eyes told Maybelle what the real problem was. They'd been working nonstop for weeks. No break, barely any help, and almost no progress to speak of.

The rebel commanders were growing impatient.

Footsteps echoed through the cavernous mess hall. Dim light from orbs affixed to the walls flickered. Red stomped toward them, his grin offsetting the sound of his large body moving through the room.

"How're the brains of the operation doing?" he asked, slinging his body onto the bench beside Maybelle.

She chuckled, taking a massive bite of biscuit and pointing a pinky at Kate.

Red looked to her friend. He raised an eyebrow. "What's wrong?"

Kate glared. First at Red, then meaningfully down at her bowl of meaty gravy. Maybelle had stopped asking about the particulars of the meat after their second meal.

Red broke into a raucous laugh. "That's it? Kid, that's what they serve, that's what we eat. You want to keep up your strength, you'll take what you can get."

"I'm older than you," Kate muttered. She did, however, pick up her spoon and force a few bites down.

Maybelle stifled a snort and looked at Red. "What's the word from command?"

"Nothing helpful," he sighed. Then he glanced up and down the table.

They were relatively alone. The other researchers still kept their distance from the only two Grey-Stars in the rebel army. Maybelle couldn't blame them. Not after some of the stories they'd heard since becoming part of the force.

"We've been reaching out, trying to make contacts with our neighbors. But Pangaea has been locked away from the world for so long... no one wants to get involved in a civil war. Especially since they don't know anything about us." He took one of her biscuits and ate it in two bites. "As far as things *here* go... command wants the counteragent before they make a move."

Maybelle shook her head, setting down her spoon for the first time since she'd gotten her food. "It's going to take so long. As we told you when we started, this isn't a simple procedure. And we only have ourselves to use as subjects."

"We could—"

"No," she interrupted. She knew what he was going to say. The offer had been made a hundred times before. But she and Kate would make do with themselves; they didn't need kidnapped Grey-Stars to complete their objective.

He raised his hands defensively and gave her a nod. "Understood."

"That's it though?" Maybelle leaned in. "They aren't even going in for rescue missions anymore?"

"They're scared, Maybelle." He rubbed a hand across his face. "The Greys have been using *suggestion* more and more. We keep running across Black-Stars with glazed eyes, unafraid of death, hacking people apart with stronger plasma bolts than we've seen before. Last report from that White-Star village outside of the capital says they've been targeting civilians. Anyone remotely connected to a suspected rebel. They're taking them and closing them off in these... prison towns."

Anger flashed across his face, followed by dragging weariness.

"Last unit to go out lost someone because their mask malfunctioned." Red grimaced. "Kid was barely twenty. Just walked right into the open. Gunned down in a second."

Maybelle swallowed. Her stomach, comfortably full a minute ago, churned. She pushed away the bowl and looked to Kate.

Kate caught her gaze. After a second she exhaled, a sad smile on her lips, and nodded.

Maybelle put a hand on Red's shoulder. "I've been thinking about a way to fix that." She leaned in. "How many *alters* do we have at the Warren right now?"

Chapter Eighteen

Present Day - Mid Summer - Abredea

Juliana paced outside the school, wringing her hands as she tried to talk herself out of this foolish idea. It wasn't necessary; she'd be gone from this place soon. She thought of the dinner she'd had a week ago. With May, and Daisy, and Taz, Anthony, and his aunt and cousin. They'd laughed, and she'd found herself laughing too. Chopping carrots and potatoes, baking them with what little spices May had left. Searing the fish Anthony had caught, picking apart the delicious pink flakes and letting them melt in her mouth.

Watching Daisy eat to bursting, her smile full after such a difficult day. Laughing as Anthony fell off his perch on the counter when Taz pushed past him for seconds. May's face, so content, so at peace with a house full of people.

Juliana's stomach clenched. If this worked, maybe she'd be able to make that sort of thing happen more often. At least, until Ms. Wolfe got her out of Abredea.

The bell rang. Parents pushed by to gather their children from the dingy brick building. Older students eyed her as they walked by.

Daisy's yelp was audible over the ruckus of people moving about. "Hey! You're doing it?" She darted forward to give Juliana a quick hug. "Good luck!"

Juliana returned the squeeze and then made her way inside. Her eyes adjusted to the dark as she followed the directions Daisy had given her. She arrived at the office, knocked on the door, and slipped inside.

An Orange-Star sat behind a long wooden desk. File cabinets crowded every wall, stacks of yellowing paper sticking out of not quite closed drawers. The woman before her looked up, a frown creasing her brow. Her bored gaze flicked to Juliana's gemstones. She leaned back, clacking a long purple fingernail against her front teeth.

"Hello," Juliana said, her most professional smile in place. "I'd like to inquire about a possible job."

The woman's eyes widened, amusement lighting up her face. "A *job*?" She looked again at Juliana's pearly white gemstones.

"Yes." Juliana took a breath. "I have all the qualifications I believe are necessary to be a teacher, or even a teaching aid for the younger classes. I'm... that is, I was a Blue-Star. My education level should allow for me to cover everything required."

The Orange-Star's smile widened, but it was not kind. "You're a Moon." She let out a laugh. "You can't teach other Moons... it's not allowed."

"I've checked the rules and regulations for Abr—for the camp. There's nothing about not being allowed to teach."

She shrugged. "White-Stars don't teach. You're not smart enough."

Sound diminished. A tunnel of wind replaced the background noise of children laughing and people talking on the other side of the walls. Juliana's heartbeat pounded in her ears, each beat pulsing heat and anger through her chest.

She exhaled through her teeth, reason leaving her as she leaned forward and planted both hands on the desk. The Orange-Star leaned back in alarm.

"I know more than anyone in your caste could ever *hope* to learn," Juliana hissed. "You could spend your entire life studying every book available to you... and you wouldn't come *close* to the knowledge I had at sixteen."

The Orange-Star's eyes widened, flashing between anger and fear. "Get out," the woman snapped. "Before I call the guard."

Juliana turned on her heel, fury propelling her away from the room, the building, and the school. By the time she reached the fountain in the square, her anger had melted away leaving her fingertips numb and her limbs heavy.

A squad of Black-Stars passed, and she straightened, eyeing them warily. They paid her no attention on their way to the half-completed barracks going up just behind the town hall. The sound of construction had harried the square for the last week, but barring a wave of mid-summer rains, the Green-Stars would be done in a few days. Captain Steel's private quarters, a bit further from the square, had already been completed.

Sunlight glistened in the water pouring from the fountain. Juliana stared, her jaw tight. A child raced past her, splashing through the mud and sticking their face under a cool spray.

She sighed. Maybe Montague would be able to do something about the school.

"*Juliana!*" She turned toward Jimmy's voice. He raced towards her across the square. Daisy, giggling, chased along behind him with Taz and Naya on her heels.

Juliana swallowed the lump in her throat and grinned down at the boy. "Hey, you ready to read?"

He nodded, jumping excitedly on the balls of his feet.

"How'd it go?" Daisy asked, panting as she came up beside them. One look at Juliana's face gave her the answer. "Sorry," she murmured.

"No luck?" Naya swung a large basket of laundry around, resting it on her hip. Juliana shook her head.

Naya glowered. "*Nacra* Orange-Stars. Always thinkin' they're better than us." She shook her head, a long dark braid whipping around her shoulder. "I've got this lot tah do," she jerked her head at the basket, "are yeh sure yer all right with Jimmy?"

Juliana smiled, the tightness in her chest loosening. "Yeah, we'll get through homework first," she looked down at the boy, "then do some reading."

Jimmy bobbed his head, eyes alight. He turned from them, bag thudding against his back as he started jumping toward his house.

"You coming?" Juliana asked Taz and Daisy. The latter nodded, but Taz had a shift at the bakery.

Daisy and Juliana followed after Jimmy, keeping up rather well as he had opted to leap his way home rather than walk.

"Do you want me to take your bag?" Daisy asked, wincing at each thud of it against his back.

"Nah," Jimmy huffed. "I've gotta practice tah help Tony with his bag when I'm bigger."

Juliana and Daisy exchanged a smile.

Ahead of them, an Orange-Star pushed a handcart with a wooden crate of mush, a bright red X emblazoned on the side, down the bend toward May's house. Juliana's gaze slid from the glinting gems on their temples—a rush of anger stirring in her belly—and settled on the Black-Star accompanying them instead.

The man looked back as they passed and Juliana averted her gaze, hurrying to catch up with Daisy and Jimmy.

They'd just settled in at Naya's house, and gotten started on Jimmy's math homework, when someone knocked on the door. Jimmy leapt to his feet before Juliana or Daisy could rise.

"Who is it?" Juliana asked.

Jimmy scurried to the door and flung it open. "My friends," he exclaimed.

Juliana's eyes widened as four children around Jimmy's age entered the house, each clutching a notebook to their chest.

"Jimmy said you could help," a girl with blonde pig-tails squeaked.

Juliana looked to Daisy; her stunned expression briefly matched on her friend's face.

Then Daisy broke into a wide grin. "Well, their teacher *is* pretty horrible. They probably need some guidance."

Stifling a groan, Juliana forced a smile and nodded to the gaggle of children. With a flurry of giggles, flapping papers, and scraping chairs, the children joined them at the table. Daisy and Juliana gave up their seats, circling as they paused to offer help, explain a problem, and occasionally stop everyone so Juliana could re-teach something that hadn't been properly explained.

An hour later they'd finished the homework and Jimmy launched himself at the small shelf in the corner of the room.

"Outside today?" he asked eagerly, clutching a book to his chest.

Juliana nodded and out they went. Her field was a bit far, so they settled themselves on a patch of green under a large tree just off the main road.

"From the beginning?" Juliana looked at Jimmy. "For your friends?"

He nodded, bobbing with enthusiasm.

She opened the book, cleared her throat, and read.

Anthony ducked through the fence, the bag on his back slowing him down almost as much as the constant checks for Black-Stars. One of the very *few* things he missed about Captain Durang and the Red-Stars—their uniforms were easy to spot.

He neither saw nor heard the guards. Their patrols fit a regular schedule, but he was extra careful these days. More eyes were on him. Black-Stars followed his movements in the square. His occasional shift in the field—his hours had not improved with Durang's absence—was accompanied by extra guards. Whether it was because Durang had told Steel about him, or because of his interaction with Steel that first day, he wasn't sure. Either way, it made life more dangerous.

Anthony dropped a few things off at his house, filling the cupboards with onions and berries. He wrapped one of the fish he'd caught in paper and tucked it inside the small wooden box on his counter. It wouldn't keep long, but he'd gut it that night and enjoy an actual meal.

Across from his bed, in the minuscule one room home, sat a large chest of drawers. He crossed to it, running a hand along the painted wood. Bright roses, red, purple, and white, bloomed from green stems and thorns spiraling up the sides. He pulled a fistful of slightly wilted wildflowers from his bag, clipped the stems, and placed them in a clear glass vase.

Then he slung the bag back over his shoulder and made his way to May's house. She was in the garden, during the hottest part of the day in the middle of summer. Her face lit into a familiar smile bringing warmth to Anthony's chest.

"May, what are yeh doin' out 'ere? It's gettin' too hot tah be weedin'."

She leaned back on her heels, her smile shifting to a squinty-eyed glare. "Are you suggesting, dear boy, that I'm too old to work in my garden on such a beautiful day?"

He laughed, taking the bag off his back, and kneeling next to her in the dirt. "I'd never dream of sayin' yeh were too old for *anythin'*."

"Indeed." She inched forward and dug her fingers into the planter box before her. From it, tomato stems shot toward the sky, squash tendrils draped over the sides, flowing to the ground, and grass-like weeds tried to eke out survival amongst the vegetables. May took hold of a weed, plunging her fingers as deep as they would go, and ripped it out by the root. "What are you up to, Tony?"

He sighed, digging out a few weeds next to her and adding them to the pile. "I just got back from a huntin' trip. Should hold everyone over for a few days. I might try and trade one of the rabbits for some flour; Naya was talkin' about makin' bread the other day."

"Hmmm," May grumbled, stretching her right arm, and glancing at the sun overhead. Sweat trickled down her forehead. "Be careful with that, you'll have to go all the way to the grocers for the trade. If the Black-Stars catch you with contraband..."

"Wha'? I'll get a few nights in the holdin' cell?" He scoffed. "I'm already down on hours. I could get caught today and not miss a shift." Heat, a combination of anger and worry, rose in his chest.

"I don't believe the new captain will settle for a holding cell."

"Whaddya mean?" Anthony raised an eyebrow.

"A man like that won't take kindly to anyone disobeying him or getting in his way. He is a different kind of threat than Durang." May pushed herself up, gathered up the pile of weeds, and walked them over to a taller box in the far corner of the garden. "Just be careful."

"Always," Anthony said with a grin.

May returned, reached up a hand, and patted his cheek. "You say that, but I never do believe you."

He stuck out his tongue and followed her inside. The house was cooler, a gentle breeze flowing through the open doors and windows. He passed her the meat and fish he'd caught, collected a few baskets of vegetables she'd harvested that morning, and took his leave.

He stopped at the usual homes along the way; fellow west-enders who had less than the Moons who lived near the square and the wall. Proximity to the city... he never understood why it meant those Moons were paid more, or why their homes were bigger. Or why most of them refused to help the rest.

He paused under a tall tree with wide branches and dark green leaves. The cool shade mellowed his temper. By the time he reached the square, baskets and bag empty except for the rabbit he was hoping to trade, the sun had begun to dip toward the horizon, giving some respite from the heat.

Anthony stumbled to a stop as he came around the bend in the road, the square splayed out before him. Across the way, at the foot of town hall and scattered across its steps, sat at least two dozen children. They rested on upturned buckets and boxes, huddled together in little groups or sitting alone, books open at their sides or on their laps.

He gaped for a moment, then strode forward to find out what was going on. He spotted Jimmy in the group, sitting on the top step with his nose in a large schoolbook.

Daisy wandered around the edge of the cluster of children, pausing occasionally to answer a question or ask one. Another ripple of surprise ran through him at the sight of Juliana doing the same. She knelt, bare knee in the dirt, to get a better look at someone's paper. With a wide grin, she clapped her hands together and rubbed the shoulder of the child she'd been helping.

Anthony blinked, losing focus for a moment as he took in that smile. He'd only seen it once or twice. It reminded him of spotting a wolf or a bear in the woods; a rare thing, and one that quickened his heartbeat.

Her gemstones glinted in the sunlight as she stood again, surveying the group. Her long blonde hair no longer hung loose; she'd braided it back and pinned it into a bun. Her clothes had changed too. She must have stopped trying for a city look and gone for practical. Today it was a pair of dark green shorts almost reaching her knees and a light long-sleeve button up. Probably to protect those pale arms from the sun.

"Come to help?"

Anthony jolted.

Daisy's laugh splintered the general quiet of the square. Several of the children turned to look as she continued to giggle, pulling Anthony to the side while he glared at her.

"What's goin' on 'ere?" he asked. He gestured to the children, though his gaze fixed once again on Juliana.

"I told you about this last week." Daisy raised an eyebrow. "Remember, I said we had too many kids for Naya's house and asked if you had any ideas where we could go."

Anthony's eyes widened. "Tha' was for *this*? I thought it was a readin', play thing for Jimmy."

"Well, sort of. It started out as a reading thing for Jimmy. Then Juliana helped with his homework." She shrugged. "Eventually his friends started coming by, then more friends, and now," she waved a hand at the children, a variety of ages, spread across the ground, "it's anyone who wants a little extra help with their school-work."

He heaved a breath, at a loss for words.

"Don't worry," Daisy patted his shoulder, "she still reads to Jimmy. Well, we take turns since most of them are *my* books anyway. And this gives Naya a chance to get more done in the evening."

She pointed and Anthony turned to see his aunt chatting with a few other women at the communal laundry basins. More time meant more money. It meant warmer clothes for Jimmy this winter; a new pair of shoes for the growing boy.

"An'… and *she* started all this?"

"Ahem," Daisy planted her hands on her hips, "I like to think I've been a pretty big help."

Anthony broke into a grin. "No surprise there, Daisy."

She gave him a playful shove and lowered her voice. "She did though. When he asked about reading, she was nervous. But…" Daisy watched Juliana with steady eyes. "Once she started, she didn't want to stop. Naya was talking about how much he was struggling with math, and she jumped on it."

Anthony eyed Daisy. "Yeh sound proud."

She shrugged. "You know how I like cracking shells. I didn't think she'd be all right around other people until winter, at the soonest."

Daisy patted his arm and went off to help another kid. Anthony started up the steps to say hi to Jimmy when boots crunched behind him.

A Black-Star paced near the fountain, gaze locked on Anthony. With a sigh, he turned and, skirting the edge of the square, made his way to the grocers. He reached the open door, glancing over his shoulder to make sure the guard hadn't followed him. The man, a stout individual with a bushy, dark mustache, and thick trunk-like legs, continued pacing around the fountain, though his gaze followed Anthony.

Anthony slipped into the store.

He stepped to the counter with a nod to Alice. "Is yer dad in?"

Alice, a girl who'd been in his class at school, gave a wry smile. "Why? Got somethin' to trade?" She gestured to the bundles of goods behind her. Sacks of flour, sugar, a basket of chicken eggs, a smaller one of duck, dried meats, spices, even wrapped sticks of butter in the small ice chest against the wall.

"I 'ope so." He leaned in. "When was the las' time yeh had fresh meat?"

Alice's eyes went wide.

He grinned. "How about a set of fur gloves? You sew, right?"

She clicked her teeth and crossed her arms. "What've you got?"

Anthony put his bag on the table and opened the top. Alice sucked in a breath at the sight of the large rabbit—his largest of the day—and licked her lips.

"Where..."

He shook his head. "My deal with yer father includes no questions."

Her gaze darted to the front window. Anthony turned ever so slightly, keeping his body between the door and the bag. The Black-Star was still there. Pacing.

"It's odd, how many rabbits get under tha' fence," Anthony said, turning back and giving Alice a raised eyebrow. "I spot one every other week or so."

She pursed her lips. "Do you?"

He nodded.

"And what do you think a rabbit this size is worth?" She leaned her elbows on the counter.

Anthony shifted. The last time he'd tried a trade Mr. Glade had taken him for everything and given little back. He hoped Alice would be a different story.

"Two pounds of flour, two cups of sugar, and a bottle of salt."

She squinted at him, lifted the flap on his bag, and studied the rabbit for another moment. "If it were already a pair of gloves, I'd say yeah, but I'll have to sew them myself. *After* cleanin' it."

Alice went silent for a moment. Anthony waited.

Finally, she turned away from him and started moving things about on the shelves behind her. She set a bag on the counter as well as a small wooden box and a glass bottle filled with white crystals.

"One pound of flour, half a cup of sugar, and one of the small bottles of salt."

"A cup of sugar," Anthony said with a nod.

"*And* you have to bring me this box back. I don't have any little bags for the sugar."

He nodded again. "Remind me to trade with yeh next time as well."

She grinned. "My father doesn't have a taste for rabbit, but mother and I do."

The hand-off was smooth. Alice took the bag to the back and emptied it of the rabbit, then returned and filled it with Anthony's goods.

"'til next time." Anthony smiled, thanked her, and made his way from the store. Outside, he hefted the bag onto his back and gazed around.

The children were collecting their things and heading home. Jimmy ran to him, giving him a quick hug before scampering off to his mother. At the top of the steps Juliana and Daisy chatted together, keeping watchful eyes on the slower moving children.

He followed Jimmy toward Naya, eager to tell her about the flour, and excited to hear when she planned on baking bread.

He halted at the sight of two Black-Stars striding toward town hall. One was the stout man who'd been pacing, the second a woman with a tight shave against her scalp. They marched up the steps, and engaged Juliana and Daisy in conversation.

Daisy shrank away as Juliana straightened and raised her chin.

With a sigh, Anthony turned on his heel and hurried toward them. As he neared the steps, Montague opened the town hall door and stepped into the evening air.

"… without a permit it's not possible. You'll have to move elsewhere," the mustached Black-Star was saying to Juliana.

"That doesn't make any sense," Juliana said. "I've read the rules, cover to cover, there is *nothing* about a study group not being allowed in the square."

The other Black-Star took a step forward, forcing Juliana to back up.

The hairs on Anthony's arms stood up. He strode around the group, positioning himself next to Juliana. Daisy was now fully behind both of them.

"What's wrong?" he asked.

"Gatherings of five people or more are not allowed without the proper permit." The female guard glanced in his direction before returning her attention to Juliana.

"That doesn't make sense," Juliana repeated, her voice cold but quiet. "That rule should apply to adults, not children."

"It isn't specified," grunted the other guard.

Juliana exhaled through her teeth. She stared at the Black-Stars, the furrow in her brow fixed in place as she seemed to struggle for words.

"Where *can* they study?" Anthony asked.

The shorter of the two shrugged. "Not our problem."

"It *should* be," Anthony growled. "It should absolutely be yer problem since yer the ones forcin' them to move."

Juliana put up a hand. "It's fine. We'll figure something out."

He turned to look at her, incredulity across his features.

"Rules are rules," she said.

The Black-Stars surveyed Juliana. She smiled. They nodded, turned, and left.

"What was tha'?" Anthony demanded once the Black-Stars had crossed the nearly empty square. The setting sun splayed red and yellow streaks across the cobblestone.

Juliana spared him a glance before gathering up her own books and papers. "What?"

Daisy slumped onto the top step, tears in her eyes. Montague eyed the three of them before stepping back inside.

Anthony hefted his arm in a frustrated gesture at the Black-Stars now disappearing into the distance. "Why'd yeh go with it? Why didn' yeh fight tha' nacra shit?"

Juliana raised an eyebrow and gave him one of the most condescending looks he'd ever received. "It's the rules. I don't have to like it, but I follow the rules… As should you."

The breath left Anthony like a blow to the sternum. His jaw locked; nostrils flared as his mouth twisted in a snarl. He turned on his heel and took the steps two at a time until his feet hit cobblestone. Without another word or look back, he strode home.

He was too angry to go to Naya's. He needed to cool off first, needed to remember that someone like Juliana—someone from such a high caste in the city—didn't think the same way he did. Didn't care about problems or people the way he did.

A whirlwind of thoughts battered him during the long walk home. He thought of the way she'd looked at him. The way she'd smiled at the Black-Stars.

He slammed his door open, ripped the bag off his back, and threw it onto his bed. The glass tinkled. He cursed.

The salt bottle hadn't broken. He put it, the sugar, and the flour on his kitchen counter.

Anthony locked the door, stripped, and stepped into the minuscule bathroom. They might not have much, but on a sunny day like today he was guaranteed a hot shower. Steam rose, melting the sweat from his face and back.

He shook his head. Naya had cut his hair a few days ago, the jagged, cropped look suited him, but he wasn't used to the lack of weight.

Daisy popped into his mind. She liked Juliana—for whatever reason. Cared for her.

First time in his memory she'd been a bad judge of character.

Still, he'd be polite. Sociable. They didn't have to be friends, but he wouldn't cause unnecessary stress to Daisy. She had enough to deal with.

The water had gone cold by the time he stepped out. He toweled off and changed into something cleaner than his sweat and dirt-stained hunting clothes. Gathering a few things from his cupboard, as well as the goods he'd traded for earlier, he headed to Naya's, hoping he wouldn't run into any blonde White-Stars on the way.

Chapter Nineteen

Present Day - Early Fall - Haven

The savory scent of bacon woke Cho. He rose from his bunk, a small cot pressed against the wall of his room. There was just enough space for a three-tier bookshelf across from his bed. Folded clothes took up the bottom two shelves; a few books, his watch, and a multitude of tiny many-colored cranes sat on the top.

Ahead was Grigoria, and the Star Office, their final destination. Their mission, to sneak in, hijack a Coding machine, and permanently change the color of their gemstones.

Cho drained the glass of water next to his watch. He'd slept. Probably longer than he should have, but his body had refused to move each time he'd woken up.

Time was odd in Haven. Ichi had a watch, similar to the one he'd given Cho—an old-fashioned thing with hands and ticking—and Elaine made sure to keep track of sunrise and sunset, matching the various lights in Haven to give the effect of night. Still, the lack of natural light sometimes made it difficult to wake.

Cho pulled on a pair of pants and a loose grey shirt. He gazed at the row of hooks on the wall between his bed and the bookshelf. Each held a hat. Most were knit, some heavy and thick to keep him warm in the winter, others made with a cool, thin material that nonetheless covered the gemstones on his temples.

He chose one of these, a grey and black stripped one which nestled over his unkempt hair and stopped just above his eyebrows. The edges, expertly crafted by Elaine, dipped low, fitting perfectly over his gems and the tips of his ears. It gave a natural look, as though he'd simply thrown on a hat.

As if he weren't hiding anything.

By the time he was dressed the smell of burned fruit also permeated his room. Cho tapped a pink crane, the size of his thumb and the newest addition to his collection, on the way out.

He wound through the halls of Haven. Colorful skirts swooshed ahead of him, and he hurried to catch up with Luna, Nova, and Claire.

The twins seemed completely recovered. They danced down the hall, Claire keeping pace between them with sturdy, no-nonsense footsteps.

"Hey," Cho said as he approached.

All three turned. Dark bags rimmed Luna's eyes, and neither of the twins had re-done their usually tight braids, but beyond that they appeared fine. Claire stared at Cho as the other two smiled and said good morning.

Her gaze was something different. A hesitant, calculating look. She didn't seem to have slept much at all. Though someone had given her a change of clothes.

Nova took Luna's arm once greetings were exchanged and, giggling something about bacon, dragged her down the hall toward the kitchen.

"So, this is the place." Claire's icy gaze left Cho as she scanned the metal walls on either side of them, looking up at the ceiling towering nearly twenty feet above.

Cho nodded. "I know it doesn't look like much, at least not right now. But it's safe. Safer than up there anyway." He gestured towards the ceiling.

Claire plucked at her shirt. It was a pale pink button-up. Likely on loan from one of the twins as they were close in size to Claire.

"I have my own room," she said, her expression thawing.

He nodded again. "Haven is huge. We have half a dozen empty rooms. People only share if they want to. Like Jane and Tommy, and the twins."

"Which twins?"

A grin broke across Cho's face. "Both sets. Jason and Samaira have a larger room than most." He shrugged. "They got first pick."

"What was this place?" Claire asked.

Cho turned to continued down the hall, and she followed.

"We think it was some sort of factory. Or maybe just a warehouse for sewer equipment. There's one room in the back completely full of old tools, empty boxes, scrap metal, that kind of thing. Ichi and Elaine spent a week clearing everything out when they found the place."

Claire's eyes widened. They passed an intersection, hallways leading to the right and left. Cho continued straight, and Claire hurried after him.

"It's huge. As big as my school." Claire's tone caused a rush of pride to flow through Cho's chest.

"It took a lot of work. Most of it before my time, but I've helped with Sky's garden and getting the tables set up since I've been here."

"How long *have* you been here?"

Cho sighed. He ran his fingers against the metal wall to his right. "Almost three years now. My... ability didn't start until I was fifteen."

Claire's blonde eyebrows furrowed. "Isn't that kind of late?"

He chuckled. "Compared to the rest of Haven, yeah." His tone went sour. "As Jason likes to put it, I'm a late bloomer."

"So, what happened?" Claire asked.

Cho glanced at her. The shielding around his power had refreshed during the night. Rest did that, it brought back his energy, and energy was what he needed to keep his defenses up. Still, he caught the edges of her emotion. Heavy with anxiety, curiosity, and apprehension. He gritted his teeth, recalling the same flurry of feelings when he'd first arrived in Haven.

"I uh..." Cho bit the inside of his cheek. "Ichi found me in Agora. He brought me here. Saved me."

Claire raised an eyebrow.

"How bout I tell you the whole story *after* we get something to eat? I don't know about you, but I'm starving."

"Luna and Nova got me something last night. They brought soup to my room. I wasn't... I didn't want to—"

"Be around a bunch of people you didn't know while dealing with this life-changing event that still doesn't really make sense to you?" Cho asked, his tone dry.

She stared at him.

He shrugged. "Been there. You remember what my ability is, right? I feel other people's emotions. Mine were... well," he grimaced, "I wasn't in a good place when Ichi found me. I spent almost a week in my room before I came out at all."

Sounds of talk and laughter reached them, and the scent of food grew stronger. Cho eyed Claire's hands. She flexed her pale fingers and then curled them in. Crunching filled the air. Ice, which had formed along across her skin, cracked, broke, and fell to the ground as she made fists.

"Don't worry too much about that." Cho winced as a wave of fear and shame slammed into him. "Ichi and Elaine will help you learn to control it. And worst case, you can always aim for Jason and hope to stop him talking for a few minutes."

A splinter of child-like laughter cut through the panic coming off of Claire. She shook her head, a nervous smile on her face.

Cho leaned toward her as they walked, the opening to the main room of Haven only a few yards away. "Remember, everyone here has been through what you're going through. No one will be angry if you lose control. And *not one* of us will judge you for being confused, or scared, or angry."

Claire's lower lip trembled as she slowed to a stop. She stared at him, her eyes bright with tears. She blinked them away, squared her shoulders, gave Cho a nod, and marched out of the hallway.

The main room of Haven was enormous. It consisted of the kitchen, a collection of tables in various shapes and sizes, Sky's garden (a marvel of plant life surviving almost entirely on her power alone), a corner of cushions and couches, a wide carpeted space in the center for meditation practice, and at the far wall a towering L-shaped staircase led to the only door in and out of Haven.

Chatter subsided as Claire and Cho entered the room. With dozens of eyes upon them, Cho nudged Claire and pointed to the left. There, a windowed wall separated the kitchen from the rest of the space. Cho took them under a wide brick archway and into the vast, bustling kitchen.

To the left were a series of stovetops, an oven, and a large flat grill. Jason and Samaira stood at the grill, each holding a spatula and growling to each other about the proper flipping technique required for the perfect pancake.

The wall across from them sported an open window through which the main area of Haven was visible. Under the window, a long, tiled countertop stretched the length of the kitchen. At the half-way mark the deep sink already held a number of dishes, and Ichi was elbow deep in soapy water.

Covering the blue and green checkered tile were plates stacked with pancakes, bacon, sausage, and even scrambled eggs. Elaine's flowery serving bowl—her prized kitchen possession—overflowed with strawberries, blueberries, orange slices, and apple chunks.

Cho's jaw dropped as he came to a halt in the entrance.

"Do you eat like this every day?" Claire gaped at the surplus of food.

Kim, a girl with black hair twisted into elegant knots, and dark freckles speckled along her deeply bronzed skin, skirted around the two of them and hurried to the counter. She held a plate in her hand, streaks of strawberry juice and bacon grease still on it. With a darting glance at Ichi, she reached up, scooped two pancakes onto her plate, and snatched a sausage. As she left, she gestured to a stack of clean plates and utensils sitting on the counter.

"Plates are there, get it before it's gone!" She giggled and pranced away, careful to keep her plate balanced even as her feet danced in excitement.

"No," Cho answered. He glanced at his brother before grabbing a plate for himself and handing one to Claire.

"You're new." Ichi turned to them, drying his hands on a towel, and plucking a slice of bacon from the stack. He took a bite, closed his eyes with a smile and chewed slowly.

Cho piled food onto his plate. Claire waited, watching Ichi.

He swallowed and explained. "We like to do something fun when someone new arrives. A welcome party of sorts to show you we're happy you're here."

"Some of us just really wanted bacon," Jason broke in from the stove.

Samaira shoved him.

Ichi laughed. "Help yourself, Claire. There's plenty for everyone. Samaira and Jason went on a little expedition yesterday evening while the rest of you were recuperating. We have a surplus... for the moment."

Cho glanced at the twins before focusing on his brother. "Did they get the coin?"

Samaira moved toward them, shaking her head. "That part of Agora is still *crawling* with Black-Stars. Plus, we need Jane to get to it anyway."

Claire's hand froze, her tongs inches above a pancake stack. She stared at Samaira; eyes wide.

"Not to worry," she said. "My brother and I know how to get around unseen. We checked it out and then stuck to a less dangerous area."

"The point is," Ichi nodded to Samaira and turned his attention to Claire, "you're here, we're excited about it, and it's time to eat." His wide grin was so welcoming Cho felt a dip in his own anxiety.

He and Claire had been the last to get breakfast. When they left the kitchen the twins and Ichi joined them, each with their own stacked plates of food. All around the vast room, children sat and ate. Laughter and conversation punctuated the soft sound of music coming from a small ancient speaker balanced at the top of the stairs. A gift for Elaine, from Jason and Samaira, on the one-year anniversary of the day they found Haven.

Claire joined Cho at an empty table. It was one of the smaller ones, round with three tall stools. Jane and Tommy sat with Luna, Nova, and a few others at a large table in the center of the space. Jane gave Cho a nod as he passed, the arguments from their botched heist having settled.

The morning passed with an air of ease Cho was not used to. The ever-present fear and anxiety were pushed below the surface as the children of Haven celebrated a new member of the family. The younger ones pestered Claire, asking about her power and wanting to show her theirs, until Elaine gathered them up and settled them all on the couches in the far corner. She pulled a massive book from a shelf and read, her clear voice ringing through the room.

Cho ate slowly, enjoying the crunch of the bacon, the sweetness of the fruit, and juiciness of the sausage, and the surprising yet pleasant addition of chocolate chips hidden in the pancakes. Claire finished before him and got up to wander the room.

His lip twitched up. Pride stirred in him at her courage.

She found Samaira. The two climbed halfway up the stairs and sat on the steps, deep in conversation. Samaira chuckled, lifted her hand, and produced a small blue flame. Claire stared, awed.

Ichi and Jason were back in the kitchen, visible in the window, one washing and the other drying the multitude of dishes produced by such a feast. Elaine transitioned the younger children from story-time to meditation. They sat in a circle, closing their eyes and concentrating on their abilities. Samaira joined them, positioning herself across from Elaine and giving the other woman a knowing nod as they began.

Kim—barely nine, crackled with electricity. Her bantu knots, almost shaped like curling roses, flickered with occasional sparks of blinding white-hot light. Blake—seven, wore his usual long pants and a sweater with the hood pulled up, but as he focused on his power the visible parts of his skin glowed with pale blue light. Cho chuckled as Tommy, sitting between the two, went completely invisible.

Claire rejoined Cho, her gaze on the circle of children. Barely a moment later, Jane lowered her tall form onto the empty stool beside Cho.

"He's getting better every day," she murmured, watching her brother reappear with a beaming grin on his face.

"He could join *our* meditation time. Kid saved our asses yesterday." Cho shook his head. "He's got more control than I do."

Jane glanced at him with a frown. "Having trouble?"

"Not right now." Cho gave her a tight smile, then looked over at Tommy again and laughed. The boy had rolled onto his back and was spinning on the ground just outside the meditation circle.

"Maybe he sticks with the kid group a little longer," Jane said with a chuckle.

They shared a moment of silence before Cho spoke again. "You're both back to full?"

Jane nodded.

"What does that mean?" Claire asked.

Jane fixed her beady black eyes on the newcomer. "We all have different kinds of powers, but there are two groups we fit them into. Ichi calls them active and passive. Tommy and me, we have active powers. We can turn them on and off, control when we use them..." She glanced at Cho. "But we get drained."

Claire looked from her to Cho. "And you?"

"My power is passive," Cho murmured, shifting uncomfortably. "I can't turn it off. Ever. It doesn't drain me to use, but I have to... essentially build a shield, or a wall, in my mind to stop it from being constant. The shield is what drains me."

"If Cho goes too long without resting his mind, his defenses fall apart," Jane said.

Cho gritted his teeth. He picked at a spot on the table with his thumbnail.

"What happens when you get drained?" Claire gazed at Jane.

"It depends." Jane glanced at her brother. He'd rejoined the group, though Elaine now sat next to him, a hand on his shoulder. "Most of the time it just means you're tired. If you go too far... You saw Luna yesterday. She went unconscious. We were all pretty low by the time we got to you." She shook her head, a grimace marring her features.

Claire wilted in her seat. Cho put a hand on her shoulder—and removed it instantly as a hammer of emotions slammed at his defenses.

"It can be dangerous," he said.

Claire turned to him.

"It's one of Ichi's most important rules. Looking out for each other, especially those with active powers. If they use too much, if they don't stop when they've reached the end of what they have..."

"Passing out isn't the worst thing that can happen," Jane finished for him.

"So mine is..." Claire gazed down at her hand. A clump of crystals formed, the ice growing in her palm, taking the rough shape of a lumpy ball. Sweat beaded across her temple. She took a sharp breath, releasing it in bursts through clenched teeth.

"Slower," Cho said.

Claire's hand started to shake.

"Breathe slower. In through the nose..."

She sucked in air.

"And out, in a steady flow. Slowly."

She let out the breath, no longer trembling as the ball finished forming. She tipped her hand sideways and the chunk of ice thunked onto the table.

"Active," Jane answered with her usual sharp voice. Her wide-eyed, impressed expression quickly morphed back to bored as Claire glanced at her. "Your power is active. Pay attention to how your body feels when you use it. If you start getting tired, not sleepy tired, but drained tired—like walking would be hard—stop."

Claire nodded. She wiped the sweat from her forehead with her sleeve. She leaned forward, resting her head on the table and taking deep, slow breaths.

"Ready for tonight?" Jane turned to Cho.

He swallowed. "We should be, right? Everything in place, all the information gathered." He glanced back at the circle. Elaine was leading the children through the final phase of their practice. They worked on different breathing exercises, each designed to help calm both emotions and powers in a state of panic or danger.

"Is Tommy coming?"

Jane shook her head, bangs flopping from side to side as a scowl crossed her face. "No. He's not... I don't think he's ready for it and I don't want him there if things go wrong."

Cho gave a shallow nod. "*I* don't want to be there if things go wrong."

She gave him a side-long look. "I was surprised when Ichi said you were coming. Him, Elaine, the twins... I didn't think we'd need you."

Cho's chest constricted. He picked at his fingers under the table, trying to find words. "I don't... You don't *need* me to come, but I can't..." He gritted his teeth. "I can't let my brother go without me. And they think it's a good idea for me to try..." He reached a hand up and touched the soft knitted material covering his gemstone.

She nodded.

A few moments later, after the children had finished their meditation, Ichi emerged from the kitchen. Claire raised her head.

Ichi clapped his hands together, catching everyone's attention. "I know the older kids need to get their practice in today, and Jason and Samaira have lessons with those of you who want to join right after that, but..." he glanced toward Cho's table, his gaze catching on Claire, "I thought it might be nice to give the newest member of Haven a formal welcome."

Everyone chattered at once, greetings and shouts of welcome. Claire blushed right to the roots of her hair.

Ichi raised a hand and the room quieted again. "Claire hasn't been here long, but I hope she's felt the warmth of our family. We are tied together through many similarities. Our gifts... our fears... our love for each other." He strode toward the stairs as he spoke.

In the shadow of the grated metal steps the wall appeared splotchy with an odd red color. A soft smile spread across Cho's face as Ichi lifted a glowing orb of light, chasing the shadows away as he put his other hand against the dark wall.

Covering the stone, visible now in the light of the orb, were dozens of red handprints. Some were close to the floor, others higher than Cho could reach. Some were small, some large, some faded almost to nothing, and a few were brighter, newer ones.

"This is our tradition," Ichi said, turning to look at Claire from across the room. "Our way of showing a clear and tangible connection to each other. To Haven. You don't have to join this wall today, or ever. That's your choice. But if you want to, you can put your handprint with ours, and forever have a home here."

Cho glanced at Claire. Her expression, wide eyed and embarrassed at first, shifted into something else. He reached out, splitting a crack in his shield as he cast tendrils of saffron power toward her.

Tears blossomed in his eyes at the sheer weight of her emotion. The line of her mouth and furrow of her brow barely contained the crashing relief, acceptance, and heart-aching wholeness.

He felt the emotions as his own, and not for the first time, he remembered the shuddering breaths he'd taken when his brother had offered him the tin of paint.

Claire slid from her stool and Cho pulled his power back into himself, closing the shield as tight as he could.

Claire took a step. She paused, turned back, and looked at Cho with wide eyes.

He nodded and stood as well. He walked with her, around the tables, past the array of potted plants, and across the room until they reached his brother.

Ichi beamed down at Claire. "Are you sure? It's all right if you want to wait."

Claire hesitated for a moment; her brow furrowed. Then she stepped past Cho and met Ichi's gaze. "I'll belong here? Even if I make mistakes. Even if I don't do what you want every second of the day? Even though I'm... I'm different."

Sorrow flickered in Ichi's gaze for a brief second. So quick, Cho was sure he was the only one to catch it.

The leader of Haven nodded. "You belong here." He knelt, looking up at her and lowering his voice so only she and Cho could hear. "In this place, what makes you different makes you special. In this place, we love you no matter what."

Tears spilled from Claire's eyes. They dripped down her cheeks as she stumbled forward and fell into Ichi's arms. He held her tight, waiting until she pulled back to stand again. When he did, it was with a smile on his face.

"Jason, you got that paint?"

Jason came forward, a shallow dish half full of red paint in his big hands. "Anywhere you want, kid." He grinned at Claire, jerking his head at the wall.

Applause, shouts, whistles, and laughter echoed through the room as Claire dipped her palm and placed her hand against the stone. She wiped her eyes with her knuckles and turned with a grin on her face.

Elaine approached with a rag, helping Claire wipe her hand and inviting her to join the meditation that would follow shortly.

Cho stood under the stairs as Elaine made sure Claire had everything she needed, and Ichi and Jason put away the paint. His mind drifted as he studied the wall. Claire had filled a gap in the center, her handprint smaller than he'd thought it would be.

He looked at his own hands. They'd grown in the last three years. He lifted fingers to his temple, rubbing the stone under his cap. His thoughts shifted to the mission ahead of them.

"Where's yours?"

Cho jumped. Claire stood at his elbow, gazing at the wall.

He cracked a smile and pointed to the upper right corner, just below his brother's. "I didn't have everyone watching when I did mine."

Claire raised an eyebrow at him.

He huffed out a chuckle. "I uh... when I was ready, Ichi and Elaine came with me, and I put my handprint up in the middle of the night while everyone else was asleep."

"Why?"

Cho clicked his tongue against his teeth. He ran a hand across his jaw and gave Claire a pained smile. "Ichi's my brother, but when he found me I," he grimaced, "I hadn't seen him for years. He was twelve when his ability developed; I was barely five."

He walked away from the wall and Claire followed him. They sat together on the stairs, Cho picking at his fingers as he talked.

"I don't know the specifics of it, but I know my parents were responsible for him leaving. I imagine it was something like what happened to you. They called for Black-Stars, or Red, I'm not sure. We were Green... our family was."

He sniffed, fidgeting on the grated metal. "Anyway, he was gone for most of my childhood. My parents pretended they didn't have an older son. When I was fifteen, I started to notice things. I'd," he cleared his throat, "get heated when my father got angry. Sad, when my mother went through one of her episodes. Someone in the market dropped an expensive vase or something and the fear that hit me..."

Cho clenched his hands together. He leaned against his knees, grateful for the pressure on his skin. "It happened more and more. At school, at home, at my dad's worksite. They sometimes had odd jobs for me but... I could *feel it.* Everything. Everything everyone around me felt."

He swallowed. "When it got bad enough, I hid. My parents knew something was wrong, and they let me take a few weeks off school. They thought I was sick. I could barely eat, but that was because of my mother's anxiety. I was running a temperature, but I think that's because my father was so angry all the time."

He stopped. Cracks formed across the wall in his mind. Closing his eyes, he breathed like Elaine had taught him, calming himself and sealing the weblike breaks.

Beside him, Claire sat patiently, waiting for him to continue.

"I must have been in my room too long, because I heard them talking. They were calling Red-Stars. Not the guard, but the emergency personnel. To take me to the hospital. Run tests." He stared at his fingernails. "It was the middle of the night. I ran. Didn't have anywhere to go, so I went to Agora. I'd spent most of my time there outside of school and I... I know the streets well."

He nodded, almost to himself. "It started raining, so I went into one of the covered markets. Hid in a corner. Fell asleep."

A shudder ran down his spine, and his jaw went tight.

"When I woke up, the market was full. And I..."

He closed his eyes, knuckles going white. Claire's fingers grazed his hand, but he pulled it away.

"Physical contact makes it worse," he explained, glancing at her. "There were people everywhere. Early morning and I was surrounded. No defenses. No way to shut it off. It... it tore me into pieces." He rubbed his forehead. "Fractured my mind into... into broken glass."

Cho bit the inside of his lip, the memory of that day gripping him and squeezing the breath from his lungs.

"By the time Ichi found me, I was in a different part of Agora. Somewhere remote. An alley I think, but I couldn't tell you where. My mind was gone. I... I barely remember those first few days in Haven." He glanced at her. "I still have nightmares about it. Being trapped. Surrounded. Unable to keep them out of my head, out of my body."

"I'm sorry," Claire murmured.

He cracked a weak smile. "It was a long time ago. Elaine has... well, they've all helped me learn to control it. Learn to block out everyone else and only feel what *I* feel."

"It's hard?"

He nodded. "A constant struggle."

Claire looked over at him. "I want to give you a hug, but that'd be worse, right?"

He chuckled. "Yeah. Hugs aren't really my thing."

Quiet fell between them for a few minutes. The bustle of the room, so large and so full of people, continued. But their little staircase was silent.

"I'm glad you're better," Claire said, meeting his gaze.

He nodded in thanks.

"And I'm glad you saved me."

He grinned. "Me too. And I'm glad Jason and Samaira are finally gonna have some competition."

She raised an eyebrow and cocked her head.

"Well, you're the only one able to shoot stuff out of your hands like they are. Fire and ice. Should be interesting."

She laughed, and he joined her.

Not long after, the two of them gathered with the other kids in Elaine's older meditation group. Ichi disappeared with the younger ones, leading them through the hallways to start the limited lessons they had during the day.

As morning faded to afternoon, and then to evening, Cho eventually left Claire's side. Luna and Nova were quick to fill the gap, pulling her toward their room and telling her she had to pick out a few outfits to wear until they were able to get more clothes from Agora.

Cho made his way to Ichi's study. There, he found Jane, Jason, and Samaira. The four poured over a map of the city. Plans were checked, double checked, and solidified into a tight timeframe.

The lights faded as the clock counted down to sunset. The children ate dinner, a meaty stew with finely chopped vegetables and thick chunks of bread for dipping.

Cho had a few bites before offering his bowl to Samaira. The flame-thrower put it to her lips and drank it like water.

Elaine and Ichi tucked the younger children into bed. They gave Luna, Nova, and a few of the other older kids instructions and a com device for emergencies. With a final goodbye, and a chorus of well-wishes from the ones standing guard Ichi, Elaine, Jason, Samaira, Jane, and Cho left.

They moved through the sewers quickly and quietly. Jason popped the grate in Agora. They snuck through the empty city streets, hats pulled low, footsteps muffled against the concrete and cobblestone.

Chapter Twenty

Present Day - Mid Summer - Abredea

T he day after the ban on Juliana's study group Jimmy had been distraught. Juliana left Daisy to deal with the others, walking Jimmy home and reassuring him it wasn't his fault they weren't allowed to meet at the square. She was still able to help him with his homework, and read to him until Anthony showed up. At which point she left.

A few days later, she strode through the square. Though it was still early afternoon—school hadn't let out yet—a summer storm clouded the sky. Rolling fields of grey blocked out the sun, only thin shafts of light breaking through.

A basket filled with tiny, round tomatoes hung from Juliana's forearm. She planned on handing them out to the members of her little study group. If everything went according to plan, she'd also have a new meeting spot for tomorrow.

She climbed the steps of town hall and pulled the door open just as the first drops of rain hit the concrete.

Thunder cracked above her. Juliana disguised her wince as a shiver and stepped into the wide lobby. Montague smiled, walking over, and reaching out a hand to her. She took it.

"Thank you for your help." Juliana followed the thin man to the seats at the far end of the room.

"Of course, Miss Juliana," Montague said. "I'm happy to do what I can. Your little group has brought a smile to many faces."

Juliana's cheeks flushed. "I don't know about that, but these kids do need extra help. The Orange-Stars," she grimaced, heat rising in her gut, "aren't teaching them correctly. I can't tell if it's purposeful or negligence, but it's wrong either way."

He nodded. "The little ones are confused and frustrated for a few years, but eventually they figure it out."

Juliana bit back a harsh retort. "There's no need for them to be confused over simple arithmetic. Someone simply needs to show them how to do it."

Montague surprised her by chuckling.

She raised an eyebrow.

He put up his hands with a kind shrug. "It's easy to tell you came from Blue-Stars. Not many others get so defensive over mathematics."

Juliana couldn't help her smile. She shook her head. "I've always loved it. My friends..." her head bobbed to the side, "not so much."

Montague gave a solemn nod. "I felt the same way about poetry."

Juliana's smile widened. She watched him gaze wistfully at one of the paintings for a moment before clearing her throat.

"Right," he said, clapping his hands together. "We need to find you a place to study. I'd love to let you all gather here each day, but we do sometimes have actual business to contend with. I fear the mayor would be rather upset if he had to court Stars from the city at his home." He leaned in, a mischievous smile crossing his thin lips. "It wouldn't give the best impression."

"This *would* be a lovely place to meet, especially on days like today." Juliana glanced out the windows. The steady drops had become a deluge of rain, pounding against the ground with occasional bursts of wind spitting water against the glass. "But the real problem is this permit issue. I haven't been able to find any information on getting one. I don't imagine it would be hard to do. It's a group of children. They can't think any level of dissent is involved."

Montague tilted his head. "You'd be surprised by what constitutes a threat to the Stars and the city." He sighed. "There was a time you didn't need a permit to grow a garden either."

Juliana's jaw dropped. "What do you mean? May has a garden..."

"Indeed. We managed to get her the permit just before they stopped issuing them. Hers, I believe, has no expiration. There are a few around Abredea, but anything larger than a two by six plot has to be signed off by a Red-Star."

Juliana frowned. "Who needs to sign off for the study group?"

Montague rose with a grunt. He crossed to the counter, picked up a file, and returned to his seat. "From what I've been able to dig up—and I'm not surprised you couldn't find anything, these records were buried—you'll need approval from the school, the mayor, and the current captain of the guard."

Juliana squinted incredulously. "Why would we need permission from the captain of the guard to have a study group?"

"Based on these documents," Montague patted the file folder, "to ensure no one is teaching things which go against the *current academic profile*."

She gaped at him.

He elaborated. "To make sure no one teaches children—especially Moon children—critical thinking, analysis, and logic."

"Why though?"

Montague straightened, pressing his long fingers together under his chin. "Miss Juliana, I'm afraid I cannot say."

"You don't know?"

"Oh, I know. I'm simply afraid, and therefore I cannot say."

Juliana sat quietly for a long moment. "That's why I can't get a job at the school."

Montague nodded.

"Is that... is that why the children born here, the Moon-borns, don't get gem-stones?"

He rose again, and this time Juliana copied his movement. "That, I'm afraid I *don't* know the answer to. But I believe it's a complicated situation."

Juliana took the papers he offered her. "When I get all these signed, I bring them to you?"

He nodded.

"And then I can have my study group?"

The gemstones on Montague's temples glinted in the light as he waved a hand over the room. "I'll help move the furniture."

Juliana thanked him, gave him half a dozen tomatoes, gathered up the papers, and left. The storm had let up. Occasional droplets of rain still plummeted to the ground, but the downpour had stopped. She wandered across the square, studying the papers before her. A bell tolled. School was out for the day.

She grimaced. This would be a good time to collect the administrator's signa-ture, but after their last interaction she doubted it would go well. Daisy though... Daisy would be able to collect that particular signature. As far as her father went, he wouldn't do anything to help Juliana, the children, or his own daughter, but if Taz asked he'd do it. He doted upon the boy, no matter how hard Taz tried to avoid him. They figured it was because Taz had gemstones, and in the mayor's mind, a chance at the city.

With a plan in mind, Juliana made her way toward the school to find her friends. Still reading over the paperwork, she didn't notice the person in front of her until they thudded against her and almost knocked her to the ground.

"What—" she demanded, the papers crumpling as she clenched them.

She looked up and froze.

A Black-Star gazed down at her. His sturdy tree-trunk frame hadn't been altered an inch by their collision.

Memory flashed through her mind. A similar interaction, but she and her friends standing tall while a Green-Star stumbled and nearly fell to the ground. His flustered apologies, and Moniqua's laughter, echoed in her ears.

She cringed.

"My apologies, I was not watching where I was going." She gave a contrite smile, forcing her anxiety down and pulling up the cordial, prim, well-educated persona she'd always worn when her parents had Blue, Black, or Grey-Stars over.

She moved to the side, but the man moved with her. She stared up at his eyes, sunken into the splotchy red skin of his face. His brow narrowed.

"Captain Steel requests a word."

Juliana blinked. Her fingers tightened around the handle of her little tomato basket. The papers shook in her hand. She swallowed, throat tight, and gave a polite nod.

"I'll follow you, then," she said with another smile.

His expression did not alter. He gestured before him, towards the Steel's office and living quarters.

"Right." Suppressing a shudder, Juliana strode forward, the crunching of boots indicating the Black-Star followed close behind her.

She folded up the papers as she went. Steel wanted a word with her. Well, that worked out because she wanted a word with him too.

She tapped her fingers against her thumb, pointer, ring, pinky, middle. Over and over as they approached the relatively small building.

Steel had built his office just behind the row of stores making up the south side of the square. The barracks for his unit also sat to the south, but closer to the main road and the rest of Abredea than Steel's domain.

The usual dust that would have kicked up once they left the cobblestone square had turned to mud from the rain. Juliana winced as the soles of her shoes fought to remain on her feet. She and the Black-Star arrived at the door to Steel's office.

She glanced back at him.

He remained unmoving.

"Am I to knock?" she murmured. A knot in her stomach hindered the calm mask she tried to wear. All the time spent with Daisy and Taz in her field, with May in the garden, and with Jimmy and the children... she hadn't needed to be the picture of a composed Blue-Star in a long time. Perhaps that was what caused the quiver in her smile.

The Black-Star reached past her and pounded a fist on the wooden door. A few seconds passed. The door opened a foot.

"I've brought her, sir."

There was an affirmative grunt from inside the room followed by, "I'm finishing up a meeting. Wait there."

Juliana bit the inside of her lip. Steel's voice carried a cold in it, a chill that sank to her bones. She shook it aside.

The Black-Star adjusted his stance, taking position against the wall, hands behind his back, gaze on a swivel.

Juliana stood before the door, on a little platform of wood and brick which had been erected with the building to limit the amount of dirt and debris that would be tracked inside. The door swung but didn't close all the way. There remained a two-inch gap through which sound escaped.

Juliana straightened as she heard a familiar voice.

"... understand you're trying to get things in order, but you *must* have patience. These are simple people. They require leadership, not cruelty."

"Of course, ma'am," Steel responded, his words stiff. "I don't intend to be cruel. However, the breaking of so many laws in this *place*," malice in the word, "such a lack of discipline..."

Wolfe spoke with the commanding tone, but the words came out soft. "Captain Steel, surely you agree the lack of discipline comes from a lack of authority. This is precisely why you were assigned the position. Our hope is for you to transform this camp into a place of betterment and peace."

There was a pause. "A difficult task, indeed, ma'am. Especially since the Moons don't view myself or my men with any trust."

"Trust is earned, Captain."

Juliana's jaw tightened. Her head bobbed in silent agreement as she took half a step closer to the door. The Black-Star, still stationed against the wall a few feet away, didn't look at her.

"I'll do what I can, Ms. Wolfe, but the people here are wild. Almost animals."

Juliana swallowed, looking down at her fingers.

"I'm sure there are a few here who want to better the community," Wolfe cut in. "Start with those born in the city. The true White-Stars. Perhaps they can help you get the rest on the same track."

There was silence for a moment, and then Steel spoke again.

"When do you plan on returning?"

Juliana's heart leapt into her throat. If Wolfe was leaving... she'd thought—hoped—after hearing the Grey-Star's voice that maybe this meeting was an update on her status.

"Not for a long while. There is much to be done. Good luck, Captain. And remember, patience with these people. Be a leader, not just a commander."

Shuffling ensued and Juliana hurriedly stepped away from the door. After a few moments it swung open. Instead of Wolfe, Captain Steel stood in the doorway.

"Enter," he said.

Juliana cleared her throat, nerves jumping in her stomach. She stepped through the door.

It took several seconds for her eyes to adjust to the darkness of Steel's office. Dark grey curtains covered the only window in the room. A lamp lit up the large desk at the far wall. Ahead of her was another door, one she assumed led to Steel's private rooms, and through which Wolfe must have left.

An ornate, comfortable-looking armchair sat behind the desk, piled high with papers and trinkets yet to be placed on shelves around the room. Before the desk, two hard wooden chairs scraped against the ground as Steel turned them out.

Juliana and Steel were alone; the guard remained outside as the door closed.

"You wanted to see me, sir?" Juliana tucked her disappointment deep down. She brought her basket around and held it before her, anxiously aware of a tear in her long shorts, the mud on her shoes, and her wrinkled dark green top.

"Yes, thank you for coming by."

As though it had been a choice.

Steel gestured to one of the wooden chairs and lowered himself into the other. Juliana crossed the room, set her basket down, and attempted to discreetly move the chair back while she sat.

"It's fortunate timing," Juliana said, "I just picked up these forms." She pulled the folded papers off the basket and picked through until she found the one for him to sign. Whatever he wanted her for, she would get his signature first.

Steel did a slight double-take. His mouth had opened, about to launch into whatever speech he had prepared, but he closed it as she spoke. The muscle in his jaw twitched, but he nodded, and she continued.

"I've been running a little study group for the younger children here. The Moon-borns, you know."

He gave a tight smile. The tattoos on his face wrinkled with his skin, giving a disjointed and unsettling look in the dark room.

"They need extra help with subjects like mathematics, reading, and their handwriting is atrocious. I'm sure you're aware a White-Star can't be a teacher. But the study group has been helping these children."

"Good," Steel said. He leaned his elbows on his knees, seeming about to continue, but Juliana plunged on.

"I'm sure you are also aware that I require a permit to continue the venture." She gave him her most cordial smile. "I have here," she unfolded the sheet requiring his signature, "the form that needs your official signature for me to continue."

His gaze flicked to the closed door leading to the other room.

"You're perhaps wary of what we are studying?" Juliana asked, following his gaze with curiosity. She reached for a loose pen on his desk. "As I said, these are young children. We've been working on addition and subtraction for the most part. The occasional division when an older student comes by." She let out a soft laugh, trying to replicate Daisy's bird-like sound. "The poor things need all the help they can get."

Her gut roiled, but she kept the smile in place. This was a game. Similar to ones she'd played countless times in the city. She might be rusty, but at one time she'd been quite proficient at it.

She pushed the pen and paper into Steel's hands. "I just need your approval, right there." She pointed.

Steel's face kept the scrunched look, but he lowered the pen to the paper and scrawled a hasty signature.

"Thank you so much. Now," Juliana widened her eyes and met his gaze, "what can *I* do for you?"

She folded up the paper and set it back atop the tomatoes. Nervous as she was, a rumble of pride coursed through her chest and eased the churning in her stomach.

"Miss Foster," Steel began.

The ease disappeared. Juliana's breath hitched. No one had used her family name since her Coding. It... it had faded into the back of her mind with other thoughts of her parents. Hidden from view because every time she pictured them tears threatened to spill from her eyes.

She concentrated on Steel, on the room around them and the ground beneath her feet and the words coming out of his mouth.

"You're a White-Star. You come from the city. You're... civilized," he let out an uncomfortable chuckle, "for lack of a better word."

Juliana's head tilted slightly as she struggled to maintain the bland smile she now had in place.

"My Black-Stars and I... we're struggling to gain a foothold with these Moons. They don't understand the purpose of rules. They can't grasp the concept of organization or community."

Juliana swallowed and shifted in her seat. She needed water. Her throat and mouth were dry, as though she'd swallowed a mountain of dust. The sadness she'd felt upon hearing her last name melted into the background as her ears thundered with the sound of her own pumping blood.

"I could use an ally, Miss Foster. I could use someone who is already part of this... Moon camp."

She disguised her shudder with a light cough.

Steel rose and strode to a cabinet against the wall. "Something to drink?"

"Please," Juliana murmured.

He returned with a glass of something amber. Juliana took a sip and winced violently as heat seared her throat. She set the glass on the desk and pushed it away.

Steel's laugh reverberated through the room. "Not used to it, that makes sense. Water then?"

"Please," she said again, quieter still.

He brought her a glass of water and she drained it.

"As I was saying, I'm well aware the Moon-borns here, and even some of the true White-Stars, have been bending and breaking the laws of the camp. We can't have that. It's important for everyone to know their place. To do what they're supposed to do. There is no order without caste. There is no peace without order."

Juliana nodded. The phrase, etched into her brain, was one she'd spoken every day at the beginning of her classes. It was written on the walls of the schools, the archways leading in and out of the districts, and scrawled across the entrance to the Star Office.

"I need you to be my eyes. You can see things we can't. Hear things we don't. I want you to let me know when you notice someone breaking the law, bending the rules, acting in a way which threatens the civilized society we are trying to build in this camp."

Juliana's fingers danced. She sat in silence for a few seconds, glad she'd had him sign her document first.

When she spoke, her voice was clear of the trembling she felt in the rest of her body. "I, of course, want to do my duty to our society. But I'm afraid I'm not sure what you're talking about. Beyond something like this," she gestured to her papers with a light smile, "where someone simply needs a permit for something, I can't think of any rule breaking I've seen. The people here are," she swallowed, "happy to follow the laws of the camp."

Steel's dark eyes—black like Anthony's but without any of the warmth—narrowed. He stood again, went to his cabinet, and poured himself a drink of that amber liquid.

"You're telling me you've yet to notice someone breaking the law? At a *camp*?" The incredulity in his voice set off alarms in Juliana's mind.

"Well Captain Steel, I've read my packet. I know all the laws and rules written into it. Perhaps there are new ones I'm not familiar with? But the woman I live with, and the few..." she hesitated at the word *friends*, "acquaintances I've made seem to live and act in the way designated for them by their status."

"They *seem to?*"

Juliana inhaled. The oxygen didn't reach her lungs. She smoothed her features, digging deep to keep her voice steady. "I haven't seen or heard of any lawlessness in my time here."

Steel turned from the cabinet and met her gaze. "You speak of acquaintances... is a man named Anthony Clearwater one of the *acquaintances* you've made?"

Juliana was sure her heartbeat was audible in the room. It had to be, with how loud it thundered in her own ears. "I know of him. We've met, on occasion."

Steel studied her. "It helps you; you know. To be helpful to me."

Juliana nodded, her skin tingling.

"I might be able to make life here easier for you. More bearable. But in return, I'd need you to pay closer attention than it appears you have been. I need consistent reports. Notes on his, and others' movements, and information about what laws he's breaking. Because," he swirled the dregs of his drink around the glass, "I assure you, a man like *that* is breaking the law. Whether you know it or not."

There was silence in the room. Steel downed the last of his drink and returned the glass to the cabinet. Juliana stared at the floor, putting every ounce of will into looking like a demur, civilized girl who didn't have a clue about the goings-on of the people in Abredea.

"I'd, of course, reward you for your time and effort. I can increase the food allotment for your household, three packets a day." A smug smile crossed his lips. "And I'm sure we can arrange some sort of stipend for you. A few coins a month, maybe more if you get me useful information."

Juliana let out a breath. A flash of rage—like lightning—cut through her fear. She struggled to keep her face smooth.

He thought an extra mush packet and a few coins a month would buy *her*? She swallowed down the rueful laugh bubbling in her throat.

"As much as I'd like to help. I truly don't know anything, and I fear I'm not close enough with any of the people here to gain you any valuable information. Not to mention," she offered up an apologetic smile, "I'll be quite busy helping the children and trying to find work."

Steel's eyes flashed, his nostrils flaring as he inhaled. His hands formed fists before he stretched out his fingers in a deliberate movement. Juliana noted his struggle to remain calm and tucked away her observation for later consideration.

"I'll be sure to let you know if I see anything out of the ordinary." Juliana lifted her basket from the ground and held it in her lap. "But I'd hate to promise information and not be able to give you any."

Steel was quiet for another moment. Finally, he said, "I don't imagine it will be easy, someone like you finding work in the camp."

Juliana tilted her head, hoping for a politely confused look.

"Soft hands, simple girl..."

She bristled, a fraction of anger breaking through her polite façade.

He smirked, his voice low. "If you change your mind, when you find it impossible to get work... when your stomach keeps you up at night and the cold bites at your toes in the winter... I'll be here with my offer still in place."

Juliana's knuckles went white on the handle of the basket. Heat flooded her cheeks. Her voice became a low hiss. "Your offer may remain until the day a new captain replaces you, but my refusal to accept it will remain just as long."

She stood, breathing fast.

Captain Steel braced his hands on the desk, eyes glinting with fury as she marched to the door and opened it.

"Miss Foster," Steel's voice trembled with barely suppressed rage, "give my regards to Mr. Clearwater and the rest of your little friends."

Juliana relented a jerky nod. Then she stepped through the door and let it slam behind her.

She marched towards the square, rolling his words through her mind to keep the anger fresh. She needed it. Once she stopped enduring the burn of the conversation, she'd feel the stomach tipping fear.

Her legs trembled.

A glance back showed the Black-Star, still posted by Steel's door, watching her. At least no one was following her.

When Juliana reached town hall, she sank onto the damp steps. She swallowed once, twice, three times to bring moisture to her throat. She exhaled a shaky breath.

Pounding feet made her jerk. She relaxed as she spotted Jimmy running towards her across the square. Behind him, Naya and Anthony strolled along at a comfortable pace.

"Juliana!" Jimmy jumped onto the steps beside her. He eyed the tomatoes. "How'd today go? Can we all read together again?"

"Help yourself," Juliana muttered, pushing the basket toward him.

Small hands plunged into the basket. Jimmy shoved a handful of the little fruits into his mouth, spirting seeds and juice out of his mouth as soon as he started chewing.

He looked up at her, a quizzical expression on his face.

Juliana sighed. "It went fine." She gave him a tight smile, chest still full of anger she was trying not to show on her face. "We can't get together today, but soon. I got what we need to make it work."

"Tha's a relief," Anthony said as he and Naya reached them. "Jimmy won't stop talkin' 'bout how much he misses yer study group."

Juliana's gaze hardened as she looked up at Anthony. She rose. "Yes, well... it shouldn't be much longer until the problem is resolved." Her jaw clenched, the memory of his words—and tone—the day the Black-Stars shut them down still fresh in her mind.

"I'm glad yer fightin' back. The whole thing is stupid."

"I'm not fighting," Juliana snapped.

Jimmy froze, fingers inching toward the basket. He stared at them with wide eyes. Beside him, Naya's gaze followed them as well. She rolled a tomato between her fingers for a second before plopping it into her mouth.

"I'm..." Juliana's gaze drifted across the square. Children were still running around, jumping through the fountain, playing together in the dirt, and waiting for their parents. A patrol of Black-Stars—three of them, fully dressed in their military gear—marched down the cobblestones toward the west end of Abredea.

Laughter faded as they approached. The children's running slowed. A mother pulled her son close, tucking him behind her legs as one of the patrol leered at her.

"I never *wasn't* going to do something," Juliana said through her teeth. "But I'm not dumb enough to pick a fight with the guard in the middle of the square."

On the steps beside her, Naya let out a snort of laughter.

Anthony clicked his tongue, his face flushing, and plunged his fists into his pockets.

"I'm handling it a different way." Juliana swallowed. A shudder ran down her spine as the fear of Steel's final words hit her again. She stepped back, putting distance between herself and Anthony.

His eyebrows twitched into a frown for a split second.

Juliana caught sight of Daisy and Taz entering the bakery. Daisy waved at her, Taz flashed his usual wild grin.

"Would you..." Juliana's jaw clenched as a brief internal battle took place. She inhaled. "Would you come with me for a moment? I need to talk to you."

Anthony raised an eyebrow and gave her a bewildered nod. "Sure."

"Jimmy," she looked down at the boy, "I'm getting the study group figured out, but it'll be a few more days until we can start meeting again. I'm sorry."

Jimmy shrugged his thin shoulder. "It's all right."

Cool relief dripped through the heat in her chest as he smiled up at her.

Naya took her hand. "Don' worry yerself too much. No one wants yeh getting' in any kind of trouble over this."

Juliana nodded. Footsteps crunched. She jolted, turning quickly only to see a family moving toward the grocers, the father's boots squelching in the mud. Juliana looked back at Naya.

"Thanks." She knelt to meet Jimmy's eye. The boy stared at her with bulging cheeks. "I'm not going to be able to read with you today either, is that all right?"

He nodded.

Naya wrapped a thin arm around her son. "He'll be all right with me for today. He's been feelin' off anyway. Yeh ought to stop eatin' those tomatoes, Jimmy, if yer stomach's hurtin'."

"Yeh don't do the voices when yeh read," Jimmy whined.

Naya rolled her eyes at Juliana. "I think ye'll survive," she said to her son.

"See you both tomorrow." Juliana picked up her basket—considerably lighter now—and descended the steps of town hall. Anthony gave Jimmy a tight squeeze before jogging down and walking along beside her.

"Whaddya wanna talk about?"

"Not here," Juliana hissed out the side of her mouth.

He gave her a startled glance. "Is everythin'... all right?"

Juliana heaved a sigh, picked up her pace, and marched the two of them out of the square.

"Are we far enough yet?" Anthony heaved an exasperated sigh. They'd crossed Abredea, passed May's house, and finally reached the field Juliana was so taken with.

Grass and flowers had already encroached upon the spot they usually laid their blankets. It had been a while since the four of them had sat together.

"Yes." Juliana turned to him, glowering. "I don't..." she sighed. "I don't want to panic the others, but you need to know that Steel is asking about you. He knows your name." She frowned, confusion in the furrow of her brow.

Anthony's jaw clenched. A shiver ran down his spine. So far, none of the people in his life—apart from Taz—had found out about his interaction with the new captain. It was only a matter of time. There hadn't been many people around, but gossip was almost a form of currency for some people.

Juliana continued. "He thinks you're breaking the law, but I don't believe he knows anything. Not yet. He doesn't have proof, anyway."

"How do yeh know this?" Anthony asked.

Juliana hesitated. She set down her half-empty basket of tomatoes and rubbed her palms across her shorts. "Steel called me into his office."

Anthony's mouth went dry. His gaze roamed her body, searching her skin for marks. He didn't find any. Still... he took half a step forward. "Are yeh hurt?"

"What?" She shook her head with a frown. "No, he wanted to talk to me. He wants..." she grimaced. "He wants me to work for him."

Anthony cocked his head to the side. "What?"

"Exactly my reaction." Juliana waved a hand wildly.

"What does he want yeh tah do?" He ran a hand through his hair, watching her intently.

"Watch *you*."

Heat—not the good kind—blossomed in Anthony's chest. "*What?*"

Juliana shook her head, blazing blue eyes wide and gleaming with something between fear and incredulity. "He thinks we're friends. Thinks I know what sort of illegal things you get up to."

"Well..." Anthony gave a half-shrug.

"Don't do that. I *don't* know anything about what you do. I don't *want* to know."

He scoffed. "Yeh don't wanna know as long as it keeps yeh fed and outta trouble."

She nodded, as though this was the most obvious thing in the world. "Yes."

Anthony's jaw clenched. He turned away, walking a small circle before coming back to face her. "Yeh 'ave so much scorn for people breakin' the law. 'ave yeh ever considered that unjust laws are *meant* tah be broken?"

Juliana stared at him.

He shook his head, anger flaring in his blood. At her, or Steel, or the situation itself he wasn't sure. "Do yeh understand what life would be for us if I didn' hunt? If I didn' break the law? If I didn' *leave* Abredea?" He rubbed a hand across his face, pausing at his left temple and massaging the scar there.

Why was he trying? She'd never understand. He sighed and let silence fall between them for a moment.

"So, yeh didn' tell him?"

"No." Juliana strode past him, toward one of the larger trees in the clearing, and plunked down against the trunk. "I didn't tell him. In fact, I told him I barely knew you and that I hadn't seen anyone doing anything illegal since I've been here."

A barking laugh broke through Anthony's scowl.

Juliana raised an eyebrow.

"How good a liar are yeh?" he asked dryly. He moved forward and sunk onto the ground, resting his elbows on his knees.

To his surprise, Juliana let out half a chuckle as well. "Not as good as you, better than Taz... and Daisy."

He laughed again. The two sat in silence for a few long moments. Anthony plucked a strand of grass, breaking it into pieces and letting them fall around his feet.

"Why does he know about you?" Juliana barely broke the quiet she spoke so softly. Her hair draped her face as she stared at the ground. She raised her eyes, piercing him with her gaze. "How does he know your name?"

Anthony ground his teeth. He broke her stare, looking at the dirt beneath his feet. He ripped the last blade of grass in half and threw the pieces to the side. "I... why does it matter?"

Juliana frowned. "When I left, Steel told me to give *you* his regards. You and the rest of my fr... my friends."

"Yer scared for the others."

"I'm not scared," Juliana snapped.

Anthony raised an eyebrow, and she heaved a sigh. Another few seconds of silence passed between them. Warm wind swirled through the trees. White and purple flower petals rained down.

"When I turned him down... when I said I wouldn't give him information, he essentially guaranteed I'll never find work in Abredea. Not as long as he's here." She cleared her throat. Her voice dropped, becoming a murmur that Anthony had to lean forward to catch. "He called me soft. Simple."

He heard fury in the shake of her words. Heard the ache, the pain of it.

Juliana glanced up at him. "I may not be the bravest, or the strongest, but I am *not* simple. And I'm not soft."

He surprised her by grinning. He recognized the expression on her face, the glow in her eyes. He caught her gaze and held it.

"Yer not scared."

She shook her head.

"Yer angry."

Pursing her lips, she nodded.

Anthony chuckled. "I understand tha'. I've been angry as long as I can remember."

More silence. Anthony shifted, turning so he sat beside her rather than facing her. This way he had a view of the forest, the mountains. He watched the trees wave in the summer wind. Birds twittered in the branches above their heads.

"How *does* he know your name, Anthony?"

He chewed on his lip, scrunching up his face in a wince. After a few seconds he heaved a sigh. "I gave it to him."

"What? *Why*?"

"He asked me."

In the corner of his eye, Anthony saw Juliana turn to face him. She stared with those lightning blue eyes. He told her what happened.

"Shit," she muttered. "No wonder you haven't told any of us. Naya is going to be furious when she finds out."

He let out another chuckle, lighter and less real this time. "Hopefully I've got a little while longer before that 'appens. I was hopin' things would settle. I was hopin' he'd forget about it."

"He doesn't strike me as the kind of person who lets go of things. Especially if he thinks you insulted him."

Anthony grunted in agreement. Breathing deep, he closed his eyes and leaned his head against the tree trunk. Life had been hard enough with Durang.

He tried to picture his uncle. Tried to imagine the conversation Dave would have with him if he were here for all this. They'd use his day off, go deep into the forest, and talk the whole thing out. Dave would have a plan.

Dave would tell him they'd figure a way out of it. He'd tell him not to worry.

They'd go to the lake again, watch the water, bring back a haul to last a couple of weeks.

Tears burned Anthony's eyes. His hands shook and he clenched them into fists. Warmth rolled down his cheeks, leaving tracks of cold as the wind kissed his face.

Juliana shifted beside him.

"Why?" he asked, breaking the silence.

"What?"

"Why didn' yeh tell him? Why didn' yeh agree tah watch me, report on me?"

She exhaled in a half-laugh. When she spoke, her voice ached of pain. "I've never met someone like Daisy before. My friends in the city weren't..." she sighed, "she's... she's something special. So is Taz. I couldn't do that to them. Or to May." There was a long pause before, "I'm not the same person I was when I arrived. And I worry what that means for my chances of... never mind."

Anthony blinked and straightened. Juliana cast him a tight smile.

"My point is, I care about them. Naya and Jimmy too. You and I don't agree on most things I think, but I know how important you are to them. I know without you their lives would be... well, harder than they already are."

He nodded slowly.

Something sat in the air between them. A heaviness, the origin of which he couldn't pin-point. Almost like he needed to say something, or she did. Like if they kept talking eventually the air would settle, and he'd be able to breathe right again.

Instead, Juliana stood. "I'm going home." She grimaced. "I'll see you. Tomorrow, I suppose?"

Anthony got to his feet as well. "Yeah. Tomorrow."

She turned, but after a few steps she paused. Glancing back, she said, "You'll be careful? Knowing he's watching you. You'll be safe?"

His eyes stung again. He pushed the burning away and tried for a version of his loose smile. "Yeh remember what I told yeh when we met, I don' get caught."

She shook her head and walked away. He waited as she disappeared down the path. He continued to wait as thunder clapped above him. As heavy droplets of rain plunked onto the leaves over his head. As they grew heavier, dripping through the canopy and wetting his clothes and hair.

The water wasn't cold, but a chill went through him anyway. Lightning flashed in the sky. The sun dipped low by the time he forced his legs to carry him home.

Chapter Twenty-One

Present Day - Mid Summer - Abredea

D aisy secured the signature from the school the next day. A mission Juliana thought would take a week or more of bribes and cajoling took a cookie from the bakery and a smile from her friend.

It probably helped that Juliana stayed outside.

The mayor was next. Taz would complete his mission during a dinner Marsterson was hosting in a few days.

Juliana, Taz, and Daisy were nailing down the final plans at May's, clustered around the table discussing exact wordage and a back-up strategy. May sat in her rocking chair—Juliana had pulled it in from the porch—knitting a pair of thick red socks for Jimmy. She pitched in every now and then, offering insight into their plan. When Daisy mentioned that her father was likely to have several drinks if given the opportunity, the old woman cackled and pointed to the top drawer of her dresser.

"If he doesn't have enough to drink, I've always got my collection of concoctions. I'm sure we can find something to loosen his inhibitions for a few hours."

Juliana's eyes widened with her grin. Taz guffawed, and Daisy seemed to be weighing the pros and cons of drugging her father.

The door was open, kitchen window too. A cool breeze drove away the summer heat. A basket of blackberries and strawberries—compliments of Anthony, and May's garden, respectively—sat in the middle of the table. Juliana's attention shifted from the plan to a lesson schedule she'd been creating.

Jimmy would be coming by soon for help with his homework. After which she'd read to him, and May too. May had asked them to move story time to her house when they started a new book. Jimmy and Juliana were both happy to oblige.

Something off caught Juliana's attention. She straightened, listening. Footsteps, too heavy to be Jimmy's, pounded toward them. She rose and crossed to the door just as Anthony raced up the porch steps.

He was drenched in sweat, hair matted to his forehead, brow furrowed in alarm. He panted as he approached, pushing past her and into the house... Jimmy cradled in his arms.

"What happened?" Juliana demanded as she followed him.

He laid the boy on May's bed, dropping to one knee and taking deep gulping breaths. May rose faster than Juliana would have thought possible and hurried to the child. She perched on the edge of the bed, hands moving from Jimmy's forehead to his chest. His usually olive complexion had gone a pale sickly color.

Daisy and Taz rose as well. They stood by the wall, watching fearfully.

"I don'," Anthony gulped, "I don' know. I waited for him after school, him and Naya. But they weren' in the square. They weren' anywhere. I went tah the house and..."

May took her knitting scissors and cut up Jimmy's shirt. Juliana gasped; her stomach knotted in horror.

Lines, sludgy green, so dark they were almost black, laced across his stomach. The skin on his chest was pale as well, the lines crawling their way up his ribcage and approaching his neck.

Anthony let out a moan like a wounded animal. He sank onto his heels, running a hand across his mouth.

"What is that?" Juliana whispered.

A tremor of relief went through her at the rise and fall of Jimmy's chest, but the movement was too uneven. He was breathing, but barely.

"A sickness," May snapped. She turned to Anthony. "Where is Naya?"

"She's," he groaned, tears seeping from his eyes, "she's the same way, May. In her bed. I brought Jimmy. It would 'ave taken too long tah bring yeh back to 'em. I didn'..."

Juliana had never seen him like this. Lost for words, yet the words came rapidly, scrambled and terrified and shocked.

May rose, bracing herself on the bed as she straightened her crooked form. She turned hyper-focused grey eyes on Daisy and Taz. "Go to Naya's. Get her and bring her here as quickly as you can. Helping them will be much easier if they are in the same place. Anthony."

Her bark was enough to bring the man to his feet.

"Go with them. Help carry her. Hurry."

The three of them raced from the room.

"May, what can I..." Juliana stared at the vein-like pattern on Jimmy's chest with disgusted horror. She blinked, took a deep breath, and concentrated on May instead. "What can I do?"

"We need to get water into him. As much, as quickly as possible."

Juliana hurried to the sink and brought back a cup. She propped Jimmy, still unconscious, onto her lap and held the cup to his lips. His eyelids fluttered but didn't open. Still, as she slowly poured the cool water into his mouth, his throat bobbed, and he drained the cup.

"What is this?" Juliana asked again.

May's back was to her. She had the top drawer of her dresser open as far as it could go. Clinking sounds of glass on glass filled the room as she shifted through vials.

"A sickness," she replied in a distracted tone. "It's in the water here if you're not careful. Every house has a filter. They're changed every year. *Nacra*."

Juliana rose, lowering Jimmy to the bed and crossing to May.

"I can't read the labels on some of these," May muttered.

"What are we looking for?"

"It'll be a pale-yellow color, should say *spidergreen* on the bottle. I ought to have several. They should be able to stop the spread. Hopefully do more."

Juliana fished through the drawer and May returned to Jimmy. She helped him down another cup of water.

"How did this happen then?" Juliana asked, plucking a vial and handing it to May.

She pulled the stopper, tilted it into Jimmy's mouth, and held his lips shut until he swallowed. Whatever the taste of the stuff, it was enough to wake him.

"Mama?" he whimpered.

"Shhh," May stroked his forehead, running circles across his cheeks with her nails. "Back to sleep little one, your mama will be here soon."

His eyes closed, but not before Juliana noted a green tint clouding the whites.

"I've never seen anything like this, May. *How*?"

May shook her head, wiping a tear from her cheek. "I don't know. I've seen this before, but years ago. Before they instituted yearly filter changes. It was rare then as well; I've only witnessed it twice."

"And the people who were sick?"

May met Juliana's gaze with a look that fractured her heart. Fear seeped through Juliana as she stared at the boy on the bed.

His small hand was clenched beside him, as though the pain of whatever this was had infected his dreams as well.

She turned back to the drawer, pulling every vial of the kind May described that she could find.

"What do we do if this doesn't work?" Juliana demanded.

"I have to see Naya. This will have affected Jimmy faster because he is young, if she's as bad as he is… We have to hope this is recent. There isn't much I can do if they've been living with it a while."

"I saw them yesterday," Juliana recalled. "Naya said Jimmy wasn't feeling well, but he seemed fine before that."

May nodded, still stroking Jimmy's face. His breathing steadied.

"Is he hot?" Juliana asked.

May nodded again. Juliana strode to the bathroom and pulled a spare towel from below the sink. Wetting it with cool water, she returned and folded it across his forehead.

"How do we..." She swallowed; not sure she wanted the answer. "How do we know our water isn't infected as well?"

"I watched them install the filter. Green-Stars. The same ones have come for the past ten years. I'm friendly with the one who does this house."

"It's government regulated?"

Before May could answer, the others returned. Anthony and Taz carried Naya between them. Daisy pushed the rocking chair out of the way as they lowered her onto Juliana's bed.

Juliana crossed, a vial of yellow liquid in her hand. The others moved aside.

With gentle fingers, Juliana pulled the edge of Naya's shirt aside. Across her bony chest tendrils of the same sluggish green jutted up from under the skin and crawled towards her neck. It didn't look as bad as Jimmy's. The lines were thinner, fewer.

Juliana lifted Naya's head. Taz moved forward, placing his hands under hers and taking the weight. Juliana nodded her thanks and let him prop Naya up as she removed the stopper, opened the woman's mouth, and gently dribbled the liquid onto her tongue.

Naya coughed and spluttered, but the *spidergreen* went down.

Taz lowered her back to the pillow. Juliana turned to May. "She doesn't look as bad as Jimmy. No fever."

May's expression flickered with relief.

"Wha' do we do now?" Anthony asked. He sat at the foot of May's bed, a hand on Jimmy's ankle. His dark eyes glinted with fear.

May sighed and rose. Daisy hurried forward and took her place, letting Jimmy's head rest on her legs. She flipped the towel, then put her fingers to his neck.

"His heartrate is steady," Daisy announced. "He's warm, but not dangerously so."

May turned in the center of the room, taking them all in with a tired gaze.

"My guess, and it is just a guess at this point, is that their house was skipped during the last filter change. None of you have had to witness this." She grimaced. "I thought I'd never have to see it again. We need to make sure this *is* in fact Spidergreen. It's presenting as so, but someone has to get a sample of their water.

Take it to Montague. There should still be old test kits at town hall. That man never throws anything away."

Taz rose. "I can do tha'. Do I just take a cupful?"

May handed him an empty vial, roughly the length and width of two fingers, with a cork stopper at the top. "It isn't dangerous to touch, but just to be safe..."

He nodded, pocketed the vial, and left. The sound of his running footsteps faded into the distance.

"Once we find out what it is..." Anthony spoke through gritted teeth. "How do we *fix* it?"

"The medicine we gave them should help slow the spread. Clean water, and food cooked with clean water, will help as well. Beyond that..." May shook her head. "I don't have any kind of cure. Everything I can make is to lessen the symptoms."

"There's nothin'?" Anthony demanded.

Daisy let out a shaky breath. Her fingers shook as she traced a pattern of swirls across Jimmy's skin. He shifted in his sleep.

"At the moment," May looked at Anthony, sorrow in her gaze, "there's nothing."

Juliana sank onto the bed beside Naya. She checked her forehead again, still no fever, and raised her shirt up to her chest. The spider-web like tendrils began near her stomach. They arched up like Jimmy's, but as she'd noted initially, they weren't as intense as his.

Naya's breathing had steadied as well; May's concoction seemed to be working. Juliana pulled a folded blanket from the foot of the bed and spread it across Naya's slim form.

They sat in silence for a long time. Eventually, Anthony rose and left. He didn't say a word, but Juliana was sure he was going to find Taz.

He'd been gone a few minutes when May spoke again.

"If it is Spidergreen, we need to keep an exceptionally close eye on Jimmy. This illness affects children more than others."

"*What* is it though?" Juliana asked. "You keep saying illness, but can you be more specific?"

May stared at her for a second, then her face broke into a halfcocked grin. "I almost forgot; we have a former Blue-Star among us. It's a bacteria. One which lives in the water pumped into Abredea."

Juliana furrowed her brow. "That should be simple enough. We get them antibiotics. A full dose of something basic should do the trick, especially if most adults make it through unscathed."

May's grin slid into a scowl. "Darling girl, you've been here a few months now."

Juliana's gut clenched, the black pit opening up and swallowing her breath.

"We're Moons, Juliana," Daisy murmured. She looked up, tears glistening in her eyes. "We don't have those things here."

"But that's *wrong*." Juliana inhaled sharply. "There *has* to be something else we can do."

"We wait," May said, her gaze shifting to Jimmy. "All we can do right now is wait."

Chapter Twenty-Two

Present Day - Early Fall - Tornim

I t was odd, walking through the city with Ichi and Elaine. Cho rarely saw them go above ground. Elaine held tight to Ichi's hand, letting him pull her along as she stared up at the night sky.

Cho led the way through a deserted Agora. The streets were empty, dark and foreboding, a chill in the air. He shivered as they edged along the wall leading to Grigoria and pulled his cap lower down his forehead.

The others wore similar coverings; hiding the swirling colors affixed to their temples. Jane was the only one who truly didn't need to hide her gemstones. Tall as she was, no one would mistake the fourteen-year-old for someone who should already have a caste.

The Star-Office sat a couple of blocks into Grigoria from the Agora entrance. The building was visible from the archway; a vast concrete structure with a small black door at the front and two Red-Stars on either side both day and night.

Appointments had ended hours ago. Cho knew this from the various nights he'd been stationed across the street, perched on a rooftop watching the movements of everyone who went in and out of the building.

"Jane," Ichi whispered, calling down their line as Cho stopped them thirty or so yards from the entrance to Grigoria.

She moved up to them. "Going through here?"

Ichi nodded. "You're sure this won't be too much? We can try to get through without expending your gift."

Cho fought the urge to roll his eyes. Jane didn't.

She heaved a sigh and raised an eyebrow. "This is the plan. We made a plan, let's just do it."

Ichi inclined his head politely. Behind him Jason snickered, and Samaira gave him a light shove.

Elaine's pearly white smile gleamed against her skin as she nodded. "Well said," she whispered, sticking out her hand.

Jane took it. The rest linked up, making sure to keep physical contact, and she took them through the wall. From there she led the way.

Cho took up the rear, keeping an eye on the path they'd made and watching for anyone following them. It took a few minutes of skirting buildings, and pausing once to avoid a Red-Star patrol car, to reach the Star Office.

They approached from the back. Where the front door was dark, crisp paint and foreboding rows of color above the frame, the rear entrance was simple metal.

"Where do we need to go in?" Jason whispered.

Jane led them to the left. They passed the door and approached the next building. The narrow alley between them was barely wide enough for two people to walk side by side. Jane pressed a hand against the concrete wall of the Star Office, brushing along it as she counted her steps.

Finally, they stopped.

Jane turned her dark eyes to the rest of them, barely visible in the blackness of the alley.

"We go through here. It should be the blood draw room. Frosted place is like a maze," she shook her head, "but there's a long hallway that leads to the nearest Coding room. This is the closest we can get to it from the outside."

Ichi nodded. He raised a hand to his temple, his finger almost itching at the wool cap on his head. "Let's do it."

Elaine's hand tightened around Cho's; he glanced at her. In the darkness her features were hard to make out. But her wide black eyes met his and he saw fear in her gaze. He gave a weak smile.

Ichi took Elaine's other hand and raised it to his lips. Pressing a kiss against her fingers, he made sure the rest of them were linked and gave Jane a tight nod.

It was like pressing through soft butter; Cho closed his eyes as they stepped through the wall. Cold hit him. He squinted, wincing at the brightness of the room. Along the wall above them a grate blew out chilled air.

Cho shivered.

The rest moved quickly. Jason and Samaira strode to each of the two doors.

"It's that one." Jane pointed at Samaira's door. "The other leads back toward the waiting room."

Ichi and Elaine moved toward Samaira. At the same time, Jason's door jerked.

Cho's head whipped around. Jason held the doorknob, keeping it from turning as his forearms bulged. On the other side of the door, someone cursed.

"We can't keep them out," Cho whispered under his breath, hurrying across to stand beside Jason. "Anything out of the ordinary will be too suspicious. Including locked doors where," he pointed to the handle, "there are no locks."

Jason snarled at him.

"There's only one," Ichi said, coming up behind them both. "Let him in. We can tie him up, and I may be able to knock him out."

"*I* can knock him out," Samaira hissed from across the room.

Cho glanced back in time to catch her smirking at Elaine. The other woman grinned with a shake of her head.

Jason let go of the door.

It burst open, the Red-Star on the other side falling through and sprawling across the floor. Jason leapt atop him as Cho scrambled around and shut the door.

He heaved a sigh of relief as the handle clicked into place. He'd seen no one in the hallway.

Waves of anger and fear slammed into his defenses; he leaned against the wall for a second, breathing hard as he fought against the intrusion of emotion.

Thudding sounded behind him.

Jason pounded his fist into the Red-Star's face. Once, twice, a third time as the man struggled in vain to rise from the ground. Jason was on top of him, straddling his stomach, pinning his arms with muscular legs.

Ichi rose from beside the scuffle, a hand-held com device in his hands. "Jason, that's enough. He can't signal for help."

Jason didn't stop. Blood spurted from the man's face, dripping down his mustache and soaking into the high collar of his uniform.

"Jace." Samaira appeared in front of him, her hand closing around his wrist as he raised his fist again. "It's enough. We have something to do. *Focus.*"

Jason sniffed, clambered off the moaning Red-Star, and let Samaira pull him to his feet.

The Red-Star rolled onto his hands and knees. Ichi put a foot under his stomach and flipped him back over.

"Moving is not in your best interest at the moment."

The man stared up at Cho's brother, terror and rage on his face as his gaze flicked to each of the people in the room. He'd remember them. He'd remember their faces. Hopefully, soon it wouldn't matter.

Glass tinkled in the corner. Floor to ceiling shelves walled most of the room. Elaine stood at one, shifting through the contents of the cabinet.

"Here," she exclaimed quietly. "Give him this."

She handed Ichi a syringe full of pale pink liquid. The Red-Star grunted and moved backward until he hit the cabinet behind him.

"Don't, please," he murmured. His voice shook, muffled by the swelling in his nose and lips.

"It won't hurt you." Elaine raised an eyebrow and met Ichi's gaze. "It'll put him to sleep for a while. Side effects include memory loss."

"Here's hoping," Ichi said. He moved toward the Red-Star.

As the man made to scurry away, Jason and Samaira each grabbed an arm. They pinned him in place.

"Find a vein," Elaine sang as she crossed the room to Jane. The two stood by the door they were to go through, watching as Ichi slapped the man's arm a few times and then plunged the needle into the crook of his elbow.

Cho gritted his teeth. Overwhelming fear pelted at him like droplets of rain. It, combined with his own anxiety, was momentarily too much for his power.

He fell against the door, slumping down as his heartbeat sounded in his ears, far faster than it should have been. Oxygen clumped in his throat, lodging in place, unable to reach his lungs.

Cho closed his eyes. He took a shuddering inhale through his nose. He focused, but his ability to concentrate on anything beyond the terror failed him.

A voice sounded outside the horrible ringing in his ears. Hands grabbed his, warmth pressing against his frozen fingers. He couldn't... couldn't open his eyes.

Something pressed against his chest. It moved with him as he breathed. Pushing down and rising up again over and over. It pushed deeper and he exhaled everything in him. When it rose up he followed it, inhaling all the air his lungs could take.

Another moment passed. As quickly as it had hit him, the fear paralyzing him vanished.

Cho snapped open his eyes. Elaine crouched before him, her black braids—beaded with sparks of silver—dangled in front of his face. It was her hand, clenched around his fingers. Her other rested against his chest. As he winced, blinking up at her, she removed it.

"Cho?" Ichi murmured from above them. Concern furrowed his brow as he gazed down at his brother.

"I'm..." Cho cleared his throat. "I'm sorry. I'm all right. I just didn't expect..." He scanned the room. The Red-Star was in the same place he'd been before, fully unconscious.

"How is your shield?" Elaine asked softly.

Cho grimaced. "It's fine," he lied.

Ichi stared.

Cho met his gaze briefly and shook his head. "It will be fine," he amended. "I'll shore up the defenses when we get home."

"Then let's go," Jane hissed from her station by the door.

Ichi took Cho's hand, pulling him to his feet. They joined the twins and Elaine as everyone grouped at the door.

"Anyone on the other side?" Jason asked.

Ichi shook his head.

They hurried through and raced down a stark white hallway. "These nacras really don't know how to decorate," Jason scoffed.

Jane chuckled.

Her laugh died as they reached the white door at the end of the hall. The temperature dropped even more here. The chill seeped into Cho's bones.

Jane grabbed the door handle and pushed. It didn't budge.

Samaira came up behind her. "That's what I'm here for," she said with a grin. Together, the two of them shoved the door. It moved an inch. Then another. With a final grunt, the thing swung forward revealing the room beyond.

A shudder went down Cho's spine.

Grated metal covered the floor. A heavy chair sat in the center of the room; large machines hung overhead. On the far wall, a one-way mirror with a door beside it led to some kind of control room.

Ichi let out a breath.

When Cho looked at his brother, he didn't see fear or anxiety. This is what they had been working toward for months. His brother had been planning it for years. Ichi's eyes were alight with the promise of the future.

He strode toward the chair. The rest followed; Jason let the door close slowly and silently behind them.

"We have to figure out the controls," Elaine said. "Decide who goes first."

"I will." Ichi met her gaze. He slid a hand around her waist, pulling her toward him and touching her forehead to his. "I will."

She nodded.

The door to the control room was locked. Jane flitted inside, undoing the latch from within and letting the rest join her. It was a cramped space. Two small stools sat side by side in front of a large panel of knobs and buttons.

The read-out screen was dark, but lit up with the Grey-Star logo as Ichi reached forward and pressed a button. A fist, closed around the flag of Pangaea, filled the screen.

Jason grunted.

"Give me a moment with this," Elaine said. "I should be able to sort it out."

Ichi kissed her cheek and retreated from the room. Jason, Samaira, and Cho followed. A few minutes later, Elaine told him to get ready.

Cho watched, wide eyed, as his brother climbed into the metal chair and removed his hat. Black hair—as coarse and unruly as Cho's—was cropped in a rumpled fauxhawk. The rainbow gemstones against his temples gleamed in the dim light from orbs fixed along the ceiling.

"Are you sure about this?" Jason asked, eyeing the machinery warily.

Ichi gave a rueful grin and shrugged. "It's this, or we never leave Tornim."

Jane stuck her head out of the control room door. "Ready?"

"Ready."

Noise filled the room. A low whirring which came both from the machines and the chair itself. Samaira gasped as Ichi rose into the air. He gripped the sides of the chair. Fear flashed across his face as clamps sprang around his wrists.

Jason cried out, but Ichi shook his head. "It's fine. This is part of it."

Still, Cho winced as another clamp latched around his brother's chest.

"A warning is coming up." Elaine's voice echoed through a small speaker above the window. "You need to stay as still as possible. Don't move your head."

Ichi raised his chin and faced forward. Serenity filled his features, smoothing the wrinkle in his brow and pulling his lips into a neutral line.

"Everyone, come in here," Elaine called. "It won't work with you in the room."

They followed her instructions, leaving Ichi alone and piling into the control room. Jane shut the door.

"Why can't we be out there with him?" Cho asked.

"The whole room has motion sensors. The machine doesn't work if the person is moving, and the sensors were picking you all up."

Jason stepped forward, watching the screen as Elaine pushed a few more buttons. "So you can pick whatever color you want?"

The beads in Elaine's hair jingled as she nodded. "There is an auto-fill that's supposed to pop up, but since we didn't go through the rest of the process, I'm able to put in what we want."

Jason shook his head.

"I bet everyone's real polite to the techs," Samaira muttered.

Her brother nodded; his jaw locked as he stared out at Ichi.

"Here we go," Elaine murmured.

The machines lowered from the ceiling. Needles slid down on either side of Ichi. Everyone gasped as the needles plunged into Ichi's gemstones.

"It's fine, it's fine," Elaine said, though her voice was strained. "This is what's supposed to happen."

Cho held his breath. Seconds passed, perhaps minutes, he wasn't sure. Eventually, the machines stopped whirring. The needles slid away from his brother's head and returned to the ceiling. The chair lowered to the ground.

With the click of a button, Elaine released the clamps.

They rushed out as Ichi stood, somewhat shaky though with a smile on his face. Cho stared at his brother. The gleaming blue gemstones pulled his gaze.

"Well?" Ichi grinned at them. "What do you think?"

"Ugh," Jason scoffed, striding toward Ichi and grasping his shoulder. "You're a spoiled boy now. I'll have to give you a harder time to keep you in line."

Ichi laughed and clapped an arm around his friend. "Here I thought this might finally get you to listen to me."

At that, Samaira and Elaine chuckled as well.

"We should hurry," Jane said.

Ichi looked to Elaine. "May I?"

Elaine nodded, her smile faltering a little as she looked at the chair. Ichi gazed at her for a few seconds.

"Got it." He walked with her to the chair, offering his hand as she moved her flowing skirts aside and climbed up. "It doesn't hurt. Just feels a little strange."

They moved into the control room and a few minutes later Elaine joined Ichi as part of the blue caste. Technically. Though Cho wondered how trying to get Ichi into the actual system would even work. He'd be allowed in the Blue-Star district, but to get a house he'd need to go through the government.

He gave a little shake of his head. None of that actually mattered. They'd be gone soon now; a grin slid across his face.

"Are you sure?" Ichi was asking Jason and Samaira.

Samaira pressed her fingers to her temple. The gemstones there glinted with swirls of green and blue. "I can't part with this. It's been who we are for so long..."

Elaine grasped her hand and squeezed it.

"I'm not going to be part of this nacra system." Jason shook his head, crossing his arms with a scowl. "We don't need anyone else done. You two can get us out and then it won't even matter."

Ichi looked at Cho.

Those tired eyes met his, so worn from trying to keep everyone safe for so long. From sleepless nights scavenging for food, staying up with the little ones as they cried over the families that abandoned them. From the constant fear that only Cho and Elaine knew about.

Those eyes, the same color as his—as *their* mother's... didn't look so tired now.

Cho nodded. "I'll... I'll try it."

Jason and Jane both sighed, but Samaira shrugged and herded them both into the control room. Cho faced the mirror and pulled off his knitted cap.

The gemstones embedded into his temples didn't gleam with color the way Jason's did. They didn't swirl with a rainbow of brilliant blues and reds and greens.

Cho raised a hand to the gemstone on his right temple, the one which had cracked down the middle on that day in Agora three years ago. The day his mind broke—and his gemstones along with it.

The color on both swirled sluggishly. Dark greys, murky greens, and faded browns twisted this way and that on his temples. The one which had split flickered, the swirling pattern fractured and faltering.

Cho trembled as he climbed into the chair.

"Are you sure we should try this?" Someone's voice murmured through the speaker.

Another person made a sound of confirmation. Cho was busy trying not to sprint as far from the chair as possible to make out who it was.

The clamps locked into place. The chair rose into the air. Needles lowered from the ceiling.

His breath came fast. Ichi's voice reminded him to hold still, to stay calm.

The needles reached his temples—

Alarms shot through the room. The machines on either side of him flew backward, joints groaning. The chair dropped to the ground; Cho's stomach lurched.

Red light replaced the dull glow from the orbs, flashing in time with the ear-splitting siren. Cho jerked against the restraints around his arms and chest, panic seizing him.

"Hold still!" Elaine shouted from the control room.

He froze. A split second later, the clasps released.

His family poured into the room. Ichi's steady gaze met his panicked one.

"It's fine. Let's go."

"Hat on," Jason shouted at Cho over the sound of the alarm, tossing him the striped cap.

Cho pulled it over his gemstones as they ran for the door. The hallway was no longer white. Red light rained down on them. The alarm blared even louder here, echoing up and down the long stretch.

Jane barreled ahead of the rest of them, charging through the door at the end of the hall as the rest piled in behind her.

The Red-Star was still slouched against the wall. Cho had a moment of confusion—who had sounded the alarm—before Jason grabbed his hand and Jane pulled them all through the wall.

Outside was different.

The summer air felt warm compared to the stark chill of the building. There were no alarms. No sirens or flashing lights. Only the darkness of the alleyway, cut with a faint beam of moonlight.

Cho leaned against the bricks behind him, shuddering and taking deep breaths. Jason looped his hand around Cho's arm and pulled. They followed the others, sprinting down the narrow alley and pausing only at the end.

Ichi glanced around the corner. "Shit. They're watching the exit."

"Other way?" Samaira asked, already taking a few steps toward the opposite end of the alley.

Ichi shook his head. "That's the front, there'll be even more."

Jane gritted her teeth. "I can do it."

Cho's stomach stirred with worry.

"We'll have to get through the entire building," Ichi said.

"It's empty," Jane reminded him, her voice low. "I get us into the first room, we wind our way through and if the door is locked, I get us through the far wall too."

Elaine nodded. "Let's do it."

Jane grabbed them again. Cho kept his eyes open this time, watching his friend's face contort with concentration, and then pain, as she moved them through the foot-and-a-half thick brick wall.

They emerged into darkness on the other side. At least it wasn't as cold as the Star Office. Cho blinked, trying to adjust to the black.

A faint glow came to life, illuminated the room. Fire danced in Samaira's palm.

They were in a storage room. Stacks of chairs lined the walls, a mop and vacuum set against a corner. Jane opened the door, and they poured out.

Cho barely had time to catch his breath as they moved again, running through the building. Jane tried door after door along the carpeted hallway they'd emerged in. Finally, one led to more light.

They came to the front lobby of whatever sort of office building they were in. The Star Office was the second building on the block, this one the first. Its front door—fortunately—faced the cross street, rather than being beside either of the Star Office entrances.

Unfortunately, the door was locked.

Jane swallowed, hand on her knees as she panted for air.

"We could break the glass," Ichi said, running a hand along the clear window beside the door.

Elaine shook her head. "We don't want anyone wondering why someone was in this building too."

"I've got it," Jane growled.

"Jane..." Ichi began.

"I said, *I've got it*."

She pulled them through.

The rest of the trip back to Agora, and then Haven, went smoother than Cho could have dreamed. They strode purposefully and swiftly through Grigoria.

Curfew had long since passed for anyone under twenty and those in the lower four classes.

Those stipulations no longer applied to Ichi and Elaine.

It took twenty or so minutes to arrive at the next nearest entrance to Agora. The gates were open, Red-Stars on either side.

Ichi strode forward, shoulders back, chin high, blue gemstones glinting in the moonlight. "Evening," he said with a sharp nod.

The Red-Stars exchanged glances, confusion on their wary faces. One looked again, his gaze going from Ichi's gemstones to Elaine's. The rest of the group followed along behind them, Samaira and Jason making themselves as small as possible. A feat given how muscular the two of them were.

Finally, just as Cho and Jane passed under the arch, a Red-Star spoke. "Evening, sir. As a... uh... reminder, children aren't allowed out after curfew, regardless of caste."

"Precisely why we're returning my siblings and their friends back home." Elaine nodded, her dazzling smile softening the Red-Star's expression.

"Have a pleasant night," the man said with a deferential smile. His gaze followed them as the group didn't slow in the slightest.

They dropped through a sewer grate a few minutes later. Jane lagged behind; her eyes half-closed as she leaned against the walls. Samaira went to her, helping prop her up and supporting her as they went down, down, down.

The massive metal doors to Haven opened with a silent whoosh of air. Beyond, curled against one of the couches at the bottom of the stairs, Luna and Nova gazed up at them.

"Woah..." they said at the same time.

They rose, meeting the group as everyone descended the stairs. Jason pushed the heavy doors closed, barring them in place with a thick plank of wood.

"You look..." Luna began, her gaze locked on Ichi's temples.

"Scary," Nova finished as she circled Elaine to get a better look at the blue gemstones.

"Still the same us," Elaine said with a smile. "But now we don't have to hide."

Ichi glanced at her. "As much. We don't have to hide as much."

Elaine inclined her head, taking Nova and Luna by the hands and walking with them back to the cushions. "How was it? Are the little ones all right?"

Ichi turned to Cho. "Brother, I want to talk with you for a bit."

Cho nodded.

"Jane?" Ichi asked after the tall girl, her form already disappearing down the hallway toward her bedroom.

She waved a hand and continued on her way. Well enough to walk to her room, far too exhausted to talk about it. Cho grinned.

"Samaira." Ichi looked at the twins. They currently stood in the kitchen, each with a, somehow already formed, sandwich in hand.

Samaira looked up through the open window, her mouth bulging with food.

Ichi paused. He glanced at Cho then back to Samaira. "First thing in the morning, let's get ready."

Her eyes grew serious, losing the glint of success she and her brother had been sharing. She nodded.

Cho watched his brother, a frown forming. He followed Ichi into the study, and then collapsed onto the thick red couch with a sigh of relief.

Ichi however, made no such move to relax. He strode to the desk, pulling out maps and papers, and pouring over them with a furrowed brow.

"What is it?" Cho asked.

"We did it, Cho. Months of planning, and this," he tapped a gemstone with his fingernail, "has finally happened. There's nothing stopping us now."

Cho blinked, sitting up as relief melted into a pool of anxiety. "You're not leaving *now*."

Ichi shook his head. "Tomorrow I'll go with Samaira, find us a transport. We might even be able to take Jane and get that coin." He paused in his movements, a thoughtful squint to his eye. "Yes. That'll have to be first. We might even be able to use some of it to rent a vehicle."

"Elaine will be staying then?" Cho asked, hope lacing his voice. "You're just taking Samaira?"

Ichi rubbed his fingers across his forehead. "No, Cho. Elaine is coming as well. If she has..." He swallowed. "If her power comes out while I'm not here..."

Cho nodded, a gnawing guilt in his belly.

"I'm leaving Jason with you."

The guilt shifted to dread. He leaned forward. "I still don't think—"

"Cho," Ichi slammed a few papers onto the table, "I can't keep having this conversation with you. He's staying. You're in charge. You need someone here who can help protect the kids if something goes wrong."

"I can't..." Cho grimaced. "I'm not like you, Ichi. I'm not a leader."

Ichiro heaved a sigh and stepped away from his map. He dragged a chair to the couch and sat in front of his brother. "Listen to me," he murmured. "You absolutely are, and absolutely can be a leader. You have it in you. More than I do, whether you believe it or not. And Jason..." he half-chuckled. "I know he's a pain and gives you a hard time. But he respects—"

"He *doesn't* respect me."

Ichi frowned. "He respects *me*. And you by extension. More than that, he cares about Haven. He's not going to do anything to jeopardize this place or these children. You should know that."

Cho swallowed and clenched his teeth. "I'm sorry, Ichi. I just... I wish you were leaving Samaria instead."

Ichi's mouth tilted into a grin. "Oddly enough, I don't want to bring the hothead on this trip."

Cho returned the grin somewhat reluctantly. "So, you leave him with me, thanks."

Ichi's laugh broke the remaining tension in the room. "I think you can handle him." He clapped a hand on Cho's shoulder. "This is going to be... this is it, Cho. A week, hopefully less, I'll find us a home. Come get you all, and we're free. Really, *actually* free."

Cho nodded, his brother's hope seeping into him like an infectious disease. Not because of his power, Ichi had more control than that. But because the look on Ichi's face was so triumphant.

"Go," Ichi said. "Get some rest. You've had an interesting couple of nights. I'm not going anywhere without talking to the rest of Haven first. And it'll take some time to get the transport ready, not to mention the paperwork we still need. Hopefully that coin will speed up the process with my contact."

Cho rose from the couch, Ichi following him to the door. They shared a tight hug, Cho clinging to his brother like a life-raft that would float away at any moment.

Elaine, Luna, and Nova were still in the main room. Sky had gotten out of bed; she lay across Luna, her head in Elaine's lap. Kim was with them as well, curled into a ball and tucked under Nova's arm. Elaine stroked Sky's silver-blonde hair as Luna and Nova murmured to her. Likely filling her in on the night's events.

It was late. Or—rather—early. Nearly two in the morning according to Cho's watch.

His bones dragged with exhaustion. The episode he'd had... He couldn't go right to sleep. He needed to meditate first, build up his defenses. Better to do it now than wait till morning.

Cho changed into a loose shirt and a pair of comfortable shorts, sat himself on the bed with his legs crossed, and concentrated.

In his mind there was a room, a circle of bricks really, with a tall ceiling and a black roof. The bricks were splintered, yellow light gleaming through the cracks. He approached, envisioned a door, and stepped through it.

A silver-platted box sat upon a plinth in the center of the circular room. He strode to it. The hinges had fractured, the lid hanging open. Saffron light, waspish tendrils of his power, danced through the air. They reached toward the cracks in the brick, peeking through and trying to find someone's emotions to latch onto.

Painstakingly, even dozing off a few times, Cho pulled each strand back into the box. He lowered the lid, poking an escaping tendril back in, and shut it. He had yet to create a lock or latch—the box alone had taken many arduous weeks of meditation—but the lid would do the trick for now.

As far as the brick went...

Cho winced as he noted the maze of cracks all around him. He'd have to patch it up. All of it.

But that could wait.

He cracked an eye open and glanced at his watch. It was almost three; he needed sleep.

Cho yanked at his blankets, settling himself snugly into bed. He reached out, clicking a button on the small orb glowing on his bookshelf. The light faded slowly. He smiled as his eyes drifted closed, the collection of little cranes watching over him as he fell asleep.

Chapter Twenty-Three

66 Years Ago - Althea - City of Pangaea

M aybelle dove aside as dirt and rubble erupted where she'd been standing. Splinters of glass showered up her arm.

"*Frost,*" she grunted, scrambling to her feet.

A few yards away Cecil, the newest member of the alter squad, stood frozen in terror as a line of Black-Stars marched toward them.

The base had fallen, that much was clear. Maybelle had zapped her squad in for a regular recon trip. "*Get the debrief, prepare for the delegates, fill them in on the plan for the next few weeks, and get Cecil used to being public with her powers,*" Red had said.

Easy.

It was supposed to be easy.

The Black-Stars raised their guns, bolts of plasma charging at the tips. Maybelle ran, rubble skidding under her feet. She threw herself at Cecil as the air surged with electricity. The smell of burning hair filled her nostrils. She blinked as she slammed into the girl.

The two of them fell into darkness.

They landed with a loud thunk, Cecil crying out as Maybelle thudded on top of her.

"Sorry," Maybelle grunted as she rolled off and up. She offered a hand and pulled the dark-skinned girl to her feet. "You can't freeze like that, Cee. They... ah, shit." She reached up and examined one of Cee's thick black locks. The end had been scorched off, the singed ruin still smoking as embers crawled up her hair.

"I..." Cecil's fingers shook as she took the lock from Maybelle. "I've got it, Captain." She closed her eyes, trembling as a bead of water formed between her thumb and forefinger. It doused the hair.

"I have to go back," Maybelle called, already sprinting down the corridor toward the armory. "Stay here, stay safe."

She'd brought them to the Warren. A safe place for Cecil, and the nearest source of reinforcements and weapons Maybelle knew of. She slammed through the door, shouts of alarm filling the room. Red's booming voice called for calm before he looked to Maybelle.

"Sanctuary is under attack. Weapons, volunteers. Now." Maybelle passed the hulking tree-trunk of a man and began unloading weapons from the wall behind him.

It took him two seconds to catch up with her words, and then he was barking orders. Rebel troops filled the room.

Maybelle holstered a plasma gun, grabbed a rifle, and turned to the room. Four rebel soldiers, each armed to the teeth, stood at attention.

Behind them, a few alters from the second squad had joined the throng as well. Maybelle met Thomas's eye. He grimaced, nodding fervently. With a sigh, Maybelle nodded back.

"All right. The situation is dire. Most of Sanctuary is dead. We were looking for survivors when Black-Stars showed up. Looks like a full unit. They're scattered around the ruins, but someone or something is keeping civilians back. Remember, we're going into the middle of a city. Do not get separated from the group. We round up any survivors we can find, we get my squad, and we come back home."

"This isn't a fight," Red boomed from her left.

She darted a glance at him. The man was holding his rifle and had a machete on his hip. Her grey eyes widened, and she opened her mouth—

"It's a rescue," Red continued, ignoring her gaze. "We get in, get them, and get out. Stay close to Maybelle. If she says it's time to leave you better get your ass in contact fast or you're getting left behind."

Everyone moved forward.

"You shouldn't be coming," Maybelle hissed as Red closed a meaty hand around her arm.

"Aww, stop mothering me," he gripped. "Let's go."

They vanished.

Barely two minutes had passed, but the battlefield changed dramatically. Maybelle had expected it. She dropped them further into the ruins of the building that had once been a major base of operations for the rebel command.

Screaming filled the air. Smoke, dust, and the stench of sweat and blood filled her nostrils. She blinked, released her hold on the soldier in front of her, and moved away.

They found two bodies on the ground. A third rebel moaned in a corner, a chunk of concrete pinning their leg.

Thomas stepped past Maybelle and shifted the tire-sized sheet of rock as if it were a pillow. He hefted the rebel by the arm and slung them over his shoulder.

The group continued on, picking their way through rubble to the sounds of crackling fire and moans of those trapped or dying.

Maybelle's heart thudded against her chest. She'd arrived with a squad of five. Had stayed with Cecil while the rest searched the ruins. And then she'd left when the Black-Stars arrived.

Where were the others? More importantly... would she be able to get them all back in one go?

A whistle split the air.

Maybelle whirled, her gaze catching on a half-standing concrete wall, barely waist high. She shot off two short whistles of her own and a head popped up.

"Captain," Trevor grunted with relief.

Maybelle sighed, her shoulders sagging as the rest of her squad came up behind him. "Injuries?" She scanned the group. Another pang of relief hit when she didn't spot any obvious wounds beyond the same cuts and bruises she sported. "Report."

"Saw you zap out." Stacey came forward, her skin glittering in the sunlight streaming down through what used to be a roof. She was the only one without any scratches. That skin, hard as diamond, made a good shield. "Figured you'd be back soon. We avoided Black-Stars as much as possible, too many to fight."

Maybelle nodded.

"This was an ambush?" Red wondered aloud as they continued along, following the cries.

"A bomb," Maybelle murmured.

They exchanged a glance.

"I think it was just bad timing." Maybelle rubbed a finger across the gemstone on her temple. It was white now. A gleaming, shimmering pearl color that matched Kate's. The two had gotten them done shortly after joining the rebellion. Grey-Stars stood out.

"What if you'd been here?" Red growled.

Maybelle shook her head. "Any of us could have been here. Which tells me they didn't know we were coming." She leaned closer to him, dropping her voice so the others wouldn't hear. "Didn't know about the meeting either, or they'd have waited for it." She returned her voice to the normal volume. "We arrived just after the blast. Caught a few crumbling walls as they collapsed," she gestured to the small beads of glass still sticking out of her left arm, "but the main blast had already gone off."

"Shit, Maybelle. You've got to get that looked at."

She shrugged—her right shoulder—and analyzed the group picking across debris.

They stopped as Thomas handed his survivor to Trevor so he could lift an unconscious but still breathing body from the wreckage.

"I should start taking people back," Maybelle said reluctantly.

Red nodded. "Won't be able to move the whole group at once?"

She shook her head. "I doubt it. I'm comfy at six, pushing it at ten, and if we tried twelve, I worry I'd leave someone behind. A few smaller trips is better. Even that..." She grimaced. "There'll be gaps."

"Get your squad out. We'll stick close to Alter Squad Beta while we look for survivors."

"I'll be back soon. Minutes, if I can manage it."

"Don't worry." Red gave her his mischievous grin, his long beard blowing in the light breeze. "I've been itching to pull the trigger on some Black-Stars since I got the desk job."

Maybelle rolled her eyes. "Thomas," she called in a loud whisper, "give Stacey that one." She gestured to the person he'd just lifted.

Stacey took the woman, cradling her like a baby, and moved toward Maybelle. Slowly, careful of the rough terrain and injured passengers, Maybelle's alter squad grouped around her. Four of her squad, two injured...

In the blink of an eye, they were gone.

It took longer than Maybelle hoped to return for the others. She helped get the wounded to the med station, prodding at her power the entire time, waiting for it to return strong enough for another trip.

They hurried through the tunnels, Alexia lighting the way with little lights sparking from his fingertips.

The Warren was massive. A cave system of tunnels, underground rivers, and caverns. Some had been carved out by hand. The newer excavations were sped along by the alters Maybelle had helped train. But most of the rebel stronghold had formed naturally long before they found it.

She'd gotten lost more times than she could count in those first several weeks. Even four years later there were moments when she wasn't completely sure she was going the right direction. Then she'd see a divot in the rock, or a design carved into an archway and know where she was.

"Left," she huffed to Alexia with a jerk of her head.

The young man—a boy really, he'd begged her to join the squad even she thought he was too young—nodded and swung down the left-hand tunnel. Stacey, Trevor, and Illena followed, supporting the two injured rebels between them.

Maybelle reached inside her mind, poking at the spark of pale purple in the very center of her. The bundle of her power was small, a densely packed sphere which spun in slow circles. It needed to be larger. It needed to spin faster before she could make another trip.

She growled under her breath and continued after Alexia.

By the time they reached the med-station she'd clawed back just enough power to get herself to the ruins. She loaded another clip of ammunition onto her belt, snatched some gel med-packs from the cabinet, and took Stacey's water—just in case.

Kneeling, she pulled from that circle of light. Her stomach surged with a falling sensation and a split second later she was crouched on bits of blasted concrete. Smoke bit at her eyes, stinging against the chunks of splintered glass still buried in her arm. She blinked, trying to get an idea of the terrain.

Red and the others were nowhere in sight. Clouds had filtered into the sky, blocking out the sun with dark shadows.

In the distance, a group of soldiers stood in a circle together. Laughter echoed across the rubble. Maybelle frowned. With slow, careful steps, she backed away from the Black-Stars. Anxiety crept into her chest.

She ducked behind a half-standing wall, poking her head out once to check that no one had spotted her.

Weight pulled at her eyelids and limbs. Fear split through her gut.

She had to find the others. Find them and get them out. Maybelle leaned her head against the concrete wall, closing her eyes for a brief moment as she crouched in place. A few deep breaths later she'd managed to close trembling fingers around the water bottle. She drank deeply.

Food. Food would help.

The ground swam beneath her.

The ruined building, a massive thing taking up a small city block, sat in a relatively remote area of the city. It had been an outpost for White-Stars coming to visit the city on weekends, a place for them to stay as a group, safe from the prejudice of the other castes.

Once the war started its purpose had changed.

The Warren was the main rebel base. It held nearly five-thousand soldiers and their families. It housed the researchers, scientists, doctors, medics, cooks, and everyone else who wanted to do what they could to help the rebellion, but were unable or unwilling to fight.

The Sanctuary, now a pile of rubble, had been their secondary base.

Maybelle thought—for a brief few seconds—about the meeting that was supposed to take place here in just a few days.

A meeting that would likely be canceled rather than postponed after the other parties learned of the attack. A meeting that might have meant the end of the war.

Tears flushed the ash and dust from her eyes.

A flicker of movement caught her gaze. The building across the street was a vehicle shop. Massive rolling doors stood open at the front, the inside obscured by darkness. Along the sidewalk on her side of the road, a row of wooden barricades had been set out; likely circling the block to keep curious eyes from seeing what the Black-Stars were up to.

She stared.

There. A flash of something white inside the shop. She watched the space for a long moment. Again, and once more.

A signal.

A fresh pump of adrenaline flew through her veins. She rose to her knee, eyes and ears alert. Behind her, the laughter of the Black-Stars still reached her. The sound dimmed as boots crunched against the ground in their direction. A new voice joined in, brisk, deep, and charged with anger.

"You've finished the search, I gather."

The inquiry was greeted with silence.

A growl echoed through the half-standing concrete walls. "How many survivors? How many dead? How many injured, too far gone? What were their colors?"

"We don't... we don't have that information yet, sir," a younger voice, shaky and hesitant responded.

Maybelle could smell the fear.

"The commander won't be pleased. Get back to work rounding up this trash. I want a full report in the next twenty minutes, and I want bodies. Live ones."

"Yes, sir."

"Apologies, sir."

"Right away, sir."

The chorus of Black-Star responses covered Maybelle's footsteps. She scurried, half bent to stay out of sight. Around another wall, under a half-fallen beam—going over would have put her in sight of the Black-Stars—and finally to the edge of the sidewalk.

A row of lightly burning hedges kept her hidden from the street, but she didn't like the emptiness at her back.

Maybelle watched the black doorway. *Wait* the signal said, the white cloth harder to see now. The sky continued to darken; thunder echoed across the city from the north.

Only a few seconds passed before the signal came again, this time telling her to go. With a gulp and a hope that they had a decent vantage point, Maybelle rose and sprinted across the road.

She didn't slow at all, moving at full speed through the doorway and into the darkness. Only once she'd been embraced by the black did she stop.

She bent, hands finding her knees, lungs taking deep gulps of air.

"Finally." Red's deep voice brought a rush of relief.

"Glad to... see you... too," Maybelle huffed, still trying to catch her breath. Her trembling fingers reached for the water again. She drained the bottle.

Thick hands passed her another. "That low?" Red asked.

Her eyes adjusted slowly to the dark, but his massive form was impossible to miss. He crouched by her side, a hand on his beard.

"Yeah. Here to the Warren is..."

"Far," he finished for her.

She nodded.

"What's the plan?" Mary, one of Alter Squad Beta, approached them with silent steps. "I'd say we've got about five minutes before the sweep gets here."

"Less," Maybelle said. "Heard their squad captain give a tongue lashing before I saw your signal."

"You can't get us out."

It wasn't a question, or a judgement, but the heat of shame and failure roiled in Maybelle's gut.

"Not yet," she said through gritted teeth. "How many survivors?"

"Six," Mary replied.

Maybelle could just make out the gold beads threaded through Mary's braids. They were spaced for battle, staggered so they made no noise when she moved her head. Her purple gemstones were nearly invisible in the darkness.

Maybelle nodded. Counting the two she'd already taken to the Warren, that made eight alive. Eight of the two dozen who had been at the base. A skeleton crew preparing the building for their guests. So many dead. Most of them untrained civilians, not planning on putting their lives on the line.

She dragged her muddled mind to the present. "I'm gonna need more than five minutes anyway. We have to get out of here. Find somewhere to recuperate for... an hour. Less if I get some food I me. Even then, I can't take us all to the Warren in one go."

Red put a hand on her shoulder. "Out of the city will do. We don't have those fancy new passes and," he reached a hand into one of the many pockets on his pants, "none of us can pull these off."

He pulled out a small blue gem; the same size as the green one on his temple and, from more than a foot or two away, the same material as well. They had twelve of them, two for each of the six foreign dignitaries scheduled to attend the meeting. People from outside Pangaea. Individuals from their neighboring countries who didn't know of a life without gemstones or castes.

At least, not from what Maybelle, Red, or the rest of the rebel command had been able to discover.

Maybelle nodded again, the motion making her dizzy. "There's the safehouse in the village. I can get us there, then take trips of two back to the Warren with half-hour breaks in between."

Red leaned in and studied her eyes. "You're gonna need a long nap after this."

Her chuckle came out as weak as she felt.

"All right then." Mary nodded. "Commander," she looked to Red, "permission to take point on this?"

Red sighed. Almost a year in and he still hadn't gotten used to people calling him Commander any more than he'd gotten used to a desk job. Though, being in charge of the entire rebellion wasn't what Maybelle would call a normal desk job.

"Absolutely," he said with a jerk of his head.

Mary lined up their group. They moved toward the front of the shop, away from the rolling garage doors.

They reached the main door, a sheet of glass with a small sign on the front reminding customers to pull their vehicles around to the back and another announcing they were closed for the day.

Mary held up a hand. The group halted as one. Even the walking survivors—who had not been tactically trained—moved with surprising cohesion.

Mary paused and closed her eyes. She inhaled, rising her hands to her chest and lowering them as she let out a slow breath. When she lifted her lids, the dark eyes had gone gold, pupils wide like that of a predatory nocturnal animal. Her ears widened a fraction, elongating as the tips became pointed.

"Here we go." Mary smiled. She tightened her hand around the doorknob and jerked it to the side. *Crack.* She pulled the door open, broken pieces of the lock tinkling to the ground.

Mary's ears twitched, angling so they faced the gap. She hesitated, then stepped outside. Maybelle followed close behind.

The group lined up along the outside of the building, keeping close to the shadows. Rain fell. Soft droplets at first, a cool mist on Maybelle's warm face. They'd gone a block when the deluge hit. Thunder cracked above them, storm clouds turning the afternoon to night.

Maybelle blinked through the thick droplets. Mary was an impressive sight. The woman paused at each intersection, each corner, using her heightened hearing and vision even through the pounding rain.

They reached the end of a particularly long alley just as another clap of thunder sounded behind them. Mary winced, covering her large ears with her hands. Maybelle touched her shoulder.

"You all right?"

Mary nodded. "Just a bit loud. This way, we're almost there."

Maybelle's forehead wrinkled in confusion. They'd traveled maybe half a mile. Not nearly far enough for her to feel safe from the Black-Star search.

Mary's golden eyes narrowed. "You forget, Captain, Althea is *my* city." She grinned, unnaturally sharp teeth glinting in the faint light from the street orbs.

Maybelle smiled. She *had* forgotten. Inclining her head, she gestured for Mary to continue. A few minutes later they darted across an open market in groups of three. The rain had come suddenly, and a few Purple-Stars were still closing down their stands, paying little attention in their hurry to get their goods somewhere dry.

Mary led them down a narrow alley, and then she stopped. A large dumpster sat near a closed metal door. Mary reached trembling fingers toward the handle. It was locked.

Maybelle groaned. One of the injured who had barely been keeping pace with the group slumped against the brick wall, clutching their leg and breathing through clenched teeth.

"What now?" Red strode forward looking at Mary.

"I'm not done yet, Commander," Mary said. She circled the dumpster and crouched down. A few seconds later she emerged with a key in her hand.

"How did..."

Mary ignored the question, unlocked the door, and gestured for everyone to pile inside. Maybelle went last, making sure the ones they'd rescued were safely in before shutting the door behind them.

They'd entered a kitchen. Wooden countertops, a double-stove with a simmering pot of something that caused an audible growl in Maybelle's stomach, flickering lights, rows of knives and other utensils lined the walls... a *restaurant* kitchen.

A wide swinging door sat opposite the group. Someone in the room beyond laughed.

Maybelle froze, her eyes going wide. "Mary..."

The door swung open. A young girl, maybe fourteen or fifteen, strode through with a serving tray tucked under her arm. She caught sight of the group. Her dark eyes went wide. Just as Red reached out a hand she darted back, scurrying into the other room.

"*Nacra,*" Red growled.

He hurried after her, Mary close on his heels. The rest of the group followed. Maybelle moved past the others, taking her place at Red's side.

The restaurant was small. Booths circled the outer walls, with cushy green seats and walnut tabletops. A narrow bar ran along the wall shared with the kitchen. The floors were pale tile, walls dark with pictures hung on every inch of space.

Red, Maybelle, and Mary stood at the front of their group, blocking the kitchen door, but doing nothing to prevent anyone fleeing out the front. Fortunately, the restaurant appeared empty of patrons. The girl, her gemstones swirling with nervous oranges and reds, had darted behind a large man.

Dark, with a shiny bald head and purple gemstones on his temples, the man stood as tall as Red and almost as broad. He wore a plain green shirt, black pants, and a dirty apron around his waist. His eyes glinted with fear as he took in their group—pausing for a few seconds on the gun Red had unholstered when they'd rushed through the door.

"What do you want?" the man asked, his voice deep and smooth.

There was a moment of silence. The soldier behind Maybelle shifted.

"We need a place to stay," Red finally responded.

The man looked alarmed.

"Not for long. An hour or two."

"If they find you here..."

Red cocked his head, his fingers tightening around the gun. Maybelle watched the man with a wary gaze. He stood near the bar, where a large kitchen knife lay next to a pile of lemons.

"You know who we are?" Red asked.

Maybelle blinked. The Grey-Stars had done a surprisingly good job of keeping the war hidden from the cities. The majority of Pangaea had no idea the rebels even existed.

Her eyes widened as the man before them held up a fist. She reached for her own gun with one hand, the other locking around Red's forearm in case she needed to move him from harm's way.

Facing his palm toward them, the man uncurled his fingers and drew a line across them with his other hand. A simple gesture, but one that matched the rebel insignia and marked him as an ally.

"I know my daughter when I see her."

Maybelle's jaw went slack.

Mary strode across the room and wrapped her arms around the man's middle. "Baba," she murmured, "it's good to see you."

A sharp inhale—half a sob—cut through the stunned silence in the room as Mary's father wrapped one arm around her back and the other in her hair. He pulled her to his shoulder for a long moment before leaning back and planting a kiss on her forehead.

Red exchanged a bemused look with Maybelle and holstered his weapon. "Good to see someone who's sympathetic to the cause."

Mary smirked, her ears and eyes slowly returning to normal. "This is my father, Dankesh."

"Dan is fine," the man said with a smile that matched his daughter's. "This is my youngest, Camile." He gestured behind him to the younger girl who hadn't lost her wide-eyed, fearful expression. She darted a glance at Mary.

"Is..." Camile swallowed, looking towards Red, "is she safe then?"

Maybelle took half a step forward. "What do you mean? Safe from the war, or safe to be around?"

Camile shrunk into herself. Behind Maybelle, the other members of Alter Squad Beta grumbled and shifted. Mary's smirk slid into a thin line.

"Both, I guess," Camile muttered.

Maybelle nodded. "Mary is one of our most skilled alters. She has control over her power that others envy. Even trains some of them. As for the war..." she turned her gaze on Dan, "we won't be here long. Black-Stars just bombed the White Sanctuary. We have survivors who need a little while to recuperate before they're well enough to travel."

Neither Red nor Mary commented on her half-truth.

Dan looked to Mary. "What would you have done if we'd had customers."

"It's pouring, Baba. We never have customers on a day like this."

Dan rubbed a hand across his forehead. "How long?" He directed the question to Red.

"An hour. Two at most. Less, if we can talk you into feeding us."

Mary, who had been watching her sister, turned to look at her father. He stood quietly for a moment. Anxiety clawed at Maybelle. Her vision blurred, her arm ached, and her energy waned. If they had to go somewhere else...

"An hour."

Red jerked his head in a nod.

Dan sighed. "Camile, get bowls for the stew. I'll heat up some bread and Mary," he glanced at his daughter, "if you want to, prep some salads."

Mary flashed a wide grin. The two sisters moved into the kitchen; Camile careful to skirt the edge of their group as much as possible.

Red reached out a hand and Dan took it.

"Dangerous or not, I can't have people coming into my restaurant and leaving hungry," Dan said with a smile. He gestured around the room. "Find a seat, water is against the far wall," he pointed to a jug with several glasses stacked beside it, "and we'll have some grub out for you soon."

He crossed to the front door. Maybelle's hand twitched to her gun. A split second later she exhaled as Dan flicked the lock on the door, flipped a sign to say they were closed, and pulled down the shades, muffling the sound of the rain outside.

Thirty minutes later Maybelle was halfway through her third bowl of spicy stew, cutting each bite with a mouthful of soft bread flavored with a variety of seeds and herbs. Her stomach yowled its appreciation of the chunks of vegetables and meat, yellow rice, and broth flavored to the breaking point.

"How're you feeling now?" Red asked between mouthfuls of food.

Maybelle painfully swallowed a large piece of bread. "Ready to move an army."

He grinned.

The two of them sat together at the bar. The rest of their group relaxed in the various booths. Most of the bombing survivors had downed steaming bowls of stew and fallen into fitful dozing. Mary had pulled Camile into helping patch wounds once everyone had eaten. Now the young girl held a quivering pair of tweezers by Maybelle's elbow as her older sister dug a second bottle of cleanser from their remaining med kit.

Maybelle winced as the tweezers pinched around a sliver of glass. Camile pulled, dropping the glass into a small dish on the counter. Maybelle sucked in a breath as Mary pressed the cleansing solution onto the bleeding gash.

"Seriously though," she groaned. "Give me another half hour or so, and a few more slices of this bread, and I'll be able to move all fourteen into the village in one go since it's so close. Getting all the way back to the Warren might not happen till I sleep."

"Not a problem," Red mumbled, stew dripping into his beard.

Maybelle winced again, though not from pain this time.

"Sorry." He dabbed at his beard with a napkin with a grin.

"Hold still," Mary demanded as Maybelle tried to reach for another slice of bread from the basket before them.

She gingerly rested her arm back in place and grunted as the tweezers went back to work.

"Maybelle." Red's voice lost its cheery demeanor as he grabbed a slice and put it on her plate. "The meeting, the dignitaries..."

She nodded. "I know. We have to tell them."

He shook his head. "They won't come. Not if we tell the truth about what happened. They were scared enough even setting the meeting before this frosted disaster."

"We can't lie, Red. They'll find out. And if we manage to make an agreement *before* they find out, we don't just lose allies... we become enemies."

He rubbed a calloused hand across his chin and sat in silence for a long moment. Maybelle took the opportunity to drain the last dregs of her stew. She sponged the remaining bits of broth with her new slice of bread and swallowed it with a satisfied sigh, followed immediately by a yelp of pain as Camile yanked a particularly odd-shaped chunk of glass from her arm. Warm liquid flowed down her skin. Mary cursed, pressed the cleanser to the wound, and snapped at Camile to get more gauze.

Maybelle turned her attention to Red as he continued speaking.

"You're right. We should send word to Sam. She'll know how to phrase it. Maybe she can convince them to come anyway. Or... maybe they'll let someone visit them, if we could get there..." He stared at the wall, his gaze distant. A few seconds passed before he cleared his throat and continued. "Need to contact her anyway, update her on this mess," he waved a hand through the air, "and let her know we won't be home till tomorrow."

Maybelle nodded. A flurry of thoughts swirled through her mind. "You worried they know about the Warren?" Maybelle stared at her glass of water, fearing the answer.

"They found out about the Sanctuary. That concerns me."

"It's in the city though, could just be watching people coming and going. And you know they've been on the Whites lately."

"True." Red sucked down half of his drink.

"Lift," Mary ordered.

Maybelle lifted her elbow, allowing Mary room to wrap a strip of gauze around the gash which had been oozing blood for the last minute.

"The only way they find out about the Warren is if someone tells them."

"Nah," Red glanced at her, "there's every possibility that we just run into the worst luck. A fly-over while a transport is leaving, carpet-bombing to sniff us out... we're hidden well enough away. But there's always a chance."

Maybelle swallowed. Her head swam; not from exhaustion, but from the throbbing pain in her arm that had finally broken through the adrenaline, the stress of the situation they found themselves in, and worry for Kate, Sam, her daughters, and everyone else she loved who lived in the Warren.

Camile and Mary finished the patch job on her arm. One or two of the cuts might leave a scar, but the rest would heal up perfectly fine. It helped, being an alter *and* a Grey-Star—she healed faster than ordinary people, and faster even than the rest of the alters.

Once everyone had eaten, and Red finished helping with the dishes, they left. Mary hugged her father, kissed her sister's cheek, and handed over the key she'd pulled from under the dumpster.

Maybelle said nothing as the rain outside washed away the tears on Mary's cheeks.

The rest of their trek went smoothly. One of the rebel soldiers pieced a chunk of wiring together in order to power their com unit, Red got word to Sam about the situation, and Maybelle transported the entire group to an empty barn in the White-Star village a few dozen miles from the city.

The musty scent of hay filled her nose. The warm sound of rain on the roof...

She counted, vision blurring near the end. "Fourteen," she murmured, a drowsy smile crossing her lips.

Then her limbs would work no more. She collapsed into a pile of hay, her eyes closing as the bliss of sleep took her.

Chapter Twenty-Four

Present Day - Mid Summer - Abredea - Town Hall

N aya and Jimmy had Spidergreen. By the time Anthony arrived at town hall, Montague had found the slip to test the water, and he and Taz were waiting for the results.

"Let me..." Montague disappeared down the long hallway, leaving Taz and Anthony staring anxiously at a stoppered vial of water. It would turn dark green in a few moments if it was infected.

Taz put a hand on Anthony's shoulder. "They'll be all right. May'll take care of 'em."

Anthony's body trembled as every worst outcome flashed through his mind. What would he do about Jimmy, if Naya... And if Jimmy didn't make it? Naya would die of a broken heart, he knew it. She'd nearly gone when his uncle had passed.

If both of them...

"*Anthony.*"

Anthony jerked, startled by Taz's tone, and the use of his full name.

"Yeh have tah ho... ho... keep it together." Taz's piercing gaze pinned him. Locked him into the present, not some blurry future where his entire family might be dead.

Anthony nodded. "We should ask Montague about filters. If it's—"

"It is." Taz pointed to the vial. The liquid had gone a sluggish green color.

Anthony moved around the counter, sticking his head into the hallway. "Mr. Montague? It's Spidergreen. D'ya have—"

He stopped as Montague bolted out of a nearby door and rushed down the hallway. He strode faster than Anthony had ever seen him move, determination creased into the lines of his face.

"I expected as much," he said in a clipped voice. "However, I just checked the records. Their house *was* marked off last year. Meaning we won't be able to get a new filter from the city."

Anthony's eyes widened, anger flashing through him.

"But," Montague held up a finger, "I happen to have a store of filters for an occasion just like this. Boy," he looked at Taz, "go tell Miss May what we're dealing with. You and I," directing this at Anthony, "will go set up the new filter at the Clearwater home. The sooner it is working, the better. I believe we ought to check with your aunt's neighbors, make sure the Green-Stars didn't skip them as well. Then we will meet at Miss May's to figure out how to best help the lady and her little gentleman."

Anthony stood, slack jawed, as something close to relief washed through his veins. He'd been alone. Since Dave's death he'd been...

He had Naya and Jimmy, and his friends, but that made him the one to fix things. The one to make sure there was food, make sure there was money for things like broken solar panels. That responsibility, the crushing weight of keeping the people he cared about away from harm. Safe. Fed. It pressed on him constantly. To the point where he felt—he knew—there was no one else to turn to.

Anthony swept Montague into a bone-crushing hug. After a second the pressure was returned, and Anthony blinked away tears.

He let out half a laugh as Taz closed in behind him, putting his cheek on Anthony's shoulder and squeezing him as well.

"All right then, gentlemen," Montague wheezed out after a few seconds. "Let's get to it, shall we?"

Three days later Anthony sat at the edge of May's bed. He rubbed his thumb against his palm, pressing until it hurt as he stared at Jimmy's pale face.

Naya was mostly recovered. Her skin was back to its beautiful bronze, her eyes alert when she was awake. She sat up in Juliana's bed to eat, drank on her own, and even managed a trek to the washroom alone earlier that day.

Her son was not so fortunate.

Jimmy's little body, already thin, had become skeletal. Lines of angry black-ish-green crawled up his neck, approaching his cheeks. He rarely woke. Feeding him was a difficult task—they managed to give him broth, but anything solid was a choking hazard.

Juliana's bare feet paced across the slatted wooden floor of May's home. Her tapping fingers kept distracting Anthony. They danced in odd patterns as she grew more and more agitated.

Naya was sleeping, May in the garden, Daisy and Taz at school. Anthony's jaw clenched as Juliana turned at the door and traced her path back to the kitchen.

He opened his mouth, to ask her to stop, tell her to leave, or announce his own departure, he wasn't sure.

"This isn't right," Juliana growled as she slammed her hand onto the wooden table in the kitchen.

Anthony jumped. He turned to her, his brow set in the furrow which hadn't faded for several days. "What?"

"This," she waved her hand toward Naya and Jimmy, "all of it. There is *medicine*. Easily accessible medicine that even Orange-Stars can afford. You don't even have to go to the hospital for it. They *sell* it in Grigoria."

Anthony ground his teeth. "Too bad we can't get to Grigoria. In case yeh 'aven't noticed, we're a little stuck 'ere."

Juliana shook her head. Her chest rose and fell with heavy, angry breaths.

"We don't have to get into Grigoria." She squinted, biting her lip and staring intensely at the wall behind him.

Anthony frowned at her. "What?"

"I need to talk to Montague."

"What?" he asked again.

Juliana redirected her stare at Anthony. "Montague. I need to talk to him." She crossed to the chest at the end of her bed and dug out a pair of faded boots.

"Why?"

"I have a theory," she grunted, pulling on the shoes. "I need to talk to him."

"He's already changed out the filter. There's no medicine at town hall, Juliana."

She turned her icy blue eyes on him, her gaze cold and incredulous. "I know that, Anthony. I'll be back."

"Wait." He rose from the bed, jaw clenching as he glanced down at Jimmy's unconscious form. "I'm comin' with yeh."

She frowned. "I don't need you to."

"I can't... I can't sit 'ere with him like this." Anthony's fist clenched at his side. "I need to get outta the house."

Juliana looked at him for a long moment. Then she turned and walked out the door. Anthony hurried to the kitchen window and called to May, letting her know the two of them were leaving, then went after Juliana.

It took a minute to catch up with her; her strides were as long as his. But he caught a glimpse of pale blonde hair and sped up.

"Why Montague?" he asked as he slowed beside her.

Juliana heaved a sigh and gave him a sidelong glance. "I saw something odd in his office."

She didn't say anything else, and Anthony bristled with frustration. He gave her a few seconds before he spoke again.

"What?"

Juliana glared at him. "I'm thinking, Anthony."

"And I'm askin' questions. Ye'd be able tah think faster if ye'd actually answer them." He didn't mean to sound so harsh, but the stress of the last few days punctuated every word.

Juliana looked as though she might shrink in. Her chest sagged for a split second, face falling. Guilt seeped into Anthony's stomach.

Then she straightened, stopped walking, and turned to face him head-on. The ice in her gaze pierced him and he almost flinched.

"Do you have any idea how many different bacteria live in our world?"

Anthony blinked. "What?"

"How many are harmless?" she asked, waving a hand through the air. "How many kill? How many infect other creatures but leave humans alone? How many live within us, harmless? How many we have antibiotics for? Which antibiotics are useful against which bacteria?"

Confusion swarmed him. The creeping, itching feeling of stupidity that had plagued him throughout his school years came crawling back. He swallowed and shook his head.

"Do you even know the difference between a bacteria and a virus?"

Anthony shook his head again, running a hand through his cropped hair.

"Well, *I* do. Or... did. I'm trying to remember things, Anthony. Things I'm sure they never intended to teach a Moon."

"Things that'll help Naya and Jimmy?"

Juliana sighed again, her fingertips dancing across her thumb. A hurt expression flashed across her face. "Yes. Believe it or not, I want them better too."

Anthony's guilt flared. "That's not—"

"Come on if you're coming," she said as she turned and continued toward the square.

Anthony growled but settled into pace behind her.

Juliana stormed through the front door of town hall, mind working frantically as she pieced together her plan.

Juliana had seen someone die. Once. There had been a horrible accident near her school a few years ago. The Red-Star medics got to the scene as quickly as possible, but not in time to save one of the Orange-Star drivers. Juliana and her friends had watched him take his last breaths.

It happened very quickly. He only suffered for a few minutes.

What was happening to Jimmy was different, and Juliana couldn't do it anymore. She couldn't sit and watch him waste away, moaning in pain each time he approached consciousness. She'd been training to be a researcher; had taken medical classes, shadowed doctors at the hospital, studied chemistry, biology, and anatomy. Maybe Ms. Wolfe would get her back into her old life. Maybe not. Either way, what she had learned would *not* go to waste.

Montague jumped as the door to his office slammed open. Juliana strode into the room, sat in one of the chairs across from his desk, leaned forward, and stared at him.

Anthony entered behind her, gently closed the door, and stood by the window.

"What can I do for you, Miss Juliana, Anthony?" Montague ran a hand over his bald head. The tufts of white just above his ears were rumpled, the baggy skin under his eyes dark with fatigue and worry.

"Do you have news about the little gentleman?"

Anthony shook his head.

"I have a question," Juliana said before he could speak.

She stared at a device on Montague's desk.

She'd been distracted during that meeting with Ms. Wolfe. Understandably so. But she'd also been correct. It was an Artificial. A mountain, made of metal, with a small pool at the bottom. Minuscule balls, small as the point of a pen, flowed like a waterfall from the top and collected in the pool. An internal mechanism made a low rumbling noise as the balls were lifted back to the top of the mountain to continue the cycle.

"Anything, Miss Juliana."

"Where did you get that?" She pointed.

Montague's neutral, tired expression flickered. Something like pride flashed for a second before concern replaced it. "Ahh, I see you've spotted my little toy."

"It's an Artificial." It wasn't a question, yet she needed confirmation. Just to make sure.

Montague studied her for a moment. His gaze darted to Anthony and then back to her. "Yes, it's an Artificial."

"You didn't bring that when you became a White-Star." She gestured to his gemstones. "They wouldn't have let you."

"How do you know?"

She shook her head in agitation. "It's illegal to bring any form of weapon or Artificial into the camp."

Against the wall, Anthony bristled at the name.

Juliana continued. "The Red-Stars at the wall search your things when you come through. They tore everything out of my bag, threw it all across the road." Her throat tightened. "They took the locket my parents gave me, because it had a holo-image of the two of them inside it."

Montague gave her a sad smile. "I'm sure it was a beautiful thing. Expensive, I imagine, coming from a Blue-Star family."

She nodded.

"I'm sure you've worked out by now that's the real reason they took it."

Juliana's jaw clenched, a shiver of anger went up her spine. She nodded again.

Montague ran a finger down the side of his little mountain. It was maybe eight inches tall, truly a marvel of craftsmanship and engineering. It was something Juliana's father might have enjoyed having in his office.

"Where did you get it?" Juliana asked. "When? How?"

Montague clicked his tongue and rose from his chair. He crossed to the door, locked it, then went to the window and pulled the curtains closed. The room plunged into darkness.

A few seconds later he lit the lamp on his desk and sat back down.

Anthony took a seat in the chair beside Juliana. "What's this about, Jules?" he asked.

Juliana raised an eyebrow at the nickname but inclined her head toward Montague. "I have a theory. If I'm right, well..." she faced the older man, "do you have a contact in the city who can smuggle things past the wall?"

Anthony's eyes went wide.

Montague wagged a finger at Juliana, but there was definitely pride on his face now. "I knew you were a smart one. Not *all* who come from the higher castes are." He sighed and leaned back in his chair. "Yes. I—at one time—had a contact within the city. We traded goods, information, and at our last meet I took this little piece as a present to myself for years of hard work."

He looked at Anthony. "Your uncle took a blade. I believe he still had it when he passed."

Anthony leaned in. "My... Dave was part of this? Why didn' I know?"

Montague shrugged. "You were young. He stopped, well, the whole operation stopped, when Miss Naya found out she was expecting Jimmy. Dave couldn't take the risk anymore. You think going where *you* go is dangerous." He gave Anthony a sharp look. "But a White-Star in the city? Even on the outskirts... it's a death sentence if they're found. I imagine that's part of why he didn't tell you."

Juliana grinned as the first piece of her plan clicked into place. "Can you contact them again?"

Montague blinked, eyes widening. "My dear, did you hear what I just said? I never ventured into the city. It is far too dangerous. Dave was the risk taker and even he had a long list of stipulations to ensure we were never caught. We only met twice a year. I don't even..." he frowned for a moment, "I don't even know if they'd still have our means of communication open."

Juliana returned his concerned frown with a hard look. "You can try."

Montague hesitated, watching her closely. Finally, he leaned forward and crossed his hands on the desk. "What are you going to do, Miss Juliana?"

Juliana swallowed. "I'm going to get some *frosted* antibiotics. I'm *not* going to let Jimmy die."

Anthony inhaled a sharp breath.

"Tha's all of it," Anthony grunted, hefting a bag onto May's kitchen table. Everything he owned, anything that might have the slightest value—he'd collected it all. He'd wanted to ask around the shops, the ones who were friendly with Naya, and get more money, more goods. Anything that might be worth enough to save his cousin.

Juliana had stopped him when he mentioned this, reminding him that what they were about to do went against over a dozen laws in both Abredea and the city. Friendly with Naya or not, no one outside of their circle could know what they were doing.

"Good." Juliana said, glancing at the bag as her fingers danced against her thumb.

He stared at her. "Where's your stuff?"

She turned, revealing a small white backpack dangling from her shoulders.

Anthony grimaced. "Tha's it?"

"Most of what my parents packed for me was clothes," she murmured.

They spoke quietly; the hour was late. Naya slept on Juliana's bed, her breath deep and steady. May lay curled around Jimmy. Her hand—the skin so thin her veins seemed to pop like his Spidergreen—rested on his chest, a silent monitoring of his unsteady breathing.

Anthony rolled his eyes but didn't say anything else about her meager offerings. He could only hope they had enough.

Montague had shooed them out of his office, saying he'd contact his man on the other side of the wall as soon as possible. It turned out that meant the very same afternoon. He'd trekked to May's house, led them out to the garden, and explained the plan.

Anthony stared at Jimmy's sleeping form, barely visible in the darkness. Thin strips of moonlight swirled in through the open kitchen window. He wished it was a darker night.

Someone tapped three times against the back door. Juliana cast a glance his direction, he hefted his bag, and the two moved outside. Daisy and Taz stood at the edge of May's garden.

"This is all I could find," Daisy said. She held out her hands, a pile of beaded bracelets and a single gold ring resting against her pale palms.

Taz handed over a bag of coins. Everything he'd saved since he got the job at the bakery.

Anthony's eyes burned. "I can't... I can' thank yeh enough."

Taz jerked his head with a shrug. "What else... else would we do? Let him... let him... let..."

Daisy clasped Taz's hand and looked at Juliana and Anthony. "You'll be safe? Both of you?"

Anthony nodded, but it was Juliana's hand on Daisy's shoulder that seemed to reassure her.

Taz slid his hand from Daisy's and pulled both Juliana and Anthony into a hug. Juliana tensed beside Anthony, her limbs stiff as her breath hitched.

When they separated Anthony looked at his two oldest friends. "It'll be all right. Promise." They stood in silence for a long moment.

"See yeh in the mornin'," Taz said with a gesture to May's house.

Daisy nodded, her arm sliding into the crook of Taz's elbow.

"See you tomorrow," Juliana muttered. She hugged them both again, patting Taz's wild hair and squeezing Daisy's arm.

Then she turned, and without checking that Anthony was with her, began the long walk toward the east end of Abredea.

Montague met them just before the turn to the square. Without a word he gestured for them to follow. They did, moving silently across the cobblestone and packed dirt, not toward the square, but at an angle, toward the wall separating Abredea from the city.

Anthony's heart raced. This was nothing like his trips into the forest—where he was alone. He glanced at Juliana. He'd have to count on her not getting them caught. The idea didn't sit well in his stomach.

They reached the wall and followed it. Lines of trees and brush obscured some of their movements. Most of the homes in Abredea were built away from the cold towering structure.

Montague brushed his hand against the concrete as they went, not as though he was searching for something, more of a caress.

"Do you miss it?" Juliana whispered. She walked between Anthony and Montague.

The older man turned his head, catching sight of his hand. He clenched it in a fist and returned it to his side. A few moments passed in silence as they continued on.

"Yes," Montague finally murmured back, his voice barely audible. "I miss it. On occasion."

"What... if you don't mind..." Juliana hesitated.

"My family were Black-Stars."

Juliana hissed through her teeth. A jolt of surprise went through Anthony. He couldn't picture Montague—the kind smile, thin stature, quiet nature—in the uniform worn by the guards around Abredea. He couldn't picture his uncle's friend sitting down at school next to someone like Captain Steel.

Anthony opened his mouth, unsure what question to ask but full of them, when Montague stopped and held up his hand.

"We're here."

Anthony looked ahead. They'd reached the point where the fence connected to the wall via large metal rings embedded in the concrete. On the other side, miles of empty space greeted them. No trees, only tall grass, and the occasional shrub.

Anthony was familiar with the view; this direction led to the fields. The twenty-minute drive offered little to look at beyond forest and mountains far in the distance.

"What now?" Juliana pressed closer to the wall, putting it to her back as though it might offer comfort.

"Now, we wait. I believe we are a few minutes early, and my guy was always a little late."

"We just stand here, in the open?" Juliana's voice held the slightest of tremors.

Anthony touched her arm. "It's not so open." He pointed to the line of trees blocking their view of the rest of Abredea. This section hadn't been developed yet. Nearly a quarter-mile separated them from the nearest house.

She nodded. "All the same... I don't like standing still."

He offered her a tight smile she probably couldn't see in the dim moonlight. He closed his eyes, pretending he was in the forest for a few brief seconds; the only place *he* was comfortable standing still.

As the minutes ticked by, Anthony kept his gaze moving. Each shadow in the trees, every gust of wind or movement of a night-time critter put him on edge. The longer they waited, the greater the chance a Black-Star would spot them. They patrolled less frequently at night, but Anthony was sure they walked every inch of the fence.

"I wish we'd had more time to plan," Juliana whispered. "Not knowing when the Black-Stars are going to walk by on patrol is..."

"Unsettlin'," Anthony finished.

Juliana nodded.

"They're here," Montague murmured.

Anthony froze, thinking for a second he meant Black-Stars. Instead, three figures approached from the opposite side of the fence. How he hadn't seen them coming, Anthony didn't know. He should have spotted them a mile away.

"Monty, that you?" Came a voice as the three people reached the fence.

"Indeed, Carthik," Montague returned. "It's been a long time."

Carthik let out a low laugh and raised his forearm, resting it against the fence. Moonlight illuminated the shape of his face. A sharp nose, pointed jaw, and a crisp cut of jet-black hair. Gemstones on his temples reflected the light. They seemed to give off a purple tinge, but Anthony couldn't be sure in the dark.

On either side of him a pair of shorter individuals stepped up to the fence. One was a woman, her hair in a high pony-tail, surveying them with an unsettling sneer. The man on Carthik's left was bald enough for the light to bounce off his skull as well as his gemstones.

"I have someone for you to meet," Montague said. He reached back, taking Anthony's wrist and pulling him to the fence. "This is Dave's boy. The one we were telling you about."

Anthony's gut twisted. He focused on the people facing them, forcing memories of his uncle into the deep recesses of his mind. Shutting out the pain.

Carthik's grin fell. The man shook his head. "I was sorry to hear about our friend. I'm glad I knew him."

Montague opened his mouth when Juliana stepped forward.

"Excuse me, all due respect, could this conversation continue at a different location?" Her voice was polite, but Anthony knew her well enough by now to hear the ice in her tone.

"You got someplace for us to go?" the woman beside Carthik asked.

Juliana's eyes widened. A chill ran through Anthony as his gaze swept along the fence; still no sign of the Black-Stars.

Chill turned to heat as the woman let out a string of shrill giggles, the harsh sound making him wince.

"You're easy," she said, scorn in her voice.

Juliana leaned in. "A patrol could come by at any moment. I assume you know that you won't be dealing with Red-Stars if that happens."

Flashes of confusion were just visible in the dark.

Carthik turned his sharp jaw to Montague.

He heaved a sigh. "We have a Black-Star guard now. I assumed you knew."

"I didn't," Carthik growled. "The girl is right. Let's move this along."

The other two moved toward the metal rings joining the fence to the wall.

"You coming this time, old friend?"

Montague shook his head. "I won't risk it. You know that."

Carthik chuckled. "Don't know why you care at this point. Can't get much worse than being stuck in there for thirty years," he tapped his gemstone and nodded toward Abredea, "right?"

Anthony exhaled sharply, a low rumble in his throat. Juliana reached a hand toward him, gently closing her cold fingers around his forearm. He glanced at her. She didn't face him, her gaze locked on what the two smugglers were doing at the wall. After a few seconds, she released his arm.

"You know that's not true," Montague said with less warmth in his voice. "It can always be worse."

"Done," the bald man said.

A second later, he and the woman shoved against the fence. It slid about six inches to the side before it stuck. Anthony stepped around Juliana and gripped the metal. With another hard push, they managed to open a gap large enough for him and Juliana to slip through.

"I can't wait for you," Montague reminded them, his voice low.

Juliana nodded to him. "We remember. If we aren't back by morning—"

"You'll be back." He smiled. "Carthik will make sure."

His friend gave an exasperated look. "You give me too much credit; Dave was always the one who made sure we were safe."

Montague looked at Anthony, now on the other side of the chain-link. "Then you'll be fine."

They tugged the fence back into place. The bald man tucked something into his front pocket. Carthik waved a hand to his people; they turned and walked along the curve of the wall away from Abredea. Juliana followed, her shoulder almost brushing the concrete.

Anthony turned to follow her, barely catching Montague and Carthik exchanging a whispered goodbye.

They walked for about fifteen minutes; far enough that the curve of the wall eventually blocked Abredea from view. Anthony was about to ask how much further they had to go when the woman—leading the way—held up a hand. Everyone stopped.

Light pierced the darkness and Anthony shrank into the wall, on alert. His rapid breaths slowed as he spotted the source, the woman. She held a device in her hand, flat with a screen like those at the school but much smaller. It was the screen that brought unnatural brightness to the night.

Juliana glanced at him, raising an eyebrow. He said nothing. A few seconds later, fear streaked across Juliana's face as a portion of the wall rumbled and groaned. She reached out again, not gentle this time as she gripped his arm and pulled him a few steps away from the noise. Her hand trembled, even with her fingers digging into his skin.

He stared at her, but her gaze was fixed on the wall. A roughly three by six rectangular opening had appeared in the concrete. The darkness of the night was nothing compared to the deep black inside the wall. Anthony glanced at Juliana. She was shaking her head, lips pressed together in a tight line and eyes wide.

Anthony gently prying her fingers off his arm and guided her hand into his. She looked at him, panic in her eyes, but she took his hand and held it as Carthik led the way into the dark tunnel.

"Go ahead," the bald man whispered, gesturing for them to go first.

Juliana squeezed so tightly Anthony lost feeling in the tips of his fingers. He squeezed back, hard enough to distract her. She glared at him, and he almost smiled. Instead, he raised an eyebrow.

Straightening, Juliana jutted out her chin and strode forward. Anthony followed; his hand still clasping her colder, smaller one.

Darkness flooded down around them. The cold and damp, seeping from the concrete, chilled him to his bones. Footsteps behind told him the other two people in their party had entered the tunnel.

Seconds ticked by. Another thundering rumble and grinding sounded, so loud Anthony pressed his free hand to his ear.

All light was gone. All sound—apart from Juliana's rapid breaths and the quick rhythm of his own heartbeat—had ceased. He swallowed, taking a few deep breaths as he reminded himself that Montague had vouched for Carthik; his uncle had worked with these people.

This wasn't a trap.

And yet...

"This way." Ahead of them, Carthik pulled a light orb from his jacket pocket. A dull glow filled the space.

Juliana's tension eased in the presence of the light. She released Anthony's hand, tucking her fingers around the straps of her backpack.

"This is..." Juliana stepped forward, staring around them as Carthik began to walk away. "Different."

She wasn't wrong.

The tunnel in the wall should have been five feet deep. It should have opened on the other side with a screeching grinding sound, revealing the warm night air and whatever horrors the city held in store for them.

Instead, Carthik descended a set of stone steps. His hair brushed against the ceiling as the stairs plunged at a sharp angle, the light receding as he went lower.

Juliana hurried after him, her footsteps echoing. Anthony followed, gliding a hand along the walls which turned from concrete to stone as they descended.

They went down and down. Long minutes passed with only the sounds of their footsteps and the weak glow from the orb to accompany them. Carthik and the other smugglers navigated the uneven stairs as naturally as breathing. Juliana slowed the pace, hesitating at larger gaps between steps, and moving carefully when they passed piles of rubble and stone.

The tunnel was worn, the steps bowed in the middle where years of boots had trod. Anthony ran his fingers through his hair. How often did these people leave the city? He spotted no cobwebs; no layers of dust and grime he'd expect from a place that hadn't been used in seven years. He expected a muskier scent, but the air here was relatively fresh.

When the two smugglers behind him began to speak in hushed tones, Anthony took it as a sign that they were allowed to talk. He hurried around Juliana, falling in a step behind Montague's old friend.

"How long's it been since ye've used this tunnel?"

Carthik barely turned his head. "Since *I've* used it? Six or seven years; my last time was just after your uncle shut things down between us. These two though," he jerked a thumb over his shoulder, "have been going on runs for a few years now."

"Montague said yeh were the top runner. Yeh mostly in charge of things now?" Anthony slowed, letting Carthik squeeze past a chunk of rock before catching up to him again.

Carthik let out a soft laugh. "Nah, I got out of the game. A few years back."

Anthony almost tripped. "Whaddya mean? How'd Montague contact yeh if yer not smugglin' anymore?"

He shrugged. "I still keep an eye out for my old friends. The business and I ended up with different interests. The person handling things now is just as capable as I was."

Anthony frowned at the tension in Carthik's voice. "So, yeh got 'em tah meet with us?"

"Yeah. Least I could do for ole' Monty."

Anthony glanced back. Juliana followed close behind him, her hand brushing the stone to keep steady. Low voices drifted in from behind her.

Anthony's gut roiled. He said nothing else, but gripped his bag with a tight fist as the stairs finally ended in a flat, narrow tunnel.

"Not much longer," Carthik said.

Anthony watched for twists and turns, but the way was straight, oddly lacking in branching tunnels and forks.

Carthik stopped before a massive wooden door. The woman pushed past Juliana and Anthony, pulling a chunky metal key from one of the pockets in her pants. She pushed it into the lock, turned the handle, and swung the door open.

Light hit them, bright and blinding. Anthony blinked a few times. The shapes came together, shadows forming people, tables, chairs, even a couch. The room before them was big. The walls were lined with tables, doors, and archways. A few people milled about, though the area could hold more than the half-dozen currently occupying it.

Orbs of light, larger and brighter than the one Carthik was now sticking back into his pocket, lined the walls, attached by little brackets mounded into the stone and brick. The smell here was more what Anthony had expected so far underground, musky, thick with the scent of people and all their sweat and dirt and soaps and clothes. His nose twitched.

Next to him, Juliana was focused on the tables. She scanned each of them, seeming to ignore the other people in the room.

A person of medium height and build approached; man or woman, Anthony couldn't tell. They wore a loose, plaid long-sleeve shirt and baggy pants. The belt on their waist held a holster. In it was a weapon, similar to the plasma-guns the Black-Stars carried, but not quite the same.

They stuck out a hand, calloused and dirty, to Carthik and the man took it. They shook briefly before he let go.

"Kendra, thanks for doing this."

Kendra, a Green-Star with russet-colored hair shaved close on the left side and braided on the right, shrugged. "It's not all for you, Carthik. I wanted to see what these ones might bring to the table." Their gaze shifted to Anthony and Juliana. Brown eyes looked them up and down, fixing on their temples a few seconds too long. Kendra chuckled. "Doesn't look like much."

Carthik turned to Anthony, his jaw tight even as he smiled. "This one is Dave's nephew. You remember Dave? Got everyone outta the way of that raid bout ten years ago. Or was that before your time?"

Juliana shifted beside Anthony. The smugglers in the room had grouped around them. The wooden door was shut. Juliana's tension radiated in the air between them.

Kendra's smile slipped. They shoved their hands into a pair of deep pockets and shrugged one shoulder. "Well, depths know I ain't as old as you. But I remember Dave. Good man."

Carthik sighed and turned to Anthony. "I've done my part for Montague, but I have to leave."

"What?" Juliana snapped.

Anthony put up a hand, he didn't want her icy tone offending these people. Not yet.

"Yeh aren't stayin' for the trade? Or the return trip?" Anthony murmured. He kept his voice light, soft, masking his rising unease.

Carthik shook his head, his brow furrowed in frustration. At Anthony, or having to leave?

"I have other responsibilities," he said. "Obligations I've had in place for a while. This was last minute, but Kendra has assured me," this he said louder, speaking to the room, "they'll treat you fairly."

"*Fairly?*" Juliana whispered.

Carthik met Anthony's eye. "I am sorry. If it wasn't important..." He grimaced. "Good luck. I hope I see you again." He hesitated before clapping a hand on Anthony's shoulder. "You look just like him, you know, back when he was your age. *Nacra* troublemaker."

Anthony nodded. He swallowed down a lump as his uncle's friend—one he hadn't even known existed—strode down a tunnel leading out of the smuggler's den.

"So," Kendra rubbed their hands together, "Carthik told me you wanted to trade. I know he worked with your uncle and that stuck up *Moon* too scared to leave the camp—"

Anthony's clenched his fists at his sides, knuckles white with the effort of controlling his anger. Beside him, Juliana exhaled, a hiss whispering through her clenched teeth.

"... but that doesn't say anything about you two, or what you have to offer." Kendra walked a slow circle around them.

Anthony stood still, used to this behavior from Red-Stars, but Juliana turned as Kendra did, watching them.

"What exactly are you looking for?" Juliana asked.

The polite tone surprised Anthony.

Kendra shrugged. "Something worth the antibiotics you want. I don't see a lot. Come, let's discuss."

They gestured for them to follow. The smugglers around them returned to their business for the most part; a few kept close eyes on Anthony and Juliana.

Kendra took them to a table in a far corner. On it were little bottles Anthony had never seen before. They looked like the vials May had, but instead of cork stoppers, they had silver caps with grey rubber circles in the center. A row of capped needles sat in a black case beside them.

"These are them. The antibiotics Montague told Carthik you want." They shook their head, planting hands on their hips. "Not cheap," a sigh, "not easy to get on short notice."

Juliana reached out and lifted a bottle.

There was a flurry of movement as people shifted, pulling weapons. Anthony darted between Juliana and the room as several guns, similar to Kendra's, were pointed at her chest.

Kendra stood before them, one hand raised in a placating gesture, the other loosely gripping the gun at their side.

"Easy," Kendra said. "Easy now. Girl's just looking at the merchandise."

Anthony's heart thudded against his ribcage so hard it almost hurt. Nothing about this was going as planned. He waited until the others holstered their weapons before he turned to look at Juliana.

She stood frozen; fingers still gripped around the bottle of clear liquid. She met Anthony's gaze for a brief second. The fear and disappointment in her eyes mirrored his own.

"I need to make sure this is what you say it is." Juliana's voice was steady. She turned to Kendra and shook the little bottle. "What I asked for *is* cheap. It is easy to get. How do I know this is right?"

Kendra gave an easy smile.

The woman who'd met them with Carthik stepped forward, sneering. "It might have been cheap at one time, but you don't live in the city anymore, *Moon*. You don't know what things cost."

Anger heated Anthony's chest. Juliana's breath hitched. From the corner of his eye, Anthony watched her features relax into an easy smile to match Kendra's.

"Where did you get them?"

Kendra reached out and Juliana handed over the bottle. "We have a contact in Grigoria. He happened to have a cache of these set aside." They flipped the bottle over, watching the small bubbles of air flip to the top. "You're lucky."

Juliana turned to the table again, taking another bottle and smoothing down a label on the side that the first didn't have. "This is the right stuff. We need two bottles."

A half-smile crawled up Kendra's face. "We might be able to part with two. Assuming you brought something worth the trade."

Anthony nodded. He hefted the bag and set it on the table next to the needles. "This is what we've got."

Kendra came up beside him, setting the bottle on the table and pushing past Juliana to get a better view of the goods.

Anthony started with his things. A necklace his mother had worn before she died, the only blade he kept in his house—barely two inches long, clothes, knick-knacks, and a small bag of coins which jingled as he set it on the table.

Kendra waited. Anthony glanced at them more than once, hoping to see a light in their eye to suggest they saw something of value. There was nothing, until he pulled out the coins.

Kendra moved forward, lifting the bag, and opening it. They pulled out a coin, held it up to the light, and inspected it closely. After a few seconds, Kendra broke into a derisive laugh.

Anthony swallowed, his chest tight. "I 'ave more." He took Taz's savings from his pocket and held it out to Kendra.

The laughter grew. They shook their head, upending the contents of the bag onto the table. A few coins pinged onto the floor. "This is it? This isn't worth anything *here*."

Juliana clicked her tongue against her teeth, the sound echoing through the room as the laughter faded. "These are the same coins used in Agora. Printed on the same metal. Worth the same amount."

"A kid," Kendra gestured to the loose coins scattered across the table, "could make that much shining shoes at the Grigoria gate for two days."

Anthony closed his eyes. Hopelessness weighed on him. Jimmy's medicine was there. Right there in front of him. His cousin's life was inches away... but impossible to reach.

"What do you *want*?" Juliana's voice was steady. The ice had returned.

"Me?" Kendra put a hand to their chest. "I just want a fair trade. I—"

"How much is a fair trade?" Juliana interrupted. "How many of these," she gestured to the coins, "are worth a little boy's life?"

Kendra's grin widened. "I knew you were holding back. These go for a little over a hundred a piece. I'll give you two for two hundred, even. Cut you a break."

Anthony took half a step back. Two hundred. Naya's busted solar panel would cost fifty. He'd saved up half that.

"Tell you what," Kendra said, running a hand across their chin. "You can have a bottle. One, for all of this." They gestured to the money and goods on the table.

Anthony cast a hopeful glance at Juliana.

She shook her head. "The child needs six doses, two vials worth, or the illness will come back."

Kendra shrugged. "Not much I can do then. Unless you've got something else."

They stood in silence for a long moment. Juliana stared at Kendra, her eyes blazing with fury.

"All right then, time to go." Kendra said.

One of their people stepped forward, grabbing Juliana's arm.

Juliana jerked out of his grip with a snarl. She turned to Kendra.

"I want all of them." Juliana pulled her bag off her shoulder. "All the antibiotics, all the needles, and..." she gazed around for a moment. "Anything catch your eye, Anthony?"

He gaped at her.

She frowned, giving him a meaningful look. "If you want anything, now's the time to speak up."

Kendra's grin was gone. They stared at Juliana and her bag suspiciously. "How do you plan on paying for all of this, little *Moon*?"

Juliana's lips curled into a smile Anthony had never seen before. It was cruel, cold. She reached into the bag.

Around them, fingers twitched towards holsters yet again. Kendra lifted a hand and movement stilled.

Juliana took out a bag smaller than her palm. It was brown, sinched at the top with a piece of string, clearly borrowed from May's stash of fabric in the bottom drawer of her dresser.

Kendra leaned in.

Holding the pouch on her open palm, Juliana pulled the string. The sides dropped. Laying against the cloth were a pair of stunning earrings.

Anthony knew little about jewelry and less about jewelry from the city, but even he could see the worth here.

They were silver. Long and sharp; they steadily widened, then came together in a point at the bottom. Embedded in the silver were blue stones. Ten on each piece. The largest sat near the bottom in the widest part of the earring, with progressively smaller stones crawling up in a line, ending with one barely the size of a pin head at the top.

Kendra's eyes gleamed. Greed emanated from the smile on their face. "Now that's more like it."

"He chooses something too," Juliana demanded. "For these. He chooses something from this room, and we leave with *all* the medicine and everything else he came with."

Kendra jerked their gaze from the earrings. "For those two little things? What—he doesn't pay anything?"

Juliana glared. "You've already played your hand. I know how much these are worth and it's more than every piece of junk you have in this room."

Anthony's eyes widened. He looked around, this time with actual interest, at the items on each table. A compass caught his gaze. It would fit in his hand, the top closed, and unlike the one his uncle had once carried, the glass wasn't shattered. He strode to the table and lifted it. A good weight.

Making eye contact with Kendra, he pocketed it.

They scowled. "You know I could take them from you. Them, the rest of the meager offering you brought. My people could kill you right now and no one would know."

Anthony tensed, as the smugglers—scavengers—around them inched forward at their leader's words.

Juliana cocked her head, her icy smile back in place. "Carthik would know."

Kendra jerked their gaze her way, an eyebrow raised.

"Montague is set to contact him when we return. An update on the child's condition."

Anthony was careful not to look Juliana's way. He kept his attention focused on the people around him, and on keeping the surprise from his expression.

A moment passed. "Fine." Kendra waved a hand. "Take it."

The people around them relaxed, and returned to whatever they'd been doing before Kendra had threatened to murder them.

Juliana glanced at Anthony. He moved quickly, sensing the same urgency she probably felt. He shoved everything he'd brought back into the bag with a brief flash of relief that he didn't have to give up Daisy and Taz's belongings.

Juliana passed him her backpack. He looked at Kendra.

"You have a case or something for these?"

Kendra, who had been staring at the earrings in Juliana's hand, their fingers inching closer as Anthony packed up his things, paused. "No."

Juliana gritted her teeth. "It's a long way back to Ab—to the camp. They're made of glass."

Kendra shrugged. "Be careful."

They reached forward, plucking one of the earrings and gazing, transfixed, at the stones.

Anthony took a few pieces of cloth from his bag—the only untorn shirt he owned and a pair of winter gloves—and wrapped the bottles up as safely as he could. Closing the lid on the needle case, he tucked them all into Juliana's backpack. She reached out her hand and Kendra took the remaining earring.

Juliana turned to Anthony as soon as the silver left her palm. With quick, yet careful movements, she shouldered the backpack and tightened the straps.

"Let's go."

He nodded. None of this had gone the way he'd thought, and he was anxious to be above ground.

"Take them back," Kendra said, leaving the room without a backward glance.

The woman who'd brought them in grunted. "Come." She turned and headed toward the wooden door.

Juliana bristled. Anthony caught the flash of anger just as she took a step forward and opened her mouth.

"Don't," he muttered, putting a gentle hand on her shoulder.

She glared at him, but the extra second between fury and action seemed to give the rational part of her brain enough time to take control. She gritted her teeth but nodded.

The gazes of the rest of the smugglers were on them as they turned and followed the woman out. Anthony was grateful for the darkness as the door closed behind them.

When she lit the orb to guide their way, she put her body between it and them, as though she might be able to leave them in the dark.

Juliana stayed close to Anthony. He glanced at her every now and then, noting a quiver to her lip, and her hands clenched protectively around the straps on her shoulders.

Their guide didn't speak to them once as they walked back to the wall. They reached the top of the stairs, standing together in the cramped space as the woman pulled out her tablet once again and typed a few buttons. Juliana watched her with narrowed eyes.

Anthony winced at the noise as the wall rumbled open, but the fresh air was a welcome relief. He followed as Juliana hurried through the opening. The tension gripping his body eased as he stepped onto soft dirt. He hadn't realized how much he hated the feel of concrete beneath his feet.

Juliana knelt a few yards away, one knee on the ground as her fingers drifted through the long strands of grass. Her shoulders shifted with each deep inhale.

Anthony turned to ask if they were returning the same way. Concrete shifted; the hole in the wall began to close, with the woman still inside.

"Yeh were supposed tah take us back," Anthony growled.

She shrugged. "Figure it out."

Juliana lunged toward the wall. "*Wait.*"

But it was done. The opening was gone except for a faint outline on the concrete.

Anthony and Juliana stood in silence for a long moment.

"Good thing yeh watched 'em take the fence apart," Anthony said. He turned to Juliana. Her expression was a cross between horror and fury.

"What?" He took a step toward her.

She swallowed and gave a vicious shake of her head. "They had a key."

"*What?*"

Juliana turned toward Abredea, staring at the long curve of the wall leading back home.

"That's how they got through the fence. There's a space for a key on this side and it undoes the bolts keeping the fence in place. They had a key..."

"And we don't," Anthony finished.

She nodded.

The darkness of night shifted, sunrise slowly encroaching from the east.

Chapter Twenty-Five

Present Day - Early Fall - Haven

C ho swam through a lake in his dream. An odd thing, as he'd never swum
before. Yet he moved through the water with grace, the sensation soothing
him. He rolled over, staring up with a smile. This was contentment. This was
relaxation. Not a single person within miles; no emotion but his own.

Something flashed into the sky above him. Cho sat up, curious, the magic of
his dream keeping him afloat. He stared into the sky, watching as a mountain
took shape among the clouds, snow-capped, towering, with smaller jagged peaks
framing it.

He coughed. Smoke filled the air around him. He surveyed his surroundings.
The crystal-clear lake, the sandy beach, and the rest of the rocky, tree-lined shore
were all obscured with smoke.

He glanced up again and jerked back in horror.

Flames consumed the mountain. Cho sunk into the water as screams split the
air. Chunks of burning trees splashed into the lake around him. His eyes and
nostrils stung. He coughed again.

And again.

And once more as he awoke, sitting bolt upright in bed; hacking and choking.
The scent of smoke hadn't disappeared with his dream, neither had his fear.

Cho scrambled from his bed, pulling on pants and boots, lacing them up with
nimble fingers and keeping himself as low as possible. Smoke hovered at the ceiling
of his room. Outside his door came the muffled sounds of breaking glass, screams,
and shouting.

Dread flooded his thought as he snatched his watch from the shelf. It was barely
five in the morning. He'd gotten to sleep at three after he'd finished meditating.

Cho grabbed a loose scarf and tied it over his nose and mouth. He reached for
the com device on his bookshelf, his fingers closing around it and a paper crane.

Pocketing them both, Cho hurried to his door and put the back of his hand to
the metal. It was cool to the touch. Whatever this fire was, the heat hadn't reached
this far into Haven. Yet.

He slipped the door open and moved into the hall. The second he stepped into open air a tidal wave of emotion slammed into him. Fear—unrelenting terror gripped him. He took hold of it, following the feeling. It came from the main room, the kitchen, and the bedrooms closest to the entrance to Haven.

He jogged down the corridor, glancing into empty rooms and banging on closed doors. Shouting from the entrance drew him forward. His room was one of the farthest from the entrance to Haven, and it appeared that most of the other children had already woken. He sped up, racing down the hall, taking sharp turns, and nearly tripping over...

Cho stumbled and stared at the boy sprawled across the ground before him. Jacob, the child who glowed. He wasn't glowing now.

A few yards away, coming from the main room, shouting continued, accompanied with screams, crackling of fire, and something banging on metal.

The noise faded into the background as Cho knelt next to the child, his heart sinking. He focused, pressing his fingertips to Jacob's forehead and drawing on his saffron power. He felt—nothing. Not fear, not the flicker of changing emotion he associated with dreaming. Nothing but emptiness.

Cho reeled back, rose to his feet and charged into the main room, horror knotted in his gut.

Ash filled the air. Through the haze, Elaine stood near Sky's garden, surrounded by children with tears streaming and noses running. Sobs echoed through the din. She clutched Sky's hand, kneeling to be heard as she spoke fiercely to the little ones, a golden silk scarf still covering her braids.

Ichi stood in the center of the room, smoke rising around him from burning tables and cushions, shouting directions to the older children with active powers.

Cho hesitated, hastily shoring up the defenses in his mind against the thundering terror running rampant through the room.

Nearly twenty feet above them all, Luna and Nova balanced on the stair railing in front of the massive metal door. Their hands were clenched together, each holding out a free palm toward the door as waves of their power pressed into the metal.

A thundering slam. The door buckled. Luna trembled and Nova shouted down to Ichi.

"*We can't hold it much longer.*"

Two other children around their age raced up the steps and stood in front of the twins. Luke and Kayla weren't related, but both had the ability to create invisible shields in the air. The air around the door swam.

That would buy them a few more seconds.

At the edge of the steps, Jason and Samaira stood ready. Their legs apart, braced, hands up, the air around their arms warping from the heat they produced.

Scorch marks coated the wall leading up to the door. On the ground, three Black-Stars lay—kicked into the corner—unconscious. Cho swallowed, how many had gotten in before the twins pushed them back?

"Claire, ice the stairs, cold as you can," Ichi commanded.

The girl, dressed in fluffy purple pajamas, ran under the steps, planted her hands on the grated metal, and closed her eyes. Frost trailed along the stairs, covering everything in a thin coat of white.

"Jason, Samaira, get ready. They're coming in with something big."

Ichi spotted Cho. His eyes went wide.

Cho hurried to his brother. "What happened? What can I do?" His voice was muffled by the scarf; he pulled it down around his neck.

"You've got to go. Get out of here with the others." He gestured to Elaine and the children, now moving toward the hallway. "The escape hatch, in the back storage room."

Cho shook his head. "What about you?"

Jane materialized beside him, clutching Tommy's hand. "I can get us out," she said. She gave Ichi a hard look. "When it's time, everyone can come to me and I'll pull us," she pointed, "that way. There's a series of tunnels only a few feet through the concrete."

Ichi nodded. "If you're sending Tommy with Elaine, he needs to go now." He glanced back, his face flashing with fear and pain as Elaine's skirts swished around the corner and disappeared.

Cho wondered if she'd already seen Jacob's body.

Tommy whimpered.

"No. He stays with me," Jane growled. She moved away, pulling Tommy toward the handprint wall. They tucked under the stairs beside Claire.

Other older children with active powers took up positions around the room. All eyes were on the door, faces and emotions roiling with determination, fear, and anger. They were ready to fight.

Cho breathed through the influx of emotion, letting the adrenaline flow while clamping down on the fear. "I'm not leaving you," Cho said, catching Ichi's eye.

His brother's newly blue gemstones glinted in the dim light from the orbs and the fires burning around the room. Ichi's jaw clenched. He glanced at the door as another slam reverberated around the room.

Luna and Nova flinched. Luke wavered, his hands falling to his sides for a moment as he struggled to stay on his feet.

"We have *seconds*, Cho. Get yourself to safety."

Shouts sounded from the other side of the door, a furious barrage of angry voices. Cho felt their fury—their hatred.

"No."

Ichi grabbed Cho by his upper arm and dragged him toward the hall. "*Get out.*"

Cho opened his mouth, and then froze. Ichi did the same, eyes briefly unfocused. Behind the door, in the sewers beyond came a wave of relief, a flash of anticipation, a bump of adrenaline. Ichi felt it too.

He turned back to the others. "*Now—*"

An explosion slammed through the room. The door flew open, the top hinge shattering as it swung, knocked into the railing and sending Luna and Nova over the side. The girls fell, their powers spent, and crashed onto the ground.

Above them, Kayla and Luke lay motionless on the landing.

Fire erupted in the doorway. Jason and Samaira moved faster than Cho had ever seen. Their limbs blurred as sphere after sphere of flames slammed into the Black-Stars pouring through the opening.

They came through anyway.

Dozens of heavily armored people stormed the gaping doorway. The first ones on the stairs slid and fell, causing a pile up at the bottom of the steps. More came, hooking ropes to the rails and rappelling to the ground.

In the seconds during which this occurred, Ichi's fear-filled gaze met Cho's. He pushed, a wordless plea, for Cho to follow Elaine and the others. Cho turned for the hallway and froze. His heart plummeted.

Emerging from the dark corridor where Elaine and the children had gone came half-a-dozen Black-Stars, with helmets down, guns drawn, and blood splattered across their armor.

"*No!*" Ichi's scream split the air.

Chaos reigned.

Children fought. Ash and soot, smoke and a barrage of lights clouded the air. A Black-Star threw something. A split second later, another explosion rocketed through the kitchen.

Cho flew to the side, slammed into the wall, and crumpled to the ground. Dazed, he shook the ringing from his ears. Scrambled to his feet.

Searched for his brother.

Spotted Ichi crouched next to a bleeding child as a Black-Star raised his gun. Cho opened his mouth. The scream stuck in his throat as the trigger was pulled.

It wasn't the plasma bolt he expected. Instead, a small projectile buried itself into his brother's back. Ichi's body jerked forward, eyes wide, mouth open in shock as he collapsed.

Cho couldn't breathe. Couldn't move. Couldn't... couldn't...

"*Cho!*"

He flinched.

"*Cho!*"

Across the din of screams, shouting, gunfire, and explosions, Jane's harsh, demanding voice broke through. Time slowed as he looked up. She stood under the stairs, Tommy tucked behind her legs. Beside her, Claire lay slumped against the wall.

Cho met Jane's eye through the smoke, through the panicked bodies. She jerked her head toward the hall to Ichi's study. Every piece of him trembled. No part of him knew what to do. He was frozen, stuck.

Then, between him and Jane, Luna and Nova shifted on the ground. They were alive. Moving. They needed help.

Time returned to normal. Cho met Jane's gaze. He nodded.

He ducked under an outstretched Black-Star arm, swerved to the side, and sprinted across the room toward the twins. In the corner of his eye, he spotted Jane and Tommy moving *through* the stairs, hugging the wall as they crept toward the study.

Cho reached the girls, skidding to a stop and kneeling beside them. "Can you get up?" he demanded.

Nova stared up at him, her eyes unfocused. Blood dripped down one of her braids.

"*Nacra.*"

Beside her, Luna braced against the ground, pushing herself to her knees and then to her feet. "I'm up. Help me with her."

They hefted Nova between them, staying as low as possible.

Children fled. The ones still standing sprinted into the hallway, desperate for escape. Black-Stars pursued, moving through Haven, hunting people down, and dropping them with their new weapons.

Fire raged. Something popped and the kitchen exploded again. Flaming rubble rocketed outward, bricks slamming into Black-Stars and Haven kids alike.

Grunting, Luna and Cho carried Nova through smoking rubble, moving parallel to the stairs as they hurried toward the study.

Samaira and Jason had been pushed back, lost the ground at the foot of the stairs. They'd been cornered in Sky's garden. Plants burned around them. Dozens of scorched Black-Star bodies littered the ground before them, writhing and screaming in agony.

Jason cackled and said something to his sister as he shot off another bolt of flames. She met his grin with her own, blue fire dancing in her hands.

She winced.

The fire in her hands died as she lifted her fingers to her neck. They came away dark. Bloody.

Jason screamed.

He screamed and screamed as she fell. The fire vanished from his hands as he caught her body, cradled her in his arms as Black-Stars bore down on them.

Cho and the girls reached the foot of the stairs. Pausing, he watched, heart already shattered and somehow still breaking as Jason held his sister. As he lowered her to the ground and stood again.

A wave of fury slammed across the room. The girls were unaffected, but the force of it knocked Cho backwards. He lost his grip on Naya, cracking into the rail of the stairs with a yelp of pain. Luna crumpled under Nova's weight.

The shields in Cho's mind shattered as Jason's rage hit him. His power exploded; saffron tendrils now free from restraint latched onto the anger and pain Jason felt. Cho's own hurt, his own fury, became indistinguishable from the pounding waves coming off the flamethrower. He rose, fists clenched as a blinding need to destroy consumed him.

A cry of pain, and a piercing fear from behind him broke through the encompassing rage. Cho glanced through the slatted stairs. Claire sat slumped against the handprint splattered wall. Blood oozed from a gash on her arm, dark red dripping down to her frozen fingertips. She cried out again, tears pouring down her cheeks.

"*Shit*," Cho muttered. Jaw clenched, he darted a glance back at the girls, then moved. Ducking back the way they'd come, he whirled under the stairs and slid one arm under Claire's back, the other hand scooping her knees. With a grunt of effort and aided by the strength of Jason's rage, he lifted her and darted back to the girls.

Luna stared at him, bright eyes shining with tears as she struggled to hold up her sister. Nova stirred in her arms. Cho couldn't carry them both.

Still beside his sister's body, Jason moved like a force of nature. A whirling tornado of flames. Bodies dropped throughout the room, scorched flesh melting and burning. Acrid swirls of smoke rose from armor and skin alike.

But the spheres of fire shrank. Jason's fury had fed an eruption of power, but he'd already been so drained. Black-Stars approached from across the room, fear of the flames no longer keeping them at bay.

"*Jason*," Cho called, grunting as he tried to shift Claire so he could help with Nova as well.

Tears streamed down Jason's face, evaporating from the heat of his skin before they fell. His gaze flicked in Cho's direction before throwing another burst of flame. It lodged into the crook of a Black-Star's neck, the man falling to the ground as he clawed at the flames in his armor.

"*Jason*," Cho shouted. He inched forward, struggling under Claire's weight. "*Help me.*"

Jason snarled. He glared at Cho, all the color and life drained from his face. There was only darkness in his gaze.

Another wave of Jason's wrath flared out and Cho's power pounced, consuming the emotion like a starving beast.

Jason half-turned, shooting off another even smaller ball of flame. This one struck a Black-Star's shoulder, leaving a scorch mark on the uniform.

"*Depths*. Jason, please." Cho edged closer.

Luna was sobbing now, pulling her sister an inch at a time toward the study as she sucked in shaky, helpless breaths.

Jason flinched. His fists, covered in soot almost the color of his skin, clenched. He stared, transfixed, down at his sister.

"*Jason*." Desperation and fear filled Cho's voice. Jason met his gaze. "I need you. Help me. *Please*."

Jason slumped. With one last glance at his sister's motionless body, he turned away.

Cho exhaled in relief as Jason hurried to Luna and Nova. Black-Stars continued to pepper them with projectiles, but between Jason's flaming spheres and Luna pushing them back in the air, none reached their target. Cho scrambled ahead, Jason and the girls on his tail.

They swung through the door. Jason kicked it closed behind them. Luna left Nova to him as she hurried behind Ichi's desk to shove it against the door.

Another burst of relief hit Cho at the sight of Jane and Tommy. They'd waited.

Jane gripped the edge of the desk, grunting with effort as she and Luna wedged it against the door.

"You can take us all?" Cho asked, his words falling over themselves in his hurry. He sagged against the far wall, adjusting his grip on Claire.

Jane nodded and put a hand around Claire's ankle. Tommy grabbed his sister's hand. Luna gripped Jane by the arm.

Something slammed against the wooden door.

Jason stood by the desk, shaking with anger and fatigue. Nova lay slung over his shoulder. He stared at Cho, agony etched across his face.

Cho felt it too, crawling through him, threatening to engulf him in despair. Threatening to drag him into a pit he'd never escape from.

Another thunderous crack as something hit the door.

His voice shook as he stared at Jason, tears burning his eyes. "We have to get them out."

Jason said nothing, but he strode forward and wrapped his dark hand around Cho's forearm.

Cho nodded to Jane. They stepped forward as one, melting into brick as the door splintered open behind them.

Nearly an hour later they emerged into the blazing light of dawn shining on Agora. Cho blinked back the brightness of the morning. He reached down, grunting with effort as Jason passed him Claire. Jane and Luna helped Nova—now conscious—from the grate in the ground, and Tommy scrambled up after them. Jason came up last and slid the cover back into place.

They stood in silence. Cho cradled Claire; her arm had stopped bleeding, but the wound was deep, red, and inflamed. Jason's cheek was sliced open. Bloody stains marked his grey shirt. Nova slumped against her sister, blood matted into her honey-colored hair. Cho sported a massive bruise across his back, the pain barely noticeable with everything else going on. Only Jane and Tommy seemed unscathed, though Tommy had yet to stop crying.

Cho glanced around. At the end of the alley they'd come up in, people bustled about their business. A man pushed a cart of melons down the street. Children scampered by, dressed in Green-Star school uniforms, bags thudding against their backs.

Above them, birds perched on the edges of the rooftops. Laundry hung from fire-escapes. Voices filtered down from windows. The movement and sound of early morning life surrounded them.

Life.

As though the entire world hadn't just ended.

As though nothing had changed since yesterday.

"Can we... have a pause?" Cho stammered.

Jane turned her furrowed gaze toward him. She glanced down at Tommy, nodded, and proceeded to sit on the ground and pull her brother into her lap.

Cho shifted, moving to set Claire against a wall. Jason stepped forward, and without a word lifted the girl from Cho's arms. He didn't look at him either when Cho murmured his thanks.

Cho sucked in a breath as the fragments of his power flitted around in a frenzy. It wanted more. Wanted to consume and feel every ounce of pain emanating from the people around him.

Jason's anger got him through the sewers, but that was ebbing now. Replaced with the same grief Cho felt within himself. A grief echoed by everyone around him.

The pain of it pressed in, scrambling through the meager defenses he'd tried to build during their trek to the surface. Cho leaned against the wall and sank down, knees cradled to his chest as he closed his eyes and tried to focus.

A choked sob escaped him as Ichi's face flashed through his mind.

He breathed, used the methods Elaine had taught him. He saw again her disappearing into the hall and the Black-Stars emerging, covered in blood.

Grief pushed against him, prying at him, pulling him apart.

"We have to go." Luna's voice broke the silence.

Cho looked up. Nova leaned against her sister. Their matching lavender dresses were torn and burned, ragged ends falling just past their knees. Nova's left ankle was swollen, dark purple and black.

Luna met Cho's gaze. "Someone's watching," she murmured. She glanced up.

Cho followed her gaze. Above them, in a third-floor window, a young woman stared at them.

Cho rose. He'd thought of a place between bursts of panic as they wound through the sewers. "This way," he muttered. He turned and walked down the alley.

Jane caught up with him, Tommy riding piggy-back with his head drooping on her shoulder. "Where are we going?"

Her sharp voice was dull, muted with sadness.

"There's a place in Grigoria."

She gave him a skeptical glare.

Cho shook his head, his eyelids drooping. He forced them open. "It's under construction. Since that fire a few years ago."

"It'll be crawling with Green-Stars."

"No." Jason stepped up on Cho's other side. He cradled Claire like a small child, her head pressed to his chest. Sweat beaded on his forehead. The slice in his cheek looked worse up close. "It was an Orange-Star training center. They did a temporary move to their own district while they fix it up, but everyone's been dragging. They don't want the Orange-Stars back in Grigoria every day."

Jane snarled. "Assholes."

Cho rubbed his forehead. "Yeah, but it gives us somewhere to go."

She met his gaze, and he thought maybe she understood. Her walls had been down since their escape, all her emotions flowing free. Her jaw clenched, eyes squinting closed for a brief second as her mental defenses returned. Not quite the unflinching shield she'd had before, but one less person's grief chipping away at him was a noticeable difference.

Jason shifted Claire and glanced at Cho. "You need a hat."

Cho's hand flew to his ruined gemstone. He'd forgotten. "Frost."

"It's fine," Jason muttered. "Side pocket." He moved closer to Cho.

Gritting his teeth—being this close to Jason sent unbearable waves of pain through Cho's already trembling body—he stepped forward and took the brown-knit cap from Jason's pocket. He backed up quickly, nodding thanks and moving to walk ahead with Jane.

He ran his fingers across the row of embroidered mountains marking the front of the hat. Elaine's embroidery. Cho's eyes burned, but there were no tears left in him.

They walked in silence. Jason fell back to keep an eye on the twins as they traversed the busy streets of Agora. Even with their scorched clothes and injuries, not many people gave them more than a second look. For the most part, they blended with the growing crowd of lower-class Stars going about their daily lives.

"You should tell the others," Jane said.

Cho jerked, glancing sideways at her.

"Remind them," she clarified. "Remind them about their mental defenses. If mine were down, everyone else's are too." She looked to him for confirmation.

He nodded.

"You can't be feeling all of this at once." Jane's eyes widened. "Losing..." She hesitated, biting her bottom lip before her gaze hardened again. "Losing what we just lost... I know what *I'm* feeling is almost too much. You're dealing with six times that."

"It doesn't matter." Cho shook his head, tugging at the side of his shirt.

"How doesn't it matter?" she demanded. "You have to be *capable*, Cho. You have to be able to lead us—"

Pain hit him. A blade, piercing his heart and dragging across his chest. "*Jane,*" he snapped. "I can't..." he sucked in a shuddering breath. "I can't..."

She glanced at him, a brief look before focusing on the uneven bricks beneath her feet. "All right."

Jane hitched Tommy up—the boy had fallen asleep, one more set of emotions Cho didn't have to feel in the moment—and strode ahead. Cho fell into the middle, offering once to take Claire from Jason, but not pushing the matter when the man said no.

It took over an hour for them to reach the correct gate into Grigoria, and another thirty minutes to walk through glistening clear and white malls and restaurants and offices until they reached their destination. Long rows of short buildings made up the majority of the block. They were metal and concrete, lacking the massive windows and whitewash common in Grigoria. Some were warehouses, holding construction materials, textiles, anything the lower castes needed for their various jobs. Others were office buildings where Green, Purple, and even Red-Stars completed the majority of their clerical work.

Cho slowed the group, skirting the buildings to avoid being seen. At the far end of the block, across from a park with rolling green hills and clusters of flowering trees, sat two burnt-out husks of concrete and wood. The acrid smell of smoke had long since washed away. Most of the roof had caved in, putting strain on the second floor, and leaving areas where access was only given to those small enough to crawl through crumbling tunnels. A few signs had been stuck to the walls, warning people to stay away in case of total collapse.

A row of black birds perched on the edge of the rooftop. A hawk flew overhead, and the crows took off, soaring in an arcing circle as Cho and the others approached the building.

Cho leaned into the closed door. It stuck. He surged back and slammed his shoulder into it. Wood splintered as the door swung open.

A plume of dust and ash flew into the air. Rodents scurried to safety as everyone moved through the doorway.

Luna and Nova moved to sit, but Cho held out a hand. "Wait, let's get further in. Away from the door."

Luna glared at him, an expression he wasn't used to on her soft face but helped Nova limp deeper into the building. They left a trail in the soot and dirt on the ground.

They explored for a few minutes, finally settling on a small room with only one window and no gaping holes in the ceiling. Cho closed the door. A stone-like weight dropped into his gut as the latch clicked shut.

Jason lowered Claire onto a faded couch and sank to the ground in front of it. He pulled his knees to his chest, head bent, face hidden from the room.

Luna and Nova huddled together in a corner. Jane went to them after laying Tommy on the ground—the boy curled into a tight ball and continued to sleep—and examined Nova's ankle for a moment before returning to her brother.

Cho watched them all. The room was full. So full.

Tommy's flickering emotions lapped against him like soft ripples in a slow-moving stream. However horrific their last few hours had been, at least his dreams were gentle.

Jane, arms folded over her brother's chest, maintained her shields. Kept her emotions from reaching him. But he saw them, in the shaking of her shoulders, the muffled breath sucked in like she was drowning.

Nova's pain sweltered out like waves of heat, a suffocating combination of fear, sadness, and anxiety.

Cho went to her, each step making him want to wince, and looked at her leg. She groaned as he felt for breaks; Luna held her still.

"Not broken," Cho murmured.

"That's what Jane said too," Luna whispered. "Are you sure?"

Cho nodded. He could explain that Ichi had taught him how to find broken bones. That his brother had given him books, shown him lectures, on the human body and emergency medical care. He didn't. Because thinking about his brother...

"Are you..." Luna stared at him. "Cho?"

He didn't respond. Just lifted Nova's ankle—as gently as possible—and placed a loose couch cushion under it. "Keep it elevated."

He moved to Jason, bending around him to get a look at Claire's arm. Blood wept from it, slow and seeping. Unlike Tommy, Claire's dreams were unsettled, disturbing. Fear hit Cho in the gut. He swallowed it down.

A break was coming. A shattering of his entire being, approaching from the distance. He knew it. Saw it.

But they had to be cared for first.

With nothing else to use, Cho ripped a strip of cloth from his shirt. He tied it, tight enough that she flinched in her sleep, over the wound. A few seconds passed and she settled into more restful dreams.

Cho backed away. Being so close to Jason was... agony. He hurried to the door. Stooped. One hand clutching his stomach.

"Where are you going?" Luna hissed.

"I need..." Bile bubbled up in his throat. "I'll be back."

Cho rushed out the door, falling into the hallway and slamming into the far wall. Beige paint cracked under his shoulder. He righted himself and ran.

He made it to a room several yards down the hall when he couldn't hold it in anymore. He vomited, choking out everything in his stomach, dry retching when there was nothing left.

On his knees, face flushed and teeth chattering from the chill in his chest. Everything wrong and broken and gone.

Gone.

Cho collapsed to the side, barely registering the impact on his already sore shoulder. He closed his eyes willing—begging—for sleep to take him. Sleep or death.

Anything to get away from this.

Light splintered through a half-cracked window. Eventually... after a long time of listening, to the world outside, to the shattering of his heart, to the stillness of this broken building and his broken mind... he sank into darkness.

Chapter Twenty-Six

Present Day - Mid Summer - Outside the Wall and Abredea

G rey light permeated the landscape. The sun had yet to rise, and even when it did, towering city buildings would keep its rays from reaching them for a while longer.

Anxiety creeped up on Juliana as she stared at the solid concrete wall before them. The wall that separated her from the life she should have had, from her parents.

Her stomach cramped with pain as she pictured their faces. She'd thought about it, while they were in the smuggler's hideout; she'd had a brief, foolish notion to run through one of the tunnels until she reached fresh air. Find her way home. Greet her parents as they rose for the day. Be held by them again.

Beyond the stupidity of such an action, there'd also been the issue of Jimmy's medicine. The backpack weighed on her. Not because it was heavy, but because if the vials broke, or if she and Anthony didn't make it back to Abredea, the boy would die.

She jumped, startled as a large bird soared overhead with a loud cry. Putting a hand to her fast-beating heart, she turned in a slow circle.

They stood at the wall, nearly half a mile from the fence they couldn't get through. In the far distance, the edge of the forest was visible across the gently rolling hills of waving grass. Beyond, she could still see the tops of the mountains. The edges of a plan began to form in her mind.

Anthony cackled, nearly doubled over with silent mirth.

Juliana squinted, planting her hands on her hips. "What in the *depths* is so funny?" she demanded.

"Tha' asshole," Anthony wiped a tear from his eye, "she really did wanna kill us."

"How is that *funny*? We're stuck out here. Stranded with no way home. If we get caught—"

He held up a hand, waving her off. "Just 'cause *they* only know one way in and out of Abredea, doesn' mean there *is* only one way in and out."

A slow smile snuck across Juliana's face. She tilted her head, hands going on her hips as she asked, "How *do* you get in and out for those hunting trips?"

Anthony clicked his tongue with a mischievous grin. "Hows about I show yeh?"

She couldn't help it. A euphoric rush of accomplishment hit her. Laughter built, bubbling in her chest until it burst from her. They'd done it. Gotten the medicine. And Anthony knew how to get them back into Abredea.

Anthony watched her with a bemused expression as her laughter faded into giggles and then a heavy sigh.

"What?"

"I 'aven't heard yeh laugh like tha'," he said.

Heat filled Juliana's cheeks. Embarrassment brought reality back into sharp focus. She straightened and cleared her throat. "We still have Black-Stars to contend with. How often do they patrol once the sun rises?"

"Every couple of hours, but tha' isn't the biggest problem."

Juliana frowned. "What is?"

Anthony gestured to the open expanse before them. "We can't get where we need tah go by followin' the fence. It's too open, 'specially now. If a patrol didn' spot us, chances are one of the field hands would."

Juliana reached her hands up, running long fingers through her hair as she pulled it back into a tail. "I thought the fields were miles away. Transports take them, right?" She closed her teeth around an elastic band on her wrist, brought it to her fingers, and tied her hair up and out of her face.

Anthony nodded, running a hand through his own shock of jet-black hair. "Yeah, but the road is right there." He pointed out, into the grass.

"I don't see anything." Juliana squinted into the distance. There was nothing between them and the tree line.

"It's there. And judgin' by the sun, the first shift'll be headin' out any minute."

Juliana's eyes widened. She glanced around, calculating the distance between them and the nearest cover with rising fear. "We're at least a mile and a half from the woods. Where are we..."

Anthony gritted his teeth. "Exactly. Once they start the shifts there's people travelin' tha' road nonstop."

"And we'll be in the open the entire time."

He nodded.

Exasperation rose in her. She heaved a sigh and gestured across the long stretch before them. "We should *go* then, right?"

Anthony looked up at her, surprise in his dark eyes. "Yeah," he said slowly.

"How long do you think we have?" Juliana asked, already striding away from the wall. She cut a diagonal through the grass, aiming for a spot between the fence line they still couldn't see, and the forest.

"Ten minutes maybe. Maybe less."

"Frost." The tips of the grass caressed Juliana's thigh. "Any chance we can hide in the grass?"

Anthony caught up with her and shook his head. "Like I said, they'll be movin' along the road all day. Black-Stars for the most part, patrollin' the route tah the fields. 'ere, this way." He pointed and angled them straight for the trees. "Faster. When we get tah the tree line, we'll be able tah move into the forest. From there we can get tah the fence with some actual cover."

Juliana followed, breaking into a jog beside him. Her throat caught. Nerves tingled at the back of her neck and the base of her spine. "*Into* the forest?"

He flashed a grin. "Yeh scared, or excited?"

Juliana swallowed and rather than answering, sped up. They ran, making a beeline for the trees. Sweat beaded on Juliana's forehead, a combination of fear and exertion making her heart slam against her chest. The backpack thumped softly against her spine.

Juliana had been wanting to be outside that fence since the day she'd entered Abredea. This wasn't exactly what she'd had in mind.

"They told us stories," she huffed, focusing on the ground beneath her feet and not looking to see if Anthony had heard her. "Stories about the wild, about why people only live in the cities now. They said it was dangerous. Deadly. Angry, aggressive animals. Everything trying to hurt you."

The two of them had kept pace so far, so she heard Anthony's laughing scoff. She bit her lip, immediately regretting it as the jolt of her running plunged her teeth into the flesh.

Any response he might have given beyond the derisive laugh was cut short as they reached what was indeed a road. Juliana understood why she hadn't seen it before. Flat, smooth dirt-colored pavement, it was nearly invisible until up close. The waving strands of grass on either side ensured it.

Juliana glanced behind them. They were maybe halfway between the wall and the forest. To the north, the road continued on as far as she could see, leading to the fields to the south, she could just make out where it connected with the fence.

And in squinting to see that, Juliana also saw movement.

She paused, for the briefest of seconds, and swung the backpack around, so it rested against her chest. Then, lungs already burning, she picked up the pace. Anthony did as well. His strides matched hers, their legs almost the same length, as the two of them raced toward the trees.

Behind them, splinters of sunlight began to paint the grey landscape in beams of gold.

Juliana swallowed hard. She sucked air in through her nose, trying not to let panic overtake her. She couldn't pump her arms like Anthony did. Her hands were clutching the backpack, preventing the glass vials from banging into each other. The trees were there, growing bigger.

She might have paused at the edge, where tiny saplings of pine and oak stood only a few feet tall, hoping to crawl out from the shadow of their brethren.

She didn't.

As Anthony pulled ahead, leading the way through a gap in the towering trees, she stayed on his heels, watching the ground so she didn't trip, focusing solely on getting out of sight.

Then they were.

Almost instantly, the unnerving feeling of being exposed was replaced with claustrophobic darkness. Juliana stopped when Anthony did and doubled over, sucking down deep breaths as her heartbeat returned to a steady pace.

Then she looked up.

She'd been to Mendax, the massive recreational site for the top three castes. She'd gone on hikes through perfectly manicured forests—every tree trimmed to just the right height, brush and detritus swept away so the ground was clear, trails marked with ropes, stones, and handholds, and beautiful animals bred to give hikers something to look at in awe as they followed the guide.

This... this wasn't that.

Sunlight filtered through the canopy. Trees entwined in and around each other, their leaves glowing green as the sun hit them. Juliana stared up, circling in place. Lost in the thin river of blue above her, peaking through gaps in the branches.

She didn't know all their names, but she recognized many of these goliaths. They were the untamed, untrimmed versions of the trees she used to play under as a child.

Beneath her feet was soft ground, a coating of leaves and pine needles, churned dirt, loosened by constant growing things plunging out of it. Her shoes sank half an inch into the mulch.

Where light reached the forest floor, emerald shoots of green erupted from the earth. Flowers in the grass arched toward the morning sun; more still twined around the trees, along with vines and ivy which crawled up and around branches, stretching between the trunks like rope bridges.

Juliana's breath caught as she watched a small furry animal scurry up the trunk of a nearby towering oak. It disappeared behind a gnarled branch. Further up, birds twittered in the leaves, hidden from sight but not from sound as their songs filled the air.

"Not quite wha' they tell yeh, is it?" Anthony asked, his voice soft, somehow matching the frequency of the forest.

"No. It's not," she breathed.

Anthony grinned. "Come on. We've got a long way tah go, and it'll be slow movin'. I don' 'ave any trails this close to the city."

Juliana nodded, still enraptured by the beauty around her. A bird, black with a red chest, hopped onto a nearby branch and tilted its head at her quizzically. After a few seconds, it lifted off and Juliana gasped at the flaming feathers under its wings.

Realizing Anthony had continued without her, she hurried to catch up. She watched the way he walked. He made noise, it would be impossible not to, but the crunch under his feet belonged here. It matched the subtle sounds made by the creatures around them.

Juliana, with her stomping boots, tripping feet, and unsteady balance, felt like an intruder.

They stuck near the edge of the forest, inside the tree line, but close enough to see and hear when the first rumbling transport truck carried a shift of White-Stars to the fields.

Anthony threw up an arm and Juliana froze. Around them, small animals scurried to safety. Birds flew higher into the trees.

Three trucks passed by, followed by an armored Black-Star vehicle.

Anthony met Juliana's gaze, his dark eyes glinting in the morning light. "We should get a little deeper into the forest. It'd be hard tah spot our movement here, but the further in we go the safer we'll be."

Juliana swallowed.

Anthony rolled his eyes. "I promise its safe. I 'aven't seen a wolf out here since before my uncle died. And tha' was miles and miles away. Further than the fields."

The eye roll sent a surge of irritation through Juliana. She glowered at him. "Fine then. Let's go." She shifted the bag and, with a quick check of the contents—no broken bottles that she could see—moved it to her back again.

Jaw clenched; she followed Anthony as he carved a path through the dense trees. They'd walked in silence for several minutes before Juliana's frustration ebbed. This was his reaction to her unease. Laughter, eye rolls, exasperation.

What would hers be, if he were thrust into the city with no knowledge, no understanding, and only relying on the stories he'd heard growing up?

Juliana caught up with Anthony as he paused, marking a tree with the knife he'd brought to trade.

"They told us the same things about Abredea," she murmured.

"What?" Anthony looked at her.

She bit her lip. "They told us things that aren't... aren't true. About Abredea."

He stopped abruptly, staring at her as understanding blossomed and a scowl took the place of his usual easy grin. "They said we're dangerous? Aggressive?"

"Violent," Juliana added with a shallow nod. "Ready and willing to hurt you at the slightest provocation."

He tilted his head.

"The slightest wrong," she explained. She ran her hands up and down her suddenly chilly arms. Shame and guilt swelled in her stomach. Shame for believing such things; guilt for joining in as one of the voices so often condemning people she'd never known.

A grimace crossed Anthony's face, a flicker of sadness in his eyes, followed by anger. He opened his mouth, clenched his hand into a fist, closed his mouth again, and turned to continue on their unbeaten path.

Juliana followed him in silence, keeping up as well as she could. The critters scurrying in the underbrush and the birds flitting through the trees distracted her from her footing.

After the fourth time she tripped and almost fell before catching herself on a branch, Anthony turned with a frown on his face.

"Do yeh wanna slow down?"

His voice, the dancing lilt she'd grown accustomed to, was different. Cold and monotone. She shook her head.

"I'm fine. There was a bird."

Anthony's eyes narrowed in an incredulous expression. "Yes." He turned and kept walking.

"Well," Juliana huffed. Heat rose up in her cheeks. "I've never seen one like it. Gold on its head and blue strips. I thought I saw more gold under the wings but I couldn't get a good look until it moved again so—"

"So yeh watched it until it flew."

"Yes." She pursed her lips.

"Yeh know, we have birds in Abredea too. Yeh've seen 'em in the trees."

Juliana grimaced, clenching her jaw. "Little brown ones, but this was different."

He stopped. Juliana almost walked into him. She halted, backing up a few steps and watching him.

"'aven't you ever," Anthony turned to her, one arm holding the bag slung over his back and the other gesturing to the trees around them, "left the city?"

"Yes." Juliana's mouth twitched to the side as irritation thrummed through her. "But we go," she sighed, "we *went* to places for Blue-Stars."

He gave a slight shake of his head and waved his hand for her to continue.

"Well, they have different..." she groaned. "I don't know how to explain it without it sounding completely ridiculous, which I realize now it is." She clenched her teeth. "They breed animals and birds so there are colorful things to look at."

Anthony raised an eyebrow, lip curled. "O'course they do."

Juliana frowned. "Listen, Anthony, I wasn't trying to offend you before. When I said..."

Anthony shook his head, his expression shifting to something more pained, hurt. "Yeh didn' *offend* me. I didn' know they said those kinds of things."

"I'm sorry," Juliana muttered.

He gave her a long look. Leaves rustled around them as the sun arched away from the horizon.

His brow furrowed as he studied her face. "Did yeh think I was gonna hurt yeh? That night we first met?"

Juliana pinched her lips together, willing them not to quiver as her nose itched and tears burned at the edges of her eyes. "I was..."

She struggled for the words; remembering the ache in her heart as she'd approached the fence. Knowing the punishment for going beyond it and not caring. Maybe some part of her wanted to get caught, wanted to be thrown in a cell to rot her life away.

Juliana swallowed. "I wasn't... I didn't care enough to think about it."

"Didn' care enough about what?" His lips parted; concern etched in his frown.

Her chin trembled. She didn't answer.

"Were yeh..." Anthony exhaled through flared nostrils, glancing around them as though searching for something to make the conversation easier. "Are yeh *scared* of me?"

Juliana shook her head, catching his gaze and holding it. "No. I'm not."

She read on him in that moment, the pain of what she'd said. The hurt she'd caused him. Her hands clenched around the straps of her little white backpack. The one holding medicine for Anthony's nephew. Medicine he'd risked his life for. Just as he risked his life each time he went hunting for his friends, his family.

"Were yeh?" he demanded softly.

"Maybe," Juliana replied. She held up a hand as he opened his mouth. "I don't remember being scared of you. All I remember is the anger I felt. The betrayal." She sniffed. This had never come up in her long conversations with Daisy. Perhaps because they'd been so close to the city. So close to the life of constant surveillance Juliana had been so used to.

Anthony nodded, watching her with an intensity that made her fidget. Her fingers tapped against her thumb. She shifted her weight, taking a few steps and waiting until Anthony joined her. They walked on and she found the words came easier while she was focused on her footing.

"I did everything right." The sentence felt real. True. For all the times she'd wracked her brain to figure out what her failing was, she *hadn't* failed. "I scored highest on almost every exam. I never stayed out after curfew. I never pulled pranks with my friends, against *any* caste." Her jaw clenched. Before her, the ground slopped down. Sticks and leaves crunched under her feet.

"They told us from the first year of school what would happen if we misbehaved. What it was like in the camps. The kind of treatment we could expect as Star born. I followed *every* rule. Every..." Her lip curled into a snarl as angry tears leaked from her eyes. "Everything I was supposed to do. I did..." she sucked in a shuddering breath and uttered through clenched teeth, "I did everything right. And they told me I failed. Told me I was worth nothing."

Her nails dug into her palms, knuckles going white as she curled her hands into fists. "So no." She cast a glance at Anthony.

His gaze was fixed ahead of them, but she saw the clench of his jaw, the stiffness of his stride.

"I wasn't scared of you. I was too busy loathing myself. Trying to disappear into the *nothing* they say I am." The last sentence was muttered, barely above a whisper. But from the quick dart of his head, Anthony heard it.

She fell silent then. Out of words she hadn't dared utter in Abredea.

They moved forward together, Anthony taking the lead when the pathway narrowed, and striding side by side when there was space enough. Juliana had no notion of how long it would take to get where they were going. Moving through the forest *was* slow. Slower, she expected, because she was there. She had a feeling he'd be moving twice as fast if she weren't.

For a long time, there was only the sounds of their footsteps between them. The sun climbed higher into the sky; beams of light brightened the forest around them. Juliana opened her mouth to ask how much longer they had to go when Anthony stopped and turned to her.

"Yeh said the Red-Stars took a locket?"

She stopped as well, glancing up at him in a moment of confusion. Then it clicked and she nodded. "They ripped it off my neck just before I went through the wall."

"Was it..." he growled under his breath. "Is tha' what the earrings were? A matchin' set?"

Juliana swallowed. More tears sprang into her eyes, and she wiped them away with the back of her hand. "Yes. A birthday present from my parents. They left the earrings for me in the morning." Pressure built in her head, just behind her eyes as the longing for her mother and father reached a pinnacle. She forced a smile.

"And the necklace?"

Her jaw clenched. "It was supposed to be a gift that night. At my celebration. But they brought it with them to the Star Office when they came to... to say goodbye."

The furrow in Anthony's brow, the sadness in his eyes, only served to flush more heat to her face. She stared fixedly at a tree just to his left. Meeting his gaze now would only bring more tears.

Still, she felt his stare. It, and the fingers he brushed against her forearm as he said, "Yeh aren't nothin'. And I'm... I'm sorry and deeply grateful for what yeh gave up for Jimmy."

Juliana bit the inside of her cheek. Sharp pain, and the metallic taste of blood, drove away the sob building up in her throat. She jerked her head in a sharp nod. Still not looking at him, she gestured forward.

They went on, the air around them warming and the dew evaporating from the tips of leaves and blades of grass. Juliana's stomach grumbled as they approached and passed the time she and May usually sat down to eat their government provided mush packets. Juliana's calves burned. Her hands stung from the many scratches where she'd braced herself on branches and scraggly trunks.

Finally, Anthony slowed to a stop.

"We're 'ere."

They'd reached a small clearing. A stream ran through, clear water trickling along the rocks. Tiny fish were just visible as their silver forms shimmered under the surface. Above them, sunlight shone down, lighting up the hundreds of miniature purple flowers scattered through the shorter, greener, grass.

Something settled within Juliana's chest. Her heart found something like solace in this place. So still. So empty and yet so full.

Kneeling, she brushed a hand through the grass to find it as soft as it looked. A flurry of small insects, barely larger than the tip of a pen, leapt out where her fingers touched the ground. Her hand twitched. She almost stood. But as one landed on her finger she marveled at the pale green color of it, the wings—so small she thought for a moment she didn't see them—translucent. It leapt again, flying back to the ground as she rose to her feet.

"This is..."

Anthony nodded, the wide, half-cocked smile she was used to back in place. "This is my favorite place in the world. Well," he chuckled, "second favorite. But the first is pretty far."

She let out half a laugh. "I can't imagine anything more... *more* than this."

His smile grew. "Yeh ready to get back?"

Juliana looked at him. They'd been up the entire night. She felt it in her bones. The adrenaline and anxiety weighed on her. Fear and relief clenched her intestines, or maybe that was her stomach expressing its displeasure at being so empty.

"Yeah. Let's get to Jimmy." She gave one last look at the little clearing before following him through the brush.

She recognized where they were the minute they came into view of the fence. "Is that..." she jerked her head to stare at Anthony. "Is that where—"

"Yeh went to read all the time? Yeah. It made gettin' in and out during the day a lot harder than it needed to be."

"How did I never know..." She exhaled a chuckle. "That night when we met. You were coming back from a hunt."

He shrugged.

"You told *me* to stay away from the fence," she said with a laugh. "Hypocrite."

Anthony grinned, scanning the stretch of fence before them. "Well, yeh'll remember that *I* don' get caught. I didn' think the same would be said of you."

She raised an eyebrow.

"Back then," he amended with a wink. "Yeh'd *better* not get caught now."

Juliana exhaled through shaky lips as her gut clenched. "Right. Not done yet, are we?"

"Nearly." Anthony pushed forward, one hand reaching behind him for hers.

She took it, letting him lead the way as they stooped low and ran across the open grassland to the fence. After the stretch earlier that morning, the fifty yards felt like nothing.

Juliana kept an alert eye on their surroundings as Anthony fiddled with the fence in a spot conveniently covered by a multitude of yellow flowering bushes. After a few seconds they slid through the fence, Juliana clutching her bag to her chest once again. Another few seconds as he did up the fence and...

Juliana stepped away from the chain link with warring emotions. They'd made it. Alive, safe, no Black-Stars in sight and a bundle of medicine in her hands. And yet, she looked at the fence with new eyes. It had always felt like a cage, but freedom had been on the other side of the wall. Not between the trees she already longed to return to.

"Come on," Anthony murmured. "I wanna get tah Jimmy."

Juliana nodded, drawing her gaze away from the mountains in the distance and hurrying behind her friend.

Chapter Twenty-Seven

Present Day - Early Fall - Somewhere in Pangaea

E laine woke several long seconds before she was able to peel her eyes open. Heavy. They were so heavy. As was her body when she tried to move. She blinked, trying to focus. Hazy fog coated her vision. Pain radiated through her head, as though a hammer drove several nails into her brain. This was worse than one of her visions; her whole body ached. Light shone down from above but looking at it sent sharp splinters into the backs of her eyes. She closed them, reaching out with her other senses.

The ground beneath her—wooden slats—moved, rocking back and forth in time with a loud clacking sound below her. She inhaled. Smoke and sweat. Old blood. Singed hair and cloth.

Elaine shifted, gingerly moving onto her hands and knees. She reached out. Warmth. Skin. She hissed, drawing her fingers back.

She cracked her eyelids. The light, blocked by her body, wasn't as painful as the first time. Through the haze she made out a face... young. Pale hair, bare temples. Eyes closed as if she were sleeping. Little Sky.

Memory hit her like a truck. She winced, smelling the fire, hearing the screams that had woken her. Ichi, not yet gone to sleep, standing quickly from his desk, eyes alert. Rushing into Haven's main room. Jason and Samaira, flanking a group of Black-Stars. Ichi, raising his hand, blood flowing from his nose and left ear as he slammed his will against their minds. Bodies crumpling to the ground.

Shouts. Shut the door. Barricade. Wake the children. *Safety. Get them to safety.*

Leaving Ichi. Her heart breaking as she put on the strong face she always wore with the little ones. Wanting to kiss him goodbye. There wasn't time.

They had a head start. The older children—still children—would give them the few extra seconds they needed to escape.

Her hand, clenched around Sky as the girl cried for her plants. Her home. Their lives.

Hope. Running down the hallway. She'd know when they broke through. She'd hear it. *We have time.* Muttering it to herself. *We have...*

They came from either side as Elaine and the children reached a T intersection. Black-Stars. Bore down upon them with guns raised. She'd turned, shielding Sky and Kim with her body as...

As it all faded.

Everything went black.

Elaine blinked through the tears now streaming down her midnight cheeks. She pushed long braids from her face and searched. Counted.

Through the dizziness and pain, and the rocking of the train car they rode in, it took a long time. She crawled, knees scraping the wood, until she found Ichi's body, felt for his pulse, found it, and then collapsed in a puddle of sobs. Samaira lay beside him, a dirty bandage on her neck but alive. They were alive.

The ones here... the ones here were alive.

Her heart sank as she rose to her knees, counting again as whatever clouded her mind dissipated from her system. She turned to Ichi as realization of their missing number crawled—unwanted—into her chest. She reached out. To wake him, or curl beside him and mourn the loss so she might be a source of comfort when he finally rose; she hadn't decided.

Rumbling jolted her upright. A Black-Star slid open a large metal door at the end of the car. Elaine got one foot under her before he raised the gun. Something familiar and sharp pierced her shoulder. She slumped. Her hand brushed Ichi's coarse hair as she fell beside him, taken by darkness once again.

Chapter Twenty-Eight

Present Day - Mid-Summer - Abredea

Jimmy's recovery was so fast Juliana almost believed he might grow up and forget the entire harrowing experience. They gave him the correct six doses. The first two were done while he was still unconscious, and Juliana realized why her parents never went into pediatric medicine when they administered the other four.

Three days after Juliana and Anthony's return from the wall, Jimmy and Naya moved back into their home.

Juliana sighed and snuggled deeper under her covers as sunlight pierced the thin curtain over the kitchen window. She'd missed this bed. Missed May's steady breathing in the night.

It was a startling realization.

"You up?" May called from the back door.

Juliana groaned and pulled the blanket over her head. "No," she said with a grin.

"If you want to be dressed before company comes over, you'd better get your butt out of bed."

Juliana laughed, tossing off the blanket and rolling from her cot. "I think we've got time."

"Still," May stepped into the room and took in Juliana's pajamas with a shake of her head, "better to be ready *before* everyone arrives."

Juliana rolled her eyes. She pulled a pair of shorts and a flowy blouse from her trunk, and crossed to the bathroom, hoping for warm water.

She paused. Hesitated with a hand on the doorframe before she backtracked to the kitchen.

"May?"

"Yes?" The old woman barely glanced at her, busy over the stove.

"You said... you told me once that I'm not the first White-Star to live with you?"

"That's right." May shifted her spatula, churning the potatoes roasting in spices and oil on the stove.

Juliana swallowed; her chest tight. "Am I the first one who was a Blue-Star?"

May stopped. She moved the pan off the heat and set the wooden spatula on the counter. "That's correct." Her brow furrowed. "Why do you ask?"

"You never had someone named Brenna live with you? Maybe thirty years ago?"

May's right eyebrow rose. "No. I've never... Juliana?"

Juliana nodded, a lump in her throat as she clenched her jaw hard enough to ache. "Thanks."

May's gaze followed her as she turned and hurried back to the bathroom.

Steam swirled around her, but it was hard to focus on the welcome temperature of the water. Shudders racked her body as tears streamed down her cheeks. After a few moments she leaned her forehead against the faded tile, water trickling down her back. With a sniff, she straightened, rinsed the tears away, and focused on the day ahead.

Naya and Jimmy had survived, but it had been close. So close, and even Juliana understood the need for a celebration.

May had come up with the plan. Juliana had told Daisy—who arrived just as she got out of the shower to help decorate—and managed to connive a few extra items from Anthony's hunting trip without him catching on.

As Juliana laid a half-full serving bowl of mush on the table, Daisy took her hand. "You're amazing, you know?"

Juliana shook her head. "It was May's idea."

Daisy sighed with a now familiar look of exasperation. "Not this." She gestured to the flowing strands of flowers on the walls, the plates of food on the kitchen counter, and the chairs they'd rearranged so everyone would have a place to sit in the largest part of the room.

"Jimmy. The medicine."

Juliana squeezed her hand. "Nothing anyone else wouldn't have done," she muttered. She turned to fetch a container of diced up strawberries.

"What is it?" Daisy asked. "What's wrong?"

Juliana cracked a dry grin. "Who said anything was wrong?"

Daisy strode forward, took the container from Juliana's hands, and set it on the table. She faced her friend. "I say. I can tell. You did it; you and Anthony got the medicine. Naya and Jimmy are all right. So, what's wrong?"

A breeze flew in through the open window, rustling Juliana's long hair before flying out the front door. Her gut tightened, a lump forming in her throat.

"I was..." she sighed and waved a hand through the air. "It's stupid. But I was closer to my parents than I've been in months. I haven't... I try not to think about them very often, but they've been on my mind since we went through the wall."

Tears beaded at the edges of her eyes. Juliana blinked them away with a forced laugh. "Foolish. I knew I'd never see them again the minute they showed me these." She pointed to the pearly white gemstones on her temples.

"You're still allowed to miss them," Daisy murmured forcefully. "You think I don't miss my mother every day? If I had the chance to see her again..." she paused, pain taking the smile from her soft face. "What you did goes beyond what most people would be willing to do."

Juliana shook her head. The words were appreciated. The hug that followed even more so, but she didn't believe it. Not after seeing the way the people here, her people, treated each other like... like family.

Anthony arrived first. He brought a pitcher of freshly squeezed juice, a sight that caused Daisy to yelp and clap her hands in glee.

Juliana gave him a squinty frown as he twirled May under his arm and stooped to hug her.

"I told you May wanted to talk about the garden. Why did you bring something?"

Anthony's laughter rang out through the house. "Jules, yeh've got a sharp mind, but yeh can' lie for shit."

Juliana's mouth fell open as Daisy and May giggled and chortled. "What? I can lie."

The other three laughed even harder.

"I *can*."

Juliana's attempt at sounding angry failed as the door burst open and Taz strode in asking, "Where's the party?"

May slapped a hand on the table with a cackle.

Juliana turned indignantly. "I didn't tell him!"

Taz hesitated for a split second in the doorway before hefting his backpack with a shrug, "She asked me to... to... to... she asked me over for tea."

Juliana planted her palm against her forehead as Anthony collapsed onto May's bed, roaring.

Taz grinned as he passed Anthony. The teasing about Juliana's deceptive capabilities came to a rapid halt as he pulled out small carton which, to everyone's excitement, held half a dozen eggs. May and Daisy went straight to work, heating pans, boiling water, and chopping their remaining onions, peppers, and mushrooms.

Montague arrived next. Daisy had been the one to invite him, so it was less of a surprise when he showed up with a tray of goodies. Cookies, in an array of chocolate, frosted, lemon, cinnamon, Juliana's mouth watered just looking at it.

Naya and Jimmy arrived last, and this time it truly was a surprise. Naya poked an uncertain head in the open doorway.

"What is..."

She barely started the sentence when Jimmy noticed the tray of cookies on the table and rushed into the room. Anthony sprang from the bed, scooping his tiny cousin into the air and spinning him around.

"Slow it down there, little man. Yer still recoverin'."

Jimmy's stream of giggles were music in the air as he was spun and plunked down on Juliana's neatly made bed.

Naya moved through the room in awe. Montague and Taz sat on the edge of May's bed, in reach of the groaning table—piled with strips of crispy meat, rolls, cookies, a bowl of scrambled eggs, potatoes, and vegetables, a similar one full of chopped fruit, and the jug of orange juice. The small container of sweetened mush had been moved to the kitchen counter where it sat pathetically during the feast.

May took up the rocking chair; Anthony sprawled across Juliana's bed with his cousin. They celebrated. Juliana savored each bite with delicious slowness, giving everyone a chance for seconds before she went back for more fruit and another half of a roll. Daisy munched the other half, giggling as they enjoyed the peace of the morning. Montague showed Jimmy and Taz tricks with a well-worn deck of cards. Anthony flitted around to each conversation, causing shouts of laughter and the occasional dirty look from his aunt when dangerous activities were mentioned.

There had been no choice but to tell Naya and May about their trek to get the antibiotics. Still, they'd left out most of the details. As everyone finished eating, any hopes for leftovers entirely dashed, Naya scooped Jimmy into her arms. She squeezed him tight and looked to Juliana.

"I can't thank you enough."

Juliana flushed. "It was..." She couldn't say nothing. It hadn't been nothing. It had been Jimmy's life. "You're welcome."

"I was there too," Anthony grumbled with a grin. He winked at Juliana as Naya gave an exasperated sigh.

"Yes, but it wasn't *your* idea," Montague broke in with a serene smile. He raised a cup of tea toward Juliana. "Our newest Moon is quite the smart one."

Juliana swallowed. She stifled a shudder and smiled instead. "Thank you."

He nodded. He'd said the same thing when she and Anthony told him what had happened. After he'd apologized for getting them into such a situation, and agreed to keep the details of their adventure to himself.

The conversation shifted and Montague left a few minutes later, saying something about paperwork. Juliana walked him to the door with another round of thanks for his contribution to their party. He waved her off with a chuckle, but she followed him outside.

"Montague?"

"Yes, Miss. Juliana? Excellent party. We should do it again."

"I have a favor to ask."

"Of course." He inclined his head.

She swallowed. It felt foolish asking. But if anyone knew...

"I was wondering if you could tell me about a White-Star who was sent here about thirty years ago."

Montague's eyes widened. He ran a hand over the bald top of his head. "I believe..." he nodded. "I believe I can do that. Do you have a name?"

"Brenna." Juliana's fingertips danced across her thumb. "Her name was Brenna. She uh... she died a few years after she was sent here."

Montague crossed the space between them and rested his spindly fingers on her shoulder. "A relative?"

Juliana nodded.

"Mother or father's side?"

"Mother's."

Montague offered a sympathetic smile. "I'll see what I can find out."

"Thank you."

He walked away, fading into the distance.

She returned to the kitchen and began washing dishes as the others chatted merrily. Daisy came to help her after a moment or two and another minute later Anthony plowed into the kitchen, demanded they stop working, and shooed them both outside as he snatched the sponge and started scrubbing.

The girls strolled through the garden. Late morning sun warmed Juliana's skin as she opened her arms for a long stretch. Beside her, Daisy yawned.

"Tired?"

Daisy nodded, covering her yawn with the back of her hand and sighing. "It's been quite a week."

"Yes, it has." Juliana gazed toward the west. Her thoughts drifted to the forest on the other side of the fence.

She frowned. Blinking, Juliana returned her attention to her friend. Daisy had lowered her arm, but something caught Juliana's eye. She reached down and closed gentle fingers around Daisy's forearm. There. She almost hadn't noticed it. A faint ring of purple marred the skin around Daisy's wrist. Her sleeved had hidden it during breakfast.

Juliana's nostrils flared. "What is that?"

Daisy grimaced. She pulled her arm from Juliana's grasp, and shook the sleeve down. "Nothing."

"*Daisy*," Juliana said, warning in her voice.

With a sigh, Daisy crossed her arms over her chest. "Nothing you need to worry about. It's fine."

"That's not *fine*." Juliana put a tentative hand on her shoulder. "What happened?"

Daisy shook her head. Juliana opened her mouth again, but Daisy held up a hand.

"Can we not? Please? This morning has been lovely. Let's keep it that way."

Juliana swallowed; anger rose in her chest. Daisy's soft gaze was dull, muted. Juliana wanted to press, to find out exactly what had gone on between Daisy and her father—Juliana was sure that was where the bruise had originated.

With a reluctant nod, Juliana pulled her friend in for a gentle squeeze. "I'm here if you need anything."

"I know," Daisy murmured, her voice tight.

As morning flowed into afternoon and the two women rejoined the others, Juliana couldn't help the return of her smile. All the same, Daisy's wrist sat at the edge of her mind. Not soon to be forgotten.

Jimmy hadn't seen his friends in over a week. It wasn't a school day, and Naya had laundry to do, so they ventured to the square together. Screams of laughter, small feet thundering across cobblestone, splashing through the fountain, the chatter of Moons as they went about their business, or just stood together talking and watching the little ones, echoed throughout the space.

Juliana brought books. When Jimmy had worn himself out in the water, he and his friends scurried to her, perched on the steps of the town hall with Daisy and Taz. She laughed, scolded one of the girls for splashing water onto the books, and got to reading.

Shade from one of the massive oaks and the balcony above, combined with a gentle breeze that rustled the pages of her book, helped chase away the sun's glare.

It wasn't a study group—which they had a permit for, but it required them to be inside. No laws were being broken; no rules bent. Still, Juliana's heartbeat quickened as three Black-Stars marched into view around the building. She paused, midway through a sentence, and kept a careful watch as they moved closer, coming up the steps and stopping a few feet away from their group.

She stood before the first one spoke. "We are allowed to be here. This isn't a study group."

The Black-Star before her, one she recognized as a right-hand to Captain Steel, waved her off. "There's a visitor. You need to clear the steps."

Taz opened his mouth, and from Juliana's peripheral vision she caught Daisy elbow him in the ribs.

"Of course." Juliana pulled forth her bright smile, softening the Black-Star's stiff expression.

He nodded, stroked his thick mustache, and turned to the other guards. "Get the others, we're ready for her."

Juliana's smile slipped. She jerked it back into place, and by the time he turned back to her, she was gently shooing children off the steps. They complained and asked if she'd continue reading in the patch of grass on the other side of the square.

The sound barely reached her through the ringing in her ears. It wasn't until Daisy gripped her arm and leaned into her vision that Juliana's gaze snapped back into focus.

"Sorry," she mumbled.

"What is it?" Daisy asked, moving with her as Taz led the children toward the grass.

"It's..." Juliana hesitated. Daisy's concerned expression drew half a smile from her. "Sorry. It's probably nothing."

Daisy raised an eyebrow.

Juliana corrected, "It *is* nothing. I..." Her words faded, lost in the noise of the squad of Black-Stars rounding town hall, Ms. Wolfe striding confidently in their center.

Quiet rippled out from those closest to Wolfe, silencing the hustle and bustle of the square. Wolfe didn't appear to notice. Her attention was on Captain Steel, who walked beside her.

They marched up the stone steps of town hall. Montague materialized at the door, holding it open as all but two of the group moved into the building. The pair of Black-Stars took up guard on either side of the double doors.

"Who is *that*?" Daisy muttered.

Juliana stared, heart pointing, throat constricted as she waited. She took half a step forward as Montague began to close the door. His gaze caught hers for a brief moment.

It was a slight movement, the shake of his head. Slight, but enough.

Tears pooled in Juliana's eyes, but the shredding she expected, the tearing, breaking ache of letdown... she didn't feel it.

She mulled it over as she turned and took slow steps toward Taz and the children. Her thoughts shifted, not to the hot showers, full belly, and other such accommodations, but to her parents. She thought of Naya. Of the heartbreaking relief on her face when Jimmy had woken up.

She stopped.

"Juliana?" Daisy turned to look at her.

"I have to do something." Juliana blinked, surprised by her own words.

"What?"

"Can you take these for me? Read to the little ones for a bit?" She reached out her stack of books and Daisy took them with a quizzical look. But her friend said nothing, simply turned and went to Taz and the others.

Juliana wiped suddenly sweaty hands on her shorts. She squared her shoulders and strode toward town hall, running fingers through her hair and giving it a hasty braid as she climbed the steps. She brushed at her face, hoping there was no dirt from the garden staining her cheeks.

The Black-Stars at the door, the same two who'd disbanded her study group, stared.

"I need to see Ms. Wolfe." Juliana's voice rang out clear and steady.

The man snorted. Beside him, the woman pursed her lips and squinted at Juliana. "Why would *you* be allowed in there right now?" she asked, jerking her thumb toward the door.

"I was asked here last time Ms. Wolfe visited the camp." Juliana's gaze darted past the Black-Stars. Montague was visible through the glass, at his usual place behind the front desk. "If you ask Mr. Montague—"

"Another *Moon*?" The man scoffed. "Why would we trust his word?"

"Well," Juliana's chin rose, hands clenching at her sides until she forced her fingers apart with a deep inhale, "your captain and a Grey-Star are choosing to meet in his domain, so he has more influence than you'd think." Her words came out icy, but she was quick to throw in a smile and a conciliatory nod.

"Beyond that, he is the one who called me here last time." Juliana bit the inside of her lip. "It's possible he forgot to fetch me for this. I wouldn't want anyone getting in trouble with Ms. Wolfe for my absence."

The woman, her cropped black hair accented with streaks of silver along the sides, clicked her tongue. "If anyone would be, it would be your little friend in there."

Juliana remained silent. A few seconds passed.

Finally, she looked at her partner, "Go ask."

"But—"

"It doesn't do any harm to ask. And I'd rather not deal with the captain if this doesn't go how they want."

The man scowled, but he opened the door and strode inside. A few moments later he returned, a deeper frown in place as he waved Juliana through the door. She nodded once more, her smile wide and, she hoped, as innocent as Daisy's as she walked past him and into the building.

Montague watched her from behind the reception desk. His tired eyes, darkened with heavy bags beneath, shut briefly. Four Black-Stars stood in the lobby and Juliana was hit with the realization that this is what Montague should have been. This man in the pressed, aged suit, with kind eyes and a weary smile. He might have been something entirely different... if not for the gemstones on his temples.

"She didn't ask for you, Miss Juliana," Montague said.

Juliana nodded. "I know. You'd have told me. But I had to... I have questions."

He sighed, rubbing the bridge of his nose. "She will see to you when she's done with Captain Steel."

Juliana's heart pounded. She licked her trembling lips. "Thank you."

"Have a seat. I'm not sure how long they will be."

Juliana sat. Her foot bounced until she realized the chair she was on squeaked with each downswing.

She shifted. Fidgeted. Re-braided her hair with more care for loose strands. The Black-Stars in the room chatted quietly together, their voices a low rumble on the edge of her awareness. Montague fiddled with his papers. Then he straightened the room.

When he'd passed her the second time, Juliana reached out and touched his arm. "Is she meeting with anyone else? Or just Captain Steel?"

Montague met her gaze and matched her whisper. "Only Captain Steel." Something flickered in his eyes. He watched her for a moment, their stares locked.

Juliana's brow furrowed and she tilted her head. The back of her mind itched; as though some thought wanted to be free, but wasn't formed enough to break through.

A door closed down the hall. Montague straightened, set down the stack of booklets he'd been holding, and returned to his post. Moments later Ms. Wolfe emerged from the hallway, Captain Steel a step behind her.

Juliana stood, pressing her hands down her shirt in an effort to straighten the wrinkled cloth. Steel moved toward his men and Wolfe turned.

Juliana's heart thundered. She smiled, tight with anxiety. She exhaled a slow breath through pursed lips, strode forward, and extended her hand. "Thank you for seeing me, Ms. Wolfe. I'm sure you are quite busy."

The Grey-Star was as put together as every other time Juliana had seen her, hair in a tight bun, streaks of grey running through dark brown strands. She wore heels, high and pointed, partially concealed by pale ivory pants. A soft lavender blouse was visible beneath the unbuttoned matching jacket.

Juliana's unease increased as she took in Wolfe's silver bracelets, and the perfection of her manicured nails. As her fingers tapped against her thumb, Juliana felt the callouses she'd built in the garden and climbing the trees in her little field by the fence.

Wolfe took her in, scanning her from head to toe before her lips split into a sympathetic smile. "I am. But I have a few minutes. This way."

She led Juliana down the hall and into Montague's familiar empty office. After a gesture of invitation, Juliana sat in one of the chairs. Wolfe perched herself at the edge of the desk, one knee over the other and hands clasped.

"What can I do for you, Miss Foster? I'm sure you've gathered that I have no news regarding a different placement for you." The crow's feet at the edges of Wolfe's eyes wrinkled even more as her smile widened.

Juliana nodded. "I understand. It was unlikely to begin with."

Wolfe held up a hand. "Now wait a minute, I've not given up and neither should you. I'm still looking for a way to get you out of here. As I said before, someone with your mind shouldn't be stuck in a place like this."

"Thank you," Juliana said, even as her stomach gave an uncomfortable lurch. "I truly appreciate everything you're doing for me. Even if it doesn't work out in the end."

Wolfe's eyes narrowed for the slightest of seconds. "Well, let's not talk about failure any longer. You wanted to see me for something?"

"Yes, ma'am." Juliana licked her lips. She twisted at her fingers, trying to sit straighter and forced a smile back onto her face. "I wanted to... that is..." She sucked in a breath and let it out. "I was hoping you would be able to get a message to my parents."

Wolfe unfolded her hands and placed them on the desk on either side of her. Her eyebrows rose as she surveyed Juliana. "That is... unorthodox."

"I know." Juliana tightened one hand into a fist and met Wolfe's gaze. "I just need them to know that I'm all right."

Wolfe blinked. The edge of her mouth twitched. She was silent for a long moment, so long Juliana worried she'd offended her.

"I know I'll never see them again," she went on. "Even if you're able to have me assigned to the research facility you spoke of, I know I'd never be able to contact them. They could never know that this," she gestured to her gemstones, "might be undone."

Wolfe inclined her head. "You are correct. Our arrangement, should it prove possible, would make any contact with your old life... *not* possible."

Juliana nodded, widening her eyes to keep the burning at their edges from turning into tears. "I don't want them to worry about me. I've..." she hesitated, "I've found people."

"You've... found people?" Wolfe uncrossed her legs and gracefully stepped down from the table. She pulled the second chair beside Juliana and sat, leaning close. "Tell me more."

Juliana was quiet for a few seconds. Possibly longer than was wise when a Grey-Star gave an order to speak, but she wanted to say this correctly. Wolfe had influence, power. Perhaps if she knew... perhaps if she were aware of the problems they faced, she might be able to help them.

"This place was a nightmare after my Coding. Coming here, it was worse than the most horrible outcome I had imagined. But it doesn't *have* to be that way. The people here, they aren't... they aren't what we're taught in the city. Not all of them at least."

She glanced up at the Grey-Star. Wolfe gestured for her to go on.

"If there were more food, or higher wages for the field hands and the miners, that would go a long way to improve the standard of living here. Homes are assigned by the people in charge, but the maintenance, for example the yearly water filter changes, aren't always handled with the most care. Recently a family got very sick because of negligence."

Wolfe's eyes widened. Her right hand rose to her lips, immaculate lavender fingernails pressing against the pale color.

Warmth rose in Juliana's chest. "The school needs work as well. New books, and a better curriculum. The children barely learn any science, any history. They struggle with basic mathematical concepts. I believe because the teachers don't care about them. They're Orange-Stars."

Wolfe closed her eyes and breathed out a sigh. "The caste system is vital for our society to thrive."

Juliana nodded with vigor.

"However," Wolfe went on, "some people do take it to an extreme. I can imagine the Orange-Star instructors not doing as well as they might if they were teaching their own."

"Exactly," Juliana agreed. "I think changing the school would be the best way to improve Abredea."

Wolfe's eyebrows drew together. She tilted her head in confusion.

"I mean, the camp," Juliana corrected. "Helping the children is an excellent first step to fixing things here. Making things better. Blue-Star schools offered meals, among other things. Children learn better when they're fed." She gave half a chuckle, which Wolfe returned. Tension eased in Juliana's chest.

"So, you did have more to discuss than the failing hope of leaving," Wolfe said. She smiled again, though her eyes flashed with something resembling irritation.

Juliana swallowed. "I did. And I thank you, for hearing me."

Wolfe inclined her head and then stood. "I will deliver the message to your parents that you are, *all right,* when I am able. It may take a while. I don't make it a habit of visiting random Blue-Stars at their homes."

"Thank you," Juliana breathed. Relief flowed through her.

"As for you," Wolfe gestured to the door and Juliana hurried to open it for them, "keep following the rules and being an obedient member of your caste. I'll work on things from my end, but any disruption here will slow things down significantly. Anything involving *you* will severely hurt your chances of leaving."

Unease twisted in Juliana's stomach for the briefest of seconds before she nodded again. "I will, thank you, Ms. Wolfe."

Wolfe gave her a warm smile. A chill ran down Juliana's back.

"I expect to have an answer for you the next time we see each other," Wolfe said. She turned and strode down the hallway into the main lobby.

Juliana stood frozen for a few seconds. Thoughts and emotions whirled through her too quickly. She struggled to sort them all. After a moment, she gave up and returned to Daisy, and Taz, and the children. They spent the rest of the day reading and chasing the children through the fountain when everyone got too hot.

May wandered to the square in the later hours of the afternoon. Taz talked the baker into lending a chair and set her up in the shade of the tree they'd been reading under. She took a turn reading after Taz had provided everyone with a particularly exuberant rendition of a story about a spider and a woman eating porridge.

May's worn voice filtered the words, transforming them from a simple story to a grand adventure. Juliana leaned against the tree, smiling as the children's eyes grew wide, as they clapped, gasped, winced, shrieked, and collapsed into fits of giggles so loud May had to pause the story to let them recover. She recognized some of the voices May used—Daisy used the same ones for those characters—and imagined a young Daisy, Taz, and Anthony, listening raptly as May read to them years ago.

Her father had read to her. He'd snuggled her close, snuck her an extra cookie, and filled her mind with stories.

The rest of the afternoon passed with Juliana in a bitter-sweet mood.

Clouds covered the western sky, the sunset lighting them up in an array of pinks, oranges, and reds as Juliana and May returned home. Anthony got back from his hunting trip shortly after. They stored the food he brought and then ate together, sending Anthony away after dinner with a bowl of rabbit stew for Naya and Jimmy.

"It was a good day," May said as the two women prepared for bed.

"Yeah," Juliana agreed. Her mind drifted to the conversation with Wolfe; the potential changes to the school. "A productive day."

May raised an eyebrow, her scar stretching and shining white. "How so?"

Juliana shrugged. "The reading, the stew, breakfast this morning. The day felt full."

May grinned at her. "Indeed."

Juliana checked the lock on the back door, cracked the kitchen window, and settled herself into bed. She pulled a thin sheet over her silken pajamas and tucked her braid to the side.

Though it was nearly ten, light still permeated the night sky. May straightened her worn pair of shorts and the loose flowing top she always wore to bed, braided her own hair, and then sat on the edge of her bed and slowly laid back.

Juliana wondered—not for the first time—how old the woman was. She had no children, no husband, that she spoke of. From what Juliana could tell, Naya was her only close friend, though other people in Abredea certainly respected and valued her.

"It was very brave."

Juliana jerked, realized she'd been staring at May, and flushed. "Sorry," she mumbled. Then the meaning of the words registered. "What was?"

"What you did for Jimmy." May sighed and shifted. "These old bones are never comfortable," she grumbled under her breath. Then louder, "going where you did was no trek into the woods. I know the risks, and I know how hard it must have been for you."

Juliana sat up, propping herself on her arm. "Did Daisy tell you?"

May chuckled. "Daisy wouldn't have told me even if I offered her an entire chocolate cake. That girl is loyal."

Juliana smiled. "She's special. I've never..." She hesitated, thinking of Moniqua, Alex, and the other friends she'd left in the city. "I've never had a friend like her. Someone I could tell anything to. Someone who looked at me like..." She scrunched her lips to the side, trying to come up with the words.

"Someone who looks at you like they trust you implicitly," May finished for her. "No matter if you feel you've earned it or not."

Juliana raised an eyebrow. "Exactly."

The old woman chuckled. "Don't look so surprised over there; I've had friends."

Juliana opened her mouth to object, but May just laughed.

"I had someone like her, a long time ago. She *is* special. Not someone to overlook, though many do." May let out a long sigh.

Juliana leaned back onto her pillow. "I don't know," she swallowed, "I don't know where I'd be if she hadn't found me."

"Well, I'm glad I suggested it then."

Juliana nearly fell out of bed she sat up so fast. "*What?*"

"You don't think she just happened upon that field of yours, do you? I've known that girl for years, Juliana. She has Taz and Anthony. But she needed someone just as much as you did. When you came along, it seemed like fate."

Juliana's chest constricted. An early memory struck her. A school room, children with multi-colored gemstones laughing and talking. The instructor, a strict Blue-Star who never forgot the morning pledge, typing words onto the screen at the front of the room. *Fate and destiny are words used by dissidents to make you question your place in society. There is no peace without order. There is no order without caste. Fate has no place in the Coding.*

She shook her head. "I've never been one for fate."

"Of course not," May muttered. "You were a Blue-Star. I know what they drilled into you growing up."

Bitterness lined May's voice. Juliana licked her lips. "What caste were you?" she asked, her voice soft. "Before."

May cackled. "That's a story for another time, dear. I'm an old woman. I need my sleep."

Juliana snorted and rolled her eyes. She lay back, staring at the wooden rafters above them. She was silent for a moment. Then, "I think Daisy's father is hurting her."

May's shifting stopped. After a few seconds she murmured, "Go on."

Juliana told her about the bruised wrist, and about Daisy's unwillingness to discuss it. "Is there anything we can do?"

"I'm afraid not. Not at the moment anyway. In a year, Daisy will be eighteen. She'll be considered an adult in Abredea and will be given a room in the apartments in the square or a house of her own. Given her father's station, I think a house is more likely."

"She has to live there for another *year*?" Juliana cringed. "There has to be *something* we can do before that."

May sighed. "I'm going to tell you something that stays between us, understand?"

Juliana hesitated for a brief moment. "Yes."

"When Daisy's father came to Abredea, he was bitter. He married Daisy's mother because she was beautiful and connected. She was also a close friend of Naya's. When Naya found out that he was hitting her, she and *her* husband, Dave, gathered a group of friends, went to their home, and taught Marsterson a painful lesson he wouldn't soon forget."

Juliana's eyes widened.

"The abuse stopped, but Daisy's mother stayed with him. She loved him, for all his faults, but we found out later she stayed because she was pregnant. A few years after that, Marsterson wormed his way into the mayoral position. All the while, Naya and Dave kept a close eye, but he never hit his wife or child. He didn't dare."

"And now?" Juliana murmured.

May shifted, tossing her thicker blanket to the foot of her bed. "Now, I don't know. Keep a close eye. If it comes to it, she can stay with us for a few nights. But, as I'm sure you remember from your close inspection of Abredea's laws—"

"She can't leave his house until she's of age," Juliana interrupted. "I remember." She heaved a sigh.

"Be there for her, Juliana. Sometimes that's all you can do."

"Yeah." Juliana rolled over, feeling less sleepy. She thought about what Anthony's uncle had done to stop Marsterson all those years ago. Then she thought about Captain Steel and his squad of Black-Stars. How would they react if the mayor was attacked on their watch?

Not well.

Juliana stifled a groan and rolled again. Heat pressed against her skin, leaving a damp stickiness she absolutely loathed. She squeezed her eyes closed and willed sleep to come.

Eventually, long after May's soft snores filled the little house, it did.

Chapter Twenty-Nine

60 Years Ago - The Warren

"I don't have time for it, Kate." Maybelle strode across the uneven, rocky floor toward the command room.

Kate followed her. "Make time, Maybelle. I *need* your help," she growled. "I've made barely any progress since we lost Jared and Rose. I'm alone in that lab, every day, trying to find the cure by myself."

Maybelle stopped. She turned to Kate, narrowing her eyes. "The cure? What about the aerosol?"

Their voices echoed across the hard packed dirt and rock walls, beams of wood fixed along the sides to aid in supporting the ceiling. A pair of soldiers moved past them, avoiding eye contact. Kate waited for them to disappear around a bend and then gritted her teeth and stared at Maybelle.

"The regular dose is finicky. It doesn't work on everyone and I haven't been able to find the common factor among the people who still succumb to *suggestion*. Not only that," she jerked her head and continued walking, "but it's taking multiple doses for the subjects it *does* work for." She shook her head. "I'm shifting focus for a bit."

"Shifting focus?" Maybelle gaped at her. "We *need* that aerosol. Without it, Pangaea will never be free from Grey-Star control."

Kate's hands formed fists as she marched ahead of Maybelle. "You think I don't know that?" she hissed back to her friend. "Maybe if you could come in for *five minutes* and look at the data, you'd understand why creating an aerosol version right now would be completely pointless. If I can *fix* the sterility problem—"

"So they can make more Grey-Stars?" Maybelle interjected, pulling up alongside Kate and glaring. "Which side are you on, Kate?"

Kate stopped dead in her tracks. Her eyes went wide, and Maybelle immediately regretted her words. She sighed, but Kate spoke before she could apologize.

"I'm on *our* side, Maybelle. In case you've forgotten, those gemstones on your temple don't have any effect on your DNA. Like it or not, you're a Grey-Star, no matter what the mirror shows." She sucked in a deep breath. Her gaze softened, sadness replacing the anger. "Beyond that, Red and I talked before..." Her lips trembled, but she went on. "He agreed with me, that we might make some progress diplomatically if we have something to offer them. A cure *is* that something. It's the only thing they'd want from us."

Maybelle clenched her jaw, grief and anger fighting it out in her heart and mind. Red hadn't told her that. He hadn't told her a lot of things before he died. As much as Sam said she wasn't responsible... if he'd told her. If he'd *brought* her...

"He recruited us," Maybelle murmured. "Trusted us. Because we said we'd find a way to stop *suggestion* from skewing the field in their favor."

"He trusted us because we said we'd help," Kate snapped, tears leaking from her tired, red eyes. She sucked in a shallow breath. "And then we *did*. We helped. We continue to help." She stared at Maybelle. "You have to remember that *you* aren't the rebellion. You're not going to win this war by yourself. You're a *small* piece of something *much* larger."

Maybelle's lips trembled. She closed her eyes and inhaled to avoid saying something she knew she'd regret. With a glance down the hall, she turned and continued walking.

Kate kept pace. They moved in step with each other, like they had walking down school hallways as children.

After a moment, Maybelle ran her hand through her hair. "I know I'm a small piece of it."

"Then sit it out every now and then."

Maybelle darted a look at her, and Kate waved a hand through the air.

"You don't have to go on *every* mission. You don't have to be part of every raid and rescue. You can take a break."

"I can't," Maybelle choked out, suddenly aware of the tears streaming down her cheeks. "If I'd been there..."

She stopped walking. She rubbed the back of her neck, her body shaking as she pictured Red, trapped under the rubble of a ruined outpost. Dying because she wasn't there to get him out. Dying because—

"Stop." Kate faced her, putting hands on her shoulders. Her cheeks glittered with tears of her own. "Stop, Maybelle." She leaned in, her forehead resting against Maybelle's until she relaxed her neck and returned the pressure.

"I could have saved him," Maybelle mumbled. "I could have—"

"Do you remember why he took a transport that day?" Kate broke in.

Maybelle sniffed and pulled her head away, shaking it as she went. "We have to get to the meeting, Kate."

"We have time for *this*," Kate insisted, her voice soft. "It's been months. You haven't talked about this with anyone?"

Maybelle shook her head, shame biting into her.

"He took a transport because those bastards in the northern outpost don't trust alters. Not because you were busy or needed a break. Because he was trying to stop the rebellion from breaking apart."

Maybelle bit her lip as Kate released her shoulders. They locked gazes. Kate took her hand.

"Maybe you'd have had time to get him out," Kate whispered. "The reports suggest that's not what would have happened. They had no warning, Maybelle. It happened too fast."

Maybelle nodded. She'd read the report. The casualty list had been in the hundreds and yet, she only registered one name.

"If I'd lost you too..." Kate shuddered.

She moved again, pulling Maybelle along with her. Ahead of them loomed a massive wooden door guarded by two rebel soldiers Maybelle knew by name.

Maybelle wiped away her tears. The guards looked so young to her, yet the guns on their hips showed they'd been personally trained by Sam. They were part of her guard, some of the only people allowed to keep weapons on them while in the Warren. Most were checked in with the quartermaster after a mission.

Maybelle released Kate's hand as her fingers itched toward her hip. She carried a blade, eight inches long with a black handle engraved with the words, *Captain Maybelle*. A gift from Red when she'd been made captain of her own squad of alters.

The blade was better for an incursion into the Warren. The small tunnels and dark rooms meant up close fighting.

She glanced at Kate with her flowy sleeves and warm fabric, perfect for long nights in the laboratory and the cold caverns of the Warren. She didn't have a single weapon on her.

"Rorty. Lou." Maybelle nodded at each soldier. Lou nodded back, reaching a hand out and pulling open the thick door.

"You're the last of them," Rorty said. She swallowed. "Good luck."

Maybelle nodded, glanced at Kate, and strode through the open door.

Tables filled the room. At the far end, Sam sat at the center of a long dais, rebel commanders of the separatist groups on either side of her. Her lip was curled, hands clenched in front of her, eyes narrowed. She caught Maybelle's eye as the two women entered and nodded. Maybelle returned the gesture, then stifled a chuckle as Sam rolled her eyes and forced on a smile.

The officers in the room were split. Elias's few dozen soldiers clustered to the right. Half that number—Tanners' men—took the tables in the center. And, nearly fifty officers, those loyal to the Warren and to Sam, sat to the left. Maybelle and Kate moved toward the other captains and lieutenants from the Warren.

A few of Elias's men watched Maybelle. She felt their gazes and met some of them when she turned her head to study the group.

Traitors.

Kate plucked at her sleeve. Maybelle blinked. She'd halted in the middle of the room. With a scowl, she continued with her friend as they took their seats.

The cavern was lit with a combination of glowing orbs lining the walls and shafts of sunlight filtering in from openings in the rocky ceiling. It had served as the meeting place for rebel leaders since before Maybelle and Kate joined the cause. Kate had only been here a handful of times, but Maybelle spent the hours before and after each of her missions in this room. She'd sat across from Red, and then Sam, as she detailed plans, failures, successes, and everything in the grey area between winning and losing.

At the main dais, Sam stood up. Her chair scraped against the wooden platform, catching the attention of those not looking toward their leaders.

On her left, a grizzled man with shaggy grey hair and a beard, leaned back in his seat, lounging as he watched her. To the right a younger man, jet black hair and matching eyes, stared ahead, surveying the Warren's officers. His gaze darted around, pausing longer on each captain of an alter squad.

Maybelle rubbed her fingers across the patch on her sleeve. A hand, with sparks flying from the fingertips announced her as an alter. Every alter squad captain displayed a patch like it somewhere on their uniform. Every captain in the rebellion, alters included, sported the rebel emblem on their chests, a handprint with three red lines cutting across the fingers. Maybelle was the only captain to combine the two on her uniform. Red's idea, to mark her as the first to captain an alter squad.

The younger man, Commander Elias, took in her patch, and then the markings on the front of her uniform. She shifted slightly, giving him a full view of the insignia.

His eyes widened slightly, cheeks flushing as his gaze rose to meet hers. She stared back at him, fury radiating through her so profoundly she was sure he felt the heat from it. She held his gaze until Sam spoke, and then turned her attention to her commander. The *real* commander.

"Welcome." The natural acoustics of the room, accompanied by her powerful voice let Sam be heard in every crevice of the cavern. "To our illustrious officers..."

Maybelle barely stopped herself from rolling her eyes.

"... and our visiting officials," Sam continued. "Commander Tanners has called this meeting. Commander Elias agreed to our invitation to host, and," she spread her hands, "now we're all here."

Maybelle raised an eyebrow. For someone who hated things like this, Sam was doing a surprisingly good job of controlling her impatience.

"There," Sam ran a hand through her cropped hair and planted her palm on the table, "an introduction and a welcome. Let's get on with business already."

On the dais, Tina—the head of Sam's guard—pinched the bridge of her nose. Maybelle concealed her smile as Commander Elias puffed up like an affronted bird and Tanners barked out a laugh.

"Right you are, Commander." Tanners' voice was as gruff as he looked. He stood, giving Sam a polite nod before staring out at every officer of the splintered rebellion. "I'll cut straight to the meat of it, because we don't have a lot of time and because, like Commander Sam, I find the fluff and pomp irritating beyond belief."

A chuckle went up from the small group of officers in the center of the room. Tanners had been close with Red. He'd seemed ready to accept Sam as commander once the votes came in, but once Elias broke apart with his band, everything fell apart. Tanners had chosen to go his own way as well.

"We have intel on an upcoming attack," Tanners said. "Black-Stars, and not the fresh-faced recruits they keep bringing in from the city. These are the ones born into the role, trained from infancy to fight."

Kate shifted on the bench. Maybelle put a hand on her leg and Kate met her eye for a second before looking back to the dais.

"They're coming for us."

Murmurs rippled through the room. Sam held up a hand and a hush fell.

"I'll elaborate," Tanner continued, "they're coming for the Dugout."

Chatter filled the air, gasps, calls, and questions shouted up to the dais. Kate turned to Maybelle, fear clouding her gaze. Maybelle squeezed her leg.

"It'll be all right. They have a plan. That's why we're all here."

Kate nodded, but her fingers shook as she clasped Maybelle's hand.

The Dugout. Second in size only to the Warren. It was the fallback location if their enemies ever found the Warren. Tanners' command consisted of a small number of officers, but the base he maintained housed hundreds of civilians. White-Stars who refused to go into the camps after being forced from their villages; lower castes who didn't want to live with the new restrictions Grey-Stars were implementing; families who fled because they'd had children pre-Coding.

Rumors going around after Red's death, and the subsequent vote to name Sam commander, suggested Elias had tried to steal the Dugout from Tanners. He'd taken a squad of men while Tanners attended Sam's ceremony and attempted to name himself the new leader of the rebellion, with the Dugout as the new headquarters.

It hadn't gone well for the young man when Tanners returned.

Maybelle had heard bits and pieces of the tales that roared through the Warren during that turbulent time. Elias leaned in and murmured something to Tanners; the man's face went red and he clenched his fist. She raised an eyebrow, wondering if the truth was more tempestuous than the rumors.

Sam held up her hand again, but only the Warren captains noticed and fell silent. The rest of the cavern continued their chatter until she cleared her throat and rose her voice above the noise.

"*Enough.*" She gestured to Tanners. "Continue, Commander."

He gave her a sharp nod. "Our information is good. Comes from a reliable source we've used many times before. They'll be approaching on the ground. Plan on raiding us, taking hostages, killing soldiers, and forcing civilians back into the cities."

"Why?" Sam asked.

"Their endeavor to relocate all the White-Stars to those camps hasn't been going well. We've had an influx of runaways. Black-stars are spending too much time trying to catch entire families who keep leaving to go back to their villages. Villages they've started burning, by the way." Tanners glanced from Elias to Sam.

From Elias's expression, he knew. Sam knew also; Maybelle had been the one to inform her after a recent mission near the capital.

Tanners went on. "We need help. We need to push back the Black-Star force long enough to evacuate the civilians."

"Where will they go?" Commander Elias inquired, his tone dry.

Maybelle's nostrils flared as heat expanded in her chest. Kate gave a soft yelp and Maybelle released her hand, apologizing under her breath.

"Many can come here," Sam replied. "Commander Tanners and I have already discussed how many we can accommodate."

Elias scowled, evidently not pleased about being left out of that discussion.

"The others," Tanners continued, "we were hoping could stay at your base until we can find a new settlement for them. Many want to..." he hesitated a moment. His gaze darted to Sam, and then to one of his officers.

Maybelle looked where he did and noted a woman with black hair streaked with red, braided and curled into three tight buns at the back of her head. She wore a uniform similar to Maybelle's. A patch on her shoulder indicated she led an alter squad. The handprint on her back—the only part visible from where Maybelle sat—carried four scarlet lines across the fingers.

Not just a captain then. A general. One of only six in the history of the rebellion. Sam had been one, Tanners too.

This had to be Aabria; a woman famed for the burn scars running from her fingertips to her elbows. Famed for the darkness of her skin, for the way it shone with light when she called upon her power. Famed for the deaths of enough Black-Star commanders that she was one of the few rebels to have their faces shown to the general public, wanted for murder and treason.

The woman gave a slight nod.

Tanners straightened, drawing in a breath as he tugged at the grey tangle of his beard. "Many want to go north. Across the mountains."

Elias scoffed, shaking his head as mutters filled the room again.

Even Sam's eyes widened in alarm before she smoothed her expression and addressed him. "Commander Tanners, we won't presume to tell you what to do with your people. But you are aware of the dangers they would face with such a trek?"

"We are aware." Tanners nodded. "The plan is this." He turned back to face the cavern, his booming voice silencing the crowd. "Three units. One to face the Black-Stars head on, two coming in from the sides to pincer them, choke them off from reinforcements, and hopefully get them to retreat."

"Hopefully," came a voice from the group belonging to Elias.

"Yes." Sam's lip curled as she shot a piercing gaze at the one who'd spoken. "We've all fought long enough to know things don't always go according to plan." She looked to Elias.

He didn't meet her eyes. "I suppose you'll want large numbers from us for this," he said to Tanners.

The older man nodded. "As many as you can spare." He looked to the room at large. "We've done many things to win this war. Lost loved ones, friends, leaders." His gaze met Sam's for a moment, and she nodded. "We've gone on rescue missions and assassinations, recruitment tours and shoot-outs. This is a chance to save more lives in one swift action than any of us have saved in..." he let out a small sigh, "*many* years."

Silence filled the cavern. Kate's fingers tightened around Maybelle's. She returned the pressure.

They both knew what Sam's decision would be. She'd have made up her mind the minute Tanners explained the situation to her. This meeting was about convincing the rest of their officers, and Elias.

"Not to mention," Sam said, her gaze drifting from one group to the next until it landed on the officers from the Warren, "we have a chance to come together.

Here and now. Show a united front to those *frosted bastards* who think they can walk over us like we're dirt. Show them what happens when they target children and the elderly. Commander Tanners' intelligence suggests the Black-Stars think this will be an easy mission. They won't expect us. And they definitely won't expect us in the numbers we can bring if we come together."

"Who will be leading this mission?" Elias leaned back in his chair.

Sam looked down at him and even from halfway across the cavern, Maybelle caught a glimpse of the roiling fury she'd carried in her since the day Red died.

"The Dugout is Commander Tanners' base. This operation will be his to run. With my full support." She met Tanners' eye.

Silence fell yet again; anxious and heavy, permeating the room.

Kate leaned into Maybelle and whispered, "Will he join us?"

"He'd better." Maybelle's hiss spread down their table, drawing several eyes to them. "We don't have the numbers without him. And he *owes us*." These last words carried venom. Around them, officers nodded in agreement, rumbling murmurs spreading through their ranks.

Maybelle clenched her hand. She sucked in a deep breath, trying to move her thoughts away from Elias's betrayal.

He'd been the one who called Red away, demanding the rebel commander come to a minor outpost in the north of the country for a meeting. Elias was the reason Maybelle hadn't been there.

What he'd done to Sam and the rest of the rebel force afterward only heightened the already soaring reach of her anger.

Something shook her.

Maybelle blinked, looked up from her clenched fist and found Kate watching her.

"You all right?"

She nodded. "Sorry."

Kate shook her head, concern in the deep pools of grey still surveying Maybelle. "I think she's done, look."

She pointed to the dais. Tanners, Elias, and Sam sat in a triangle. Sam leaned back in her chair as the two men continued their discussion. Maybelle recognized her body language. The hooded gaze, crossed arms, and locked jaw. Sam was done talking. She was ready for action.

Another minute passed before the men pulled their chairs back into position. The rumbling voices in the cavern quieted as each commander stood.

"We have decided." Sam raised a hand and indicated the men on either side of her. "We do this together. Prepare yourselves and your soldiers. This mission takes place in three days' time."

Maybelle's mouth went dry.

The next few hours were spent planning. Units were assigned and officers given their orders.

In the organized chaos, Maybelle slipped away from the alter squad captains—arguing about who would have to be with Elias's group—and Kate—discussing plans with medic units—and made her way to General Aabria. The warrior stood at the dais, bent low over the table, looking at a map with Commander Tanners.

Sam sat beside them, her focus on a tablet in her hands. Over her shoulder, Tina gave Maybelle a curt nod. She returned the gesture and climbed the stone steps to join Sam at the top.

"You ready for this?" Sam asked without looking up.

"I am. I'm wondering if they are."

Sam's jaw clenched. Beside her, Tanners had stopped moving his hands across the map. He wasn't looking at them, but Maybelle felt his attention.

"They'll be ready," Sam sighed. "We need them, Maybelle."

"I know." She shifted her weight, leaning to the side and glancing out at Commander Elias and his people. "I don't like it."

"I don't think any of us like it," came a low silky voice, edged with heat. General Aabria straightened, her dark gaze on Maybelle. She took in the insignia on her chest. "Ahh, the famed first captain of the alters. It's an honor."

Maybelle shook her head, putting a hand to her chest. "The honor is mine, General. Your skills on the battlefield are impressive to say the least."

"My skill with this…" She held up her hand. The skin, dark as any of the caverns in the Warren, glowed with red light, swelling up her hand and forearm.

From where she stood, Maybelle felt the heat.

"… or this." The same hand moved to her holster, light fading, heat vanishing in an instant.

"Both," Maybelle said with a smile. "I hear you're a marksman second only to this one." She jerked her thumb toward Sam and her friend chuckled with a shake of her head.

Aabria's upper lip curled into a sneering grin which might have seemed scornful were it not for the gleam in her eyes. "I heard you were funny," she murmured, her voice making Maybelle wonder if her power had burned her throat in the early days of her training.

"I'm a lot of things." Maybelle shrugged. The smile slid from her lips. "Do you really mean to cross the northern mountains?"

Aabria nodded. "The real conversation starts now I suppose. Yes. I mean to take my people across the mountains." Her smile became serious and determined.

Something stirred in Maybelle. Concern drifted through her stomach, but also a flash of anger. "The danger… leaving Pangaea… why?"

"I'm tired of fighting for a land that doesn't want me. I want something new. I want to *see* what the rest of the world is with my own eyes." She blinked, long eyelashes resting for a moment on her high cheekbones, and she let out a soft sigh. "I know the danger, Captain. What is life without danger, without risk? What is it worth if you don't fight for it?"

"Well said," Sam murmured.

The heat in Maybelle's stomach eased. She nodded. "I take it you won't be in this fight with us?"

Aabria shook her head. "I wish. I'll take out a few Black-Stars on my way through their blockade, don't you worry." Her gaze went dark, lips falling into a tight line as her nostrils flared. "And I'll be back."

Maybelle tilted her head.

"Someday." Aabria gave a half shrug. Her eyes blazed with red light for a brief second. "I will return."

Maybelle nodded. "Hopefully to a different Pangaea."

Aabria held out her arm and Maybelle took it. Her fingers closed around the scarred skin just above Aabria's wrist. They exchanged a final nod, and then she and Tanners moved away from the dais.

"You'd never met her before?" Sam inquired as Maybelle watched them walk away.

"No," she shook her head, "I don't know why. Our paths never crossed."

Sam sighed and rose from her chair, setting the tablet on the table. "Because you're two of the strongest alters we have. I doubt there was a span of more than a few minutes that you've both been in the Warren. Besides, she sticks to the Dugout when she's not on assignment."

Maybelle's gaze drifted to Elias.

"You can't trust him."

Sam growled. The sound drew Maybelle's attention back to her friend. Sam's hand was clenched into a fist, the tattoos across her forearm bulging.

"That's what my instincts say too," she uttered through gritted teeth. "Every inquiry... each investigation cleared him. He didn't have anything to do with Red's death."

Maybelle ran a hand through her hair. "I know. All the same..."

Sam nodded. "Fortunately, we have a large enough force that we don't need to pad it with his people. Tanners will get the extra help from them, and us." She blew out a sigh. "The Dugout has so many civilians..."

"You're worried we won't be able to hold them off long enough for everyone to get out?"

"That's part of it," Sam started down the steps and Maybelle followed, "but I'm also thinking about our own numbers. If something happened here..."

Maybelle waited, but Sam didn't elaborate. Instead, the two of them followed one of the narrow corridors off the main room, Tina in step behind them. They reached a small antechamber, an office of sorts, used by Red and now Sam as a workspace when they didn't feel like trekking all the way back to their quarters after a meeting.

Sam pulled Maybelle inside. "I want you to do something for me."

Maybelle's chest went heavy. She tilted her head. "What?"

Sam crossed the room to her desk and plucked a frame off the wood. A stone sank into Maybelle's gut. She had an idea of what was coming.

Sam returned to her, forcing the picture into her slender hands. Red took up most of the background. He'd hated that picture, the way his mouth was open in his usual roaring laugh, one of his eyes half-closed and a bit of lunch still in his beard. Sam stood to the side, a rare soft smile on her face. Her arms were around Penelope's shoulders, clutching her eldest daughter as she laughed along with her uncle. In the center of the frame Kate was facing the camera while wrestling with four-year-old Jamie. Maybelle's arms were outstretched, reaching to catch Jamie, a wide smile on her face.

A soft crown of flowers rested on Penelope's head. Her tenth birthday and Maybelle and Kate's third year in the rebellion.

"Sam..."

"I need you to stay with them," Sam said. Her eyes, those same piercing eyes which had look at Maybelle with such hatred and malice the first time they'd met, glistened with tears. "There's something in my gut, Maybelle, something telling me they can't be left alone."

"They won't be alone," Maybelle reminded her. "The guard will be here. Kate will be here. And you and I will be on coms the whole time."

Sam sucked in a breath, taking the frame back and staring down at the glass. "It's not the same. Not like having you here. If something goes wrong..."

"Sam, I need to be with *you* in case something goes wrong." Maybelle's heartbeat quickened. Letting down her friend like this... it wasn't what she wanted to do. But she'd learned her lesson when she let Red go on a mission without her. It wouldn't, *couldn't*, happen again.

"I want you here. Able to get them out at a moment's notice."

Maybelle swallowed. She cast a glance at Sam's guard. Tina slipped out the door, closing it behind her.

"No." She caught Sam's eye and forced herself to hold the gaze.

Chapter Thirty

60 Years Ago - Northern end of Pangaea - Near the Dugout

T hey had a good vantage point at the top of the hill, sunrise lighting up the world behind them. It gave them a slim advantage, but they'd take what they could get in this battle.

The world seemed so still now. Waves of wind blew the grass around them, flowing over dusty rolling hills, patchwork forests, and a deep ravine trickling with water after the storm two nights ago.

Maybelle refamiliarized herself with the battlefield, going over maps and plans, scouting every tree and rock and hill. The entrance to the Dugout sat behind them, at the edge of a forest of thick pine and crumbling boulders. The base zigzagged through rock and stone, spreading like webs from its center point to cover nearly three miles of tunnels. Behind them, at the end of the longest shoot of tunnels, sat rows and rows of trucks ready to transport civilians to the Warren and Elias's compound.

General Aabria's people were already on their way to cross the northern mountains. The rest of the civilians in the Dugout waited for the distraction. The Black-Stars knew where the Dugout was; the risk of moving everyone early was too great.

Maybelle closed her eyes, breathing in the scent of dirt, wild jasmine, and sweat and fear from the soldiers around her. It felt as though time stood still for a moment, as though no scout would sound the alarm, and no squadron of Black-Stars would be arriving at any minute.

Rumbling filled the air. A few soldiers cried out. Their captains called for quiet as the ground shook beneath their feet.

A piercing whistle sounded in front of them, coming from the gap between two large groupings of trees. It was one of two places the Black-Stars could approach the Dugout without crossing the ravine or razing a forest. Intelligence had assured them it would be the Black-Star's main point of egress.

Heads turned as another whistle splintered through the air to the right of them. Maybelle's eyes flew open. A shudder ran down her spine as she looked north. Beside her, Sam cursed.

Maybelle pulled the blade from her thigh, loosely rolling the grip through her fingers. "So much for the intel."

"We still have a plan," Sam reminded her. "Elias's soldiers will handle it."

"If they don't, we strike head on and then get surrounded," she murmured, voice too low for the soldiers around them to hear.

"I know." Sam glanced around.

They stood at the front of hundreds of soldiers, the majority of their force. The rest were helping with the evacuation or protecting the Warren. Others were helping with the evacuation, the rest stationed at the Warren.

Sam grunted. "Red was always better at this."

Maybelle reached out her free hand and clasped Sam's shoulder. "You trained these people. You know our capabilities better than anyone. If you say we're going to win... we're going to win."

Sam nodded. She furrowed her brow, straightened her shoulders, and turned to face the front line of soldiers. They held guns, blades, med-kits, and explosives. Sam's gaze scanned the ranks as she spoke.

"You all know why we're here. This is our chance to save thousands of innocent lives, and to take a *bite* out of the Black-Star force."

There was a ripple of nervous laughter and shouts of agreement.

"These people have destroyed your homes," Sam shouted. Her voice road the wind, soaring across rows of soldiers, feeding the mounting tension and anticipation. "They've killed people love, taken our freedom, stolen our choices. Now they try to take back the ones we've saved."

A shudder ran through Maybelle. Fury mounted in her as she remembered her capture by the rebels and the images they'd shown her and Kate. The truth they'd revealed, like pulling a curtain she'd never bothered to check behind, like taking off a blindfold she wore in willful ignorance.

Ahead of them black vehicles approached the narrow gap between the thickets. Trees and vines, jutting rock formations, and sharp stone funneled them into a bottleneck.

The com in Maybelle's ear beeped.

"Looks like six rows, four vehicles wide, coming in first. Another fifty trucks behind them. The rest are waiting to come through the trees on foot," Stacey reported.

Maybelle scanned the tallest trees in the thicket. The woman had skin hard as a rock, but was still light enough to scamper to the top of a swaying pine to get them the information they needed.

She pressed a finger to the device. "Numbers?"

"On foot... a lot, Captain. I think we're looking at more than twenty-five hundred."

Maybelle danced on the balls of her feet; fists clenched at her sides. They were three-thousand strong. Every soldier they could spare was prepared for the battle, some hidden, some ready for an open fight, and some helping with the evacuation.

Lavender sparks burst from her core. Power surged down her arms, tingling the tips of her fingers. She hadn't teleported in days, conserving every ounce of her energy for this moment. This battle. This chance to not let what happened to Red happen to Sam.

Her commander strode up the line. "Will we *bend* to their will?" Sam shouted into the crisp morning air.

The soldiers shouted back, "No!"

"Will we *break* in the face of their tyranny?"

Louder this time, more ferocity, "*No!*"

"Will we let them *destroy* everything we have worked to build? Will we roll over like *dogs* to their *masters*? Or will we *fight*?"

Maybelle broke the line, turning to stand next to Sam as she shouted in echo, "*We fight!*"

"*WE FIGHT!*"

"*WE FIGHT!*"

"*WE FIGHT!*"

Over and over the rebel soldiers shouted their response. Sam looked to Maybelle.

"I can't convince you?"

Maybelle shook her head. "I'm not leaving your side, Sam."

The two turned to face the forest where, through the trees, the front of Black-Star convoys were emerging. Four-hundred yards away.

Three-eighty.

"... I made a promise, you know," Maybelle murmured as she and Sam, and every rebel in their platoon, knelt into the grass.

Three-sixty.

Sam glanced at her, eyebrows drawn together in a silent inquiry.

"Penelope came to me, after Red." A soft smile crossing her lips at the memory. "I told her I wouldn't leave you."

Three-fifty.

Sam shook her head with a grimace.

"You raised her well, Sam." Maybelle laughed. "She turned out just like you."

Sam opened her mouth, but the convoy had reached the marked line, so instead of responding to Maybelle, she shouted, "*Brace!*"

Maybelle ducked, curving her body away from the trucks.

An explosion shook the air. Then another, and another. The sky went dark with smoke. Heat burned the air before them as chunks of metal and flame flew in every direction. The ground trembled as more transports plowed through the ruined wreckage of the first line.

There was movement in the trees. Maybelle's eyes narrowed with concern. Stacey swung from a towering oak and landed on the hood of a transport. Above her, tree branches were alight with flames.

Seconds later, coming from further away because he didn't have her diamond hard skin to protect from the explosions, Thomas raced into view. He ran to a second truck in the line. It moved at an angle, one tire popped from driving over blasted metal. He sprinted, keeping pace with the vehicle, reached out, grabbed the metal just above the popped wheel, and yanked upward.

Screams sounded, barely audible to Maybelle and the front line, as the truck went onto its side wheels. There was a split second when it balanced on two tires before it rolled, crashing down and slamming into the transport beside it.

Pride roared in Maybelle's chest. This was the Alter Squad Alpha, *her* alter squad.

She should be out there with them, neutralizing the Black-Star's main advantage—those frosted transports.

Her gaze darted to Sam.

Sam sensed her looking. Without taking her eyes from the battlefield, she said, "You know, you could get in there and be back to me before the Black-Stars reach our line."

Maybelle's right cheek quirked up in a half-grin. Her fingers clenched around her blade, eight long inches of steel glinting in the morning sun.

She focused on the last truck in the second line, weaving its way through the wreckage. She blinked.

Scents, sounds, and lighting shifted. Abruptly, the morning sun dimmed. Heat intensified, along with the smells of burnt flesh, engine grease, and singed wood and metal.

The men on either side of her gasped. One reached for a microphone on the dash. Her blade sank into his heart before his fingertips brushed the buttons.

The driver screamed and scrambled for his gun. He lost his grip on the wheel. The front right tire hit something. Maybelle lunged forward as the truck tilted. Black gemstones glinted in her vision as she fell atop the man, her knife sliding through flesh, finding the gap between rib bones, and puncturing his lung.

The truck continued to tilt. She blinked again.

Maybelle stood atop the hill, Sam to her left, Tina to the right as the three of them surveyed the field. The first line of trucks smoked and burned. Her alter squad had taken out the second wave.

Now the third line of Black-Stars approached. Massive wheels navigated around and over the detritus of their fellow vehicles. Screams overtook the sounds of fire. Black-Stars crawled from overturned trucks, rose—staggering—to their feet. Some advanced, but most retreated to find a medic or a new transport.

Maybelle bared her teeth as one of the trucks got past the last line of explosives. She clicked a button on the small device in her hand. An instant later she appeared, stumbling as the truck under her feet slammed on the brakes. Black-Stars surrounded her, lining the benches in the bed of the transport, weapons clenched in their hands as they waited to arrive at the front.

She dropped the device, and by the time the first Black-Star lifted her gun, Maybelle had vanished.

Back on the hill, she watched as a Black-Star transport—the one which had so skillfully avoided their traps—exploded. Beside her, Sam grinned.

"Nice."

She crouched atop an overturned rebel vehicle they'd dragged to the battlefield ahead of time. The area was deliberately strewn with debris, giving rebel soldiers hiding places from which they could observe the battle, pick their targets, and ambush them.

As Maybelle did now.

The field had shifted. Black-Stars emerged from the trees, engaging in direct combat. Clusters of rebels picked away at them, firing from cover.

She glanced south. An alter squad waged furious battle with a group who had tried to follow the ravine, circle around, and cut them off. She wasn't sure which squad was handling the problem until a burst of vines shot from the ground. The Black-Star progression halted as soldiers found themselves tangled in a thorny mess of angry plant-life.

She grinned.

Maybelle couldn't make out the battle raging to the north. The eastern forest, housing the Dugout, and the western thickets created a narrow channel of rolling hills. Whatever Elias was doing over there, it was holding off the second force of Black-Stars. For now.

Smoke rose above the trees, nearly filling the sky like storm clouds.

She shook her head. Narrow the focus. Look closer.

A massive man, Black-Stars barely visible through the mess of black tattoos covering his face, had lost his helmet as he seared across the battlefield. He strode forward from the thicket bottleneck, moving around strewn chunks of metal and burning wood.

Men and women fell, holes blasted in their chests as he shot off round after round of plasma. Spare cartridges covered his belt, a crisscross of them going over his chest as well. The gun itself was nearly as big as the man. It was a two-handed weapon, designed to shred its enemies with no remorse.

Maybelle flattened herself against the door of the upturned vehicle. She scooted back and leaned her head over the edge. Sam stood below, her back to the fractured solar panels on the car's roof, a weapon in one hand, the other pressed to her earpiece as she shouted instructions over the sound of plasma bolts firing. Her guards took down a group of Black-Stars who had gotten past the front line.

"I don't give a *nacra*," Sam bellowed. She lifted her gun, stepped around Tina, and fired. Forty yards away another Black-Star fell. "Get them out of there *now*."

An earsplitting scream drew Maybelle's attention back to the goliath.

Maybelle's sucked in a breath and took a few extra seconds to gulp from her canteen. With a grimace she rose, took sight of the monster's position, and blinked.

She missed.

He'd moved in the fraction of a second it took for her to zap from one space to another. She fell; hit the ground with a grunt that left her breathless. A roar ripped through the air, and she rolled.

Above her, a massive boot came down where she'd been a second before.

Scorched skin hit her nostrils. Smoke filled her sinuses as she inhaled.

"Nacra," she groaned. She got her arms under her, knife still clenched in her hand, and rose to all fours.

Something slammed into her. Pain erupted across her side. Her body flew several feet, crumpled as she landed in the dirt again. Mud now. Wet with blood.

She scrambled to her feet as a fist the size of a dinner plate connected with her face.

Everything went spotty. She hit the ground again. Fury howled through her veins and her power growled within her.

She zapped and landed on top of the truck she'd been watching from. Shaking her head, her vision cleared.

There. The man had released the butt of the gun, letting it dangle as he scanned the area around him, confused.

Where had she gone?

Maybelle grinned.

In his moment of confusion, she launched. Flew off the truck and zapped on her way down. The momentum from her fall carried through as she slammed into his back. Her legs wrapped around the trunk-like torso. Her arm flung around him, aiming for the front of his neck. She screamed into his ear. Her blade slid. Caught on his armor.

He reached a meaty hand back, howling and spitting as he caught hold of her tight braid.

Her knife found purchase.

She pulled, dragged it with every bit of muscle she'd built up over the last ten years. Swung her whole body backward.

She felt the moment her blade hit his spine, his bones the only thing keeping her pinned to his back. Then even they gave way.

She hit the ground. Tumbled and frantically rolled as his body came crashing down on top of her.

She screamed as he landed on her leg. Fear. Not pain.

Well, not much pain.

She kicked and pushed and grunted as she freed her leg. The beast lay sprawled on his back, neck ripped open, blood coating his armor. The gun lay on the ground, far too heavy for her to lift, but she made a mental note to tell Thomas to find it.

If she saw him again.

She'd lost track of him after they'd taken out the transports, and hadn't been able to get ahold of him on the com.

Fear curdled in her gut.

Maybelle found Stacey's body in the path of corpses the monster left in his wake. No burns, no cuts, no holes in that beautiful, still glittering skin. Her throat had been crushed. Maybelle gently closed Stacey's eyes, a cascade of memories burning an ache in her chest. Shots rang out in the distance; she had to find Sam.

She jogged across the battlefield. The movement, steady and even, served as all the rest she'd get, all the rest she needed.

Maybelle bared her teeth as she passed the truck she'd launched from. Sam was gone. She pushed down a jolt of fear and kept running.

She made her way east, scrambling around stacked trees, trenches, and anything else the rebels could use as cover.

A cluster of rebel soldiers raised their weapons as she hurried past. She stopped, whirled around, and knelt. One had a bandaged arm. Another sported gashes across their cheek and shoulder. Small burns marred them all.

"The commander?" she demanded.

One pointed further east. "You're not far behind."

She nodded, the flush of relief dying quickly. "You're doing great," she said to the group. She rose.

"How much longer can we hold them off?" the youngest looking of their group, a redhead with swirling gemstones and wide emerald eyes, asked. "They keep coming." He swallowed.

Maybelle crouched back down. She dug deep and pulled up the same smile she'd used on Kate each time their lives seemed to be spinning out in front of them. "We're saving how many lives today?"

"Reports said six-thousand," the soldier muttered.

"*Six-thousand.*" She nodded, letting her pride shine through. "In one day. And taking out a fair number of the enemy as well."

The redhead nodded. One of his comrades sat straighter. Hands tightened around weapons, gazes grew steely.

"We hold this line." She jammed a finger into the ground. "We hold it while the ones who can't fight get out. And then we retreat and leave the Black-Stars fumbling and confused while we celebrate our victory."

They nodded. Maybelle scanned the field. No movement, yet. She had to find Sam.

"Hold the line," she said.

Maybelle rose, blade out and ready as she moved across the open rolling hills.

Barely a minute later she stumbled across a circle of bodies. Blood and water mixed together into a sludge that clung to her boots. Black gemstones glinted on the temples of the fallen, maybe a dozen men and women, without a mark on them. Some had their eyes open, empty and glazed over. Blue lips, swollen throats...

She took a hesitant step.

Her chest constricted, knuckles going white as she clenched her blade. Cee lay in the center of the circle, beads of water still trailing from her fingertips. A gash cut across her soft features. It ran from forehead to chin, slicing through her amber eye and marring her beautiful face.

A flicker of memory ran through Maybelle's mind. Another broken eye. A long time ago.

She swallowed down her vomit, bent to close Cee's good eye, and continued east.

Maybelle found Sam and her guards crouched behind a chunk of concrete in one of the trenches they'd made the day before, nearly halfway between the Dugout entrance and the front line.

Her throat went dry. Where six had circled her commander, two now remained.

She'd nearly reached them when she spotted movement thirty feet away, behind a stack of logs. She picked up the pace, circling Sam's position to get a better look.

A Black-Star stood, hefted back his arm, and flung something. Blinking red light glowed on the small device.

It wasn't something she'd done before. As much as she enjoyed her power, enjoyed learning to fight, to defend herself and others... As much as she enjoyed risk, this was...

She zapped. Timed it perfectly. Her body floated for a brief moment, suspended in the air next to the hand-held bomb. She grabbed it, twisted in the air, and threw.

She zapped again. Her momentum didn't let her land gently. Her body slammed into the ground in front of Sam. At the same instant, an explosion went off behind their cover.

Pain shuddered through her shoulder. Maybelle gasped. A yowling shriek erupted from her as she rolled, clutching her upper arm. Sam knelt beside her.

"Hold still, *nacra*," she snarled through gritted teeth.

"So sorry," Maybelle gasped. "I suppose I'm making too much noise as well?" She winced as Sam helped her sit up, dug hands under her armpits, and dragged her back against their cover.

The commander's guards took up flanking positions, heads on a swivel.

"Thirty feet," Maybelle grunted, catching Tina's gaze. "I only saw one. Explosion might have got 'em."

Tina nodded, crouched, and went to investigate.

"As a matter of fact," Sam murmured, but her focus was on Maybelle's shoulder. "Dislocated. Ready?"

"No—*frost*." She bit through her lip. Blood ran across her tongue. She spit the metallic liquid onto the dirt.

It landed next to a flower. She growled.

"How're we doing?" she asked.

Sam's brow furrowed. She handed over a canteen. Maybelle waved her off, took her own from her waist, and drained it.

"There was a cave-in."

Maybelle's eyes narrowed. "What does that mean?"

Sam ran a hand across her forehead, staining her skin with red-tinged mud. "The civilians haven't been able to escape."

Maybelle exhaled, and a shudder ran through her body. Her blood chilled as bile churned in her stomach. "None of them?"

Sam shook her head. "A few. A hundred, maybe. They cleared about half of it a few minutes ago."

Maybelle let out a groan that had nothing to do with her injured shoulder. "Any other good news?"

"Elias lost the line."

Maybelle exhaled, eyes wide, fear lacing her veins. "That explains the guy throwing bombs. We're surrounded?"

"Tanners is holding them off." She paused, putting a hand to the small black com device in her left ear.

Maybelle waited, watching her.

It was surreal. The calm around them. This small sliver in the center of the battlefield, somehow quiet. Plasma guns went off in the north and west. The next line of Black-Stars would be approaching soon. They'd slammed into the rebel force in perfectly timed waves since the first transports had been destroyed.

She didn't know how many had been killed, how many Black-Stars were still to come. She'd stopped getting reports from her squad about five minutes ago. She shut away the rush of emotion that came with that realization, locking it up tight so it wouldn't distract her.

Maybelle rubbed a hand across the back of her neck, shaking off the sweat and rolling out her bad shoulder with a grimace.

She stared around them. The grass no longer waved in the wind. Blood and bodies held it down, grinding it into the dirt.

"Tanners is dead."

"*What*?"

Sam's brown eyes were wide, her lips trembling. "He took a shot to the chest. Minutes ago. Their line fell. Black-Stars are headed towards us from the north." She paused again, tilting her head with an unfocused gaze. "No. They're waiting."

"Waiting for what?" Maybelle moved into a crouch, wiping her blade across her shirt before sticking into the sheath and pulling her gun.

"I'm not sure. His remaining forces are pulling back to the Dugout. They'll hold the entrance as long as they can. We'll stay here; keep the Black-Stars from getting more reinforcements."

Maybelle nodded and stood.

Sam reached up a hand and she took it, pulling the commander to her feet.

"How many do we have left?"

"Last report?" Sam took her own weapon from her holster, checked the cartridge, and cracked her neck. "Half."

Maybelle's stomach lurched. On either side of them, the guards, Rorty, and Tina exchanged glances.

"They're still coming," Rorty murmured.

Sam nodded. She looked to each of them, steel in her gaze. "This went from a distraction to a last stand. Let's make it worth it."

Maybelle perched atop the tallest tree, above the Dugout entrance, high over the forest. Her gaze slid over the battlefield.

With how much blood was down there, it was surprisingly colorless. Beige and gold, from the rolling hills. Black, from the uniforms of those who had fallen.

So many had fallen. On both sides.

The Black-Stars had given up approaching from the south. A muddled thicket of thorny vines and bushes had swallowed the ones who tried.

Most of the bodies lay strewn across the northern passage. Rebel forces, eliminated with cold intent. Sundered by the massive trucks that now formed a line, blocking escape in that direction.

Maybelle seethed.

Before her, she could make out dying fires from the explosions she and her alter squad had caused. The ruined trucks completely blocked any form of transport approaching from the west.

Her own soldiers had been funneled to the center of the battlefield by the Black-Stars who'd made it past the line. She pressed a finger to her com.

"Just south of your position, I've got a small group. Looks like they're hunkered down in one of our trenches. Two grenades should do the trick."

"Affirmative."

A pause. Movement below.

"Confirm twenty yards to target."

"Confirmed."

A few seconds passed and then the trench of Black-Stars exploded. Dirt, body parts, and shredded chunks of wood flew in every direction.

"Kill confirmed. Keep moving that direction. I see two more clusters, about that size. Might be able to cut a path to some reinforcements of our own near the ravine."

She clung to the tree. Watching, reporting, directing, and confirming as Sam and a squad of rebels cut through the Black-Stars foolish enough to hunker down behind enemy lines.

Minutes passed. Her hands itched. Scraped from the bark, sticky from the sap. A breeze kicked up and she clasped both arms around the trunk. The tree swayed, rocking gently in a way that might have put her to sleep if she weren't eighty feet in the air.

Her stomach lurched from the rocking, as well as the scents below. Burned flesh, putrid smoke, and the stench of blood wafted into her nostrils. She blinked rapidly, tears forming to clear out the ash and dust clouding her vision.

Her gaze caught on the thickets to the west.

She blinked again. Gripped the edge of her shirt and pulled it up to rub her eyes. Everything swam in a haze.

No. The ground closer to her was clear.

That movement, though. In the trees, like ants swarming through blades of grass...

She raised a finger once again to her com. Spoke with a trembling voice, and then zapped back to the ground.

Maybelle's hand shot out a fraction of a second too late. Her fingers, sticky now with blood, wrapped around the back of Tina's shirt.

When they zapped behind cover, she nearly fell with the weight of the woman's dead body. Sam cursed, fury etched into the lines of her face.

"What do we do?" Rorty asked. "What do we do, what do we do, what do we do?" Her voice devolved into a panicked whisper. The gun fell from her shaking fingers.

Maybelle grunted with the effort of gently laying down Tina's body. She stood quickly, grabbed the front of Rorty's shirt and slapped her across the face.

Rorty gaped and blinked.

"I don't have time for you to have a break down." Maybelle pointed a finger at her.

Rorty nodded.

She stepped away, darting a look beyond the truck they'd hid behind. Black-Stars marched toward them. Rows of men and women, locked in step, plasma rifles at the ready. They'd emerged from the trees in an endless wave, marching so close it had been easy to cut down chunks of them at a time.

Still more came. A dense wall of force encroaching ever closer to the soldiers they'd scrounged into a final line of defense. To hold the middle ground between the thickets to the west and the entrance to the Dugout.

Shots fired, someone screamed.

"Stay down!" Sam shouted. She leaned out.

Maybelle grabbed the back of her jacket and yanked as a plasma bolt whipped past her head. "What are you doing?" she demanded.

"They need to get behind cover," Sam snapped.

Maybelle shook her head and leaned her back against the truck. She looked out behind them. Her heart sank.

"They are," she whispered.

Sam followed her gaze and uttered a sound like a wounded animal.

Approaching from the east was another contingent of Black-Stars. They marched across the bloody grass and mud, the corpses of rebels and Stars. And above them... in the sky...

"*No*," Sam groaned.

Hilo-carriers soared across the horizon. They neared the entrance of the Dugout, just at the edge of the forest, and they dropped their cargo.

Maybelle acted without thought. Her fingers gripped the fabric of Rorty's uniform, while her other hand wrapped around Sam's wrist. Her commander opened her mouth, but it was too late.

The three of them landed on the other side of the ravine as the bombs hit. Explosions rocketed through the forest and across the battlefield. Black-Stars and rebels alike were blasted by the force.

From where they stood, nearly half a mile away, Maybelle took a staggering step back as the shock wave hit them.

"*Depths*." Sam lifted her gun and then dropped it and fell to one knee.

"What..." Rorty looked from Maybelle to Sam. "What just..."

Maybelle shuddered. She closed her eyes, turning from the blazing fires consuming the forest. Consuming the innocent lives of everyone in the blast radius.

Something crackled in her ear.

She stepped further from the battlefield, and pressed a finger to the com.

"*Maybelle? Maybelle!*"

"Kate?"

Sam looked up as Maybelle uttered the word, confusion in her voice.

"*Finally. Shit. Maybelle it's... it's bad.*"

"What are you talking about? Have you gotten any reports from the civilians coming out of the Dugout?"

Sam stood, putting a hand to her own com. She gave Maybelle a nod as she found their frequency.

"*It's not... if you can... you need to come home.*" Her voice was thick, full of tears.

Maybelle frowned. Glanced at Sam.

A thundering crash sounded in her earpiece.

"What the *frost* was that?" she demanded.

"*That's what I'm trying to tell you.*" Kate's voice trembled. "*They found the Warren, Maybelle. They're here. The Black-Stars are here.*"

Chapter Thirty-One

60 Years Ago - The Warren

Maybelle moved. On instinct she wrapped her hands around Sam and Rorty's wrists, sliced open the world, and they fell.

They landed in the Warren's largest cavern. Heat from a thousand bodies pressed in on them. Maybelle stumbled when they appeared, lost her footing, and nearly went down. Sam gripped her under the arm and yanked her upright.

"Sorry," Maybelle mumbled. Her vision blurred for a moment. She shook it off.

"Kate," Sam called. She pulled Maybelle through the throng of civilians. Most recognized their commander and moved to the side. Others called out questions. Rorty took up her duty, moving people back and reminding them to give Sam space. She was crying.

Many of the lights along the walls had gone out. Others flickered and sputtered. Darkness seemed to be trying to overtake them.

Maybelle scanned the crowd as they moved toward the middle of the cavern. Three towering pillars formed a triangle to help keep the ceiling stable.

These people were elderly or young. Children sat with their mothers, grandparents, or guardians. Maybelle took in countless scrapes and cuts. Burns. Bruises. Ripped clothes and heavy coughs.

Her brow furrowed; chest tight.

They passed one of the naturally formed pillars, carved by rebel artisans into a complex piece of art. In the center, surrounded by the last of Sam's guard, were her daughters. Sam ran to them. Jamie wrapped herself around her mother, clinging to her as Sam embraced Penelope.

Rorty joined the other guards protecting the commander and her family.

"What's going on, Kate?" Maybelle asked as they embraced.

Kate sniffed. She gestured. "This is all I could get out, Maybelle. Sam," she turned to their Commander and friend, "I'm so sorry."

"What do you mean?" Maybelle's stomach sank.

Kate opened her mouth to answer. An echoing boom reverberated through the cavern. The ceiling shook; rock and debris fell. Screams erupted, fear—pain—panic.

Maybelle's eyes were wide as she looked to her oldest friend. "They breached?"

Kate nodded. "An hour ago. We couldn't get through to anyone on the coms. It was... it was a slaughter. We barricaded the doors, but..."

Another blast hit the ceiling.

"They're dropping bombs," Maybelle murmured.

Kate nodded; her lips pinched together as tears sprang from her eyes.

Maybelle looked at her hands. They were a mess of scrapes and cuts from the trees, branches, catching herself on metal as she scrambled through wreckage, and burns from pressing her hands to scorched flesh as she tried to stem the blood flow of a fellow soldier.

Her fingers trembled. Her body shook. Hours of fighting. Of zapping all across the battlefield.

She gazed out at the people remaining in the Warren. So many innocent lives... So many.

"You have to get them out."

Maybelle turned. Sam stood behind her, prying Jamie off of her neck as she pushed Penelope towards her.

"Mom, no." Penelope shook her head, fury and fear vying across her face.

"You will *not* die here," Sam snapped, her finger poking into Penelope's chest. She turned to Maybelle. "Get them *out*. Please."

Even as she said it, her voice broke. She pulled again at Jamie, but the eleven-year-old screamed and buried her head against Sam's neck.

"Mom." Tears slid down Penelope's cheeks as another blast rocked the ceiling. "Where are we even going to go?"

"Maybe it's best if we end this together." Kate put an arm around Penelope's shoulder.

Maybelle realized then how much the girl had grown. She'd witnessed a decade of these children's lives. Penelope's gemstones swirled in a spiral of scared reds and sad blues. She was only seventeen.

"No."

Everyone turned to Maybelle. She cleared her throat and spoke again. "No. We aren't giving up. We have fought so hard for so long. There has to be *something*."

Kate reached out a hand, caressed Maybelle's arm.

"Is there any way out?" Sam asked, directing the question to her guard.

Tavi stepped forward, already shaking their head. "We had to barricade every entrance to the cavern. Even caved in a few. Black-Stars have us completely surrounded." They swallowed, running a hand across their cropped sapphire-colored hair and lowered their voice. "They aren't accepting surrender."

Sam bit her lip. She nodded. Eyes glistening, she turned back to Maybelle. "We can't—"

She jerked away. "No." She looked from Sam to Kate, fury bubbling in her gut. Her hand cut through the air. "*No*. We aren't giving up. We *can't* give up."

"Please, Maybelle. Please take my girls."

"I'm not going," Penelope said with a sob. "I'm not going without you, Mom."

"Sam," Kate murmured as her own tears fell. "Can she take *anyone*?"

Maybelle's legs trembled. Their voices, the arguments going on around her, faded away. The next crash above them barely registered. She glanced up. Cracks like spiderwebs crisscrossed along the red and brown rocky ceiling.

Within her, at the core of her being, her power flitted and flickered. It spun slow and small, a tiny orb of drained ability.

This wasn't right.

This wasn't right. Or fair. Or...

The world isn't fair, Maybelle. That's why we're here. To sow order in the chaos. Peace in the castes.

Who had said that? Her mother? A teacher somewhere along the way? A Grey-Star.

Heat flared in her belly. A Grey-Star who thought they had the right to control others. Thought they alone could bring balance to the world.

But it *wasn't* balanced.

Lavender light exploded within her. Fury, at the lies, the loss, the trials they'd gone through, burned from every inch of her being.

The core of her, the center of her power and her person, shook and sparked with uncontrolled energy.

Maybelle's legs gave out. Her knees slammed into the ground, but she didn't feel the pain. Images flashed through her mind; Red, Cee, Stacey, Tina, the soldiers they'd lost over the years, the people they'd been able to save, the people they hadn't...

Energy coursed through her. She closed her eyes. Concentrate. Focus.

Pull.

In her mind, flaming tendrils of lavender flowed through her body. They rose from her chest, crawled down her arms, caressed her cheeks.

Someone gasped. The sound pulled her back to awareness. A scream followed. She opened her eyes.

Her body was alight. The purple glow of her power had, for the first time, left her skin. It floated above her arms. She raised them, tilting her palms toward the ceiling in shock. Confusion muddled purpose for a split second and the tendrils spluttered.

A hand touched her shoulder. Kate knelt beside her. Looked her in the eye.

The first person to look her in the eye when she'd discovered this power.

"Breath," Kate whispered. "Breath and concentrate."

Maybelle nodded. She filled her lungs. On her exhale, purple light arced into the air.

It flowed from her hands, spiraled up, then shot out like a wave in every direction. A glowing bubble of lavender light. So bright. Too bright.

"Oh," Kate murmured.

Maybelle winced. Tremors of pain ran through her limbs. Her palms burned like they were pressed against heated iron. Her skull cracked, splintering pain stabbing into her brain.

Voices tried to break through to her. Screams. Shouts. She couldn't... couldn't *hear* them and *do this* at the same time.

The ceiling above them shuddered. A whistle, high and piercing, filled the air.

"It's coming." Kate squeezed her shoulder. Gentle pressure. "You can do this, Maybelle."

Tears flowed from her eyes, blood from her nose and ears. She sucked air in through clenched teeth and tore open the world.

The ceiling broke. The falling sensation came.

She stared up. Watched the cavern crumble and drop. She closed her eyes. She didn't want to see the end.

She was cold.

Death. Was death supposed to be cold? The chill went through her pants, soaking her knees in frigid moisture. Her arms ached above her head. She dropped them to her sides; her hands brushed something stiff and cold and crunchy. Crunchy ice.

Maybelle cracked her eyes open. She winced back from the blinding light, lifting a hand to protect her eyes.

Snow. She recognized the source of the light. It was the sun, reflected against the snow.

What...

A hand squeezed her shoulder.

Kate.

Maybelle jerked, turning to find her friend. The movement sent shooting pain through her entire body. It felt as though her head would explode. Her chest seemed to cave inward, pressing against her lungs, pinching her spine.

She was there. Kate's hand, those soft, slender fingers meant for science, not weapons, slid down Maybelle's arm until it reached her own hand.

They intertwined fingers and Kate pulled Maybelle against her. "You did it," she breathed.

Maybelle barely heard it. She had closed her eyes against the light, reassured by Kate's presence.

"Maybelle?"

She jerked as footsteps crunched against the snow. The sounds drove daggers through her head.

"Kate, is she..."

"She'll be all right," Kate murmured.

Other voices pushed through Maybelle's muddled mind. She couldn't make out the words.

"Give us a minute," Kate said, louder.

Maybelle whimpered as Kate drew away and pulled her to her feet. She stumbled. It hurt. It all hurt.

"Maybelle."

She recognized the voice. Sam's voice. Not the pleading, hopeless sound she'd heard in the seconds before the cavern collapsed. Sam's real voice. Confident. Powerful. Dangerous. The voice which had hauled her from bed at four in the morning for combat training for six straight months.

Maybelle kept her hand raised and peeled open her eyes.

She blinked rapidly. The splintering pain faded. As did the brilliance of the snow. Her gaze focused and she gasped.

Mountains stretched before her. Rounded snow-capped tips, frost coating every rock and tree with a dusting of white. They stood on a cliffside, water rushing through a canyon hundreds of feet below.

Towering pines rose up around them. The scent hit her nostrils, so coated with smoke her fingers came away black as she wiped snot and blood and tears from her face.

The sight was amazing to behold. The trees, the jutting faces of rock peeking out underneath the thin coat of snow. But as Maybelle's eyes adjusted to the light and the cold, new tears filled them.

People.

Sam, clutching both her daughters and staring at Maybelle in awe. Tavi and Rorty, and the other members of her guard, with equally wide eyes, fear and relief competing for dominance in their expressions. Beyond them, more people. Hundreds more.

Maybelle turned to Kate. "I... I did it?" Her own voice sent another stab of pain and she winced.

Her friend nodded, tears trickling down her creamy brown cheeks.

"You did it," Sam said. She took a hesitant step forward, pulling Penelope forward—Jamie still clinging to her torso. "You saved us."

The words spread, caught in the wind as they were echoed in rippling waves by the people around them. Bodies pushed forward. Kate put her hands out, holding off the approaching crowd.

"Wait, please. She needs rest."

It was Sam's barking shout of "*Enough!*" that stopped them. Stopped most of them.

A woman pushed through the crowd. Tear tracks cut through soot and dust; her dark hair glistened with sweat and rubble.

"Why?"

Her voice was ragged, as though screams were all it had known for some time now.

"I... what?" Maybelle stammered. She looked to Kate, confused.

Kate half-shrugged. "What do you mean?" she directed to the woman.

"Why did she do it?" Anger and hate radiated from her.

Maybelle took half a step back. Spots danced at the edges of her vision, her limbs barely able to hold her up.

"Why did you *do* it?" she demanded, glaring at Maybelle.

"To save us," Maybelle whispered. "I..." she glanced at Kate again, then Sam, "didn't I save us?"

"You did," Sam said with conviction. She pulled her daughters to her, clenching them tight.

"*No*," the woman before them spit the word at Maybelle. "My baby." Her gaze flickered briefly toward the sky. "My little girl." Her glare returned to Maybelle, piercing her. "You left my little girl."

The words hit like a blow to the chest. Maybelle shook her head, but even as she did, her gaze was scanning, counting.

There were hundreds. Hundreds of people scattered across the mountain side. There had been thousands in that cavern.

Maybelle couldn't breathe. She opened her mouth, sucked in a cold breath. "Please," she shook her head, fresh tears running down her cheeks. "I didn't know. I don't know what I was doing, or... or how to control it."

"Then you shouldn't have done it," the woman seethed. She whirled around, waving her hand through the air. "My baby is *dead*. Because of you."

Kate stepped between them, her eyes narrowed in anger. "She saved your life, all these people's lives. I am sorry for your loss, but we would all be dead now if she hadn't saved us."

"Then we should have died," the woman spat. She shoved Kate aside.

There was a flash of silver. Sharp pain sliced through Maybelle's face. Warmth flooded the left side of her neck and shoulder. Someone screamed, and then everything went black.

Maybelle's eyes drifted open slowly. The room was warm. Above her, a dark wooden ceiling was made visible by the beams of light filtering in from a dirty window against the far wall.

Her head rested against a soft pillow. A thick, scratchy blanket covered her body. Her uniform had been replaced with a white cotton shirt and clean underwear. Wincing, she pushed herself up to sitting, her legs still under the blanket.

The left side of her face itched and tingled. She brought a hand to it and found a thick bandage. It started just above her hairline, extending to the bottom of her chin. Her peripheral vision on the left side was blocked and blurred by the bandage.

A door opened behind her. Her hands jerked to her waist. No blade. No gun. Her gaze darted around frantically for her weapons.

"You're awake," a familiar voice caressed her ears.

Maybelle slumped into the bed; her frantic movements drained her.

Kate hurried to her side. She sat on the edge of the bed, lips pursed with concern.

"Yeah—unhh—" her words were halted by a sharp sickening pain. The skin on the left side of her face no longer itched, instead her flesh felt like it was ripping apart.

Her head spun with pain. She stared at Kate, fear on her face. How bad was it?

"Don't talk."

"What happened?" Maybelle spoke through her teeth, moving her mouth as little as possible. The words still sent shooting pain through her jaw and up to her temple.

"That woman, the one from the Warren, she went crazy. She slashed your face with a knife. The cut was so deep." She paused. "If it had been half an inch to the side, we'd have lost you. As it is, you're lucky she missed your eye."

Maybelle took a shuddering breath. It too sent waves of pain through her face.

"The others?" she asked. Her hands clenched the bed sheets as she focused on breathing through the pain. "How many?"

"They're safe." Kate looked around the small room. "You got..." she hesitated. At Maybelle's glare, she continued.

"You got hundreds out. Insane, really. That you're still alive."

"How many left?" Maybelle grunted.

Kate shook her head. "Maybelle, that's not—"

Maybelle slammed a hand against the wall beside her, tears in her eyes.

Kate sighed and glanced around the room, running a hand through her hair. "We estimate another thousand were left behind. Based on reports, it seems like that wave of yours made a bubble and some people... they were on the wrong side."

Agony ripped through Maybelle's chest. Her lips trembled. She clenched the blanket until her knuckles went white. Sobs forced their way out. The bandage on her face absorbed some of the tears, the rest flowed freely as she bent over, trying—failing—to keep in the screams.

Kate sat with her. One hand on her shoulder, the other rubbing her back until the sobs ebbed and finally subsided.

"Sam and the girls are safe," Kate murmured.

Maybelle looked up.

"We all split up. Some people snuck back into the cities. They're hiding with family until they can work their way back into the system. Most of us are in the other camps. Sam and the kids went to Calida. It's big. The one Red used to live in back in the day. They have a couple contacts."

Maybelle sniffed and wiped the back of her hand under her nose. It brushed the bandage. She winced. Then she tapped Kate's hand and pointed at herself and then Kate.

"We're in the camp outside of Tornim. It's just us and a few others."

Maybelle looked around the room and raised her eyebrow at Kate.

"We live here, temporarily. They're building more houses for all the new White-Stars coming from the city. We'll blend right in when they all arrive. Until then, we're sharing with an older couple who lost a son in the war."

A shudder ran down Maybelle's spine. She swallowed; her throat dry. It was over. The rebellion had failed. She'd failed.

At least Sam and the children were safe. And Kate.

The two sat in silence for several long minutes.

Maybelle took Kate's hand. "I want to see it," she murmured.

Kate looked at her, sadness in her eyes. "I don't think that's a good idea."

"Kate," she said, wincing at the words. "Please."

Kate sighed and gritted her teeth. Then she stood. She left the room, returning a moment later with a mirror.

"Hold this."

She gently pulled the pieces of tape off Maybelle's face. The bandage slowly came away. The air stung as it caressed her wound.

Maybelle held up the mirror, her eyes widening in horror. The gash started an inch above her hairline. It drove down, deepening as it went until it reached her gemstone. It must have glanced off. There was a small nick, barely visible in the stone itself, and a space between it and her cheekbone where the knife dove back into her flesh. It dug in, deeper as it followed the curve of her jaw, leading from the bottom of her gemstone to the edge of her chin.

A decade of fighting. Ten long years and she only had a few cuts and burns to show for it. But this... she'd have this for the rest of her life. A reminder of the lives she's lost. The people she'd failed to save.

She laid the mirror face-down on the bed and sank into the mattress. She turned away from Kate, closed her eyes, and tried to erase the gruesome image from her mind.

Chapter Thirty-Two

Present Day - Late Summer - May's House

J uliana chewed happily on the last bite of her lunch. A sandwich. Fresh bread baked by Naya, strips of smoked meat Anthony brought in from his last hunting trip, even cheese from the grocers. She and Daisy had continued their study group and as the days passed, parents had started offering what they could as a thank you for helping their children.

May had given Juliana a little wooden box to keep the coins. They'd feasted on muffins offered by the baker's eldest daughter. It seemed that even though Juliana had no chance of getting a job at the school, or anywhere else while Steel ran things, she'd make do with what she had.

"When is Anthony getting back?" she asked as she wiped her fingers and carried her plate to the sink.

"A few hours." May heaved a satisfied sigh. She leaned back in her chair, fiddling with the end of her long braid. "He still joining us for dinner?"

"That's what he said this morning," Juliana replied as she snatched up May's dish as well and washed up.

"It was sweet of you to make the deliveries this morning."

Juliana shrugged. "Daisy and Taz are at school. I don't have much going on in the mornings. Besides," she dried her wooden plate and put it in the cupboard, "I like staying busy."

May nodded and stifled a yawn. "I'm coming with you to the square today."

Juliana turned from the sink; her eyebrow raised. "Why?"

May glared at her. "Because I want to, that's why."

Juliana raised her hands and turned back to the dishes. "Sorry."

"I'm tired, Juliana," May grumbled. "I want to get out of the house. A walk will wake me up."

"You could always take a nap."

May scoffed. "I'm an old lady, not a toddler."

Juliana laughed, finished the dishes, and held May's arm as the two of them made the long trek to the square.

Sun streamed down on them, breaking through gaps in the clouds which had covered the sky since the morning. Familiar faces were scattered through the square. Juliana's morning routine had shifted since Naya and Jimmy had gotten better. She'd started going with Anthony to deliver the goods from May's gardens—as well as whatever contraband food he had from the forest.

A few people waved and stopped to say hi. To May, but also to her. They found Naya with her group doing laundry. Juliana left May with Naya; the two laughing together as Naya sank a pair of stained trousers into the warm soapy water in the laundry bin.

She moved across the square, a frown crossing her face as she noted the fountain had been shut off. Perhaps because of the coming rain.

Daisy grinned at her from the steps of town hall. "Inside today?"

Juliana nodded, taking her into a half-hug as the two of them strode toward the door. "I have a feeling it's going to get wet later. Don't want the books to be ruined."

"I had the same thought," Daisy giggled as they stepped inside. Spread out before them, their study group—nearly two-dozen children of varying ages—sat strewn across the furniture in the lobby.

"Taz joining us?" Juliana glanced around.

Daisy shook her head. "He's got an extra shift this afternoon. Apparently, he's been doing good. He should be getting more shifts in the upcoming months."

Juliana grinned. "That's going to go straight to his head."

Daisy laughed.

Montague gave them a nod as Juliana moved through the small crowd. She ruffled Jimmy's hair as she passed. He stuck his tongue out at her.

The memory of him, laying in that bed, his olive skin deathly pale, spiderwebs of green/black veins spreading across his chest—her breath hitched. She hesitated, then drew him in for a hug.

Jimmy squeezed her and then plunked himself onto his chair and pulled out his math book. "This was really confusing today."

Juliana grinned and crouched.

As she helped with his math, more children from his class asked questions. Soon enough, she stood at the front of the room giving the lesson over again. Light streamed in from the windows. Warmth from the late summer sun kept them comfortable as wind rustled the trees outside.

Daisy wandered the room, taking her time with individual children while Juliana took on the majority of the group. An hour passed. Children filtered out of the room as they finished their work. Afternoon faded.

Juliana and the remaining members of the study group—Jimmy and his friends—read a book together. Daisy helped pack up their things and everyone descended the steps of town hall.

Jimmy's friends went to find their parents. Juliana, Daisy, and Jimmy crossed the square to find Naya and May still at the laundry station. The clothes were done, damp cloth folded in baskets, waiting to be hung overnight on the clothes-line behind Naya's house.

"Do you want me to walk home with you?" Juliana asked May.

The old woman shook her head, pulling her grey braid in front of her with a half-smile that stretched her scar. "I'll walk home with Naya and Jimmy. They're going to be joining us and Anthony for dinner."

Juliana grinned and turned to Daisy. "You want in on this?"

Daisy laughed. "Let's see what time Taz gets off. Maybe."

They said their goodbyes and hurried to the bakery.

It was nearly five o'clock. The day shift would be ending soon and there was a line of people out the door waiting to get bread to go with their dinner servings of mush. Daisy slipped in and Juliana followed.

Taz stood behind the counter, a towel thrown over his bony shoulder. Flour caked his apron and sweat coated his brow. Still, that toothy grin was in place. He laughed as a customer said something, grabbed a paper bag from behind the counter, and stuffed a few sticky buns inside.

Daisy and Juliana waited a few minutes, but it quickly became clear Taz wouldn't have time to talk. Daisy slid forward, pushing herself in front of the next person in line long enough to tell him they were having dinner with everyone at May's that night.

Taz grinned and nodded, then apologized to the person behind Daisy and hurriedly got their order going.

Leaving the bakery and linking arms, Daisy and Juliana strode together across the cobblestone, headed for May's.

They'd barely passed the fountain when Juliana paused. She tilted her head. "Do you hear that?"

Daisy didn't answer. She stared ahead, having caught sight of the commotion Juliana had heard. Juliana followed her gaze to the source of the noise.

Her stomach dropped.

Three figures moved toward them. Two Black-Stars, marching down the cob-blestone path with a third man between them. He seemed barely conscious. His feet dragged behind him, sending up a swirl of dust.

"Oh no," Daisy exhaled; her hand tightened around Juliana's arm.

The figures entered the square proper and the Moons in the area gaped in fear and confusion. There were more shouts as Black-Stars, two dozen of them, appeared from behind buildings and out of the shadows. Some stalked through the square, dragging people from buildings with shouts for everyone to gather. Others ventured further into Abredea, their calls growing distant as they called for mandatory presence in the square.

Juliana went unsteady for a second, clinging to Daisy as the three men moved past them.

Anthony. His left eye swollen almost shut, blood dripping from his nose, staining his grey shirt in red patches. He was conscious and favoring his right ankle as the Black-Stars dragged him toward the steps of town hall.

A flash of terror cut through Juliana's gut; one of the Black-Stars holding him also carried his hunting bag.

Daisy and Juliana exchanged fearful glances. "What do you—"

"I don't know," Juliana murmured. She detached herself from Daisy's arm. "But I'm going to find out."

Daisy nodded and cleared her throat, wringing her hands. "I've got to find Taz. He might—"

"Do something stupid," Juliana finished. Her friend nodded and disappeared into the gathering crowd.

Juliana sucked in a deep breath, squared her shoulders, and followed Anthony. He struggled to keep up with the Black-Stars pulling him, but he stumbled, and they did not slow as they crossed the square.

Juliana broke into a jog, pushing past the people who'd already been pulled from the various shops and buildings around the square.

"Stop," she called, softly at first, then louder. "I said *stop*. Wait, please." She straightened as a Black-Star—not one of the ones holding Anthony—turned to face her.

Juliana cleared her throat. "I'd like to know where you're taking that man." Her tone left no room for question. No expectation for anything but a clear answer.

The Black-Star snorted. She shook her head and tapped the black stone on her temple. "You don't give orders, *Moon*. You'll find out soon enough anyway." With a cruel grin, she turned away and followed the guards with Anthony up the stone steps of town hall.

Juliana growled. Fear wormed through her stomach, wriggling and fighting to overwhelm her. She pushed it down, her gaze locked on Anthony until he disappeared into the lobby she'd left only half an hour ago.

Montague was shoved out of the building a moment later. He shook his arm, trying to dislodge the hand holding him. He snapped something to the Black-Star and the man let go.

Montague turned to face the growing crowd and swallowed.

Murmurs filled the breezy afternoon air. Questions, demands for answers, anger at being pulled from their homes on orders from Captain Steel.

Juliana's fingers drummed against her thumb as she heard this over and over through the crowd. *Orders from Captain Steel.*

Her gaze met Montague's as he looked out at them from the top step. Upon catching sight of her, he moved forward. There were less people closer to the front.

"What's going on?" Juliana demanded in a hoarse whisper as Montague joined her.

He shook his head. "They wouldn't tell me. Orders from Captain Steel, whatever that means."

"They had his bag," she murmured.

Montague shot her an alarmed look. His pressed suit hung as limp as the day they'd met, cut and tailored, yet ill-fitting. He took off his wire-framed glasses and wiped them on his shirt. "I fear this will not go well for our friend."

Juliana frowned. She opened her mouth to speak, but her words were cut short.

Above them, on the second story balcony that looked out over the square, the door groaned open. Captain Steel stepped out first. Juliana's stomach churned with fear and anger at the victorious smile on his face. He threw an arm up as if he were presenting something glorious for them all. It reminded Juliana of Marsterson's own presentation when Steel had arrived in Abredea.

She stared up at him and as more shapes moved through the door, her throat went dry. Two Black-Stars pulled Anthony through. They shoved him toward the edge near Steel as the Black-Star captain grinned out at the people still filtering into the square.

Anthony regained his footing. He stood tall beside Steel, a scowl on his face, but no fear to be found in his expression.

They waited.

Juliana fidgeted with her fingers, heart pounding, neck aching as she stared up at them. Steel didn't once look at Anthony, his black gaze fixed on the crowd, flitting around as time passed at an agonizingly slow pace.

Juliana's couldn't stand the waiting. She turned to Montague. "What are they doing?"

"They're bringing everyone." Montague gestured to the flocks of people around them. "This is going to be bad."

She clenched her jaw. "The law states his punishment if they found him on the other side. Three weeks in solitary confinement for the first offense."

Montague uttered a pained grunt. "This isn't going to go the way you think it will, Miss Juliana." He swallowed. "You must do nothing."

"What?" Juliana's eyes narrowed. "What do you mean?"

Montague gazed at the Black-Stars and Anthony, twenty feet above them on the unused balcony. "I mean that this will not be what you expect. Nor will it be just. But you *must not* interfere. It will only be worse if you do."

Juliana gaped at him. Her gaze darted back to Anthony. He stood straight, looking out over the crowd below. She glanced behind them, wishing she could see May and Naya through the crowd. Hoping Jimmy was with them. Hoping Daisy had gotten to Taz.

Steel continued to scan the crowd, his brow furrowed.

Her chest tightened. Three weeks in solitary.

They would run out of fresh food quickly, but she had her coins from the study group. She knew how to get in and out of Abredea. She'd pick up the slack while he served his time. She might not know how to hunt, but she knew what kind of mushrooms he found. Knew what the onions looked like, what the berries smelled like. Knew how to find the stream, and, how hard was it to set up a net?

They'd survive. She'd keep Naya and Jimmy, May, Taz, Daisy, all of them fed while he was locked away.

So why was anxiety roiling in her stomach? Why was fear turning the blood in her veins into shards of ice?

Steel's gaze found Juliana and Montague. A few seconds passed and then he raised a gloved hand. On his right middle finger, a large silver ring glistened, illuminated by a ray of sunlight streaming down from a gap between the clouds.

Silence spread through the crowd in a ripple, starting with those closest to town hall and moving out, until the only sounds in the square were the wind and occasional whimpers from some small child. A lone bird circled overhead.

Steel lowered his arm. Juliana's hands clenched into fists at the sight of his smile. At the way his gaze flicked to Anthony and the smirk grew, and at the way he looked out at the White-Stars with scorn laced in every glance and movement.

"This man—"

Juliana flinched as Steel's voice reverberated around them, his shout loud enough to reach the back of the crowd.

"—has broken the law."

Murmurs rose up; Steel waited for them to quiet.

He went on. "He was caught. Caught with this."

He reached out and a Black-Star handed him the hunting bag. Steel tossed it off the balcony. It smashed into the concrete steps below, contents spilling out. Onions bounced down the stairs and rolled across the dusty cobblestones. A hare fell limply onto the ground.

Anthony snarled. The Black-Stars grabbed his arms to keep him in place.

Juliana inhaled. "They didn't catch him outside the fence," she breathed.

Half a step behind her, Montague leaned forward and whispered, still staring at the scene playing out before them. "That won't matter."

Juliana opened her mouth to ask how it could possibly *not* matter. Steel's harsh voice cut her off.

"Illegal food. Evidence of wrongdoing and lawlessness. Two weeks solitary confinement." His tone grew dark.

The clouds overhead shifted. Shadows replaced the warm beams of sunlight. A chill went down Juliana's spine.

"I warned you," Steel continued. His gaze flicked to Anthony. "I warned all of you what would happen if you continued to defy my rule and *forget your place.*"

Anthony growled. The sound spread, from the front of the crowd to the back as White-Stars hissed and spit their disapproval of this statement.

"Oh," Steel's eyes glinted as he looked out at the crowd. He spread his arms. "You think because you have lived with no enforcement of the law, that you are above it? That you are above your station? That these," he jammed his finger against his black gemstone, his violent sneer twisting the tattoos on his face, "don't matter here?"

He took a step back, away from Anthony, then whirled and backhanded him across the face.

Anthony lurched out of his captors' grips with the impact. He stumbled but remained upright. The crowd gasped. Juliana stepped forward, fury pounding through her at the... the *wrongness* of this.

Bony fingers gripped her elbow.

"You must not interfere," Montague hissed in her ear.

Juliana's hands trembled at her sides as above, one of the Black-Stars used the moment to press on Anthony's shoulder, shoving him to his knees. Juliana's breath came quick, her jaw clenched.

"I assure you..." Steel moved closer, putting a leather clad finger to Anthony's bare temple.

Anthony jerked his head away from the touch.

Steel shook his head with disgust and said, his voice cold with malice, "...they do."

He gripped the front of Anthony's shirt and pulled him to his feet. Anthony's chest heaved.

"Do you have anything to say before you face your punishment?"

Anthony worked his jaw, lips pressed tight together as he winced. Then, with Steel inches from him, he spit a glob of mucus and blood into the man's face.

Steel recoiled in fury, releasing Anthony's shirt and wiping at his cheek with angry slashes of his gloved hand.

"Yeah." Anthony's voice carried as well. He grimaced, as though moving his jaw was painful, but a wry, crooked grin split his lips. "If yer gonna get tha' close tah me, brush yer teeth first."

A combination of laughter and low moans went through the crowd. Juliana's eyes widened as Anthony winked to his fellow Moons.

Montague's grip on her elbow went lax. She glanced at him. The old man shook his head slowly, a pained expression on his face.

Juliana looked back in time to see Steel's face contort into a mask of wrath. He gestured, and the Black-Stars on the balcony grasped Anthony's arms, twisting them behind his back and forcing him into a half-bow.

The first blow hit Anthony in the gut. Juliana winced at the thud. Her fingers flew to her lips. Steel swung again. Anthony was nearly ripped from the Black-Star's grip as Steel's fist connected with his face. Blood dripped from his swollen left eye.

Rumbling went through the crowd of White-Stars. Calls for him to stop, for mercy, and for the law to be enforced as written. Black-Stars stationed around the edges of the crowd and on the steps of town hall drew their weapons.

Tense silence descended. Above their heads, above the platform where Steel had lost all reason, thunder clapped, and rain began to fall.

Juliana glanced around; someone had to have the power to stop this. But all she saw was her own horror mirrored on the faces of the Moons around her.

Anthony grunted, the sound reverberating around the square. Steel's fury had no end. Spit flew from his mouth as he pummeled Anthony, now limp in the Black-Stars' grips.

Someone in the crowd sobbed. It sounded like Naya.

Rain dripped down on them, large droplets slowly turning the dust-coated cobblestones to mud.

Juliana rounded on Montague. "Is *this* what you thought it would be?"

The man flinched away from her, and from the carnage on the balcony.

He shook his head. "This is... more."

"We have to *do* something," she murmured fiercely. "This can't be allowed to happen."

"There is nothing we can do," he replied.

She glared and he shook his head.

"It will only make things worse, Juliana."

She almost didn't hear Montague's low murmur over Steel's blows.

Juliana sucked in a cold breath of air, shutting her eyes against the helplessness. This was happening. This was actually happening. This brutal, vicious display of power.

Her mind flashed to history lessons, discussions of what the world was like before the plague. Before the Grey-Stars saved them from total destruction. Back when this sort of thing was allowed.

It wasn't allowed now. It wasn't supposed to be.

Something broke in Juliana. The piece of her that had been holding on, clinging to her old life, shattered. This was *wrong*.

"This is not the law," Juliana hissed. Her eyes snapped open. "This cannot be allowed to happen." Montague's fingers slid from her elbow as she stepped forward.

The crowd barely moved as she pushed through.

"*Stop*," she shouted with every ounce of the power she'd once had as a Blue-Star.

There was a ripple in the crowd. The people around her stepped back, for their own safety, or to get out of her way, she didn't know or care. She made it to the bottom of the steps and came face to face with a Black-Star. She ignored him, her neck craned, her focus on the balcony.

Steel froze, fist midway to Anthony's swollen face.

He glanced down at her through the rain. His gaze shifted. The hazy fury dissipated, replaced with focus.

Something slammed into her cheek. Pain; earsplitting, blinding as she reeled and fell to the side with the force of the impact. She threw out her hands. A sharp cobblestone edge sliced through her palm as she caught herself.

She blinked and shook her head, vision spotty, ears ringing. Rain drenched her; dripping hair framed her face and blocked her from clearly seeing the Black-Star towering over her kneeling form.

Above her a familiar lilting voice shouted. She clambered slowly to her feet. It took a few seconds for her legs to stop shaking.

She shook her head again and brushed the hair from her face, wincing as rain hit the cut on her palm. She raised fingers to her stinging cheek, and they came away red with blood.

The Black-Star stared at her. Juliana's lip curled as she regarded him. There should have been fear. Fear causing her hands to shake and her chin to quiver. Instead, blistering anger filled her veins.

"*Enough*," Steel's barking voice broke through the last of the ringing in her ears. "Stand down, Collins."

The man who'd struck her looked up with something like contempt on his face. The expression on his face morphed to worry as he looked from his captain back to her. With the slightest nod, he stepped aside.

Juliana straightened and looked up at the men on the balcony. Anthony was slumped against the stone carved railing, his face swollen and bloody, one arm draped over the edge, the other clutching his stomach. The Black-Stars who'd held him stood close. Steel shook out his right hand, flexing and curling his fingers as he gazed down at her through the rain.

Juliana pushed her anger down, as deep as it would go and poured honey-coated pleading into her voice. "Please," she called up to them. She sucked in a deep breath; the movement of her mouth sent a sharp sting through her cheek. Her gaze darted to Anthony for a split second. Relief pooled in her stomach as he met her eye and his mouth twitched into half of a broken grin. She turned her focus back on Steel. "Please, Captain. We all know the law. Two weeks for contraband items. Not..." she gestured toward them with a shake of her head, "not this."

Steel considered the back of his bloodied glove. He took a step toward Anthony.

Anthony straightened—somewhat—and took his arm from the railing. He wavered on his feet as he faced the captain, his left arm still clutching his ribs.

Steel reached out and wiped the back of his glove on Anthony's shirt. He waved a hand at the Black-Stars standing inches from Anthony. They moved back, leaving Steel and Anthony alone at the railing.

Juliana exhaled through barely parted lips.

Steel stared down at her. She met his gaze, trying to keep the malice from her face. He turned away, one hand lifting to his ear as he cocked his head, apparently deep in thought.

Anthony wavered on his feet once Steel's attention shifted. He put a hand back on the railing to steady himself.

Only a few seconds had passed, but Steel's expression had returned to its usual upper caste superiority as turned back to the crowd. He looked down at Juliana and inclined his head.

"Of course. The law shall be upheld. Two weeks solitary confinement for possession of contraband items." He waved a hand over the crowd and glanced at a few of his Black-Stars. "We are here to uphold the law, after all."

Anxiety spiked in Juliana's stomach. She swallowed and nodded as his gaze turned back to her.

Behind her, murmurs went through the crowd. Shuffling feet suggested movement. Yet Juliana kept her eyes fixed on the balcony.

Steel gripped Anthony's shoulder.

He grimaced, but made no move to resist as Steel pulled him close.

Steel's mouth slid into a grin. He leaned in and murmured into Anthony's ear, his beady black gaze still locked on Juliana.

Anthony's dark skin went pale, and his hand clenched at his side. Steel released him with a shove.

Anthony's fist was a blur, moving so fast Juliana's didn't realize what was happening until his knuckles slammed into the captain's jaw.

Steel reeled and staggered back. Stepped forward again, his hand closed around the front of Anthony's shirt.

Juliana's legs carried her forward as time seemed to slow.

Steel's locked eyes with her for a second that stretched and stretched. His teeth gleamed as a smile flashed across his face, his jaw already red from the blow.

He shoved.

Anthony flew backwards. One hand reached out, grasping at the air as he fell... fell...

Juliana didn't know if her voice joined the screams, the volley that drowned out the sound of Anthony's body as it collided with the concrete steps below.

She reached him before he went still. Knelt beside him.

Tears would be in the way here. She shoved them deep as her fingers, wet from the rain, scrambled to find a pulse. There was blood on the steps beneath him.

There.

Anthony's heartbeat. Thudding against her fingers as a low groan escaped him.

She shifted, putting her body over his face to block the rain pooling in the crease of his closed eyes. She scanned his limbs and torso. The right leg, broken in at least two places. Her hands traced his chest. Cracked ribs, possibly broken. Something was wrong with his right arm. She didn't know if the shoulder was dislocated, or if his humerus was broken as well.

The heartbeat. She kept going back to the heartbeat. It still pulsed and—as she checked it a third time—everything around her seemed to speed back up again.

Rage surrounded her. The White-Stars howled their fury. A familiar voice reached her through the crowd.

"Get out of my way," May snapped.

Juliana turned. Daisy and Taz helped May to the steps even as the Black-Stars at the door tried to move towards them.

A wave surged forward. White-Stars charged the steps, flowing around Juliana and Anthony. They blocked Steel's people, linking arms as they moved in front of Anthony.

May groaned as she knelt beside Juliana and gave her a look that made questions unnecessary.

"He's alive," Juliana panted. "Broken leg, possibly arm. His chest..." she swallowed. "At least cracked ribs, maybe fully broken. And he's bleeding somewhere..." her voice cracked.

She glanced at the pool of blood mixing with rainwater and dripping down the steps.

"Not too much," May murmured. Her hands, gnarled and spotted with age, sped across his body with expertise.

Juliana glanced up. The shouting around them was muffled to her ears. Montague stood at the top of the steps, facing a Black-Star. His finger pointed at the man's chest, and he spoke with a vivacity Juliana had never seen in him.

"He has a chance." May gripped Juliana's wrist and met her gaze with grey eyes as intense as the storm above them. "We need to get him home. Away from this," she jerked her head at the flurry of activity around them, "and onto a bed. I have to set these bones. We need to find the bleeding and stop it."

"Are you..." Juliana choked back her fear. "Are you worried about internal bleeding?"

May glanced up. Juliana followed her gaze. The slotted balcony railing, nearly twenty feet above them, had become an outlet for the rain. Rivulets fell onto the ground around them.

"I'll be able to figure that out when we get him home."

Tears burned Juliana's eyes as Daisy sucked in a breath. Behind her, Taz rose from where he knelt, blood and mud soaked into the knees of his pants.

"Stretcher," he shouted to the White-Stars behind them.

A blur of shapes quickly coalesced into a group of men running forward with a set of thick blankets between them.

"Careful," May barked. "Move him slowly; do not disturb his head or neck."

Daisy took charge of that. She dug her fingers into his coarse black hair, and cradled his head in her small hands as the men—friends of Anthony's from the field and people he delivered food to—carefully lifted his body. Taz and Juliana slid the blanket stretcher beneath him.

On Daisy's count of three, the men lifted, grunting as they carefully hauled Anthony up from the ground, and carried him down the steps and through the crowd of White-Stars toward the main road.

Juliana put a hand under May's arm as the old woman clambered to her feet.

A shot rang through the air.

Juliana wheeled around as everyone froze. Steel still stood on the balcony, arm raised, pointing his plasma gun into the sky. He glared at her, a grim look of fury smeared across his face.

"He owes me two weeks," Steel's shout rang through the square as he lowered his weapon.

A rush of anger like nothing Juliana had felt before slammed into her. She stepped away from May. Snarling, she shouted back, every bit of her malice biting through her words. "He could still *die*. *Frost* your two weeks."

Steel shook his head and lowered the gun, pointing it at her chest.

Her heartbeat thundered in her ears, fear and rage fighting for dominance as she glared at Steel.

The Moons surged forward. Fists slammed against the windows of town hall. The Black-Stars on the steps had retreated indoors. Steel blinked as he took in the scene below.

Juliana waited, her fingers trembling with fury.

"He's already broken," Steel hollered down. "Worth nothing." He holstered his gun with a sneering grin. "Patch him up—if you can."

He waved his hand through the air in a tight circle. The Black-Stars around the square disappeared, melting into the shadows leaving nothing and no one for the White-Stars to target with their rage.

Juliana caught sight of Montague, appealing to the White-Stars at the top steps. He would fix it. He'd calm them down and stop them from giving Steel an excuse for more violence.

She turned from the square and hurried after May and Anthony.

Chapter Thirty-Three

Present Day - Late Summer - Abredea

N aya and Jimmy caught up with Juliana before she reached May's house. The storm had subsided somewhat, the downpour replaced with gentle drips. Naya's eyes were puffy and red. Her lips trembled as—without a word—she let go of Jimmy's hand and pulled Juliana to her.

Thin arms wrapped around her torso. There was a hitch of breath, and then Naya was sobbing into Juliana's already soaked shirt.

Juliana hesitated. Her heartbeat had only just begun to slow. Her breath not quite steady as images and sounds played on repeat in her mind. She swallowed.

A small pair of arms hugged her left leg. Jimmy squeezed. She didn't know if he understood. As smart as the boy was, she hoped he didn't grasp the extent of what happened. She hoped Naya kept him from seeing what had been done to Anthony.

Juliana wrapped an arm around Naya, the other closing around Jimmy's thin shoulders. They stood together in the rain. No words. Only the pressure of each other to keep the fear at bay.

A long moment passed before Naya let her go. Jimmy moved closer to his mother as she stepped away.

"Thank yeh," Naya murmured. Her soft voice, the dancing lilt to her words that sounded so much like Anthony's, felt at home with the light fall of the rain.

Juliana shook her head. "It's my fault this happened."

Naya frowned.

Guilt twinged in Juliana's chest. "Montague told me what would happen if I interfered. I did it anyway and..." she gestured helplessly toward May's house.

The urge to run there, to sprint through the door and make sure he was all right, warred with her desire to never find out if he wasn't.

"Steel was killin' him." Naya reached up and put her slender fingers against Juliana's face.

Juliana winced. The cut across her cheek had been completely forgotten. It burned where Naya touched it.

"Steel wasn't gonna stop," Naya continued. She lowered her arm. "We need tah get that patched up."

Juliana grimaced at her word choice. Steel's voice reverberated through her skull and she turned toward May's.

"It's not me I'm worried about," Juliana whispered.

Jimmy clasped his mother's hand between both of his and tugged her down the path.

They followed the boy, sloshing through the mud until they reached the tiny front porch. Rain splattered against the hanging glass bottles sending up a chorus of tinkling notes.

Juliana fell back as they reached the wooden steps. She followed Naya up and waited as the woman gently pushed open the door.

Inside was a flurry of activity. Daisy carried a bundle of sopping red fabric to the kitchen sink. Taz stood at the stove, heating a large pot of water. The men who'd carried Anthony to safety hesitated in the background, seeming unsure if they should leave or not.

And there, on his side and facing the wall on May's bed... Juliana's breath caught at the same time Naya gasped.

They'd propped up Anthony's leg. The makeshift splints told Juliana they'd already set the bones. It was wrapped, tight yarns of cloth holding everything in place. His arm hadn't been tended to yet—there was a more pressing issue to deal with.

His shirt was gone and, on his back... Juliana knew enough about human anatomy to understand how severe the damage was.

A red and swollen indentation stretched from just below the ribs on his right side, down to his hip bone on the left. It must have been the first point of impact on those stone steps. Blood flowed from a long, jagged slash following the trek of the bruise.

May stood at the edge of the bed; she folded a clean cloth and pressed it to the wound.

Anthony made no sound.

Juliana panicked for a brief second before deciding it was probably best he didn't feel what was happening right now. She turned to Naya.

"Jimmy shouldn't be here."

Naya didn't look at her. Her terrified eyes were fixed on Anthony's back. Blood had already seeped into the sheets and mattress beneath the man.

Daisy rushed over the took up putting pressure on the wound as May dug through her chest of drawers, pulling out a needle and thread.

"He's so pale," Naya muttered and her gaze shifted to her son.

Jimmy had been on that bed not long ago, before Anthony brought home the medicine.

Juliana took hold of Naya's arm. "You need to get Jimmy out of here." She looked to the others. Daryll, a man with a tattoo on his inner wrist, wrung his hands together as he turned his attention to her. "All of you, unless you have a specific way to help, need to leave. We need room to work."

Naya nodded, tears streaming down her face.

Without another word, Juliana strode to the kitchen, and began scrubbing soap onto her hands with scalding water. The cut on her palm burned and stung. But it wasn't bleeding. She wrapped it with a strip of white fabric laid out on the counter. Taz stepped forward and tied the cloth in place.

When she turned, only Taz, Daisy, and May remained. She went to May. "What can I do?"

Taz hurried over and set a tray of sanitized suture tools on the bed. May held up a curved needle, thick black string dangling from the end. "My hands are too old for this, Jules."

Juliana clenched her jaw and nodded. "I can do it." She took the needle.

"I know some stitching," Daisy whispered.

The room was so silent. So still.

"Have you done a suture before?" Juliana asked, not unkindly.

Daisy shook her head. "Just mending clothes."

Juliana leaned forward, putting her shoulder against Daisy's for a brief second. "This is different."

Daisy swallowed and nodded.

Juliana's fingers shook as she studied the needle.

Taz moved to the head of May's bed. "I can hold his... hold his... hold..." He grimaced.

"His arm," Daisy murmured. She gave Taz a ghost of her usual smile. "That will help a lot."

Taz took hold of Anthony's right arm, already stretched to the side, and gently raised it above his head.

"I'll ask for pressure as I go," Juliana said to Daisy. "Don't leave."

"Wasn't planning to." Daisy adjusted her angle, cloth at the ready.

Juliana sat just behind Anthony, her hip pressed against his upper back as she leaned over him.

May crossed to Juliana's bed. Her face, lined with age, looked older than Juliana had ever seen it. Her skin was nearly the color of her scar; sickly off-white.

"Stop me if I'm making a mistake," Juliana said, glancing at May. "I've only done this twice, and never on an actual person."

Daisy and Taz both exchanged a look.

Juliana pretended not to notice as she sucked in a breath, bit her lower lip, and bent toward the jagged slice cutting across Anthony's back and side.

Blinding light pierced through Anthony's eyelids coating everything in red. He raised a hand and pain flashed through his side. He winced, putting a hand to his forehead as he pried his eyes open.

Everything danced before him in a jumble of blurred colors. There was movement, but when he tried to focus on a shape the space behind his eyes ached.

"Hey," he moaned.

Each breath was painful. Every time his chest expanded it felt like a spoke stabbing him in the ribs.

He closed his eyes, sinking into darkness.

He was on his side, right leg in a cast and propped on a stack of pillows. Everything hurt: his face, his chest, his back. He opened his eyes and tried to sit up, but it felt as though red-hot blades were stabbing him all over. With a grunt, he leaned back onto the soft blankets beneath him.

"Anthony?"

He knew the voice that breathed his name.

The room around him slowly came into focus as he blinked through the pain and the haze jumbling his mind. Juliana's face swam into view. She rose from her bed and settled herself on the chair beside him.

"Where..." He wanted to ask why, but the word came out wrong.

"May's." Juliana leaned toward him. "Are you in any pain?"

He flashed a half-smile, an attempt to comfort her.

Her eyes went wide. "Hang on," she murmured. She rushed into the kitchen.

He glanced around. It was evening or morning; he couldn't tell with curtains drawn over the window at the front of the house. Red and orange light filtered in under the edge of the pale fabric.

He was supposed to have dinner here. He frowned, confusion pushing in on his mind. The pain had settled into a dull ache over every inch of his body. His right arm... Anthony rubbed his stiff shoulder. He remembered this feeling. He'd dislocated the same shoulder once before, falling from a tree when he was sixteen. His uncle had pressed him against an oak, popped the joint back into its socket, and taken him home to rest. He'd had nearly three weeks of slow movements, stretching, and May's burning ointments before he could use it properly again.

Juliana returned carrying a steaming mug of something that smelled like wet socks and mint.

"Drink this," she said, sitting in the chair and holding the cup to his lips.

"I was afraid yeh were gonna say tha'," he groaned.

The corner of her mouth twitched up.

His grin spread. "Wha' is it?" he asked, trying once again to rise. He didn't make it more than a few inches before pain made him wince.

"Stop." Juliana put a hand on his shoulder and gently pushed him back down. "You'll rip the stitches."

Anthony's eyes widened, questions pouring into his head.

She cleared her throat and moved the drink closer. "It's tea. Mixed with some of May's medicine. It'll ease the pain for a while."

Anthony let her pour the foul-smelling concoction into his mouth. He spluttered and coughed. It tasted worse than it smelled.

Juliana actually smiled this time. She let out a chuckle and continued laughing as she took the cup and returned to the kitchen. There was a pause. A hitch.

A sob.

Anthony struggled to sit up. "Jules?"

She came back with another cup and tears on her cheeks.

"What..." He leaned toward her and then hesitated as he felt his wound stretching. Settling back, he asked, "Jules, what is it?"

She handed him the cup. "Water."

He huffed out a chuckle and took it. "Not what I mean, but thanks." He regarded her as he drained the cup.

She swallowed. "We weren't sure when you were going to wake up."

Anthony studied her. He handed the cup back and she placed it on the ground before folding her hands in her lap and watching him.

"How does everything feel? Any pain in your leg?"

"Juliana," Anthony gestured up and down his body, "what happened?"

Her tear-stained eyes went wide. She sucked in a shallow breath. "I don't..." Almost absentmindedly, she traced a cut marring her cheek. "I don't know where to start."

He hadn't noticed the wound before, the sunset bruise, probably close to a week old, surrounding an inch long jagged scab along her cheek bone.

He went cold. "How long 'ave I been asleep?" he murmured, fear clutching him.

Juliana bit her lip and closed her eyes. When she opened them, the hard expression he was used to snapped back into place.

"You've been unconscious a little over a week."

His jaw dropped and he sat up further.

Juliana's hand returned to his shoulder. "Don't. Stitches."

"Jules how... wha' in the *depths* is goin' on?"

"What do you remember?"

Anthony shook his head, sorting through a flurry of images and sensations as he worked to recall his most recent memories.

"I was huntin'." He stared at the window, watching the fabric blow with the breeze. "Came back no problem and then..." He frowned.

"A Black-Star," Juliana prompted softly.

He nodded; voice quiet as he worked to remember. "Right. There was a Black-Star on the road. Thought it was odd, they don' usually come out so far." His brow furrowed. "He said something. I don't..."

Frustration flared at the slow return of his memories.

"He saw the bag," Juliana murmured. "I don't know what happened. I wasn't there."

Images flashed through his mind. Thick arms, slamming him into a tree after he'd refused to go with them. Dirt turning to cobblestone beneath his feet as he tried to stand, to walk as they dragged him along.

Anthony looked up. "They took me to the square."

Juliana nodded. "They brought everyone, every Moon in Abredea not working a shift. The Black-Stars dragged them out of their houses. To..." she ground her teeth, anger flashing through her eyes, "to witness Steel's show."

Anthony's gaze went distant as he remembered the stairs, the balcony, a crowd in the square, Steel, and his stupid speech.

He half-grinned at the image of his bloody spit splattering across Steel's cheek. Then he looked up to find Juliana crying again.

"Jules, I'm 'ere. I'm fine. Why..."

She gaped at him and shook her head. Long strands of blonde hair fell in front of her face. "You came so close, Anthony." Her voice shuddered. "So close to..." She pursed her lips and furiously palmed the tears away.

"I didn't know you cared so much," he joked.

"Oh, *frost* you," she snapped.

He blinked in surprise.

"I'm sorry," she groaned, rubbing slender fingers across her forehead.

He reached up, wincing, and took hold of her wrist. "Juliana," he pulled it toward him, turning it so he could see her palm, "what is this?" He pointed to the bandage, holding her fingers when she tried to close her hand. "And, what is tha'?" He gestured to her face.

She shook her head. "It doesn't matter."

"It matters to me," he growled. "When did this 'appen?"

Juliana watched him a long moment before she gave him a bitter smile. "I don't want to tell you."

"What? Why?"

"If you don't remember what happened... I don't want to bring that back to you."

Anthony didn't let go of her hand. He traced the bandage. It was small, clean, tightly wrapped.

"Steel went..." He kept his gaze on her palm as more of it came back to him. "He went insane. I remember the look in his eyes. He wanted tah kill me." He let out a rueful chuckle. "Guy can' take a joke."

Juliana spat out half a laugh and shook her head.

Anthony frowned. He moved a hand to his stomach, his chest, his face. "He was killin' me..." he looked to Juliana for confirmation.

She grimaced. "He was vicious. Barbaric."

"You..." he recalled her voice sounding from below, the strength and fury in her tone. "Yeh stopped him."

Juliana pulled her hand away, more tears pooling in her eyes. She clenched her jaw, her words barely audible as she murmured, "I made it worse."

He scoffed. "Not possible."

"Anthony." Juliana heaved a sigh and wiped at her tears again. "If I hadn't... if I had left it alone, he wouldn't have pushed you."

There it was.

The piece he'd been missing. The chunk of memory he hadn't been able to access until she said that. The explanation for a broken leg, dislocated shoulder, what had to be cracked ribs, and a slice along his side bad enough for stitches. The reason he had been unconscious for over a week.

"Off the balcony," he muttered.

"Yeah."

"I landed on the steps?"

"Yes."

They sat in silence for a long moment.

Her fear made more sense now. Her tears.

He swallowed, wondering how Naya was doing. Jimmy, Daisy, Taz, and May, all of them thinking he might die. All of them going without the food he brought, for a full week. Fear crept into his chest.

But something still didn't make sense.

Juliana stood. He reached out, clasping her wrist again.

"Don't. I 'ave more..." he twisted his lips to the side, unsure of how to ask her to stay.

She hesitated, then sat.

"This isn't yer fault, Jules." He waited for her gaze to meet his.

She stared at the blanket instead. "Montague told me not to interfere. When Steel started beating on you, he told me it would be worse if I got involved."

"Yeh think tha's why he pushed me off the balcony."

She nodded.

Anthony licked his lips and forced a grin. "Tha's not why, Juliana."

She frowned and finally met his gaze.

"He shoved me off tha' balcony because I punched him." He released her wrist. "Yeh've read the laws. What's the punishment for attackin' a Star higher than yeh?"

Juliana nodded slowly. "A month."

"And attackin' one of the top three?"

There was a second of hesitation. "Decided by the highest authority present," she whispered.

Anthony's cheek twinged, but he forced the smile to grow anyway. "Steel decided throwin' me off a buildin' was my punishment." He shrugged—and immediately regretted it. "Tha's not on you."

The guilt melted from her shoulders. She inhaled, her chin quivering.

His fingers brushed across the back of her hand. "It's not yer fault."

"I thought," she hesitated, "I thought I almost got you killed."

He chuckled. "Nah. As usual, I got myself into trouble." He met her gaze. "Nice havin' someone tah get me out of it though."

She laughed. A real laugh this time. One which filled the house, shaking her body and pulling painful laughter from him as well.

The back door flew open.

Anthony caught a glimpse of Taz's dirty blond hair before his friend disappeared again. A hollering shout reached them.

"*He's awake!*"

Juliana stood. "I'm not getting in the way of this."

Anthony gave her a wide-eyed look. "Do I need tah be worried?"

She cracked a wicked smile and gave him a half-shrug.

Seconds later, Taz rushed into the room, nearly tripping as he ran up to Anthony's bed and sat beside him. Daisy strode in behind him, hands to her mouth, giggling and crying at the same time.

May entered behind her.

Anthony's heart swelled as the old woman hurried to his side and took up Juliana's empty seat. She put a hand to his forehead, her lips pressed tight together.

"I'm going to get Naya," Juliana murmured. She slipped out the front door before Anthony could object.

He stared up at the woman who'd helped raise him. The woman who'd taken him in when his mother died and tried so hard to keep him out of trouble. He took her thin hand between his.

"May, I'm..."

"Don't you dare apologize for a thing," May croaked. She glared down at him.

His lips trembled, eyes burning. He sniffed and nodded. "Thank yeh."

She ran a gentle hand down the side of his face. "You had us scared for a minute there, child."

Daisy nodded, crouching on the ground beside May's chair. "How are you feeling?"

"I'm all right," he said. It was truer this time. Whatever he'd drunk had eased most of his pain.

"What'd he say?" Taz asked. "Tah get yeh tah hit... hit... hit him like that?"

Anthony's throat went dry. He smoothed his face, but caught May's eye and knew she'd seen the panic in his expression.

"I don' think I've ever seen yeh swing that hard," Taz continued.

Anthony smiled tightly and lied. "I don't remember."

May gave a slow nod and Taz shrugged saying, "That makes sense, yeh did fall pretty hard after."

Daisy, however, met Anthony's gaze with weary, red-rimmed eyes.

He gave her a tiny shake of his head. A plea to let it go, discuss it later.

Daisy considered his briefly, then her familiar smile returned. "Well, now that you're feeling better it's time you started pulling your weight. You'd better get ready to read a lot of books. Jimmy knows you can't walk for a few more weeks and he's expecting story time every day."

Anthony opened his mouth to object, but was silenced by the front door opening. Naya and Jimmy rushed in, the others making room for them.

He made the effort to speak; reassured Naya, joked away Jimmy's fears, and tried to listen as his friends filled him in on what he'd missed during the last week. Fatigue pounded at him and the pain was returning. When he laid back against his pillows, favoring his hurt side, May shooed everyone out of the house.

When the door closed, he thanked her. He still had questions; concerns that needed to be addressed. He tried to focus, to keep his eyes open so he could make sure his family was safe and fed. And to make sure Steel hadn't followed through on his whispered promise.

Juliana gave him a soft smile as sleep overtook him. "I'll tell you everything when you wake up, Anthony." Her smile flickered. "So, make sure you do."

He sank into darkness, a crooked grin still on his face.

Chapter Thirty-Four

 Present Day - Early Fall - Abandoned Warehouse in Grigoria

C ho rubbed his aching shoulder. Pain radiated from the joint, even two days after it had hit a brick wall, after he'd used it to slam through a locked door. He stared at the cracker in his hand. A dry square, salty enough to make him thirsty, thin enough to melt onto his tongue.

The burned-out warehouses in Grigoria had proved to be a good plan. No one had disturbed them. In her search for Cho, Luna had found a cabinet with dry goods in it. She'd also found Cho, unconscious, next to a pool of vomit.

Jane brought around their water. A single bottle split between the seven of them and refilled at the park in the dead of night. She sat next to Cho on the dirty green and brown checkered carpet, her gaze on Tommy for a long moment.

The boy was struggling. The combination of grief, shock, and boredom sent him into fits of uncontrollable shaking, sometimes losing control of his power, going invisible without meaning to, and scaring the frost out of Jane when he did.

Cho's chest was heavy with the weight of Tommy's pain. Only seven, and he was faced with losing most of his family, having nowhere to go, and being on the verge of starvation.

"We need to go out," Jane murmured beside him.

Cho darted a quick glance her way before looking down at his hands. He said nothing.

"Cho." Jane touched his shoulder. She seemed to be trying for a gentle approach, but a jagged severity seeped into her words. "We're running out of food. We need water, clean clothes," she looked at Clair, lying on the filthy couch, "and medicine."

Cho followed her gaze, his jaw clenched.

Claire had woken long enough for them to get some food and water in her, but she'd been in a haze. The gash on her arm oozed puss and blood. Cho had cleaned it after Luna found him, but he feared the damage was already done. The skin bubbled with bright red blisters of infection and she'd developed a fever.

Jane was right. Something had to be done.

Cho leaned against the dirty wall behind them. "Jane," he struggled to speak, grief choking him. "I can't. I can't go out there."

"I know." She gritted her teeth. "You have to remind everyone about their defenses," she hissed barely above a whisper. "They're killing you."

His eyelids fluttered closed. It didn't matter. He couldn't explain it to her, but it didn't matter. It was done. *He* was done. Broken.

All that mattered now was making sure the others would survive.

"I can go," Jane said. "I'm taking Tommy."

Cho dragged his mind to the matter at hand. "Jane, you can't steal the kind of medicine we need for Nova and Claire."

She glared at him. "I don't need to *steal* anything."

Confusion broke through the steady levels of pain and grief he'd grown used to.

She let out an exasperated growl. "Cho, we have almost five-hundred coins sitting in a box in the sewers of Agora."

Across the room, Jason looked up.

Cho stood and paced, thinking.

Morning sun pierced the sky outside, shafts of light breaking through the blinds on the window.

He turned to her. "You'll go?"

"So will I," Jason declared as he pushed to his feet. "Someone needs to be here with Claire and Nova, but I can keep Jane and Tommy safe." He met Cho's eye with the same empty gaze he'd had since his sister fell.

"And me." Luna stood as well.

Nova, resting on a stack of cushions behind her sister, sat up with worry on her face. "But—"

"We *have* to get supplies for your ankle," Luna interrupted. "If you're going for the coins," she glanced at Jane who nodded, "you'll probably need me."

"Need us," Nova snapped. She planted her hands on the wall and pushed herself to her feet.

Waves of anticipation and fear and pain cascaded off of her. Cho closed his eyes, bracing internally as the wounds in his mind and heart deepened.

"You can't go," Cho said to Nova.

She stared at him; eyes wide as tears pooled in them. "I can't sit here while *she* goes." She gestured to Luna. Her lips trembled, as she gazed at him with pleading eyes.

Cho opened his mouth, but hesitated as Jason crossed the room to Nova. He bent, put a hand around her blackened ankle, and squeezed. Nova yelped, lost her grip on the wall, and slid back to her cushions. Cho moved toward her, but Luna was faster.

She glared at Jason as he stepped back. "Why would you do that?" she snapped, kneeling by her sister.

He waved a hand at them both. "You can't stand on it. Can't walk on it. What will you do if we have to run?"

Nova burst into tears.

Jason cursed and ran a hand across the top of his dark hair. He swung in a circle as a muscle in his jaw twitched. With a grimace, he knelt in front of the twins.

Luna scowled at him.

Jason looked to her, then set his gaze on Nova. "I won't let anything happen to her."

"You promise?" Nova sniffed, shaking as she clenched Luna's hand and glanced up at him.

Her voice was so small; Cho was hit with how young she was as well. She and Luna both, barely twelve.

Jason cocked his head to the side and a shadow of his old smirk slid across his face. He held up his hand, a small orb of flame materializing above his palm. "I promise."

Cho might have smiled. Might have let his shoulders ease, let his chest take a full breath, let himself sleep for more than an hour at a time. Might have—if he hadn't felt the true emotion beneath Jason's attempt. The raging fury, like a storm of fire. The grief. Sorrow so deep Cho had to constantly fight to keep himself from drowning beneath the darkness.

Cho crossed to Claire and felt her forehead. "She's still too hot. Go. But be careful. And be quick."

Jane met his gaze with a sharp nod. She, Tommy, Luna, and Jason made a quick plan and left.

The main door of the building closed, the sound echoing through the abandoned halls. Nova glared at Cho, but as he settled onto the cushion beside her, she leaned into his chest and let him put his arm around her.

He winced at the movement in his shoulder and breathed through the thundering fear she felt for her sister. Cho leaned his chin on her frayed, blood crusted braid, and held her as she sobbed into his shirt.

Chapter Thirty-Five

Present Day - Early Fall - Tornim

J ane clenched Tommy's small hand like a lifeline. It was.

She glanced down at her brother as they scurried behind Jason and Luna, rushing through the streets of Grigoria. He met her gaze. His eyes—the same shape and color of their father's, but without the cruelty—were wide.

She threw on a grin, masking her worry to protect him the way she always did. He offered a hesitant smile back.

Jason held up a hand for everyone to stop, darting his head out from behind the corner of a white-washed concrete building. His dark hair and swirling gemstones were hidden by the brown knit cap he'd lent to Cho after their escape. The one Elaine had embroidered with mountains.

Jane's jaw tightened, her fingers squeezing Tommy's hand until he yelped and she loosened her grip with a murmured apology.

It wasn't fair that she'd never gotten a chance to thank Elaine and Ichi for all they'd done. Taking her and Tommy in, teaching them control, giving them a home, and trusting her. Ichi had trusted her, treated her like an adult. She'd gone on missions for him, with him, and now he was gone. Her lip curled into a snarl, resolve hardening in her gut. She'd justify that trust.

"We need a change of clothes," Luna murmured. "We look horrific. And probably smell pretty bad too."

Jane nodded. "Once we get the money. I don't know about you, but I don't have any coins on me."

They both looked to Jason.

"What?"

Jane glowered. "How much do you have?"

He frowned at her. "What are you talking about?"

"Come on," she snapped. "I was there. I know you took a handful of coins from the crate before we hid it. Let's use that to get ourselves some clothes and we can move a lot faster."

He swallowed and ran a hand across his forehead. "I spent it."

Luna sighed and returned to keeping an eye on the street beside them. It was early still, and a rest day for most workers. The breakfast restaurants they'd passed a few minutes ago had been full, but the rest of the city seemed to be sleeping in.

Jane's lip curled. "How can you have spent it already?"

Jason glared back. "None of your business. Let's get the *frosted* coins and get what we need and get back."

Jane bit her tongue to keep from saying something she'd regret.

"We're almost to Agora anyway," Luna murmured.

Jason nodded. "Let's go then."

Tommy glanced up at Jane as the other two darted around the building. "Are we..."

"We're all right." Jane gave him a tight smile. She crouched down. "Things are hard now. Everyone is hurting. But I promise nothing is going to hurt *you*."

Tommy swallowed. Her heart broke a little as he straightened his thin shoulders and gave her his best 'grown-up' nod.

They hurried after the others.

Two days had passed. It felt like a lifetime, yet nothing had changed.

The Red-Stars at the gate gave them long looks.

Luna had redone her braids and washed her dress as best she could. Jane found an oversized sweater to throw over her blood-stained shirt. She'd rolled the sleeves up to her elbows, sweating already, but at least it covered the worst of the damage. Tommy had soot and dirt on his clothes, but no blood, so she wasn't as worried about him.

Jason had the cap, but beyond turning his shirt inside-out, there was little to be done about his wrecked clothes. Scorch marks dotted his shorts and—even inside-out—the blood from Claire's wound was still visible on the light grey of his shirt.

"All right," Jason muttered as they passed through the gate. "Jane, it's you."

She led the way, skirting the edge of Agora until they reached a quiet alley with a large sewer grate next to a pair of garbage cans.

"We go down here," she said.

Jason grunted as he heaved at the crisscrossed ring of iron. Luna approached, facing her palms toward the grate, and scrunching her face in concentration. A few seconds passed and then, slowly, the heavy chunk of metal began to move.

"That'll work." Jane stepped forward when the grate was halfway open. "We don't all need to go down. I'll take Tommy and a few bags, and pass the coins up to you."

Jason sat on the ground, panting and rubbing his palms where the metal had dug into his skin. "You want to split up?"

Jane shook her head. "I want someone up here keeping watch."

Jason stared at her for a long moment. Then he nodded. "Be careful."

Jane didn't respond as she released Tommy's hand and jumped down the hole. Her boots landed in a half-inch of water. The splash reverberated through the hollow tunnel.

She glanced up and grinned as Tommy's head blocked the light pouring in from above. "Let's go," she called.

He backed in, his shoes finding purchase on the top rung of the ladder. He went slow and steady, just like she'd taught him, until he hit the half-way point. Then, without warning, he launched himself at her.

Jane snatched him out of the air and swung him around before planting his feet firmly on the wet ground.

"Are you all right?" Jason called down.

"Fine," Jane replied. She smirked at her brother. "You've gotta warn me next time."

He laughed. The sound eased some of her tension. "No, I don't, you always catch me."

Jane rolled her eyes. "Listen, kid, I'm going that way." She pointed to the wall behind him. "You're staying here. When I get back, you'll pass the bags I hand you up to Jason. We wanna do this fast, so climb back up there, about half-way... perfect." She smiled. "I'll be right back."

She melted through the wall.

Cho had told her once, what it was like to ride along while she used her power. Like sliding through wet cement. It wasn't like that for her. For Jane, her power was freedom. She'd never been in an open field surrounded by nothing but blue skies and miles of emptiness in every direction, but she imagined it would feel the way she felt when she went through a wall.

Not including having to hold her breath.

She passed through the thin outer layer of metal, and the two feet of stone beyond it, and inhaled again when she emerged into cool darkness. Her lungs rejected the stale air—a cough cutting through the silence.

Her stomach dropped.

There was no light in this little room, the door blocked by debris, where she'd stashed a massive chest filled with coins. She'd had an orb last time she'd been there; now the dark was absolute.

Jane's breath came in shallow pants as she clenched and unclenched her fingers. It would be so easy to melt back through the wall behind her and return to the light. Return to Tommy and the others, steal a light orb, and come back.

Unwelcome memories from long ago, before she'd taken Tommy and fled, seeped to the forefront of her mind. *Shouting voices. Screams. Her hands scram-*

bling for a way out. Searching above her for the lock on the wooden floorboards. Her eyes, unable to adjust to the suffocating dark of the tiny basement.

Jane slammed her fist into the wall behind her. Pain radiated through her hand, pulling her to the present. She clenched her jaw and pulled different images forth. Black-Stars, storming her home. Black-Stars, killing the people who'd become her family. Black-Stars, coming for them now—coming for Tommy.

Jane grunted in frustrated fear, stepped away from the wall and felt around in the darkness without outstretched hands. She found the chest and jerked at the lid. It didn't open.

She pulled at it again. It opened fine before, what... Her hands traveled the length of the box and she nearly screamed in frustration. Something had fallen on it, some piece of debris in the room must have been dislodged when they'd placed the chest here.

She shoved, but it remained unmoved. Furious tears slid down her cheeks. With a resigned sigh, Jane rolled her neck and pushed her hands through the top of the chest.

It was tricky work, keeping her arms fluid to be inside the lid, but making her hands solid enough to pick up the coins. Sweat beaded on her forehead. She sucked in breaths through her nose, grudgingly following Elaine's breathing protocols for extensive use of active powers.

She filled a bag, pulled it free, and plunged in with another. She wanted to rush. The thought of Tommy alone in the sewer, waiting for her... but she couldn't. Not without risking cutting her arm off at the elbow.

Seconds passed. Minutes ticked away as she filled the second bag, then the third, fourth, fifth. Her power dwindled, draining fast with this level of concentration. She set the last bag on the chest, heart pounding, and a headache splitting her skull.

Jane scooped the bags into her shaking arms, anxious to return to the light. She backed up until the wall hit her back, closed her eyes, and sank into freedom.

Clothes were first and much appreciated. Jane twinged at how accustomed she'd grown to the clean environment in Haven. Some part of her begrudgingly enjoyed

Elaine checking on Tommy to make sure he'd bathed, eaten, and changed. It was nice, just being his sister sometimes.

They wandered through a little second-hand store. Jane chose an ivory top with sleeves cropped at the elbow and a pair of thick brown shorts that wouldn't look spectacular on her but would last.

She talked Tommy out of the neon orange shirt with metallic flames on the back. Instead, they chose slightly more muted colors and grabbed extra of everything to have with them for later.

Jane grumbled when Luna asked for help picking something for Claire, but she gestured to her pick of the fabrics her friend held up. They left Jason to shop for Cho. The back of the store had a collection of bags and accessories. Jane tossed a small backpack, covered in pictures of little animals, to Tommy. She grabbed a thick black canvas bag, Luna took two identical lavender ones, and Jason took three more for himself, Cho, and Claire.

They changed in a dead-end alley, taking turns watching the front.

Food was next. Agora had medicine, but what they needed for Claire was in Grigoria. They'd get it on the way back.

They moved through an outdoor market, pockets jingling with coins as they grabbed everything they could reach. Jane reminded them all to try and stick to food that would last. By the time they emerged from the last colorful umbrella, their backpacks were bulging with food, toiletries, water bottles, first aid supplies, and Jason had a handful of blankets strapped to the bottom of his bag with two belts.

It was late afternoon and the day had gone from warm to hot. Jane's new shirt stuck to the small of her back as they made their way through Agora. Tommy clung to her hand. His feet stumbled on the concrete as they hurried down a set of steps toward the main road that would lead them to the closest Grigoria gate. From there all they needed to do was find one of the massive shopping malls frequented by the higher castes and convince a pharmacy to accept coins rather than the usual virtual credit.

Jane and Tommy followed close behind Jason as the group moved between two vehicles parked along the main road that circled Agora. Jason held up a hand. She froze, tugging Tommy to her when he tried to keep moving. Jason's gaze darted back at them, his eyes wide and alert.

Jane's pulse quickened and she glanced around.

Two Red-Stars at the gate was not unusual. So, what was causing Jason to...

Four more Red-Stars joined their fellows. Behind them came Black-Stars. Not just any Black-Stars. These men and women—almost a dozen—sported scratches, burns, and bruises.

Fear shifted to fury, then back again as Tommy's hand trembled in hers. Jason took Luna's hand in his and turned to walk parallel to the street rather than cross it. Jane followed suit.

Striding close behind Jason and Luna, Jane murmured out of the side of her mouth, "How did they find us?"

A muscle in Jason's jaw twitched. "They didn't. This is a sweep. Maybe they're looking for anyone who escaped. Maybe this is something else."

She shot him an incredulous side-eye.

He shrugged. "I didn't say it was likely. Just possible."

Jane shook her head. "If this is at every gate... I can pull us through a wall, but I'm spent."

She fell silent at the sound of footsteps behind them.

Jason kept walking. Jane's long legs kept up with his brisk pace, Tommy and Luna nearly jogging to keep up.

"If we get split up," Jane muttered, "meet at the warehouse. You have enough to get the medicine?"

He nodded.

"Me too."

They exchanged a glance. Jane's own anger, a burning fury she'd carried for years—magnified by the raid on Haven—reflected in Jason's eyes. She missed the humor usually found in them. She missed Samaira.

"We shouldn't split up," Luna said, panting as her short legs pumped alongside them.

"I don't plan to," Jason growled.

Behind them, thudding footfalls turned to thundering steps. Jane glanced back. The Black-Stars had broken into a run.

"*Go,*" she commanded.

They turned off the main road. Jane and Tommy took the lead, moving left and rushing down a narrow alley between apartment buildings. Jason and Luna hurried behind them.

They shot out of the alleyway and onto a busy street lined on both sided with art. Jewelry, vases, paintings, and musicians. A symphony of sound and color.

Jane darted to the side. Tommy scrambled with her, his small form squeezing between people to stay as close to her as possible while they ran.

Shouts went up around them, from the shopkeepers, and from the Black-Stars bursting into the street behind them. Jane glanced back in time to see a beefy man in full military gear slam into a table and send a cascade of blown glass shattering onto the street. She grinned and faced forward. Her gut twisted in fear.

Another group of Black-Stars stood at the end of the row of stalls, weapons drawn, watching and waiting as Jane and the others hurtled toward them.

"Take my hand," Jane shouted to Jason.

His large hand clasped around her free one. She tightened her grip on her brother and then veered, pulling them through a stall. The slender glass trees with elegant necklaces dangling from their branches didn't move an inch as they passed.

They came out in the next row of stalls, but Jane didn't dare release Jason's hand. If even a part of him or Luna were still *inside* something... it was too crowded here to risk it. She kept her power flowing, even as the energy in her body grew faint, and led everyone toward a gap in the buildings around them.

Jane flinched as a loud voice rang through the air, demanding they halt. She ran, keeping her grip on Tommy even as they reached an open section of road between the market and the restaurants.

A shot rang out.

A chunk of cobblestone inches from Tommy's leg exploded in shards of shrapnel. Jane screamed as a sharp corner of stone ripped through her shorts and pierced her thigh.

Tommy cried out as well. Jane saw the blood dripping from his arms and the tears in his clothes. Bright light flashed for a split second of time and her mind lost every thought except keeping her brother alive.

She hoisted Tommy into her arms and ran with every ounce of strength in her body.

He thudded against her, his shoe scrapping against the rock still embedded in her leg as she sprinted, not daring to look behind her. Nothing existed except her and the road. She mapped out a route in her head. A right turn, two lefts, through the back kitchen of that little sandwich shop, another right and she'd come out in a small square with a fountain. There was a playground. A popular place for lower caste children to play. A good place to hide. They made the right, and the first left.

Bolts of fear shot through her. Black-Stars. Half a dozen, at the entrance to her next turn. They marched toward her. One shouted and she turned.

Terror gripped her heart as she put her back to the enemy and flew down a different alley. Figured out a new route.

People strode past her, staring briefly at the fleeing children, but largely ignoring the hunt playing out in the artisan neighborhood of Agora.

Jane panted with exertion, a frustrated groan escaping her as another path dead ended in more Black-Stars. They were running out of ways to get out. She brushed a hand against the stone wall beside them, finding it unrelentingly solid.

"Tommy," she huffed, out of breath and shaking from the weight of her brother and the weakness of her gift, "can you do it?"

He murmured, nearly unintelligible against her shoulder, "Yeah."

"Can you hold it for a few minutes?"

"Yeah."

Jane grimaced. His power had been irregular since they'd escaped Haven. She bolted down a busy street, loosing herself in the hustle and bustle of Orange, Green, Purple, and Red-Stars going about their business.

This was one of the wider streets in Agora. Colorful murals of famous locations in Pangaea decorated the uneven walls on either side. Evenly spaced stones jutted out a few feet apart from each other, the design leading half-way up the two-story wall. A painting of the Capital rippled against the texture; the blue of the ocean clashing against the glistening white of the jewel of Pangaea.

On the other side, bricks did the same, little squares sticking out from the wall, warping the image of a sparkling lake lit up with fireworks above the trees around it.

They stood in a thoroughfare between the artisan neighborhood and an area with more restaurants and clothing stores. Dozens of people walked through here, maybe...

Hope died and realization struck as she spotted black gemstones at the far end of the doorless—alley-less—walkway. They'd been herded here.

She wheeled. If they could go back before—but she'd barely made it two steps when the Black-Stars who'd been on her tail from the beginning stepped into view.

"What do we—" Panic split through her. She wheeled again. Her gaze traveled the crowd, searching frantically for Jason and Luna. They'd been... hadn't they been behind her?

They were gone. She and Tommy stood alone. She backed up, leaning against the wall behind them with a silent, desperate plea to the silver ember of power left in her. It wasn't enough.

Tears sprang from her eyes. She sucked in a deep breath. Then another. Tommy leaned back and looked at her. She couldn't work up a smile. Couldn't do anything but adjust her hands under him to stop him falling backward.

"I'm ready," he said.

She glanced either direction. The Black-Stars were moving in, herding people out of their way and blocking off the street as they went. Emptying the area and limiting the witnesses.

Jane looked at her brother and nodded.

He closed his eyes. Like vapor melting into the air, her brother seemed to dissolve before her eyes. Only his weight, and the feeling of him wrapped around her, reassured her that he was still there.

She glanced at her feet and saw only the ground. "Good job," she murmured in his ear. "Move around to my back."

He scrambled around her side as she moved her backpack out of the way. He settled into position, and she tucked her arms under his knees.

She moved with quick silent footsteps away from the place they'd vanished. Black-Stars shouted in fury and confusion at the disappearance of their inevitable prey. Jane pressed up against the stone wall as Black-Stars encircled where she and Tommy had just stood. They were still too close, but there was nowhere else to go. She breathed through her mouth and rubbed her thumb against Tommy's ankle to reassure him, silently hoping he'd stay quiet.

"*Nacra* bullshit," a tall Black-Stars grunted. He turned, waving an arm at a few stragglers. "Get them out of here. *Now.*"

Four of the Black-Star group broke off, ushering pedestrians away and taking guard at both ends of the road.

"What the shit was that?" a Black-Star woman with long, dark green braids asked. "Where did they go?"

"*Frost* if I know, Vanessa," the tall one growled. "Maybe teleported. Maybe went invisible. Maybe turned into a nacra rock." He gestured to the ground.

A younger-looking man beside him kicked at the pebbles on the sidewalk.

The tall one turned, a grimace of incredulity on his face. "You're an idiot, Stevens." He looked back to Vanessa. "These freaks can do almost anything. I don't even..." he pulled off his helmet and ran a hand through damp, matted blond hair. "I'm not supposed to be here," he grumbled.

The woman—Vanessa—turned to the other Black-Stars. "Start at either end of the thoroughfare. Link hands and walk toward each other, meet in the middle. If they turned invisible, they can't have gone far." She looked at the tall man, now leaning against the wall and rubbing his pale face. "I'll get on with support and tell them to shrink the perimeter. We know they were here seconds ago. If they're still here, we'll find them."

He heaved a sigh and nodded. The Black-Stars, having hesitated once Vanessa finished speaking to them, seemed to take his movement as an order. They marched to either end of the walkway, leaving him and the woman in the center.

Jane glanced around. No escape presented itself to her.

She'd have to make one.

She tapped on Tommy's leg, softly, without sound. He stirred. She squeezed his legs for a brief second and he tightened his grip around her, his knees squeezing against her waist.

Jane turned, gut twisting at the thought of his back to the Black-Stars instead of her. She faced the wall, the image of the Capital towering above her.

With a deep breath she grabbed the stone with her fingertips and hefted. She clenched her jaw to keep from grunting as she climbed, feet finding purchase on the textured wall.

Behind her, the Black-Star's conversation leaked into her perception.

"... covering for Lexi," the tall man was saying. "I don't..." his voice shook. "After the raid? I'm not cut out for this shit. I trained to fight *people*, *humans*, not these frosted *freaks* of nature."

"What happened, Greg?"

"Got in my head," Greg muttered.

Jane's hand slipped. She winced as a rough edge of the stone shredded the skin on two of her fingers.

"What do you mean?" The Black-Star's voice carried a concern Jane never thought she'd hear from one of them.

The Black-Stars on either edge of the thoroughfare moved toward them in a line, running their hands along the walls.

Jane swallowed and kept climbing. Tommy's sweaty hands clenched around her throat. The chunk of stone in her thigh ached, blood dripping down her calf and pooling in her sock.

Fear gripped her, pushed her through the pain in her fingertips.

"I was one of the first through the door," Greg said. "Something happened to me. I can't..." his voice broke, "I can't really explain it. Like I was screaming, right? But no sound came out. Pain like nothing I've felt before, but all in my head. Not a mark on me when I woke up, 'sides the bruises from falling down the stairs."

"They're dangerous," Vanessa growled. "No wonder she put so much man-power into finding the rest."

Jane's feet were nearly five feet off the ground, but not high enough to evade the sweeping hands of the men headed towards her. It was slow going. Tommy wasn't as little as he used to be.

The two Black-Stars talking crossed the road. Jane leaned her forehead against the wall as they came to a halt a few feet from her injured leg.

Greg shook his head. "A waste of time and energy," he grumbled. "We should be aiming to kill, not capture."

A chill went through Jane.

"Orders are orders, Greg," Vanessa sounded apprehensive.

"We caught enough of them for those Blue-Stars in Dolor to run their *nacra* experiments. Rounding up the last handful won't make a difference."

Jane's heart leapt into her throat. She bit through the skin of her lip, tasting the salty, metallic tang of her own blood. Pins and needles raced along her skin.

She exhaled, slow and smooth, and hefted them up one last foothold. Tommy trembled on her back. She leaned her cheek against his arm, silently begging him to hold on a little longer. Her power flitted and sparked, the revelation of the Black-Stars' words acting as kindling for the ember still inside her.

The Black-Stars reached their commanders. A hand brushed, inches below her ankle. Blood pooled in her shoe. Fear scratched at her throat.

"Nothing, Captain," one of the Black-Stars barked.

Vanessa nodded. "Get on the coms and widen the search. We're finding these freaks."

"They don't have anywhere to go," Greg said. "Let's cast the net."

Drip.

Jane's stomach lurched as the sound reverberated around them. Vanessa glanced around, frowning. Another drop of blood hit the ground. Pain spiked through Jane's fingers.

Greg knelt. He put a finger to the ground as a third drop fell from Jane's shoe. It landed on the back of his hand.

He looked up. Squinted right at them, but Tommy maintained control of his power. The Black-Star stood. Reached out. His hand brushed the bottom of her foot.

Jane gritted her teeth, pouring everything she had left into making the spark grow.

His fingers swiped the air, closed around her ankle.

"Hold on," Jane commanded.

Tommy's grip tightened around her neck and waist. Jane sucked in a breath as the Black-Star holding her yanked. Jane released her hold on the stones. They fell back, still invisible.

She closed her eyes, the spark of her power roaring into silver flames as she pushed deeper than she'd ever gone before.

Her foot slid from Greg's grasp. They plummeted toward the ground. Through it.

Jane dropped them through three levels of sewer tunnels before they hit the ground with a thud. The world around them was pitch black. Near her, Tommy shifted.

"Jane?"

"I'm here," Jane reassured, her voice weak. Pressure thundered in the space behind her eyes, weighing down her lids until all she wanted was to consume the darkness and sleep.

Instead, she pulled a small orb from her bag. She flicked a switch at the bottom and a warm yellow glow spread a few feet in every direction. Just enough light to keep the dark at bay.

Tommy sat against the wall not far from her. Jane scooted next to him and lifted an arm, making room for him to snuggle in and lean on her chest.

Dirty brick walls formed the tunnel; old architecture that had been built over and forgotten. The tunnel stretched in both directions. The black almost reaching out to pull her to it.

Her head drooped and she caught sight of a jagged shard of brick sticking out of her left leg. Red stained her skin, fading to a rusty orange in the yellow light from the orb. She needed to tie it up. Put pressure on the wound.

Don't take it out.

She blinked, staring sleepily at the wall across from her. Ichi's voice echoed in her mind.

Don't take it out. Not until we get you somewhere safe.

"We are safe," she mumbled.

Tommy looked up at her.

Jane glanced back at her wound and Ichi returned again. A memory, that's what this was. A memory of the first time she'd met him, except that wound had been a slice of glass embedded just above her elbow.

She swallowed. She had to stop the bleeding but taking out the object would only make it worse. That's what Ichi had taught her that day. She dislodged her brother and dug through her bag for a strip of cloth, but before she'd found one, Tommy handed her a roll of gauze. She stared at him for a moment, then took it and wrapped it several times around her leg.

Blood soaked through the white fabric. She took a few shallow breaths, gripped either end of the gauze, and pulled. She screamed. Pain erupted in her leg; spots of light danced across her vision.

She tied it off and leaned against the wall, panting and swallowing. Trying to breathe through the excruciating hurt in her leg.

Seconds passed, ticked on until they turned to minutes, until Jane lost track of time entirely. The bleeding slowed and stopped. Tommy leaned on her once more, this time curled into a ball.

"Jane..." Tommy whispered.

Jane jerked awake and glanced down at him.

"Were they telling the truth?" he asked. "About... about the others?"

"I think so, Tommy."

"So they aren't..." Tommy sat up, staring at her.

"They're alive," Jane murmured. The revelation, and realization that she and Tommy were the only ones who knew, pushed her to sit up. She stood, shouldering her bag as her fury, that constant friend she kept in her heart, pulled her back from the deep recess in her mind.

She said it again, "They're alive."

Tommy scrambled to his feet, clenching the small orb in his hand and sending shadows of his fingers across the walls around them.

"They're alive." Jane's hand closed into a fist. She reached the other out and Tommy took it. She gave him a tight smile, her mind already mapping the way through Agora. She limped forward, her smile sliding into determined frown. "We have to get back."

Chapter Thirty-Six

Present Day - Early Fall - Abredea

"How bad is it?" Anthony murmured.

Taz stood over him, cleaning the stitched-up gash sprawling across half his back and around his side. The room was empty apart from the two of them, the perfect time to get some real answers.

Since waking up a week ago, Anthony had seen how thin his friends were. He'd asked how things were going and received the same bland answer from Naya, Juliana, and May each on separate occasions. Things were fine, focus on resting up. Focus on healing.

He'd ask Daisy, but she hadn't been coming by as often as usual.

He grimaced as Taz gave him a wide-eyed glance. "Taz," Anthony grumbled. He winced as Taz pressed antiseptic onto his stitches.

The cloth came away clean this time. They'd been fighting back an infection since he'd woken up. He hadn't gotten a full night of sleep since he'd pulled out of his unconscious state. The pain from his many injuries woke him. Pain and fear.

"I'm not..." Taz set the cloth aside and put a fresh bandage on the wound. "I'm not sure what... what yeh..." He looked away with a grimace, avoiding Anthony's eye.

Anthony put a hand on Taz's arm. "Tell me."

Taz sighed and nodded. "It's bad."

Anthony pushed himself up, grunting with the effort before he settled himself upright against the wall. Taz moved a pillow under his injured leg and sat at the foot of the bed. He ran a hand across his face, fingers lingering at his gemstones.

"Steel increased the guard," Taz mumbled. "They're hur... hurt.... They're findin' reasons tah hurt people. They blocked the last shipment of goods tah the square. The baker is... is out... is out of flour. Everythin' got more expensive. Most people are only eatin' the mush packets right now. There isn't anythin' extra."

Anthony ground his teeth, anger burning in his chest. "This is insane. He's starvin' people 'cause of me."

Taz shook his head. "I think it's about Juliana. About her standin' up tah him."

"What makes yeh say tha'?" Anthony leaned his head against the wall. All he'd wanted was to keep his family fed and safe. He closed his eyes, weariness washing the anger from him.

"He's havin' her followed."

Anthony's eyes snapped open. He straightened and peered intently at Taz. "How d'ya know that?"

Taz shrugged. "She had a plan. I was gonna keep watch while she went tah get food."

Anthony's eyes widened with horror. "She left Abredea? Alone?"

Taz shook his head. "That's what I'm tellin' yeh. She couldn'. Every time we turned around there was a Black-Star. They're ev... evv... they keep showin' up. Everywhere."

Anthony exhaled through pursed lips. "Are they on *you* that way?"

Taz shook his head again.

"Daisy?"

Another no.

Anthony frowned. It made sense for Steel to be furious with Juliana for undermining his authority. But he'd won, hadn't he? Thrown Anthony off a building for *frost's* sake. What more did he want?

"Plus, they called her to town hall today," Taz stood and took the cloths and old bandage to the kitchen.

Anthony nearly fell off the bed. "When? Why?" he demanded. He scooted himself to the edge of the bed and—with a grunt of pain—hoisted himself onto his good leg.

Taz turned around. "Whaddya think yer doin'?"

"I'm goin' tah town hall. She can't be *alone*."

Taz rushed back to him, put hands on both his shoulders—Anthony winced—and pushed him back onto the bed. It wasn't difficult with Anthony barely balanced on one leg. His stitches flared with pain as he hit the mattress.

"She's not alone," Taz reminded him. "Montague is there. Other people too."

"Who?" Anthony demanded.

Taz ran a hand through his ragged locks of hair. He opened his mouth, closed it again, and sat beside Anthony on the bed. "It was rough while yeh were out," he finally said. "But I think," Taz hesitated, "I think it was maybe somethin' Abredea needed."

Anthony raised an eyebrow. "Abredea needed me tah fall off a buildin'?"

Taz flashed a rueful grin before resuming his contemplative frown. "No. People are actin' different. Some are really scared. More than they were before everythin' happened. But others..." he rubbed a thumb against his gemstone, "they're stickin' together more. A couple of the men who helped you that day told me tah let 'em know if Steel tries anythin' else. They've noticed all the guards. They're watchin' Juliana too."

Anthony's eyes stung with tears. He squeezed Taz's shoulder in unspoken gratitude.

Taz hand covered Anthony's and he squeezed back. "Black-Stars came here while yeh were unconscious. Before we even knew if yeh'd wake up again." He sniffed and rubbed the back of his hand across his nose. "I've never seen anythin' like it. People saw 'em marchin' and came tah help. They blocked the door. Dozens," his voice broke, "tah stop 'em gettin' at yeh."

There was a moment of silence before Taz continued. "I thought... I thought they were gonna shoot. But there were so many of us. The Black-Stars stayed a full day but after that... they never came back."

Anthony grabbed his friend and pulled him into a tight hug as emotion broke over him. Sweeping waves of love and gratitude overwhelmed his fear and anger. He thought he'd been alone since Dave died, but hearing this...

"Thank you," he whispered, his tears soaking into Taz's shoulder.

Juliana strode through Abredea with her head held high. The desire to hunch her shoulders, and melt into the trees, was strong. She wanted to go back to her field, sit under a tree. Maybe borrow a book from Daisy and share a strawberry picnic with her friend.

She gave a little shake of her head. Not in a hundred years would she have thought of those as simpler days. It was different now.

Her skin crawled as she felt eyes on her, again. When she glanced behind her, a Black-Star, about twenty yards back, met her gaze with a sneer.

Tailing her had to be a boring job. She'd spent the last two weeks helping May with the garden, doing what she could for Anthony, and delivering carrots, tomatoes, peas, blackberries—the small ones from the garden, not the massive juicy wild ones—and any other produce they managed to coax from the dirt.

Her plans, to sneak out of Abredea like Anthony did and help keep everyone fed, died before she'd made her first attempt. Steel had doubled the regular guard and was having her followed.

Juliana entered the square. Her footsteps echoed across the deserted cobble-stone. The fountain hadn't turned back on since Anthony's beating. The bakery was closed. The backer had run out of goods around the same time anyone who could afford them ran out of coin. The grocers remained, but with the cost of everything, Juliana was amazed they bothered to keep their door open. Even Naya's group of laundry ladies had ceased their regular trips to the communal bins.

She clutched an empty basket to her side. It might have been smarter to go straight to town hall when she found out Ms. Wolfe wanted to meet with her rather than making her deliveries first. Smart didn't feel as important now. Not when so many people were hungry.

Montague watched her approach from the top of the steps. His gaze flicked to the Black-Star behind her, and his bushy eyebrows narrowed.

Juliana shook her head. Montague saying anything to them wouldn't help at this point. There was nothing more he could do.

A shudder ran through her as she passed the dark stain on the middle section of the steps. The image of Anthony, sprawled, broken, and bleeding slammed into her.

She hurried up the steps, smoothed her grimace into a smile, and thanked Montague as he opened the door for her.

"I expected you earlier," he said as the door closed. He flipped the lock.

The Black-Star assigned to her rushed up the steps. He reached the top, tried the door, and heaved a sigh. Shaking his head, he leaned up against one of the stone pillars, gaze fixed on the door.

Juliana turned from the glass window and walked to the center of the lobby. "I had deliveries to make this morning."

He nodded. "I understand."

She waited, but he didn't continue.

"She's not yet arrived?"

He shook his head and took off his glasses. "I notice the study groups haven't returned."

Juliana plopped her basket on a chair. Her mouth twisted to the side in frustration. "Steel has people following me everywhere I go, every day. He's looking for any *nacra* excuse. I'm not putting a group of children in the middle of that."

Montague nodded as he used his dress-shirt to clean his glasses. "I don't disagree. Captain Steel has..." He replaced his glasses, pushing them up his nose with his middle finger and sighed. "I won't say he's *becoming* unhinged, because I believe we both saw the moment he cracked and lost all reason."

The thudding sound of Steel's fist, slamming into Anthony again and again echoed through the air.

Juliana nodded.

"But I do believe he has lost sight of his purpose here." Montague crossed the lobby and stepped behind the U-shaped counter.

Juliana followed him as he flicked a switch on a small round speaker. Music...

Tingling flowed down her arms and legs, like pinpricks of ice were melting under her skin. Tears formed in the corners of her eyes. Her father had played this song on his days off. The two of them would bake in the kitchen as he warbled off-tune to the jaunty melody.

Montague turned to her and studied her face. "Miss Juliana, are you alright?"

Juliana swallowed and sniffed. "I'm fine, Montague. I didn't realize this was allowed." She gestured to the speaker.

Montague gave half a shrug. "I found it tucked away in the attic."

Juliana sank onto the armrest of the closest couch. Outside, the Black-Star still watched the front of the building.

"What do you mean, 'his purpose'?" she asked.

Montague carried the speaker over as he sat beside her. He lowered his voice and she had to lean in to hear him over the music. "I don't think it's a coincidence that the new captain arrived shortly after you did."

Juliana furrowed her brow, puzzled.

Montague went on. "He has had an interest in you for quite some time now. He..." Montague fiddled with the buttons on his jacket, his cheeks reddening. "He's been asking about you from the start. Always with the warning not to mention any of our conversations to you, of course. But he has been curious of your comings and goings. How you're adapting to life here."

Juliana shook her head. "This doesn't make any sense. I..." she hesitated, frowning and dropped her voice to match his, though unsure of why. "Ms. Wolfe was at my Coding."

Montague gave her a sharp look.

"She said she wanted to bring me to work with her." Juliana stared at the floor, her mind working through several curiosities. "When I was placed here, she said she'd try to get me out."

Montague exhaled and rubbed his fingers across his sweaty forehead. "That's impossible, Miss Juliana."

She nodded. "I understand how foolish it was to hope for, but at the time I did."

"Not any longer?"

Her fingers tapped against her thumb as she hesitated to find the correct words. "I don't think there's any chance of me leaving this place. But I don't..." She sighed. "I don't see it the way I used to."

Montague regarded her for a long moment before he nodded. "I experienced something similar when I was your age."

"Perhaps Steel is working more closely with Wolfe than I thought. I knew they had dealings. I overheard her reminding him to be lenient after he first arrived."

Montague scoffed. "Clearly the man didn't listen to that order."

Juliana grimaced.

"It could be he's keeping an eye on you because of Ms. Wolfe, but I'm wondering why," Montague said.

"It could have been to make sure I didn't break any rules. To ensure I wasn't acting like a Moon. But that doesn't make sense now," Juliana replied. "I told Wolfe at our last meeting that I knew how unlikely it was I'd ever leave. I asked her to make sure my parents know I'm all right. I don't think..." she hesitated, clearing her throat, "I don't believe she is still trying to orchestrate my removal."

Montague rubbed his chin with a perplexed expression. "She will be here soon, I expect. I wanted to have this little conversation before she arrived. You deserve to know how long the captain has been looking into you. Whether it's a coincidence or not is for you to decide."

Juliana nodded. "I appreciate it, Montague. I appreciate everything you've done. For me, for Anthony." She smiled weakly, her mind busy filtering through every conversation she'd had with Wolfe and wondering why she had been asked to meet with her today.

"Be careful, Miss Juliana. I don't believe things are going to get better for a while." He stood and lifted the speaker, giving her a pointed look. "Watch what you *say* and do. I, and many others, have grown fond of you." There was a pause. "I also wanted to let you know, I looked into your aunt. Brenna." He shook his head as she opened her mouth. "I have no record of her death. Nor was I able to find anything about her being sent here. According to Abredea's records, no one by that name ever passed through the wall."

Juliana frowned. "Is that normal? Missing records like this?"

"I was here thirty years ago, but I'm afraid I'd not yet taken up my post in this hall. I can't say how careful or accurate the last hall master was."

Juliana nodded.

He switched off the music, and as he did Juliana noticed for the first time a small tattoo on the inside of his left wrist. She got a brief glimpse of a set of mountain peaks but missed the details when he straightened his jacket and strode to the front door.

"Montague," Juliana called as he reached for the lock.

He hesitated, glancing back at her.

"Did you give Steel what he wanted?"

Montague's face went taut for a second. He gave her a tight, apologetic smile. "Only at first, Miss Juliana. Only at first."

She nodded and slid down her armrest and onto the couch, settling in to wait for Wolfe.

Wolfe was perched on the edge of Montague's desk again. A matronly figure, her grey eyes, watching Juliana with more intensity than was in her smile. Her gemstones swirled like a storm as they regarded each other.

"You've heard what happened?" Juliana murmured.

"It was quite unfortunate." Wolfe's voice rang out, clear and sharp. "I understand one of your friends got into some trouble and was badly hurt. He's recovering?"

"Does Captain Steel work for you?" Juliana asked over the end of Wolfe's question.

Wolfe shifted her rigid shoulders. "I'm not sure I understand the question. He is a Black-Star. All Black-Stars work for Greys."

Juliana forced a deferential smile onto her face. "I meant you specifically. I had assumed he was a general contractor, working for the city in their efforts to... aid the camp."

"You'd be correct," Wolfe replied. Her smile brightened for a moment.

Juliana's emotions fluctuated as the air in the room warmed. Her brief calm was shut down by the memory of Steel shoving Anthony off the balcony. "He has been... extreme in his enforcement of the laws here."

"Indeed."

Juliana fidgeted in her seat. "Things need to change here. There isn't enough food. Children are going hungry; people are angry and scared. This can't be allowed to go on."

Wolfe regarded her for a long moment. "I agree, children mustn't be in such conditions, however, there is little I can do to remedy the situation. Unfortunately, most of these people have brought these problems upon themselves. The young man, for example, was caught with contraband food. Such actions must be punished, or else others will follow the example."

Juliana opened her mouth to clarify the situation, but Wolfe continued.

"Now, I understand Captain Steel had a heavy hand when dealing with the situation, but the boy did strike him."

Juliana clenched her hand by her thigh, careful to keep the fist hidden.

Wolfe went on, "I don't disagree, my dear, with your assertion that things here could be better. But I am not the one to make it so. I'm not in charge of this camp. Captain Steel is."

Juliana cleared her throat. "Something needs to be done, Ms. Wolfe. There has to be someone with the ability to do *something*."

Wolfe's eyes glinted. She rose from the desk and dragged a second chair next to Juliana's. She sat, leaning forward on the armrest, and gazing into Juliana's eyes.

Juliana fought the urge to lean away.

"It could be that there is already someone here with the *ability* to do something. Someone with the *ability* to change things." She reached out and put a hand on Juliana's forearm. "Maybe you're just the person to do so."

Juliana's brow furrowed. Her mind buzzed as the plan she'd been concocting, the idea she'd been stirring around since Anthony had fallen, solidified. She *could* do something. She would.

It wouldn't be in the way Wolfe meant; obeying the law, making nice with Steel, or helping the next generation of Moons learn to bow to the people above them. And it would take someone with authority to manage a few of the obstacles in her way.

"I think..." she hesitated, wanting to make sure she got her point across clearly. "I think doing *anything* will be difficult while Captain Steel has so many Black-Stars in the camp."

Wolfe leaned back, an eyebrow raised.

"I only mean," Juliana clarified, "he has flooded the camp with guards. I can't do my study groups with the children. The baker and grocer can't get their supply shipments. Anth—" Juliana swallowed down a shudder, "my friend is no longer a threat. He was seriously injured and will be recovering for several more weeks."

Wolfe put a hand up; her immaculate fingernails filed into perfect half-moons. "I don't believe you know what you're asking of me."

Juliana angled herself towards Wolfe, slouching so she was looking up at the Grey-Star, subservient. "I'm not just asking; I'm begging you to do something to help us. Even a return to the standard number of guards would be a start at returning to normal, everyone following the rules, everyone getting enough to eat."

She moved her hand around her back and dug her fingernails into her palm. With tears in her eyes, she went on, "Without order, there is no peace. Without caste, there is no order." Juliana stared up at Wolfe. "Let the White-Stars do what they're meant to do. Let them tend the fields and work the mines; let them live quiet lives here, away from the rest of society."

Wolfe studied her for a long moment. Juliana couldn't get a read on the thoughts behind those stormy eyes, but she caught a flicker of a smile. Finally, the woman rose from her chair. She crossed to the window and turned back to murmur, "You're right, of course. The captain does seem to have gone slightly overboard with his form of justice."

Juliana clenched her hand even tighter and gave a slight nod.

"I will do what I can, dear girl. But remember, you're the one with the *ability* to make real change happen here. You're the one who can help your friends."

Juliana blinked. Her mask slid a fraction as confusion flitted across her face. Then she nodded and forced a submissive smile. "Thank you, Ms. Wolfe. You have my gratitude."

Wolfe chuckled as she strode to the door and pulled it open. "I'll have your debt as well, if I manage to convince Captain Steel to calm his forces."

Juliana's smile tightened, but she nodded again. "Of course."

An hour later, Juliana rapped on the back door to the mayor's house. She glanced at her palm. Angry red lines marked where her nails had dug into her flesh. Her jaw ached from keeping it clenched, keeping herself from telling Wolfe what she really thought of Steel's *slightly overboard form of justice.*

Even now, a low growl bubbled in her throat. She scowled. There was no justice in what Steel had done.

She'd begun to understand that there was no justice in Abredea when Jimmy lay dying. The fact had solidified in her mind as she'd stitched Anthony's gaping wound until the thread was stained red.

The door swung open. "What do you want?" Mayor Marsterson glared from the dark interior hallway.

Juliana gave him an equally respectful look. "I want to see Daisy."

"She's busy," Marsterson grunted.

Juliana's lip curled. "I don't care. I want to see her. Now."

Marsterson blinked. His face flushed scarlet and his eyes bulged in fury. He spluttered for a second then said, "Listen here, girl. You don't give orders to me, or anyone else. You may have been worth something in the city, but that's not the way things work here." He smirked. "I'd have thought you'd figured that out after what happened to your friend."

Heat roared through Juliana. She gritted her teeth, sucked a breath, and called into the house, "Daisy? I need to talk to you. It's important."

Marsterson's smirk slid from his face. "I told you. She's busy."

"I don't give a *frost* what mindless chore you gave her today," Juliana snapped. "You can say all you want about how much I'm worth, but the people you're responsible for are starving. Maybe try to solve a problem for once instead of making things worse."

As she finished speaking, the stairs to the right of the door squeaked with Daisy's light footsteps. Juliana grimaced as Daisy came into view, her usually rosy cheeks gaunt and pale, bags under her eyes, lips dry and chapped.

"Hey," Juliana murmured. "I have something to discuss with you." She glared at Marsterson. "If you have the time."

Daisy swallowed as she reached the door. She stood at the frame, between her father and Juliana. "Father, I've finished what you asked me to do. I'd like to go with my friend."

Marsterson grunted.

Daisy closed her eyes, her face falling.

"May and the others will be pleased to see you," Juliana injected. "She's missed your visits." She raised her eyes from Daisy to Marsterson, catching his gaze and holding it while she spoke to Daisy. "You know how fond she, and Anthony's friends, are of you."

Marsterson cleared his throat and shifted. He ran a grubby hand across his shirt, leaving a grease stain on the crisp white cloth. "Go then," he grumbled, "but be back soon. You have dinner to prepare this evening."

Daisy's eyes went wide. She glanced at Juliana before nodding and—not meeting her father's eye—darted out of the house.

They strode through the square, Juliana moving at a pace that had Daisy jogging to keep up.

"What was that?" Daisy asked as they left the cobblestone for hardpacked earth and flowing trees.

Juliana gave half a shrug. "I miss you."

"Not *that*," Daisy chuckled. "I mean, how did you get him to let me leave with you?"

Juliana rolled her eyes and snarled. "That man should have no say as to when and where you go."

Daisy's smile fell. She was quiet for a while as they walked together, their pace slowing once they were a little further from her house. She fiddled with the pocket of her amber vest. Her dress—cream colored on top with flowing green skirts, had seen better days. It was stained. Spots of white where bleach had dripped onto it, a few tears, clearly mended with care.

"Daisy." Juliana paused as they reached the turn-off to May's house. "We can go to May's. Everyone *does* want to see you. We've missed you. But I need to talk to you about something else first. Somewhere private."

She glanced back down the trail. A Black-Star, a new one, was about fifty yards from them, overly observing a tree.

"All right." Daisy followed her gaze. "Where do you suggest?"

Juliana grinned. She reached out and took her friend's hand. A shudder of anger rippled down her spine at how bony Daisy's fingers were. Still, she gripped her hand and pulled her toward the place they'd met.

A few minutes later the two emerged through the thick, overgrown bushes and trees into their little field. Juliana closed her eyes and inhaled. Jasmine... mint... pine... the scents drove the anger from her limbs.

Wind ripped through her hair, stirring the trees around them. Under one tree lay a blanket, a basket, and a thin notebook.

Juliana walked towards it, pulling Daisy along.

"Jules, you didn't have to..." Daisy's shoulders slumped, her body shook with sobs.

Juliana pulled her close, wrapping slender arms around her too-thin torso. "Of course I did," Juliana whispered. "It's what you'd have done for me."

Daisy cried into her chest for a long moment. When her sobs subsided, she pulled away.

Juliana glanced behind them. The Black-Star wasn't in sight. Either because he'd lost them, he'd gotten uncomfortable at the tears, or he'd been called back. She hoped for the last of the three but wouldn't bet on it.

She and Daisy settled onto the blanket and Juliana pulled the picnic basket toward them. It wasn't full as it had been in the past, but there was the last of the bread, a few apples, some sliced carrots, and a bit of cheese.

Daisy shook her head, silent tears sliding down her cheeks, as Juliana fixed her a pitiful version of a sandwich and handed it over. "I'm sorry, Juliana."

"Why?" Juliana's eyes widened as she leaned forward and took one of the apples.

"You did all this for me, and I haven't been there to help with Anthony's injuries." She sniffed.

"That's not your fault." Juliana's voice was sharp though she tried not to snap at her friend. "You aren't to blame for your father being a piece of shit."

A hint of Daisy's old giggle bubbled up and out, the tinkling sound like that of a songbird.

Juliana grinned. "There it is."

"What?" Daisy asked before biting into her food. She moaned, chewed far too quickly, and swallowed it down.

"Your laugh," Juliana murmured. She took a bite of her apple and munched on it slowly as Daisy shook her head, cheeks flushing.

They ate in silence for a few minutes. Juliana took her time with the apple, waving off Daisy's offers to share the rest of the food. Her stomach ached with hunger. It had for days now. Mush packets for breakfast and dinner, and a portion of produce from May's garden to sustain them the rest of the day... it wasn't enough.

She grabbed the notebook and pencil, and got to work as Daisy licked the crumbs off her fingers.

"What did you want to talk about, Juliana?" Daisy asked softly, watching her draw.

Juliana held up a finger as she bit her tongue. It had been so long since she'd seen a map of the city, even longer since she'd seen one with Abredea included on it. After a few minutes she'd managed a somewhat clear representation of Tornim, the main roads, Abredea, and the surrounding fields and forest.

"Sorry." Juliana leaned back with a sigh. "I had time to set this up, but I wanted to get you here, so I didn't get this done." She waved the map through the air.

"What is it?" Daisy scooted closer, her thigh brushing against Juliana's as they studied the paper together.

"It's the key," Juliana said with a grin.

Daisy raised an eyebrow and Juliana laughed.

"I have a plan, Daisy. One that'll make everything better, I promise." She stared out at the mountains. She had a better understanding now, of that itch Anthony spoke of. The itch to be back in the forest.

If Wolfe came through on the Black-Stars, if Juliana was able to get the other information she needed without raising suspicion, if she had the guts to pull this off...

She'd be out there, among the trees, soon enough.

Chapter Thirty-Seven

Present Day - Early Fall - Abredea

T hree days after Juliana's talk with Wolfe, she stood with Taz and Daisy watching the extra Black-Stars march back through the wall. This time they would not be returning in the morning.

A crisp chill filled the evening air. Juliana wrapped her hands around her arms, grim satisfaction on her face as the men and women disappeared from view. Many of them did not look unhappy to be going.

Taz turned to her as the wall began to slowly slide closed. "When do we... we... do we..." His lip curled. "Is it time?"

Juliana nodded and turned from the wall. She walked through the square, her mind running through the information they'd gathered in the last few days. "It is. I think..." she swallowed, "tomorrow morning, in fact."

Daisy darted a wide-eyed glance at her. "Already?"

They settled onto the steps of town hall. Juliana glanced toward the glass doors, unsure if she should fill Montague in on their scheme.

She still hadn't told Anthony... a problem she'd remedy that night. She shouldn't. Daisy and Taz would support her if she decided not to. But it felt like a betrayal—going into his forest, his sanctuary—and not letting him know.

Maybe Montague would cover for them. Maybe he'd try to talk her out of it. Maybe—and it was a nasty little voice in the back of her head that said it—maybe he'd tell Steel.

Juliana shook her head, sending the thought from her mind. He may have reported on her when she first arrived, a piece of knowledge that still stung, but he'd stopped all that. She didn't know exactly when, but certainly before he'd helped them get into the city. Before he helped them save Jimmy.

"Yeah," she finally replied.

Daisy and Taz looked at her.

Juliana lowered her voice. "I know it's a risk, and I'm telling you, I can do it myself. You don't have to come. Either of you."

Taz scoffed and flailed a hand through the air. Daisy put her fingers around Juliana's forearm and gave a little squeeze.

"We aren' about tah miss out on this," Taz said, a little too loud for Juliana's comfort.

"Shh." She gave him a meaningful stare and he nodded sheepishly.

"He's right though," Daisy murmured, a sly smile on her soft face. "Even if it wasn't about being there to help, there's no way either of us are passing on this chance."

Juliana nodded. Her palms were damp with sweat, heart beating faster than she was used to. She inhaled, breathing out through pursed lips as she took in the excitement on her friends' faces. She understood a little better now, why Anthony had never brought them. That excitement worried her.

"All right then." Juliana rose from the steps and dusted off her pants. "I'll see you both tonight."

They stood as well, Taz straightening to his full, lanky height and giving her a sharp nod. Daisy turned to go but Juliana reached for her arm.

"Hey." She swallowed. "Are you sure—"

"Don't," Daisy whispered fiercely. "Don't ask me if I'm sure this is what I want. I'm sure."

Juliana raised an eyebrow and released her friend's arm. "I know it's what you want, but I don't want you—"

"Getting into any trouble," Daisy interrupted again. "I know. It's my decision, Juliana. Let me make it."

Juliana nodded. But when Daisy turned to go, she pulled her back again into a tight hug. "Be careful getting out tonight."

Daisy returned the pressure without hesitation. When she moved to go, Juliana let her. Juliana squared her shoulders and strode through Abredea. It was time to take care of that last problem.

She went over her list of reasons why he couldn't come with them, muttering to herself as she swung her empty basket through the air. She reached the steps to May's. The glass bottles hanging from her roof twinkled as the sunset reflected off their many colors.

Juliana squared her shoulders and stepped through the door.

Anthony struggled to contain his excitement as the door squeaked open. Juliana stepped into the room, he flung his hands wide and shouted, "Ta-da!"

To his disappointment, rather than looking exited that he was standing, indeed walking through May's house, Juliana's eyes were wide with alarm.

She hurried to him, putting a hand on his arm and scanning him. "Should you be out of bed? What about your leg?"

He laughed off her concern and turned at the front door to do another lap around the house. Slower than he was used to, wobbling a bit on the uneven foot of his cast, but moving nonetheless.

He watched her as he went, waiting for her eyes to light up.

"How..." Juliana sank onto her bed.

May, sitting at the kitchen table with a ball of yarn, her knitting needles flashing, said, "He's been practicing every day while you're out of the house."

Anthony shot her a frown. She gave him a wry, one-sided grin. She paused her knitting, taking a moment to rub at the top edge of her long scar. It seemed to bother her more during changes of the season.

Juliana glanced between the two of them. "You've been walking?"

Anthony nodded, concern stirring in his stomach. "For about a week now. I can get tah Naya's withou' much trouble. I didn't wanna show yeh 'til I had it down." He swallowed.

Her expression was not what he expected. She looked upset and anxious. She leaned against the wall behind her bed, tapping her fingers against her thumb in a steady pattern.

He hobbled over to her, trying not to look like he was trying too hard. "What's wrong, Jules? I thought yeh'd be 'appy about this."

He heard the disappointment in his own voice, and Juliana must have heard it too because she plastered a forced smile onto her face. "I am. I'm happy for you, Anthony. You're back on your feet faster than expected. Well done."

He chewed on his thumb nail.

Juliana sighed. She darted a glance at May who was back to her knitting and pretending to ignore the two of them.

"I wanted to talk to you about something," Juliana murmured. "Wanna..." she grimaced, "go for a walk?"

Anthony pushed off the dresser where he'd been leaning. "Sure." Maybe she'd explain what her problem was.

"Don't mind me," May called as they walked out the front door. "I'll just be here knitting until dinner I suppose."

Juliana cracked a smile at that. She stuck her head back in the door while Anthony slowly made his way down the crooked wooden steps. "Did you want to join us, May?"

"Oh no darling, I'm tired."

Anthony caught the end of May's cackle as Juliana pulled the door closed, turned to him, and rolled her eyes. He laughed. She joined him at the bottom of the steps, and they automatically began moving west, toward the forest.

He felt her stare. Felt those dazzling blue eyes piercing him, analyzing. They walked in silence for a few minutes. Anthony set the pace and watched the ground with a wary eye to avoid anything that might trip him up. After a while, when she didn't stop staring, he halted and turned to her. "Wha' is it?"

Juliana sighed with half a smile, but there was worry in her eyes. "I had a whole speech, but you've ruined it."

"What?" Anthony furrowed his brow, confused. He moved a few steps to the side and leaned against a tree to take some weight off his leg.

She followed waving a hand through the air as if to shoo away his frown. "I have a plan, Anthony. One that has a chance to change things."

He raised an eyebrow. "Change things how?"

She shook her head. "All you need to know is..." she exhaled through her nose and he caught a glimpse of the frustration hiding behind her smile, "it involves leaving Abredea again. Going into the forest."

Alarm flared through him. A chill went up his spine. He opened his mouth, but Juliana held up her hand.

"I'm going," she declared. "Tomorrow morning, before dawn."

"Juliana," Anthony spoke across her words, "yeh can't leave Abredea right now. It's too dangerous."

She arched her eyebrows and nodded, a sly grin on her face. "It *was* too dangerous."

"What changed between now and yesterday tah make it less so?" he demanded.

"Steel cut back the guard."

Anthony's breath caught in his chest. A flare of pain went through the slowly healing wound along his back and side. His leg handled walking around just fine—the cast was well made. But the rest of him felt the effort. "Why would he do tha'?" Anthony breathed. Fear cut through his curiosity.

Juliana gave a noncommittal shrug. "It doesn't matter why. The important thing is that I can get out a couple hours before dawn."

"Why though?" Anthony caught her gaze and held it. "What're yeh doin', Juliana?"

She ran slender fingers through her flowing blonde hair. The summer sun had bleached it even lighter. It had also resulted in a splattering of freckles across her shoulders. He'd found himself counting them each time she'd changed his bandage over the last few weeks.

"Do you wonder where the baker gets his flour?" Juliana asked. "Or where the grocer gets their goods? How fabric and yarn and tools and shoes get into Abredea?"

Anthony shrugged. "They come from the city, same as everythin' else."

Juliana shook her head. "It's not like with the mush packets. They're manufactured in Tornim, in one of the factories in Grigoria. I'm talking about a shipment of food." She leaned in as he shook his head, still not understanding. "Trucks, Anthony. Most of the things that come into Abredea, and into the city itself, are shipped via trucks."

Anthony's eyes widened. He watched her as realization hit. Watched her eyes narrow, lips twisting into a sly smile. He cocked his head. She nodded.

"Oh shit."

Juliana laughed as Anthony pushed off the tree and took a step toward her.

"A whole truck, Jules?"

She nodded again. "And not one of ours. One headed for the marketplace in the city. They have..." she sighed, a wistful look coming across her face, "the most wonderful things you've ever tasted."

"Yeh wanna steal a truckload of food meant for the city," Anthony breathed.

Juliana glanced at him, her grin faltering. "I thought you'd like the idea."

"Like it?" he crooned. "I'm mad I never thought of it before. When do we go? Yeh said in the mornin'?"

Juliana turned from him, and Anthony's heart sank.

He stepped after her, his cast catching on a rock, and nearly fell before he steadied himself. She faced him and he straightened, hoping she hadn't noticed.

"Anthony..."

"No." He held up a finger. "I'm not sittin' this out. Are yeh jokin'?"

She gestured to his leg, her eyebrows narrowing, nostrils flaring. "Are *you*? You can barely walk, Anthony. How are you supposed to keep up?"

He scoffed. "I know those woods, Jules. I'll be just as fast as yeh, if not faster. Besides, it's too dangerous for yeh tah go alone."

Her lips slid into a thin line, whitening as she pressed them together. "I won't be going alone."

His eyes widened. Another flash of alarm went through him. "Taz?"

"And Daisy."

Anthony shut his eyes. Years. He'd spent years telling them no, putting their safety ahead of what they wanted. What he wanted. Because of course he wanted to bring them. Of course he wanted his closest friends to share the place he loved more than any other.

"But look at what happened tah me," he said aloud.

Juliana blinked and looked at him. "What?"

"Yeh can't take 'em. What if yeh get caught? Steel did this tah me." Anthony gestured to his body. "What will he do tah the three of yeh?"

"We're going, Anthony. Someone has to *do* something. I won't sit here while people starve." Her jaw tightened, a flash of guilt and shame flaring through her eyes. "Not again."

Anthony exhaled, his anger dissipating in the wind. "Jules." He hobbled forward and put a hand on her arm. "What yeh didn't know when yeh lived in the city isn't yer fault."

She stared at him, her gaze hard. "A lot of things aren't my fault, Anthony. That doesn't mean I don't have an obligation to try and make them better."

Anthony's mouth lifted into a half-grin. He squeezed her arm before letting his hand fall to his side. "I know what yeh mean."

They returned home as the sun set over the mountains. An agreement had been made. One that didn't make either one of them entirely happy, but it was good enough.

Dinner consisted of mush packets and roasted carrots. Anthony downed it with his usual enthusiasm, but he stared at the bowl for a long moment after he'd finished eating. A plan was wiggling into his mind.

He lay on Juliana's bed and grinned up at the ceiling. A few hours of sleep would be smart, but his mind couldn't get past the anticipation and excitement about what was coming.

Anthony rolled onto his good side, and rubbed his thigh just above his cast. He'd get through the fence; he'd make it into the forest. He closed his eyes and focused on his breathing. He wouldn't slow them down.

Two hours after midnight, Juliana rose from her make-shift bed on the ground, stretched with a silent groan, and slid on her boots. She hadn't slept. How could she? When so much depended on this going well. When getting caught...

Fear gripped her chest and she reached for the door. Part of her wanted to go then and there, leave, carry out her plan without endangering the others.

Anthony stirred behind her.

Juliana pulled her fingers back and hurried forward. As Anthony sat up, stretching and wincing as his right arm went over his head, she knelt and pulled a thick bundled cloth and a bag from under his bed.

"How long 'as tha' been there?" he hissed.

Juliana raised a finger to her lips with a warning glare.

Anthony rolled his eyes and flung back his covers. Juliana moved into the kitchen, gingerly setting the bundle on the table, and pulling things from the cabinets. The backpack she'd taken when they got the medicine for Jimmy was no longer white. She'd dyed it a few days earlier, the better to blend into the forest. The dull brown bag filled up quickly as she mentally checked off the items on her list.

Behind her, Anthony silently pulled on a shirt and laced up one boot. He tucked his pant leg into the boot, the other leg was cut just above the knee so it fit over his cast, and stood up.

Juliana caught his eye as she pulled on her backpack. "Ready?" she mouthed.

He nodded and clumped toward her. She winced with each thud of the cast hitting the floor, but May didn't stir.

Juliana let Anthony lead the way. She scooped up the bundle of cloth and followed him out the back door and into the garden.

Juliana couldn't help the grin that slid across her face after she silently closed the door.

Taz leaned against one of the trees that lined May's garden. He looked at ease, moonlight streaming down around him, a cocky grin in place, arms crossed as he surveyed them.

She should have known he'd get there early.

Anthony hobbled to him and they clasped forearms, Anthony drawing Taz toward him for a quick hug. Juliana joined them and patted Taz's arm.

Her fingers trembled with nerves as her friends looked to her. "Almost time," she whispered. She met Taz's eye. "Is Daisy on her way?"

He gave half a shrug, eyebrows drawn together in a concerned expression. "I don't know. We said we'd meet here."

Juliana nodded and turned to watch for Daisy who should be walking up any minute.

Her nagging fears and anxiety grew as she stood there, arms crossed tight over her chest—Taz had offered to carry the bundle. Fortunately, it didn't take long for Daisy to arrive.

Juliana exhaled and went to meet her friend. They hugged, and Daisy gave Taz and Anthony a quick squeeze as well. Without a word, the four of them turned toward the mountains and made their way to the fence.

The moon was nearly full above them. It lit the way, causing contradictory feelings in Juliana. She was grateful for the light; they'd move faster with it. But they were also more visible.

Tiny claws of tension snagged at her.

But they did it. They made it to the fence. Juliana double checked for Black-Stars and—with none in sight—the four of them scrambled through. It took Anthony a few extra seconds. Juliana held her breath until he'd reached the other side and slid the chain-link back into place.

Night in the forest hit in a different way. Juliana sucked in a trembling breath as they stepped together into the trees. Moonlight cascaded down, beams of white illuminating the spaces between the branches above them. The flowers had closed, their petals pulled together like little blankets covering a snuggled-up child. But the ivy... the crawling tendrils of shadowy green stood out in the darkness.

Juliana paused a few feet into the trees. She closed her eyes and inhaled, sucking in the scents of the dirt, the oaks and pines, the air. All of it enveloped her; a mystical combination of comfort and nerves as she embraced the natural chill of the night.

On either side of her, Taz and Daisy gawked with wide eyes.

Anthony limped forward, pushing his way through the vegetation until he found the trail. His voice carried to them, gentle like the breeze and soft as silk. "This way."

Juliana followed, Taz and Daisy close behind her as they reached the path Anthony had formed over years of hunting.

Juliana's eyes widened at how quickly the forest had reclaimed the trail. "Have you ever been away this long before?" she murmured, squinting through the dim light at Anthony.

He shook his head, black hair flopping into his eyes. He brushed it away. "Nah. I think a week was the longest. This," he gestured at the shoots of grass under his feet, "is new."

She nodded. "All right well, let's go. We have a while, but I want to get in place."

Taz punched Anthony in the arm.

"What the *frost*?" Anthony yelped, rubbing his bicep.

"How could yeh *not* bring us out 'ere before now?" Taz demanded. He waved an arm through the air, his fingers brushing against a few overhead leaves. "This place is amazin'."

Juliana cracked half a grin and Daisy's giggles filled the air.

"Let's get goin'," Anthony grumbled.

The others followed him as they headed north, toward the farming fields and the main road leading in and out of the city. It took almost two hours to reach the spot Juliana had shown Anthony on her hand-drawn map and, even with his hobbled leg, she knew they were faster with him than they'd have been without.

She leaned in as they maneuvered around a set of fallen trees, rotting into mulch beneath their feet. "I'm glad you can walk."

Anthony shot her a wry grin. "Yer glad yeh didn't leave me behind, huh?"

Juliana glowered. "Of course I am. I never wanted you not to come, but if you were still bedridden what was I going to do, carry you?"

Anthony raised an eyebrow.

Juliana laughed and gave him a light shove. "Come on. We have work to do."

They reached the edge of the woods and peered out into a foggy grey-lit morning. The moon approached the horizon. Ahead of them, nearly a hundred yards away and barely visible amongst the whisps of fog rising up from the grass, stretched a smooth paved road. One end led to the city gates where Juliana knew Red-Stars stood at attention, waiting to let in the city's shipments. The other led north, miles and miles of nothing between it and the next city in Pangaea.

Juliana crouched on the forest floor, undid her backpack, and pulled out a few apples, four metal stakes, and a notebook filled with her calculations. "Breakfast," she announced, tossing the apples around.

"Thanks," Taz mumbled around his first bite.

"We have to be careful about this," Juliana said.

"As opposed tah everythin' before now, which was not careful?" Anthony gave her a wicked grin.

"Eat your apple," Juliana commanded dryly. "Seriously, we have to pay close attention. Once the truck goes over that," she gestured to the bundle of fabric Taz had set on the ground, "I have to get there fast. Everyone else should stay here—"

"No," Taz said.

At the same time Anthony said, "Nope."

They glanced at each other. Taz went on, "We already agreed, Juliana. Someone is comin' out there with yeh."

"Someone who doesn't have a broken leg," Daisy muttered, giving Anthony a side-long glance.

"Hey—"

"All right," Juliana cut off his objection. "Taz, you can come with me, as planned. But you *have* to listen to me. If I don't get this right..."

"You'll get it." Daisy put a hand on her shoulder.

Juliana nodded her thanks. She finished her apple, wiped sticky fingers on her shorts, and hefted the bundle. "Let's go."

Taz and Daisy followed her, hunching down as they ran towards the road. When they reached the pavement, they knelt and carefully unrolled the fabric. Together, the three of them gingerly lifted it and spread it over the road.

Juliana had traded her favorite shirt in exchange for the three dozen nails embedded in the cloth. Some were bent, others rusty, and a few she'd had to toss as they were too short to do any good anyway, but what they had would work.

Once the thing was in place, they sprinted back to the trees.

"Now," Juliana huffed, hands on her knees, "we wait."

Thirty minutes passed. The four of them chatted, Juliana becoming quieter as time dragged on. She wrung her hands and fidgeted restlessly.

"Hey," Anthony sat beside her on a fallen tree, "it's comin'. We knew we'd 'ave to wait a while."

She nodded, her stomach clenching with a combination of hunger and nerves. "I know. I just... the information came from the shop-keepers and..."

"Yeh don't know how reliable it is?" he prompted.

"It's not that," Juliana objected. "I don't think they were lying. I just know things work differently in the city. Maybe their shipments come at a different time of day."

As the words left her lips, a rumbling broke the silence of the early morning. Juliana leapt to her feet. Anthony's hand closed around her wrist and gently brought her back down.

She sat, elbows nervously perched on her knees as the truck approach.

It was smaller than she'd expected. Not necessarily a bad thing, given where they needed it to go. According to the intel she'd gathered, this was a shipment of raw goods, and a few pre-made items, for a multitude of restaurants in Tornim.

She leaned forward as the front tires reached their cloth. The truck didn't slow. A thunderous pop hit the air, followed by another, and another, and another. The truck didn't screech to a stop. It rolled on shattered tires, slowing...

Slowing...

Juliana was on her feet before it came to a stop. Taz ran right behind her as she sprinted toward the vehicle. She yanked at the front door of the cab, heart in her throat as the final piece of the plan slid into place.

A wash of cool relief flowed through her. The cab was empty. As she'd expected... hoped? The thing was entirely automated.

Now it was time for her part. The part of this only she could do. Because only she had been trained in Blue-Star tech and software.

She climbed onto the hard wooden bench where a driver's seat would usually be and pulled forward a keyboard and command screen. Red lights flashed above her. Diagnostic warnings flew across the screen. The truck's automated scanners picked up on the problem and a message began to form across one of the side screens. *Tire ruptures. Emergency stop. Awaiting assistance.* Along with the geographic coordinates of the truck's location.

Her fingers flew across the keyboard.

"Juliana, what're yeh—"

"Not now, Taz," Juliana snapped. She glanced at the side screen. The message was seconds from being sent.

Her mind raced, excitement pounding through her. This was like her tests. A chance to prove herself. To prove she belonged.

Five seconds. But she was in the messaging system.

Three. She split the message. *Tire ruptures. Emergency turn-around. Shipment delayed.* Sent to Tornim.

One. *Tire ruptures. Within acceptable parameters for continuation. Slowed shipment.* Sent to the truck's city of origin.

Juliana leaned back and wiped the sweat from her forehead with the back of her hand. It was done. Well, that part was done.

She sighed and went back to work. The tires were shredded, but the rims were intact.

Juliana disconnected the truck's access to city frequencies and turned off the implanted tracker and rear camera. Then she programed a path for the truck to take. One that would lead it along the edge of the forest until it found an opening, then it was to make a turn and get as far into the forest as it could.

The trees were dense, but there were plenty of clearings and little openings in the trees were a smaller vehicle like this one might be able to hide. Especially if it was covered with fallen brush.

Juliana hit *enter* and jumped from the cab as the truck rumbled to life again and slowly veered off the road and into the grass.

Taz rolled up their spiked fabric and carefully slung the bundle over his shoulder. He followed Juliana.

The two of them trailed the truck, brushing flattened grass back to its height and smoothing tire tracks in the loose dirt. Juliana waited until the truck reached the trees, then hurried back to the road for a quick check. She surveyed the landscape. Apart from the vehicle slowly rolling along the tree line everything looked normal.

She breathed a sigh of relief. By the time she caught up with the truck, Anthony and Daisy had joined Taz.

"How long will it be outside the trees?" Anthony asked. He watched the vehicle with worried eyes. "We're approachin' the fields and they'll be gettin' busy in the next hour or so."

Indeed, beams of gold had replaced the low grey light, and the sky had taken on its bright blue hue.

"Not long," Juliana replied. "It's programed to find a space and turn."

"Ahh," Anthony nodded, "should be the next couple of minutes then."

Juliana raised an eyebrow at him, and Anthony shrugged.

"I know the woods."

She laughed.

The truck's pace was slow. It rolled gingerly over roots, rocks, and gnarled branches. The tires flaked off as it went, the metal underneath warping and denting with each hard bump. Daisy and Juliana collected the scraps of black material.

They stuck close to the trees, falling a bit behind the vehicle with Anthony's limp and the pauses to clean up evidence. Another wave of relief hit Juliana when, as they rounded a particularly sharp edge of forest, the truck had disappeared from sight.

Taz uttered a low squeak, but Juliana just chuckled and pointed. Between the trees and moving even slower, the truck was still rolling along. It had found a small stream. The tires bridged it, two on either side where the trees made room for the trickling water.

Daisy giggled. Anthony shook his head, his half-grin lighting up his face.

They continued on as the truck followed the stream's path. A few minutes later it turned again, struggling as it angled the broken tires across the water. Branches cracked above as the hard rounded back shell forced its way under a few low hanging trees and into a small clearing.

There, the engine sputtered a bit and shut off.

They stood in silence. The sounds of the forest, silenced by the rumbling of tires and the humming of the solar powered engine, resumed. Birds, silent on their trek out, took up their tunes.

Taz hurried to the back of the truck and started trying to figure out the door, but Daisy only had eyes for their surroundings.

Juliana watched her friend exhale, turning in a slow circle as she stared up. Beams of light poured through the canopy above. Daisy's hair, braided back on both sides before becoming one long braid down her back, seemed to shimmer with red and gold as she spun. She pointed, gasped, and caught Juliana's eye as a green bird with a golden chest alighted upon a nearby tree and cocked its head at her.

Warmth buffeted Juliana's side as Anthony slid up next to her. They stood at the edge of the clearing, the stream at their backs and the future of Abredea before them.

"Yeh did it," he murmured.

Juliana glanced at him.

He cocked a half grin. "Ready yah crack into this thing open, or did yeh wanna have some mush for breakfast first?"

She shook her head with a snort. "Absolutely not. Give me a second."

She hurried around the side and back to the cab. Now that the truck had found its spot, the front camera needed to be disabled as well. It was quick work.

Juliana strode back as Anthony hobbled up to Taz.

Taz ran a hand through his hair and glanced at the two of them. A thick padlock rested in his free hand.

Juliana raised an eyebrow.

"I've b.... be... I practiced." He gave a sheepish grin.

Anthony laughed again and slapped him on the shoulder. "Well, go on then. Open the *nacra* thing. I'm hungry."

Taz dropped the lock and reached for the heavy handle. Juliana joined him. The two heaved, metal scraped, and the handle shot up. Juliana grabbed one side of the door, Taz the other, and they pulled it open.

Daisy's hazel eyes went wide. "Ohh," she murmured.

The rest of them stared at the contents of a Tornim food transport. Sacks of flour, rice, lentils, potatoes, and onions, each stamped across the front with their contents and restaurant destination. Sealed metal boxes were marked as varieties of cheeses. Juliana spotted containers of strawberries, melons, apples, peaches, peppers, squash, garlic, ginger, and more. A standing rack took up the left wall of the truck. It was strapped in, six shelves stacked from bottom to top. Juliana's mouth watered as she gazed upon the pre-made pastries destined for some shop in a Grigoria mall.

Taz's stomach rumbled, the sound loud enough to send a flock of birds fleeing from their nearby tree.

Anthony cackled. "Someone get up there and bring me somethin' tah eat."

Taz obliged. Juliana gave him instructions as he went through the boxes and pulled out smaller packages of goods and a tray full of pastries.

They sat together in the clearing. Time slowed as they filled their bellies; Juliana reminded them to go slow and not eat too much. She introduced them to coffee, passing around a jar of ground beans and laughing as each of them winced at the smell.

She promised to make them some in the morning and a jolt of excitement went through her at the thought of May's reaction to a fresh pot of coffee complete with cream and honey.

Taz burped and flopped onto his back with a deep sigh. Anthony joined him, laying back gingerly with one hand on his side as he stared at the sky above them. Daisy leaned back on her elbows. The rosy glow of her cheeks was back. Juliana's heart warmed at the smile on her friend's face.

They rested a long time, probably longer than was smart. But as they walked back to Abredea, a heavy box of food between Juliana and Taz, and thick bags on both Anthony and Daisy's backs, Juliana realized how much they'd needed this, the food, the sense of success, all of it.

They went slow, coming back into Abredea. Alert eyes, careful movements, and good timing kept them from being found.

Juliana and Taz covered the shiny metal box with a thin sheet Juliana had tucked into her pack.

"We'll have to bring more bags next time," Juliana huffed as they moved toward Naya's house.

Taz nodded, his face red with effort.

When they reached Naya's, Anthony went in first. His aunt's thin frame filled the kitchen as they carried in the box and bags and set them on the ground. Her eyes blazed, brows narrowed.

"Wha'..."

Taz and Daisy both moved back to the door at her tone. Anthony stepped forward with both hands up in a placating gesture. At the table, Jimmy stared at them all, the homework in front of him forgotten.

"... did yeh do?" Naya strode forward. She reached out, her red, chapped hand closing around the box lid and lifting. She let out a little gasp. The lid shut with a thud.

"I can explain," Juliana said.

Naya stared at her, alarmed. "How did yeh do this? Did yeh bring him with yeh?" she demanded, gesturing at Anthony.

Juliana let out a little sigh. "You know him well enough to understand why I couldn't leave him here."

"I'm standin' in the room with yeh," Anthony growled.

"If you'd been caught..." Naya breathed, she shook her head, glaring at Juliana.

"I knew the risk." Juliana stared her down. Her heartbeat thundered in her ears.

The hurt in Naya's eyes shot beads of regret through her, but her gaze also caught the sharp edges of the woman's collar bone, the sunken eyes, and hollowed cheeks of someone who had been hungry for weeks. It caught sight of Jimmy, staring at the box with wide eyes.

Naya sighed, pressing fingers to her forehead. "No one saw yeh?"

Juliana shook her head.

"An' no one else knows?"

"No, Naya." Anthony stepped forward.

The muscles in his back tightened as he stepped on his cast. Juliana's brow creased. How long had it been hurting him?

"No one knows. No one saw. Now we just need a place tah store it all." He put his hands on her upper arms and bent his head to catch her eye. "This is the kind of score Dave always talked about. If we do it right, this'll keep us fed for months. This can change things 'round 'ere."

Naya clenched her jaw.

"Mama?"

They all paused, turning to look at Jimmy.

"Is there..." he glanced from his cousin to his aunt. His wide eyes gave the impression he was worried he'd get in trouble. "Is there somethin' tah eat?"

Naya exhaled and closed her eyes. Her expression caused a new kind of burning ache in Juliana's chest. Slowly, Naya nodded.

Taz moved forward, lifted the lid, and pulled a pre-wrapped pastry from the top of the box. "Try this, little guy."

Jimmy nearly inhaled the thing, even with Juliana and Naya telling him to take smaller, slower bites.

They got Naya to eat as well. Anthony sat her at the table and fixed a sandwich for her.

Juliana's gaze kept darting back to him. She found herself watching where the fabric of his shirt brushed against his side and back, waiting for it to come away wet with blood. He'd ripped some stitches. She could tell, from the way he leaned on the counter, the stiffness of his arm as he dropped it casually to his side.

Going to Naya's first had been more than just a stroke of genius on Anthony's part. He'd known his uncle well. After eating, heaving a few more sighs, and cursing under her breath, Naya had them lift a heavy wardrobe away from the wall beside her bed. A wooden trapdoor sat in the ground where the thing had been.

It was a storeroom. Small and stuffy, it had plenty of room for the dry goods they'd packed into Abredea. Enough supplies to last a couple of weeks if they kept it to themselves, less if they shared with other struggling families in Abredea.

They said goodbye to Naya and Jimmy. The woman didn't quite smile as she gave Juliana a one-armed hug.

Anthony bent to lift the remaining heavy backpack, but Juliana grabbed his wrist. He glanced up; mouth open. She shook her head and shot a pointed look at his side.

Anthony nodded and relented, straightening up and leading them out the front door.

"What's n... ne... ne... Where to?" Taz asked.

Juliana shifted the straps of the bag. A smile settled onto her face. "Let's spread this around a bit. We aren't the only people who've been hungry."

Anthony caught her eye and the two shared a grin. Daisy and Taz moved ahead, linking arms and leading the way to the closest home they were friendly with. Anthony fell into step beside Juliana.

"Your stitches?" Juliana murmured.

"How'd yeh know?" Anthony whispered back.

She shook her head. "Let's not tell Naya, yeah? I don't want to see what she does to me if she finds out I let you come *and* you ripped your stitches."

He laughed. "I won't tell her, as long as yer the one tah patch me up."

She raised an eyebrow at him.

"May has cold hands."

Laughter burst from her. She cackled for a long time, long enough for Daisy and Taz to pause at the side of the road to wait for them. Anthony chuckled along with her, letting out the occasional wince as he inhaled.

The sound tickled through her. Little sparks of warmth spread out from her chest, through her whole body, fueling the smile she couldn't seem to shake.

Chapter Thirty-Eight

40 Years Ago - The Camp Outside Tornim

"Come here, you little troublemaker." Maybelle chuckled as her four-year-old scurried around the house.

Her youngest, the baby, slept soundly in her crib.

Kate laughed, her hand gently caressing her swollen belly. "When is he starting school?"

"Not for another year." Maybelle sighed. "It's a bit hectic." As she said it, Dave fell from where he'd been climbing up the dresser. He landed on his butt, sprang to his feet, and immediately switched to climbing a different piece of furniture.

"You love it." Kate grinned at her, a knowing gleam in her eyes.

A warm smile crossed Maybelle's lips. "I do."

"Peaceful life suits us." Kate stretched out her arms and picked up her knitting. The pink baby bonnet was almost half-way done.

"It certainly does."

Maybelle's little boy ran over and climbed into his mother's lap. She ran her fingers through his thick black hair. Dave picked a peach out of the bowl on the table and took a big bite. Yellow juice slid down both sides of his mouth, coming together in one big drop at his chin. Maybelle took a cloth napkin from the new kitchen table—a bit plain, it needed some paint—and wiped away the sticky juice.

Kate paused her knitting, a frown on her face as she cocked her head to the side. "Do you hear that?"

A faint buzzing sound came from Maybelle's dresser. She lifted Dave, balancing him on a hip as she opened the various drawers.

A small white communications earpiece, from long ago, buzzed in a bottom corner. Maybelle's jaw tightened. She swallowed and set Dave down.

She picked up the com and carried it back to the table. She set it down and stared at it.

"What's that, mama?" her son asked, following her.

Kate's eyes went wide. She leaned forward, resting her knitting on the table and giving Maybelle a sharp look. "You kept it? All these years? You know how *dangerous* that is."

Maybelle planted a kiss on Dave's forehead. "Go play with your blocks, baby."
She sat at the table, watching the still buzzing com. "I know. But what if something happened? What if someone needed us?"

"Those people stopped being your responsibility the day you saved their lives and they thanked you with that scar," Kate hissed with a curled lip.

Maybelle ran her finger down her face. The scar was half an inch wide at its largest. It ached when the weather turned cold.

She shook her head. "That wasn't Sam, or Rorty, or the girls; it was one distraught mother."

She picked up the com and held it to her ear.

"*Oh, please tell me you can hear me. Please, please tell me you can hear me. Hello? Is anyone there?*"

"Who is this?" Maybelle asked. The voice was lightly familiar, but not one she could instantly place.

"*Maybelle? Is that you?*"

"Who wants to know?" Maybelle looked at her son.

"*It is you, finally. I've been reaching out to so many... it doesn't matter. Maybelle, it's Penelope... I need your help.*"

Maybelle put a hand to her chest, eyes wide. The familiarity clicked. Sam's oldest daughter; all grown up she sounded so much like her mom. Maybelle listened intently. When Penelope finished speaking, she leaned back against her chair and rubbed her fingers across her forehead.

"We shouldn't get into too much more detail over an unsecured com," Maybelle murmured to Penelope.

Kate frowned at her, concern lining her face.

"Someone took Jamie," Maybelle said.

Kate's dark face paled. Her hands moved protectively over her baby bump.

"Who's Jamie, mama?" Her son raced around, spreading his arms like a bird.

"An old friend, sweetie." Maybelle focus returned to Penelope. "I need an hour. Where are you?"

"*I'll meet you outside Calida, by the main road.*"

"Stay hidden. I'll be there soon."

Maybelle took the com out of her ear and slowly set it on the table. She stared at it, gaze unfocused and mind a haze. Of all the things someone might have contacted her for...

Kate stood up, wobbling for a moment before she balanced herself, and gave Maybelle a hard look. "What are you going to do?"

Maybelle sighed. Her fingers went to her scar again, trailing it from the tip of her forehead to the edge of her chin. "Penelope is in Calida, and she needs my help. Someone took her sister, and she knows where. She wants me to teleport her in for a rescue."

"Ahh..." Kate looked at a loss for words.

Maybelle didn't meet her friend's eye as she muttered, "I'm going."

"Can you even zap that far?"

She crossed to her dresser, digging through the top two drawers for the other elements of their lives as rebels that she'd stored away. "We're going to find out. I've been able to get to the forest with no trouble so far."

"The forest is substantially closer than Calida."

Maybelle sucked in a deep breath. "I have to help," she said through clenched teeth.

"Then, I'm coming with you." Kate took a deep breath and squared her shoulders.

"Kate." Maybelle rolled her eyes and looked pointedly at Kate's belly. "You can barely stand on your own, let alone be transported on a dangerous journey that might end *very* badly."

Kate waddled over to her and leaned in close, her forehead wrinkled in an angry frown.

"You don't owe anyone anything, Maybelle. You have two children and a husband who need you here."

The front door swung open.

"Daddy!" Dave raced into his father's arms with a giddy laugh.

Maybelle's husband took one look at Kate and his wife and swung Dave in a delicate arc before planting him back on the ground.

"What's goin' on?" Tony's thick, lilting voice danced across the air like a melody.

That voice was the first part of him she'd fallen in love with. It seemed like forever ago. It had been twenty years since the rebellion failed; since she and Kate had locked themselves in with the other White-Stars to hid from Black-Star kill squads hunting down the remaining rebels.

Maybelle had spent a long time shut away in those early days. Mourning their loss. Mourning their friends. Mourning her face.

Then, ten years ago, she'd met Tony.

"Maybelle thinks she's going to go on a dangerous mission," Kate growled.

Maybelle sighed. Tony looked at her, bemusement in his smile and arched eyebrow.

"Can I talk to you outside, dear?" Maybelle jerked her head toward the backdoor. "Dave, be good for Aunt Kate."

Dave nodded, Kate glowered, and Maybelle and her husband walked outside.

"What's goin' on?" he repeated. Concern filled his deep voice. Dark calloused hands rubbed across her creamy shoulders, stroking up and down her arms.

"I got a call." She shook her head, two sides of her heart in conflict. "Someone from my past."

"One of the rebels? Was it Sam?"

Maybelle gave a half-hearted smile. "Her oldest daughter. She said Jamie was kidnapped."

Tony pulled her close. Her cheek pressed against his chest; the beating of his heart filled her with warmth.

"She needs my help to get her sister back."

He didn't pull away and it reassured her. Instead, he squeezed her tight before moving to look her in the eye.

"I fell in love with yeh for a lot of reasons, May. One of 'em is how much yeh help people. Yeh 'ave to help people." He gave her a wry grin and shrugged. "It's who yeh are."

She gazed into his dark eyes. For the last decade those eyes had been her sanctuary. His understanding shown through them.

Maybelle laced up her old boots. They'd sat in the back of her wardrobe since Kate had taken them off of her unconscious body all those years ago. Her blade—the one she'd used at their final stand, went at her side, the holster looped onto her belt.

She gathered everything else in a backpack. Her com, a few clothes, some vials of a mixture that would speed up the healing process if Jamie was injured, some food, and her husband's favorite hunting knife—for luck.

Maybelle hugged Kate and listened as her friend whispered a demand for her to come home safe. She kissed her husband, his passion matching her own. Then she planted gentle lips on her sleeping daughter's forehead, swept her son into a fierce hug, and stepped out the door.

She walked to the edge of the camp, slipped through a break in the fence and headed into the woods. A few minutes later she closed her eyes, concentrated hard, and fell into nothing.

Maybelle gasped as blinding light slammed against her eyes. She squeezed them shut, her head pounding. Noise thundered in her ears, driving spikes of pain into her brain. She leaned against a tree, thankful she at least seemed to have landed in the right place.

She was on the edge of Calida, one of the largest cities in Pangaea. It was almost twice the size of Tornim and its camp was rumored to be much worse than hers. There were more people, the houses were older, dingier, and the fence was higher and actually reinforced.

She'd arrived a good thirty yards from the road; woods and wilderness around her. She waited and caught her breath. After a few moments the ground crunched behind her. She wheeled as a gasp hit the air.

Penelope had aged. It shouldn't have been a surprise, but for some reason Maybelle had been expecting the teenager she hadn't gotten to say goodbye to, not the middle-aged woman standing before her.

Almost forty, Penelope was as short as her mother, but with darker hair and softer eyes. She wore heavy clothes, a long button-up, the sleeves rolled to her elbows, and thick pants with large boots. A small tattoo was visible on her forearm; twin birds, one red and one gold, surrounded by a thin purple circle.

She moved forward through the trees, her stride as sure as her mother's. "I can't believe you're here." A brief smile flickered across her face. "It's been so long."

Maybelle smiled. She pulled Penelope into a hug. "It has. Where's Sam? What happened to Jamie?"

Penelope looked down. "Mom died last year."

Maybelle's chest constricted as a pang of regret shot through her.

"It was peaceful, she just..." Tears glistened in Penelope's eyes, and her mouth twitched. "She went to bed and... and didn't wake up."

Maybelle nodded, her lips pressed tight together. Tears itched at her nose and eyes, but there wasn't time for it. She'd mourn her friend when she returned home. "Tell me what happened with your sister."

Penelope moved her hands, flexing and cracking her knuckles as she spoke. "Jamie was taken last night. I didn't see it. I was working. But they contacted me today."

Maybelle frowned. "Give me details."

Penelope bit her lip. "It was a man." She rubbed her jaw before clenching her hands together. "He said he wants you... in exchange for my sister."

All the oxygen left Maybelle's lungs. Her lips parted, mouth dangling open in disbelief. A few seconds passed before she sucked in a deep breath. Then another.

"He knew my name?"

Penelope nodded.

Someone knew she was alive. Another rebel with a vendetta against her? Or someone from the other side… If the Grey-Stars had Jamie, then they knew she hadn't died. Her whole family could be in danger.

Penelope took half a step back, her hands up as she watched Maybelle intently. "He wanted me to lie, to trick you into coming. But I know you. I knew you'd come anyway. I knew you'd help me even after I told you." Her voice shook. A tremor ran through the words, giving away her trepidation.

She hadn't known. She'd hoped.

It was the hope that stopped Maybelle from having even a second of hesitation. She nodded. "Of course." A half-smile flashed across her lips; the remains of the warrior within her stirred. She wished Sam were there. One more mission for the two of them.

Maybelle rolled her shoulders. Her body still ached from the teleport. Calida was a long way from Tornim. "Where are we headed? I might need to take a few minutes before zapping again. You said you know where she is?"

"Yeah." Penelope nodded and pulled a thick sheet of paper from the satchel at her side. She unfurled it, revealing a map, and pointed to a spot not far from Calida. "He's holding her at the Warren ruins." She paused and swallowed. Fear crossed her face. "I think he's insane."

Maybelle tilted her head, a furrow in her brow.

"He kept talking about you. Rambling on the com. He said you took his honor, and this would get it back. He said… he said 'isn't it fitting that we meet where you should have died'." She shook her head. "But I don't know how he knew about us. We never told anyone we fought for the rebels. Mom was insistent."

Maybelle's stomach clenched. Her gut churned with knowing, with the understanding that a future she thought she'd escaped was still very possible. She brushed it away. Shoved the worry and fear into a deep recess in her mind. Now was not the time. Still, a chill seeped through her at the thought of what could happen to her family.

"We'll worry about that later." Maybelle took hold of Penelope's hand. "Let's get your sister back."

Maybelle closed her eyes. It had been over a decade, but she knew exactly where she needed to go. The familiarity of zapping to the Warren lingered in her bones.

She stumbled on their arrival. Her landing put them a few yards into the forest, away from the ruins of the Warren. Her vision blurred, chest tight. She wobbled and crouched, leaning back as her butt hit the ground. She swallowed, rested her arms on her knees, and took a few slow, deliberate breaths.

"Are you all right?" Penelope knelt to meet her eye. Concern laced her voice.

Maybelle nodded and cleared her throat. She pulled a bottle from her backpack, opened it, and gulped down a few mouthfuls. "My power hasn't been the same. Not since the mountain."

Penelope looked around, her dark eyes wary. She pulled a handgun out of the waistband on her pants. It was old, like the ones the rebellion had used. Designed for metal projectiles, not plasma bolts. They'd been all but eradicated after the rebellion. Melted down.

"Where did you get that?"

Penelope turned it over in her hand. "I stole it off one of the guards in the camp. They use 'em to kill animals in the fields. Plasma bolts are a fire hazard in the summer, so they use these." She turned toward the ruins. "Are you able to move?"

Maybelle nodded and reached out a hand.

Penelope pulled her up with a grunt. "Let's go."

They stuck to the tree line and kept quiet as they circled the massive, crumbling crater that had once been their home. She hadn't seen it since that day. Hadn't been back since those desperate moments when she stared up at a shattering stone ceiling. When her power had taken control and erupted from her.

Maybelle's head ached, but the pain in her heart overshadowed it. The tunnels and halls they'd once laughed and run through were gone. Grass and weeds sprouted from every flat surface. Small trees stretched into the air, trying to reach the height of those deeper in the forest. Sections of stone, brick, and wood lay scattered around, their surfaces rotten and crumbling.

The crater was huge, and not as sunken in as Maybelle had imagined. Most of the Warren had collapsed straight down, but there were tall pillars, stretches of stone wall, even a doorway, still intact. The uneven levels made visibility difficult.

Maybelle breathed silently through her mouth; ears focused on any change in the steady sounds of the forest. They rounded a particularly dense section of collapsed wood. Maybelle froze.

"Let me go. My sister's gonna kill—" a woman shouted. Her words were interrupted by a thwack. She moaned.

"Shut your mouth," a man hissed. His voice should have been quiet, but it reverberated through the space.

There was another thud of fist on flesh and the woman yelped.

Penelope trembled next to Maybelle. Her eyes blazed with fury. She clenched her gun with both hands and made to run forward.

Maybelle grabbed her arm, holding it tight. She spoke softly, but fast. "Stop. We go down slow. So we see him before he sees us."

Penelope exhaled through flared nostrils. She met Maybelle's gaze and nodded.

They reached the edge of the crater and made their way down. Rain had fallen recently. The rocks were slippery, and mud slid under their boots. Maybelle lost her footing halfway down. She grasped at a twisted set of roots sticking out of the dirt wall. It was enough to catch her, but as she stepped away her side was coated with muck.

When they reached the bottom, the ground squelched under them with each step. Maybelle grimaced, but there was nothing to be done about it now. Ahead of them was a narrow opening between a half-collapsed wall and a molding pile of burned wood. They paused at the edge, Maybelle beside the wall and Penelope crouched behind the wood.

The man spoke again, though his muttered words were unintelligible. Maybelle bit her lip and shifted just enough to get a glimpse around the wall.

The opening led to a cavernous space. No ceiling, but high stone and mud walls on all the sides Maybelle could see.

Jamie was on her knees, hands bound behind her back, heaving deep breaths. A mature woman had replaced the little girl Maybelle remembered. She bared gritted teeth, her eyes matching her sister's in color and fury. A bruise blossomed across the right side of her face. Blood dripped from her mouth and nose.

She sucked in a breath and spit, a glob of mucus and blood landing on the mud in front of her.

Maybelle leaned a little further. Where was...? Ah...

The man paced a few yards from Jamie; his face hidden from view. He spoke to himself, sometimes shouting a word or two. He held a plasma gun in one hand. As he turned, walking back toward them, his face came into the light and Maybelle covered her mouth to keep from gasping.

Ben. An older, wilder version, but still Ben. He wore his uniform. The crisp edges were wrinkled now, the shiny leaves on his shoulders dull and dirty. His hair was peppered with grey. A little over thirty years had passed since they'd seen each other. Since he'd called her a traitor and attempted to blow up the rebel base she and Kate had been taken to.

She ducked back and looked at Penelope. The woman's eyebrows were drawn together, her mouth a thin line as she waited.

"I'll distract him," Maybelle said, her voice just above a whisper. "You get her out of here."

Penelope gave a firm shake of her head. "We leave together, or we don't leave at all."

Maybelle shoved away the fear clawing at her chest. "I have things I need to find out from that man. If you have a chance to get her out, *do it*."

Before Penelope could respond, Maybelle stepped out. "Ben."

He turned. His head twitched and his eyes lit up as he took her in.

"Ha," he shouted, then he laughed. The sound was high and demented. He twitched again. He brought his gun up and held it next to his head, tapping it against his forehead.

"Maybelle?" Jamie's ragged voice expressed her confusion.

Maybelle moved to the side, trying to draw Ben's gaze away from the opening as Penelope stepped into the space.

Relief flashed across Jamie's face. "I knew you'd come," she said.

Penelope gave a tight, reassuring smile.

"Shut up," Ben shouted. He pointed the gun at Jamie, and everyone froze. "Shut up," he said again, his voice lower. He stared at Maybelle. He moved the gun again, continuing to tap it against his grey gemstone. "Is that you? Is that Maybelle? Not so pretty anymore."

"Yes," she said softly. She felt no pity for him. There was no room in her heart for a man who betrayed her, a man ready to slaughter innocents to get ahead. But she had to keep him talking. She had to know. "Ben, what happened to you?"

His shrill laugh broke through the stillness of the ruins once again. "What happened? What happened to me? You, you, *you* happened to me." He paced towards her.

Maybelle held her ground, but he stopped a few yards away.

"You ruined *everything*," he screamed the last word.

Everyone jumped. From the corner of her eye, Maybelle saw Penelope slowly inch her way toward Jamie.

"You." Ben shook his head. He ran his free hand through his hair, leaving streaks of blood and muck amidst the shaggy locks. "You warned them about the bomb. I know you did. And it *ruined* me." The hate in his eyes bored into her.

"I didn't do anything to ruin you." Maybelle's voice was low. She took a step to the left, turning his focus away from Jamie and Penelope. "I did what I did to save lives. Innocent lives. You'd have killed them all."

"To win the war," he spat at her.

Her fingers curled around the handle of the blade at her hip, just out of his sight. "There were children in those tunnels." Maybelle's lip curled in disgust, her even tone flickering with long cold fury. "You never cared about that, did you? The only thing you ever cared about was getting command to notice you."

"They did notice me," he shrieked. He flung his hands through the air. Spit flew from his mouth, his voice trembling. "They noticed me *fail* because of you. I was stripped of my rank, my title, *everything*!" He wheeled as he spoke, pacing through the mud. "I tried to explain," he inhaled through clenched teeth. "I told them who was really to *blame*. I told them whose fault it was. And they," he giggled, the sound even more unsettling than his screeching laugh, "they called me crazy."

Maybelle took a step toward him, inching the blade from her sheath. He leveled his gun at her. She hesitated. Released the handle of her blade as she slowly raised both hands into the air.

"You. You're the reason I was kicked out. *No one* thought you were still alive. But I knew. I knew the whole time." He leaned toward her, only a few feet away now, his eyes gleaming, maniacal. He licked his cracked lips. They curled into a grin. "Do you have any idea the things I had to do? To convince them to let me look for you?" He took a shuddering breath. "Everyone still thinks I'm crazy... but now I have proof." His grin slid into a malicious sneer. "I have proof you're still alive."

He twisted, fast. Raised his gun and trained it on Penelope. "Back up," he snarled.

Penelope, only a few yards from Jamie, took a step back. Her gun remained clenched in her right hand.

Maybelle caught her gaze for a brief second before she turned her attention back to Ben.

He walked to Jamie. Caressed her cheek with a muddy hand before he grabbed her hair and yanked her head back.

Fear gripped Maybelle's throat, constricting her voice and breath.

"Wait," Penelope shouted, panic in her voice. She put up her free hand. "Wait, please."

Maybelle shook off the choking terror and took a step toward him. "Stop, Ben." Her voice was rough, as hoarse as it had been since she'd used more power than anyone before could remember. Since she'd done the impossible and saved both of these girls and their mother and countless others. "Let them go," Maybelle said, stepping through the mud. "You have me. You don't need them now."

"I never *needed* them." He spat at the ground. "They just made it easier to find you." His sneer twisted, becoming crueler.

"Who else knows, Ben?" Maybelle took another step toward him.

She stopped, hands out, as he pressed the muzzle of the gun against the skin just under Jamie's white gemstone.

"Who else knows I'm alive?" Maybelle asked. Keep his attention. Keep him looking at her. Feel for it, the power barely stirring at her core. It flickered, darted about half-heartedly. Concentrate. "Who's looking for me?"

He tilted his head sideways, giving her an incredulous look. "Everyone. Everyone you stupid girl. Everyone knows you're alive, and they're all looking for you." His eyes seemed to glaze a bit as his chest swelled. "But I found you first." He glanced down. "Which means I don't need her anymore."

The first shot was quiet. A crackle of plasma, the thud of Jamie's body, the smell of her burning hair. The second blast shook the air. It accompanied a scream of anguish. The impact of Ben's body on the ground was significantly louder than Jamie's. He had further to fall.

Maybelle's stomach clenched. Her vision went foggy, her mind reeling. She stared down at her hand where crackles of purple light sprang up from the wrinkles in her skin. Tears cleared her eyes.

Penelope's screams split the air. They went on and on. She dropped the gun and ran to her sister, lifted Jamie's body and rocked back and forth, screaming. Moments passed and her cries turned to sobs, her sobs to shaky breaths, and then stillness.

Maybelle clenched her hand closed, the lights going out in her fist. She sank to her knees. Ran fingers up and down her scar. She sucked in breath after breath as the reality of what just happened settled into her brain.

Jamie was dead.

Ben was dead.

Ben knew she was alive. *Who else knew*? Who else might be looking for her?

He had said everyone, but he was... was he lying? Was his mind too gone for those words to be trusted?

Her family. Was her family safe? Her babies... her husband... Kate?

She licked her trembling lips and stood. She walked to Penelope and touched the younger woman's shoulder. Penelope flinched.

"We have to go." Maybelle spoke with a soft voice. Her *it'll be all right* voice. The one she used during the war when it would absolutely *not* be all right.

"I'm not leaving her here." Penelope's ragged voice shook with despair. "Not leaving her with him." She shook her head, her eyes shut tight.

Maybelle walked around Jamie's body and knelt down in front of Penelope. Her hands, chest, and face were covered in Jamie's blood. The rest of her was coated in mud.

"No. I don't think we should leave her either."

Maybelle glanced at Ben's body, the small hole in his forehead, a trickle of blood running down his face. The answers she needed had died with him.

She clutched Penelope's shoulder in one hand, Jamie's wrist in the other. Then she blinked and took the sisters home.

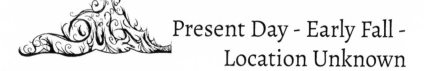

Chapter Thirty-Nine

Present Day - Early Fall - Location Unknown

R ed and orange danced together, the flames casting shadows in the already dark room. A flicker of blue popped in and out of existence in the center of the roiling heat.

Samaira closed her hand and the fire died in her palm. Her eyes adjusted to the thick blackness. Only two points of light now broke the cold dark.

Milky blue beams filtered through a high slit window in the far wall, and on the other side of the room Jacob's body lay unconscious in a metal cage, his skin glowing faintly.

Without the hot smell of her fire, the stench of sweat, blood, and fear made its way into Samaira's nose and throat. She sat, cross-legged, knees rubbing the edges of her cramped cage. Rage burned through her, threatening to overwhelm her senses. She took a shuddering breath and pushed the thoughts of her brother from her mind.

A lone door stood at the end of the room, shadows on either side. Cages, an assortment of sizes, lined the other three walls. A fourth row of slightly taller and wider cages ran down the center of the room; these held multiple children.

The high ceiling made the darkness seem vast, looking up was like staring into an abyss.

Samaira had woken before the rest, just after being shoved into her cage. She'd watched as nameless men carried her family in, pushing the unconscious children into thick-wire cages. She'd counted them.

The children around her still slept. When they woke, they too would realize were missing. How many had died in the raid.

She clenched her fist. Her eyes burned as the faces of the dead swam before her. Claire, the new girl Cho had rescued. Samaira had been looking forward to helping her ice ability grow and go toe to toe against someone with opposite powers. The twins, Luna and Nova; she'd helped train them in their powers. Tommy and Jane; she'd tried so hard to protect her little brother. Ichi's brother. Ichi's heart would break when he realized Cho wasn't with them. Samaira closed her eyes. And, Jason...

An emptiness spread through her heart. It was pumped through her body with each beat, numbing her, extinguishing every light within.

She sat in silence. The light through the window changed. The blue faded into grey, and then a bleak yellow. The children stirred.

Elaine sat up in her cage. She brushed long black braids back from her face and rubbed her eyes and forehead.

Samaira watched in silence as her friend straightened as much as possible in the cramped cage she was in and surveyed the room.

Elaine turned to look at her—the only other body sitting up—and tilted her head, a question in her eyes.

Samaira shook her head, jaw clenched, hands twisted together as she barely kept her rage and pain in check.

"Do you see *anything*?" Samaira whispered, trying not to plead.

Elaine's lips quivered. Silent tears rolled down her cheeks as she bit her bottom lip and sucked in a deep breath. She shook her head.

They were too far away to touch. Too far to hold hands as they had done on the terrifying nights before they'd found Haven. Samaira wanted to crawl into her friend's lap as she had done when they were both children. When Elaine, only twelve, had kept her and Jason safe and warm against the rain, the wind, the threat of this exact outcome.

So they cried apart. Elaine's tears triggered a flood from Samaira. She brushed the first few away, fury tearing at her insides. The sun rose as the two women released their pain in silent sobs to keep from waking the others.

Minutes ticked by. Samaira's eyes dried. She moved and stretched, shifting her body as much as possible in the tight space.

Elaine was not alone in her cage. Long after her tears stopped coming, Lily and Kim woke. They huddled against her. Murmured questions and hushed sobs reached Samaira's ears even as she tried to tune them out.

Elaine brushed her fingers through Lily's hair, the girl's head resting on the silky skirt coving her thigh. Her other hand massaged Kim's scalp between her rose-shaped bantu knots.

A slow melody drifted through the air. Elaine's gentle voice rang through the room as she sang an old lullaby.

Samaira closed her eyes. Let the song take her back in time.

When Elaine finished the first, she sang another. Then another. By the time she'd uttered the final notes of the fourth song, the rest of the children had woken, and light from the window had chased away most of the shadows.

Ichi sat in the cage next to Elaine. Middle row, closest to the door and alone in his enclosure. Samaira watched him from her position halfway down one of the side walls. He straightened with a groan and gazed around their prison.

Samaira gritted her teeth. She called another ball of fire to her palm and stared into the flames, avoiding her friend's eyes. Ichi would see it soon. See who was gone. She didn't want to see his face when he realized.

"Hey." Ichi's calm voice cracked the silence that followed Elaine's song.

"Morning," Elaine replied. The tremor of fear in her voice offset the casual greeting.

"How are you doing?" he murmured.

"The children are scared."

"Do you know how long we've been here? Where's Cho?"

Samaira looked up. Elaine shook her head urgently and tapped her temple. Samaira leaned her head back against the cage. Ichi would go into her mind now, and he'd find out without having to count, who was missing.

Ichi nodded and closed his eyes for a moment. A few seconds passed, and then he took a shuddering breath. "What happened?"

A longer silence this time.

Ichi swallowed a few times and exhaled. "Everything will be all right." He looked around the room. He caught Samaira's eye. There was a furrow in his brow and a devastated expression on his face that he tried to smooth into something calm.

The blind, bitter, fury in Samaira's heart flared. It was a lie. Nothing would be all right. They'd die here. Ichi only gave them false hope.

She shook her head, lips curved in a grim expression and let the flame die in her hand.

Seconds later the door burst open. Light flooded the room. Samaira grasped the links of her cage and scrambled to her feet. Her body hunched at an odd angle to fit in the short metal box. Her dark eyes scanned the entrance to the room.

Three men entered.

Elaine went rigid, her eyes glowing with golden light. Lily and Kim moved to the back of their cage. Elaine's head twitched. She gasped.

Ichi stood as well, his taller cage allowing him to stand at full height. "No." He looked from the men, back to Elaine, panic in his gaze.

"What did she see?" Samaira called. Fear laced her voice; she put a clamp on it. She stiffened her body, flexed her bicep, and rammed her shoulder against the door of the cage.

Ichi didn't answer.

The three men—two Black-Stars and a Blue-Star—stayed near the doorway. The Black-Stars wore matching uniforms. Simple black pants, long-sleeve shirts, and boots. Utility belts carried a communications device, restraints, and a long, narrow metal stick. No plasma-guns that Samaira could see, nor the new weapons they'd had in Haven.

The Blue-Star stood a little ahead of the other two. They flanked him and, though he was a lower class, he carried an air of authority, like he was the one in charge. A billowing white lab coat, thrown over a button up shirt and a pair of jeans, accentuated his pale skin. He paused a moment at the entrance, his gaze scanning the lot of them.

"Ichi," Samaira called. He knew what Elaine saw. He'd read her mind as she'd had her vision.

The Blue-Star strode forward. He stopped in front of Elaine.

Samaira slammed her shoulder against the door to her cage again.

"Perfect," the man exclaimed. He clapped his hands together once before turning to the Black-Stars. "Get her." He pointed to Elaine.

The light in the room seemed to dim. Samaira's mouth went dry as Ichi launched himself against his cage, rocking it an inch off the ground.

"*No*," he shouted; his voice echoed off the concrete around them.

Samaira clenched her jaw to keep from shouting again. She felt along the seam of her cage, searching for any kind of weakness in the metal. Finding nothing, she rammed her body against the door again.

The two Black-Stars walked forward. The Blue-Star stepped to the side as they opened the cage door, reached in, and took hold of Elaine's arms. Her eyes were glazed, the color had dimmed to faded gold. She was still in her trance. Still looking ahead in time.

Kim and Lily shrieked and cried. They scratched and hit the guards, pulling at Elaine's arms in a desperate attempt to keep her with them. One of the men planted a palm against Lily's chest and shoved her back. She slammed into the metal at the far end of the cage. The Black-Stars slammed the door shut.

"Stop." Ichi leaned onto his cage, fingers clenched around the metal. His voice shook. "Take me instead, please. *Please*. Let her go."

Samaira trembled at Ichi's pleading tone. She'd never heard such helplessness from her friend. She sucked in a breath and called a ball of flames to her palm. She increased the heat as far as she dared, the color shifting from orange to bright blue. Then she pressed her hand against the hinges of the cage. She glanced up, watching the scene unfold before her as she worked.

The Blue-Star grinned and moved in a slow circle. His gaze flicked from child to child, cage to cage before he glanced back to Ichi. "What about her instead?" He pointed to Sky's cage.

She shrieked and curled in the corner.

Ichi's balled his hands into fists, his arms shaking as a muscle twitched in his jaw.

"Or this one?" The Blue-Star gestured to Jacob, who scrambled backward as far as he could go, whimpering.

A growl escaped Samaira's throat. She switched hinges.

"No?" The Blue-Star chuckled as he approached Ichi's cage. He leaned in with a smug grin. "Too bad. I suppose we'll have to stick with what we've got. For now."

He turned and walked toward the door. The Black-Stars followed him, dragging Elaine between them.

She'd started to come out of the trance. Her feet found purchase on the ground, and she looked around, confusion in her eyes.

Samaira closed her hand. The fire went out. She launched the entire weight of her body against the cage.

A shattering crunch reverberated around the room as she broke the hinges. The door hung crooked, barely held together by its lock. Samaira stood in the aisle; bare feet spread apart in a fighting stance. She brought her hands up, flames appearing in each palm.

The effort of producing the fire surprised her. She hadn't noticed the drain while heating the hinges. She took two sharp breaths as the men at the doorway turned, shifting Elaine with them.

"Let her go," Samaira said through clenched teeth.

The Black-Stars' eyes widened. Fear flickered across their faces.

Samaira poured a little more power into her palms, letting the fire grow noticeably larger.

The Blue-Star, hand on the door frame as he waited for his captive to go through first, looked Samaira up and down. A half-smile crossed his face, blue eyes glinting. "Ahh, that's a new one." The smile disappeared. "Lawrence," he called through the open door, "more men."

Samaira took three steps forward, then froze as six more Black-Stars pushed into the room.

Elaine's scream echoed through the room as the men rushed Samaira.

She shot off her flames. One grazed a shoulder. The other she didn't see, but smelled scorched cloth. A blow caught her across the side of the head. She fell sideways into a cage.

The children inside screamed.

Samaira came back up swinging. Bone crunched beneath her knuckles. She kicked out. So many bodies. Vision fuzzy from the blow. The side of her foot connected with something soft.

Someone retched.

They were on her. She raised her arms, shielding her face as a fist caught her in the stomach. Another against the back of her head. A boot flew toward her.

Everything went dark.

"*Samaira.*" A familiar voice floated through her dream.

"*Samaira!*" The urgency pulled her. Up and away from the meal her mother had just set down. Away from the laughter around their table as Jason told another joke their parents laughed too hard at.

She didn't want to go.

Light flashed on the other side of her eyelids. They flared red for a brief moment. She cracked her eyes open, squinting through her lashes.

"Samaira, please. Please wake up."

She struggled to consciousness, and a wave of pain hit her. Her head ached, and blood crusted across her upper lip and chin. Her right arm felt as though someone had tried to jerk it from the socket, and her chest and stomach felt like someone had used her as a punching bag.

She blinked a few times as the light shot splinters of pain through her already throbbing head. A moment passed before she was able to see where she was.

Directly in front of her, a flat sheet of black glass took up most of the wall. White brick made up the rest of the chamber she was in. A glance to the right showed a white door, still open. Men in black muttered to each other in the hallway outside. Glowing white orbs were placed in brackets where the ceiling and walls met.

She tried to take a step forward, but she couldn't move. Panic flared through her chest as she jerked her arms and legs. Restraints held them in place. Thick nylon bound her to the wall. She had maybe two inches of movement in her hands. More restraints wrapped around her torso. They'd been holding her up while she was passed out. Now they kept her tight to the wall behind her.

A needle stuck out of her left arm. Blood ran through a thin tube and into a bag hanging from a metal hook. There was something else, stuck on either side of her neck just under the jaw line. She couldn't see it.

Ichi stood to her left.

She could turn her head, at least.

Similar chords and wires were hooked up to his restrained figure. He was awake. He stood straight, his bare feet planted firmly on the cold tile floor. He stared at her, a beseeching expression on his face. When she met his gaze, he sighed.

"Finally." He slumped, looking relieved. "I wasn't sure..." He pulled at the nylon around his wrists, but they were as tight as Samaira's.

She gave a hoarse chuckle. "Takes more than that to keep me down."

Ichi didn't smile. He shook his head, tears growing at the corners of his eyes.

"What happened?" Samaira cleared her throat. Her dry tongue stuck to the roof of her mouth. A fuzzy sensation went through her head.

"They knocked you out."

"I figured," Samaira said.

Ichi shuddered. "They took Elaine. Samaira, I don't... I don't know where she is. What they're doing to her."

A chill went through Samaira. Before she could respond, the Blue-Star walked into the room.

"Nothing, yet," his cool voice interrupted their conversation, sending another wave of seeping cold down Samaira's spine.

Ichi jerked on his restraints, his teeth gritted, the tears gone.

"Now that we have you two hooked up," he glanced at Samaira, "and conscious. We can begin."

"*Don't you touch her,*" Ichi spat.

The man flashed white teeth at them. The edges of his nose wrinkled, eyes glinting with excitement.

He ignored Ichi and looked to Samaira. "We know what *you* can do."

Samaira growled and twisted against her restrains. The effort sent searing pain through her right arm. "You have no *idea* what I can do."

To her fury, the Blue-Star chuckled. "All in good time, I'm sure." He turned to Ichi. "What about you?"

"You don't want to know what I can do." Ichi's voice was nearly unrecognizable. No warmth. No comfort. Cold. Unforgiving. Dangerous.

Samaira glanced at her friend.

"Tell me, Keith," Ichi tilted his head, almost quizzical.

The man's eyes widened.

"Do you think this will make you wanted?"

Keith licked his lips and darted a glance at Samaira.

She soothed her features, and smiled that cocky grin she'd learned from her brother, as Ichi went on.

"Youngest son of a mother who loved your sister more. Always had to prove yourself. But you were *never quite good enough*. Not when you graduated top of your class. Not even when you were elevated to a higher caste during your Coding. And now..." Ichi narrowed his eyes, leaning as close to Keith as his restrains would allow. "Now you're trying to prove you can do *this* job. Trying to prove you belong, you deserve to be a Blue-Star."

His voice went darker still and Samaira knew he wasn't only speaking aloud. His voice was inside the Blue-Star's head. Echoing as though he were in a cavern of darkness.

Keith's breath quickened as fear took root. He swallowed and glanced to the door.

"You haven't changed, Keith," Ichi said. "You haven't grown. You're a sad little boy, trying to make mommy love you."

Keith's brow furrowed as fury replaced the fear.

"She never will, Keith." Ichi's voice did not waver. He stared into the Blue-Star's eyes and gave him a cruel smile. "You can't hide your thoughts from me. You have no secrets." He dropped his voice to a whisper. "I see what scares you."

Ichi slumped against the wall, breathing hard.

Keith swallowed. Beads of sweat had formed across his brow. He brushed them away with the back of his hand, curling his fingers into fists. A few seconds passed, and then he shifted his shoulders. Shook his head and clenched and unclenched his hands. Finally, he met Ichi's gaze again, fury burning through his eyes. "And I see what scares you."

Samaira's heart plummeted.

He crossed the small room in two strides, tapped the black glass, and stood back. The glass cleared, the room next door becoming visible.

All the oxygen left Samaira.

"*No*," Ichi cried out. His voice was back to normal. His body shook.

Elaine sat, strapped to a large metal chair. Tears streamed from her eyes. Metal clamps held her arms, legs, and chest in place. Needles stuck out from her up-turned wrists, pumping blood from her body into clear cylinders behind her.

A shadow of a bruise was etched across the right side of her smooth, dark face.

The Blue-Star crossed back to Ichi and leaned close to his ear.

Samaira jerked on her restraints again, but Ichi only had eyes for the woman he loved. He stared at her through the glass, despair on his face.

"You've been in my head. You must know I like chess," Keith murmured, inches from Ichi's face.

Ichi darted pleading glance at their captor.

"Tactically..." Keith smirked, hesitated, and shook his head, "making *me* angry? Not a smart move."

He turned and strode from the room.

Samaria snarled as he passed, trying in vain to reach him. To latch her hands around his skinny neck and squeeze until his eyes burst.

"Don't do this," Ichi called. "*Please.*"

In the other room, two different Blue-Stars walked around in quick, efficient movements. They prepared instruments, shuffled papers, and tapped on their tablets. Both had to be decades older than Keith, but he strode into the room with the confidence of a person in charge.

Four Black-Stars joined them. Two circled the room and then stationed themselves near the door, out of Samaira's sight. The other two stood behind Elaine.

Keith came to the window. He tapped it with his forefinger and spoke. His voice reached them through speakers high in the walls.

"She can't see you." He glanced at Elaine.

"Take me instead, please," Ichi shouted. He pulled against the wall. The restraints held fast. "*Let her go.*"

"Ichi?" Elaine's shaky voice was barely audible. She looked up, brilliant black eyes searching for him. "*Ichi?*" More frantic this time.

Keith chuckled and tapped at something beside the window. "And now, she can't hear you. But..." His smile grew.

Samaira trembled, tears burning at her eyes.

"... you *will* be able to hear her."

He hit another button. The glass went black.

Ichi screamed. The sound pierced Samaira. Tears fell as she shared in her friend's anguish.

A low moaning sounded somewhere in the room. Samaira glanced around, trying to pinpoint the source. It came from the speakers.

"No," she whispered.

As the realization hit her, a sharp scream sounded. The speakers amplified it, but they'd have heard it through the wall. Samaira's blood ran cold.

Ichi snapped. He yelled. Thrashed. Like a caged beast he yanked at the restraints with no thought of his own safety. The needle in his arm dislodged and fell to the floor.

Elaine's scream ended. They heard her panting breath as a curt voice announced subject 1109 lacked resistance to extreme heat. Cold would be next.

"*No,*" Ichi screamed.

A ragged whimper sounded above them. "Stop... please..."

Tears poured from Samaira's eyes as she listened to Elaine beg them to stop. Elaine, who saved her and her brother from capture, torture, and likely death when they were only seven. Elaine, who showed her how to twist her hair into tight knots against her scalp, to keep it out of the way during a fight. Elaine, who taught her to control her flames. Showed her they were a part of her. Her closest friend's lover. *Her* friend. Her *sister*.

Elaine's voice tore through her like sharp blades. Everything went white. Samaira's vision, her hearing, seemed to go as she took a deep breath and opened her clenched fists.

Flames erupted from her palms.

Ichi's shouting stopped.

Samaira opened her eyes. He stared at her. The broken look in his eyes shattered her heart.

She pulled from her core. From the depleted source of her power. As it grew within her, roaring for freedom, burning bright... she pushed. Flames shot up her wrists. The nylon around her arms caught fire and melted. The material left hot red welts across her black skin as it fell away.

Another scream came through the speakers.

"Hurry," Ichi whispered.

Samaira unclipped the restraints at her ankles. She did the same for her friend. The two of them ripped the nodes from their necks and arms and raced to the door. There was no handle. No hinges.

Tears streamed down Ichi's face as his fingers grasped the edges of the wall.

"We have to get her, Samaira. We have to get her out." His voice shook.

Another scream tore through the air.

"*No!*" Ichi turned, ran to the window, and slammed his fists against the glass. He leaned into it, punching over and over.

Samaira watched, helpless, as her friend bloodied his knuckles trying to reach Elaine. She frowned. Squinted at the glass. Glanced back at the melted nylon restraints. Maybe...

Samaira grabbed Ichi's arm and heaved him away. "Stop. This isn't getting us anywhere."

"We can't do nothing," Ichi shouted at her, wrenching from her grasp.

Samaira reached out and snatched the front of Ichi's shirt. She dragged him around so they stood face to face and glowered down at him. "*Nothing* wasn't what I had in mind. *Get behind me.*"

She shoved Ichi against the back wall and faced the darkened window.

She reached deep inside again, grasping at the power waiting for her. It was faint. The flames had been dim even before her last burst of power. The trauma of the last few days. Losing her brother... her friends... the lack of food, sleep, the constant fear. All of it took a toll on her strength.

She concentrated. Focused intently on her hatred. On the fury within. Pushed the fear from her heart.

Another scream sent a shiver of rage down her spine. They would not kill her sister too.

She took a step forward, knees slightly bent, body angled, prepared to fight. Her hands rose to her sides. She opened her fists, and flames burst into life.

Her chest rose and fell. She brought her hands up, wrists together, and launched her open palms toward the glass.

A funnel of fire shot forward. Heat blasted through the room.

The tint on the glass crackled and burned. It faded, crawling away as the glass itself began to melt. Her body shook. Tears ran down her cheeks.

A shattered scream erupted from her.

The flames reached an uncontrollable size. The window bent and buckled. Cracks formed around the edges. As the last of Samaira's energy flooded from her hands, the window shattered.

She slumped. Sucked in exhausted breaths. Barely on her feet. Barely conscious. Someone screamed.

She looked up as Ichi raced past.

"*No!*"

Elaine sat in the chair, the restraints still in place. Blood ran from her right eye. Burns and scratches and welts covered her arms. Nails were missing from one of her hands.

Keith stood to the left of Elaine's chair. A strange device was hooked to her gemstone. Metal tongs grasped the smooth edges. A flat sheet of metal pushed against her head, circling the stone.

Samaira stumbled forward. It was all happening too fast.

Ichi had just reached the low lip of the shattered window.

Keith glanced at them.

He smiled and flicked a switch.

Elaine screamed. The machine pried her gemstone, at shocking speed, from her head. Her eyes closed. She slumped, blood pouring from her temple.

Ichi sliced his hands climbing over the short wall. He ran to Elaine, falling to his knees before her with a cry of anguish. Tears flowed from him as he reached up to touch her face.

The Black-Stars descended upon him.

Samaira stood frozen at the window's edge, hands covering her mouth as gut-clenching horror overwhelmed her, staring at Elaine's bleeding form.

Chapter Forty

Present Day - Early Fall - Grigoria Warehouse in Tornim

H e couldn't breathe.

He tried. Gulped in air like a drowning fish. Jason's words faded into the background as Cho trembled at the window. Jane and Tommy hadn't returned.

His fears kept coming true.

Why did they keep coming true?

Jason and Luna had arrived a few minutes ago. They'd burst into the building, out of breath and in a panic.

Never get separated.

That's what Ichi had always told them. It's what he'd drilled into everyone before every excursion to the surface.

Cho clenched his shaking hands. He should have reminded them.

In the corner of the room, Nova clutched her sister, wrapping protective arms around Luna as she sobbed into her shoulder. Claire was still passed out on the couch. Jason glanced at Cho, his dark eyes hooded and hard to read.

Jason crossed to the couch and knelt next to the girl. From a pack on his back, he pulled ointment, gauze, and a thin bottle of pills. "Help me with her?"

Cho jerked at Jason's rough voice, but it was enough to pull him from the window. He joined him at the couch. Together they cleaned Claire's wound, coated it with a healthy dose of the ointment, and wrapped it with the clean gauze. She stirred a few times during the cleaning process, but slept through the rest of it.

"She needs this." Jason shook the bottle. The pills clattered around inside. "So does Nova."

The twins perked up in the corner. Luna crossed to them and took a round green tablet from the bottle.

"Wrap her leg as well," Cho murmured. "It'll heal faster if she doesn't accidentally move it wrong."

Luna nodded and pulled a thicker bandage from her own bag.

"You need to eat," Jason said. "And change."

Cho stared at him. The weight of Jane and Tommy missing pressed against his chest. Bile rose in his throat. "I..." He grimaced. "I can't. Not until they get back."

Jason pulled packages of neatly wrapped food from deeper in his bag. He set them along the windowsill—the only flat surface in the room besides the ground. A pair of pants followed, and a shirt. He tossed the clothes and Cho caught them on instinct.

"It's been days," Jason said, his voice flat. "You should change and eat."

Heat rose up in Cho. Jason could pretend all he wanted, but Cho felt his fear. Felt the anxiety, the terror, the guilt.

Cho felt them too. Some of the feelings it his own, some belonging to his friends who *still* had not put their mental defenses back into place. Having Jason and Luna back without Jane and Tommy was bad. And—and Cho hated himself for the thought—the return of their emotions brought him lower than he'd thought possible.

The reprieve, only Nova and an unconscious Claire in the room, had been a breath of fresh air.

Now he couldn't breathe again.

Jason went over to Nova and Luna, taking a handful of breakfast biscuits with him. The scent of melted cheese, freshly cooked meat, and steaming bread, brought a growl of life to Cho's stomach.

He went into the hallway to change into the clean clothes.

"... are we going to do?" Luna's soft voice carried out the cracked door.

"We wait," Jason replied. "Jane can handle herself. She and Tommy will be here. We just have to wait."

Cho's gut twisted. He buttoned the jeans and tossed his sweat stained, bloody shirt onto the floor.

"What then?" One of the twins asked.

There was a pause. Cho clenched his new shirt between his hands.

"Then we do what Ichi wanted. We follow Cho. We get somewhere safe, together."

Cho shook his head at the sincerity in Jason's voice. He wasn't supposed to be sincere, supportive. He was supposed to be a smart-ass. A jerk who tried to steal Cho's hat and made fun of his broken gemstones.

"We follow Cho?" One of the twins again, Cho couldn't tell which one.

Another pause. "Yeah. He got us out of Haven. Without him..."

Cho's teeth hurt with how hard he was clenching his jaw. He couldn't breathe again. He tried to swallow. His mouth was so dry.

Above him, the gentle tapping of rain echoed across the roof.

Cho turned. He strode down the hall and worked his way through the crumbling building until he made it outside.

The park across the street was empty. Beams of sunlight flashed through the rapidly moving clouds, reflecting in the raindrops on the grass and causing them to glitter. What had started as a sprinkle quickly shifted into a downpour.

Cho stared as puddles formed in uneven patches along the road. The rain matted his hair against his forehead. He leaned against the grey stucco of the building, slid down the wall and sat on the wet asphalt, tilting his face towards the sky. Could the rain drown him?

He didn't know how long he sat there, droplets of water thudding onto his skin, washing away the soot, dirt, blood, and days of sweat. He shivered. Pulled on the clean shirt, though it was as wet as the rest of him now.

"Hey."

Cho jerked. Snapped his eyes open and stared up at Jason.

His dark eyes were still cold. No trace of the fire that once lit them up, no matter what he pretended with the others. Cho could feel the truth.

He didn't respond.

"We need you in there, Cho. While we wait for Jane and Tommy."

Cho shook his head and glared at the ground. "What makes you think they're even alive?"

Jason took a step toward him. He crouched, forcing himself into Cho's view. "Because it's Jane. They'd need more men than the city *has* to take her out." His laugh was forced. Laced with the same fear that gripped Cho's heart.

Cho grimaced. He rose to his feet and pushed away from the wall. Away from Jason. "Stop it."

Jason rose behind him and followed as Cho continued to walk away. "Stop what?"

"Stop faking it," Cho snarled. "I can feel it, Jason. I can *feel* the fear in you. The pain. Don't *pretend* you aren't terrified they're already dead."

Jason went silent. His footsteps stopped.

Cho stopped as well. His arms shook at his sides. The anger. The hurt. He was drowning. Drowning with nothing. No way out...

The tumult of emotion from Jason faded.

Cho frowned. He turned, squinting at Jason through the rain.

Jason moved toward him, hands in tight fists at his sides. "I forgot."

"What?" Cho demanded. He swallowed, pushing through the muck of emotions roiling through his power. He filtered them as he stared at Jason and realized they were his own.

"I've had my defenses down this whole time," Jason said. He took another step forward. "You've been..." he grimaced. "Since the raid?"

Cho tightened his jaw.

"I'm sorry," Jason muttered.

The sound barely made it to Cho through the pounding rain.

"Listen," Jason gestured back to the ruined warehouse, "I'll talk to the others, remind them to put up their shields again. But we need you in there. We can't... we need a leader."

"It's not me," Cho growled.

Jason took half a step back. A wrinkle appeared between his eyebrows. "What do you mean, not you? Ichi said—"

"I don't care what he said," Cho spat. He bit the inside of his cheek as a flurry of sadness swept through the anger he'd dredged forward. Anger he'd used to hide the rest of his anguish.

"Cho..." Jason tilted his head.

It was that gesture, and the sincerity in his gaze, that broke the dam.

"I can't do it." Cho trembled. "I can't, Jason."

"What are you—"

"I *broke*," Cho shouted. His voice echoed across the empty, rainswept street. The memory of that day, three years ago, of his mind shattering into a million pieces, the weeks, months it took to put himself back together... "You *have* to understand, Jason." Cho's voice shook as tears mixed with the rain on his cheeks. "You were there. You saw how... how *weak* I am." He hated the pleading in his voice. Hated knowing he'd never be as strong as the rest of them. As his brother.

Jason took a step toward him, but Cho held up his hand.

"I can't be like him." Cho's voice cracked. "I can't lead them the way he would if he were still..." he choked on the word. A sob ripped from him. "If he were here."

Tears streamed down his cheeks. The rain that had been hiding them petered out.

Jason stepped forward and Cho didn't stop him this time. The sorrow was too much. Everything else faded into the background as the loss of his brother tore through him.

Jason's hands found his shoulders. Cho fell as Jason pulled him in; collapsed against his hard chest. Solid warmth met him. Jason's arms wrapped around him as shuddering sobs wracked his body.

They didn't speak. Jason offered no words of calm or comfort. He just held him. Held him and let him pour out the grief. His breath kept a steady rhythm by Cho's ear. In and out. The beat of it somehow pulling Cho from the pit of despair he'd been trapped in and centering him in this time. This space. This moment of relief.

Cho ate.

The two returned to their hideout to find Nova on her feet, wobbling around the room with a grin on her face.

"I can do this," she sang as she hobbled toward the food, one hand steadying herself against the wall.

"Take one." Luna shoved a biscuit into Cho's hands as the men stepped back into the room.

He took it, unfolding the brown wax paper that had kept it warm and finally allowing his hunger to be satiated. He ignored the satisfied nod Jason gave. Instead, he strode to Claire, still chewing, and sat at the edge of the couch.

"Hey," he jostled her uninjured shoulder.

She stirred.

He shook her again and gestured for Luna to bring over another biscuit. She obliged and, by the time Claire was sitting up, a bewildered expression on her tired face, Cho had a clean bottle of water, food, and meds waiting for her.

Once she'd been settled, nestled against the side of the couch with her wounded arm cradled against her and food in her hand, he rose and paced the perimeter of the room.

"How long has it been?" he asked Jason.

"Probably a couple hours now." Jason plucked a sticky bun from the windowsill and took a bite. "I say we give them another hour."

Cho nodded. "Jane knows more about Agora than any of us. If they had to hunker down and hide, we wouldn't find 'em anyway."

Luna murmured her agreement and then ordered her sister to sit down. Nova obeyed, slightly pouty, and drank the water Luna handed her.

"If they aren't back in an hour," Cho continued, "I'm going out. Just me." He put up a hand as Jason opened his mouth. "I know Agora too, and I'll be able to cast a net."

"What?" Claire asked from the couch.

Cho turned to her. "My power. It... it likes to latch onto people's emotions, but I can also get a read on a room. Or even a building. I'll feel it if I'm close enough to sense her shields." He gave a rueful smile. "No one else in Agora will be using mental wards to protect themselves. She'll stand out if I can get close enough."

Nova grunted and Cho looked back at the twins. Luna had blanched, her face pale and almost a sickly green color. She stared at Cho with wide eyes.

"I didn't..." she glanced at her sister, then Jason, then Cho again. "I haven't been... hang on." She inhaled through unsteady lips and blew the air out again, closing her eyes and sinking into the cross-legged position they used during meditation practice with Elaine.

Almost instantly, Cho felt her shield go up. Nova's too.

Claire was still an open book of raw emotion, but as the twins closed their minds, Cho's chest expanded with relief. His power, manic, excited, and roiling like a storm, settled as the amount of emotion to consume lessened. It wasn't under control, not the least. He'd need days to get his own walls back up, to cage the saffron tendrils that even now reached toward Claire.

He yanked them back.

As everyone took another helping of food and rinsed off in the bathroom down the hall, Cho settled himself in a corner of the room and thought about what came next. They needed a place to go. Somewhere safe. That had always been Ichi's dream.

From what Jason and Luna had said, Black-Stars were crawling all over Agora. Still, if they gave it a few days things would settle. It would be too suspicious for the rest of the city otherwise.

They'd wait a week or so, get in touch with the person Ichi had gone to for papers, and find a way to get out of the city. Together they'd search. Find an old village from before the cities had pulled everyone into them. Fix up a house. Live.

There were holes in the plan. But it was a *plan*. A step forward. Something to keep him from sinking back into that pit.

Cho gathered the others to fill them in. Before he could get out the first sentence, something thudded at the front of the building.

Jason was at the door before anyone else had risen. Spheres of fire caressed his palms as he slid into the hallway.

Cho closed in behind him, gesturing for the others to stay put.

They moved down the hall. Jason ducked under a broken beam, eyes forward. Cho followed. His heart thudded against his chest. Hope and fear coiled tight in his stomach.

"I've got enough going on without you lighting me on fire. Put that out, will you?"

Jason closed his fist as Jane stepped into view, Tommy at her side.

Cho exhaled in relief. "You made it."

"'course," Jane scoffed. "It's us."

Cho's grin slid away as he took her in. Tommy under one arm, not for protection, but to support his sister's weight. She limped, blood oozing from a dirty bandage on her thigh. Scratches covered her forearms and hands.

Cho moved past Jason and swooped under Jane's other arm. "What happened?"

Her cocky grin wavered as she met his gaze. "Cho..."

He hesitated, her weight on his shoulder, head twisted at an odd angle to meet her blazing grey eyes. "What is it?"

"They're..." she swallowed. Her gaze darted to Jason, then back to Cho. "They're alive, Cho."

His heartbeat thundered in his ears. He frowned at her. "Wh—"

"Ichi, Elaine, Samaira... everyone." She stared at him, her gaze piercing. "They're alive."

"The question is, when do we leave?" Cho paced before the couch.

Jane sat next to Claire, a clean bandage around her thigh, ointment on her cuts, a bottle of water between her legs, and the last biscuit sandwich—half-eaten—in her hand. Tommy was in front of her, resting on the floor with a fruit pastry clenched in his fingers.

Jane had filled them in between getting cleaned up and eating. Tears came first. Planning was next.

Cho knew about his brother's plans. They had the money. They had Ichi's contact in Grigoria who could draft the papers for their escape. The problem was gemstones.

Jason hadn't gotten a caste. Cho couldn't. No one else in their group was old enough to pass for an adult. They had to find a way to get past the Red-Stars, but as Cho racked his brain for any feasible idea, he came up empty.

"We could paint Jason's?" Luna suggested half-heartedly.

Jason raised an eyebrow. "With what, exactly? Nothing sticks to these things." He tapped the gemstone on his temple. The last few days had seen them swirling with dull grey, dark greens, and shades of brown. After hearing his sister was alive, they had returned to the usual spinning rainbow of color Cho was used to.

Luna shrugged. The initial elation they'd all felt when Jane told her story had faded. They were left with the sinking realization that rescuing their loved ones was a long way off.

First, they had to get out of Tornim.

"The guy with the papers," Jane said. "He does this sort of thing, right? Gets people out?"

Cho nodded. "That's what Ichi heard. Not sure how true the rumors are, but he was at least able to get paperwork for everyone in Haven to leave."

Jane cocked her head. "That's not a simple thing. Maybe we talk to him, right?"

Cho chewed on his lower lip. "It's worth asking." He heaved a sigh. "I'm going. I'll be back soon."

Jason put up a hand, stepping in front of the door as Cho made to leave. "You shouldn't go out there without back-up. They're looking for us, remember?"

Jane grunted and pushed to her feet, standing a bit lopsided on her injured leg. "I'll go."

"Absolutely not," Luna snapped.

There was a brief pause as everyone stared at her. Even Nova looked surprised.

Luna gritted her teeth. "You're injured. Nova is injured. Claire almost died."

"What?" Claire glanced around, eyes wide with alarm.

Luna waved a hand dismissively. "Jason, Tommy, and I are the only ones physically able to keep up if something goes wrong."

Jane opened her mouth, eyes narrowed.

Luna plunged on, not letting her interrupt. "Tommy's powers are drained." She crossed her arms and glared at Cho. "It's me or Jason. But he's right. No one should be going anywhere alone."

Jane sank back onto the couch with a satisfied expression, and took a bite from her sandwich.

Cho rubbed his forehead. "I don't want to put anyone else in danger," he murmured.

Luna strode across the room and stood in front of him. She stared up, tired, pale eyes holding his gaze. "We're always in danger, Cho."

"It's part of being what we are," Jane said around a mouthful of sandwich.

Cho glanced past Luna for a moment and caught Jane's eye. She grimaced, then nodded and flicked her gaze toward Luna.

"Jason," Cho turned to him, "you stay here. Keep them safe."

Jane gave an audible scoff and Jason flipped her off. Claire snorted.

Cho and Luna collected the coins left over from their purchases—still quite a bit—and left.

Cho pulled the embroidered cap down over his ruined gemstones as they stepped into late afternoon sunlight. Clouds drifted overhead. Thick and grey, they routinely blocked out the sun and cast cold shadows across the ground. Even still, puddles of water from the downpour an hour ago slowly dried out. By the time Cho and Luna reached the more populated area of Grigoria, the ground beneath their shoes was relatively dry.

"Where are we going?" Luna asked after thirty minutes of walking.

The quickest way to the towering office building, in which Ichi's contact kept an inconspicuous set of rooms, was through Agora. It was in the bustling wealthier half of Grigoria; nestled against the Blue, Black, and Grey districts and away from the warehouses and factories generally occupied by Orange and Green-Stars.

Cho avoided every entrance to Agora. Instead, they took the long way, walking the boulevards of Grigoria in a wide circle around the heart of the city. They kept to busy streets. Lower castes drove, picking up fares or commuting to work. Blue-Stars, Black-Stars, and even Grey-Stars strolled along on the sidewalks. It was a bustling mass of people arriving and departing, shopping, working, laughing, talking, and leaking bursts of anger or sadness or joy.

Cho swallowed at Luna's question. His focus had been split between mapping an inconspicuous route to the man's office and keeping his power in check.

He flinched as they moved past a car pulled to the side of the road, the front wheel off its axel and the Orange-Star in the driver's seat pounding the steering wheel as a Red-Star patrol approached.

"Stay close," he muttered through gritted teeth.

They continued on, getting past the whirling emotions of the situation. Cho turned, taking them further into Grigoria, leaving the road behind as they entered a sprawling park. Concrete paths wound through flower beds; neatly trimmed trees and bushes offered shady spots with clean benches for people to relax.

Cho pulled Luna to one of the benches and sat. He leaned against the wood, hand clenched around the armrest as he sucked in a few deep breaths.

"Cho?"

"I just..." he closed his eyes. Breathe. Focus. Slowly, he pulled his power back. The tendrils of yellow, which had been drawing every emotion they passed into him, shrank inward. They returned, at an agonizingly slow pace, to the small box he pictured in his mind.

The wall was still broken, crumbling bricks and dust coating the ground around the container he'd created to hold his power. Still, closing the lid on the swirling saffron whisps brought *some* peace.

"Sorry." He opened his eyes. "I needed a... anyway. We're headed there." He pointed.

A large building, six stories tall with thick glass windows and cream-colored walls, loomed in front of them across the park.

"That's not what I expected." Luna folded her hands in her lap.

Cho almost chuckled at her straight posture, raised chin, and immaculate braids. She was the picture of an upper-class child.

"Let's go." Cho stood.

Ten minutes later they'd made it through the lobby, up to the sixth floor, and paused before a pale wooden door with a foggy glass window consuming the top half. Black letters across the glass read: *Trading Post, Offices and Records of Carthik Nidgel*.

"Trading Post?" Luna asked.

Cho nodded. It was one of the larger Purple-Star businesses. Most of the caste kept to their little shops and restaurants, but a few of the wealthier families had business which spanned multiple cities. The Trading Post was one such company. In Tornim, they owned half a dozen smaller stores in Agora, and one of the large malls in Grigoria.

Cho reached up; a shiver ran down his spine. He took a deep breath and knocked.

Almost a minute passed. Cho clenched his hand to keep his fingers from trembling. Beside him, Luna went up on her toes and back to her heels over and over. The black orb in the far corner of the hall—one of a dozen they'd spotted in the building—had a little blinking red light that sent shoots of nerves through Cho's gut.

He tugged at the edges of his cap.

The door swung open. A tall man with sharp features, maybe in his mid-forties or fifties, stood before them. A coif of jet-black hair was slicked against his skull. Purple gemstones glinted at his temples. An artificial tattoo covered much of his neck, the geometric design disappearing beneath his black suit-jacket.

The man had opted away from the bright colors currently in fashion. The shirt under his jacket was a pale blue grey. There was no tie, the jacket open and a bit wrinkled.

He rolled his shoulders as he raised an eyebrow at them. Bags under his almond-colored eyes, creases on his face, and a rumpled chunk of hair on the side suggested they'd woken him from an afternoon nap.

"Who are you?"

Cho cleared his throat. "Are you Carthik?"

The man raised an eyebrow. He glanced at the door. "Yes."

Cho stood a little straighter, trying to imbue himself with his brother's confidence. Luna gripped the edge of his shirt sleeve.

"My name is Cho. I'm Ichiro's brother."

Carthik's gaze darted up and down the hall. "You'd better come in then," he muttered. "Quickly."

Cho swallowed, reached out a hand for Luna's nervous fingers to grasp, and walked them inside. Luna's hand squeezed his as she stepped in behind him.

"Where is Ichi?" Carthik asked as he closed the door and slid across a heavy metal bolt.

"He's not able to meet with you today." Cho glanced around the room.

It was a large set of rooms, but they felt cramped. Wooden boxes and bins cluttered most of the front. An open doorway led to an actual office space, with a wide metal desk, a couch—on which a balled-up blanket and pillow were perched—and a set of chairs accompanied bookshelves and piles of paperwork.

"That wasn't my question." Carthik slid off his jacket and tossed it across one of the boxes. He rolled up the sleeves of his shirt, folding them just below his elbows.

Cho stared at the man. Ichi had met with him. Elaine too. But no one else had gone to those meetings. Ichi trusted Carthik... to a point.

Cho released his power. Anxiety hit him. Saffron tendrils spiraled, latching onto the fear, unease, and genuine concern leeching from Carthik. He was worried. For himself? For Ichi? Cho wasn't sure.

"He's alive," Cho said.

The emotion shifted. Relief. Worry still present, but definite relief. It hit Cho through his power but was impossible to see on the man's face.

He nodded. "That's good. Still not my question."

Cho reeled in his power. Concentrating on the task at hand would be a hundred times harder while trying to separate his emotions from Carthik's.

Still a little behind him, Luna squeezed his hand.

Cho swallowed. "He was taken."

The alarm that flashed across Carthik's face also slammed through the residual connection Cho still had with him. He took half a step back.

Luna stepped forward, keeping a tight grip on Cho's hand. "Most of Haven was taken. Black-Stars."

Carthik cursed.

Cho finished shoving his power back into its box. The echo of Carthik's emotions still lapped against his mind, but he didn't feel them as his own.

"When?" Carthik demanded.

"Days ago," Cho replied. "We thought they were dead."

Carthik cursed again and strode forward.

Luna ducked behind Cho, but the man went straight past them and into his office. Cho followed, gently tugging Luna along.

"I have most of what he needed." Carthik moved around the desk and leaned over, rifling through a stack of papers. "He hadn't given me names yet," he pulled out a few thick sheets with delicate writing, "but I have everything else filled out."

Cho gritted his teeth. "Can you reuse them?"

Carthik frowned. "What do you mean?"

"We don't..." Cho stepped further into the room. "We don't need as many now. Only seven of us escaped."

The papers slipped from Carthik's fingers. He sank into the chair behind him, a hand going to his forehead.

The room fell into silence for a long moment.

"I'm sorry to hear that," Carthik said. "I know Ichi was in a hurry. I worried when I didn't hear from him, but I know he was also pressed for the money he needed."

"We have the money," Cho cut in.

Carthik looked up at him. Then at Luna. He blinked. "Please, have a seat you two. I'm sorry I didn't offer before. You... you took me by surprise."

Cho moved forward and took one of the soft leather chairs before the desk. Luna released his hand, somewhat reluctantly, and perched on the edge of the other.

"We still need our papers," Cho said.

"You're leaving the city?"

Cho nodded.

"I take it you've got something in the upper echelon under that hat?"

Cho glanced at Luna, confusion crossing his face.

"He's asking if you've got the gemstones we need," Luna murmured.

Cho sank back into his chair. "No."

"Then Elaine wasn't captured?" Carthik asked. "I take it Ichi managed his little foray into the Star Office since he got word to me that he was ready to go."

Cho rubbed his hands together and bit the inside of his lip. "They were both taken. We don't..."

"You don't have anyone with a fixed caste?"

Luna shook her head, the delicate braids flopping around her shoulders.

"Well," Carthik leaned back in his chair and folded his hands across his stomach, "that does present a problem."

"That's something we wanted to discuss with you." Cho scooted forward, resting his forearms on his knees as he gazed at the man before them. "My brother mentioned you were in the smuggling business."

Chapter Forty-One

Present Day - Early Fall - May's House

A nthony lay sprawled on his side across May's bed, his shirt lifted to his armpit, forearm resting on his forehead as he heaved a sigh. "This is the fourth time you've checked, May."

The old woman, hovering above him with a clean piece of unnecessary fabric, scowled. "This shouldn't be possible, Anthony. What did you do?"

Anthony gaped at her. He turned his head, craning to catch Juliana's eye at the dinner table. "Will yeh tell her? I didn't *do* anythin'."

Juliana shook her head. "I'm with her," she said. "This is beyond even what Blue-Stars medics can do."

Anthony blinked. He hadn't known that. All he'd known is that over the past week the itching at his side and back had stopped. The slice quit hurting. His leg quit hurting. His arm—the right one which had ached nonstop since it had been pulled from the joint—had quit hurting.

For some reason, he was the only one not complaining about it.

"Something changed, Anthony. This should still need stitches. It should be scabbing over, not healed already." May sank onto the bed next to him as he lowered his shirt and sat up. She brushed away a strand of grey hair, her hand landing on his arm. She gave him a hard look. "You've always healed quick, but something is different. I want you to tell me what it is."

Anthony shrugged—it felt good to do it without concealing a wince. "We've had decent meals for the past week and a half. Could tha' be it?"

At the table, Juliana chuckled and took a bite of her lunch. Lentils, seasoned with an array of spices Anthony had never tasted before. Rice cooked with flavored broth. Meat, mushrooms, and onions with a smoky tang he'd found odd at first, and now couldn't get enough of.

His bowl sat cooling next to hers, waiting for May to finish his examination.

"Can I get up now?" Anthony asked.

May sighed. "How's your leg?"

"Same as the rest," he shrugged, "just fine. In fact," he licked his lips, anticipating a fight, "I asked Montague tah set up gettin' the cast removed."

Juliana's spoon thunked against her bowl. She coughed a few times and downed a large gulp of water.

"Anthony," May's eyes widened, "it's far too soon for that. Breaks like yours take months to heal. Not weeks."

He tightened his jaw. Complaining about her concern felt childish and rude. Still, she and Naya had been fussing over him like mother hens ever since...

His eyelids fluttered closed as the memory of falling struck him. He grimaced. Then he frowned. A thought occurred to him. Maybe this had to do with the plan he'd enacted once they'd successfully brough back the food from the stolen truck; a plan he'd shared with Taz and no one else. Why? He wasn't entirely sure. Though it probably had something to do with the mother hen situation.

"I uh..." He shifted against the wall.

May gaze at him expectantly. At his hesitation, she raised an eyebrow. Her scar stretched against her wrinkled skin, and he realized why she would be so familiar with how fast wounds as bad as his healed.

Guilt caused his stomach to clench like a fist.

"The food thing," he said, "is the biggest change. But when we brought them back I..." he glanced at Juliana.

She watched him with furrowed eyebrows, her meal momentarily forgotten.

"I stopped eatin' the packets."

Juliana's face creased into a frown of confusion, then a frown of understanding, then an outright glare.

May on the other hand just looked puzzled.

"We can stop eating them?" Juliana demanded.

"Not technically," Anthony replied with a sheepish grin.

Her lower jaw jutted to the side in a bemused grimace.

"What?" He held up his hands. "I've had tah swallow down that nasty shit for as long I can remember. No choice. And not just 'cause they're required, but 'cause without 'em there just wasn't..." he trailed off.

Juliana shook her head, the grimace sliding into a half-grin. "I can't fault you for anything except *not telling me*. You think I want to keep eating them?" She gestured to her still steaming bowl. "When we have this now?"

May rose from the bed and crossed into the kitchen. Anthony's witty retort died in his throat as she walked away.

"May?" He stood as well, still wobbly on his cast, but now it was because of the bulk rather than pain.

May leaned against the counter. Her fingers found the edge of her scar at her forehead and trailed it down, tapping gently along the shining white skin. "A week?"

"What?"

She faced him; stooped and wrinkled but commanding a tone that made him stand straighter. "You've been going without the packets for a week?"

"Since we came back with the first haul. Little over a week." He nodded.

She stared to the side; her gaze distant as she looked at the corner of the room. "This is..." she shook her head and fell silent.

Juliana and Anthony watched her for a long moment before they exchanged worried looks. Still, they remained quiet.

Eventually she gave Anthony another hard look. "That was a foolish thing to do. If they catch you, they'll—"

"Throw me off a buildin'?" he said with a crooked grin.

Juliana shook her head. "You have got to stop making that joke."

"Never."

May slammed her palm on the kitchen counter and they both jumped. "That's enough. This isn't funny." Her chest rose and fell with heavy breaths. Pink tinged the pale skin of her cheeks; her dark eyebrows drew together in a frown. "Juliana, you should stop eating them as well. Tell the others. Taz. Daisy. I'll see if I can talk Naya into it, but..."

"It's a lotta risk for her right now," Anthony said. His aunt was having enough trouble dealing with storing their stolen goods beneath her house. "What's goin' on, May?"

"Why would he heal faster because he stopped eating them?" Juliana murmured. "No one in the city would be able to heal that fast."

May swallowed. She strode across the room and reached a hand toward Anthony's face.

He blinked. She pressed her palm to his cheek; her cold fingers warmed as she held them to his skin. Grey eyes met his black ones, and she seemed to pierce him with her gaze. The furrow in her brow reminded him so much of his uncle.

"I want you to be very careful, Anthony."

Anthony frowned; a chill went down his spine. "I'm careful, May, really."

He expected a snort or laugh from Juliana, but she stayed quiet, watching them.

May stared at him for a long moment. Then she patted his cheek and turned away.

Juliana raised an eyebrow at him. He shrugged back. As May moved through the kitchen and out the back door, Anthony joined Juliana at the table and pulled his bowl over. He dug into the delicious meal.

Juliana grilled him on the mush packets as they ate. He explained how he'd put them down the drain and put the packaging back into the wooden crates that were switched out every week. He admitted that Taz had been doing the same and using his house to empty the packets since he was still in the group home.

Juliana finished her food, crossed to the counter where a bowl of mush packets sat waiting to be eaten. She took half of them and began the process of squeezing the grey lumpy mixture down the drain.

"Do you really think your leg is healed?" she asked.

Anthony leaned back in his chair, stretching his hands over his head and enjoying the lack of flaring pain in his side. "This is fully scabbed over and startin' to scar." He gestured to the gash she'd re-stitched only a week ago. "It doesn't 'urt to walk on anymore. I'm done hobblin' around, Jules."

She smirked and shook a bit of mush off her hand with a grimace. "All right then. I'm not going to stop you."

He laughed. "If yeh even could."

She turned. With a threatening wave of an empty packet, she glared at him. "Oh, I could. You think Montague would listen to you over me?" She shook her head, locks of bright gold hair falling across her shoulders.

Anthony rolled his eyes and clambered to his feet. "Do yeh 'ave the list of houses for today?"

Juliana tossed the third empty packet back into the bowl and wiped her hands on a dish towel. "Yes." She glanced at two heavy bags in the corner of the kitchen. "We'll need to do a run to the truck soon."

His face lit up in a wild grin. "Tomorrow? I'll see if Montague can get this thing off this afternoon."

Juliana smiled back as she shouldered one of the bags.

Anthony followed her out of May's house and down the twisting path to their first stop. He hadn't gotten his hours back in the field. The foreman claimed it was the injuries, the leg. But Anthony didn't have any hopes of finding work again once he had the cast off. No one dared cross Steel in that way.

Still, he cracked a smile as he followed Juliana to the door of their first stop. Things were changing in Abredea. Whatever had sent away the extra Black-Stars had brought a sliver of hope back to the Moons. That sliver had blossomed when they'd started handing out the food.

He didn't know how long it would last. Nothing seemed to these days. But he'd enjoy it while he could. This feeling of happiness. This contentment that finally, he was able to do something to really help.

"You 'ave tah get Anthony outta here," Naya's hoarse voice murmured in Juliana's ear.

Juliana glanced at the woman, fear etched across her face, hand clutching Jimmy's as the boy stared ahead with trembling lips.

They were in the square, a week after Anthony had gotten his cast removed. Light afternoon rain drizzled down on them.

May, standing to Juliana's right, gripped her arm. "Naya's right. Get him away, as quickly and as far as you can."

Juliana bit her lip. Anthony stood a few feet ahead of them. His back was taut, hands clenched into fists, practically vibrating with fury.

All the way across the square, up on the steps of town hall, a family of White-Stars were being held by Steel's men. Owen stood tall, but fear etched lines across his features. His daughters stood with their mother, huddled against her skirt as a Black-Star gripped her a little too close.

The children were bruised, flecks of blood on the older one's dress. Lillian, the mother, had also been struck when the family was dragged from their home.

Steel stood before them all on the top step, facing the residents of Abredea. He hadn't called the White-Stars out this time. He wasn't making an example of them. This was about simple, brutish punishment.

Juliana's own hands trembled as she tried to block out Steel's cold voice.

Owen and Lillian had been one of a few families in the western end to refuse the food Juliana and the others offered. Fear stopped them. Fear that Steel would find out, that he'd know they'd associated with Anthony. He'd know they took what had to be illegal goods—though Juliana and her friends hadn't told a soul where they'd gotten the bags of flour, rice, spices, and potatoes they'd passed around.

Instead, their youngest daughter had reached a breaking point of hunger. She'd walked past one of the field trucks, scrambled up the back, and stolen an apple.

For that... Juliana clenched her jaw as Steel finished his speech and turned toward Owen.

"Take him away." Naya gripped Juliana's arm, shaking her from the anger muddling her mind. "Please."

Juliana glanced at Anthony. Watched as he took one step forward. Fear clamped an icy grip around her chest.

She strode forward, Naya's hand slipping from her arm. She reached out. Her hand slid into Anthony's.

He was trembling. Still, the contact broke his stare. He glanced at her.

She closed her fingers, interlocking them with his, and tugged.

He glared.

"Anthony," she murmured, stepping close. "There is *nothing* you can do to help right now."

His nostrils flared and he shook his head, looking back to the steps of town hall where Steel was pacing around Owen.

"He hates you." Juliana pulled again on Anthony's hand. "Anything you do will make it worse for them." She swallowed. "He won't kill them. He has no need to."

There was a pause, a brief moment where she thought he'd stay, or rush the steps. Instead, he relented as she tugged. With reluctant movements, he allowed her to pull him around, lead him through the crowd and down the road as the thuds of fist against flesh began.

Naya was right. She had to get him away. His hand tightened around hers and she picked up the pace.

They were nearly the same height; running with him didn't feel unnatural. They moved through Abredea quickly. Juliana kept her grip on his hand. Even as they reached the field. Even as they got to the fence, slipped through, and raced to the forest.

She didn't stop until they reached the small clearing he'd taken her to on her first trip into the forest. Months ago. When Jimmy had been on the verge of death, and they'd done the impossible to get his medicine.

They'd done the impossible again when they brought in the food for Abredea. Yet, injustices like today's in the square were still happening.

Juliana slowed to a stop in the center of the clearing. The brilliant green grass fluttered in the soft breeze. The clouds hadn't reached here yet, the storm moving slowly. Tree branches waved gently around them, the leaves on some turning orange and gold as they days grew colder. Sunlight shone down through gaps in the leaves. Ahead of them, the little stream babbled away, flowing over rocks and around bends as it cut through the clearing.

Seconds passed. Juliana waited. Anthony's calloused palm tightened for a moment, then he released her hand. He turned away, every muscle tense with anger.

"Anthony," Juliana said.

He shook his head, pacing the clearing. "We should 'ave stayed. We should 'ave done somethin'."

"Anthony."

"*No*," he snapped. His hands curled to fists as he reached the thick row of trees surrounding them. "I should 'ave *done* somethin'."

"What could you have done?" Juliana demanded. "They were going to punish Owen no matter what. What could you have *possibly* done to help the situation?"

He didn't answer. He stood with his back to her, his shoulders shaking. A moment passed with only the wind making any sound.

Juliana took half a step toward him, not knowing what to say. What to do.

An anguished cry split the air and Anthony swung; his fist connected with the tree in front of him.

Juliana froze, her heart aching as he pummeled the rough bark of the tree over and over. Flecks of blood flew through the air. Anthony's shouts, splintering with sadness, fury, faded to sobs.

Juliana gritted her teeth against her own tears and strode forward. She took hold of his arm as he raised it again.

He jerked back. His dark eyes met hers with wild confusion.

She tightened her fingers around his forearm. "Anthony. Stop."

The confusion cleared. His face was reddened and puffy, heavy bags under his eyes, tears streaked down his cheeks.

"What did you do?" she murmured. She lowered his arm, cradling his hand in hers.

The skin was torn. Ripped down to the bone in some spots. Blood oozed from his knuckles and he winced as she moved his fingers for a better look.

"I don't..." Anthony swallowed.

"Come here." Juliana led him to the shallow creek and knelt at its edge.

Anthony grimaced and let out a low moan as she cupped a handful of water and dribbled it on his injured hand. Flecks of bark and dirt had burrowed deep into his skin. They didn't budge as she rinsed his hand.

"This is going to hurt," Juliana muttered. She didn't wait for Anthony's response, but plunged his hand into the clear creek.

He yelped as the water stung his bare wounds. She rubbed, as gently as she could, slowly teasing the detritus from his bloodied hand.

"I was almost seven when they took me from Dave and Naya's and put me in the children's home." Anthony winced again as her thumb brushed against a particularly deep gash.

Juliana paused in her cleaning. She looked up at him, but he stared at the water before them, his eyes unfocused, his voice flat.

"The man who ran the place didn't like kids. He didn't 'ave any kind of patience and he thought..." a low growl sounded at the back of his throat. "He thought it was funny when we were hurtin'. I ran away every day. To my mum's house. Technically it was mine after she died, but I couldn' stay there 'till I was old enough." He shook his head. "I ran away every day for almost seven years 'till they stopped botherin' tah come for me. That's when I told May about him. After I was outta that place and he couldn' hurt me anymore, I told her wha' he was doin', and she put a stop to it. She made sure he never went near that place again."

Juliana stared at him, horror in her gut, her heart a lump in her throat. "That's why when Steel first arrived. When the little girl..."

Anthony nodded; his jaw tight. "When he tried tah hit her I lost some sense, I guess." He finally met Juliana's eye. "I swore to myself I'd never let another child be treated that way. I'd never let it happen if there was somethin' I could do tah stop it." His lips trembled and his voice shook. "Those kids," he looked away from Juliana, "if anythin' 'appens to 'em..."

"Anthony." Juliana lifted his hand from the water and rested it against her knee. Blood and water seeped into her pants, sending a chill down her leg. "There was nothing you could have done."

He clenched his free hand into a fist and swallowed hard.

"I'm serious." Juliana moved her hand to his chin, gentle fingers lifting his gaze to hers. "If you had tried anything, Steel would have had you. He probably would have killed you this time. And he'd have hurt them far more than he's hurting them now. Only because *you* got involved."

She dropped her hand as tears slid down Anthony's cheeks. He stared at her for a long moment. The two of them sat in silence at the edge of the creek, birds twittering above them, water lapping upon rocks.

Finally, he nodded. "I can't stand bein' 'elpless."

"I know." Juliana's fingers took up their steady tapping. "When Steel was..." She grimaced and cleared her suddenly hoarse throat. "When he was hurting you..." She shook her head. "I kept thinking, after, what I could have done differently. What I could have said. I kept thinking that if I'd only stepped forward sooner maybe... maybe you wouldn't have gotten so hurt."

Anthony's dark eyes, black even in the clear light shining down on them, flickered for a moment. He stared at her, and then shook his head. "Nah." He gave half a grin. "He threw me from that balcony 'cause of me, not you."

"Why did you do it?" Juliana broke in. She hadn't meant to ask it, but now seemed the right time if there was any. "Why did you hit him?"

Anthony's face flushed. "He..." His jaw tightened; a muscle twitched along the sharp edge. "He said some things. Threatened Jimmy and Naya, and..."

Juliana frowned. "What?"

Anthony glared down at his hand. He flexed the fingers with a wince and blood began to ooze once more. "And you."

Juliana blinked. Anxiety, laced with fury, flooded her. Her hands trembled. She stared at them, following Anthony's gaze and studying the ripped flesh across his knuckles.

"He laughed at the idea of yeh all starvin' while I rotted away in a cell. He said when someone gets 'ungry enough, they'll do almost anythin' to get somethin' tah eat."

Juliana shook with anger. She looked at Anthony. His face was red, his body tense, his gaze still fixed on his hand.

She inhaled, the fresh scents of the woods filling her. On the exhale, some of her rage left her body. Not all of it, but enough.

"I don't think he foresaw hijacking a truck as one of the anythings," she said with a sly grin.

Anthony met her gaze as she chuckled. His chest fell, broad shoulders relaxed. He huffed a breath, then broke into a grin, then his laugh split the air. He brushed his free hand through the long dark locks surrounding his face. "No, I doubt he did," Anthony said. "People 'ave a history of underestimatin' you, Jules."

She shrugged.

"Really."

Heat flushed her face, and she lifted his hand to distract herself with inspecting his wound for more debris.

"Jules," Anthony murmured.

She swallowed. "This needs to be cleaned more before I wrap it."

"Jules." He reached his free hand across and took hold of hers. "I know it was hard for you, comin' 'ere."

A shiver went down her spine. Memory of that day, the locket ripped from her neck, the deep black hole in the wall, the horror of seeing her gemstones gleaming pearly white.

"But I'm..." he ducked his head, forcing his face into her down-cast view. Drawing her gaze up as he locked eyes with her. "I'm really glad yer here."

Another shiver. Different. No memories flooding her mind this time. Instead, heat slammed across her chest and stomach.

She took a breath. "I think..." Her brow furrowed as she dug through her head and heart to determine if she was about to tell the truth. "I think I'm glad I'm here too."

The half-cocked grin she'd grown so accustomed to split across his earnest expression. They sat quietly for another moment. Juliana swallowed a yearning she couldn't quite explain. Anthony still held her hand, the callouses on his palm and fingers rough against her softer skin.

On her leg, his other hand still bled.

"Shit," she muttered, breaking from his gaze. "This is going to hurt again."

He nodded.

Juliana took her hand from his and as gently as possible, lowered his back into the water. The clear liquid swirled and darkened with blood as it flowed downstream.

She watched the water. Frowned. It *wasn't* flowing downstream.

A swirling eddie of bloody water had formed. Ignoring the laws of physics, it circled Juliana and Anthony's hands.

A shudder went through Juliana. From her core, the very center of her chest, heat blossomed. It traveled up, warming her, and flowed down her arms.

Her hands shook.

"Wha'?" Anthony had noticed the water as well. "Jules, what's..."

He fell silent.

Blue light—electric and bright—seeped from Juliana's fingertips. She recognized it instantly as the warmth which had gone through her, manifesting in thin tendrils which swam through the water.

Juliana's eyes were wide. She stared, transfixed.

The light touched upon Anthony's knuckles. It pulled back, just for a moment, before sliding up and caressing the ruined skin.

Juliana's arms trembled. Her head swam as the skin on Anthony's hand begin to heal.

"Jules?" Anthony's voice sounded distant. It echoed in her ears as though she stood on the other side of a long tunnel.

New flesh grew, covering the patch of white where his bone had been visible, fusing together the jagged gashes across his fingers. Dirt and bark seeped into the swirling water.

The blue light faded. Anthony's hand was healed, clean skin in place of what had been ripped and bleeding only a moment before. The bloody water moved away, picked up by the flow of the stream once again.

An ache built in the back of Juliana's head.

Anthony pulled his hand from the water. He stared at it. Flexed his fingers. Tightened his fist. Then gazed, open mouthed, at Juliana.

Still on her knees beside the creek, she swayed. The pain spread, seeping forward through her brain until it pierced just behind her eyes. Everything swam in shadow.

She opened her mouth—to scream or tell Anthony she was about to pass out—but no sound came. Her eyes fluttered closed. Her suddenly heavy body tilted. She sank into darkness.

Chapter Forty-Two

Years Ago - Abredea

Maybelle leaned into her husband's body. He wrapped a comforting arm around her, his other hand coming up to wipe away her tears.

Anya, her daughter, squeezed her hand and planted a kiss on her cheek. Then she moved across the circle of mourners.

In the center lay a plain wooden box, Kate's name delicately carved into the surface. A wreath of wildflowers rested at the foot.

The sky grew dark, sunset casting an impressive show of light and color against the clouds. Maybelle smiled through her tears; Kate would have loved this sunset. They'd sat together almost every evening over the past few months as the sickness grew in her friend, watching the sun go down.

She gazed across the casket at her son and daughter, on either side of Kate's daughter. She was fifteen now, a beautiful, kind, thoughtful young woman. Close friends with Anya and not-so-secretly dating Dave.

Kate died young—at least for their kind. Still, the years they'd spent in the camp hadn't been unhappy ones. It took her a long time to get pregnant. Three miscarriages, two stillbirths, and she'd finally had her baby girl. Not long after Maybelle's own daughter's first birthday.

Pregnancy had made her weak and the birth left her in bed for months. But she'd loved little Naya with all her heart. Maybelle did too. Her son slid his fingers through Naya's, closing around her hand and pulling her into him as she began to sob.

Their group was small. Kate's husband, hand on her casket, tears running into his thick beard. Maybelle and Tony, their children, and a few remaining friends from the days of the rebellion. Time did not treat them the way it had treated Kate and Maybelle. They had said goodbye to most since the rebellion had ended.

Maybelle leaned closer to her husband, breathing in the comfort of his scent. Tears flowed down her cheeks, along her jagged scar, and dripped onto the russet dirt beneath their feet. It was hard to feel alone, surrounded by her family...

But Kate had been by her side since they were children. Since that first day in class, the two of them intent on making mischief and keeping each other out of trouble.

She sucked in a shaky breath and exhaled half a chuckle, half a sob. Tony shifted, pulling her close to his chest. She leaned into his sturdy frame, closed her eyes, and cried. Grateful he was there with her in this moment.

Chapter Forty-Three

Present Day - Early Fall - Underneath Tornim

"You're sure about this?" Jason murmured into Cho's ear as they trudged along behind Carthik.

Cho grimaced.

Jane hobbled along beside Luna, leaning on her for support. Tommy clenched his sister's hand. Claire walked slowly, her eyes hazy and unfocused, clinging to Cho's arm. Jason carried Nova on his back, his backpack across his chest. Her ankle was still swollen and dark, even after the medicine.

Ahead of them all, Carthik strode down the dimly lit tunnel. This was a different part of the sewers, one Cho had never seen, even with all of his exploring in and under Agora. Then again, they weren't under Agora now.

"I'm sure this is our only way out," Cho hissed out the side of his mouth. "Neither of us have the gemstones to get through the gate, Jason."

"I know," Jason said. He had an almost apologetic expression. "I'm just checking in. I don't trust any of this."

"Me neither," Cho admitted. He glanced ahead. Carthik had paused for the fourth time to wait for them to catch up. "Still, it's our best shot."

Jason nodded. Nova met Cho's eye from Jason's back.

"I can't walk," she whispered, "but I can still fight if we need to."

Cho clenched his jaw and gave her a grateful nod. His heart ached.

A fight was coming no matter how this portion of their journey played out. Even if Carthik wasn't going to betray them... their family was alive.

"We're here," Carthik's thick voice interrupted Cho's thoughts.

Cho stepped forward, leaving Claire to lean on Jason. Ahead of them was a cement wall. Thick, flat, and without any visible door. "What now?"

Carthik reached for the wall. He pressed a small square in the upper left corner.

Cho's hands flew to cover his ears as a deafening, harsh grating sound echoed through the tunnel. The wall ahead of them shifted. It inched to the side, an opening appearing along a seam in the middle of the concrete. The doorway grew to about four feet wide and stopped. Darkness lay beyond.

Cho stared at Carthik.

The older man met his gaze with wary eyes. "This is where it gets tricky. Stay quiet while I talk to them. Keep yourselves as small and inconspicuous as possible."

Cho swallowed and nodded. Claire took his arm again.

Carthik pulled an orb from his bag, flicked a switch to turn it on, and walked through the opening.

Cho glanced at the others. Jane met his gaze and jerked her head in a small nod. Jason heaved a sigh and nodded as well.

Cho followed Carthik.

The other side of the wall was more tunnel. Shorter this time, made of stone and brick. As they moved forward, lights became visible in a cavern beyond.

Carthik darted a glance back at them before he stepped through, shutting off the orb in his hand and sticking it back into his bag.

They emerged into a large room, maybe twice the size of the main room in Haven. Tables lined the walls, gaps left for doorways and open tunnels. There were chairs and a couch, encircling a rectangular heating box. Stacks of crates, barrels, and lumpy bags took up space along the far wall—on either side of its singular physical door.

A collection of people lounged about the room.

Cho took a breath as everyone entered behind him and poured more energy into his mental defenses. Hints of emotion drifted toward him, but his saffron power was clamped down.

"I thought you were joking," came a voice from the couch. An androgynous figure rose, sturdy frame, red hair shaved close on one side and braided back against their skull on the other. They wore thick, multi-pocketed pants, a black tank-top, and heavy boots.

Cho tightened his grip on Claire's arm as he spotted the holster on their hip. His gaze flicked around the room, and he swallowed. Each person carried a weapon. Each non-Black-Star person. A life sentence in a prison up north—worse than the camps...

That was the punishment for anyone without black gemstones on their temples possessing a gun.

"The coin I gave you wasn't a joke," Carthik called back, striding into the room.

Around him, men and women closed in. There were maybe a dozen. A chill went down Cho's spine.

"You've got to admit," the person stretched with a groan, "shuttling a bunch of brats isn't what you're known for. I figured the coin was for whatever we were really seeing you about."

Carthik shook his head. He reached back a hand and gestured for Cho and the rest of them to move forward.

With a glance at Jason and Jane, Cho obliged. His footsteps, and those of his friends, echoed against the stone walls.

"I was honest with you, Kendra. Just passing through to get them on the other side."

Kendra slunk forward, like a cat prowling around a mouse. "Interesting." They flashed a set of white teeth. "Why do the kiddies need to leave the city?" Their gaze moved from Cho, standing at the front of the group, to Jason. "Ooh, you're not a child, are you, boy?"

Cho's gut twisted at the expression on their face as they moved closer. He gritted his teeth and opened a crack in the wall holding his power in check. Saffron tendrils sprang forward, latching around the lust, amusement, and greed leeching from Kendra.

Jason remained silent. Cho glanced at him, reading the apprehension on his face. Over his shoulder, Nova's gaze darted around the room, her eyes wide.

"A child, not yet through the Coding," Carthik said.

Kendra had crossed the room and stood between them and their smuggler. Cho shifted his arm, circling Claire's waist in case they needed to move quickly.

"Really?" Kendra inched closer, staring unabashed at Jason. They circled him, forcing Luna, Jane, and Tommy to move to the side. Their eyes glistened as they turned back to Carthik. "He looks old enough for it."

"Look again." Carthik's voice was steady, but Cho's power picked up his growing anxiety. "His gems are as unsteady as your aim."

There was a flicker of movement. Cho stepped back, nearly bumping into Jane, as hands twitched towards holsters all around them. Half a dozen people moved forward; two stepped in front of the wooden door.

Kendra's gaze darted to Carthik. The man smiled and cocked his head. Kendra snorted and then laughed. The sound shattered the tension in the room.

"Fair enough," Kendra said, backing away from Jason. Their hands went into their pockets as they strode toward Carthik. "Still, this doesn't seem like the kind of thing you do."

"I'm branching out," Carthik muttered as Kendra circled him instead.

"A hundred." Kendra shook their head. "That feels..." They pulled a familiar bag from one of their pockets.

Cho attempted to keep his surprise from his face. It was the bag he'd given Carthik the day before. The payment he'd brought to their meeting, in the hopes that the man would be able to find a way to smuggle them out of the city.

"... low."

Cho's breath caught.

Anger flashed across Carthik's face. He turned with Kendra as they moved around him. "It's what we agreed upon. I gave you the head count. We agreed on a hundred for passage through."

Kendra shrugged one shoulder. "Now I've seen 'em though." Their lip twitched. "They look old enough for the adult rate."

A shiver went down Cho's spine. They didn't have anything else.

Carthik's jaw clenched. He looked at Cho, a furrow in his brow.

"Unless..." Kendra turned away from Carthik, their gaze fixing again on Jason. "We can always do an exchange."

Cho stepped. He didn't do it on purpose, didn't mean to move his body in front of Jason's, and almost regretted it as he had to tug Claire along with him to keep her upright. But it happened. He moved, straightening as he stared at Kendra, trying to keep his expression neutral as fury roiled through him.

Kendra laughed. "Relax, child. I hire plenty of people to work for me. I'm simply suggesting he," they jerked their head at Jason, "work off what it costs for you to go through. After that he can join you."

"No."

Kendra's smile flickered and faded, a sneer replacing the easy expression. They turned to Carthik. "No?"

"No," he repeated.

"I have something."

Everyone stopped and turned. Jane stepped forward, walking on her injured leg but giving no sign that it hurt. Behind her, Tommy clenched Luna's hand, fear, and confusion in his eyes.

"What could you have to offer me?" Kendra said.

Jane's lip curled into her usual snarl. "There's a box. A box of coin in the sewers in Agora. It's where we got that." She gestured to the bag still in Kendra's hand. "It's hard to get to. Which is why we haven't gone back for more. But there's at least double what's in your hand."

"Right," Kendra scoffed, "and you'll tell me where it is if I let you leave."

Jane shrugged. "It's an easy score. We did the hard part. You just have to pick it up."

Kendra hesitated. Their gaze moved around the room, watching their people as murmurs began to fill the space. The idea of hundreds of coins, sitting ready and waiting in a sewer tunnel, was tempting.

With a final, appraising glance at Jason, Kendra nodded. They looked at Carthik. "You've got a smart group here. Sure you don't want 'em working for me? Might be useful."

"I made a deal to get them out. That's the only reason we are here." Carthik's tone was polite, but Cho felt the cold fury in his words as much as he felt his own heated blood.

Kendra waved a hand. "Fine then. Girl, give me the location and you can leave."

Jane hesitated. She caught Cho's eye. He nodded.

There was a moment of stillness in the rest of the room as Jane crossed to one of the tables and drew a simple map for Kendra. The cross-streets were easy enough, but getting to the room with the chest in it was more difficult. Explaining how to access it without mentioning their powers...

Cho was impressed with Jane's ability to lie.

Kendra straightened, folding up the piece of paper and sticking it into their back pocket. They pointed to a woman leaning against a table and then to the door. The woman stood with a scowl.

"See you soon then, Carthik. Don't get into too much trouble out there, kiddies." A sneering grin slid across their face again and Cho couldn't help his grimace.

Kendra's people opened the massive wooden door against the far wall. The woman Kendra had called up went first. Jane strode through after Carthik, still giving no sign as to her injury. Cho waited as Luna and Tommy followed her. He jerked his head as Jason motioned for him to go first.

With a glare and a sigh, Jason moved through the doorway, Cho and Claire close on his heels.

Carthik flicked on his orb before the door closed behind them. With a glance at their group, he turned and followed the woman down a long stone tunnel and up an uneven flight of stairs. Jane joined Luna and Tommy at the back of the group. Cho glanced at her once, caught sight of the pain on her face, and then the glare she directed at him.

"Almost there," Carthik murmured.

Anxiety seeped through everyone's defenses. Cho felt it, embraced it because along with that anxiety was a sense of purpose. A feeling of excitement. Hope.

They reached the top of the stairs and came face to face with a massive concrete structure.

The woman stood to the side, lifted the tablet of glass she'd been carrying, and clicked the surface. It lit up.

"Give us a second," Carthik said. Then he turned to Cho. "This is it."

Cho glanced at the wall ahead of them.

Carthik nodded. "Once you go through there, you'll be outside the city."

Cho nodded.

Carthik moved to the side, away from the woman. Cho followed him, the others close behind. "You'll want to make for the forest. You're less likely to be spotted there. Do you..." his gaze roamed over their group. "Do you have a plan for when you get there?"

"We have to find the others," Cho whispered.

Carthik gave an approving nod. He rifled through his bag and pulled out a map. "I dug this out for you." He unfolded it.

Cho leaned forward, Jason and Jane coming up on either side of him to get a look as well. He recognized the map from his school days. It was Pangaea. The entire country, laid out before them. Ocean to the west, mountains to the north and south, a massive river and desert expanse to the east. And Tornim, nearly in the center with a smaller range of mountains just west of them.

Cho cocked his head. The map was marked. Small points of red ink dotted three areas. One moderately close, the other two very far from their city.

Carthik pointed, his scarred finger brushing one of the points. "I took the liberty of marking a few places you might check first."

Cho met his gaze with wide eyes.

"I've heard rumors," Carthik said. "We all have. Research facilities running experiments, tests. We think they're trying for a weapon. I can't..." He grimaced and glanced at the woman standing against the opposite wall. "I can't help you beyond this," he gestured at the wall, "but if you find them—*when* you find them—head south. Get to the mountains if you can. There are... well, get to the mountains if you can. You might find help there."

Tendrils of saffron power danced through Cho. They reached out, caressing the regret, the anxiety, the hope seeping off the man before him. He cared. He wanted them to succeed. The power of his hope, his genuine desire to do more and the frustration that he couldn't, brought burning to Cho's nose and eyes. He blinked back the tears and nodded.

"Thank you for this. We didn't... I can't pay you for this."

Carthik waved his hand, folding up the map and handing it to Cho. "You've paid enough. I wish..." his gaze flicked to Jane and Nova, "I wish your brother had trusted me more. We might have managed this from the beginning. Though," he sighed and glanced again at the woman who was now clicking her tongue with a sneer on her face, "I understand why he didn't. The farming fields are to the north. You might have luck finding a transport there."

Jason cracked a grin. "Now you're talking."

Carthik chuckled. "Be careful. They have Black-Stars running the patrols these days." He nodded at the woman. She tapped her tablet, and they all covered their ears as the massive concrete before them ground to either side. Cool air hit them. It was dark still, the sun not yet risen enough to light the sky.

"Thank you, Carthik," Cho murmured.

The man nodded. "Good luck."

Cho stepped out, the others close behind him.

Long blades of grass came up to his knees. The dirt beneath his feet was soft. It sank under him, cushioning his weight. The air was clear, crisp, and slightly sweet.

The wall slid closed behind them. Carthik stood on the other side, watching until the last few inches cut him from sight. With him, went the light from his orb.

Cho blinked in the darkness. He and the others put the wall to their backs as their eyes adjusted. Moonlight danced across the sky. Stars, slightly obscured by the clouds, twinkled through the dark.

"Well then," Cho breathed. He glanced around. Ahead of them was an expanse of grass leading to the edge of a large outcropping of black shapes. The forest.

"Let's go," Jane said. She started forward, limping, but leading the way with Tommy by her side.

Cho and Jason exchanged a glance.

"Hardest part is done, right?" Jason said with a half-grin.

Cho looked toward the forest. He inhaled, the cold air sending a shiver down his spine. "I don't think so. I have a feeling the hardest part is a ways off still."

Jason chuckled. "Yeah. I figured you'd say that."

They moved together, slowly making their way toward the forest, away from everything they'd ever known. One step closer to getting their family back.

Chapter Forty-Four

Present Day - Early Fall - May's House

"What *happened?*" Anthony demanded. His expression was fierce, his voice harsh.

Juliana inhaled the steam from her jasmine mint tea. She sat at May's kitchen table; her gaze locked on the old woman. Her tone was soft as she murmured, "If anyone knows what's going on, it's you, May."

Only a few hours had passed since their time in the woods. Anthony had carried Juliana until she regained consciousness, then helped her get back through the fence and to May's. A half-eaten plate of food sat before her. Between it and the tea, she no longer felt dizzy and lightheaded.

Her confusion had yet to fade.

Anthony had filled May in while Juliana ate and took long, slow sips from her tea with trembling fingers. May listened raptly, leaning against the kitchen counter. Until Anthony got to the part about the glowing blue light emitting from Juliana's hands. Until he explained the sensation of watching and feeling his skin stitch itself back together, growing over an open wound and healing.

May hurried forward and took told of his hand, examining it closely. She glanced at Juliana. Then she sank into one of the kitchen chairs with a hand to her chest.

"May?" Anthony said. "Juliana passed out. She could 'ave been hurt. What is goin' on?"

May shook her head. "I never..." She met Juliana's gaze for a brief moment. "I never thought I'd see another one."

Juliana's chest heaved with anticipation and anxiety. She watched May intently. "Another *what?*" Anthony growled.

"Another *alter*," May replied. "And sit down, you're making me anxious with all that pacing."

Anthony blinked, the furrow in his brow lessening as he reluctantly lowered himself into a chair.

Juliana leaned forward. "What's an alter?"

May sighed. "This is a long tale."

"We have the time," Juliana said. She glanced at Anthony. "Was I really responsible for fixing his hand?"

"I believe so." May nodded. "I wasn't there, and I've never met someone with healing abilities, but from Anthony's description, yes."

"There are more people like this." Juliana examined her fingers—cold and lightless—before she settled back in her chair, cradling her mug.

Again, May nodded. "I should back up. Explain what else is going on before we dive too deep into alters."

Anthony grunted. "Any kind of explanation would be great at this point."

May chuckled. She rose, shaking hands pressing onto the table to support her weight. Once she'd straightened, she crossed to the tea kettle and poured herself a mug of tea. "It starts a long time ago. Centuries, maybe."

Anthony raised an eyebrow.

"Over a hundred years ago," Juliana whispered.

He nodded and May went on.

"I don't know the specifics. I doubt anyone does at this point. But what we do know is someone wanted power. They wanted to create a soldier with enhanced abilities. Physical prowess beyond anything they'd seen before."

She blew on her tea and took a sip before returning to her seat. "That's when the experiments began. People. Tortured, twisted, maimed, for the sole purpose of expanding some territory or another. Some country demanding more power." May shook her head. "They didn't achieve their goal. But they unleashed something else. They created people who live decades longer than the average human. People with a strange ability. People who could turn someone's will. Warmth seeps from them. A desire, a *need* to please them rises up and is nearly impossible to fight."

Something in May's description caused the little hairs on the back of Juliana's neck to rise. She frowned, her fingers tapping against the side of her cup. "Are you..." She glanced at Anthony and then back to May. "Are you talking about Grey-Stars?"

May ran a finger around the rim of her mug. She nodded. "I am."

Juliana exhaled through pursed lips. "That's... I remember feeling it." She looked at Anthony. "There was a woman—a Grey-Star at my Coding appointment. And I've met them through upper caste functions." Her eyes narrowed; mouth parted in disgust. "Is that how they gained control?" She stared at May. "They use this power on us?"

May's smile was the saddest Juliana had ever seen it. "Some Grey-Stars believe they are using their *suggestion* to keep the peace." She shook her head. "I'm getting side-tracked. There is more." She met Juliana's eye. "You learned about the plague in school?"

Juliana nodded. "Most of the people on planet were killed. The Grey-Stars brought Pangaea together, saved our country from the fate that befell the rest of the world."

Anthony snorted. "What?"

Juliana glanced at him. "You weren't taught that?"

"We didn't learn anythin' about the history of Pangaea. They explained the caste system. Told us there are dangers in the wild. White-Stars were criminals, and when it became too dangerous for 'em to live in the villages beyond the cities, the camps were built for us."

Juliana scoffed. "That's not..." She swallowed and shook her head. "In the city we're told the White-Stars were moved to camps because they were hurting people."

"Let me finish *my* story," May cut in, "and then you can exchange notes on your history lessons." She turned back to Juliana, "As I said, the people who created the Greys wanted physically perfect soldiers, not soldiers who had the power to control people's minds and live longer than anyone else. They kept up their work." Her scar twisted and glinted white as a snarl split across her lips. "Grey-Stars were imprisoned for many, many years. Until, one day, the researchers made a mistake."

"The plague," Anthony said.

She nodded. "They started something they could not control. It killed billions of people. Infrastructure crumbled, governments toppled, and the people who suffered the most were those living ordinary, simple lives." May swallowed and took a shuddering breath. She sipped her tea. "Your history wasn't entirely wrong," she directed at Juliana. "The Grey-Stars did pull Pangaea from the depths of chaos and ruin. They used their power to build what we have today."

Juliana shook her head. Her hands clenched her mug so tightly her fingers were white. Anthony reached across the table. His hands—so much warmer than hers—rested on her wrist. She met his gaze, saw the betrayal she felt echoed in his dark eyes. Her grip softened.

"What does this 'ave tah do with Juliana?" Anthony asked in a low voice.

"Ahh, yes. The heart of the matter." May smiled. "The plague did many things when it changed this world. One of them, was altering the DNA of the people who survived."

Juliana's eyes widened. She glanced at Anthony. He shrugged.

"Over the generations, certain people have... presented abilities. They usually emerge during moments of heightened emotion. Times when the blood is rushing, heart pounding, fury or fear or rage coursing through them." She cracked a grin. "My power emerged when I was taken by the rebels."

"Power?" Juliana said.

"Rebels?" Anthony said at the same time.

The two exchanged a glance as May's grin spread. She sucked in a deep breath, winked, and disappeared.

Juliana jolted back from the table. She glanced around the room, heart racing frantically. "May?"

Beside her, Anthony sat with wide eyes, staring at the spot where May had vanished, her empty chair and mug of tea all that was left.

A cackling laugh sounded from the door to the garden. "Over here," she croaked.

Anthony pushed back his chair and hurried through the kitchen. He returned a few seconds later, May leaning on his arm as she hobbled back to her seat. Her laughter grew as she took in their faces.

"We called ourselves *alters*," she groaned as she leaned back in her chair. Her skin was paler than it had been a few seconds ago. Her hands shook as she rested them on the table. She sighed, her expression turning wistful. "It's been a long time since I've done that."

Juliana gaped. "You have... you can..." she squinted, trying to think of the word, "teleport?"

May laughed again. "My friends called it 'zapping', but teleportation is the technical term."

Anthony stared at May. "That's amazin'." He frowned, circled the table and sunk back into his chair. "Why did yeh never..." he licked his lips, brow furrowed. "Why didn't yeh use it to leave? Tah hunt?"

May raised an eyebrow at him. "How do you think I got the dirt for my garden? Or the seeds for my plants? Who do you think put that hole in the fence, young man? I was walking those trails in the forest long before your uncle was born."

Something flickered in the back of Juliana's mind. A thought she couldn't quite grasp.

"There was a time," May continued, "when I could go almost anywhere." Her smile faded.

"Were you always so tired after?" Juliana asked. "Will I always..."

May shook her head. "No. If it had been a simple scrape, you'd have been fine. But broken bones, torn flesh, an injury like that... I'm guessing it took a lot to heal."

"What's making you so weak now?" Juliana said.

"I overextended myself. Years and years ago. There was... I was part of something that did not end well. A lot of people died. My power split from me for a moment, consumed me, and in doing so, I managed to save many lives. But there was a cost... More than one." Her fingers drifted to her scar. She stroked the tight white skin, tracing it down to her jaw. "I was never the same again. My ability, my power, was greatly weakened."

A heaviness settled on Juliana's chest. The three of them sat in silence for a moment before May's hand returned to her tea and she gave them a forced smile.

"Add on my old age and well, it makes sense that going further than a few feet tires me out." She looked to Juliana. "The more you use it, and I mean use it within your capabilities, not overdoing yourself like today, the stronger you'll become. I've never met someone able to heal, but if you're as strong as I think you'll be, it won't take long for you to do what you did today with little effort."

Juliana couldn't help the soft smile creeping across her face. She thought of Anthony, sprawled against those concrete steps, blood pooling beneath him. If she'd had this before... But she had it now. That was the important part.

"Why now?" Anthony asked.

May grimaced. "I believe it has something to do with how quickly you healed from your injuries. Those packets... I have no proof," she shook her head, "no evidence that I'm right, but I believe there is something in them that suppresses our abilities. It would explain why I've seen so few alters these past decades. And it makes sense," she sighed. "I was working to figure out a way to suppress the Grey-Star's *suggestion*. They'd have found a way to keep alter abilities hidden."

"But yeh..." Anthony frowned. "Yeh said yeh zapped into the forest before."

Juliana's eyes widened. She inhaled through parted lips. "You're a..." She glanced to May's temples. "You were a Grey-Star? Your genetic make-up is slightly different, so whatever is in the packets wouldn't have worked on you the same way."

May met Juliana's eyes and stared into them for a long moment. "You really are one of the smartest women I've known."

Juliana swallowed, her throat suddenly thick. Pride swelled in her chest.

"Yes," May pulled her long hair forward and sectioned it into three pieces, "I was a Grey-Star. A long time ago."

Anthony exhaled. "How did... what did... May."

May chuckled. "It's all a very long story, Anthony." Her smile fell. "And one I probably should have told you before now. When your mother died I..." A flash of grief, intense and vivid, went across May's face. "I wanted to tell you then, but I was still so scared. And then Dave—" her throat caught. A sob took the place of whatever words she was going to say.

Realization struck Juliana like a blow to the gut. She stared, from May to Anthony as little details clicked into place. Their expressions, the way they stood, the way she'd talked about his childhood, his mother. The way she and Naya were close. The way she doted upon Jimmy.

"No," Juliana breathed. She met Anthony's eyes and saw the confusion in them. Her chest compressed. She gaped at May. Her heart thundered against her ribs. "Why doesn't he know?"

Anthony swallowed. "Jules, what are yeh talkin' about?"

May shook her head, tears flowing down her cheeks. "So clever." She gave Juliana a sad, rueful smile. Then she turned to Anthony. "When the rebellion ended those of us who survived hid in the camps. Some managed to filter back into cities. But most of us..." She grimaced. "That's not so important now." She sucked in a shuddering breath. "I had a life here, after a time." She gave a little nod. "Kate and I, she was my closest friend, we had lives. Lovers..." She pursed her lips, a fresh set of tears cascading from her grey eyes. "Children."

Anthony pushed away from the table, leaning back in his chair as understanding took over his expression.

"Kate had Naya." May smiled. "And I had Anya and Dave."

Anthony rose. He strode across the kitchen to the door. The muscles in his neck twitched, his hands clenched and unclenched. When he turned back to face them, tears glistened in his angry, hurt eyes. "Why did yeh never tell me? You or Naya? Why keep it a secret that I 'ave a grandmother? Did yeh..." He swallowed, bracing himself on the counter. "Are yeh ashamed of me?"

"No," May exhaled. "Never. I..." she closed her eyes, pain etched across her face. "I have much to tell you. To start, the reason you never knew was to keep you safe."

"Whaddya mean?" Anthony murmured.

She told them. She started at the beginning, with her time as a Grey-Star. Her upbringing, her service as a medic in the military. Her capture by the rebels.

Anthony returned to the table and sat. Juliana heated another kettle of water.

May told them about a man named Red and a woman named Sam. A fellow Grey-Star who joined the rebellion with her, Kate—Naya's mother. She told them how the rebellion ended. How it imploded with death and treachery and betrayal.

"I met a man here, a decade after everything ended." She sighed. "I'd kept to myself, you know. Just me and Kate for a long time. And then she fell in love and I..." she smirked. "I had to leave the house every now and then and I found him. Or he found me." She looked at Anthony. "You have your grandfather's eyes." Her smile grew. "His hair too."

Anthony ran a hand across his face, his features twisted in a way that caused Juliana's heart to ache. "Why though?" he demanded. "Yeh still 'aven't explained why I never knew about him. About you."

May nodded. "I'm getting there."

She told them about the call from Sam's daughter. The help she'd asked for. The man who'd been waiting. Hunting May the whole time.

May swallowed as Juliana refilled her tea. "Ben died before I got any answers. Grey-Stars..." She grimaced. "Many of us can't have children. In the past few generations, many have been born without *suggestion*. I was a traitor to my people. But beyond that... I had powers. And *two* children." Her lips trembled as she shook her head. "I knew what they'd do to Anya and Dave if they ever... If they found me, found out about my children, we would suffer a life of torture and experimentation. They'd tear us apart to find out how I have the power I have. To find out if my children had power equal to Grey-Stars."

More tears flowed from May's eyes. She wiped them away and sat in silence for a long moment, sipping from her tea and staring across the room.

Juliana looked to Anthony. He'd barely moved while May spoke. One hand rested on the tabletop, the other across his lap. Juliana reached out. Her fingers brushed against the knuckles that—only a few hours ago—had been a bloody mess.

Anthony caught her gaze. His lips twitched at the corners. Half of a broken smile as he gave her a shallow nod.

"I lived apart from my children and my husband for the remainder of their lives." May's jaw was tight as she spoke. "Most of the people who knew Kate and I from the rebellion had long since passed. We kept to ourselves here. Tony kept the home we'd built near the square, and I moved here." Something glinted in her eyes, a memory that brough a soft smile to her lips. "We were happy still. Through it all, my children knew me. As they grew older, they understood the need for caution. They understood why they called me May in public and Mama when we were alone." She swallowed.

Anthony moved his hand across the table toward his grandmother. Her lips trembled as her gnarled, wrinkled fingers were covered by his.

"I don't know if you remember," she murmured. "But you stayed here after Anya died. While Dave and Naya were trying to figure out keeping you. And then off and on before the Red-Stars took you."

"I remember," he said. "I remember yeh singin' tah me. After she died. Yeh sang me tah sleep."

She heaved a breath. "I tried so hard to keep you at your uncle's. But I'd lost my *suggestion* long before then."

Anthony stood and pulled May to her feet. Her stooped form barely reached his chin as he tightened his arms around her. She embraced him as well. Stroked his head as he cried into her shoulder.

Juliana quietly rose from the table and crossed the kitchen. She shut the door behind her, holding it until the latch closed before she walked through the sprawling garden. Her mind swirled. Emotions slammed against each other like waves fighting the wind in a storm.

Anthony's grandmother.

She shook her head with a grin. They'd have to have a dinner to celebrate. In a few years Jimmy would be old enough to keep the secret. She'd talk May into it. Into letting them be a real family again.

Ache slipped through the happiness in her chest. Her fingers went to her throat, to the spot her locket would have rested against her skin. She wanted to see her parents' faces. How much time would pass before she forgot what they looked like?

Tears burned at the edges of her eyes. She shivered. Rubbed her hands up and down her arms as she looked to the west. The sun was split in half by the horizon. A few more minutes and darkness would fall. The early autumn air would grow colder still.

What did winter look like here?

"Jules?"

Juliana turned. Anthony stood at the doorway, his eyes red, but a contentment on his face she'd never seen before.

"The family's all right."

Juliana tilted her head, a brief moment of confusion crossing her face.

"Owen and Lillian. Steel gave Owen a lashin', but tha' was it. May says they're back at home, some people are bringin' 'em food."

She nodded. "Good. That's good."

There was a pause between them.

"So, dinner?" he said. "I told May we want tah hear more stories from the rebellion. I'm curious about the woman with diamond skin."

"That sounds great."

He hesitated. Then he stepped outside, letting the door fall shut behind him. "I don't think..." He swallowed and took another step toward her. "I don't think any of this would 'ave come out if yeh weren't here. I wouldn't 'ave known. Maybe ever."

She looked at her hands. At the fingertips that had channeled the blue light, the warmth inside her manifested into something real. "I wish I'd had this before. When Steel was hurting you."

His lips slid sideways into his crooked grin. "Yeah, that makes two of us."

She met his dark gaze. Behind her, the sun dipped below the mountains. The bright yellows and oranges in the sky shifted to reds and purples.

"I think... if it weren't for you, I'd never have found this." Juliana glanced at her fingers again. "This power." She bit her lip. Her heartbeat pounded at an impossible rate.

Anthony took another step. His hand moved to her arm, resting gently against her skin. "I meant what I said before. I'm really glad yer..." He paused and swallowed, inches from her.

Juliana leaned forward—they were nearly the same height—and pressed her lips against his. Then, wide-eyed and breathing fast, she moved away and hurried inside, her lips burning from where they'd touched his warm skin.

Chapter Forty-Five

Present Day - Early Fall - Abredea

Juliana strode down the dust-coated cobblestone road toward Daisy's house. Her fingers tapped against her thumb, heart pounding. Anthony would meet her at the fountain. He was fetching Taz.

They'd stayed up most of the night, prying story after story from May. She'd told tales of the rebellion that Juliana almost didn't believe, they were too fantastical, too impossible. Then again, just yesterday, she'd healed shattered skin with blue light from her hands.

May also told them about Anthony's family. His grandfather—and name-sake—who started the family tradition of hunting, with help from May. His mother, responsible for the delicate paintings on all of May's furniture. Dave, and his penchant for getting into trouble, even as a little boy. A trait Anthony inherited.

Anthony had reluctantly gone home in the early, dark hours of the morning. Sleep dragged at them all as he said goodbye to Juliana and May on the steps of the porch.

Juliana reached Daisy's front door and banged on it with a closed fist. It was early. The sun glinted on the horizon, barely peaking over the edge of the city wall.

Someone shouted inside the house. Something crashed to the ground.

Juliana gritted her teeth. She clamped her hand around the doorknob. It was unlocked. She shoved inside and strode down the front hall. Sounds were coming from the kitchen. Cursing. Slamming.

Juliana burst through the swinging kitchen doors. Her hands clenched into fists, hate rushing through her.

Daisy stood by the sink, a broken dish on the floor at her feet. She'd dressed for the day, loose pants, and a pale lavender top. Her hair was done up in a braid, a bit of flour on her cheek. On the counter before her sat a lump of half-kneaded dough. Daisy was shaking. Her jaw was red, a small cut on her lip and a drop of blood on her chin.

Marsterson leaned with his palms against the long kitchen table. He was in shorts, bare chested and screaming at her.

The rage in her expanded. It consumed her. Heated her chilly hands and flared like a fire in her chest.

"Daisy." Her voice shook.

Daisy looked at her, surprise in her tear-filled eyes.

"Come on." Juliana stepped forward, her boots crunching on the broken porcelain. "Come with me."

"She's not going anywhere," Marsterson snarled.

Juliana ignored him. The majority of her was thrashing, screaming to attack. To make him hurt the way he hurt Daisy. To claw his frosted eyes out. A tiny sliver of her brain remained in control, tethering her rage to the knowledge that once she got Daisy out of that house, she could heal her lip. That once they got to Anthony and Taz, Daisy would be safe, warm, and loved.

She reached out. Daisy took her outstretched hand, her gaze locked on Juliana.

Juliana clasped her hand tighter as they walked down the hall, Marsterson's heavy footsteps thudding behind them. Daisy's fingers trembled in hers.

They moved through the still open front door. Marsterson reached the doorway and called after them. Juliana barely registered his voice. Fury buzzed in her ears, drowning other sounds.

Daisy didn't speak as they hurried into the square. Anthony and Taz were waiting for them at the still dry fountain. Anthony took one look at the two of them and strode forward.

"Wha' happened?"

Juliana shook her head, biting her lip with a grimace. "Let's get out of here. I'll explain later."

Daisy glanced at her and the tears which had been waiting to fall, finally did.

"Daisy?" Taz hurried forward, taking her free hand. "What's wrong?"

Juliana met Anthony's gaze with a fierce look. "Not here."

He nodded, turned, and led the way as the four of them moved through Abredea toward the field, the fence, and the freedom waiting for them in the woods.

"Is that the first time he's hit yeh?" Anthony growled.

They had reached the clearing where Juliana healed his hand the day before. She sat against a large rock, rubbing soft circles on Daisy's shoulder blades. Her friend nodded with a sniff. She rubbed her palm across her cheeks where the tears had yet to stop falling.

"It's not the first time he's hurt you, though," Juliana murmured. She met Anthony's gaze and saw the fury there.

Beside him, Taz paced the clearing, rolling his neck and clenching and unclenching his fists. "I'm gonna kill him. I'm gonna rip out his heart. I'm gonna—"

"Taz," Anthony interrupted. "Give it a rest, it's not helpin'." He gestured to Daisy.

Their friend sat next to Juliana, her knees tucked into her chest, sucking in shallow breaths, and shaking her head. "I didn't..." she sniffed. She cleared her throat and pressed against her closed eyes with both hands until Juliana took her wrists and pulled them away.

"You didn't do anything wrong," Juliana said, her voice cold.

Daisy shook her head. "I know. I know he's a piece of shit. I know I don't deserve any of it. But..." she heaved a shaky sigh, "there's also nothing I can do about it. I'm stuck there for another year."

Juliana met Anthony's eye. "There might be something we can do, but let us worry about that."

Daisy glanced at her. Her face was red and puffy, her lip swollen, a hollow look in her eyes. "What..."

"Jules," Anthony cut in, "do yeh want tah show our friends what yeh discovered yesterday?"

Juliana nodded, grateful for an excuse not to talk about what they were going to do to Daisy's father at that moment. They'd find a time to talk it over with her, and make sure she was all right with what needed to happen to stop him ever touching her again, but this wasn't it.

"What?" Taz asked as Juliana rose to her feet.

She reached out a hand and pulled Daisy up as well. They stood together, the four of them in a circle in the cool morning air. "This is... going to be strange," she murmured.

Daisy gave her a wary look. "Is everything all right?"

Juliana nodded. "Just... hold still for me, will you?"

"Yeah." Daisy glanced at Anthony.

In the corner of her eye, Juliana saw him offer up a reassuring smile.

"Anthony?" she said.

"Yeah?"

"Catch me if I pass out again?"

He chuckled. "Always."

A flutter went through her chest at that. At the warmth of his voice, the growl in his throat, the way his tongue danced around the word.

She pushed it down. "Here we go."

Sucking in a breath, Juliana turned to face Daisy. She closed her eyes, reaching inward the way May had explained it. Reaching into her mind and her heart and feeling for a core of heat. Of power.

There.

She felt it more than saw it. Felt the heat. The raw energy. A swirling ball of chaos and light. In her mind's eye it spiraled, shaped itself into an orb. She reached out, a tentative piece of her prodded the lightning-blue sphere.

It burst. Light and energy and crackling power rushed her body. Heat spread through each limb even as she tried to tighten it, control it.

Juliana breathed deep. She slowed her mind. Slowed the whirling vortex within until it settled back into the orb. This time she didn't prod. She pulled. Pinched two invisible fingers together and drew a spark of blue light from her core.

She opened her eyes. Her thumb and forefinger were pinched before her, clinging to something that wasn't there. She felt it though, in her arm, her hand, her fingertips... that warmth.

Parting her lips with a shaky breath, she reached toward Daisy.

Her friend stared, eyes wide as Juliana held out her hand and hesitated, less than an inch from the cut on Daisy's lip.

She pressed a finger to the wound. Blue light flowed, caressing the cut, melting into Daisy's skin and giving it a blueish tinge as it rolled through the bruise on her jaw.

Before their eyes, Daisy's cut healed. Her lip returned to its normal size, the black and blue chunk of sore flesh reverted to its freckly tone. All that remained of her father's strike was a small drop of blood on her chin.

Juliana took a staggering step backward. Her mind spun, her vision hazy, but only for a moment. When she regained her footing, she didn't feel the exhaustion she had the day before. Instead, her limbs felt stronger. Her mind sharper. Elation spread as she took in her friend.

"That's what we wanted to show you," she panted. "Turns out, I'm more than just a pretty face."

Anthony broke into a grin. Taz stared, his gaze flicking between Juliana and Daisy with shock across his freckly face. Daisy watched Juliana, her mouth parted, her breath shallow, a furrow in her brow.

Fear trickled down Juliana's spine. She swallowed. It hadn't occurred to her that her friends might be scared of her new ability. Of the strangeness of her. A familiar anxiety grew in her stomach. Different. She'd spent a long time trying not to be different.

Her fingers tapped against her thumb as she stared at Daisy, waiting for a reaction.

Daisy shook her head, licked her lips, and exhaled with a smile. "That was..."

"*Amazin*'," Taz shouted.

Juliana chuckled in relief.

Daisy drew her into a hug. "That was incredible. How did... what?" she giggled, the sound filling the air. "Jules..."

"I know," Juliana said with a smile. "We have," she glanced at Anthony, "a lot to tell you."

Juliana and Anthony filled Daisy and Taz in as the four of them began the long trek to their stolen truck. Juliana had worried the food would go bad, but the solar panels on top kept the refrigeration unit powered.

Daisy and Taz took the news of the existence of people with powers, government conspiracy, and even the revelation about Anthony's family rather well. There was a lot of gasping, Taz slamming his hand across Anthony's shoulder in excitement, and a few tears as they explained what May had told them. As they realized their lives were the way they were in part because of the rebellion. Because of a chance at peace and equality which had failed.

Daisy took Juliana's hand as they moved through the trees, tears on her cheeks again. This time for the lives of people they'd never known.

They were a few minutes from the truck when Anthony paused. Taz almost stumbled into him but caught himself at the last minute.

Juliana's smile faded. She stepped forward, letting go of Daisy's hand and coming up next to Anthony. "What is it?"

He held up a hand. His head cocked to the side, a frown on his face. "There's somethin'—"

His words were cut short by a ball of fire shooting past his head close enough to singe his hair.

Daisy screamed. Taz pushed in front of Anthony, trying to move him out of the way. Anthony grunted, gripped Taz's upper arm, and heaved him to the side.

Juliana glanced around, searching for the source of the fire which had hit a large tree-trunk and disappeared with nothing but a scorch mark in its place.

"Who's there?" Anthony called, his voice sharp.

There was a long moment in which nothing happened, then figures stepped through the trees. Juliana frowned, her anxiety shifting to confusion. They were children. Most of them, at least.

A little boy, maybe Jimmy's age. Two girls, one on either side of him, the tall one with short dark hair limped as they moved closer. The other, with soft sandy blonde braids looked terrified. A man, dark skin and hair, with a girl identical to the one with braids on his back. Her ankle, sticking out the front as she clung to him, was wrapped with fabric. Ahead of them all, a boy, almost old enough for the Coding it looked like, stepped forward with a blonde girl clinging to his arm. His gaze was fierce and wary.

"Who are you?" the boy asked. "What are you doing out here?"

"We could ask the same," Anthony said. His tone had softened. "Yeh aren't from Abredea."

"Where?"

Juliana nodded. "They aren't." She frowned at the youngest looking girl. There was a bandage wrapped around her arm, faded blood dried onto the dirty gauze. "They're from Tornim."

Anthony's eyes went wide. He took half a step back.

"How would you know that?" the girl with dark hair demanded.

"Because." Juliana looked at her, taking in the limp, the way she clenched the little boy's hand. The way he held tight to hers as well. "You all have gemstones. White-Stars born in Abredea don't."

Gazes flicked to Anthony and Daisy's bare temples.

"You're from the camp?" one of the twin girls asked.

Juliana nodded. "And you're from the city. So, what are you doing out here?" She studied the oldest of them. The dark-skinned man had a tattoo across his forearm and was definitely old enough to have gone through the Coding, yet his gemstones were a blaze of swirling color. The other one who might be old enough had a knitted cap pulled low on his forehead, a shock of black hair sticking out the sides.

The man carrying one of the twins met her gaze with narrowed eyes. He raised his free hand and flames blossomed in his palm. "I think we're the ones asking questions right now," he said.

"Woah," Taz murmured. He took half a step forward, but Anthony kept a grip on his arm.

A surge went through Juliana. A rush of excitement. Another one like her.

The boy in the knit cap winced. "They won't hurt us," he said.

Juliana faced him. "No, we won't."

Beside her, Anthony kept his gaze on the fire.

"I'm Cho." He gave a sharp nod. "Jason and Nova, Jane and Tommy, Luna, and this is Claire." He gestured to each of them in turn before looking back at Juliana. "And you are..."

She hesitated for a brief second before offering up a smile. "Juliana. This is Anthony, Taz, and Daisy."

Daisy stepped up to Juliana's other side. She tilted her head. "Can you all do that?"

The girl with the limp—Jane—scoffed.

Juliana glanced at her. "Do you all have powers?"

Cho fidgeted at the head of their group. He glanced at Claire, barely conscious and wavering even as she clung to him.

Juliana stepped forward.

The children from the city acted as one. They moved together. Jason's ball of flame grew. Jane pulled Tommy behind her legs. Beside her, Luna seemed to grow a few inches. Juliana's blood raced as she glanced down and noted that the girl was no longer touching the ground.

Juliana put her hands up in a placating gesture. "I'm not going to hurt you." She took another step, meeting Cho's eyes as she reached slowly toward Claire.

Anthony didn't move forward, but Juliana felt and heard him shift behind her. "She's an *alter* too," he said. "She might be able tah help."

"How can she help?" Jason growled.

"What's an *alter*?" one of the twins asked.

Anthony chuckled. "Give her a chance and see."

Juliana swallowed. She'd only meant to check Claire's temperature, see if one of May's concoctions might bring down any fever. But at Anthony's words, the whirling blue orb at the center of her being lit up.

Cho watched her with wary eyes. She gave him a soft, reassuring nod and reached for Claire. She winced as her fingertips touched the girl's skin. She was hot. Clammy and trembling. Juliana—with all the care and patience she could muster—slid her hand up Claire's arm to the bandage just above her elbow.

Juliana inhaled through her nose, closed her eyes, and breathed out through pursed lips. Internally, she touched the edges of her power, caressing the blue light within and feeding it through her chest and down her arms until it buzzed with warmth in her hands. She opened her eyes.

Her vision had changed. Warped images, like she was looking through water, or staring at an oddly textured painting, swam before her. Claire glowed with frosty white light. Beside her, Cho gleamed like the sun, tendrils of yellow wisped away from his skin and were pulled back in a steady rhythm.

There. On Claire's arm. No light glowed where the bandage lay. Juliana gently undid the wrapping—noting the blue light coating her own skin as she did so.

Beneath the bandage were two images. In Juliana's regular vision, slightly underlaid by this new one, a jagged slice ran from her shoulder, twisting around to the front, and ending just before her inner elbow. The glowing light emanating from Claire dimmed here. Shadows seeped from the wound, clouding her skin and blocking out the light.

Murmuring penetrated Juliana's concentration. Whispered voiced grew louder. Concerns, demands, all foggy and distant compared to this shadow overtaking the girl.

Juliana breathed deep again, urging her power to flow. It did. Swirling blue strands of light, like rivulets of liquid or mist, caressed Claire's wound. They flushed through and around, circling the girl's arm and shunting the darkness away.

The shadows faded, gone like darkness at dawn. In their absence, Juliana's power moved to the cut itself. Shiny red skin bubbled as puss oozed from the open wound. A shard of metal, small and long and buried deep, rose from her skin, and dropped gently onto the forest floor. The infection gone, Claire's skin returned to its normal color. The cut began to heal.

A flicker of pounding went through Juliana's mind. She hesitated, pulled her power back for a moment as she focused on her own mind, on her own energy level. She hadn't reached the exhaustion she'd felt with Anthony, yet.

She returned to Claire's injury. Moments passed. Long and slow as she poured her energy into knitting skin together, sewing nerves back into place, and shooing away the fever heating Claire's body.

The final piece of new skin grew over the wound. Juliana released Claire's hand and took a staggering step backward. Strong arms caught her around the middle, keeping her upright as she blinked away the bright fuzziness obscuring her vision. She sucked in a few breaths. Got her feet under her. Gave Anthony a nod of thanks as he stepped away, releasing her with a wink.

Pain thudded in her mind, just behind her eyes. Her stomach growled, demanding sustenance. She bent, hands on her knees as she inhaled too fast and let out a little cough.

Daisy's floral print pants appeared at the edge of Juliana's vision. A small hand rested on her upper back, fingers rubbing in little circles at the base of her neck.

The pain in her head eased a bit.

"Thanks," she muttered.

Another moment passed, and then she straightened. The eyes of each child from the city were on her. Jason's fire had gone out.

Claire stood beside Cho, no longer leaning on him, blinking and gazing around with a frown on her face. "Where..." she glanced at Cho. "What's going on?"

Cho studied her arm without answering. Then he looked at Juliana. "You can heal."

She nodded.

Cho pursed his lips for a moment, a frown creasing his brow. "Can you..." he glanced back at Jane and the girl still on Jason's back. "Can you help them too?"

Juliana licked her lips. Her mouth and throat were so dry. She sucked on her tongue, trying to bring moisture back. "I—" she paused as her stomach heaved. She exhaled. "I can... just not right now."

"She needs tah rest first," Anthony explained. "Food?"

Juliana nodded.

Cho looked to the rest. "Do you all have abilities?"

Daisy shook her head as she took hold of Juliana's arm. "I don't. Neither do they." She gestured to Anthony and Taz. "At least, not that we know of."

Cho nodded. "Will you be able to return, so she can help the others?"

"We aren't goin' back tah Abredea, if that's yer concern," Anthony replied. "Yeh can follow us." He scanned their group. "We can all get somethin' tah eat and talk a bit. I 'ave questions."

"Us too," Jane snapped.

Juliana's lips twisted in a brief smile. "Don't trust us?"

Jane's gaze darted to Juliana. In it, Juliana recognized the same fear masked as anger she'd had when she was first coded as a White-Star.

"Not a bit," the girl said with a glare.

"Jane," Cho sighed. He looked at Anthony. "We *do* all have abilities. If you turn on us, you'll find out what they are."

Anthony hesitated. He met Juliana's eye.

She gave half a shrug. They couldn't leave these children alone in the woods; two of them still injured. They carried bags, but there was no way they had enough food to last more than a day or so. And, given what she knew about the city, about leaving it, and about the caste system... whatever reason they had to be out here, they wouldn't be able to go back.

"Yeh mean there's somethin' better than fire-guy over 'ere?" Anthony jerked his thumb at Jason.

To Juliana's surprise, a smile flashed across the man's serious features.

Cho smiled as well. "Maybe you'll find out." He pointed at the forest. "Lead the way."

Anthony smirked and led the way, in the opposite direction.

Juliana fell into step with Anthony, Daisy still holding her arm. They moved slowly. Juliana wanted to think it was purely for the sake of the children behind them, but she had a feeling Anthony was taking it easy for her as well.

"That was impressive," Anthony murmured as they walked through the trees.

"You've seen me heal before," Juliana said. She pushed a branch out of her way and glanced behind them.

Taz was walking with Jason, a stammering stream of questions flowing from him. The man answered with dry, one-word responses, his expression bland and solemn. Taz was not deterred.

Juliana smiled.

"It was different this time," Antony said. "Yeh looked controlled. Like yeh knew what yeh were doin'." He chuckled.

Juliana gave him a squinty glare. "It helps having some pointers," she said dryly.

He grinned at her. They continued on and his grin faded. "Yeh think yeh'll have the strength tah help those girls?"

A shiver went down Juliana's arms. Daisy tightened her grip, giving her a concerned look.

"I think so." Juliana licked her lips. "Some water, some food. Give it an hour or so and I think I'll be able to heal them." She glanced back again.

The flame thrower's sour expression had softened. He leaned in to say something to Taz and her friend laughed.

Juliana walked the rest of the way in silence. Daisy kept her balanced as they strode over the buildup of leaves, sticks, rocks, and branches. It didn't take long for them to reach the clearing and the truck. When they did, the children from the city stuck close to the tree line.

Juliana plunked down onto a fallen tree trunk.

Daisy settled next to her. "Why are they out here?" she wondered aloud. "Do you think they went through the gate?"

Juliana shook her head. "I don't see how. Maybe with a power we don't know about. But not like this." She gestured to the children, clustered together as Anthony and Taz went to open the truck. "You have to have a caste to go through. Only the top three are allowed to come and go as they please. Everyone else needs specific paperwork. Permission to leave the city and a date for their return." She plucked a piece of bark and broke it apart between her fingers. "Even being Blue-Stars, my parents had to get documentation for me each time we left."

"They can't come into Abredea," Daisy murmured. "I don't want to think about what would happen if Steel found them."

Juliana shook her head. "No, they aren't looking for a place to stay. There's a reason they're here. It took work to get out of the city. There's a reason they took the risk. A purpose."

She glanced at Cho. He had pulled his group together and was speaking to them in a hushed voice. His gaze darted to her, and their eyes met for a brief second.

Jane shook her head, her hand going around Tommy's shoulder. She glared at Cho and made a slashing motion with her hand. She gestured to the trees, hissing out her argument as Cho waited.

Beside her, the twin—Luna—put a hand on her shoulder. Jane grimaced. Juliana looked away as tears glinted in the girl's eyes.

"All right," Anthony called from the far side of the truck. "Time tah eat."

He and Taz came into view pushing the storied cart that had once held rows and rows of pastries. The top shelf was still covered in an assortment of sugary confections, but they'd also stacked slices of bread, cheese, meats, fruit, and more onto the bottom shelves. Taz helped with one hand, the other carrying a jug of amber liquid Juliana recognized as the cold tea they'd found last time they'd brought in a batch of food.

Daisy crossed to where the men stopped and pulling food from the racks for herself and Juliana.

A few yards away, the children from the city gaped.

"Plenty for everyone," Anthony said.

Jason was the first to come forward. He moved toward Juliana and gently lowered Nova onto the tree next to her.

By the time he walked to the cart of food, Anthony had stacked together two massive sandwiches and planted a pastry upon each. He handed them to Jason.

The taller man nodded his thanks and returned to Nova. "Here, eat."

Nova took the food. Jason leaned against a tree near her, taking a massive bite from his sandwich.

His bite released the flood gates. The other children hurried toward the cart. Taz and Anthony moved out of the way to let them make their own meals. Daisy returned to Juliana and handed over what she'd taken.

"Did we look like that?" she asked, watching as a jumble of hands grabbed for anything they could reach.

Juliana laughed. "We were worse. I remember the stomachache on our way back to Abredea after our first picnic." She lifted a slightly stale peach pastry to her mouth and took a bite, savoring the flavor and the ease it brought to her head as she swallowed.

"They don't get to eat like this very often," Jason muttered.

Juliana turned to look at him. Out of the corner of her eye she caught Nova, scarfing down her sandwich like it might disappear. "There's food like this in Tornim."

Jason swallowed his bite and let out a hoarse laugh. "Not for us."

Cho walked over to them, also choosing to stand while he ate. "We had stuff like this sometimes; when there was coin for it. Priorities lay elsewhere."

Juliana went to lick a bit of icing off her finger, noted the blood on her hand, and wiped it on the grass instead. "What caste are you from?" she asked.

The others glanced over. Jane stared at Juliana, but the rest watched Cho.

Daisy handed her a cup and Juliana downed the tea while she waited for Cho's response.

He chewed for a moment, swallowed, and said, "None."

Juliana raised an eyebrow.

He shrugged. "It doesn't matter what caste we came from. None of us are going back. We aren't going through the Coding and most of us haven't lived in a district in years."

"I was a Red-Star," Claire said.

Cho gave a little bow of his head. "Claire is the newest of us. We got her to Haven just before—"

He fell silent. A muscle in his neck twitched, his jaw tightening. Shadows drifted across his eyes.

Juliana frowned as she took another bite of her sandwich, not pressing the matter just yet. She had a hundred more questions, but for now they should eat. She could heal the girls' ankles. Get them able to walk again. There would be time for questions later.

"Before what?" Taz asked as he bounded over and plunked himself onto the grass at Cho's feet.

Juliana held back a snort as Daisy giggled next to her.

"Let 'em eat," Anthony laughed as he strode over from the cart and leaned up on a tree next to Jason.

The others filtered over as well, choosing to sit or stand as they downed a healthy amount of food. Claire rolled and stretched her arm between bites and gazed around with wonder in her eyes. "Where are we?"

"The forest," Cho answered. "Outside the city."

"How long have you been out here?" Juliana asked.

"Since yesterday morning," Cho said. "We've been waiting for the right time to take a transport from the fields."

Anthony straightened, his gaze darting to Juliana before he looked to Cho. "Tha's a bad idea."

"He didn't ask your opinion," Jane snapped.

Juliana glared at the girl. "You're in *his* forest. You're gonna get his opinion whether you ask for it or not."

Anthony hid a grin behind his hand as he met Juliana's gaze and raised his eyebrow. She rolled her eyes.

"Why is it a bad idea?" Jason asked, licking his fingers before wiping them on his jeans.

Anthony dusted his hands off as well, little crumbs falling to the grass. "Black-Stars guard the field hands. They do six tah twelve-hour shifts and every-thin' is accounted for. Everythin'. My guess? Yeh steal a worker transport one of two things'll happen. They'll catch yeh right away, 'cause each one has a trackin' device embedded in the engine. Or they'll assume one of the Moons took it and they'll beat the shit out of everyone workin' the shift and probably their families too. *Then* they'll track yeh down."

Jason glanced at Cho. A look passed between the two of them, one Juliana couldn't put a name to.

"We'll need to talk it over," Cho said.

Anthony gave half a shrug, but his face was tense. Juliana read the concern there. For Cho and the others, but also for the White-Stars who would most certainly be punished if a truck went missing during their shift.

They finished eating in relative quiet. Juliana stood when she'd finished a third cup of tea and tried walking. Her feet stayed under her, steady and firm against the forest floor. She wandered into the trees a bit, using their trunks as handholds before she returned to the group. Anthony was watching her closely. She grinned, stretched, and looked from Nova to Jane.

"I think I'm ready to give someone else a go. Who's more hurt?"

Anthony held up a hand, his head tilted.

Juliana glanced at him from the edge of the clearing. Her heartbeat quickened at the intensity on his face. "What is it?"

Anthony looked at Jason, then Cho. "Is there someone else with yeh?"

Jason frowned and twisted, planting his feet as a ball of fire appeared in his palm. Cho shook his head, shifting to stand closer to the younger children.

Anthony put a finger to his lips. "There's someone here," he murmured.

A footstep sounded behind Juliana. She half-turned. Pain slammed across the back of her head. She swayed, her vision went black, and she fell.

Chapter Forty-Six

Present Day - Early Fall - Forest Outside Abredea

A nthony watched Juliana as she stood, picked her way around Daisy, and wandered into the forest a bit. She flashed a smile at him when she turned back to the group and a surge of heat rose up in his chest. A buzz thundered through his nerves.

They hadn't talked about the kiss. The gentle brush of her lips against his. He smiled back.

He paused. The hair on the back of his neck bristled. His cheek twitched as sound reached him. Not the quiet chewing, not Taz or the little boy shuffling around. A footstep on the forest floor.

Another.

He warned the group and reached up to gesture for Juliana to move forward. To come away from the edge of the trees.

His eyes widened. Behind her, towering over her slender form, a Black-Star appeared from behind a thick, towering oak. Their gemstones were obscured by the thick black helmet covering their face. They wore a matching black jacket—the Black-Star insignia on the arm—pants and boots. Anthony caught sight of a gun at their hip before his gaze locked on the thick round club in their raised hand.

Time slowed.

Everything around Anthony seemed to move at a fraction of its usual speed. The club came down. The sound of it cracked across Juliana's skull and rage like he'd never felt slammed through his body. Heat surged at his core. Hate and fear and fury comingled and became a roaring beast within him.

Something snapped. A bone. His bone.

He glanced down. His legs had gone numb. Arms too. Dark hair—no—fur... sprouted from his skin, coating his arms as his fingers shrank into his palm, thickening as he stared at them in horror. His back legs no longer held his weight and he fell to all fours.

There should have been pain.

His jaw elongated. Teeth sharpened and grew. Ears twitched as fur covered their now pointed tips.

There was no pain. Only the roiling pocket of darkness in his chest, spreading. Consuming his thoughts. His vision sharpened, focused on the Black-Star who stood—transfixed—over Juliana's body.

Anthony's head jerked. He narrowed his eyes. The scent of her blood reached his nostrils.

Juliana's *body*.

A growl rumbled deep in his chest, and he opened his jaws as it rose up from him. Not a roar, but a howl of fury. His powerful legs, stronger than they'd been seconds ago, sank down a fraction before he pushed off.

He sprang forward, soaring over the tree-trunk. A flash of heat went by his head. The Black-Star dropped the gun they'd been reaching for. A cry split the air and the smell of scorched fabric hit Anthony's sensitive nose.

Then he was on them. His front paws slammed into their chest. They shot backward. His jaw widened. Someone screamed. The sound cut off as he closed his teeth around warm flesh. Blood spurted across his tongue. Blood and flesh and bone crunched between his vice-like jaws.

It was over in seconds.

He released the Black-Star's neck as darkness swirled back into his chest. His mind returned. His stomach twisted.

Anthony stared down, still with the strange new eyesight which focused on the blood oozing from a broken, shattered neck.

He backed away. A low whine split the air. He turned.

Behind him, in the clearing with a stolen truck and a cart still stacked with food, stood Daisy, Taz, and the children from the city. They gaped at him. Jason's fire had gone from his palm.

Anthony took rapid, deep breaths as he tried to focus. How could he focus? He was covered in fur.

Panic crested over him like a wave. It crashed down. The whining grew louder, and he realized it was coming from him. From the vocal cords in his throat, currently incapable of speech.

He couldn't talk. Couldn't stand.

"Hey."

He jerked back, head twitching to take in Cho, stepping toward him with slow movements. His cool, tawny-brown hands held up in a passive gesture.

"It's all right, Anthony," Cho murmured. "You're you again. You can come back. Breathe."

Anthony's form... the wolf's form... trembled. He inhaled through his snout, the strangeness of his dry nose briefly distracting him. He licked it. The tang of blood coated his tongue again.

Bile rose in his throat.

"Breathe," Cho said again. He took another step.

Anthony took one as well, backward, into the forest. His gaze darted to Juliana, still on the forest floor between him and the clearing. His heart raced. Another low growl seeped out from between his teeth.

"It's going to be all right. *She's* going to be all right. Remember yourself." Cho's voice floated through the air. Calm. Sure. At ease with the impossible strangeness of the situation.

Anthony closed his eyes and inhaled again.

"Think of your friends," Cho said. "Think of your home. Your face. Your hands... that's it."

Images flashed through Anthony's mind. Taz, laughing with an open, joyous expression as they walked through Abredea. Daisy, reading in the field, her soft face at peace in the afternoon sun. Naya and Jimmy, pulling him to the dinner table after a long day in the fields when all he wanted was to sleep. His hands pulled back the string of a bow. His fingers tied a knot in one of his fishing nets. He looked up into the mirror on his mother's dresser. A scar on his temple. He thought of May's voice; a lullaby from his childhood. His grandmother. He thought of Juliana. Of their first meeting at the fence. Of what she'd given up to save Jimmy, the last connection to her family. Of the heat on his lips as she'd kissed him...

"There you go." Cho's voice cut through his thoughts.

Anthony opened his eyes. Cool air brushed against him. He was on all fours, Cho crouched before him. He looked down. Hands. Human hands on the ground beneath him. He sat up, leaned backward, and sank onto his heels.

He stared at them. His hands. Callouses where they'd been. Scars and scratches still in place as though nothing had changed. As though they hadn't been clawed paws seconds ago.

"Ahem." Jason cleared his throat.

Anthony glanced up. The others were looking away.

"Here." Jason lifted his bag from the ground where he'd dropped it and fished out a pair of pants. "We're almost the same height."

Anthony's eyes widened. He glanced down. Every inch of his dark russet skin was exposed. "*Nacra*," he growled. His voice was hoarse. Heat bloomed in his cheeks.

He caught the pants Jason threw to him. He stood, positioning the fabric over himself as he moved a few yards and ducked behind a tree. He pulled on the pants. They were about an inch too long, but they covered the important bits.

He returned, uncomfortably aware of the sticky blood coating the lower half of his jaw and neck. He swallowed down the rising bile in his throat.

A flood of relief hit him as he stepped back through the trees. Juliana leaned against the tree trunk next to Daisy. Still unconscious, but her chest rose and fell in gentle movements. Daisy held a cloth to the back of her head. Blood matted her blonde hair.

"She's stopped bleeding," Daisy said as Anthony moved forward. To her credit, she didn't back away like the others. Neither did Taz, quietly standing beside her.

He pretended not to notice. "Maybe she heals quick too."

Daisy nodded. "I think so. Head wounds usually bleed a lot more than this." She examined Juliana's head and sighed. "Yeah, it's already clotting."

She met Anthony's gaze. Tears pooled in her eyes, her hands trembling as she pushed up from the ground and stood before him. She sucked in a shaking breath and glanced down at their friend. "I thought..."

"Yeah," he nodded, "me too."

She reached out a hand and he took it. The pressure of her thin fingers sent another shot of relief through him.

Taz stepped forward, a damp bit of fabric in his hands. "Yeh should c.... cl... Yeh should cl..." he inhaled through his nose. "Wipe it off."

A rumble of nausea went through Anthony's stomach. He took the rag from Taz and wiped away the blood splattered across his jaw and bare torso. He gave his friend a grateful nod. Then he turned to the Black-Star.

Jason crouched over the body. He met Anthony's gaze. "He's dead."

Waves of haze clouded Anthony's vision. His hands shook as he cleaned the blood of the man he'd killed off his skin.

The clearing was silent for a long moment. In the space of quiet, Jason pulled the gun from the Black-Star's limp form and tucked it into his bag. He took the club as well before returning to the rest of the group.

"What now?" Daisy asked, her voice soft. She met Anthony's eye, and he knew she was thinking the same thing he was...

He'd never be able to go back. Abredea couldn't be his home anymore.

"What I want to know," Jason said as he carefully wrapped food from the cart in wax paper and tucked it in his bag, "is who he was following." He jerked his head at the Black-Star.

"It might 'ave been you?" Anthony asked.

Jason shrugged.

Cho stepped forward, glancing at Juliana and then back at his people. "We ran into a little trouble getting out of the city. I wouldn't put it past the people who got us through to turn us in if it meant they got paid."

Anthony nodded. "I know the type. There's a strong chance he was followin' us. Abredea is run by Black-Stars now. And their captain doesn't like me much."

Behind him, Taz snorted, choked, and coughed.

"That's an understatement."

Anthony wheeled at Juliana's voice. He hurried to her side as she shifted, straightening in the grass and lifting a hand to her head.

"Ow," she mumbled, glancing up at him. "What happened? Where's your shirt?"

Daisy's sigh of relief was everything Anthony felt. He put a hand under Juliana's arm and helped her up enough to sit on the tree.

"Are yeh all right?" he asked.

"Are *you*?" she demanded, taking in the bits of blood still on his neck.

"It's not his blood," Jane said. She stepped forward with a wince and sank onto the tree beside Juliana with a groan. "It's his." She jerked her thumb behind them.

Juliana looked at the Black-Star and her throat bobbed with a hard swallow. "You..." she glanced at him.

"Killed him... yeah." He tried not to put too much into his expression. Tried to keep his fear from showing.

She hesitated, then nodded.

"He has powers too," Taz cut in, moving forward and crouching next to Juliana. "He turns in.... in... into... well, I don't really know what it was."

"A wolf," one of the twins said. They'd moved closer too. All the children from the city had. They stood together in a tight circle around Juliana, the injured girls on either side of her.

Juliana's eyes widened. "A wolf?"

Anthony half shrugged, a chill going through his veins. "I've seen 'em before, but I couldn't exactly see myself."

Juliana gave a dazed sort of nod. A moment passed in silence, then she furrowed her brow, her eyes clearing and a focused look coming over her face. "Was that one of Steel's men?"

"We don't know," Daisy murmured.

Anthony's stomach protested what he was about to do. "Let's find out," he said.

He crossed to the body and, with trembling fingers he hoped no one noticed, he lifted the visor. A ripple of guilt, anxiety, and grief went through him. He recognized the dead man before him. One of Steel's. One of the ones who'd marched him to the top of town hall. Who'd held his arms behind his back as Steel beat him.

He swallowed, a metallic taste on his tongue. "He's from Abredea," he called back to the group.

He returned and stood beside Cho with his arms crossed over his chest.

Cho shifted. He winced. He clenched a hand and then shook his head as he crossed their circle to stand beside one of the twins.

Anthony's gut churned. He glanced at his hands. They were clean, no evidence of the blood he'd spilt. Flecks of it were dried to the skin of his chest. Still, he felt—for some reason—that his hands should have been red. They should have been sticky and matted with the life he'd taken.

"If he's been followin' us from Abredea," Taz turned to Cho, "then he heard about yer plan to steal a transport."

Jane cursed.

"We need to talk," Cho said. He grimaced. "Just us Haven kids for a moment."

Anthony nodded, lost in other thoughts.

"Of course," Daisy said with a soft smile.

The children left their circle, Luna helping her twin, and Jason offering a hand to Jane as she hobbled across the clearing.

"Anthony," Juliana murmured, "you can't go back to Abredea. When Steel finds out..."

"I know." He clenched his jaw. Naya and Jimmy and May flashed through his mind. He rubbed a hand across his chin, widening his eyes to keep the tears at bay. He looked from Daisy to Taz to Juliana. They'd be all right without him. They'd survive. Juliana, he knew, would ensure it. No matter what it took, she'd take care of them all in his absence.

Juliana tilted her head, squinting at him. He met her gaze and the tears he'd been holding back leaked from the corners of his eyes.

He blinked, surprised as her expression shifted. She glared at him. Jutted her lower jaw to the side and stood with hands planted on her hips.

"Jules," Daisy said in a worried voice, putting a hand on her friend's arm.

Juliana pulled away, still staring at Anthony. She took a step forward. "You think..." she scoffed. She held up a hand, pointing a finger into his chest.

He swallowed now, unease filling him.

"You think you're leaving on your own?" she asked.

Anthony's brow furrowed. He glanced at Daisy and Taz before his gaze returned to her blazing blue eyes. "I..."

She scoffed again. "Anthony. You can't go back. That doesn't mean we can't go with you."

Anthony's eyes widened. He took half a step back, shaking his head. "No. I won't put yeh in tha' position."

She stepped after him, the intensity of her gaze thrilling and terrifying at the same time. "You aren't putting us—me," she amended with a quick glance at the others, "in any position." Her lips curled into half a smile. "I've been looking for a way out of Abredea since we met."

Anthony swallowed.

Juliana shrugged. "Now I've found one."

"I'm coming too."

Anthony looked at Daisy and his chest swelled. She stared at him, her gaze as fierce as he'd ever seen it.

"Don't tell me not to," Daisy said. "There's nothing for me in Abredea. Not with you all gone."

"Same," Taz cut in. "I'm comin'."

Anthony shook his head. "We can't all go off and live in the forest."

"Why not?" Taz asked. He ran a hand through his cropped sandy hair, making the ends stick up as a wild smile lit his face. "Sounds like fun."

"They'll be after me, for starters," Anthony said. He looked at Juliana. Read the determination in her gaze. A surge of fear went through him once again. Not that she'd hate him, or be afraid of him, but that he'd be leading his friends to a dark, twisted fate. That he'd get them all killed or worse.

Anthony shook his head again, stepping away from them with a grimace as he clenched his hands. "This is a bad idea—"

"Steel won't stop coming after you," Juliana interrupted. "He'll hunt you down. You stand a better chance with us than alone."

Anthony sighed. He didn't want to agree with her. It didn't make sense to agree; he knew the forest, knew how to survive, knew enough to find some hidden place in the mountains to hunker down until Steel moved his search somewhere else.

At the same time... the thought of facing it all alone.

Juliana gave an angry shake of her head. Her hair fell across her face, and she brushed it away with a hurried hand. She moved closer, standing inches away as she looked him in the eyes. "Black-Star helmets have cameras in them."

A stone sank into his stomach. His lungs constricted.

"What do you think Steel will do to the rest of us if we go back to Abredea now?" She glanced at Daisy and Taz, a few feet away, watching them. "You aren't helping any of us by trying to leave us behind."

His fingers stopped trembling as her hand found his. He glanced down. Her cold, calloused fingers laced between his and squeezed.

He licked his lips and nodded.

His gaze flicked to the side of the truck. Cho and Jason rounded the corner, deep in discussion.

"—be able to help."

"—too dangerous."

Juliana turned to them. "I think it's time we had a conversation about why you're all out here."

Cho nodded.

Jason cocked his head. "Mind if we get away from the dead body first?"

Daisy and Taz gaped at him. Anthony caught his eye and noted the faint twitch at the edge of his mouth.

"Pack up as much as you can." Juliana gestured to the truck. She turned to Anthony. "And we should get a few crates together. Maybe drop them at the fence if we can."

"I wanna..." Anthony gritted his teeth. Anticipation clenched at his gut. She wasn't going to like this. "I need tah go back."

Juliana's eyes widened.

"Not for long," he added quickly, "but I 'ave tah say goodbye tah Naya and Jimmy. Give 'em what I can." He inhaled. "Maybe see about Montague protectin' 'em."

Juliana bit her lip.

"I know it doesn't make sense," he said. His chest heaved. "I know it's not the smart move. But I have tah, Jules."

Juliana closed her eyes for a few seconds. When she opened them again, they were glistening with tears. "It makes sense, Anthony." She caught his gaze and held it. "I know what it means to need to say goodbye."

Chapter Forty-Seven

Present Day - Early Fall - Abredea

T he Haven kids were surprisingly helpful when it came to taking loads of food to edge of Abredea. Even with Juliana still healing from her own injury and unable to help the remaining wounded girls, they made themselves useful packing up boxes of supplies.

Anthony slid through the hole in the fence, pulling one of the massive boxes behind him. Juliana slithered through next, pushing a second box through and helping him as they pushed the crates to one of the trees at the far edge of the field. They covered them with brush and strode into Abredea.

Daisy and Taz had stayed in the forest. Their group were the only ones Taz would have said goodbye to. As far as Daisy... Anthony didn't press her on it, but he was sure she didn't want to run into her father and lose her nerve.

"I'll be quick," Juliana said as they reached a fork in the road. She had things to get for her and Daisy, and she wanted to say goodbye to May. "Don't forget to tell them goodbye for me, all right?"

Anthony nodded. "You'll ask Montague?"

Juliana squeezed his hand before letting it fall. "Yeah."

He turned down the beaten path to his home, a heavy weight on his heart. He wanted to say goodbye to Montague himself, to thank him for everything he'd done. But there wasn't time.

Anthony walked through the door to the one-bedroom home he'd kept since he was fourteen. The painted dresser sat across from his bed as it always had. He brushed a hand across the wood. He supposed he knew his mother had painted it. Or, at least, he'd always assumed it. But knowing it. Knowing she was May's daughter. She'd painted. Created.

He'd been so young when she died. Tears sprang to his eyes. He'd planned on hearing more stories from May. More tales about his mother and uncle, his grandfather, the rebellion.

He sniffed and wiped at his nose. He washed the crusted blood off his chest and neck, opened one of the drawers, and put on a faded green shirt. Hurrying to his bed, he reached under and pulled out his thick, canvas hunting bag. He filled it with clothes, blankets, soap, tools, his raggedy spare pair of boots, and carefully folded together a bundle of all the food in his kitchen to lay on top. He tucked a bag of coins in the corner pocket, everything he'd saved to replace Naya's broken solar panel.

With a final glance at the dresser, he left.

He jogged to Naya's, painfully aware that with each second ticking by, it was more and more likely that Steel would learn of his guard's death and begin the hunt for him.

"Wha'..." Naya gasped as he hurried through the door, closing it behind him and leaning on the wood with a sigh.

"Hey," Anthony said.

Jimmy sat at their little kitchen table, coloring with the home-made wax crayons Daisy had melted together a few weeks ago. "Tony," he called. He jumped from the table and raced across the room to cling to Anthony's legs.

"Hey, little man." Anthony swallowed down the lump in his throat. He met Naya's gaze.

"What's wrong?" She wiped her hands on a dish cloth and set it on the counter. "Anthony?"

Anthony took a deep breath. "I 'ave to go."

"Where?" Jimmy asked.

Anthony forced a grin and ruffled the boy's hair. "Nowhere for yeh tah worry about." He looked at Naya. "It's safer if yeh don't know. Somethin' happened with one of Steel's men. I don't wanna tell yeh. I don't wanna put yeh in danger." His voice shook.

Jimmy took a step back and stared up at his face. "Are yeh comin' back?"

Anthony took Jimmy's hand and walked him further into the house. He set his bag on the table and knelt to look his cousin in the eye. "Yeah. I'll come back. I don't know when. But I will. I promise."

Tears beaded at the corners of Jimmy's eyes. The sight shot a pang of guilt through Anthony's heart. He looked up at Naya.

Her cheeks were wet with tears even as she wiped them away with her thin, tired fingers.

"I brought yeh some things." He stood and pulled the food from his bag. He pressed it into her hands.

She backed away, shaking her head. "Where'll yeh go? Don't yeh need..." she inhaled, trembling.

"No," Anthony said. He forced his voice not to shake. Pushed every ounce of calm he could into his tone, into his expression. He set the bundle on the kitchen counter and took Naya's hands. "I don't need anythin'. There's plenty in the truck."

Jimmy leapt forward and latched himself to Anthony's leg. "I wanna go too."

Anthony closed his eyes. He tightened his hold on Naya's hands. Hands that wiped away his tears, bandaged his scrapped knees, held him through cold nights when he woke up screaming for his mom. "Listen, I don't 'ave a lot of time. There are two crates in that little field Juliana likes tah go to. They're hidden by some brush under a tree, but there's plenty there for you and Jimmy. It will last a long time if yeh do it right."

She nodded.

"There's also this." Anthony pulled his hands away and took the bag of coins out. "Yeh've got a busted panel." He pointed to the roof.

Naya's eyebrows narrowed in confusion.

Anthony shrugged, half-apologetically. "I didn't wanna tell yeh 'til I had enough to replace it."

Naya put her hand to his cheek. Then she slid it around his neck and pulled him into a tight, stooped hug. He held her close, inhaled the scent of home one more time.

"I really will be back," he murmured into her neck. "I promise."

Naya sniffed as he pulled away and brushed away a fresh set of tears. "I know. You and yer uncle," she chuckled, a sad smile on her lips, "yer good at keepin' promises."

Anthony hiked his hunting bag back over his shoulder. Jimmy still clung to his leg.

He knelt again and put a hand on his cousin's arm. "Yer readin' by yerself, right?" he asked.

Jimmy nodded, wiping his palm under his nose.

Anthony grinned. "Yer too smart, kid. Listen," his gazed darted to Naya for a brief second, "Juliana has tah come with me, so she won't be able tah read to yeh anymore. But yer gonna read. When yeh get really good at it yeh can start readin' tah the other kids, right?"

Jimmy nodded again. He frowned. "Juliana's leavin' too?"

Anthony's lips twisted into a forced smile as he tried not to let Jimmy's tears dig into his heart. "Yeah. Daisy and Taz also. But like I said, we'll be back. All right?"

Jimmy cast a tearful, scared look at his mom. Naya nodded with a tight smile.

Anthony's gut burned. He stood, gently pushing Jimmy towards his mother. "I love yeh both." He turned and paced to the door, his chest tight and a thick lump in the back of his throat. He pulled the door open.

"We love yeh too, Anthony," Naya's voice broke as she said it.

Anthony nodded. He let the door fall closed as he strode away.

"*Frost*," he muttered to himself as he hurried to May's. Juliana would have already been there. She was hopefully nearly done in the square, collecting clothes for Daisy and talking to Montague.

Anthony picked up his pace.

He turned onto the main road that ran through Abredea. Captain Steel walked up the street toward him, twenty yards away. Anthony's heartbeat raced, sweat beading across his forehead as he hitched his bag and continued forward, attempting for a nonchalant stride.

"Stop." Steel's black gloved hand planted itself against Anthony's chest as they were about to pass each other.

Anthony gritted his teeth. He thought of Juliana, of how cold and collected she'd been when they faced the smugglers in the city. "What can I do for yeh, Captain?" he said.

Steel sneered. He glanced around, looking behind Anthony. "Where are you headed without your friends?"

Anthony sighed. "Deliverin' some clean clothes to an old lady... Captain." He forced out the word, the deference expected. Forced himself to ignore the memory of Steel's breath on his ear, whispering what he'd do to Anthony's friends while he was in solitary. Steel's fist, clenching the back of his shirt, leaning him over that balcony. Pushing him off.

Steel raised an eyebrow, his twisted sneer still in place. "Watch yourself, boy. That little *bitch* won't always be around to get you out of trouble."

A shudder went through Anthony. He swallowed and bit down a response which would have gotten him dragged into the square again. Instead, he offered a shallow nod and moved to step around the man.

Steel raised his hand again, this time giving a shove as it hit Anthony's chest.

Anthony fell back half a step. He clenched his hands at his sides. Every ounce of will pouring into keeping a lock on his tongue, and his fists.

Steel laughed. He lowered his hand and spit onto the ground in front of Anthony. He leaned close, like he had on that day, and muttered into Anthony's ear, "You won't be so lucky next time you cross a line. I'll be waiting."

Anthony managed to stand still as Steel walked off, toward the town square. He inhaled, muscles tight, fingernails—short as they were—digging into his palms. When the sound of Steel's footsteps had faded around a bend, he continued.

It was luck. Luck and a matter of time until Steel realized his man was missing. How long had a Black-Star been tailing them? Did Steel hate him that much, to allocate man hours to constant surveillance?

He sped up, jogging down the winding paths until he reached May's house.

She was waiting for him at the front step. May held out her arms and he fell into them. "Come inside," she murmured.

He obliged, following her into the house and sinking into a chair at the kitchen table. May set a mug before him, steaming with fresh tea. Juliana's usual mug, the one with a chipped handle, sat on the counter.

"Juliana told me what happened," May said. She settled into a chair across from Anthony and met his gaze, holding it with those stormy grey eyes.

"I..." Anthony's voice shook. "I didn't mean tah kill him, May. I never meant..."

"I know." May nodded. "I know." She looked down at the table and traced her fingers along the painted foliage, tapping her thumb against a bright bird's wing. "There's something someone told me a long time ago." She shot him half a grin. "Red, right before I formed the first alter squad."

Anthony lifted his mug to his lips and sipped the sweet jasmine and mint tea.

"There was an attack on a medical unit. Kate and I, along with a few others, were transporting medicine to an outlying village. They'd been helping us for a while and a sickness was going through their school." She shook her head, a flash of anger drawing her scar taught and white across her skin. "I killed a Black-Star. Stabbed him in the chest with the small blade I kept for emergencies." She swallowed and spread her hands, staring at her open palms. "It felt like I couldn't wash off the blood, even hours later when we'd completed the mission and returned to the Warren."

Anthony nodded. His hand went to his jaw, his neck, where he could still feel the gore and blood even though he knew there was none.

"Red talked to me then." She met Anthony's gaze. "There are things we have to do to protect the people we care about. Sometimes those things aren't... good. Sometimes saving the people you love means killing. Those deaths will stay with you. And they should. You have to decide if you can live with it." She reached across the table and took his hand. "If you can, then remember why you're fighting, and it'll help ease some of the ache that'll keep you up at night. If you can't, do what you can for those who do fight."

Anthony licked his lips. "You did. Yeh fought."

May nodded.

"Yeh remember all of 'em?"

She hesitated. Sighed deeply and stared up for a moment. "There were enough in my time that I don't. I don't remember each face. I don't have a number in my mind." She gave him a sad smile. "I don't think I've ever gone through and tried to count the ones I've killed. But I know who I saved, and that's what lets me sleep." The smile spread, becoming true and reaching her eyes as she looked at him.

"I'm sorry I 'ave tah leave," Anthony murmured. His lips trembled. "I wanted tah get tah know yeh." He let out a little chuckle. "As my grandmother, that is."

She nodded. "I know."

They sat for a moment. The stillness calmed him. His grandmother's hand holding his, the scent of her tea, the warmth of her home, it seeped into his chest and heart, settling the ache within.

"Those children," May said, "the ones from the city, Juliana said their family was taken."

Anthony nodded. "They're on their way to find 'em. We..." he cleared his throat, "we're goin' too."

She smiled. "Good." She moved her hand from his, taking a drink from her tea. "I knew there must be others, but I had no idea they were so close." She met his eye. "I'm glad you're helping them. Be careful. Take care of each other."

He nodded.

She rose as he did, moving from the table and pulling him into a surprisingly tight hug. She only came to his chest, her grey hair falling down her back in the long braid he was so used to.

"The people you're up against," she said as they separated. "They want power. Control. They think the best way to get it is to keep everyone in their place. People like *us*, we're dangerous because we can fight back. We *do* fight back. They know it, and they'll do whatever they can to stop us. To cut us up and find our power."

Anthony stared at her. The fringes of fear, not for himself, but for what they faced, tickled the edges of his mind.

She smiled and ran a hand down his arm. "I wish I could have seen you transform. I knew a few who could shift back in the day. It's a special gift."

Anthony's jaw tightened. He blinked back tears and swept her into one more hug.

The door behind him burst open, slamming against the wall with a deafening *thwack*.

"Thought I'd find you here." Steel stood at the doorway, plasma gun in his hand, fury on his face. "Crossed the line. *Frosted animal*," he spat.

Anthony pushed May behind him, his gazed fixed on the gun in Steel's hand. He reached behind his back, fingers grasping the handle of the blade tucked into his waistband.

"I knew you were some kind of freak," Steel growled. He shook his head and raised the gun.

"You'll want to *think* before you do that." May's stormy grey eyes glinted as she stepped beside Anthony.

He shifted, putting his body half-way in front of her small frame.

"Really?" Steel cocked his head, his eyes glinting with fury. "*I* think I want to kill him and be done with it. You murdered one of my men," he spat at Anthony.

"Yeh don't care about yer men," Anthony hissed. His heart thudded in his ears. Nerves buzzed against his skin. "Yeh don't care about anyone."

"It doesn't have to go this way," May said. Her voice shook with fear.

"Shut up," Steel interjected. His gun wavered, twitching toward her for a brief second. "I..." he hesitated. A light glinted in his eyes, a realization. His gaze and gun fixed on Anthony. "Where is she?" he demanded.

Anthony noted May out of the corner of his eye, still half-covered by him. He shifted to the side even more, hoping to get her completely behind him.

"Who?" May moved again, keeping her line of sight on Steel.

"The girl." Steel glanced around the room. "Did she return with you? Or is she still in the forest with those little *nacras* from Tornim?"

Anthony's frown deepened. "Why d'yeh care?"

Steel grimaced. "That's no concern of yours. Tell me where she is, and I won't kill you where you stand."

"Yeh'll take me to a lab and strap me down for experiments instead?" Anthony shook his head. "I'll pass."

Steel's free hand clenched at his side, but his gun hand remained steady. "I can find out without you," he snarled.

Anthony tightened the grip of his blade. One opening. One chance...

"Why?" May asked.

Steel's gaze darted to her and then back. "Why what?" he snapped.

"Why do you need her? Why did the Grey-Star take interest in a Moon?"

Steel's eyes went wide. Alarm flashed across his face before shifting back into that snarling frown. "It's none of your concern."

Anthony remained still, heart thundering against his chest, as May spoke again, her voice harsh.

"That Grey-Star knew... didn't she?"

Steel said nothing. His gaze remained on Anthony; gun still pointed at his heart.

"She knew Juliana had power. Is that why she was sent here?"

Steel swallowed.

Anthony pulled the blade from his waistband in a smooth motion, keeping the hand behind his back. The other he held up in a vain defense that would do nothing stop a bolt of plasma.

"What d'yeh want with her?" Anthony growled.

"*Enough,*" Steel shouted.

Anthony jerked. Behind him, May didn't so much as flinch.

"You're coming with me, boy. I'll find the girl. But for now... I'm sure Dolor could use another body for their experiments." He lowered his gun half an inch. One hand moved toward the black cuffs at his hip.

Anthony reacted. Elbow forward, hand straightening over it in a fluid motion. His wrist flicked. The movement so familiar. Almost as though Steel was one of the many trees Anthony had sunk knives into over the years.

The blade whirled through the air. Lodged into the flesh just below Steel's right shoulder. His body jerked back, feet stumbling against the doorframe. Fury and pain lit across his face as he roared.

He lifted his gun.

Anthony watched Steel's fingertip twitch. The muzzle of the gun lit up as a bolt of plasma discharged. Nothing went through his mind. No last thought. No dying declaration.

The air before him fractured and warped. Someone was there. A figure was in front of him.

Plasma struck and May crumpled to the ground. Anthony's breath caught. This wasn't right. She was behind him. She was safe. He turned. His grandmother wasn't next to him anymore.

Roiling fury slammed through him once more. Fur erupted down his arms. He blinked, and his vision was once again that of a wolf's.

He fought it even as grief broke across him. He fought to control the animal threatening to break out of him.

He rushed forward.

Steel stood at the door, smoking gun, bleeding from his shoulder, briefly stunned by the unexpected change in targets.

Anthony slammed into him. Used his full body, and the strength of the wolf, to propel the much larger man into the door. The solid wood cracked, but didn't break. Steel grunted, winded. Anthony grabbed the gun from his hand and flipped it.

Steel opened his mouth. Fury erupted from him in a shattering screech. He swung. Connected with the scar on Anthony's side.

Pain blossomed against his rib cage.

Steel's second swing caught him in the jaw.

Anthony stumbled back. Shook his head and felt the roar of the wolf, trapped inside him, snapping to be let out. He shoved forward, slamming Steel against the door again and this time swinging as he did.

The butt of the heavy gun cracked against Steel's skull.

The sound echoed against the wooden walls. Everything went silent. A glassy sheen rolled over Steel's dark eyes. He swayed. Blood slid down his forehead, followed the lines of his nose, and dripped from his chin.

His body hit the floor.

Anthony dropped the gun.

He turned and fell to the ground beside May.

She was still alive. Wheezy breaths shuddered through her, unsteady and forced. Her stomach...

Anthony swallowed back an urge to retch.

Her stomach was a scorched mess of blood and charred flesh. As she exhaled, flecks of blood flew from her open mouth.

"No, no, no," Anthony cried. He lifted her head, slowly, and pulled her into his lap. "May?"

Her eyes, wide and staring, focused on his face. Her lips curved in a grin. "Your eyes," she muttered, "mine do that too. White though."

"What? May, hold on. Hold on, yer gonna be all right." He bit out the words as tears pooled and flowed from his eyes. The wolf vision faded, the fur on his arms seemed to dissolve away. He stared at the ruined flesh of her stomach. Blood dribbled, the flow slowing as she went pale.

May shook her head. A cough split from her lips, blood flying across the floor. "I don't think so, Tony. Not this time."

"Why'd yeh do that?" Anthony sucked in a terrified breath as he clung to her. "You didn't need tah do that."

She chuckled and winced. "Taking risks... runs in the family." She smiled again. "So does that temper." Another cough racked her body.

Anthony bit his trembling lower lip. "You can go," he murmured. "Teleport tah Jules. She can help yeh." He sniffed, glancing at the wound, and wincing against his own lie. "She can heal yeh."

"Shh." May's hand found his arm. She clung to him. "It's time."

"It doesn't 'ave tah be," Anthony said. His voice broke. "*Please.*"

"I'm not," May choked out, "strong enough to get to her. And she'd kill herself fixing this mess." She gestured with her free hand to the scorched wreck of her body.

"But yeh can't die," Anthony pleaded. "I can't lose you." A shuddering sob ripped through his chest. "May..."

"Shh, quiet, boy, I have things to say before..." She grimaced.

Anthony fell silent. Pain and determination flashed across her face.

"There's something..." she inhaled a ragged breath, "more going on. I thought..." Her eyes fluttered closed, but with a wince, she forced them open again. "I thought it was done when they won, but there's more... you have to help those children. It's going to get worse unless you can stop them."

Anthony nodded. "We will."

"Juliana," May's grip on Anthony's arm weakened, "they want her. Keep her... keep yourself safe. Have to... someone you... trust..." Her words faded, becoming nearly unintelligible as her eyes went hazy once again.

Anthony nodded again. His tears dripped into May's hair, her head nestled against his chest.

"Please don't go, May. *Please*."

Her eyes flicked open. She gazed at him. Her hand released his arm and reached up to touch his cheek. "I'm glad..." she inhaled a shallow breath, "I'm glad... I didn't have to... lose you too..."

Her eyes slid closed as the air left her body. She did not breathe in again.

A ragged cry filled the home. Grief, fury, loss, and helplessness poured into the air with the sound of heartbreak. Anthony's body shook as May's hand fell from his cheek. He held her close, rocked on the ground as he sobbed.

Everything she'd done. Everything she was. Gone.

Through tears, he watched black fur erupt across his flesh. His nails lengthened, fingers shortening, his palms becoming thick pads.

With another roar he pulled himself back in control. He stared down at May. Brushed aside a stray hair with his regular, human fingers.

For a long moment he cradled her in his lap as he sobbed. When the tears faded, he lifted her onto her bed. He pulled a blanket over her and folded her arms across her stomach. As though she were sleeping. As though the blood on her face was paint. The mess of flesh hidden by a comforter covered in flowers.

There should have been more.

More he could do for her.

But as he straightened, he caught a glimpse of Steel's body. Blood seeping from his head and shoulder, slumped on the ground near the door.

Anthony didn't want him in the same room as his grandmother. However, putting him in the back felt like a betrayal to the garden she'd so lovingly cared for. And dragging him out front had a good chance of attracting too much attention.

He took a spare blanket from the dresser. He took hold of his blade, and yanked it from Steel's body. Blood dribbled from the wound. Anthony scowled and flung the blanket over Steel's crumpled form.

He returned to May. Bent. Kissed her forehead and whispered a thanks for everything she'd done.

Anthony's bag slammed against his back as he ran west. Red dust coated his shoes, sticking to his grandmother's matted blood. He burst through the trees into the field where Juliana was waiting.

She stood under the branches of a towering oak. Its leaves had begun the transformation from green to gold. Her brown bag bulged on her back, another bag of supplies at her feet.

"Ready?" she called, hefting up the bag and hurrying to him. She hesitated as she got nearer. "What's... Anthony?"

He closed his red, puffy eyes and shook his head. "We 'ave tah go, Jules."

"What happened?" she demanded. Her tone left no room for waiting.

Still, he couldn't do it. Couldn't say it. Tears tracked down his cheeks. He pressed the back of his hand against his mouth, wishing the pressure would ease the pain. It didn't.

Juliana stared at the blood on his palm. She looked back the way he'd come, realization dawning in her striking blue eyes. She swallowed. "Who?" she whispered.

His lips trembled. He forced them open. "May."

Juliana reacted as though she'd been struck in the gut. One hand flew to her mouth; she dropped her bag and pressed the other against her stomach as tears sprouted in her eyes. "No..." she looked at him, horror in her gaze. "How?"

He shook his head and bit the inside of his mouth. Blood spurted, coating his tongue with a metallic taste, and sending pain across his raw senses. "We need tah go. I'll explain everythin' when we get to the others."

Juliana turned, like she wanted to go back into Abredea. "I can help." She glanced at him, forehead wrinkled, grief etched across her face. "I can heal her, right?"

Anthony exhaled a shaking breath. He shook his head. "It's too late, Jules. She's gone."

Juliana inhaled several shallow breaths, her body quivering. Her hands clenched. Jaw tightened. Eyes narrowed to thin slits of cold blue. She grabbed her bag off the ground, nodded once at Anthony, and made for the fence.

Anthony reeled for a moment, lost at her sudden shift. But he followed her.

The two moved in silence through the space between fence and forest, then traveled through the trees. Juliana led the way, taking them deeper and deeper.

The dense trees finally opened into the clearing where they'd left the others to wait.

Anthony dropped his bag onto the grass as Daisy, and Taz, and the children from Haven looked up. He sank to his knees. Daisy and Taz hurried to him, each putting a hand on his shoulders and anxiously questioning him.

"May is dead," Juliana said.

The Haven kids glanced at each other. Taz cursed. Daisy burst into tears.

Juliana looked at Anthony and though her gaze was fierce, he thought he saw a hint of softness behind her eyes. "What happened?"

Chapter Forty-Eight

Present Day - Early Fall - Forest Outside Abredea

M ay was dead. Steel too.

Juliana dug her nails into her palms, biting back a fresh wave of tears. She walked at the back of the group, letting the children from Haven follow Anthony, Daisy, and Taz.

Alone. She just wanted to be alone.

Like she had been when she first came to Abredea except... she clenched her jaw. She hadn't been alone then either. May had been there. An unwelcome presence at first, but a presence. One that stayed with her through her temper, her insolence, her fear and anger, her rash words and misplaced hate.

Juliana lifted her hands, staring at whisps of blue emanating from her fingers. She knew, with the logical part of her mind, that she wouldn't have been able to help. Anthony had been clear when he told the story. Juliana understood the damage a full energy plasma bolt did. Still...

She paused to suck in a deep breath through her nose, keeping the bile at bay.

They shouldn't have split up. Should have stayed together, gone to May's together. Her conversation with Montague, picking up Taz and Daisy's things seemed so meaningless now. She'd wanted to help.

She stumbled, caught herself on the branch of a pine, and glanced ahead. Jason walked ahead of her, one of the twins dangling on his back.

Juliana grimaced. She wasn't strong enough to help those girls yet.

"Hey."

Juliana startled. Daisy stood a few yards away, having popped out from behind a tree when Juliana stopped walking.

"I've been waiting for you to catch up," she murmured.

Juliana stared at her.

"It's not your fault this happened," Daisy said.

"People keep saying that." Juliana clenched her jaw.

"That doesn't make it less true." Daisy took a step forward. "I know you, Jules. I know you want to have been there. I do too. But we can't know if it would have changed anything." She swallowed.

Juliana shook her head, fresh tears burning her already tired eyes. "I was so cruel to her..." She sucked in a breath and exhaled through her lips, trying to keep the tears in. Her gut roiled and tightened with unbridled guilt and grief.

Daisy brushed aside a lock of brown hair that had escaped her braid. "May loved you. And she knew how much you loved her."

"How can you know that?" Juliana sniffed and rubbed furiously at the tears on her cheeks. "How can you know?"

"Because we all love you." Daisy stepped closer; her voice stronger than it had been in weeks. "Because you saved her grandson's life. Both their lives. Because you help people, Jules. Just like she did."

Juliana took the hand Daisy offered, their fingers interlocking. Daisy squeezed and Juliana returned the pressure. Her stomach eased. Not much, but enough to get her moving. They followed the unused and overgrown trail Anthony had led them down.

"I can't believe she's gone," Juliana murmured.

"I know." Daisy nodded, brushing a hand across her face to wipe away her tears. "It hasn't completely hit me yet, I think. It took a while when mom died."

Juliana tightened her grip on her friend's hand. "I think she would have wanted us to help these kids. Even if we *could* go back."

"Yeah," Daisy said. "I think so too."

They walked in silence for a long time. Wherever Anthony was taking them was hours away. The group stopped a few times, letting the children rest, drinking water, and snacking on a package of crackers.

After a couple hours, Juliana examined Jane's thigh. The cut was deep, but not infected. She healed it.

Standing made her dizzy for a few seconds, but she went to Nova anyway and looked over her ankle as well. It was worse. Her odd power vision showed a bruise on the bone itself.

"I'll take care of this tonight, or tomorrow morning," Juliana promised.

Nova nodded. Her sister, Luna, gave Juliana an appreciative smile. "We're sorry about your friend."

Juliana swallowed and gave her a tight smile.

They continued on. The day stretching into evening, wind picking up through the trees. As the sky switched from brilliant blue to a soft purple and red, Juliana—still walking behind everyone—found Anthony sitting on the side of the path.

"What are you..." she glanced ahead. The trees thinned out in front of them. A faint rumbling sound of water reached her ears. "Where are the others?"

"We're here," Anthony responded dully. He gestured ahead. "They're out there." He closed his hand into a fist. "I just... I couldn't..."

Guilt washed through Juliana's stomach. She hadn't been able to look at him all day. He hadn't had the chance to wash May's blood off his face and hands.

She went to him, sinking onto the fallen tree beside him. Bark scratched at her thighs through her shorts.

"She wasn't... she wasn't supposed tah be in front of me, Jules." His voice broke.

Without looking, Juliana took hold of his fist, letting him slowly unclench it before she pressed her palm to his. Why this movement, this interlacing of their fingers, brought her comfort she wasn't sure.

"She was behind me. I made sure," he glanced at her, "she was behind me. And then..." He heaved a breath, shaking his head.

"She used her power," Juliana filled in for him. He'd left that part out when he gave the group the explanation of what had happened.

He nodded. "I didn't... I couldn't..." He stared at her.

"It wasn't your fault." Juliana reached out and touched the part of his face that was clean of blood. "She chose to save you. It was—" her throat caught, but she carried on, "it was her decision." She tightened her grip on his hand. "There was nothing you could do" she breathed. Her chest constricted and more tears formed in her eyes. "Nothing any of us could do."

Anthony gazed into her eyes. He gave her hand a gentle squeeze.

She offered up a small smile. "Come on." She stood, pulling him up with her. "Let's go see this lake of yours."

Grief pitted in her stomach, a small dark bead of it feeding off her rage and fear. But as Anthony followed her down his trail, it fell further away, deeper within her, fading from her immediate sight.

As they came through the trees, Juliana's breath left her in a low sigh of awe.

The sun sunk behind towering rocky mountains. A waterfall was just visible across a glistening lake, responsible for the low rumble they heard. Gentle wavelets licked the rocky shore on their side. Fish rippled the surface of the lake, leaping for insects. Above them, massive birds circled in the sky. A quarter-mile away, a small stream cut through the forest.

"How did you find this place?" Juliana whispered to Anthony.

Ahead of them, the others seemed frozen, beholden to the beauty.

"My uncle showed it tah me, years ago." Anthony chuckled. "Always talked about findin' a way tah build a house here. Leave Abredea for good."

"This is a nice spot," Cho said. He turned to them. "We can stay the night here, discuss our plans. Figure out where to go next."

Juliana nodded. She squeezed Anthony's hand as Cho turned and began directing people on where to start a fire and lay down sleeping rolls.

"I'm glad you brought us here," she murmured.

"Me too," Anthony said. "I forgot how beautiful it is."

The sky was clear, the air warm for that time of year. Between their small fire and the blankets they'd brought, it would be a comfortable night. Talk was minimal as they ate and settled in to sleep.

Juliana lay down, reaching her hands above her head in a stretch.

High over their heads, a red-tailed hawk soared through the sky. His feathers glinted in the light of the moon as he landed in the treetops, keeping a close eye on the people below.

After a moment or two, Anthony stretched out beside her. They stared up at the stars, silent. Juliana's mind was a blur. She tried to get it to stop, to slow the thoughts rapidly firing through her brain.

Slowly people fell asleep. Taz's light snoring filled the air, and a small smile crossed Juliana's lips. Her arm fell to the side, and a few seconds later, a warm, calloused hand found hers. Their fingers intertwined.

Her mind settled. Her heartbeat fell into an easy pace. She drifted, exhaustion suddenly clinging to her bones and dragging her down.

Juliana slipped into sleep, her hand still in Anthony's. Safe, if only in her dreams, from everything coming after them.

Chapter Forty-Nine

Epilogue - Many Years Ago - Abredea

May strolled across the main square. She waved to Kate, standing with her daughter on her hip next to the bakery door.

May stopped beside the fountain and glanced in the direction they'd be coming from. He was running late, and she worried for a moment.

Then she heard Dave's excited yelp and a grin spread across her face. Tony's deep booming voice thundered behind their son, telling him to slow down.

Dave came into view, running as usual. He got halfway across the square when he tripped and face-planted. May hurried forward, but he sprang right up and finished sprinting toward her as his father and sister rounded the bend.

"Hi, little man," May said, wrapping her arms around her handsome six-year-old.

He grinned up at her, then went to play in the water.

Her daughter came running toward her, short four-year-old legs not letting her move quite as fast as her brother. Her long dark hair bounced against her shoulders in beautiful tight curls.

She was about ten feet away when she shouted, "Hi, May!" at the top of her lungs.

Then she came closer, and May knelt down. Anya wrapped little arms around her mother's neck and whispered.

"Hi, Mama."

May lifted her daughter, clutching her tight. Her husband smiled at the two of them, the sight of his face bringing her the warmth it always did.

"Dave," Tony said. His son rushed over to his side, his eyes wide, and a big grin on his face. They walked up to May and Anya, and the family made their way west, down the crumbling street toward the fence.

"Where are we going today, Mama?" little Anya asked.

"Today, my love," May smiled, her fingers brushing against Tony's hand as they got further away from the square, "we're going to have an adventure in the forest."

The End

Thank You

H ow do I even start this? I have so many people to thank for this dream finally coming true.

I'll start close to home.

My husband, thank you for the constant support. For picking up the slack, giving me the time and the space, and helping me every time I need advice, even though this isn't your cup of tea. I love you, and the girls. I know I say it all the time, but we really do make an amazing team.

For my mom and sister, you two are wonderful. The first people to read this. My sounding boards and brainstorming partners. My best friends. Without you this wouldn't have been possible.

To my dad and the rest of my family, your support is felt even from across the country. I love you all.

To my llama gals, I never thought I'd find a group like this. New, but beautiful and everything I've been looking for in a group of writers and a group of friends.

To my D&D group, you guys are the best. Having a creative outlet that isn't specifically book writing is insanely helpful. I'm so incredibly grateful to know you all and I can't wait to see where our friendships and adventures take us.

My editor, those cuts were worth it. You were absolutely right, as usual. To my cover artist, and the other artists who have worked on art for this story, I can't tell you how much I appreciate your ability to bring my vision to life.

To Dana, Katie, Caty, Tori, Erin, and Sam, your love of this story motivates me to write. Thank you for being some of the first people to read Hope and Lies, and some of the strongest voices urging me forward.

To Tracey and Margaret, it may seem small to you but your advice was extremely valuable to both myself as a writer, and this book as a whole. I cherish our friendship. Thank you.

To my friends at the Y, without the amazing childcare you all provide this book would have taken much longer to finish. Likely years longer. Having my girls in a safe place, with people I trust, gives me the emotional security to focus on the writing and getting the story on the page. That, plus the support and encouragement I get from you all, means the world. Thank you.

I'm sure there are others. Dozens more people who I could and should be thanking. This book is over a decade in the making. I started writing it when I was fifteen, and it's releasing a week before my thirtieth birthday. It's been tweaked, adjusted, re-worded, and re-written so many times. I think I needed to be here, in this place and this time with these people for Hope and Lies to be the way it is now. I think I needed these years of waiting to decide to take the plunge, leap off the cliff, dive in.

The last person I'd like to thank is you. You, the person reading this, who got through the book and even a little further. I hope you enjoyed these characters. I hope you love them like I do. I hope you're excited to see what comes next. Thank you for reading.

A Glimpse of Book Two

Chapter One - Present Day
- Dolor Research Facility

The far window of Wolfe's office overlooked a series of open-topped exam rooms. The tinted glass allowed her a view of most of the experiments going on at any point in time. She paced along the window now, her gaze catching on the occasional burst of flame, spark of electricity, or plume of frost.

These children were powerful. Far too powerful for their little bodies and less capable minds. Wolfe clicked her immaculate fingernails against each other. Across the large office, the metal door slid open. In the shadowed darkness of the room, a figure stepped in and slunk to the corner behind Wolfe's mahogany desk.

Wolfe gave no notice of the movement beyond a brief wave of her hand. She inhaled through her sharp nose, a river of frustration coursing through her. If that man didn't hurry up...

Her hands clenched to fists just as a tinkling bell rang from her desk. She straightened and strode across the thin carpet, wheeling around the desk, and clicking a button embedded in the wood.

A holo-screen lifted from the desk, the image of her top Black-Star flickering for a moment as he moved in and out of frame. The bandage around his bald head was bloodstained and in need of changing. Twin dagger-shaped tattoos curled down his cheeks to the edge of his jaw.

"Report." Wolfe leaned against the desk, heart hammering against her ribs.

"I'm sorry, ma'am."

Her lip curled as heat filled her gut.

Steel went on. "There is no sign of the girl, or her friends, in the camp. My men have scoured the surrounding woods and fields, but—"

"What of the footage," Wolfe demanded. If he were there, in the room with her, she'd pour enough *suggestion* on him to break his mind. His shame at failing her would know no end. "Your men have been tailing her for months, surely you know where they're headed?"

"No, ma'am." Steel ran a leather-gloved hand across his face. The skin under his eyes were heavy with dark bags. As he stepped away from the camera for a moment, another bandage across his shoulder became visible. He returned quickly. "We do know they met up with others. Seems like your secondary squad didn't manage to capture all the children from the sewers."

Wolfe snarled. "Rich of you to judge, Captain Steel," she spat. "Given your inability to keep track of *one* girl."

He flushed. His head bowed in acknowledgement as a muttered apology rumbled from his lips.

"Speak no more of it," Wolfe said, raising a hand to cut him off. She sucked in a breath and thought hard. "If those children are with Juliana, they are your responsibility now. Get some frosted Reds into the camp, get your men together, and *find her*. I expect frequent updates."

A second wave of tinkling bells filled the office, the sound slightly harsher than the first call. Wolfe's gut clenched with fear she quickly masked from showing on her face. Behind her, the figure in the corner sucked in a breath.

"Do not fail me, Steel," Wolfe murmured through gritted teeth. Her Black-Star captain gave a sharp nod, pressed his fist to his chest, and was mid-bow when she shut off the call.

The tinkling sounded again, the high pitch, along with the words glowing across the holo-screen, announcing who it was without Wolfe needing to answer.

She sank into her chair, smoothed her hair, and sat as straight as her back would allow. Then, with a glance to the corner and a swallow, she accepted the call.

"Chancellor, to what do I owe this honor?"

"Cousin." Chancellor Jackie Collette smiled from the screen. Her teeth were naturally sharp, the canines standing out each time she spoke. Her greying hair was dyed dark brown. Still, no amount of color could hide the wrinkles at the edges of her eyes or the permanent crease along her nose from a life-time of scowling.

A chill ran through Wolfe as Collette leaned back in her own office chair. The windows behind her desk showed a picturesque scene of the sea. Capital City sat along the coast, plentiful in beaches, cliffs, and fresh seafood. Wolfe had been raised in that place, and hated every time she had to return.

"We have a council meeting coming up," Collette said. "You will be in attendance?"

The question was pretense. Wolfe was on the council, and therefor required to attend every meeting.

"Absolutely, Chancellor."

"Good, good..."

Collette went quiet for a moment and Wolfe clenched her hand under the desk to keep her emotions from showing on her face. The Chancellor of Pangaea, and her cousin, did not call via holo-screen for something as mundane as this. Something else was coming.

"You will have the opportunity," Collette finally said, "to present your latest findings at the meeting. The council is eager to learn of your progress."

Here Wolfe's bland mask faltered. She blinked and let out a little breath. "Chancellor, we've only had the newest batch of subjects for a week. Surely the council doesn't expect—"

"There are members on the council who question your efficiency, Minerva. There are some who wonder if your efforts are too time consuming. We've had reports of stirrings, people speaking out against the caste system, again. Possible recruiters for another rebellion."

Wolfe's eyes widened.

"Nothing I'm worried about," Collette waved a nonchalant hand, "but the council has been newly motivated to desire the might you promised. You've had a long time to complete your assignment." Her palm pressed into the wood of her desk, eyes narrowing as she leaned forward. "One wonders if you aren't wasting time and resourced with your little experiment."

The figure in the corner behind Wolfe shifted and Collette's gaze moved. Her lips curled into a cruel grin.

"Tell me, Minerva, has the girl's power emerged yet?"

It was like standing under a waterfall. The cold running down her back, the pressure pounding across her shoulders. An image flashed through Wolfe's mind. Juliana standing before one of her unimportant little friends, blue light emanating from her fingertips as she healed the girl's lip. Steel had sent it that morning. A victory, quickly soured by the discovery that Juliana, and her friends—one of whom was also an alter—had disappeared.

Wolfe forced the image away, keeping her face passive. "Not yet, Chancellor. But I am certain we will have progress soon."

Collette leaned back in her chair. "Perhaps you were wrong, Minerva. Perhaps the girl didn't inherit the power."

Wolfe cleared her throat. "I have confidence in my hypothesis. I believe she will be stronger than anything we've seen before."

"She'd better be." Collette looked away for a moment. Someone in the room spoke to her, something about her next appointment.

Wolfe waited, sweat making her hands damp and clammy.

Collette turned back to her. "As I was saying, you destroyed the last healer we encountered."

Behind Wolfe, the shadow made a small sound, like the whine of a muzzled dog.

Collette continued. "If the girl doesn't reveal her ability soon, you will step in and bring her to Dolor."

"I *will* complete my mission, Chancellor. I *will* get the power you seek." Wolfe nodded.

Collette shook her head. "Any fool with a gun can have power over life, Minerva. I want power over death. And since you squandered our last opportunity for that power... I expect you to be more careful with it this time."

Wolfe bit back the mix of fear and anger stirring in her gut. "Yes, Chancellor. I understand."

"See you in a week."

Collette ended the call.

Wolfe sat rigid and still for a long moment. Then, with no warning, she let out a shriek of rage. She rose, slamming her hand onto the desktop. With a rush of blinding fury, helpless and unappreciated, she ripped the holo-screen from its weak hinges and threw it to the floor. The carpet wasn't soft enough to rescue the fragile glass and the thing shattered into pieces.

Wolfe's heels crunched across the glass as she strode toward the door. Without turning back, she said, "Get that cleaned up." Then she stepped through the door and went to find her head of research.

If Collette wanted power, they'd get her power. No matter the cost.